SEVEN OF SWORDS

SEVEN OF SWORDS

LEWIS HASTINGS

This edition published in Great Britain in 2020

by Hobeck Books Limited, Unit 14, Sugnall Business Centre, Sugnall, Stafford, Staffordshire, ST21 6NF

www.hobeck.net

A CIP catalogue for this book is available from the British Library.

ISBN 978-1-913-793-18-0 (pbk)

ISBN 978-1-913-793-17-3 (ebook)

Cover design by Jem Butcher

http://www.jembutcherdesign.co.uk

Printed and bound in Great Britain

Seven of Swords logo © Russell Budden

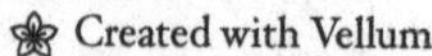 Created with Vellum

BY LEWIS HASTINGS

From the Seventh Wave trilogy:
Seventh
Seven Degrees
Seven of Swords

The fourth Jack Cade novel:
The Angel of Whitehall

Autobiography:
Actually, The World Is Enough

ARE YOU A THRILLER SEEKER?

Hobeck Books is an independent publisher of crime, thrillers and suspense fiction and we have one aim – to bring you the books you want to read.

For more details about our books, our authors and our future plans, plus the chance to download free novellas, please sign up for our newsletter at **www.hobeck.net**.

You can also find us on Twitter **@hobeckbooks** or on Facebook **www.facebook.com/hobeckbooks10**.

NOTE ON THE SEVENTH WAVE TRILOGY

My most detective-worthy readers will note that the number seven features in my writing; I met 'her' on the seventh and the trilogy is in seven parts. When I started the story there was only one book. Then it grew, and grew, so if you are finding yourself immersed in this book and wondering why there is a Part Four without a Part One, or Two, or Three... Now you know, you might want to park this one up and start with *Seventh* (Parts One and Two), then move on to *Seven Degrees* (Part Three) and then return to this book. Case solved...

Lewis

*Give me the child until he is seven
and I will give you the man*

Aristotle

$$
\overline{\qquad}
$$

PROLOGUE

$$
\overline{\qquad}
$$

London, 2nd January 2015

ANOTHER BRITISH CHRISTMAS HAD COME AND GONE. AS it did every year and would continue to do so for as long as people were allowed to celebrate it without feelings of guilt in my green and pleasant homeland.

There had been an economical snowfall as I recall – just enough to create delight and chaos all at once, but not quite enough to cause concern at the leading bookmakers, who secretly prayed for rain on Christmas Day, instead of having to contend with an obscene, weather-based pay-out for a traditional but rare white Christmas.

People were ambling back to work and what they classed as normality; boxes had been stowed in lofts, decorations carefully wrapped and stored, until September, possibly early October, when the chaos would all start once again. For this year, I was glad it was over.

Don't misunderstand me, I have always enjoyed Christmas. Without children it could never be as magical as I perhaps wanted it to be – I guess that's where the nephews and nieces made good on their promise to lighten my bank balance, for the must-haves of the silly season.

What I missed most about the season of goodwill – other than the rare opportunity to overly-embrace a girl under the mistletoe was the weather. Crazy, I know.

Now I found myself living in the southern hemisphere where the weather is arguably more clement and yet I missed, no, yearned for those dark mornings and darker evenings, where the wind could slice you in half and the air of a December night find itself so chilled that one's breath could fracture as it exits the safe haven of the lungs.

There is also something ethereal about the tranquil and silent state that the mere threat of a snowfall brings.

And mist – or fog – I never really understood the difference. I missed the...fog. Not for the green-grey Dickensian spell that it casts upon the streets – of London in my case – but for its ability to allow you to progress at a slower speed than society and life normally and currently demands. Whether on foot or in a car, you have to slow down, to watch out for the others; sound is enhanced at the expense of vision, and normally the whole experience can best be described as strangely comforting.

At least I find it to be a place where I can actually be alone.

Judging perfectly where that person will head and passing, without words, stepping, drifting into the veil until only stifled footsteps give away the presence of another approaching human is a subliminal thing.

It happened to me only weeks ago.

I had walked out of Scotland Yard – the ludicrously iconic home of the Metropolitan Police, an organisation that periodically over the preceding ten years had become my professional foster parent.

It hadn't been a long day, or even week. It had been months of getting up early and heading home late. Of losing weight. And sleep. Of gaining ground and losing more. Two forward, three back, sometimes four.

As the albeit unwitting leader of the team that named itself Breaker, after the police operational name targeting a crime syndicate, I had been offered the chance to head to London and offer some expertise in the area of Eastern Europe. They, 'The Met' and as such my unintended new employers had seen fit to promote me – the street cop from the east Midlands of England.

It made no sense, but no one challenged it. It became apparent that I had friends in high, or possibly low places.

I was actually keen to retain my rank of sergeant – the best job in any force. But someone, in some place, thought differently.

In my cynical mind, there was always an agenda.

That was ten long years before. December 2014 had proven to be a cathartic month. I was able to succeed in what the Buddhist tradition preaches – the Third Noble Truth – the art of letting go. And it felt good. I had closed the office door behind me, taken the many flights of stairs and braced myself as I walked into the brightly lit, festive night air.

I had walked away from a career as a police officer. It was actually as easy as that.

Being independently 'wealthy' helped, of course. The money that had come my way in a drunken foray in Hong Kong had provided a future income, and selfishly I had no one to share it with. Until she arrived into my life and brought with her the Four Horsemen of the Apocalypse. And now, they had a Fifth, and it was called Greed.

The criminal syndicate who called themselves the Seventh Wave had been dissected, imprisoned and disrupted – but their successors were waiting for the call. In the world of organised crime there is always someone willing to take a risk, to fill the void.

Their leader was once again in a fortress – this time with no hope of acquittal. He had something I wanted, and vice versa. We were connected, inexorably, and there was only ever going to be a painful conclusion. For now, our only point of difference was that I was free to roam the globe, and he was backed into a corner and brooding. With his connections, hidden wealth, influence and lust for revenge – and an avaricious nature I had never managed to understand, he was beyond dangerous.

Sitting in a putrid, poorly lit cell, he was a caged animal.

And he blamed me for all that was wrong in his life.

I prayed every night that he would never survive his incarceration.

Technically, having walked away from the United Kingdom, from policing and from the problem itself, I was no longer able to legally pursue the group that had caused me and others so much anxiety. That was until a woman from a government department in London had approached me and made it quite clear just how much I was needed – "Forget rank, forget your past, build a team of people you trust and send me the bill," she had said. Or at least words to that effect. I chose to interpret them in a way, which for once, suited me – and my agenda.

"You work for me now and whether we like it or not, those people that keep you awake at night hold the aces and we need them back, nicely tucked away in their box before the damage is irreparable."

"And should I decide to say no?"

She smiled. "You won't Mr Cade. It's not in your interest, and it's certainly not in mine. And, for the record, I will do absolutely anything to keep you onside."

Those who I thought of as enemies had actually become allies, and conversely some of the very people I knew I should have faith in were to become my most dangerous enemies.

'Keep them close, Jack.'

It was on that December night in 2014 that my life collided with one of those people that instinct said I could always trust. She appeared through the mist on a much-travelled walkway across the Thames. Our eyes met and for a brief second, we were unified once more.

There was a visible scar.

On her exquisite features.

Mind over matter. I had wiped the blood from her face.

She was dead. I saw her die – watched the life ebb from her eyes. I knelt on that unforgiving tarmac surface and I held her hand up until the point where instinct said I had to go – now. As much as I had denied it, I knew they were back, hunting me in my adopted home and though it tormented every sinew I had to close her eyes and let her go.

The figure on the bridge, in the mist, simply could not have been the girl that walked brazenly into my beach-side life on that cloudless day and allowed me to stare through the thin veil of her summer dress and into her life. But it was her. I knew it.

Her scarred hand delivered a message that night, in the sodium-lit haze, on that bridge, in that city – succinct. Its instructions were clear, it said:

'I am alive, Jack. Come and find me. But be careful who you trust. With love.'

She didn't hear my reply, which was even more laconic.

'I'm on the way. And you – Elena – have some questions to answer.'

PART FOUR

CHAPTER ONE

Winter – Pazardzhik Southern Bulgaria

PAZARDZHIK IS A CITY SITUATED ON THE BANKS OF THE Maritsa River, southern Bulgaria and the capital of the province.

To the north and alongside Road II37 – The Trakia Highway – on the edge of the city, bordered by agricultural fields, is a faded, cream and peach-walled structure. Its outer walls adorned with posters that depict men employed in various trades, which appear conventional until closer inspection reveals that each male is a prisoner, repairing a wall, or amusingly, using a high-profile power tool to give the impression he has just broken down the walls of his cold and characterless cell.

Advertising had taken on a new stance in this part of the world.

The Bulgarians had a sense of humour. That much was true.

Sitting at intervals alongside the II37 are towers, and barbed wire and palisade fence tops, designed to tear human flesh on contact. To the north west, a river and another to the south. A long-forgotten car dealership occupies the boundary to the east and a petrol station – the first indicator of life beyond the walls, its yellow and blue insignia and a brightly lit canopy marking it out as the only beacon on what was otherwise always a depressing drive out of the city.

An unmarked side road off the Trakia Highway reveals a different vista, gone are the pastel shades of peach and magnolia that so depict the outer margins of the city. Grey, featureless and towering walls of stone exist among an outer cordon of off-white metal panels, the inner boundary topped by a walkway along which guards patrol. More wire.

In the foreground rusting hulks of abandoned machinery lay dormant, never to serve man again. They had a purpose once. Like the inhabitants of the building. Once.

At the heart of the structure is an ostensible three storey building, flanked by an administration block. To the north, a solitary, bright yellow security office, large enough for one or two in the winter. A rudimentary barrier of red and yellow provides a minimal divide between those at liberty and those, not.

On the face of it, to a passing visitor or enquiring mind, Pazardzhik Prison is like any other. A place outside of which society deems itself to be safe.

A sign in blue Cyrillic lettering greets visitors. Its meaning is a mystery to a western eye and with a degree of flexibility might say, 'Welcome to Pazardzhik Prison.'

A more reasonable translation might be, 'Pazardzhik – The Lock.'

The lock. There are no romantic similes. The word conjures up polished steel, cold brass, a metallic depriver of liberty. The end.

For those entering its walls the words probably say, 'Welcome to Hell.'

. . .

Inside, much further inside in fact, those same scanning eyes might land upon other faded and red-painted letters, high over the door of the most notorious wing, clinging for life, to the distempered and flaky white walls: Живей с мечмирай от меча.

Loosely translated, it read: *Live by the sword. Die by the sword.*

No one could remember who had written it up there, or how he got there, out of sight of the guards, but he did and he would forever be a folk hero. It was a male, for this was a place inhabited only by the male of the species where women were welcomed for only one reason.

No one could name the artist, for he died in his cell, a cold and solitary death. Ice on the walls. Even the damp mould had frozen.

And no one would ever remove his work, least of all the deputy commissar who saw it as a double-edged sword indeed. Remove it and cause a riot, allow it to stay and remind the men of its meaning every day.

In Pazardzhik you lived however you could, fought for your life, and never took your eye off your opponent, not once. Down in the bowels of the building, without glass or even a window, daylight was a luxury and tobacco was worth more than gold. Class A drugs were considered a death sentence – for those inmates that possessed them, or those that smuggled them through the daunting outer main doors. But still it arrived. Alcohol too, when not distilled on site in ways that defied ingenuity.

Fresh fruit and clean water were worth more than that gilded nugget itself.

This was far from a conventional place, where conventional prisoners were sent. Below the three stories, visible and open to visitors and priests, lay a subterranean network of cells that were little better than an underground ghetto. It was said that the Bulgarian prison system had somehow avoided the attention of its government for decades. The buildings from the sixties, not just at Pazardzhik, were considered to be in a deplorable state, with living and sanitary conditions beyond questionable. Some cells in the worst quarters of the system had no sanitary facilities, making them worse than some third world institutions.

Obsolete, overcrowded, lacking in security and medical facilities, housed among old, past tense buildings, now awash with heroin; contrary to the rules. Inmates existed in a few square metres per person – again contrary to what society deemed fit.

But it was a prison after all. Why should they have rights?

The European Courts had been repeatedly pressed by humanitarian groups, all to no avail. According to those groups, Bulgaria might well have been a despot African nation, not a developing country only hours from Europe's central administration centre.

They were learning; the government assured those that listened. They were investing, and only the very worst of society would be housed in the older establishments.

Pazardzhik was a forgotten place where the inmates had given up caring and the staff less so. In the summer it was unbearable, endlessly hot, everywhere. In winter, death was considered a better option.

One man knew the prison well. Constantin Nicolescu had spent only a few desperate months there many years before.

It was 2002, may have been three. Time was a commodity he had no control over, so he never wasted any more worrying about it.

A prisoner of the Bulgarian government – locked away, underground, the result of his opportunistic offending, a burgeoning burglar, he had been caught; young and naïve. He soon learned. Learned to love his fellow man – it provided for temporary stimulation and currency, his choice being lower-tier drugs which would one day lead to a heroin addiction that ruled his life.

Constantin had learned to map the building in his mind. He knew every corner, dark or otherwise. With his eyes closed. He knew who to talk to and who to avoid. Showers were rare, once a fortnight at best. He avoided them too.

He knew the way to the prison wing office, in broad daylight. And it was there that he read the signals correctly. That the man who stood proudly before him, immaculate shining boots and newly issued epaulettes, the man before him with buckling legs, biting his lip to avoid detection, the man upon which Constantin was committing an act that would have seen the officer dismissed in disgrace, sent to prison himself, would one day become a most useful commodity.

Abused, malnourished and disinterested Constantin had lost faith in everything and everyone until he met the only beacon of hope in his pitiful and illegitimate career. It was November; he had no idea what year, or week, or day – they were all one back then in his alcohol-bewildered mind. It may have been raining or even snowing. The sun would not have been shining, that much he knew. It never did in that part of the world.

· · ·

Fourteen or fifteen years later, he lay in a cell in Britain, staring at the graffiti-laden walls, with its orthodox light green paintwork, which he recalled was designed to bring a calming influence. He marvelled at the light that flooded in from a two-by-two glass block window to the outside world. He knew his cellmate was awake, pretending to be asleep.

This was the Hilton in comparison to Pazardzhik. The beds were five star. The cell even had a toilet, with paper and a basin with warm water. As comparatively luxurious as it was, he had no intention of becoming a long-term resident, he would be gone by the morning. A plan to head south – to meet up with his leader. A man he owed his life and existence to. He had been his salvation. It seemed like yesterday that he had carved the deep blue sign of lifelong affiliation into his cold skin.

Now, in the winter of 2015, they would meet again. Constantin had planned to repay the debt, arranging to strike a deal with the very man who had convinced the Romanian government to release Stefanescu into their custody – to punish him for his sins. Deputy Commissar Andonov.

The Romanians were intrigued and delighted by the offer and sent one of their own in exchange for five Romanian nationals – whose charge history combined would not create a tenth of the disorder that Stefanescu had. If the Bulgarians really wanted to punish him for his legacy of attacks upon their nation, then so be it. He was out of their hair. The sooner, the better.

For Constantin it was tangible – his dream-like thoughts had such substance, as if it was that morning. He could almost taste the place on the tip of his tongue, its stench filling his nostrils. He was there again, in that subterranean hell-hole.

He could taste Deputy Commissar Andonov too.

Nicolescu had kept low on the radar, served his time in Pazardzhik, back then in the darkened days that he considered a part of his past. He had moved on, quickly, across Europe to Germany and Britain without ever looking back. It was where heroin had first got a grasp. Sold to him by a whore whose throat he should have cut when he had the chance. In her defence, she didn't do what many would have done; abandon him, naked and penniless in a cheap hotel with questionable sheets, mould-encrusted bathrooms and tacky carpets. She had standards this girl, this nameless, shameless and pretty young thing, now pock-marked, with collapsed veins and shrunken cheekbones and no doubt dead.

He recalled how he had left her in a five-star hotel, curled into a foetal position, soaked in sweat and doused with alcohol, awash with class A narcotics, paid for from his illicit earnings as a commercial burglar. He was adept at it too. She had exploited him for the now. Another leech. He had to move on. Anywhere was better than Pazardzhik.

'Do not ever forget that, Constantin.

The one freezing shower he had taken that winter's morning, around seven, had proven to be cathartic in more than one way. Another inmate was in the block, showering alone. Two more, stood at a distance were obviously aware of the male – connected. He wasn't of a large build, muscular, but not what Constantin would later describe as impressive in stature. Yet he struggled to take his eyes off him. Not for any other reason than he had a look, a presence, a sense of divinity. He was for Nicolescu the nearest thing to God that he would ever experience. He knew he was a fellow Roma; no words were needed to confirm that.

It was then he saw the tattoo. The simple arcing mark on his right wrist. He had heard stories, in Romania, out on the streets, in the Roma community and certainly here, in Pazardzhik. They talked of the image of a blue wave, a sense of belonging to a better thing, a brotherhood, but more. Its leader was not a large man physically, but they told of his sheer presence among men. They said his bloodline was pure gypsy – those that thought the word offensive to the Roms said it with vigour.

Gypsy!

They almost spat the word out.

They said he was the leader of Primal Val – The First Wave.

They said he was the King of the Gypsies. He knew better than to associate with this title, for it was not what it seemed to the uninitiated. In Romani folklore, the holder of the title was often considered to be nothing more than a liaison between the Roma and the Gadje, or the non-Romani. The King would often place himself at risk of arrest rather than bring harm to his people.

As such, he refused to be associated to the title.

He saw himself instead as the King of Men.

The curving black streak on his wrist confirmed it. As he stood in the shower, frigid water cascading off his honed body, the scene in monochrome played out before the older man who stood, staring.

Yes, there it was, the black wave. That simple linear mark, drawn in a prison, using only rudimentary tools under the light of a scarce match.

The best Constantin could offer, as he stood before him, naked and intimidated, was, "Sastipe!"

To the uninitiated it was a foreign language – to the men in the shower block it was pure Romani. The Indo-Aryan language of the travelling people.

The dark-haired male turned to face Nicolescu. Comfortable with his surroundings and the intense cold. He showed no sign of fear. He dried himself with the miniscule piece of cloth supplied by the prison, thought deeply, then spoke.

"Sar san?" *How are you?*

"Mishto, palikerav tut." *I am well.*

"Soi t'jiro nav?" He was staring into his eyes now. *What is your name?* This was not the time to lie.

"Miro nav si o...Constantin." *My name is...Constantin.*

The male with the black tattoo extended his stare, raised an eyebrow. He needed more.

"...Nicolescu."

"Loshalo sim te maladjov tut." *Pleased to meet you.*

Nicolescu bowed slightly, keeping his eyes on the group.

"Me vi loshalo sim." *The pleasure is all mine.*

The male smiled. He had cold, hooded and black eyes, olive, pock-marked skin, a strong, straight nose and thick black hair that shone with blue-grey hues. His hair was matted to his head, still cold, still wet, but the colours were striking, like that of a bird, similar to a Magpie, better still a Jackdaw.

"No, Constantin Nicolescu, the pleasure is all mine." In English. For he spoke at least five languages.

"Come." He beckoned.

Constantin began to walk, desperately afraid of what would follow.

The male threw the cloth to one side, and as naked as his new associate, held open his arms. Constantin stepped forward and waited to hear his neck crack, to feel the home-made shank driving up and into his spleen. But it never came.

The male held him in a strong embrace. Whispering into his ear.

"They call me Alex − King of Men. You have heard of me?"

He nodded. "Of course."

"Speak up. Let them hear you. I am looking for someone to work for me, someone who knows of many ways to kill and steal. They tell me you are the one. Is this so?"

"Yes. I am that man."

"Good. I always need honesty. I am pleased that you wish to join us."

Nicolescu nodded, feeling that he had no choice but equally that he had nothing else to cling to.

"Then give me your wrist."

'What now?'

Was this the moment he feared? Blood on the walls? His life washing down a drain in a country he could never call home?

Alex Stefanescu held the wrist, dried it with the cloth and summoned one of his aides. A basic metal spike appeared, rinsed under the cold water and then run across the skin on the inner side of his wrist. Too shallow and the homemade ink would not adhere to deep and he would probably bleed to death.

"Come to my cell later. We will add the ink. Yours will be blue, like these proud men beside you. Primal Val accepts you into its family. We live by the sword, but never die by it my brother. That is a fool's game. OK?"

"OK. Thank you."

"Don't thank me yet. You have no idea what I need you to do. Let us just say we shall drink Tuica together in my club, very soon − and then you shall travel to London and become rich. But first you need to get me out of here."

He laughed, a cackling bird-like laugh. It was a sound colder than the stone room they stood in, on a winter's morning in Pazardzhik, alongside the Trakia Highway, in the winter landscape that was Bulgaria.

Constantin was good to his word – to his orders. It was only days later that he had engineered an escape from the place the government considered escape-proof.

Alex Stefanescu told him that he would forever be in his debt – at the very least he assured him he had a job for life and should never have to worry about money again. Quietly he trusted the drunk as far as he could kick him, but he knew how capable he had become; reading books, endlessly studying ways to cause the very chaos that Alex craved, and yet cautiously watching from the corner of his eye in case the man whose life he spared ended up being his murderer.

That was then. He had barely aged and was still in good condition for a man who had abused his privileges. For a man who they had been hunting for, for so long. A man hated by the authorities who barely knew where to incarcerate him, let along how to deal with him. Solitary confinement just made him a martyr and increased disorder in the prison system tenfold.

As he walked around his two-by-two cell, Alex Stefanescu could only smile. It was in a cell just like his many years ago that he had initiated so many fine men into what over time had grown from the small team called the First Wave into the fabled strongest event of the oceans, *Septal Val* – the Seventh Wave. A group so organised, so well led, that it had caused fear and chaos across Europe. Interpol held files too thick to bind. Police forces from Spain to Britain wanted him for a smorgasbord of offences.

. . .

He had taken twenty years to create an empire in his Romanian home – where the authorities were happy to allow him to co-exist. Money talked. Girls too, and he had plenty of those from around the world. Pretty girls, attracted to crime and criminals. It never ceased to amaze him how this happened so often. He had lost count of the amount of women he had slept with; European, African, one particular Australian, Roma, Gadje, all different but all manipulative.

They were cunning, and he admired that, so he rewarded them well. Those that abused the privilege weren't abused or beaten, but killed – in ways that even shocked him. In time he had drowned them, dragged them along deserted mountain passes and starved them to death.

But he had a heart. He was charitable, ever looking after the meek. And he had a daughter. And a wife. Once.

That was until he had been caught. Again. The British had helped the Spanish and Bulgarians to capture him. Better to get him off their radar. The man they called Johnnie Hewett had betrayed him. He had allowed him into his home. What type of sociopath would do that? Open his home to a stranger? Give him a bed for the night? He asked of anyone that was prepared to listen.

It was all an elaborate game.

He knew, of course, that as soon as Hewett had served a purpose he would have met his demise either at his own hand or by one of his teams. Dumped in a forest, or buried in the dunes on the west coast of France – that was a favourite. Or just dropped down a sewer, head first.

He was surrounded by betrayal – it was just varying degrees of treachery. Did these people not understand that trust was the élan vital of the Roma people? They knew nothing. You remained loyal, or you paid the price. And blood was not necessarily thicker than water. It wasn't difficult.

And Cade. How he had made himself look so important to his bosses – to his government. Once a lowly police officer until he had met with Nikolina – Mrs Alex Stefanescu. And his beautiful daughter, Elena.

Jack Cade. He would kill him one day. He had missed the chance. Should have let the assassin called Valentin play with their lives for a while, then flick the switch.

The rest of the hangers-on would be dealt with by his team – piece by perfect piece. But Cade was his, and he had spent many months dreaming up ways to end his infuriating life and those that he loved and that loved him.

And then, there were the others – the key pieces on the magnificent chess board. They still owed him, and he intended to cash in.

And what of his dear little brother Stefan? Surely he was still loyal, despite the elaborate stories that he wove around his audience; a web, spun, delicate, but so very strong.

His daydream came to a crashing end.

"Prisoner! I am talking to you."

On the top floor of Pazardzhik Prison, Alex Stefanescu found himself manacled and stood loosely to attention before the deputy commissar.

He smiled and nodded and made pleasant small talk.

Miroslav Andonov was a career prison officer. He had joined the glorious service at the age of eighteen and had risen rapidly through the ranks. Just one more step to becoming Commissar of his own prison. Over the years he joked that he was one of the few that hadn't been able to escape Pazardzhik, having stayed there for the majority of his service. He enjoyed the challenge that so many had declined. He also knew that to date no one had escaped and survived to boast to their friends and families.

He had hunted them down. And that made him a rising star.

He shivered as he looked out of his office window. God alone knew what it would be like to be on the run out there, and he knew he also needed to get out soon, to start afresh, somewhere new.

Bobov Dol or Sofia were the places he craved, the flag-ships of the service, not this desolate shit hole. His words.

"Mr Stefanescu, you know that I have a duty to keep you away from the people of Bulgaria? That the people you call your own don't want you back? I must also protect the government from your illicit trading in drugs and firearms and people?"

Stefanescu frowned.

Deputy Commissar Andonov held his hand aloft. "Wait, I have not finished yet."

The Jackdaw nodded, a delicate movement only, with a half-smile on his lips.

"And above all, to protect you from yourself. We agree?"

"Of course, Deputy Commissar. A point, if I may? I do not deal in drugs or firearms. Look to the north and south for those commodities, but please sir, do not suggest that is how I made my millions. You have a very difficult job to do and one, may I say, that you do very well, and have always done very well, with compassion for the people of your wonderful country and my fellow prisoners, and above all the glorious people, outside those cream-coloured walls."

He took a moment to stare beyond the deputy governor, a chance to see green fields, sky, clouds and a river.

"Enough prisoner Stefanescu. Do you not think I can see

through your sneering sarcasm? You will do well to remember who is in charge here!"

Stefanescu, heavily shackled, picked deliberately at his fingertips, dropping pieces of skin onto Andonov's pristine scarlet carpet.

"The last time I looked it was Commissar Vanchev."

Another half-smile.

"You are the most despicable person I have ever met prisoner Stefanescu. You have no idea about society or civilization. What lies outside those walls is beyond you and always will be. I will stake my career on it. You will remain a prisoner, here at Pazardzhik for as long as I live." He stood, leaning forward, hands palm down on the oak desk. The discussion had been ended.

"As is your wish, Deputy Andonov. Was it not Dostoyevsky who said 'the degree of civilization in a society can be judged by entering its prisons'?"

Andonov had no idea who had uttered those words, and frankly he did not care. He was successful, not educated.

"I am not interested in your words of wisdom. You will leave now. Go back below with the other rats."

Turning halfway towards the office door, Stefanescu stopped, standing his ground.

"But sir, you summoned me to your office. Did you not? What was it that you had to discuss with me?"

He had blindsided the man he considered an enemy and a weak one.

Andonov looked up, and into his eyes, beyond to the guards, looking for signs of insolence.

He tried to show no weakness. He had learned that on Day One.

"Yes. Indeed. I chose to call you here to say that I have appealed your sentence – due to your behaviour, and the way that you incite such violence in my prison. You will serve another three years."

Andonov now wore the half-smile.

"But my behaviour has been exemplary."

"I disagree. This conduct meeting is over." He nodded to the three guards.

For Stefanescu, it was time to lay his cards on the future Commissar's table.

Aces, four of them, one by one, dropping onto the polished oak desk, among the photographs of his wife and children.

The first ace was the diamond, Constantin Nicolescu. The name alone caused a microscopic show of recognition. His eyes narrowed.

The second, a cold winter's day as a junior officer in a quiet rest room known affectionately and ironically by the staff as The Club.

The third, the ace of hearts, an act of exquisite pleasure performed for and upon him by a man he had tried to forget. He was a prisoner, for God's sake.

The fourth, the ace of spades, was the set of grainy photographs sitting in an unopened envelope, postmarked in a place he had never heard of.

Constantin's timing had been as exquisite as his sexual talents.

"Sir, you may wish to open the letter that is sat on your desk. The one with the red stamp upon it. Yes, that one. I can go if you would like me to. Or perhaps I should stay. So we can talk..."

He watched Andonov open the envelope with his precious long-service paper knife. Then saw his eyes close once more.

"...Alone."

Andonov's mouth filled with bile. He swallowed it and spoke.

"Guards, you will leave me with prisoner Stefanescu for one minute. I will be fine. Go." He ushered them away with a sweating palm.

The door closed as the three staff exited, knowing better than to listen at the door.

"You have something to say, Mr Stefanescu?"

"No, Deputy Commissar. I do not. I have nothing to add."

"Good. Are these the only copies?"

"Roma are trustworthy people, Miroslav. Unless you deceive or betray us. You have my word that you now own the only copy."

"So if I burn them, I hold the ace card?"

"Yes. But I suspect you are also a man of honour. And besides, allowing me to walk out of here would actually help you. Wouldn't it? You could restore order quickly. Or, if I wish I can show you who actually runs this prison. Are we in agreement?"

Andonov played chess too and knew when he was beaten. He tore the photographs into eight pieces, placed them into his ashtray and set light to them, watching the green and yellow flames and knowing that the man in front of him who held his fate in his shackled hands had for reasons unknown allowed his career to continue.

It was all a wonderful game. He turned towards the window, not wishing to look into Alex's eyes. It made the act less of a betrayal.

"You will escape from here Friday. I cannot let you walk away. It would finish me. You understand? Please allow me that honour?"

"We have an agreement, Mr Andonov. I assure you I will never return to your prison again, nor my people, nor my team. I assume you will leave the front door unlocked?" Now his smile was complete.

He turned and hobbled towards the door.

"Good luck with your promotion and please send my kind regards to your lovely wife Katerina and those pretty girls."

At ten o'clock on the Friday morning, Mr Alex Stefanescu, dressed in the uniform of a prison guard, walked along the service corridor of Pazardzhik Prison, through four sets of doors, into an awaiting truck and left the inner walls and his past where it belonged. His heart barely missed a beat.

He waved as he passed by the yellow gate lodge, with its blue painted welcome sign, which contained two guards sheltering from the cold. For Alex, the day was as warm and bright and full of good fortune as any he could recall.

The deputy commissar would ensure his superiors and the media that no stone would remain unturned, that he would spend the rest of his days hunting down the leader of the Seventh Wave. His reputation depended upon it.

But Alex knew the truth.

So easy. One act. One photograph. One admission.

Everyone had a price.

Of course he had another copy.

He was free. He had left behind his past. His past had died. And when a gypsy dies his family asks for forgiveness, for his sins, for every and anything that he may have done. Gypsies fear the return of the dead, that they might haunt the living. He needed forgiveness.

What was left of his family forgave him, a few cousins here, an uncle there. His parents had lay in the ground for many years, unable to exonerate him – they had died at his hands. Brutal and pointless, he needed to teach them a lesson about respect and he did so in one of his many, growing and quiet episodes of rage. His own parents had sold him to the authorities for a few thousand Leu – had let them tie him to a cold, damp bed for weeks on end, covered in bed sores and filth, until he could hardly walk. And they called him a sociopath?

There was his brother Stefan. His one final opportunity would come soon – blood is thicker after all.

And finally, his pretty girl, his beautiful little Elena, the union of one true night of love with his beloved Niko. He never once doubted that she was his – her strength was incredible, her mind so active and her eyes, those opaline windows to her soul, were pure gypsy. They said that she had deceived him – and therefore she too had to die.

He had always said that he alone could order her death. When and only when he decided, he was after all the King of Men.

He did not fear her return. She had her chance and like her mother had betrayed him. His brother had given his word, had said that he had watched the blood flow from her body onto the isolated country road.

She was gone, unless somehow she could be reborn.

Perhaps she had met with her mother? The dead and lascivious reunited.

His mind was racing. He considered himself sane. The rapidly burning psychological file at Pazardzhik disagreed. Even his name lingered among the ashes, taunting their arsonist as he stood in the freezing rain in a quiet corner of the prison seeking warmth from the embers.

Beware the Necromancer – the medium, the witch, the fore-teller of the future. To die and return is to become feared, and she must surely be put to death. It said so in the bible.

He had studied it as a child. Forced to, but he admired its wisdom, appreciated its words.

'They shall be stoned and their blood shall be upon their own heads.' *Leviticus 20:27*.

She was gone. Curses and magic were the bedrock of Romani folklore but as loyal as he was and as Christian as he considered himself he believed none of it.

She would never return to haunt him.

He opened a new SIM card, slid it into a cheap phone, made a call, lowered the window and dropped it out onto the highway where it shattered before being destroyed by a following car. In another kilometre he snapped the SIM, then flicked it out of the window too, watching it arc over the railings and into the verge.

He wound the window back up to keep out the cold, nodded to his driver, a man who also wore the mark, then made himself as comfortable as he could. It was a seven-hour drive, due north through the Central Balkan National Park, avoiding Sofia and the main cities en route to Craiova.

They boarded the Nikopol car ferry for the eight-minute journey from Bulgaria to Romania across the River Danube.

In seven hours he would be home, with his people, in his own bed, surrounded by his opulent belongings, a glass of Tuica, a roaring fire and the start of his return to notoriety.

CHAPTER TWO

Heathrow Airport, 13th January 2015

THE WORLD'S GREATEST AIRPORTS ARE ALWAYS BUSY, AND London Heathrow was no exception in the post-Christmas high shoulder – one of the busiest times of the year at any airport.

The man that slipped quietly through the rental drop-off and check-in experience at Terminal 3 knew how to navigate his way around most airports – they had a common theme and once you had studied it, it made the initial process easier.

Under six foot, still in good shape, casually dressed but sharp in the right places, he knew how and what to say to the ground staff. He'd paid in advance for a premium economy seat and now stood in front of a twenty-year-old with bloodshot eyes and a wish to be elsewhere, he said the right things.

"Must be awful having to be so bloody nice to everyone all the time?"

The young woman looked up from the British passport

and saw that the face matched the image. She smiled the first and probably the last smile of the day.

"Isn't that the bloody truth?" She was a local girl with a broad London accent and skin as black as charcoal. Her smile, once it formed, was infectious.

"Where are you flying to today...Mr Cade?"

"Australia."

"Nice. I must go one day. For now, I've only been to two places in my whole life, Nigeria and Heathrow!"

"Then you must make it a goal. You are in the right industry after all. Get a job as a flight attendant. You'd be ideal with that smile."

"Do you know what? I will do that. Thank you. You are the only person to actually treat me as a human today. Just hold on a minute, would you?"

He did. Checked his cell phone for messages and cleared some old ones.

John 'Jack' Cade – or as he was now more commonly known in the much-guarded inner circles as ex-Inspector Cade – Metropolitan Police.

An old colleague of the smaller force, further north in Nottingham that Cade had originally joined, had once said, 'There's no such rank as 'ex', Jack – when you leave, you leave.'

That colleague was correct, to a point. When you do finally decide to walk away, to leave the 'job' you sever all physical ties, but the job never really leaves you.

As he stood at the fourth check-in desk from the right at T3 on that bitterly frigid day he couldn't help but scan his surroundings, watching for the next available threat to form. He looked into the eyes of off-duty cops doing the same thing. He knew, they knew, no words said, it's how it was.

He was lost for a while, just people watching, wondering how the wonderful gift of global travel had become such an intrinsic part of terrorism and the similar valiant efforts to eradicate it.

Couldn't the bastards just let people get on with their daily lives?

The two men leaning against the pillar, one trying not to draw attention to himself, the other doing a better job. Law enforcement? Or goal-driven attackers just waiting for a window?

North African, at a guess. Wrong place, right time. Two uniformed and armed police staff were approaching them with the same thought, both ready to engage, the lead with his hand overtly on the handle of his Glock 17.

They were in their faces quickly, taking control, pointing to the ceiling, allowing their targets to know that they were being watched. Harmless pickpockets or anxious carriers of IEDs, they were a threat. Heathrow had a reputation to uphold. Cade was impressed with the response – or rather, the preventative approach to policing.

Damned if you do and a complaint if you did.

"Mr Cade?" Her voice was now like molten chocolate. Smooth and sweet, and it brought him back to the land of the present.

"Sorry, I was gone then. Too many late nights…" He lied.

He looked at her name badge, "Adaoma."

"I know that feeling. I was absolutely wasted last night. I really shouldn't drink when I am up so early. I really shouldn't." She yawned and favoured her eyes.

"Indeed. It gets to us all. Nice name, by the way. What does it mean?"

"Oh, thank you. It means virtuous…although between you and me." She bit her lip playfully, "I was *far* from virtuous last night – know what I mean?" Her laugh erupted and Cade couldn't help but join in.

"Best I don't comment then! You are however a very

lovely young lady and I thank you for making this part so much easier than normal. I wish I was twenty years younger! I may not be back for a while, so take care of Britain for me."

He slid his case onto the conveyor, tapping it for luck. The combination locks dialled in with his chosen number 0845 and a freshly attached bright orange sticker declaring it to be priority luggage.

"Have a good life Adaoma."

"You too Mr Cade, don't forget to turn left."

Her words were lost but as he walked away, into the growing crowd he looked at his boarding pass and smiled. Business class, on Emirates, London to Sydney. She was indeed virtuous.

He stopped at a café, ordered a coffee and a pan-au-chocolate and checked his phone once more. Three minutes later the coffee and pastry were on Adaoma's desk and Cade had made his way to departures.

As he queued at the aviation security screening point he felt different, not alone, just different. It took a while to reach the business end of the operation, as he slowly moved forward, emptying his pockets of loose change and other bits and pieces, whilst all around him people panicked over nail clippers and liquids, aerosols and gels. For years he had been on the other side of the fence – a watcher, an observer, looking for trouble. Now he was being observed, physically and via an all-seeing network of cameras and sensors and trying to avoid trouble.

He got through the whole process in minutes, avoided the 3D body scanner and the inquisitive blonde bloodhound with her hand held detector. He was through, technically off British soil, in limbo and now just like everyone else – waiting.

He stopped in the brightly lit duty free outlet and picked

up a bottle of Givenchy Neo – the tones suited him, mandarin and bergamot, not overly exuberant and on his skin it lasted at least long enough to be enjoyed by someone else, up close, personal.

He took an escalator up to the Emirates business lounge and having received a beaming smile from the concierge gravitated towards the most comfortable seats, grabbed an English Breakfast tea and a bowl of muesli with chopped fruit and then picked up the freshly folded copy of the *Daily Telegraph*.

The sports pages showed the usual mix of Premier League highs and lows. He noted that Leeds United had lost, again. Next season would be their year. The middle section was bolstered by equally positive and negative business news but a small headline on the front page, bottom right, turn of page, caught his eye.

Criminal leader escapes from Bulgarian Prison.

It was the type of headline that attracted Cade's attention – always the police officer. He was about to flick the page over to see what chaos page two brought when he halted and re-read the first line of the article.

Bulgarian authorities are hunting for the man they call the Jackdaw...

The last word hung on his lips like a cigarette clings to its host.

Cade picked his phone from his jacket pocket and pressed two.

"Jason. It's me. Our man has escaped." It was arctic cold. Both his voice and his demeanour.

He waited for the inevitable bout of non-diagnosed Tourette's-induced language, which never came. Instead there was silence, albeit Cade knew his former partner was still there, absorbing the information.

"Still there, mate?"

"Yep. Jesus Jack, they said he was inside for twenty years. He's got more bloody lives than my mother-in-law's ginger tom. How? Where?"

"Don't know the ins and outs mate but from what I read in the *Telegraph* he was en route from his usual suite at his favourite Cat A prison at Pazardzhik to the newer prison at Sofia when he escaped. That's pretty much all it says other than he was once Britain's most wanted criminal, etcetera."

"Just superb. You know what this means, don't you?" The younger and latterly Detective Chief Inspector Jason 'Ginger' Roberts sounded excited.

"No, Jason, I don't but I suspect I am about to be enlightened."

"It means the old team can re-form, because as sure as I can play the piano, he and his team will be out and about causing chaos and looking for revenge. He blamed us don't forget."

"He did, but he's a shrewd operator, Jas. He won't come anywhere near the UK."

"Maybe not, but with all your European connections you could lure him out, the sprat to catch the mackerel and all that."

"Jason it's been a few years since I worked in Europe, some of those connections will be long gone, and besides, unless it has escaped your attention I am no longer a police officer, for the Metropolitan Police or Interpol for that matter."

"Fair point. But surely you still harbour a grudge against him for what he did to Carrie and how he killed Clive back in 2004? I know I do."

"Perhaps, probably. But I have had to move on Jason, let sleeping dogs lie and all that. Right now I'm sat in the Emirates business class lounge and eventually heading to the Great Barrier Reef. I have a date with an old friend."

Roberts was distracted for a short moment, ever the excitable puppy, he wanted to know more.

"Ooh, pray do tell all to your old Uncle Jason."

"Should I trust you? Are you one of the six degrees of separation, Jason?"

"Jack. I thought we were lifelong buddies? Anyway, you told me it was seven degrees, just like I told you that the most powerful wave was actually the ninth, not the seventh."

"You didn't answer the question...buddy."

"Yes. You can always trust me."

"I know, it was rhetorical. Before I answer it, you must answer one for me. No, make that three."

"Go on."

"One. I know it was a while ago now, but do you think we ever got to the bottom of Operation Breaker? You know, who was who in that zoo and who we could trust?"

"No, but I wouldn't mind resurrecting it again, I'm bored Jack and I've got more staff now, some new really top-flight officers just looking for a project. Just say the word..."

"Thanks, agreed, there were too many loose ends. In the ten years I was away I never managed to figure out what was so important about the documents, what they meant, who had which copy and why – and above all who was set to gain from it. But I know they came for her in New Zealand and in turn that added me to their list of targets."

He stopped, cleared his mind.

"Two. Why are you wearing an orange shirt to work?"

Roberts had no idea how Cade did it. Someone must have sent him a text.

"It's tangerine."

Cade paused to listen to an announcement. "Jason, it's orange and I have to go, a fold-down bed and an endless supply of female international charm awaits me aboard an

Emirates flight to Dubai and Sydney. Those crew are dripping in expensive perfume and agendas. I'm a single man with needs. Be good and let's agree to stay in touch over these new developments. Ring me if you feel you need to. Oh, and ring JD – let him know, if he doesn't already. He likes to keep his finger on the pulse. And send my regards to Carrie, would you?"

"Sure, anything else whilst I'm at it boss?" Roberts was joking but could sense there was an unasked question. "Was there anything else before you lower yourself into the lap of a deliciously hot flight attendant, Mr Cade?"

"Of course, the most important question!"

"Oh, I'm all ears Jack."

"Can you play the piano now?"

"I can Jack, it's very much black and white now. Listen, fella, look after yourself and stay out of trouble." He was about to hang up when his own burning question resurfaced.

"Christ, Jack you almost got away with it, you cunning bastard."

Cade was smiling as he stood to walk to the gate lounge and step onto the A380 super jumbo to Dubai.

"Jason, do hurry up man, I'm about to board flight 007 – how cool is that?"

"Oh yes, very. Come on Jack, stop trying to deflect, who are you meeting and where?"

"I wondered how long it would take that eager mind of yours! I'm heading to Sydney and then north to the exquisitely beautiful Whitsunday Islands where I'm meeting an old friend."

"You said, although you didn't explain why, but I doubt you'll tell me, so I'll settle for who?"

Cade decided on the blunt approach. "Elena Petrova. Catch up soon my friend and don't forget to pick that jaw up off the deck..."

Before Roberts could respond Cade had cleared the line, switched to flight mode and walked along the air bridge, through the door of the Airbus and turned left.

"Welcome aboard Mr Cade may I get you a drink?"

The voice was soft but suggestive and Latin, possibly Spanish. Its owner was regulation slim, white teeth, tanned with a head of well-cut hair. Her badge said she spoke three languages.

"I'd like a twelve-year-old Aberfeldy, but I'm guessing that is pushing things a little?"

"Not at all. Ice? I'll be back shortly."

The flight attendant handed Cade his drink, smiled and tended to another passenger. She was as smouldering as the scotch and he struggled to take his eyes off her.

"Is there anything else, sir?"

"No, I'm fine thank you Sofia. But thank you for asking."

She spoke with her eyes. A subtle flick of the brow, three successive blinks. "My pleasure, have a lovely flight." She knew.

It was far too soon. 'Stop now, Jack – you need a break from chaos and pretty girls.' He laughed at the notion, remembering where he was heading and who he was going to meet.

For all of his talk about encouraging sleeping dogs to lie, Cade couldn't rest. Roberts was right. They needed to be ready.

Removing a small laptop from his carry-on luggage and accessing the free wi-fi on board, he began to type an email. It wasn't without risk, accessing what for all intents and purposes was an open network. If his enemies were on board the same aircraft, then good luck to them.

The email was addressed to Jason Roberts, John Daniel and the woman who had assured him that he could contact her day or night if the need arose: Sassy Lane, the Secretary of State for Foreign and Commonwealth Affairs – the message's prime target.

'In summary, ma'am, I need your complete support. We all know that Stefanescu still holds too many aces, that his team are diverse and mobile, and now, with what I perceive to be a credible threat, he has means and motivation. I don't know what that is yet, but he is out and on the run and if their operation is anything remotely like their last, it will be exponential and we need to be ahead of the game.'

He re-read what he had written so far,

'In closing, I need the following people to form a team in London, with your total backing, financially and otherwise. I will return to London from Australia as soon as I am able to, however, the meeting I intend to hold may just return one ace to our pack. I need this to remain close hold ma'am, if necessary at TS level, but at the least between myself, Jason Roberts, John Daniel, the Op Breaker team, including additions as I see fit, and finally, respectfully, yourself. No one else should be party to this. It is about trust.'

He re-read the message three times, altered one word, added a red exclamation mark, as much encryption as his simple system would allow, and finally hit send.

He got comfortable, created patterns in the condensation on his glass, emptied it, slipped on some noise cancelling headphones and decided to sleep on the first leg.

He was gone before the wheels were up and the aircraft slipped out of British airspace and headed across the English Channel.

CHAPTER THREE

IT WAS FIVE HOURS LATER, TWO-THIRDS OF THE WAY INTO the flight to Dubai that Cade woke. His headphones had done their job, shielding the incessant drone of the four massive engines that propelled the aircraft across Europe and toward the Middle East.

As he had many times before he found himself asking questions for which he simply had no answer.

He ran them through his mind. Many of them were subliminal – almost constantly gnawing at his subconscious. Ten years had lapsed since he first left his wife for a new and arguably more interesting life. He had no idea what Penny, his long-divorced first wife, was doing and frankly didn't care. He wished her no harm. When they had first met things were fine and he had to hold onto those thoughts alone. He had heard on the familial grapevine – one that he had tried to also divorce from – that she was doing well, running a team of men in a new business somewhere in the east Midlands. He laughed at the notion of her sleeping her way to the top. Of course she did. It was what she did best.

. . .

When Cade had left the Metropolitan Police for the first time, as a serving officer, he had vowed never to return, but time, place and circumstance all aligned to draw him back into the heart of one of the most dynamic cities on earth and if he was completely honest, he missed it – missed the chase. The bell curve of chaos and success since he had first arrived was alarming; exciting, but alarming. But with the right people supporting him and a few notable bosses leading the way he knew that he had made the right call.

However, he hated leaving with so much unfinished business at hand. He was given a subtle ultimatum, as subtle as being told he had a week to live and that 'sorry, the news should have been delivered seven days prior'.

He couldn't recall who had said it, but the words resonated.

'We feel that now is the time to leave London, Jack. For your sake and the sake of the organisation.'

His planets had become misaligned, Mercury and Venus at odds, and with his boss John Daniel offering wise counsel, he decided to make the professional leap of faith and head to Lyon, France where a liaison role at Interpol's prestige headquarters was waiting. His desk literally had his name on it. All he had to do was pack and go.

What happened in France – and where it took him over the subsequent years was a series of events all on their own, each separate and yet linked through their own varying degrees of separation.

Heading away happened – he felt he had no choice. But he did so not under a cloud but with the words of one or two of his most senior confidantes ringing in his ears.

'You can always come back. One day.'

· · ·

That was early 2005. It took the best part of six months to mourn the old life. He stayed religiously in touch with Roberts and Daniel and watched from afar how some notable figures from Operation Breaker had sorted their differences and gained a foothold on the ladder to success.

People like Johnathan Hewett – the devil-made-good of the British Foreign Office, and ironically the man Cade had to thank for his role in France. Cade never knew whether to trust him; call it male intuition, but the government did, and that appeared to reach ministerial level. What was good for the goose and all that. Hewett operated in a different world, one which was trying to keep pace with the global developments that looked likely to impact upon Britain. Cade considered him an equal, but knew he would never reach the same heady heights.

Where did Hewett sit on the ladder, near the bottom rung, able to reach out to help a friend, or perched perilously near the top where one reach too far would bring him crashing to the ground?

He made it look far too easy and had edged his way to the top, gaining ground and adding friends that he could influence and in turn could impact on his career. Had he got away with it or was he genuinely good at his job?

Then there was Stefan Stefanescu. Now there was an altogether different case. More twists than a cough candy and a love him/hate him aftertaste. He had appeared on the Op Breaker radar as the ruthless co-leader of the Seventh Wave criminal syndicate, and importantly, the brother of Alex Stefanescu – the Jackdaw – arguably Europe's most-wanted.

His degree of separation had become apparent when he had become the gamekeeper, having been a successful poacher for so long. He was now an ally, according to the British. So much of this was 'need to know' and Cade needed to know more than anyone else, for he held him accountable for so many deeds.

Blood was always thicker than water and when Cade had been lying on the coarse surface of a rural New Zealand road that fateful day, propping up his newly acquired girlfriend, stemming the flow of blood and praying for her salvation, he saw in her body language that Stefan was – by two degrees – responsible for her death.

Whilst no one had witnessed it, it was apparent that Stefan had been in the car that had deliberately caused her high-speed demise. He had walked up to its remains, held her wrist, feeling for a weakening pulse and had turned on his immaculate heels and left her to die.

He would later confess his horror at having to leave her – after all, he had said in a secretive 'trial', recognise it or not, she was technically his niece. He loved her. That fact has escaped many.

He argued and counter-argued that the initial crash was supposed to be a distraction, a chance to recover the documents that she was carrying and hopefully steer her back onto the right path, steer her away from the risks involved – to learn to trust him for the duration, as, he said, they had the same goal.

Her injuries were never meant to be.

He said, if anyone was prepared to listen, that if someone have been watching the incident, they would have seen him smile as he held her wrist, shed a tear, the pulse was weak, but she had a pulse and she had her mother's tenacity and he knew with help on the way that she would survive. That was the cause of his 'heartless smile'. He loved her. No matter what any court dare state.

Internal bleeding had nearly claimed her. She was pale, clammy and breathless before becoming unconscious. The inbound air ambulance – guided by the calm voice of an unknown British male – had found her in time.

He was right; she did have her mother's genes. And it looked as though the New Zealand authorities were quickly weighing up the severity of the crash, as flying below the bright red and yellow chopper that day was a dark grey one, approaching fast with men in the doorway. Like Cade, Stefan knew he had to leave the scene – and leave he did, but he saw them approaching, looked back in the tinted mirror of the Rolls Royce Wraith, the leviathan luxury car that carried them to Auckland, and its airport and separate seats on unconnected flights, home.

There was Sassy Lane and Michael Blake from the British Foreign Office. Surely, of all people, they were to be placed into the trustworthy pile? But whilst he found Lane to be good to her word, Blake concerned Cade on many fronts – he just wished he was able to prove his doubts. Something about leopards and spots, but without a reason to double check his reservations, he would have to wait.

The outstanding members of the Seventh Wave caused him little concern, so many years later they were memories, albeit a few were still capable of raining on his parade. However, the majority of the capable ones were either dead or in custody.

The man the Romanians called *Copil de umbra* – real name Valentin Niculcea, had practically disappeared off the face of the earth. He'd cashed in his IOU from the British, packed his meagre belongings and fled from the place he had called home in the provincial village of St Helene, France.

Submerged beneath the pack ice, no one knew where he might surfaced, but surface he would and he had promised Cade that in the event of him requiring his future services he only had to put an article on the Metropolitan Police website with his name in it – announce he was wanted. It really was that simple. And besides, it would make him smile. And that was a rare event.

Constantin Nicolescu: A name to genuinely strike fear into Cade's heart. He was the true wildcard. Not even Alex, his leader and ten year long source of income, trusted him. But then Alex trusted only one man.

Cade had feared that Nicolescu had surfaced in New Zealand, on that moderate left-hand bend. He couldn't prove it, but if instinct were to be followed it meant Nicolescu was alive – that his mistress heroin hadn't claimed him, and above all that whilst he was alive and anywhere near his loved ones, he was still a threat.

Cade's old employer knew this and put things in place to alert staff, but this was a man who feared only one thing – the hatred of his fellow human being, and that made him a tangible threat. Full stop.

This left two names. John Daniel, now retired and happily living on the Pacific coast of New Zealand, running a restaurant and living the proverbial dream. Cade had come to both trust and respect his old boss – but there was one question he had never got an answer for. Given the Breaker team's involvement in myriad crimes committed by the Seventh Wave, and the government insistence that the operation must come to an end, despite its growing success, did Daniel know more than he was prepared to divulge?

Was he still connected to the business-end of the Metropolitan Police? Did he know that Stefan Stefanescu was in-country in New Zealand and hunting for his own niece?

If he knew so much, could he have stopped the circus from coming to town? Or was he just the same as Cade, a pawn on a virtual chessboard?

Daniel had said once, during a frantic moment, that he knew where Cade was. He meant geographically.

He knew where Cade was. How?

He needed to ask him before too long, if indeed Daniel would ever answer such a set of questions. Had he been briefed higher up the chain? UK eyes only? Was it really that sensitive?

Was he part of the inner sanctum that knew the answers?

What stopped Cade from asking was a genuine friendship, and he valued that more than any answer. Yes, let sleeping dogs slumber. Let them be.

Elena Petrova was the last and always would be. She had arrived, not by chance into Cade's life, carrying a burden and a document or two, none of which made any sense and she had fought her battle with the Four Horsemen of the Apocalypse on that immaculate morning, in a fast car, on an isolated road in a far-flung country. And time would show that she had been the victor.

Where had she been in the time between, who had cared for her and where? How had they shielded the news of her survival from everyone? What was her role? Who was she?

As much as Cade had fallen for her. He had explored her from almost every angle, run his fingers through her glistening hair, lowered his lips onto hers, stared into her pristine eyes until they blurred and repeatedly felt her respond to him in a way no woman ever had. He was left with that one question though, and it haunted him. Not just the police officer in him, but the man.

Who was she?

She had more questions to face in two minutes than a Mastermind contestant. And it would be nowhere near as enjoyable as the past. He felt that those days, whilst sweet, were very short-lived indeed.

In twenty or so hours he might be able to ask her those questions himself. If indeed she was where she said she would be:

Catseye Lodge – Whitsunday Islands on the 17th January 2015.

He still had the note tucked into his wallet.

He had no idea where Catseye Lodge was until a rapid search of the internet had literally guided him up a quiet road on a pristine island off the coast of Queensland. The search had allowed him to drive up the road, scanning and zooming from the safety of his laptop until he found the white gates on a road called One Tree Hill. He could go no further than the gates as privacy rules prohibited such an intrusion, but what he saw were rooftops and palm trees and a location that quickly used up superlatives.

And blue sky, and blindingly white beaches.

The home he had observed on his screen was there, it existed. He felt uneasy about visiting alone and knew from research that the island had no regular police. It was very much a case of risk versus consequence. What was the worst that could happen? She could kill him with kindness.

Now that would make a fitting epitaph.

Here lies Jack Cade, eternally recovering from a night of lust.

He shook his head to clear the data from his short-term memory.

His itinerary was routine Cade: sensible and well-planned. He had no intention of wondering up One Tree Hill in a golf buggy − for that was the de rigour transport choice for the island, pressing a button and announcing his presence. That may have been the norm for a normal person, but to Cade it smacked of recklessness.

She had not contacted him to say she was alive. That, and that alone was the least she could have done. As pretty as she was, as captivated as he was, questions needed to be answered.

Day One on Australian soil was a stand down in Sydney. Darling Harbour, to be precise, a simple room in a nice hotel, with a very comfortable bed and a pool. He knew the perils of long-haul travel, and when he arrived in the islands, he knew he had to be on top of his game.

Day Two would be in Queensland, a meeting with an old colleague. Local knowledge didn't come any better.

Day Three would hopefully be an unannounced arrival into Hamilton Island and a chance to observe and counter-surveill before he pressed the button on that white gate with its stone pillars.

He closed his eyes once more, waking when the wheels of the A380 announced the arrival of flight 7 into Dubai. A few hours later he would be back on board the same aircraft and probably sat in the same seat. It gave him nearly seventeen hours to contemplate his future.

CHAPTER FOUR

New Zealand, twelve months earlier

"So gentlemen, you all know the drill? Any questions?"

There never were any. That was what training and the Seven Ps ensured – among other things, a lack of piss poor performance.

It was a pretty if not surprisingly cool morning at the defence force base twenty miles south of Auckland. Two Airbus NH90 helicopters, flown by the Royal New Zealand Air Force, were warmed up, checked, re-checked, loaded and ready to depart.

Their passengers, as was often the case for a small country which dutifully shared its defence responsibilities, weren't from the Air Force but from the New Zealand Army, specifically 1 NZSAS.

Two teams of five men, dressed in their choice of battle clothing and carrying what they needed as individuals, and as a group, carried out last-minute checks, waited for their

NCOs to join them and then one by one boarded the helicopters, took their places and watched as the ground left them behind.

Another day, another exercise.

Lifting quickly away from the base and out across country, flying low, their initial task would be to carry out live fire drills at a location only minutes away and then re-board, back to Papakura, their spiritual and regimental home, where there was an expectation that they would cause organised chaos at the Killing House and finally home in time for tea. No medals.

They carried out the initial phase three times before the helo headed south across the Coromandel Peninsula towards the Pacific Ocean. The briefing was clear; having been dropped off in the Pinnacles, a stunning range of mountains in the North Island, the team would carry out a speed march across terrain that for them was considered easy and later meet up with the RNZAF at a predetermined rendezvous.

In its day this area was renowned for logging and gold mining, the ground still full of the precious ore – but shrewdly left for future generations by its current guardians.

An average male could carry out the walk in two to three hours. The team were expected to march and reach their RV in half that. Hydration would be the key to setting a fast pace. They could eat like kings later.

'Feint heart never won fair lady gents' – the words of the operation commander. Like its closely held ally, the British SAS, the local regiment guarded its operations, equipment and men with a vigour displayed by organisations that could be counted on the fingers of one hand. But what it prized more than anything was its reputation.

'It's all about doing it well and safely these days, gents. Let's not forget the latter in this wonderfully PC world in which we now find ourselves. As much as I fucking adore you bunch of losers I do not wish to mislay any of you, nor do I expect to find the slightest hint of what looks like paperwork on my desk this evening. Safe journey, see you at the debrief. End of friendly and loving chat.'

The teams knew each other intimately – in that they had got naked, fought alongside each other, got so pissed they couldn't stand and knew that when it counted they could reach out in a smoke-filled room and find their teammate waiting. It was a loyalty rarely experienced by the average man – or woman.

Scott McCall was one of those men. Now nearly thirty-seven he had been an almost stereotypical failure at school, however, when it came to self-preservation and tactical thinking he was as bright as the buttons on his regimental tunic that shone on the day he had passed out as an Infantryman.

Over the next four years he did what he was told, when he was told. He jumped when asked. Not for him the life of a basic soldier. He applied for and qualified as a member of D Squadron (Commando) as soon as they had been heralded as New Zealand's domestic counter terrorist force. Its new badge attracted him, in part due to his Scottish and Maori origins – black, with silver ferns; at its centre a taiaha, a famed Maori close quarter weapon positioned in what was known as popotahi or 'ready to strike'. That appealed to him enormously. And he appealed to the army as a future leader.

He worked hard, striving for the front but never aspired to the headier heights of a commission. He wanted to remain a warrior, not someone bound to an office by virtue of their success.

He served the unit well and when he applied for the next logical step – the Special Air Service – no one was surprised. That he qualified joint third was even less of a shock.

As one of their youngest ever members, he relished the role and acquitted himself well as a quiet man, physically fit, known for staying out of trouble, making his ancestors and his father proud. He had achieved the rank of corporal and that suited him and his career path.

Like any man, he had a weakness. It wasn't women, although it needed to be said that with his ever-tanned skin, taut body, thick head of coal-black hair and bitter chocolate eyes, in this branch of humanity he never struggled. The mystique of whether he served in such an elite unit was justification enough for a night of physical and breath-taking sex. There was always a girl hanging around a bar somewhere nearby. It seemed he just needed to ask.

He didn't need drugs – despised them. His job provided adrenaline in super tanker loads and he had seen the damage caused among his community and his family by the myriad commodities available to the buyer with the correct amount of money. Gambling was a fool's game. He had no mortgage, for he had no home, he had a car but it was basic. Why attract attention? He had good clothes and a nice watch, but the unit provided the latter, and if it got broken, they would just supply another.

What he had, what he valued more than anything else, were three sisters who he adored and protected. There was nothing they couldn't or should not ask for. When their father had passed away, he had become the de facto head of the family and that suited him greatly.

He was rarely more than half an hour away from them; the exception being when he was deployed overseas.

Heading away to fight for the people of another land in 2002, he had made a promise to return. Aroha, Mary and the youngest and prettiest, Kora prayed each night that he would come home, alive.

It was in Paktia Province, Afghanistan, that Scott McCall first came to the attention of the elite.

Special Forces teams from around the world had combined their might and training as part of Operation Anaconda. McCall was the first to volunteer to support the operation in any way he could. He saw it as a chance for a nation to recover its identity, and for a man who came from a mixed marriage, he understood that better than most.

What he saw scarred him. It scared him too but he never once stopped to think of himself, carrying colleagues in conditions that the man in the street would simply refuse to tolerate. Like many he was affected for the rest of his life, but he sheltered his memories from everyone, including the doctors.

Life in the McCall family home had become financially untenable when Peter McCall had passed away. He worried not for his son – he was a survivor, but his daughters struggled, without their mother who had died young; living together in one basic home, on basic wages in a rapidly growing city where property prices were ever increasing and not far from the place that would become their big brothers' military base.

McCall had the answer, and it was simple. Cashing in his stability as a means to an end. Selling his financial soul to the devil was how he saw it. His credit rating was high, and he took out the first credit card to pay for a memorable Christmas. By the second he had five, all to their limit, so he took out a loan and between the family members only one person knew how desperate things were.

Legitimate loans became a thing of the past. Interest rates rose as leaches drank the last dollar from the McCall home. At thirty-seven he was broke and almost suicidal with worry.

All he had to do was discuss things with his welfare officer and a plan could be created to help – the regiment protected its own. But he had his pride, and besides, the current situation was just another bridge to cross, and that's what a member of the finest regiment in the country did each and every day.

'Just another bridge, Scottie.'

He had decided to sever links with the army as soon as he could. His thinking was becoming irrational. He needed to earn more to clear the debt and dishonour. As heart breaking as it was, there was a way. His skills and courage could help. He could offer a service to the local criminal gangs, or travel overseas and earn three times what he owed, just by looking after some faceless billionaire or his wife or her kids. But a hundred thousand was a lot of money in any currency. There had to be a faster way.

He hated his thoughts that intruded upon his every waking moment. Work was the rare exception where he could escape.

On board the NH90, he stared down at his beloved Aotearoa – the land of the long white cloud. She was without a doubt the most beautiful place on earth. He'd fought for her and her people. He felt he was owed his pride at the very least. There had to be a better way than living day to day watching the interest outstrip the original loan.

As the helicopter landed he had reverted to professional mode and was already out on the ground, sweeping the terrain, guiding his men towards their first target. It was easier than reality.

He was accurate with all of his weapons, seeing them as an extension of his own body. He could fire and reload whilst most of his peers, equally experienced soldiers, were still clearing their magazines.

An hour and twenty minutes later he had driven them as hard as he dare, setting a record back to the rendezvous. Moments later the first of the NH90s appeared and McCall ushered the team on board.

Text book.

He checked his weapons and his favoured possession, a knife. Double-edged it was ever-honed, and he had a reputation with it that earned him his nickname – Mack – for no one was known by their real name in the regiment. That much the general public was allowed to know.

They gained height before the pilot dropped down the valley heading south east for State Highway 25A. The plan was to take a fast horseshoe detour across the terrain, back towards the Firth of Thames and home. It was a great experience for the aircrew to hug the land and trees, to almost feel them brushing against the fuselage.

As they began to bank and follow the highway McCall's attention was drawn to the presence of a red and yellow MBB-Kawasaki twin-engine helicopter approaching their airspace quickly and reducing altitude.

"You see him, Tommy?" McCall was scanning the ground with a pair of Fujinon gyro binoculars.

The younger air force pilot had seen the other aircraft long before McCall but he appreciated the extra sets of eyes. He tilted their larger aircraft for a better view and went into a circular search pattern.

"Copy. It's Westpac Rescue. Thanks, Mack. Looks like he's heading down there..."

The two crews spoke to each other via their open comms. It transpired that the rescue team was heading for a critically injured occupant of a car that had rolled on the main road below them.

"Westpac One, Westpac One, this is call sign Zulu One-Four."

"Zulu One-Four, this is Westpac One. Go ahead, sir. We have you in visual."

"Received. You have priority, however, can we be of assistance? We have three experienced but woefully under-employed defence medics on board."

"Received, thank you. Driver is believed to be status one. We are looking for a decent landing spot. Terrain looks a little hostile for us. Closest ground medics are fifty minutes south and nearest LZ for us is half a K away, and the road is not an option – looks like my passengers are going to be walking. However, if you can support any quicker than us, then yes, we would be grateful. Over."

"Received, Westpac One. We will see if we can assist and locate a place for you to land, worse case we'll leave it with you."

The pilot turned to his colleague, then took another look at the terrain.

"Not happening. We'll leave it to them."

McCall shuffled forwards in the Air Force machine.

"Tommy, worse case that could be one of ours down there. It's a good experience for all of us. Get it down onto the road, just to the right there." His leather-gloved finger was pointing. "Come on, brother, are you man or mouse? I thought you guys were the elite?"

"Mack. Need I remind you that this is an eighty million dollar aircraft? When it comes to report-writing, I'm more cute little rodent than man. And I'm not biting onto your elite hook."

McCall was persistent. "There's a patrol vehicle arriving. He'll soon get the message if I start waving at him. Come on, Tommy, live a little. Go home knowing you have made a difference. Actually earn a bloody medal for once, eh?"

McCall knew it would grate. They'd served in a few places together and the comment, although light-hearted, hit home.

"For Christ's sake, Mack, you'll be the death of me."

"And she could be dead before any of us get to her."

"She?"

"Yes she, I can see her through these quite clearly. Could be your kid-sister. One of the most attractive blood-soaked arms I've ever seen."

Flight Lieutenant Tom Maynard was regretting the moment he lifted off from his temporary base. The team he was working with always caused him issues – but they were so damned infectious in their enthusiasm – for everything.

"My kid sister doesn't drive a Porsche. But you get your wish. If this gets out, I will never speak to any of you again. Clear?"

"Crystal. If it gets out, you'll always get a job in the army – we are always on the lookout for cooks and storemen..." McCall winked at the co-pilot who couldn't help smile.

This was wrong on so many levels, and they all knew it.

The NH90s second-in-command came from a long line of military personnel, one of whom had saved lives in the United Kingdom at a commercial airliner crash on a major motorway. He told the story only once. By the time conventional medics had arrived, those that would survive were evident, as opposed to those that weren't. Simply marking their foreheads was enough to prolong the lives of men, women and children.

Pilot Officer Michelle Best looked across at her boss.

If all they could do was land next to that road, administer some morphine and 'Foxtrot Oscar' then their day would have improved.

She switched the radio channel so that only she and her boss could communicate and spoke in a clipped tone.

"Come on, boss. What's eighty million between friends?"

The NH90 landed in a hail of dust, but well clear of the road. It was a landing the rescue team on board the civilian aircraft were unprepared to risk, but one the military made on a regular basis after risk assessing the ground, adopting a hover and allowing staff to leave by jumping or roping down. They even had a winch if things got really complicated. Risks were risks. Both crews respected each other's abilities in this area.

The first two military staff were running to the vehicle, the third towards the Highway Patrol officer who was doing his best to triage on his own. He had already closed his lane down and an approaching logging truck driver had seen the issue and used his vehicle to close the northbound lane.

"Where the bloody hell did you lot come from?" The question was yelled over the whine from the engine of the impressive grey helicopter to his right. The boy in blue to the dark-haired, brown-eyed man in green.

McCall put a strong gloved-hand on the officer's shoulder.

"Sent by the man upstairs brother, sent by God. One of my team will help you wave at traffic."

They shook hands.

"Jeff. Good to meet you."

"Nice to meet you, Jeff. Any ETA for a ground ambulance or fire brigade?"

"I've been here as long as you mate. You look like you know what you are doing. I'll leave that bit with you. I've updated my comms as best I can. I'm on my own here, nearest back up is at least half an hour away. I'll start getting some cones out and grabbing some imagery, looks serious, not much I can do for the poor girl. She's unresponsive."

"Roger that. Do me a favour chief?"

The patrol officer was already jogging away. "Go ahead."

"Keep your camera stowed until we've gone?"

The longer hair, the three-day growth, the lack of a name and the quality of his kit should have been the clue. They were all the same. They looked physically different too. And confident beyond the norm. He smiled and tapped the front pocket of his body armour.

"Staying right here. Right here."

With a thumbs up, McCall joined his team.

"Well?"

"Well, she's pretty boss. And pretty fucked if I'm honest, she's not heading in the right direction that's for sure. And the car stinks of smoke."

"Nothing? No signs? You sure?" He knew the stench of black powder emanated from the multiple airbags.

McCall was the most experienced medic on the team having been there, done that and got more than a few T-shirts. He quickly took control.

"Tell the helo we won't be long. We achieve miracles in five minutes or we bugger off. Five OK? No longer."

He started the timer on his green-strapped G-Shock and dropped to the ground and pulled himself into what was left of the car. The build quality of the German coupe was renowned, but the structural integrity had been fully tested when it had rolled repeatedly. The cabin was in complete disarray, as cabins of vehicles always are after a high speed, violent collision. Once neatly stowed, here and there, possessions now littered the furthest reaches, stained roof linings and ripped and shredded flesh. There was a smell familiar to him.

He grunted and twisted until he was face to face with the woman.

His teammate was right, she was striking; covered in blood and dust and pale-faced fear, she was quite the most beautiful woman he had ever seen.

"Now then my lovely, how did you end up like this, eh? You must have a pulse somewhere. I know you can hear me. So it's time to get a little personal. No offence, miss."

He ran his fingers across a number of points on her body where he knew he could find a pulse. The carotid was made difficult by her position, on her side with her head tilted, a few attempts were futile. The radial was non-existent. She was bent awkwardly, so the abdominal aorta was equally pointless as an indicator of life.

"Apologies love, I normally like a bit of foreplay – and prefer for my girlfriends to be conscious..."

He lifted her dress and cut through her underwear.

He pressed the middle finger of his left hand onto the femoral vein and closed his eyes. Waited.

"Come on...come on." He blanked everything else out of his mind. "There!"

He wiped a swab across her skin and then another over his hands, then called out to his teammate.

"Green needle and morphine."

He knew there was no way he could or should move her. With time against him and her awkward position he could be causing myriad other problems, but for now he could just keep her from entering through the proverbial Pearly Gates and having a chat about graciousness.

The large needle entered her body and propelled the pain-killing drug straight into her veins. Dark red blood seeped back into the syringe. He extracted it slowly and pushed his finger onto the exit wound.

"A plaster if you would be so kind."

He held the adhesive in place and waited with her, twisted, trying to maintain his own comfort whilst he watched for a signal from her unconscious body. And there it was. This girl was a fighter.

And she had heard everything for the second time that day. She would remember his voice anywhere, as sweet as Manuka honey.

"OK, my lovely. Whoever you are, hopefully that will allow you to fight another day." He checked his watch then ran his hand along her left arm, partly to comfort, partly to see if she had a significant other. It was wrong, but what an introduction it would make when he visited her in hospital.

"Hi. I'm the dark knight that saved you..."

What he found in her left hand was a folded piece of paper, four sheets to be accurate. The back was blood-smeared and almost glued to her fingers. This thing was important, that much was clear.

She heard every word.

She held onto the paper, as if her life depended upon it.

She had sought it out with her bruised and bloodied fingertips; through rapidly closing eyes and the vice-like grip of death, she had found it.

And she heard the new voice – his expression was so calm, polished, reassuring. So very close. His breath upon her eyes. He even reeked of confidence.

She felt his solid hands upon her, touching her, pressing, hunting for a sign of life, then pulling at the paper until it was gone. Her lashes knitted together once more than she slipped further into the void. His voice would remain one that she would remember for a lifetime.

. . .

He prized the document from her hand and unfolded it. A quick scan stopped him in his tracks. What was this report and why was a woman in her twenties on a deserted New Zealand road holding it? And what was its real value?

It was at that moment that Sergeant Scott McCall, New Zealand Special Air Service, chose to sacrifice all to protect his sisters.

He saw the value of what the girl held, saw it in any currency. He just needed to find a buyer and the first clue was in the name on the top right, written in smudged graphite.

Jackdaw.

'I have no idea who you are Mr J but we need to talk. I need to find you.'

He turned his head from side to side looking for other evidence. He was now damned if he did and damned if he didn't. Hung for a sheep as a lamb, or whatever his father used to say.

McCall re-folded the papers and placed them into his cargo pocket, taking care to close the seams tightly. He regretted it already.

"For the girls. No other reason, Scottie." His words hung in the air, mixing with the diminishing stench of black powder, cooling liquids and blood.

He started to extricate himself. He was shuffling across her body and back out onto the road when she shuddered – not awake but now further from death than she had been.

"Jack!"

And she was gone again. Unconscious, but breathing.

He had no idea who Jack was, but McCall considered him a lucky man. Somehow he couldn't correlate Jack and Jackdaw. Were they one and the same?

"I'm going now, miss. You'll be just fine." He paused,

knowing that his inbuilt morality had collapsed for the first time in his life. He held her cold hand for a second.

"I'm sorry, miss. Truly."

The Westpac medics arrived at the scene and were quickly briefed by McCall's team.

"Looks like the boss has got her stable. Bloody hero, as usual."

The comparatively young trooper smiled, slapped the medic on the back and said, "Leave it with you, mate. We have places to go and maidens to seduce."

He yelled to McCall, "Five!"

His wrist throbbed gently, his watch reminding him that time was indeed up.

In five minutes the helicopter had landed on rough terrain and its occupants had stabilised a complete stranger. Saved her, possibly. As they gained height and turned away McCall felt nauseous. It wasn't from the visual disturbances created by the aircraft, the torque or impending sickness.

What he held in his pocket disturbed him greatly.

His father would hate him for betraying his integrity – but he would understand. Wouldn't he?

It was for the girls.

'And that made it acceptable', he whispered to no one but himself, staring down at the ground that blurred as the helicopter gained altitude.

Within the hour the rescue helicopter had arrived at Middlemore Hospital, south of Auckland. It was used to dealing with almost everything when it came to trauma.

The Emergency Department doctor took one look at her and raised his eyebrows. He knew.

"Did you do this?" Looking at the paramedics.

"Partially, yes. But she had some help from a guardian angel who happened to be passing by."

"Then she's a very lucky girl. Who is she?"

"Now that's more difficult. No one has a clue."

CHAPTER FIVE

Nottingham, England, 14th January 2015

"Name?"

"Mr Lee?"

"And do you have a first name, Mr Lee?"

"Yes."

"And what are the chances of you divulging this today?"

"I have no idea what that word means."

"Do you understand what the word enlighten means?"

"No, sir. I don't."

"Right. What about 'the truth'?"

As tempted as he was David Beggs was bound by the rules and knew, like any other custody sergeant in the United Kingdom police that the Police and Criminal Evidence Act had been created to protect both him and his many customers.

He recalled with fondness how things used to be. Sat there on an elevated stool, looking down on the man placed before him by a pair of battle-hardened constables, who were now wishing they had never met the aforementioned Mr Lee.

Beggs took a long considered swig of his dark brown, twice-heated tea, placed the mug back onto the heavily stained cardboard coaster and started again.

"OK. This is how it's going to be Patrick. My name is Sergeant Beggs. I'm the custody sergeant. What I say goes."

"So you're the boss man?"

"That's right. Over everyone else in this building, my love."

"So you can get me a cup of that tea if I asked nicely?"

"I could."

"And will you be doing?"

"I might."

It was going to be a long night.

The male in Cell Two shifted, tossed and turned and cursed the moment they had closed the door loudly behind him. The pale green plastic mattress that lay on the concrete plinth, that just about warranted the term bed was the most uncomfortable thing he had laid on since his time in a mainstream British prison. In comparison to this place, HMP Wormwood Scrubs seemed more like the Hilton.

He despised everything around him. Everyone. Except his fellow prisoner. He knew there was an order, a scalar chain of command in any custody area. He looked through the edge of the steel spy-hole that separated him from the relative space and sanity of the custody area.

This new man, standing at the sergeant's desk, trying his best to manipulate him. He was no stranger to a cell or a prison. It bled out of every pore.

Five foot eight, medium build but with broad shoulders

and broader fists. His red-and-white checked, long sleeve shirt hid a forest of self-made tattoos and scars. His black business trousers, slightly too long, seems worn away, draped over a pair of working boots and held in place by a brown leather belt, made larger over the years. Hair, thick, golden-red like a freshly harvested corn field and a face that could tell a hundred stories, some of which were questionably true.

It was said that the eyes were the window to the soul. Patrick Lee's were deep green and smiling. But they were a long way from Ireland and hadn't seen the truth in years.

The caged tiger in Cell Two walked another circuit. He wiped a smear of blood from his nostrils. He should have been quicker. The drunk had reacted quicker than he expected. But then any man would have done if he knew that what followed was to be his last hour on earth.

The tiger had no idea what time it was, nor did he care. Where he was heading time was his greatest enemy. Boredom his nemesis. If they didn't have a library he had decided to end his life. It was easier. Without study, without knowledge, or the very limited friendship of one specific person, his life was pointless. He no longer needed the mind-altering drugs of his past, what he needed was freedom, and right now, on whatever day of the week it was, wherever he was, in the middle of England they held the key.

If he was unable to get away, then he would slowly saw through his wrists with the sharpest-edged implement he could find.

At the custody desk Patrick Lee looked up at his keeper and waited for the next question, whilst his two captors looked overtly at their watches and calculated whether their day had been ruined, or fortuitously that their bank balance was about to be enhanced. A cunning overtime plan, one of them called it. And if PC Tris Robertson had his way, every arrest would be on the last day of his working week, a few hours before he was due to head home; for an arrest at the eleventh hour rewarded in so many ways.

Arrests on the last day of seven similar shifts were the very best, the most lucrative. Tomorrow a new team would be on duty with its own agendas and characters. They would have their own arrests and issues to contend with.

For the ever-jovial Robertson, this arrest had been different.

The very last thing he wanted was to spend hour after futile hour trying to identify a member of the travelling community. Some called them gypsies, or diddicoys, others less-favourable names. He often used a fishing analogy when describing his many interactions with the humble gypsy. He found, for professional reasons, that it was more convenient.

'Now squire, envisage catching a magnificent salmon? Indeed. Now, imagine when the silver beast approaches from the depths, towards the shores, and you learn with some amount of horror that it is in fact an eel...absolutely! A bloody eel, messing up your tackle, twisting and turning, trying to get off the hook. That there is your humble traveller. The most slippery eel of all.'

It made sense to anyone gifted with the powers of a constable. Sometimes it was just better to let them go – let them off the hook. But Lee was different. He had a few warrants in his name and Robertson and his partner Phil Brown knew that if they played their cards correctly, they could be home within the hour, having accrued four hours overtime. All they had to do was correctly identify their man.

And that task was often not as easy as it sounded for the honourable non-gypsies, or gorgers as they were known among the travelling community.

It was Beggs's turn to try again.

"Right, Mr Lee. It's time to play again. Do you have a date of birth and an address?"

"I was born on a Wednesday if that helps?"

"Oh, it does. Enormously." Sarcasm was Beggs's strongest suit.

"But as for an address. I move around a lot, wherever the mood or the work takes me. I'm a traveller, sergeant, not settled like your good self. A free spirit. A true Romany." Lee had a strong Irish accent and yet neither Beggs nor Robertson were confident that he had ever set foot in the Emerald Isle.

"So we are saying no fixed abode then Patrick?"

"If that means what I think it means. Yes."

Beggs rubbed his eyes. As the custody sergeant of the Meadows Police Station, in the southern half of the city of Nottingham, things were always busy. It was just varying degrees of busy.

Familiar excrement – alternate day.

He took another sip of his now-cold tea.

"OK fella, last chance. What is your date of birth?"

"I'm twelve and so is me, father!" It was a joke, but Beggs had lost his sense of humour.

"Mr Lee you are detained for the purposes of executing these warrants. Someone from the Metropolitan Police will come and fetch you tomorrow and you can be out of my hair. Sleep well. Cell Two, please gents and don't give him a bloody cup of tea until he confesses to everything."

"As is your wish, sergeant." Robertson looked at his

colleague and tapping his wallet, winked. "Home in time to imbibe a refreshing and delicious ale, I do believe?"

Lee was remonstrating as Robertson guided him robustly towards his bed for the night.

"He said he was going to execute me!"

"Yes, he did. But not until the morning. He drew the long straw. I was gutted. Anyway, here we are sir, the canal-view suite awaits. I shall try to rustle up a frozen sandwich from the last millennium. Don't forget to swipe your rewards card before you leave us. Thank you for choosing the Nottinghamshire Constabulary, we do appreciate you have a choice."

Lee stopped as they got to the cell door. It was quite common. If he was going to fight, it was now. The final frontier.

He leant towards the officer who was now visibly backed up by his colleague.

Whispering, his index finger subconsciously shielding his words, he said, "I have something to tell you."

"Oh, do please tell. Is it the lottery numbers? Or my fortune? I bought some lucky heather from one of your team once, did bugger all to improve my life or luck. And the pegs were no better. This had better be good. I am all ears."

"I'm not from around here." Lee opened with this and continued with an equally ambiguous, "But I know lots of people."

Brown countered with, "Absolutely fascinating, Mr Lee. Goodnight."

The door was opened with an impressively large steel key as Robertson and his long-term colleague guided Lee into the darkened space.

Lee braced himself against the doorframe and looked up

at the taller officer. Now he was belligerent and stronger than any ox.

"I *need* to tell you something. It's important. I have to tell you before I go back to prison." He was hissing his words, spittle landing on Robertson's black body armour.

"Mr Lee, can this wait until the morning?"

"No, sir. It cannot."

He exhaled. "Go on. Do enlighten me."

"That means tell. Your man there said it earlier. I learn quickly. I may not be able to read or write, but I'm not stupid. Would you agree?"

"Oh, I would. I am so glad you told me this. Goodnight."

"No! Stop. That was not it. I know about a job that is going to happen in London, soon. If I tell you, will you let me go?"

"No. I can't do that. Now, if you wish to tell me all about this mythical job, then I am still all ears...if not..."

"No, it's fine. I'm not going to be treated like an idiot. If Mr Roberts hears about this, he'll be furious."

Robertson looked at Brown. There was a chance of some overtime here. Brown nodded. Ever the Yorkshireman, he knew that the age-old saying about pennies and pounds was eternal. Out of sight of Lee, but in his mate's peripheral vision, he did a little jig and rubbed his large hands together.

He was due to retire soon, like many of his colleagues he'd served the public well, and thirty years had passed 'like that'. He had a brother in the adjoining force. Similar build and length of service. His hair wasn't a patch on his luxuriant main. And Phil was the better looking of the two. Naturally. And in his eyes he had joined the better force.

Nottinghamshire was one of those provincial forces that had a reputation borne out of sheer bloody-mindedness and hard work.

His had been a great career, he'd joined the force when it

was still allowed to be called one, back in the late seventies. He'd lived through the strikes and the massive changes and had enjoyed every day. He was a little broader nowadays. His once-immaculate black hair, which he convinced the girls was from his Italian heritage, was also now a little thinner. A few grey companions to their black neighbours, here and more often there. But his eyes still smiled, and he was a good cop and a better person. Always.

However, things were changing, society, and with it policing too. He could no longer live in the past, but for now he may as well make hay whilst the sun still shone.

His slightly younger partner was about to close the cell door for the night, turn the solid metal handle, twice checking it was closed, peer through the spyhole, dim the lights and head home. But the similarity to his own name piqued his interest. After all, what was another hour at double time and an extra day off?

"And why would this legendary Mr Roberts be furious?"

"Because I am his informant."

"So he's a police officer?"

"The top man. Scotland Yard."

"Impressive. And what exactly do you want to tell him?"

"DCI Roberts always lets me go. It's the arrangement we have. We both win that way."

"Well, the Nottinghamshire Constabulary does not work like that Mr Lee, we have standards you see. Best I ring your Mr Roberts and ask his opinion. Is there a broad theme to your information? Or is it just a medley of lies and betrayal?"

"There is and unless I receive the emancipation that I seek, then this conversation is over."

"Crikey. Less than an hour in our custody and Bob Marley is channelling through your Irish blood. I'll go and hunt down your DCI, but he will not be happy being rung at this hour, I'm sure."

"Oh, he will be. Trust me?"

"As far as I could throw you."

Lee, a career criminal, knew when to call it a day. If the copper was good to his word, then he would ring Roberts. All he could do now was lay down and wait at the end of what had been a long day. He was hungry but first things first. He unzipped his jeans and guided the hot, dark-yellow, pent-up and odorous urine into the basic stainless steel toilet.

Leaning against the green-painted block wall with his left hand he finished his task with the other, shook it vigorously until the last drop fell into the utilitarian bowl and then turning, as he put his pride and joy away, introduced himself to his cellmate.

He held out his hand, "Patrick Lee. And what would you be in for?"

The male leaned forward slightly but refused to shake the offered hand.

"Did your mother not teach you to wash your hands afterwards?"

The voice was unusual, European, slightly rasping, his words passing over fractured teeth and arid lips.

"I never met her, I'm sorry, I didn't catch your name."

The face moved into the available light.

"My name is not important."

"My uncle is the tenth richest man in England. My name is Patrick Lee and I am *very* important."

"I know you told me and I heard the sergeant talking to you. Now, if we are going to get along you really need to improve your game Mr Lee."

Heavily accented, morose, angry.

They would get along fine, or Lee would quietly throttle

him in the cell whilst everyone else slept, and then claim, in a sweat-stained panic that he has been attacked by the foreign maniac, just as he had the last time that Mr Roberts had come to his aid – negotiating with a judge, stating in no uncertain terms just what a valuable resource Lee was to the Metropolitan Police.

But he knew it would be a long night without another word said, so he tried again, ever the talker – he had the genetic gift of the gab.

"So, are you a Romany like me, my friend?"

His voice filled the room from the dark recess of the bottom bunk. "We are all gypsies in the end, Patrick. I am descended from the travelling peoples of the North Indian Subcontinent and yes, my way of life and my work means I have to keep moving, either that or the xenophobic hatred tracks me down, time and time again. You will say we are alike, as I sense the gypsy in you too. The only difference is I made something of myself and you are just a thug."

Lee sniffed through a twice-broken nose. His Irish accent now more evident. "Is that so? Well, you don't look that bloody successful roight now, Mr feckin' Romany. You know I've punched people in the mouth for less than that!"

"Of course you have. But please, don't do that to me or I will end up sliding bits of your anatomy under the door to feed the other zoo animals." He rolled his sleeves up, deliberately, one turn at a time.

"You appear to be confusing your brute strength with my wisdom."

Lee would normally follow through on his threats. He was, it was said, afraid of only one woman and one man, and that was, in turn, his mother and God. He was a proud individual with a long family history and a reputation as a member of the British bare knuckle fighting circuit. But this man was different and Lee feared his voice and he feared what he saw.

"So, you see my tattoo and things change? Interesting, then it would appear that the people I work with have at least gained some respect among your community." He then just as carefully rolled the sleeves down again, taking time to fasten the buttons, just so.

"OK. To show I am a man of honour, I will tell you my name. I am Constantin Nicolescu – son of Nicolae and a proud Romanian. I am, as you saw, a member of the group known as the Seventh Wave. Our leader..."

"Jackdaw?"

"Ah, his reputation really does precede him I see. Yes, to you Jackdaw, but to me, one of his most loyal soldiers he is Mr Alex Stefanescu – quite simply the brightest star in a galaxy of criminals."

"Yes, his name is known throughout our community from Eastern Europe to England – as far as Appleby Horse Fair. OK, so I'm impressed and not a little shit scared. To be honest, I didn't realise." Lee was on edge. It wasn't the man in front of him that concerned him. He could deal with him with one punch.

"Oh, you didn't realise and of course that makes all the difference. I should allow you to allow yourself to be strangled by me, slowly, until you beg for forgiveness, your eyes bulging with fear. But that would be most boring. You see, when I kill people Mr Lee, I do it in such a way as to make even experienced police officers vomit. Or I destroy the body with chemicals, or even better, explosives. Simple. Understand?"

Lee nodded.

"A hundred Euro would enable me to track down your family and kill them one by one. Burn them alive, smother them with acid, cut pieces off their helpless bodies and bury them in a hundred different places. Each day posting a piece to you, until you get the hint. I could fill their homes with poisonous gas, use chemicals to disfigure them, so bad not even the rescuers would bother to save them. Should I continue?"

"OK, OK, so you have my feckin' attention. What do you want?"

"Good. Now, I need you to do something for me."

Constantin outlined his intentions over the course of two minutes. Slowly, deliberately, and with no margin for ambiguity.

"No. I am not prepared to do that. Mr Roberts has been good to me over the years. Call it honour between men."

"He is a police officer, Patrick. And members of the travelling community do not trust them, and they do not trust you. But you pretend he is your friend?"

"I didn't say he was my friend, I said he had been good to me. There is a difference. I always get what I need from him."

"I am glad to hear this. Any moment now that kind police officer is going to come back here and ask you to accompany him to a phone. You ask your charitable police friend to carry out my request or there will be a hundred Euro note with you family's name written across it."

The cell hatch opened.

"Mr Lee. Turns out you do have friends in high places after all. Step back as I open the door. You OK, look like you've seen a ghost?"

"No officer, not at all. I'm fine. Your man here was showing me his tattoo. That's all. I'll be fine. Take me to the phone, please."

CHAPTER SIX

LEE PICKED UP THE PHONE, ITS HANDSET WAS HELD together with a grubby wrapping of sticky tape.

"Hello."

"Patrick, it's DCI Roberts." He vigorously rubbed the substance of the day from his red-rimmed eyes. "What's happening up there?"

"I got picked up on a warrant boss. My own fault, I should have given false details and prayed that the coppers wouldn't suss me."

"Why change the habit of a lifetime?"

"Fair point. Look boss, I've gotta get out of this place. You know how they screw me up. I need to go, now..."

Roberts sensed an urgency in Lee's voice, one he wasn't used to.

"You OK Paddy?"

"Other than being in custody and facing a few months in the big house, yeah, I'm absolutely fine."

"Alright, well, for the record, I asked. Now, what have got to tell me? Make it good and I'll see what I can do for you. No promises Paddy. You understand?"

"I understand, sir. You've always been straight with me."

He started whispering, turning his back on the custody staff. He cleared his throat as he watched a drunk being wheeled into the waiting area, Lee could smell the alcohol from where he was stood.

"Mr Roberts, I've heard something big is going to happen in your city. Our city. It's big, bloody big. Almost unbelievable."

"Well Paddy, on average half of everything you tell me is a lie and the remaining fifty percent is dubious so this had better be good." Roberts took a sip of a lukewarm coffee and sent a rapid text message to his wife.

It's me. I'm going to be late. Sorry.

Patrick Lee had spent his entire criminal career balancing the truth with its direct opposite, of living in a sterile cell and constantly moving on, of dealing with the xenophobia and hatred and of knowing that people disbelieved him, even, on the rare occasions that he was actually telling the truth.

He knew even now that Roberts wouldn't believe him.

"Mr Roberts, I heard that a group of men are going to hit London hard. The banks probably, but there was something else." It was his opening gambit, and so far the police officer hadn't stopped him in his tracks.

Roberts looked at his watch, working out how long the casual chat with one of his longest-running informants might take, and how long the drive home would be – finally coming to the conclusion it might be better to sleep in the office. The black leather chair had accommodated a few of his predecessors over the years. It was looking promising.

He leant back as far as he could and placed his gleaming leather-soled shoes onto the desk. "Do go on."

"The team is Eastern European." Roberts felt the hook, the industrially honed barb. Ten years, maybe longer since he had last felt the reaction deep inside his stomach. He ran his fingers across his forearm, stopping to favour a dark red scar, a reminder of the shattered bones that once lay beneath, a legacy of being chained to a cold metal pole, deep underground in the capital.

"Bastards."

"Sorry?"

"Forget it, just talking out loud. Keep talking, tell me what you know."

"So you are interested?" Lee's hopes were building. Perhaps he might soon see the kids and their mother after all.

"Yes. But I need detail."

"Well, I heard a man talking about the tower and jewels." As he uttered the words, they sounded ludicrous. No one would believe him.

"A tower or *the* Tower? If it's the latter, you know this sounds ludicrous, don't you? Repeat what you heard. Slowly."

"I understand. I surely do sir yes, but you have my word, he said the Jewel of London – the safest place in the capital. And that means the Crown Jewels. The Queen's stuff. Doesn't it?"

"Yes, Paddy, I know who bloody owns them! But they've been secure for hundreds of years. Not since your Irish brother Thomas Blood tried to steal them in the sixteen hundreds has anyone had a proper go. And he was as much use as a chocolate poker."

Roberts knew that the Crown Jewels were the most protected pieces of metal and glass on the planet. Bombproof glass, sensors, locks the size of a small country and hundreds of CCTV cameras, constantly monitored by the Tower Guard. It was nonsense. In situ, now in the Jewel House, they had remained within the Tower since the thirteen hundreds. Moved twice, cleaned regularly, admired by millions, valued almost beyond belief and never stolen.

"Look, you said the Tower, then you said the Jewel of London. What exactly did *he* say? Think, man."

"Look Mr Roberts, it's been days since I slept properly, these bastards have given me a half-cooked frozen meat pie and a cup of tea with nowhere near enough sugar in it. And to cap it all, I haven't had a shit since Wednesday. Do you know how that feels? You should try it sometime."

The detective chief inspector was tired too, but he acknowledged that at least he got to go home.

"OK Paddy, what's it to be. The Tower or the Jewel? Or would you settle for a shit?"

They both laughed, the ice was broken.

"The Jewel. He said the Jewel and OK, I probably put two and two together and came up with four, which is pretty good for someone who never went to school."

They both laughed again. "Patrick Lee, you are a bloody nightmare my son. Leave this with me and I'll do my best to get you out by the morning. Worst case, I'll send a few of my lads up to collect you and bring you home rather than sticking you in a prison van. Deal?"

"You have yourself a deal, boss. Sleep well, regards to Mrs Roberts. She's a lovely lady."

He'd met her in the street with Roberts once. Soho. October, it was raining, which meant the meeting was thankfully short. He was right; she was lovely, the silver-tongued bastard.

"She misses you daily. Sleep well too, do avail yourself of the facilities before it's too late and kindly put the nice constable back on the phone, I need to have a little chat with him, you know, sort out your little problems as always."

"Thank you, sir. I owe you."

Lee handed the phone to Robertson, who had been indiscreet in his eavesdropping. He wiped the mouthpiece with the edge of his police sweater and spoke.

"Sir, PC Robertson, how may I help?"

"Is that lying bastard still stood near you?"

"Yes."

"Get him back to his cell. I'll hold."

Roberts took a second to look around the office, once the home of his great friend John Daniel, retired chief inspector and the man considered responsible for putting him on the police map. He began to pick the pointless white bits from under his fingernails, place them onto his lips and fire them around the room, each time seeing how far he could reach.

"Sir."

Roberts sat up so quickly the seat nearly toppled.

"Do go ahead, my son, tell me about Lee, what has he been saying and what are the chances of getting him out on bail for me, Pray tell. I am like Dumbo...all ears."

"He's been alright to deal with, to be fair, no different to the usual run-of-the-mill traveller. Demanding, demonstrative, loud, and unbelievable. Literally, unbelievable. He was OK actually, mentioned you as I was bedding him down for the night. He looked like he had seen a ghost. As I brought him to you he mentioned something about the other lad in his call, about a wave and how he wanted to move cells?"

Roberts stood up. The room closed in. He fixed his gaze on a team photo, a long-forgotten image of his initial training.

"A wave? Right, stop. Slow down, go over what he said. Word for word."

Robertson uttered the words so slowly they were in

danger of appearing sarcastic. But he sensed their importance.

Roberts continued. "I hear you. Who is his cell mate?"

"Hang on, I'll read his name to you." He nodded to the custody record, sat with a pile of others. Slipped the phone onto his shoulder and leafed through a few bits of paper.

"Here we go. His name is Constantin…"

"Nicolescu?"

"Yes, boss. Spot on. How did you know?"

"I didn't but there's only one Constant in my life and his name ends in Nicolescu. Bastard smashed my forearm with the sole of his boot. Left me to die on a tube train a few years ago."

"Nice. I'll get that added to his custody record." Robertson slid the creased paperwork across the desk and nodded to his multi-tasking custody sergeant who leant across and wrote 'Monitor regularly/assaults police' in black biro before slipping it back into the pile ready for the morning shift.

"I don't swear often, but you watch him like a fucking hawk or he'll escape. Do I make myself clear?"

"Crystal boss."

"Why is he in custody?"

"Fighting, well to be technically correct, aggravated burglary. Nearby flat about half a mile from here. Ex-soldier lives there, bit of a drunk, often talks about the old days and how he helped us to do our jobs. Problem is boss, this place we call our professional home is so full of Walter Mitty characters that you literally couldn't make it up."

He laughed a tired laugh. "I bet. But I am one hundred percent interested."

"Your man travelled up to our patch from London, apparently. Some score to settle from the past. Out on bail, unbelievable given what he said he'd been banged up for?

Magistrates these days will believe anything. Said he wanted to rid his past of a witness – something like that, I can't really understand what he is rambling on about. Talked about killing Francis so that all the loose ends were neatly tied. Asked to make a call to a female called Thomas and has refused to eat. I suspect he's on the gear, heroin at a guess. He looks like a living skeleton."

The line was quiet. "You still there boss?"

He was.

"I am. What's your first name?"

"Tris."

"Well Tris, if you've got a few minutes I'll tell you a story. It all starts a long, long time ago in a place called Kent."

Roberts outlined the Op Breaker days, how Constantin had become the unchained assassin for Alex Stefanescu and how, even ten-plus years later, the past still haunted the Breaker team and its members, who had dwindled, one at a time. Three dead now, all apparently unconnected, but none considered routine.

"And Mr Cade is still with you?"

"No, sadly not. He's from your force, as I mentioned, but we didn't hold it against him. He's currently somewhere at thirty thousand feet chatting up a cabin crew member, having become a consultant to the British government."

"Very nice. Good to hear your story boss, but respectfully it's time for me to call it a day. Anything else you need from me?"

"No Tris, I think we are done." There was something, but it wouldn't gel. He was about to say goodbye when he looked back at the ceremonial picture of himself from his training days, resplendent in the dark blue uniform, boots shined to within an inch of their lives. The whole future ahead of him.

"Francis?" He paused. "Francis?" He said it again, and

then the light became illuminated. The scorched photograph in what was left of dear old Edward Francis' home, all those years ago. The terraced family home in north Kent, decimated by what first appeared to be an accidental gas explosion.

"Just before you go. And bear with me, Tris. Your aggravated burglary victim. He's not called Dave Francis, is he?"

"Yes, as it happens. Your intuition is spellbinding, sir. Any chance you know this week's lottery numbers?"

"No. And call me Jason. Just bear with me one more second." He ran the ideas around in his head. "Have you got Mr Francis' phone number?"

"I have. Would you like it?"

"No, I need you to ring him. I'll hold. Ask him what is father's name is – and importantly if he knows a man called Jack Cade."

"As you wish, sir. I'll put you on hold, apologies for the brutal lift music."

The phone rang six times. An old Blackberry, barely able to operate now, given to him by Jack Cade at a time when discretion was the better part of valour. Cade had paid for its upkeep, too. A real gent, that one. Even through the haze of an alcohol-fuelled decade he had kept it charged, just in case. He may have been a drunk, but he was a disciplined one.

Francis shuffled barefoot across the sparse lounge floor and looked at the display. It was late. He really couldn't be bothered to field some annoying bloody insurance call. But his analytical mind couldn't allow the 'Caller withheld' to pass by unchallenged, and besides, no one ever rang him on this phone. He pressed the green button.

"Yes?"

"Mr Francis? Please don't hang up. It's PC Robertson from the Meadows Police. How are you feeling?"

"Bit late for a welfare call. What do you need?" Once the tactical operator, always the tactical operator.

"I'll cut to the chase. I've got a DCI from the Met Police on hold. I've been talking to him about the man that broke into your place tonight. I have two seemingly random questions for you if I may?"

"You may." He tipped the scotch down the tarnished steel sink and eased the cold tap on decanting water into the glass. He needed to drink more of this and less of that.

"OK. What is your father's name?"

It stopped him in his tracks. His hand shook subtly, spilling some of the water.

"Was. Past tense Constable. He's dead. Died in an explosion in Kent. 2004. Edward Francis. Second question?"

"Do you know anyone called Jack Cade?"

He tipped the water down the plughole and with his right hand opened and poured a double from a supermarket red-labelled bottle.

"Now there's a name from the past. He was one of yours. The only one I ever trusted, present company excepted. What's the connection?"

"I have no idea, sir, but I'll try to find out. Stand by."

Robertson picked up the desk phone.

"OK boss, or should I say Jason? His dad was called Edward Francis, dead now..."

"Died in an explosion. Kent. 2004. Go on."

"And, yes, he knows your Mr Cade."

"A classic case of six degrees of separation, Tris. I've still got it." He clicked his fingers together. "And I have never lost it!"

Roberts knew more about Dave Francis than most people. Cade had talked about him fondly, and his skills as a thoroughly trained intelligence officer, and importantly how he had salvaged Cade's early career. And he knew that if

Constantin had managed to track him down, he was vulnerable. His stomach twisted like a wet flannel. His intuition was calling out from the rooftops of London.

'They are back.'

"Boss, what do I tell David? He wants to know what the connection is between Constantin and his old man – Edward Francis."

"That's simple. Tell him he is. And tell him to pack his bags, tip away that cheap scotch and get to your place. In fact, get someone to fetch him. Keep him away from Constantin Nicolescu at all costs, issue him with a travel warrant, and put him on the first available train to London. Tell him he's employed again."

"As you wish, sir. I'll let the duty inspector know we might have a guest overnight who isn't in our custody. Oh, and one last thing, Patrick Lee mentioned the female called Thomas? In case you've forgotten? Seemed important."

"It is, more than you'll ever know. Thanks mate, I owe you one. Goodnight."

"Before you go boss...what about Lee?"

"See if you can bail him to me, would you? If not, stick him in a van with the rest of them, he's come up with a priceless story that holds no water with me. But I suggest you segregate him from his cell mate or one of them will end up dead."

"Good talking to you sir, sleep well." He took the last words of the faceless, but pleasant voice at face value.

"Tris, I've changed my mind. Hold Francis there, somewhere secure. I'll send a car first thing. Don't let him out of your sight."

Robertson still took the comment about Lee and his cell mate as a joke – a tired one but not one to be taken seriously. He opened the pale green, graffiti-laden door and guided Lee back into the cell where his companion for the night was already sound asleep.

"Please, sir." He hissed his plea to a weary police officer, wanting nothing more than a quiet ride home and his wife and his bed. Preferably in that order.

Now Lee was desperate. Laying what he considered a royal flush onto the card table.

"But he said the tide will turn."

"Did he? That's grand. You'll be fine. Go on."

"He said the bird has flown the nest!"

"Marvellous. I hope he has a wonderful time. I need to fly as well or Mrs Robertson will see to it that the door to her veritable bodily paradise is forever locked."

The door closed with its familiar metallic thud, the steel handle confirmed the lock was in place for the night and with a gentle tap on the door Robertson walked to the plywood radio cabinet, slipped his Motorola into the slot marked twenty-four and headed for the locker room.

"See you in four days, Sarge!"

Constantin smiled in the darkened room. He could hear the English traveller's heart beating. Lee thought they were connected, drawn together by their ancestry, felt that their origins would protect him. He was wrong.

Lee failed to sleep for a moment, he spent most of the night leaning against the cell door, whilst on the worn green plastic mattress next to him Constantin slept like a baby. Tomorrow would be a new day and Constantin was quietly optimistic about it – in fact he couldn't wait.

A few hundred miles south Roberts grabbed a pen and piece of paper and made a brief things-to-do list before he could drive the equally quiet commute, back to the edge of

London and home. It was late, and he needed to be as sharp as one of Carrie O'Shea's pencils the following day. The list was interspersed with bullet points and arrows and inane late-night doodles, but the importance was paramount.

He rested the silver-barrelled pen on the paper, then started writing.

Ring Lucy Thomas.
Ring Carrie O'Shea.
Sort out Francis.
Ring Jack.
Sleep!

He switched the office light to off, closed the door and headed for the stairs, wearily walked down to the ground floor, so tired he misjudged a few steps, left the building and slumped into his car.

Late night music guided him north. He missed most of the familiar landmarks, only realising so when he pulled onto the drive of his comfortable suburban home. He leant back into the driver's seat and let the last lines of the familiar song wash over him, exhaled, exited the car and walked towards his front door.

Tomorrow would be a long day. Tomorrow, for Detective Chief Inspector Jason Roberts was now less than ten minutes away.

CHAPTER SEVEN

Scotland Yard, London, 15th January

ROBERTS WAS BACK IN HIS OFFICE, FIRST THING, DRESSED to kill in a blue suit, pink shirt and navy tie with pink dots, Armani belt and an oversized watch. His black shoes were as shiny as they were the day he had joined the police.

'Says a lot about a man,' a chief inspector had once said to Roberts and his intake at Hendon Police Training College. It was a phrase mirrored across England and Wales, at a time when the UK police forces still had regional training centres.

Roberts adjusted his tie, wiped the top of his shoes across the back of his trousers and walked from his office to the briefing room. The Ops Centre of Scotland Yard had never lost touch with the operation known as Breaker, its people had just moved on, to new pastures, new hunting grounds.

Breaker was now a perennial business as usual operation for the Metropolitan Police, rolled out quickly when the slightest hint of financial crime was so much as murmured in the great banks and trade centres in arguably the most important centre for monetary trade on the planet.

Syndicates from across Europe had continued to target the UK – there were so many possible targets and countless victims and the methods of operation had grown, become viral, to the point where now even the big four banks were having to share data and intelligence with the police, UK Border Force and the Inland Revenue. An act hitherto unheard of.

If Breaker staff weren't looking at financial crime and its perpetrators, it was short-term secondments to support other units – firearms the week before, Albanians the week before that, Yardies two months prior. Their ability to support and confront criminal entities was becoming legendary, backed up by the recently formed Specialist Crime and Operations team known as SCO19.

Roberts' unit were, what the Met called, a Tactical team – able to deploy to a problem. Their reputation had also grown. But not without cost. The memorial wall was growing and Roberts needed to contain the activity in that area, where and whenever he could.

At the heart of all criminality as money. Follow that and you couldn't go far wrong. 'Show me the money' was a by-line for the team.

"Morning, you retched shower! No, please don't stand. No, seriously, how are we all?"

Roberts' people were sacrosanct as far as he was concerned. No one touched them, not unless they had gone to or through him first. And that was why his team was the one everyone wanted to join. Young, upwardly mobile detectives, through to pre-retirement old-school officers that still had a passion for doing the job well, they all wanted to get into the hearts and minds of the public via their targeting of criminal syndicates.

The team had come a long way since they had been rapidly established under the guidance of a northerner, Jack Cade and the debonair and highly respected boss called John Daniel, who had since retired for a better life, running his restaurant in a terribly picturesque part of New Zealand.

Roberts often harked back to those days but knew that the past had to remain there – nevertheless no one could take the experience away from them. He realised that his team has learned it in bucket loads from Cade and Daniel. And now, there was a whisper on the floor that Cade might one day return.

"Right, let's start this off with the quiz." Roberts had commenced each shift in this way, along with copious amounts of tea – and the right biscuit – since he had taken over. The junior staff member fired up the computer and projected the questions up onto the screen. Fifteen questions and no less than one hundred percent was expected. Occasionally, if they really put their heads together, they scored ten.

"Question One: Where does Saddam Hussein keep his spices?"

The team had heard it before but allowed their leader to regale them with his punchline.

"In Iraq!"

A collective groan ensued.

"In a rack. You see, it's a play on words?"

He knew. They knew.

The usual sarcastic cheer erupted, followed by a down to business attitude that epitomised the group. In charge and always leading, with a subtly-hardened edge since the days he had been brutally assaulted on an underground train was Roberts – stood at the front of the room scanning for alertness and ready to throw out a series of questions, not unlike his fabled science teacher Mr. Walton.

He cast an eye over the room, quickly conducting a head count. He did this every morning, the mother hen making sure that all her chicks had come home to roost.

Cynthia Bell wasn't there that morning. Her usual diligent activities included taking notes and analysing as she did best, and she was always first in. She had been with Roberts since day one and was arguably one of the best analysts in the business, let alone the police. She had a soft spot for Roberts that was never sexual, and so they got along like the best of siblings – and he protected her from all types of harm – and with his wife's blessing.

He made a note to check where she was. She had no discernible family. Doctors probably, but she was never ill.

Carrie O'Shea entered the room eating a croissant and drinking a takeaway black coffee from across the road, her favourite haunt since Cade had forced her there years before. Her hair had grown slightly, she'd long favoured the shorter cut but had lost interest when she knew her and Cade would never amount to anything. She could always hope.

The gym had become her saviour, that and long walks through the city she adored, often by night. There wasn't a corner she didn't know. If Cynthia Bell was the Princess of Data, then O'Shea was the Queen of All She Surveyed.

It had taken her years to recover from the attack that had almost claimed her life. Cade and Roberts and a twist of fate had saved her. Her stubbornness, too. However, her obstinate approach to Cade also saw him make a decision to move on, leaving her in his wake, drowning. She had been given an olive branch but had snapped it in two. A move she regretted every day she woke and stared down onto the Old Queen Street mews, where she still lived a fortified lifestyle and from where she had once dragged a surprisingly-hesitant Cade upstairs to her bedroom.

Nil carborundum desperandum. Wasn't that what Cade had said once over coffee, that morning that she was thinking of leaving the Yard?

God, she missed him.

"You're alive then, Carrie? I tried ringing last night."

"No, boss I'm a fucking mirage. Course I'm alive. Living the dream me."

He whispered, "Alex has escaped from a Bulgarian prison. Stay closely in touch with me day and night. Any issues, we get you into protective custody – no exceptions. It will all blow over, but for now, we take no chances. Understood?"

"Boss." She understood implicitly.

It was standing room only on an already busy morning. Twelve more detectives had joined the team. Four had left – policing was like that, cycling and recycling. If you stayed around for a while, the same faces re-emerged. Roberts' favourite Detective Dave Williams had also endured since day one; now one of the three team leaders, he had seen many changes but leapt out of bed every day, trying to make a difference. He had three more years before retirement and refused to be one of those staff that equated that to thirty-six more pay days. Retirement would surely follow, but for now Williams was fit and healthy and as far as he was concerned, the moment he gave it all up would be the start of his demise.

Roberts had a vacancy for a detective inspector and was eying up the potential among his three detective sergeants, two males and a female, and two were ferociously competitive. Williams had been up front, 'I'm happy with my lot. It's not for me governor, but thank you. Let one of the other two have a go.'

The first was DS Nick Fisher. Fisher was the nearest thing to permanent heart failure for Roberts and the previous six managers that he had all but broken. What Fisher didn't know about tactical policing wasn't worth knowing. He'd started in the West Midlands Police when that force was still trying to rebuild its reputation, following the dissolution of the Serious Crime Squad and the media frenzy that surrounded its demise.

A devout Lancastrian, Fisher had been a Royal Marine, short term, but the beret and the esprit de corps had never left him. He was what even his dear mother called a hard bastard. Brilliant and inquisitive blue eyes that wouldn't have been out of place in a falcon, scanned and watched for the slightest sign of weakness, but they smiled too and his sense of humour was legendary. Sharper than the proverbial axe.

He had a sense of purpose that saw him walk from A to B in a stance that meant he leant forward a few degrees, as if doing so would mean he reached his destination quicker than anyone else. He said he kept his hair deliberately short and what he had was greying-blond. His face was a roadmap, formed by the stories of his life and its resultant pressures; what he hadn't done to get a conviction – all above board – was hardly worthy of note.

He dressed well, never afraid to be bold, and had remained devoutly single. There had been plenty of women, two at once on one memorable night in the Balearics, but that was another story.

He knew that he needed to leave the Midlands force and had headed south, making a new name for himself in the overt world of crime squads and firearms. The greatest challenge for Roberts was restraining what Fisher called professional swearing. He struggled to rein in the expletives at the best of times, but when the clock was ticking and the end in sight it was akin to being in a Bangkok brothel when the US Sixth Fleet had arrived in town. If he didn't know a swear word he would make one up and they were often interspersed with real words.

His briefings were a challenge. His briefings to command were a bloody nightmare. And yet when in front of command or politicians, or once a delightful female Secretary of State, he was as eloquent as the next man. He had a switch did Nicholas Joseph Fisher, a pity no one knew where it was.

He'd used the middle name Joe many times as an alias – always use something real in your cover story. He had once even called himself Joe D'Etalle – a tweak of the law enforcement term Joey Details or false names. Whatever he did, he did well and his team would follow him to the ends of the earth. In his direct opposite, he had an equal. And he loved her, but had never summoned up the courage to tell her. Never could. Never would.

DS Bridie McGee was also a career police officer. Contrary to her name she had been born and bred in south Yorkshire and had joined the police pretty much straight after attending Canterbury University, in a city she grew to love, the home of the famous cathedral, inside a walled citadel, a place of pilgrimage and her home for three years.

She had studied English and had fallen in love with study. Like Fisher, she had met a few people that she had been attracted to, one or two had made it to her bedroom, but she was always waiting for the right partner to come along. Married, for a short time and soon divorced, she became wed to her job.

She was captivatingly pretty, in a girl next door way – but that somehow made her even more attractive to Fisher.

Short-haired, she had a perfectly rounded face and a smile that could light up the moon. It was her eyes though that were her primary weapon and she could melt him from across a room with a sideways glance or a deliberate look. Their eyes darted back and forth at every opportunity but not once had anyone noticed.

She felt the same about Fisher. Those looks were not for anyone else. But she sensed a feeling that she would never truly get to know him – unless she left her current husband and he, the job.

"Bridie, you and Team One have a new job. I need you to get out on the ground, talk to the homeless and find out what they know about Eastern Europeans."

"Yes, guv. A question if I may." Her Yorkshire accent had softened but was always evident, especially when she became animated.

"Go ahead."

She leant forward slightly. "Is anyone actually collecting intel on this group, or are you still bearing a grudge from years ago?"

It was a fair question given the lower volume of ATM and point of sale attacks. A few amateur gas attacks had happened further north, and in one case a team of Irish travellers from a nearby site had literally dragged a bank machine from the wall of a post office in rural Derbyshire. They would spend days trying to cut it open and all for a few thousand pounds.

"Bit of both Bridie. On one hand, I will never stop hunting them down, on the other we've had a little bit of detail late last night when you were tucked up in your deluxe goose down duvet with Mr McGee."

"Care to elaborate boss?" It was Fisher.

"No. What DS McGee and her husband get up to in their own home is their business."

"I meant…"

"I know what you meant Nick, keep what's left of your hair on. No, I can't. Not yet. Needless to say, things might change. In fact Nick, get out in a car with Bridie will you, go and lift a few cardboard cities, turn over a few moist blankets, offer a few quid here and there."

"You said moist boss. Fucking disgusting."

"Get out DS Fisher and take the lovely Mrs M with you. And when you get back, come and see me before you go off duty. We need to talk. Both of you."

"Guv." It was the standard ending to any directive.

They quickly briefed each of their teams, then headed to the Scotland Yard car park to collect a pool vehicle. Another year and the iconic police building would be gone, sold to the highest bidder for upmarket accommodation. Someone in Abu Dhabi had considered it a snip at three hundred and seventy million.

Roberts walked back towards his office, bumping into Liz Staveley, the executive assistant.

"Elizabeth, you are looking rather scrumptious today! Lovely dress!"

"Thank you, sir. Tea is it, and a gingernut?"

"Piss off Liz, I was being nice. Look you haven't heard from Cynthia, have you?"

"No, sorry. Do you want me to check the duties?"

"Please. Let me know sharpish. Not like her."

"You worried boss?"

"Quietly Lizzie, yes. Call it male intuition."

Ten and a half thousand miles away, Cade had touched down in Sydney. It was a city he liked very much. Laid back but cosmopolitan enough to be trendy and dynamic.

His taxi took him the more interesting way from Kingsford Smith Airport to Darling Harbour. The cab pulled into the foyer area and the jovial Somali driver lifted Cade's luggage out and shook his hand, taking more cash than he asked for. He had been polite and interesting. His life story, condensed into a twenty five minute ride had been enough to convert into a thriller. Two bachelors' degrees and an enquiring mind should never have been captaining a cab around one of the great cities.

Cade walked through the blue-glass rotating doors into reception. The Sofitel had been recommended by his friend and mentor, John Daniel. The staff were discreet, polite, professional and across both genders, attractive. That explained one reason JD favoured the place.

The receptionist looked up, in her thirties at the most, a typical Aussie stereotype – fit, evidently healthy and attractive. Her name was Issy.

"Good afternoon, Issy. Jack Cade, one night in one of your harbour view rooms. How's your day going?"

"Welcome to the Sofitel Mr Cade. My day is good thanks. Started with a swim and a surf. How much better could it get?"

"Lucky thing. Mine has been a hellishly long flight from London, but at least it's a tad warmer here! How's the pool today?"

"Warm and inviting." She flashed another smile as she processed his room details and took a copy of his passport. No wedding or engagement ring. Tanned. Toned. Stop it Cade.

"Great, then with your blessing I'll be in there in half an hour!"

"I'd join you, but the manager wouldn't be impressed!"

"Haha I bet. Tell him it's all part of the customer service."

"It's a her, and best not. And she's definitely not your type. Nor mine."

"Oh. Point taken. Your secret is safe with me." She was lovely. The last time he had flirted with a hotel employee, she'd also had blonde hair and Irish eyes. He wondered how Elizabeth Delaney was and whether she had ever looked out from Room Eight in the same way.

"Oh sorry, I forgot to mention, I have a guest later on. Can you get a message to me when she arrives?"

"Sure. Do you want us to make up the room for two people?"

He smiled. Or was she offering to stay the night?

"No, sadly not Isabel. She's an old acquaintance. But I will be using the restaurant, could you book me a table for two? With a view?"

"I can. Consider it done. There's your room cards. You have a Luxury room with harbour views as requested. Enjoy the bath. And it's Israel." Blonde hair, brown eyes and a triathlete's body.

"Dad, serve in the Middle East?"

"Nope." She smiled and closed the guest folder, her attention drawn to a newly arrived couple. "Hello, my name is Issy. Welcome to the Sofitel."

Clever girl had left him wanting more.

He declined the porter and headed to his room, flashed the card against the door and walked in, searched every part of the space he would call home for the night, checked the bathroom, the back of the door, opened the fridge, opened the complimentary spring water and stood for a moment admiring the view as he emptied the bottle and dropped it in the bin. Around the corner was the bathroom, with a bath, big enough for two, overlooking the harbour. If only.

Fifteen minutes later he was unpacked and laying a blue and white striped towel on a sun lounger next to the infinity pool. The air temperature was still in the late twenties. It felt wonderful when he plunged beneath its cooling surface and swam up to the wall where he breathed in the panoramic view of one of the world's great harbours.

The air bubbles were fizzing around his tired body as he lowered himself below the water and sat on the bottom for a while, exhaling slowly.

In a few hours, he'd get ready to meet an old friend.

In London, Liz Staveley walked from her office to Roberts' larger home from home.

"Boss, I know it's early but you got me thinking about Cynthia. I don't think she's had a day off sick or otherwise since I've worked here. Does Carrie know anything?"

"No. She said she thought she seemed fine. Nothing out of the ordinary. Busy, but then we all are. I'll try ringing again. Get Carrie, would you?"

O'Shea arrived, a light tap on Roberts' door, and she was in, dropping her takeaway cup into his bin and pointing to a chair.

"Yes, grab a seat, mate. I may need your help. Got a funny feeling." He dialled, tucking the phone receiver into his jawline. Answerphone.

"Cynthia darling. It's your boss here. We are a bit worried about you. If you have run off with an Arab sheik, that's fine but can you send me a postcard. It's still early, so you may surface yet. Ring me. Jason."

"Couldn't you have just asked her to ring you?"

"I guess." He looked at her, and she picked up on his concern.

"What is it, Jason? Talk to me."

"Shut the door."

Sitting again, she said, "Go on..."

"I didn't want to alarm you, but I spoke to a snout of mine last night. I've worked him for years. A traveller who I first locked up in my probationary days. He's given me some A1 intelligence over the years and since I registered him he's come good on many an occasion."

"And?"

Roberts exhaled slowly. "And late last night he rang from a custody suite in Nottingham. He'd been locked up for some nonsense bloody crime and started throwing my name around like confetti. That was fine, but it was what he said me that stopped me in my tracks."

Roberts outlined what he had been told.

O'Shea's face paled. An altogether wonderful time had passed since she had heard the names. She felt her stomach knot and her fists clench. She gripped hold of her own hand and squeezed until her knuckles whitened.

"You OK?"

"No. But I'll be fine. So what's this about the tower?

"I have no idea, Carrie. I think it's a red herring. But I can't afford to discount it either. My waters tell me there will be action in this fair city any day now and my betting head says its ten to one, odds on that a man with a black tattoo is involved. It's been way too quiet. It's also been a bloody long time since we locked them up Carrie and retribution can be sweet and apparently best served cold."

"You think they would come for us?"

"No, not at all." He wasn't convincing. "But I wouldn't be surprised if they take another pop at our banks. They've moved on since then, smarter, more techno, and with Alex Stefanescu at the helm they could really be looking to make their mark among the other criminal syndicates in town." He realised what he had just announced.

"He's out?" O'Shea's simple words were cold and demanded an answer. "Why didn't you..."

Roberts raised a hand. "Because you didn't need to know until we confirmed it. Jack spotted a headline in the bloody newspaper of all places. Said he'd escaped whilst being moved from one prison to another. Bulgarian authorities were hunting for him, he's using a network of associates etcetera."

"And what does Jack think about it?"

"He thinks it's all a cover. Thinks our man Jackdaw was causing so many issues inside that it was easier to just open the back door and let him walk."

"Never. No government would sign off on that."

"Wouldn't they?" He rubbed his face, removing the last of the night's sleep from his eyes.

A hundred and twenty miles north, the Meadows Police Station custody area was beehive-like; staff arriving, staff leaving, sergeants handing over the bountiful captures from the night shifts, working out who could deal with who and who got the short straw – normally a stolen car full of juveniles who knew more about the law than their captors.

Breakfasts, of sorts, were offered along with the standard 'builder's' teas – of milk and as many sugars as could be immersed into the stewed liquid being presented with glee to the waiting criminal guests.

Constantin Nicolescu looked at his cellmate.

"You know what to do?"

"I do, but I don't want to do it Mr Nicolescu. I'll be in more bloody trouble than I am already in."

"No, you will not. It seems that you have friends in low places."

With the handover almost complete, the night shift sergeant made sure that his replacement knew where the worst of the worst were held, who was staying, who was leaving and whether there were any medical or suicidal cases that needed attention. Then he clicked save, then restart and began to think about the joys of sinking into a warm bed when everyone else was begrudgingly heading to work.

"Usual cocktail of society's finest. We've got two banged up together, both travellers, make sure you get the right bloody one – you know how devious they can be."

"Takes a clever bastard to get one over on me, mate."

"Indeed. I'm just saying be careful." He pointed to the screen with the end of a well-chewed biro. "Now, one is heading to court here, the other to London, on bail after some DCI from the Met intervened last night and managed to convince Dave Beggs to talk to our inspector. I've got a travel warrant sorted so he can catch the train straight there. Oh, and we've also got another overnighter, not in custody, in a side office for his own safety apparently, being collected by some Met staff. All very hush-hush. Best you don't ask. Right, any questions?" He was almost through the door.

"None."

"Right, Mr Lee. I am Sergeant Farmer. I can see with that injury to your mouth you are struggling to talk. I don't suppose you want to tell me how it happened?"

Lee shook his head.

"Fair enough. I'm flat out busy with a full house and five juveniles in a stolen car who I could do with you giving a good talking to...you know, tell them the error of their ways?"

Lee smiled an awkward smile and shrugged his shoulders.

"Your call, but I'll be writing up the custody report to

support the fact that I asked. How does the other fella look?"

"Better than me." His words were slightly slurred, but it was all he said.

"OK, you are bailed to attend Bow Street Magistrates on the twenty-fifth of January, year of our Lord two thousand and fifteen. You know the penalty for not turning up?" The male before him nodded.

"Good. My advice is to be there or you'll be looking over your shoulder. You clearly have friends in high places in London. Sign here. Here's your train ticket."

He took the train ticket and signed on the dotted line.

"And don't be coming back, I'm short-staffed and I've got enough to do without more bloody paperwork."

He nodded again, walked through the grey-painted windowless door, towards another, waited for the buzzer to sound then entered the main reception area which was already full of people wanting to report crimes, lost property and enquire about their loved ones who for some reason had been detained by the police overnight.

The pretty counter clerk with a dark brown bobbed haircut looked up, took a deep breath, scribbled her pen onto a pad to check whether it would last the shift, and beckoned the first of the day's visitors.

"Next."

A male dressed in someone else's oversized hand-me-downs nodded to the two suited staff in the queue. He was constantly pulling the trousers up and around his waist and stepping from side to side. He looked sixty but was probably in his thirties. Homelessness did that to you.

"They can go first, sweetheart. I've got all day. And besides, I know a detective when I see one."

The two Metropolitan Police staff walked confidently up to the counter and showed their warrant cards.

"DCs Hawker and Dayton to see your duty inspector please my love."

"We've been expecting you, gents. Good journey?"

"Rest day, less than eight hours' notice. It was exceptional thanks."

"Cup of tea?"

"And they say northern hospitality is dead! Love one. Breakfast would be great if you have a canteen?"

"We do. Alistair, can you watch the counter for me I've got a hot date with two dishy detectives from London?"

They walked from the reception through another grey, anonymous door and into the lift. "I'm Angie. I run the place. At least I may as well. I'll get you up to the canteen and introduce you to our inspector, he's called Darren Fletcher – a good man and I know he can't wait to get rid of your secret passenger!"

"After you." They both looked as she confidently walked into the lift. Cute. Playful. And probably married.

An hour later they were ushered back downstairs to a side room where their newfound guide introduced them to David Francis.

"Here you go, gents. This is Mr Francis."

He looked up, scanned them both and for old time's sake took a last look at the ever-so-lovely Angie, then stood, steadied himself and shook their hands.

"Francis. I have no idea what is happening here but let's go shall we?"

"Sounds like a plan, Mr Francis. You got everything?" He looked and saw that for Francis, everything was a simple black back pack.

"Yep. I've got all I need to survive."

They were on the M1 motorway heading south thirty minutes later.

"So what's your connection to DCI Roberts?"

"None. My connection is more six degrees. Your DCI used to work with a man called Cade. They were investigating a criminal group a few years ago – one of whom killed my father. At least that is what Cade told me, and I trust Jack Cade more than any man I have ever met, and that includes my military days."

Over the next hour Francis outlined how Cade had rescued him from an alcohol-laden and early death just by dropping in during his patrols, putting the kettle on and allowing Francis to vent. Cade discovered that far from being a reclusive drunk, the man was actually a premier league intelligence operator. Abandoned by all who knew him.

There were Walter Mitty characters out there. Every cop had met them, but this man in their unmarked Vauxhall had the scars and cynicism of many years to back up the impressive collection of operational T-shirts. He had, as they say, walked the walk.

Having battled through the all-day commuter traffic, the trio arrived at the security barrier of Scotland Yard to be met by Jason Roberts.

Dark grey suit, light grey shirt and an orange tie with a matching handkerchief.

Francis got out first, again judged his surroundings, then nodded to Roberts. "You must be Ginger? I guess you know who I am? So, why am I here?"

"Long or short version, David."

"Short. To the point. And sweet."

"The man that tried to attack you in your home is called Constantin Nicolescu. I suspect he tried to kill your father some years ago. He is a member of the Romanian criminal syndicate known as the Seventh Wave. He also tried to kill me on a train a few years ago. Therefore, we have a mutual hatred. My team, with the support of Jack Cade, locked most of the group up back in 2004, including their leader, one Alex Stefanescu."

Francis was taking it all in, filtering, triaging, retaining what he needed to keep for the future.

"Things elevated, David. Governments became involved, stuff way above even my level started to happen. People we thought we could trust became people we couldn't. Innocuous bits of paper became more valuable than diamonds or gold. And I can see you processing this and wondering where you fit in?"

"You are a smart man, Jason. And please call me Dave."

"Dave, it is. And thank you. Cade is in Australia at the moment, long story. Things have happened since you last saw him. Frankly, we will never have enough time to recap, but needless to say what we thought was dead and buried has been resurrected, and right now I have a horde of criminal zombies shuffling through my city. I can sense it. My problem is, I have no idea what their next move is. And that sir is where you fit in."

"So what exactly are you saying? I've been taken out of my home and forced to come down here to do what?"

Roberts remembered when he had first set eyes on Francis, or rather a faded, heat-curled facsimile of a young and hopeful soldier. The Francis he looked at now looked older than the image of the bright young man, staring back at him from the floor of his uncle's demolished house in north Kent. He had lived a hard life, and it showed, but there was an intensity in his eyes and the way he spoke that indicated he was also seeking vengeance.

Cade said he was good. If they could keep him sober all the better.

"Look Dave, if Jack Cade rates your skills then I do. For now, I need you to avoid Messrs Daniels and Beam. Grab yourself a desk and we'll get you whatever you need. You will be working with Carrie O'Shea – go easy on her at first, she's your equal, and when it comes to knowledge of London, she has no one to touch her, and for fuck's sake don't try it on with her. Tomorrow I'm hoping to introduce you to Cynthia Bell, she's a geospatial genius. What she can't do with maps isn't worth mapping."

"So who's paying for this?"

It was a fair question.

"Fair question, Dave. Not my budget, that's for sure. We'll put you into some nearby accommodation, give you a cell phone and clear you for access to this place. For now, let's just say the British government is funding your stay."

What he didn't say was that he had no idea whether this was true. He did know, however, that he may need to use Francis as bait. He also conveniently forgot to mention that Francis had just spent the night sleeping next door to the man that had killed his uncle. Metres away. Keep your enemies closer still and all that. It was easier that way.

CHAPTER EIGHT

In Nottingham, Constantin Nicolescu walked out of the impressive archway, with its gloss black door standing sentinel below a blue police lamp. He dragged in a lungful of cold morning air, turned left onto Station Street and walked with confidence away from the police station, clutching a ripped-open polythene custody bag and a train ticket to London.

He emptied the minimal contents and dumped the bag into a concrete bin. He had no idea where he was heading other than to find someone with a phone or better still, an internet café. Anywhere that would allow him to link up with his team. He was on the move. Hunted.

It had been that easy. Exploiting the principle that many hands made for mistakes, he had waited for the right moment, swapped with Patrick Lee and stepped forward when he was asked for. The overweight early-shift custodian had asked Lee a question to which he answered in Romanian. Lee had been needlessly practising it all night. It meant nothing to him, but it certainly wasn't the Queen's English.

The custodian looked at Nicolescu. "I heard you had fallen out with your cellmate. Then you must be Mr Lee."

The crooked, blood-stained smile that he got in return and a grunt of 'I'm fine' was all he needed. The quicker the uniformed civilian cleared the cells, the quicker he could grab some breakfast. He hadn't eaten for two hours.

Candy from a baby. The subsequent reports would take days and an enquiry much longer.

Lee now found himself a victim – of fear. An unusual experience for a man who had led with his fists for so many years. Nicolescu held the full house on fear though and Lee hoped that another call to his friend Mr Roberts might allow him to be treated with compassion. He didn't hold out much hope. How would a man in his position even begin to understand the hierarchy among the travelling people of Europe?

The call to arms was rapid, it always was for any 'escapes custody', as it was known the world over. The call from the custody sergeant to DCI Roberts was more difficult. He held the earpiece a few inches away but could him clearly.

"He's done *what?*" Roberts was incredulous.

"Promise me you have every man and his proverbial land shark hunting the streets of Nottingham for Nicolescu? Do you know how dangerous that man is? What sort of three-ring circus are you running up there?"

"Sir, I'm sorry, we were busy and your man was convincing. I take full responsibility for this error."

"Error? It's a right fuck up, sergeant. Where's Robin Fucking Hood when you need him? No, forget that, he was bad too. The Sheriff of Bloody Nottingham."

He took a second to gather his thoughts. "OK, no point in falling out. We need to act together. Get your duty inspector to ring this number when he's come down off the ceiling will you?"

"And what about Mr Lee? He says he was forced into it. They look similar in the half-light..."

"In future, may I recommend turning the bloody thing on? As for that caravan-dwelling bastard, tell him from me that I'll be forcing something up his arse the next time I get my hands on him, probably my unlubricated truncheon. Jesus Christ, what a mess. Send my best wishes to Friar Tuck. At least he was a decent spoonerism..."

The sergeant let the senior man rant, apologised again, hung up, then added a second charge to Nicolescu's record of escaping custody. A warrant would be issued. All they needed to do was find him.

Nicolescu had turned left again, quickly covering ground and away from the railway and police stations and the CCTV that accompanied them. He had Lee's wallet and a few tacky pieces of jewellery, but they had a value and might become useful. He never had a taste for gold sovereigns but he knew their worth and the one mounted on Patrick Lee's ring, gifted by his father for his twenty first, was worth a few hundred at least.

Halfway along the street he stopped at a brick-built arch. Derelict, a legacy of the old railway system that once brought people and products into the city. Now a temporary shelter for a few more weeks before the developers moved in, and the homeless moved on.

He beckoned to a figure in the shadows. 'Come here.'

The male brushed the cardboard covering from his poorly clothed body, eased himself onto his feet and put a hand into his right pocket. He felt the knife and was reassured.

Constantin held up his hand. 'No need.'

He spoke in broken English. "I am not here to steal from you. I want to give you something in a trade for information. We are brothers. OK?"

The male was nineteen and trusted no one. Not even the people he shared the archway with, those that drank themselves to death and the others who inhaled glue from a shared carrier bag until life and its problems evaporated.

"No one gives me anything without wanting something in return, and you are no different. What do want? Sex? Forget that, I'm too sore. Yeah, shocking ain't it that a man would do that for a few quid or some drugs. I'm nineteen, homeless, hungry and have nothing and no one, so do me a favour, fuck off and leave me alone before I stab you to death. No, wait, if I do that at least I'll get fed and have somewhere dry to sleep."

He removed the knife from his pocket. His thousand-yard stare lengthened as he walked towards the man with the accent.

The chink of metal onto the grubby brickwork stopped the younger male in his tracks. It was gold. And valuable. So what *did* this man want in exchange?

He bent to pick it up, never taking his eyes off the older man. It felt cold in his already chilled hands. He rubbed the metal between his thumb and forefinger. It was probably the most valuable thing he had ever possessed. That and his dog.

"It is worth money to you, no?"

"Yeah. It is, and I've got it now, and you haven't so piss off and don't come back."

Nicolescu tossed the train ticket to the boy.

He unfolded it. It was a chance to get to London. It wasn't his home city; he was slowly dying in that one, without a roof or regular food. Why rot to oblivion here? The capital was the place to go. Better to exist in the big city where it was warmer and there were more night shelters and opportunities.

"OK, you have a deal man, I don't know what you want, but I have nothing to give."

"A mouthful of your drink and one coin from your begging collection is all I ask. That, and your clothes. Then, I will, as you say, piss off and leave you alone."

The boy knew the man had escaped from somewhere, but had no idea he was still so close to his captors. He undressed slowly, his aching limbs impeding him. He was covered in sores, and Nicolescu knew he probably suffered from scabies too. Wearing his clothes was not without risk, but it was necessary and he prayed that if his skin did crawl, it would only be for a short time.

He looked at the boy and felt pity for him, stood there in a dirty, damp Victorian portico, forgotten by his family in a city that passed him by every day.

Now, the same boy, wearing Nicolescu's clothes felt almost human. He held out his hand, which was filthy, long nails, underlined with grime.

"What do else do you need?" he handed his bottle over, having respectfully wiped the rim as he collected what possessions he had and put them in the cleanest carrier bag he could find.

"I just need a phone."

The boy laughed. Leonard Simon Barker, nineteen and destitute, actually laughed.

"You think I have a phone?"

"No. But you may know where a payphone is. I must not be traced."

"There's one a hundred metres from here. Right outside the police station."

Nicolescu allowed himself a moment of levity, too. The next few days would be far removed from anything humourous. "Thank you, brother. Travel safely and good luck."

They shook hands. The prey and the preyed upon, for a short time they had an alliance. Constantin waited for the younger man to exit the tunnel, then followed about twenty paces behind him, running the single coin between his fingers as the boy did the same with the ring. As they reached the payphone, Barker thanked his lucky stars, crossed the road and never looked back.

The Romanian picked up the phone and followed the onscreen instructions, hearing the only coin he had eagerly consumed by the machine.

"It is me. I need to be collected. Quickly." He was told to wait a moment. Every second was painful, his paranoia was returning and his breathing increased in pace, he knew he was starting to panic.

"Hello. You still there?"

Looking around. At people, going places, all looking at him, at a police officer entering the station – it was just a matter of time.

"Yes. Go on." His reply was hurried.

"Get to the end of the street, cross the main road, there is an old track that leads to a dead end. We will pick you up there in two hours. Silver car. Get in the back and lay down. Say nothing. We will bring you to London."

He was walking along the one-way street before the call had been ended, shuffling, apparently homeless but very much untraceable.

And very much ready to visit old adversaries. It had been too long.

CHAPTER NINE

TWENTY-FOUR HOURS PASSED. CONSTANTIN WAS BACK, near London, in hiding. He brought skills and a mind-set that was worth more than the pitiful rewards they gave him. His knowledge was plentiful – myriad skills farmed from books in libraries right across the British prison system. Chemistry, biology and medicine. For a failure from the poorer parts of Craiova, he should have been considered a great success and been given the freedom of the city. Instead, he remained a broken, bitter and capable prodigy.

"Eat, brother. Shower too, you smell worse than the municipal dump outside our home town. Then we have some work for you, which we think you will enjoy."

Constantin had no idea who the new male was. He didn't trust him, and that was reciprocal. He had a job to do. Alex was the one man he responded to, for Alex had kept him alive and rewarded him. He needed to. He had to.

"I need you to send a message to an old friend, Constantin. How you do it is entirely up to you. But please, do not be too pleasant."

. . .

"OK, everyone gather around." It was Roberts in a non-playful mood. His team had read the briefing paper he had signed off. His best analyst O'Shea had written it the night before and now stood up and started talking.

"Our target Nicolescu is on the move, foolishly bailed by an overworked team up north. In isolation, this means one man is out there and potentially problematic. As a group, with him as their hired help, this is not good. We all need to focus from this moment on."

O'Shea covered the history, the injuries and fatalities, and laboured on the aspect of hell-bent revenge.

"Word is that the group have re-formed, are better equipped and trained, and one source even suggests that Alex Stefanescu is in-country. We have nothing to support this and have expanded our intelligence network to include all border agencies and GCHQ."

This stopped a few of the wiser staff in their tracks.

Nick Fisher held up his hand and spoke without waiting to be asked. "Hold on, Carrie. GCHQ? What are the Doughnut brigade doing involved in this?"

The name was a colloquial reference to the shape of the building that housed Britain's most classified signals intelligence network. Created during the Second World War and located at Bletchley Park, it achieved fame for its role in breaking the Enigma codes used by the Germans.

Now housed at specially constructed buildings in Cheltenham, a few hours to the west of London, it now employed six thousand people and consisted of signals and cyber intelligence teams. Its linguistics component was also considered among the best in the world.

"Are we talking ECHELON stuff here? Well? Are we?" Fisher looked at the boss, then back at O'Shea. "I think if ever there was a fucking time for need to fucking know it was now." He sat back and waited, allowing the Tourette's to lessen.

O'Shea looked at Roberts, who looked around the room, then nodded.

"Team, the only people cleared to TS level on this floor are myself, the governor and Cynthia. It's how it is. Intelligence staff has to be cleared to this level. I will not be discussing anything other than I have to. End of."

"And that lady does not even begin to answer my question."

"He's got a fair point, guv. Let's lock the bloody door here and get some answers. This does not strike me as a bunch of Eastern Europeans running around and nicking a few quid from bank ATMs anymore."

She looked around more to garner support from her team than anything else.

"What's going on? Nick and I were out for hours the other day and came back with bugger all but a need to scrub ourselves vigorously in the shower." There was a cheer which DS Bridie McGee skilfully ignored. She also wanted answers.

Roberts took in enough air to start speaking, allowing his lungs to fully inflate, then exhaled, loosened his tie and began what for him felt like a eulogy.

"Folks, listen in and listen well because I will never be saying this again. I have looked each one of you in the eye and counted the faces. Therefore, if this leaves this room, worst still your lips, we won't just be having the Commissioner's boot up our arses we will probably go to prison." He held the last note.

"Late last year former Chief Inspector Daniel, ex-Inspector Cade and I were privy to some information that no one other than Assistant Commissioner Johnson and a few select members from the Foreign Office knew about." He let that sink in too.

"Extremely close source evidence indicated that the criminal group the Seventh Wave had come into possession of some documents. These documents had been stored where the nation keeps its diamonds and pearls."

"Hatton Garden." It was Fisher. A statement made, if nothing else to show he was listening.

"Yes, Nick. The very same. Secure as the bloody Bank of England, apparently, but perhaps not as safe as the Tower. Quite why they didn't put the bloody things in there is beyond me." He paused, something was playing with his cerebral cortex, dropping some bait into the water and waiting for the float of consciousness to dip.

"Anyway, it wasn't, and the team got away with diamonds, which as you know were recovered. But they also got away with documents that related directly to the demise of Europe and the monarchy."

He picked up the desk phone. "Lizzie, can we get some strong coffee please, enough for about twenty people?"

"Sure thing, boss. You need me to join you?"

"No. Thanks."

The last few sentences had drilled home, so he continued.

"Jack and I were up to our nuts in secrets last year, some of which we may never divulge until we are sat dribbling in a high-winged chair in a nursing home. But what you do need to know is that those documents have been split. Stefanescu has one set and the others are somewhere else."

"Shit, boss. The monarchy? That could hit our revenue really hard."

"Yes, it could Bridie, but the departure from Europe... this could hit our shares, our businesses, our trade, our defence programme. Need I go on?"

"But guv, there was always a chance we might one day leave Europe. Wasn't there?"

"Yes Bridie, I agree. However, it's not why – but how. The government does not want to leave. If they put it to a vote right now, I think the rank-and-file Brit would vote yes to leaving. And he might not think it through. And it could bite us on the governmental arse."

"But it might not." Fisher was interested, and off the record would vote to leave. "I still don't understand why the government chose to hide the bloody things in a jewellers."

"Why does the US hide its silver near West Point military academy?" It was a throwaway line designed to give Roberts breathing space.

"There's more to this, isn't there, guv?" It was McGee again.

"Sadly, yes. And that is why I am creating a new team, from today, with the blessing of the Secretary of State. I'm bringing Jack back in as a tactical advisor and our old DCI John Daniel too. Carrie and Cynthia will remain as our intelligence analysts. Bridie, Nick, you will work with your current teams to gather intelligence and investigate. Operation Niko is classified as confidential, which encompasses all of you. Anything over that will be restricted to the aforementioned. This is just about as high as any of us will ever reach in our careers. Me included. We make sure our comms are brief, informative and timely."

Roberts took a quick gulp from a bottle of water, remembering one more introduction.

"Team, apologies. This is Dave Francis. Jack tells me that what Dave doesn't know about the darker side of intelligence can be written on the back on an ant. Consider him cleared, consider him a friend. And if he asks any weird questions, just answer him. He reports to me for now, to

Jack when he returns. Any questions? If not, today is Day One and we go from here."

"I've got one boss." O'Shea looked sullen.

"Yes, Carrie?"

"Where is Cynthia?"

He had no idea.

"I honestly don't know."

The Wells Fireworks Factory – or what remains of it – is south of the River Thames, east of the River Darent and minutes from the impressive Queen Elizabeth Bridge that spans the mighty Thames and joins Kent to Essex and thus the regions to London.

Started in the eighteen hundreds by Joseph Wells, the factory was the foremost manufacturer of display fireworks in Britain and remained so until cheap imports from China slowly eroded the marketplace and caused Wells' demise. He left behind a legacy of outbuildings, scattered across a desolate part of the tidal approaches and, for obvious reasons, isolated from the general population.

The buildings, once partly destroyed by German V1 flying bombs, were now derelict, their lives smothered by purple buddleia, invasive brambles and stinging nettles. Over the years a few interested parties had looked at buying the place, children had explored it and generally speaking everyone ignored the site that was once the hub of the industry. Logistically speaking, it was ideally located to the river and the growing road networks. Now, some hundred and thirty years later, it provided the perfect place for the team to hide. No one looked, no one cared.

A long-departed graffiti artist had once daubed white paint onto the walls of an explosive store: 'No one will ever know I was here.'

He was right.

She lay on the bench. Cable tied and gagged. There was no point in blindfolding her as they cared not whether she could identify them in the future.

They had taken her in a simple operation that required minimal planning and limited resources. There was no long-term seduction or online capture. They waited until the other tenants had gone to work early, and kicked her door in. The only surveillance they had conducted was on the approach to the street, the building and the doorway. Not one camera watched over the occupants. In a city that arguably had more close circuit television scrutiny than any other, it was unusual. For the three men employed by Alex Stefanescu, it had been a blessing.

He had conducted a broad internet search of derelict buildings in London, but each had its own issues. They were either being renovated or partially occupied by the homeless. What he needed was a derelict site that would not be developed any time soon and one which no one would bother to visit. Ever. In Joseph Wells he found a friend. In Constantin he had a thinly controlled sociopath.

The aging silver Vauxhall Senator arrived at the palisade metal gate. It waited a few seconds, then entered. The gate closed behind them and they drove along overgrown roadways to the larger of the buildings. It had been a long day.

Driving across country, through the Eastern counties, down through the Fens, into Norfolk, Suffolk, then Essex. Avoiding all motorways and major A roads. It was deliberate but had added many hours to the journey.

Constantin was hungry and needed water. His drug habit

was always close to the surface, but alcohol helped. The swift taste of the acidic brew in the railway arch in Nottingham had helped alleviate his thirst and put him off forever. He had to avoid all types of addiction, except that is the one they paid him for.

Pain.

He walked into the off-white building with its pitched roof and broken windows. The team had made themselves at home with beds in old store rooms that were watertight and intact. They had everything they needed to survive a few weeks. A generator provided power and carried out its duties without a soul hearing it. There was enough food for all. Water, too. No alcohol, and only one person had a cell phone.

They would stay here until Phase Two.

"These are for you." The younger male handed a holdall to Constantin. He opened it and saw it contained new clothes, shoes, washing kit and painkillers. Alex knew him well. He was addicted to opiates in any way he could get them. His rotting teeth ensured he was in pain, every day and all night. It drove him to distraction. Inflicting pain upon others helped.

He put the holdall into a spare room and declared it off-limits to all. They knew of his reputation and agreed.

"Where is she?"

"In there. Do you not wish to change out of those filthy clothes first?"

He smiled. "No, and you will accompany me. And then you will learn why. Did you get all the stuff I asked for?"

The younger male nodded. He would always remain as just that, the 'the younger male'. Alex had decreed that no one on the new team would be named, all the better to provide what the police called plausible deniability. For when they got arrested, as some would, the police would ask questions. They would buckle eventually, their techniques and laws were pathetic. No one could match the resilience of a travelling man.

"Good. Come on let us go and visit her."

She was immobile, but as soon as she sensed their presence she stiffened, ready. She had no idea what they had planned to do with her, and in one way that made things worse. Just get it over with.

"Hello. I am Constantin. We haven't met, but you know me, or my name I am sure. Your friend Carrie lives because of me. I have the power to hold your lives in..."

He rummaged for the word.

"Abeyance."

Her eyes were darting around the room, looking for others, looking for an escape. Her wrists were raw. Her shins too. She was fully clothed, at least they didn't plan to strap her to a wooden frame and slowly drown her, naked, like they had that poor girl Nikolina.

He removed a large-bladed tool from the bag and looked at her. Most humans would try to detach themselves from the event. Constantin was captivated by her terrified eyes. If his victim had been a male he would have been aroused.

For Cynthia Bell, drowning seemed her best option.

CHAPTER TEN

In the Sofitel, Darling Harbour, John Cade was waiting for his dinner guest. They had last met many years ago, he a Liaison Officer for the British Police at Interpol's Lyon Headquarters in France and she, his equivalent from the Australian Federal Police.

Kim Helston was twenty-nine back then and what the police called a blue flamer, one who was destined to rise through the ranks quickly. A natural blonde, she epitomised the Great Australian Outdoors. She ran, she rode, she swam. And she could drink any man under the table. Except that is, a man called Jack, who sat opposite her at work and shared sideways glimpses, a passion for hunting international criminals and great humour – he called it banter – she called him a Galah, whatever that meant.

She was tanned, as most Australians seem to be, even in the winter. She had smooth thighs a supermodel would kill for and double espresso eyes that he wanted to dive into. But theirs was a platonic relationship, one that never moved beyond outrageous flirtation and a genuine mate ship. Sometimes relationships suffered if they went further.

She stood in the doorway in a simple navy blue shift dress and matching shoes. She still looked physically fit, her legs shapely and toned and her hair, tied in a simple ponytail had lost none of its lustre.

"My God, you look amazing." He held her close to him and she reciprocated. She smelt good too. So did he.

"I see you still wear Givenchy, Jack."

"You don't miss a trick you fox."

"It was our job, wasn't it? I take it you have booked a decent table in the best restaurant in the hotel, view over the harbour?"

"Of course. You know me."

"I do. Predictable, though. Come on, let's go somewhere else."

And they did. A simple Italian on the waterfront, noisy and full of atmosphere. She ordered the wine: Witches Falls Syrah.

"Any good?"

"I hope so, Jack. The vineyard I set up with John makes it." She smiled a winning smile.

"You've done well, Kim. As patronising as it may sound I am proud of you."

"It does. But from you, I'll accept it."

The waiter arrived and offered to pour a trial sample for the lady. She declined. "It's fine. Trust me?"

They ordered from a brief but authentic menu, chatted and sipped on the wine until their food arrived.

Cade acknowledged the deep red liquid. "It's very good."

"Thank you. From a man who drinks as much as you I'll take the compliment."

"Cow. I'll have you know I hardly touch the stuff these days."

Theirs was a relationship that could recommence in minutes, as if they had worked with each other the day before. Theirs was a chemistry, a recipe that lacked one essential ingredient. At least that is how he recalled it.

She held her wineglass in both hands, looked over the top, beautifully, her head slightly to one side and said, "So come on old man, what do you want? You don't just arrive in the Lucky Country and front up and ask a gorgeous and very married girl out to dinner. What is on your mind, you marvellously British man?"

"Where do I begin?"

Over the starter and main course, supported by the rest of the bottle, he outlined what had happened across the water in New Zealand, the year before.

"So this is the same group as back in London, in 2004?"

"Yep."

"And that time in Europe?"

"The same."

"And they are still operating? I thought you had put them all away for the rest of their naturals?"

"So did we, but a judge died here, another retired there, money changed hands, and before you can say they've all escaped and re-formed, they had. Dessert?"

"No, I'm stuffed. More wine?"

"Ditto. I'll get the bill."

"Go halves? Please?"

"No. Not a hope in hell. As you say I'm marvellously British and if I take a gorgeous and annoyingly married lady to dinner, I bloody well pay."

He joined her, held her hand so she could stand, in case the bottle of her wine had taken effect. He should have known better. She grew the bloody stuff!

"Fancy a walk?"

"Is that the pre-cursor to 'fancy a coffee'?"

"Come on, Kim, you know me better than that."

"Shame." She laughed. "Come on, let's go this way. It's darker."

They walked arm in arm for an hour, his jacket around her shoulders.

"So what is the plan when you get to the Whitsundays? You going in alone? Need some backup?"

The thought hadn't occurred to him.

"I hadn't given the thought any...thought, Detective Inspector Helston. I was planning to just rock up to the house and put her across my knee."

"Then what?"

"Talk about the first thing that comes up?"

"Cade, you are incorrigible. Seriously, you need to be careful. This lot nearly killed you before, and you lost members of your team, and the girl, Carrie. Is that not warning enough?"

"But I trust her. And that counts for something. Come with me, if you feel it will make a difference."

She stood against some railings overlooking the Opera House, flicked the screen open on her Galaxy and looked at flights from Sydney to Hamilton Island.

"Credit card."

He handed it over.

Four minutes later, she was on the same flight as Cade.

"We go tomorrow."

"But what about John? Your husband."

"Yes, Cade, I know who I am married to thank you."

She put her arms around him and pressed her head into his chest so she could hear his heart beating. She smiled. The wine had begun to take effect.

"This is surreal, so you are actually coming with me? I don't know what to say." He held her head, stroking her hair. It was the most physical they had ever been.

She pulled away, laughed, her head falling backwards, clapping her hands together.

"I love it when I am in control of Mr OCD."

"OCD. Me? I bloody well don't think so," he replied, straightening the hem on her dress. "And anyway you live in Queensland, it's miles away from here. You need to pack. What are your plans?"

"The Sofitel?"

His thoughts were normal masculine ones, but her answer surprised him. "My hotel?"

"Oh, it's your hotel now, is it? Yes, I mean the Sofitel. Do you have a problem with that? You have a luxury king sized bed, big enough for two, in a room with a corner bathroom and a large bath, also big enough for two, overlooking the harbour? What goes on tour, stays on tour. Correct?"

"Allegedly one hundred percent. But Kim, I am surprised, flattered, but surprised."

She held his hand and guided him back towards the hotel.

"You'll be surprised when you pick up the bill tomorrow, Jack. I've got exactly the same room as you."

In Dartford, in another dimension and in accommodation that was the polar opposite of the Sofitel, Constantin listened to a bird singing in a nearby tree. A song thrush. Beautiful. It reminded him of his brief childhood; a melodic, peaceful sound was all he could hear. Actually, that and the distant thrum of cars and lorries continually crossing the Thames was all he could hear, especially when the wind blew in from the east. But then he listened again. There was a pitiful sigh, a whisper of fear. It was her.

He ran his fingers through her hair and stroked her

cheek. It was a moment of misplaced compassion before he started.

"Hold her arm."

The local anaesthetic flooded into her. He owed the wretched cow that much.

He was no longer the ex-prisoner, fascinated by chemistry, the hired killer with a ferocious heroin addiction. He was Constantin Nicolescu, surgeon.

Her brain flooded with worry and questions for which she had no answer.

'Where were her saviours? She worked for the bloody guardians, where were they now? Where was her big brother? Why didn't her departed mother send a message from the grave? Someone? Please...'

The blade cut through the outer layer of skin. It was razor sharp. At first she felt nothing. But then the nerves started to send their frantic signals back to her brain. Pain. There was no other word for it.

More localised drugs. This was a first for him, too. He needed to keep her stable.

The blade began to saw through her wrist. They could hear it. He looked at the younger male as it severed the veins, nerves, tendons and muscle. He cut deeper and pushed down, as a chef cuts into a tough piece of meat or a Halloween mother forces her blunt knife into a child's faceless pumpkin.

He was fascinated by what he saw, stopping briefly to examine his work and what lay beneath.

He pulled at the limb. It wasn't as clean as he had hoped. The text books had lied. She had passed out. Her arm no longer fought him, so he took the opportunity to detach the hand from the radius and ulna, rocking it back and forth until it snapped free. When he looked at it, at liberty from its host, he felt a sense of enthralment. Almost waiting for it to move.

Had he not have fitted the junctional tourniquet, she would have bled to death. The military medics were the saviours of so many casualties with their battlefield discoveries. He knew he'd read almost all of their books. He screwed down the pressure ball onto the artery and the bleeding, at least the voluminous flow, stopped. The site still bled, and he was covered in it, hands, arms, trousers. Sticky and sweet, a tang of aluminium, drying quickly in the air.

"See? This is why I do not change yet." It was supposed to be amusing, but the younger male was retching. Who was this butcher before him?

All he had to do now as pray the younger male kept her alive. Hemostatic bandages were rammed into the void and instructions were given very clearly in their mother tongue. Technology might save her, he said. That and her will to survive.

"I need to leave her with you. Keep that limb elevated and change the dressings like I showed you. If she dies, it will be your fault."

He began to wonder whether he had taken on too much. His reputation was out on a limb – a bit like Cynthia – he laughed to himself.

'Nicolescu the surgeon. What would mother think of me now?'

He went from the rudimentary operating theatre, through the main accommodation area that included cooking facilities, en route to another room.

Once there, he found what he was looking for. He stopped and looked down, realising why the others had stared at him so intently. It was garish, surreal, hideous but fascinating. In his left hand, was hers.

Opening the second holdall with his master hand, he found what he needed. He reverently placed the severed hand to one side and then emptied a box of cheap candles into an old saucepan that was sitting on a portable gas stove that the team used to cook their meals. He then slowly watched as the wax filled the pan to halfway.

As the wax became an opaque liquid, he produced a piece of white card from the bag, together with a permanent marker. He began to write.

Jack. 'He will not spare when he takes revenge.' AS.

The message was biblical, chosen by a man who had learned its contents at an early age. It was exactly what he had asked for. Constantin knew better than to meddle with the words.

The molten wax was poured into an old can, which was then placed into a pool of cold water. The hand was lowered into the wax as it started to set. The congealed blood mixed with the whitening wax as he slipped the message between the fingers. The last important part was the wick.

He stood and watched as the candle formed, becoming whiter by the second. It soon solidified, the base colours swirling red and white. It was almost artistic. Ensuring it was sufficiently cool he admired it once more, and unable to see through it, content with his work, he lowered it into a presentation box. He was satisfied. Almost happy.

"Boy!" He called out to the other room.

"Put this box into another, mark it fragile, and have it couriered to this address. Go to the next town and do it. Pay cash. No conversations other than the bare minimum. No mistakes." The young male nodded and took the package and headed for the nearest town in another low value but legal car, bought from a side street for cash.

The surgeon thought about his patient once more, wondering whether she was still alive, and importantly, what he would do with her next.

Cade had successfully guided a slightly drunk Helston back to their hotel. Through the foyer to a knowing smile from the blonde surfer, into the lift and to the door of her room, four away from his.

"Your room, ma'am."

She was more affected by her own product than she realised.

"Oh, thank you kind sir." She tried to bow but stumbled. It had been a long time since anything like this had happened.

He held her up against the door frame and flashed her access card across the reader.

Easing her into her room, he noticed that she had already unpacked, she was nothing if not prepared.

"Coffee, Jack?"

It was tempting. But he knew to say no.

"Thanks, Kim, but I had better say no."

"Jack Cade, are you blushing? I was offering you coffee, nothing else."

He could only reply, "Come here you. It's been a long day."

He pulled her towards him and held her. She felt good. She looked great, still fit, and she reacted to his hug by pressing her face into his neck and kissing it. He could smell her hair, he inhaled and could feel himself becoming aroused. So could she.

"It's been a very long time, Kim. You know when we worked in France..."

She put a finger up to his lips. "Say nothing."

She moved her face and kissed him. He kissed her, gently. She sighed, closed her eyes and kissed him again. The kiss and the physical embrace lasted a minute.

"I need to go Kim." He held her, not at arm's length, but it may as well have been.

She smiled, kicking her shoes off and turning her back to him.

"Unzip me, would you, inspector?"

The klaxon in his mind was screaming stop!

He walked the few paces to her, unzipped the dress and slipped the straps from her shoulder.

"I have to go. Now."

"You certainly do. Sweet dreams."

As she walked away the dress dropped to the ground, revealing black knickers, no bra. Her toned body looked even better than he could have ever imagined. She glanced back across a tanned shoulder and smiled, then collapsed onto the bed, face down, and as he stood and watched her, she drifted into a deep sleep.

He walked to the side of the bed, pulled the covers up and over her legs, did what most men would do and ruefully studied her body, looked at her underwear. It was far from cheap and possibly selected for the evening. Possibly not.

With his mind revolving like a cyclone, he ran his hand over the lower part of her back, walked his fingers up her spine towards her neck, where he paused, brushed her hair from her face and placed a kiss onto her neck, then tapped her back, it was saying goodbye as best as he could.

She responded by lifting her arms up and under the pillow and letting out a gentle and relaxed sigh. It was obvious she felt secure in his company.

Cade felt comfortable too − as he pulled the covers up and over her naked back, he paused again.

Should he stay, or should he go?

Pulling the curtains closed and turning off the light he began to regret his decision.

"Ever the gentleman, Cade. Ever the gent." He closed the door, securing it twice and walked to his room smiling. He had either missed the opportunity of a lifetime or dodged a bullet. He would never know.

Minutes that felt like hours slowly evaporated as Constantin paced around the derelict outbuildings. Brambles and vines were growing around them, suffocating the life out of the old place. He was sensing a feeling that he too was being throttled by guilt. It was unlike him. Perhaps age was reducing the years of neurosis and evil? He was waiting for the next call from Alex. The Jackdaw had been freed from his cage and Phase Three would soon commence.

Alex had chosen to brief only his most important people, his brother Stefan, his lieutenant Artur Gheorghiu, and to their surprise Constantin. Alex knew that in Constantin he had an assassin, a surgeon, a chemist and a bomb maker. He also knew that employing him was not without risk. He had seen and heard of the destruction he had caused and realised that one day he could become feral – biting the hand that had fed him since the dire day he had been recruited by the *Septal Val* – the Seventh Wave.

Another nameless male, in his late twenties with three days' growth, appeared in the semi-shade of the doorway. He was holding the team's phone.

"It is for you, sir."

Constantin rubbed his hands together vigorously to remove more of the dried blood, lifted the phone to his ear and spoke.

"Yes." It was deliberately clipped. He had been warned.

"I am moving as planned. The Queen Bee to the hive. Have you sent the message – exactly as I asked?"

"Exactly."

"Good. Now we can begin to have some fun. You know what to do?"

"Yes. Of course. Do I have your permission to start – today?"

"As long as you don't allow them to find us and put us back in those terrible places – then yes – do as you wish and with whom."

He heard him say 'girl, come here and teach me things' before the line cleared. It was obvious that now he was out and free again, he was making up for lost time. He hoped she did exactly as he said, for the last one that disappointed him was still decomposing on a mountainside in Spain – dying, where he had dragged her behind his car and rolled her down a rock-strewn slope, terrified and still alive.

CHAPTER ELEVEN

They met as arranged in the Atelier restaurant, the heart of fine dining at the Sofitel, Darling Harbour.

She had got up early and run, in the opposite direction to Cade, taking in the cooler part of the day and marvelling at the sunrise. Back in her room she took advantage of the deep bathtub, sinking into it and watching through the full height window as the world dragged itself out of bed, like ants down below scuttling here and there, and heading to their place of work.

She did the same once. In fact, she started her police career a stone's throw away from where she now lay, partially submerged in perfect surroundings. Like most police officers, she started on the beat, the real way to learn the noble art; walking everywhere, talking to everyone until she knew the whole beat area and importantly, what made it tick; who, when, what, how and why.

She knew where. In fact, she prided herself on knowing the lay of the land better than any of her peers. And the bosses saw this in her too. She became a detective at a time when such roles were considered unlikely for a woman, then promoted to sergeant within a few years.

Detective Sergeant Kim Helston was the first of her kind to implement a new approach to victim related policing and became what many considered a legend in the area of investigative approaches to serious crimes against the person. Within three years she had made it to detective inspector, transferred to the Federal Police and was told to never look back.

Life and her career were blossoming. She met a likely husband via the job – obviously – but things became sour when he was investigated for fraudulent expense claims, and on his way down tried to drag her with him. His peers felt there was enough mud to stick and avoided her like the plague. She was innocent beyond belief. But mud stuck and her partner was guilty.

She offered her resignation six months into the investigation into what she saw as an attack upon her credibility and integrity. It was then that a senior manager, the one who had actually recruited her into the Criminal Investigation Branch, saw an opening that he knew would benefit all.

"Ever been to France, Kim?"

"No, sir."

"I hear it's very nice at this time of the year. There's a desk with your name on it. You can leave in a month. Take some time off between now and then. Au revoir."

For many, it was an enforced departure. For DI Kim Helston, it was the break she needed. Once in France, at Interpol's HQ she blossomed; the pruned-back rose allowed to flower again. She learned about international crime and criminals, syndicates, stolen artwork and child custody cases, borderless crime, fraud and people smuggling. But best of all, she learned about wine. In particular, she discovered the complexities and delights of Syrah, in a region famed for its success. Why not take the opportunity to learn a new skill?

A seed was sown that would germinate years later at Witches Falls, ten thousand two hundred and eighty miles away. Exactly.

And, although she had never admitted it to him, she made another of her greatest discoveries; Inspector John Cade. Jack, to his friends.

And here she was sat opposite him, dining on fruit and muesli and sipping tea.

"Is that how you retain such an amazing figure, Kim?" Cade said, gesturing to the breakfast with his spoon.

"Depends, which part you mean Jack?"

"Well, the fruit I guess."

"I meant my figure. I guess you saw enough of it last night to decide?"

"I did. But Kim you need to know..."

"It's OK. I know. I woke about half an hour later to find myself semi-naked and covered up. Ever the bloody gentleman!"

Cade was still undecided. Lost opportunity or bullet dodged?

"I'm teasing you, Jack. Come on, you know me well enough. Thank you for being that perfect gent. Most men would have at least had a grope. Here, try this, it's good for you." She offered a spoonful of fruit, which he took.

Things were back to normal.

"Bacon?" He offered a forkful.

She sipped on something green. "No. Thank you. Most kind. So last night. Tell me you didn't at least take a look?"

"As I covered you up, I marvelled at the delightful shape of your arse and those delicious dimples above your hips. I wanted to slip my hands underneath your body and feel just how pert your breasts were. There, happy now?"

She was actually quite shocked. "Jack! Is that true?"

"No, Kim, it's not."

She looked vaguely disappointed.

"Well OK, I may have had a feel of your tits. Right, come on, we have a plane to catch."

He dodged a slap, headed to reception, and paid the bills. It was the least he could do for an old friend who was willing to drop everything for him, including her knickers. He was still glad she hadn't. It was better that way.

"Taxi will be here in twenty. I'll see you back down here, I've got a call to make."

She breezed through the reception area and slid in between closing lift doors, looking back and winking at him as the automated female announced where she was heading.

"You are very naughty." He said out aloud as the phone was answered in the UK.

"Jack, you old devil. You must have read my mind. How are things?"

"Cut to the chase, Jas. What do I need to know?"

"Long or short version?"

"Short. I've got ten before the taxi takes us to the airport."

"Us?"

"It's a longer story than yours. Crack on mate."

"OK. Dave Francis is here, at the Yard. I've hired him to do some analysis on your recommendation, that and the other bits that you said he was a genius at."

"OK. I'm sure I'll find out why when I get back next week. But in the spirit of collaboration, good call."

"In short, his place was burgled. One hell of a fight. Guess who the offender was?"

"No idea. The reincarnated Kray Twins?"

"No. That would have been more believable. Our old friend Nicolescu."

"Jesus Christ. Any better news?"

"Well yes, he got arrested by the local force."

"Wonderful! And there's a 'but' about to be inserted here, isn't there?"

"So to speak Jack…" Roberts paused then spat it out.

"He's escaped. Off the face of the bloody earth."

"Brilliant. And the good news?"

"There isn't any. We think Alex is on shore. Either that or he's coming. A few bits of chatter we've picked up on the wires and from a few trusted sources. We are playing with the big boys since Hewett seduced the Secretary of State. We just need a direct signal to confirm our suspicions."

"It will be subtle, Jason."

"Alex Stefanescu subtle?"

"Yes, trust me. If he's looking to step up a gear, he'll do it in phases, then hit us hard when we are at our weakest. Look for a subtle message. He has a lot of unfinished business, as do I."

"OK. I'll bow to your greater knowledge. What will you do if you ever meet him?"

"Ha. I have many plans that visit me in the wee small hours. The latest was cuffing him to a freight train."

"Nasty, would hurt being dragged along the track."

"And the other hand would be cuffed to the one heading the other way."

"Oh, now that is entertaining! So either way you win." He put on a muffled voice, pretending to be an announcer at a British railway station.

"The four forty from Nottingham will be calling at Leicester, Luton and St Thomas' Hospital!"

Cade had to laugh.

"The only other thorn in my side, or rather a sickening worry, is that Cynthia hasn't turned up for work mate. She's never taken a days' leave, let alone sick leave or even been late."

"And you are thinking what?"

"I'm trying not to panic. But I think something has happened."

"Done all the usual checks?" It was a rhetorical question to Roberts, who was a smart operator.

"And more besides. Seriously getting concerned now but trying to keep it on the old down low."

"Then put her out as a missing person, Jason. You have to."

"Yeah, I know, was trying to convince myself she'd turn up."

"She will."

Cade had no idea where. He swallowed some bile. The group that he had spent years chasing did that to him. On the surface he was calm, the archetypal swan. Under the water he paddled like a duck on acid, desperate to get to where he was heading. He had learned to hate the group and their leader in particular.

'Cade is a simple man. Very calm, no skeletons, he can be trusted one hundred percent to do the right thing, when asked.'

Words uttered in a meeting in an office where power was worn as a badge of rank, an office that housed the very people likely to lose the most. And words he was likely never meant to hear.

Cade had listened, he had no option in the exulted company. His internal dialogue returned.

'Calm? No skeletons? Maybe. Simple? Thanks, I think. Angry? Beyond its very description. It has taken ten years, maybe more, and in those years I have gained nothing but contempt for Alex and his band of brothers – but those in power, on my side, that live selfish and despicable lives. I trust you even less.'

As he left that meeting he heard a voice he trusted say to one he didn't.

"Unexploded bombs are no less powerful as time goes by. On the contrary, they become less stable and more dangerous. In this respect, Jack Cade is no different. Treat him with disdain by all means. But be prepared, somewhere down the line to pay the price."

"A threat, sir? Do you threaten me?" Said the first faceless voice to the second.

"No. I warn you. Nothing else, just a warning."

To Cade, it felt like yesterday. Where had the time gone and how had he ended up where he was? Fair questions that revisited him as he was about to head to one of the most beautiful places on earth, with an equally alluring woman, to meet one he had fallen in love with.

Through varying degrees his life came back to visit, occasionally to upset and now and then to play with his subconscious.

"All passengers for flight JQ846 to Hamilton Island, please now go to departure screening."

It was a simple message, and one echoed across the airport and the world. Every minute. Of every day.

Cade and Helston joined the aircraft, both turning right as there were no other options on the Airbus A320.

"Two hour flight to paradise, Jack. Shame we are not on holiday. So, what are your plans?"

It was a reasonable question from one friend to another, even more so from a former DI to her equivalent.

"Honestly Kim, I have two plans. Plan A, roll up to the house and ask her what the hell she was playing at..."

She sensed the gap. "And Plan B?"

"You've already second-guessed me, haven't you?"

She had. They buckled in and watched the New South Wales coastline disappear as the Queensland beaches came into view before they turned north east and across open water towards the Whitsundays.

CHAPTER TWELVE

IN NOTTINGHAM, AT THE BLACK LION to be exact, Tris Robertson was at his usual chair, in his local haunt, enjoying time away from work so much more than attending to the miserable needs of others, when inconveniently his phone rang. He allowed its rhythmic buzz to continue until curiosity got the better of him.

His partner and off-duty drinking companion was quick to point out that they were very much off duty and prematurely enjoying the fruits of their recent enhanced-rate overtime.

Phil Brown ran his fingers across his throat in a mime that said, 'Don't answer! It'll be your wife!'

Robertson looked at the white writing on the black background. The name Lenny meant he should answer the call. The time of the call added some weight to the fact that he had to. It was what informants and their handlers did. Dedication, beyond the call of duty.

"Yes. This had better be good. I am about to imbibe an entire flagon of foaming Nun's Pride at the Grand Chat Noir."

The voice on the other end sounded out of breath – panicked.

"Hang on, I'll go outside."

Once in the car park he put the phone to his ear.

"Go on. Good to see you haven't sold the phone I bought you."

"Look boss, I met him when he came to the arches. He swapped my clothes for a gold ring and a train ticket. I couldn't lose. All he wanted was a coin to make a phone call. I didn't trust him enough to lend him my phone. It was weird. He was odd. I know I'm hardly purer than the driven snow boss but..." The words were hurried but made sense.

Robertson cut him off. "Need I remind you I am off duty and that I had just tasted the simplest offerings from an impure nun upon these tender lips?"

"What? Look, it's no laughing matter boss. He scared me. I've not slept since. I sold the train ticket to another homeless lad."

"And the gold ring?"

"I pawned it for fifty quid. I'll give it back. I know it wasn't mine, but I needed to eat. I don't want anything to do with this, I'm trying boss, you know I am, I just need a break. You trust me, don't you?"

He chose not to answer. "Lenny, calm down. Who are we talking about here?"

"A guy. Older than me, think he'd just been bailed from the station or escaped. Russian he was."

"In a hurry? I'm sure he was if he'd just escaped!" Robertson knew it was no time for humour but couldn't resist.

"Boss I'm trying here."

"Fair enough. Go on." It was then he stopped and rewound the conversation.

"Stop. Russian?" Robertson scanned his environs, checking for eavesdroppers.

"Yes, boss. He took my clothes and said he was heading to London."

"Could he have been Romanian?"

"How the fuck would I know I've never been further than Derby. Do they sound Russian, these Romanians?"

"Yes, to you they do. You say he was heading to London?"

"That's right. But I'm smart, Mr Robertson. I followed him. I didn't believe him and I wanted to make sure that if the shit hit the fan, I wouldn't be knee deep in it. He couldn't go to London, cos I 'ad his train ticket and he 'ad no money. So I knew he was lying."

"So where did he go?"

"About half a mile down Station Street, across London Road – you know the old railway station – over the canal?"

"I do."

"There, boss. That's where he went. He hung around for a while until an older silver Vauxhall picked him up."

Robertson had forgotten about his pint now. This was a chance to redeem his force – for word had got out quickly that Constantin had escaped and no force liked to be humiliated, especially by the Met.

"And would you have got any of the registration number?" Robertson waited to be disappointed. Fingers tightly crossed.

"I did. I always wanted to be a copper. But the old man forbid it. This is my chance, eh?"

"Possibly, yes..."

"EW and it had the numbers 04...and E and S and S."

Robertson leant against a nearby Mini. The boy had just quoted back the plate, verbatim.

"Did I do well, boss?"

"I'll be sure to let you know Lenny. Good lad, and do me a favour? Have you got any of that fifty quid left after feeding yourself?"

"Yes."

"How much?"

"Forty-six pounds."

He'd spent four pounds on food. Homeless and starving, he still knew how to budget.

"Keep it. It'll be our secret. OK? Now, another act of kindness if you may? Use some of it to get a bus to your place. I'm sure your parents are beside themselves with worry Lenny. Go home. Whilst you still can. And you can keep that phone too."

He took a breath, cleared his head, then rang his station.

"Sarge. Don't ask why. I need you to get into the custody record of a prisoner called Lee. We locked him up on a warrant the other night. I need the phone number of the DCI from the Metropolitan Police and I need it now."

Provided with the number, he dialled, then nodded to his partner who was over-acting, pulling faces through the pub window and pretending to finish the abandoned pint.

"Roberts."

"Boss. Don't hang up. PC Robertson from Notts Police. We spoke about gypsies, tramps and thieves the other night."

"Oh yes. Just before you let my bloody prized target leg it down the street with another man's identity and a grin bigger than a Cheshire Cat!"

"Sir, respectfully, that wasn't down to me. I'm ringing you off-duty."

Roberts' interest piqued. "Touché. Fair enough. Do go on."

"I run an informant in the city. Homeless lad. Says he met your man not long after he escaped. Described him well. Said he was heading to London. They swapped clothes. Anyway, long story short – he followed him to a car."

"Praise the Lord above. Tell me he can describe the vehicle?"

"He can go one better. He got the registration."

"Tris, if ever there was a time where it was appropriate for two heterosexual males to open mouth kiss then it would be now. I owe you. Who do I write to?"

"You don't boss. Let's just call it an act between brothers in arms, shall we? But if I'm ever in the capital, I'll expect you to buy me a pint to replace the one my erstwhile colleague has just downed in front of me."

"Consider it a debt of honour. Top man. You have no idea what this is connected to. Keep my number. Next time you are down this way, I'll take you to a proper boozer – the Sanctuary. It's where real men drink and I normally have a shandy."

"Hello CAD room, PC Ellis."

"DCI Roberts from the Operation Niko team. I need an urgent broadcast of the following registration, across the Met area – and ideally Essex and Kent too. If sighted staff are to contact you in the first instance, then me on this number. Do not stop the vehicle, consider armed response. Occupants wanted for aiding an escaped prisoner and in connection with an international crime syndicate."

"Consider it done, sir." Keith Ellis looked down at the notepad and transcribed the figures into the PNC2 system. The vehicle was stolen, from Essex, a week before. He added the commentary and commenced a broadcast across the main channels, reaching out to area and traffic staff all over the city of London and its furthest reaches.

. . .

Roberts leaned back into his sofa, stacked a few cushions behind his head and watched a drama unfold on the television. His wife brought in a coffee, a long black, no milk, some sugar. He felt more at ease, knowing that at the very least they had a start point, and with a syndicate like the Wave he knew that was a significant development.

As he allowed the drama to wash over him, he couldn't help but smile and grimace at the past. Chases, shootings, assaults, murders, poisonings and the surreal world of transvestitism all rolled up into a recipe for disaster – itself more than enough for any TV drama.

"Transvestites!" He threw himself up and off the light grey sofa.

"What's that, love?"

"Christ, sorry, pause this will you? I've got to make a call and now."

Roberts had begun to drift back to the past when his photographic mind had centred upon the list on his desk, in his locked office, in the iconic police HQ which had been his professional home for longer than he could recall. There, on the note at the very top of the list, it said in clear and over-written black letters: Ring Lucy Thomas.

"Shit, shit, shit." It was hardly eloquent, but it summed up his concerns.

"How could I have forgotten?" In actual fact, Roberts had spent over ten years trying to forget the first time he met Lucy Thomas – codename Harrier. It was a long story, in fact there was no short version other than to say that Lucy wasn't exactly everyone's idea of a woman.

They had met, with Jack Cade, when one of the team had heard that Lucy had been entertaining a potential target of Op Breaker – the team created to fight Eastern European organised crime. The prettily named Lucy Thomas had indeed built up a client base across the fair city of London –

all males, the occasional heterosexual, an experimental couple and an old war veteran that she visited for tea, biscuits and nothing else. She was the epitome of discreet.

Roberts couldn't actually recall what her real name was. It mattered not. What mattered now was saving her life. He even referred to her as a woman, and she referred to him as 'Jason darling'. It was wrong on every angle, but she was a great informant and via knowledge that had surprised him had saved Carrie O'Shea from a fate worse than death. The Met Police owed her.

"Answer the phone, you crazy bitch."

She did.

"Oh, Jason darling. I love it when you talk dirty. How are we this evening?"

"Lucy shut up and listen."

"Oh dominant as ever!"

"Quiet. I am fine. You are not. I need you to pack your bags, travel light, and change back to being a man if you have to. Either way, be ready to go in an hour. And do not answer your door to anyone except me."

"And would it hurt you to tell this little birdie why?"

"Constantin is out. He's spent a night in a cell babbling in his sleep. And the highlight was what he intended to do to you. Quote: If I can't have her, no one can. I've seen this before with him. Need any more convincing?"

Roberts couldn't begin to understand the relationship that Nicolescu had made with the middle-class call girl, but he knew what love and lust did to the male of the species.

"I'll meet you in the foyer in under an hour."

Roberts mouthed to his wife 'sorry'.

He heard the reply. "Under an hour."

. . .

He got into his own car and drove as fast as he could, south east and ignoring red lights where possible. He dialled the control room and asked for a local unit to attend the area – keep eyes on but avoid the property itself.

'How long does it take to drive this far at this time of the night? Where are all these bloody people going?' He muttered between clenched teeth and whitening knuckles as he negotiated traffic and deliberately broke the law.

Lucy Thomas was what could best be described as an interesting character. Brave and foolhardy. Bright and breezy. Professional, filthy, but cautious. Reckless yet compassionate. Influenced by money. Demanding to be loved for what she had become. And now worried. Who did she trust the most? The man that rang her when he needed something? Or the one who called when he wanted something?

The silver Vauxhall had left the Dartford location an hour before. Zigzagging across south west London until they reached a side road off Camberwell Road, turned right, then kept going. Heading north, then west, avoiding cameras where possible, side streets all the way in. They arrived, and the driver was told to wait.

"Stay here. There will be three of us when we return. We head straight back to our current home. No questions. Do not speak with the new passenger. It is a woman. You don't need to know anything else."

The younger male was stood three metres away from Constantin. On the fourteenth floor, waiting, interested to see what was going to happen next.

He tapped on the door with a familiar tune.

Thomas froze. Tried to stop breathing. It was him. She

knew that series of knocks anywhere. Then there was the voice. Eastern, exotic and familiar.

"Lucy. It's me. We have to go. They are coming for you. You have to trust me. We have five minutes." Nicolescu had no idea that Roberts was racing towards them, and that he had back-up in the form of two staff.

The clock was not ticking for him, but for Cynthia Bell – his captive audience of one who was potentially bleeding to death. He needed to keep her alive. He knew how. He'd read the book, turned the top of the page down as a marker. He just needed a donor.

"Come on. Come fucking on. For crying out loud."

'Traffic at this time? Didn't these bastards have homes to go to?'

Roberts changed down to second, gripping the wheel and letting it slip as he turned corners. It was contrary to everything he had been taught.

His arm muscles pounded, the bones that the toothless bastard Nicolescu had stamped upon as he lay manacled to an underground train years before were screaming out at him.

He knew he was getting close, he could almost smell him.

He dialled Thomas' cell phone. No answer. In a way, that was a good thing. Roberts would cross the river soon and then with a good run he'd be at her apartment in under ten. Local police were bound to be there any minute.

"Lucy. We have to go, my dear. Now." He tapped gently.

She slid open the spyhole and looked. There he was. The man who had made her his own, from the very earliest days.

She loved him, yet detested him too. Adored, his compassionate soul, despised his drug-fuelled demons.

"I'm coming." The urge was too great. For all the information she had given Roberts and his blue-eyed partner, for saving that girl O'Shea's life – not a penny. For a working girl, money was everything. And despite what Roberts had said, Connie Nicolescu had never harmed her. Was now to be the first time?

She opened the door. He hugged her, took her bag and introduced her to the younger man.

"This is Andre. He is my driver. Come, we must leave. I need to get you to a place of safety. Trust only me."

It was a lie. It all was. He knew she had betrayed him.

They reached the car, got in and headed south – blending with traffic. Thomas sat back and saw another man, counted that she was outnumbered three to one. And yet with him there she felt safe.

The first police unit arrived seconds later. As instructed, they waited outside in the street. For all intents they may as well have been a hundred miles away.

The Vauxhall turned left, second left, right and straight on, a different route but equally anonymous.

Roberts was at the flat three minutes later. He took the lift, followed by one of the two uniformed officers, asking the other to take the stairs. Rank had its privileges.

They got to the hallway. "Anything on the stairs?"

"Nothing boss" said a breathless constable who decided that now would be a great time to start smoking.

"Wait here."

He approached the door and knocked. A nearby door opened.

"Wasting your time, guv. She left with two blokes about five minutes ago. Bloody door has been banging all night.

We all know what she gets up to, filthy cow. Each to their own though, eh? Night."

"Wait." Roberts had his brown shoe in the doorway. "Two of them?"

"Yep."

"Description?"

"You Old Bill?"

"No, I just get a kick out of hanging around with men in uniform. Yes, I am a police officer. A DCI as it happens."

"Crikey, not seen one of you round here since the last murder."

"Look, I'd love to chat, but what did they look like?"

"Swarthy. Black hair. Druggies, probably. Needed a good meal. One was younger, the other one, older, he did all the talking. Seemed pretty friendly with her. Even called her dear, which was nice. Anyway, Coronation Street is on. Anything else?"

"No. You've been outstanding, say hi to Ken Barlow for me."

Roberts leant against Thomas' door. It was open. He beckoned to the staff who approached, drawing their spray and batons.

He pushed open the door and entered, remembering the last time he had done so. Nothing. Lucy Thomas never allowed anyone into her home without a fanfare. She was gone.

So now all he had to do was find her and Cynthia Bell. Any more good news?

CHAPTER THIRTEEN

With occasional and deliberate stops the Vauxhall finally got back to the old fireworks site.

"This is remote Connie. Pretty. But remote." Thomas was trying her best to sound confident.

"It is. We need to keep you safe. Away from everyone. Come on."

He held her hand and lifted her gently out of the car, picking up her bag and guiding her towards a doorway.

As she entered the darkened room, she felt the first barb of the Taser hit her skin. She tried to scream but failed, convinced she was saying something she could only offer an extended moan. The pain was not intense, but it was rapid and soon over. Her whole body was rigid, her legs cramped and as she fell forward, landing in an undignified position onto the concrete floor where she relaxed. Her wig had slipped and her make-up had slithered, now smudged and unattractive. It was a low point in her career. She thanked God above that no one was filming her.

The probes were still in her back and attached to the Taser.

Plasticuffs were wrapped around her wrists and tightened with a rasping sound.

Who would do this to her? Had they got Constantin too?

Carried like the carcass of a dead animal she felt genuine fear for the first time in her life. It worsened when she saw the man she trusted stood at a bench, alongside another similar structure. She could see another person lying on it, strapped down, immobile and pale. She was probably dead.

"Constantin please..."

He looked at the two males. "You know what to do."

They lifted her up and onto the bench and secured her to it, level with the other person who she could see was a female. They then started cutting away her sleeves. Silver-grey tape was wrapped across her lips.

Nicolescu looked at her. Did he feel hatred towards her or pity?

Had she betrayed him or herself? Did she need to die?

His head was awash with questions. For now, what she needed to do was keep her unintentional roommate alive. He hoped that everything he had read about this moment would work. He stared at the yellowed pages of a manual. It had to be a manual, there was no room for higher-level communications and the internet was taboo.

He had no idea how they had got the book, or the equipment that was on the nearby table, but he admired their skill and tenacity in providing him with everything from his shopping list. Strong gypsies all of them.

He opened the book which dated from the First World War and began to read, avoiding the frantic eyes of Cynthia Bell and Lucy Thomas.

The two males stepped back – quite unsure what was going to happen.

"I need light. And peace."

He nodded from one to the other. "If this works, we keep her alive. If it doesn't she bleeds to death too. Either way I have to try, as our surgery didn't quite go to plan. At least we have plenty of land on which to bury them." He smiled at Bell who was willing herself to die.

"OK. I first need to make an end-to-end connection between the donor – this person here who I used to love. And the patient, this person here who actually means nothing to me."

It was as if he were performing a lecture, or a TED Talk video to medical students.

"Right. I need to cut here, next to the elbow. This vein just...here...and slide this in...like this."

The first male passed out.

"Now comes the difficult part. There may be some blood."

Bell was trying her best to scream but instead made desperate muffled, gagging sounds.

The younger male watched in awe. He had never seen anything like it in his sheltered life.

"Sir. How many times have you done this?"

"Only once. Right..."

He passed a suture through the radial artery in Thomas' wrist then clamped it. He slid a short metal tube into the gap and threaded the artery through it, pulling it back to form a cuff. He secured it in place. It was surreal. He was actually smiling.

He told the boy to add extra pressure at the junction of Bell's elbow. He had the tourniquet if necessary but that seemed to even up the odds a little too much. He worked better under pressure.

With the blood flow stemmed he prepared Bell's vein. Then, when he was satisfied that the unions were in effect clean and 'watertight' he joined them with a rubber tube.

There were easier ways than this. But the book he had only showed this one untried and latterly precluded method. This was brutal and had its origins hundreds of years prior.

If the blood flowed and did not clot too quickly, he would succeed in his aim – to keep Bell alive long enough to send another message.

Thomas' heart pumped the blood around her body, through the cannula and into the tube. The rhythmic pulse did its job admirably, forcing her universal Type O blood into Bell's famished veins.

Bell visibly improved, almost grateful, she accepted the life-giving donation, conversely hoping it was the beginning of the end.

Thomas watched as her own blood left her, wondering where she would be in the next few hours and why this had happened. She should have listened to Roberts.

It took longer than he thought but Constantin had succeeded in keeping Bell alive. The wound where he had removed her hand would probably never heal in the conditions in which he had found himself, literally operating. But that was acceptable. She was what he saw as a casualty of war. He gave her morphine and watched her settle, her eyes closing, praying to never open them again.

He removed the cannula from Thomas' wrist, held a gauze pad on the small wound, then added a decent sized plaster. Tapped her on the face and nearly said thank you. For now, she was alive too and useful.

Roberts rang a few people, spoke to the control room then headed home. There was nothing he could do. He hadn't felt as professionally anxious in years. Why couldn't these people just go somewhere else, and annoy someone else? In classic negotiation operations he knew that if they had Bell in their captivity, sooner or later there would be a message of some form. He wasn't sure however why they had taken Thomas – and what for.

Torture? Fun? Revenge? Help? Perhaps she had converted to their way of thinking? Money talked. She could talk under water. Unlike Niko, his mind whirred.

'Stop now. Stop. Seriously Jason stop.'

He slipped into bed knowing he had to be up and awake and on top form again. His team would need a briefing on what had happened, and he needed to elevate this to the next level – probably higher.

He needed Cade back in the country too.

He closed his eyes and endured a half-sleep until four when he lowered himself out of bed and forced the shower nozzle onto pulse and stood there trying to make sense of the night before. His head nodded, eyes closed. He was back on the tube train, hearing the bones shatter in his forearm. The sound of them snapping brought him back to life with a jolt.

He drew pictures on the steamed-up glass and tried to use it as a whiteboard – brainstorming, but nothing transpired. All he could do was draw a bloody wave. He needed to be at work, surrounded by people that understood. He adored his wife, but she hadn't got a clue about the brutal way of life that surrounded him. 'It's better that way' he said as he rinsed the shower glass and stepped out.

He shaved, cleaned his teeth, kissed his wife on the hand and left. It was just after five.

Bell had made it through the night. Thomas was in a stronger condition and trying to remonstrate with anyone that would listen now that the duct tape had been removed.

No one could hear her, so she could shout as loud and long as she wanted to.

"Hello Lucy." Nicolescu walked into the room, rubbing his eyes.

"How did you sleep?"

"I didn't. I needed to go to the toilet. You cannot keep us like this."

"I can. There is a hole in the bench. Just do it, we will hose you down."

"I've seen animals treated better than this."

"That is because I admire animals. They are loyal."

"Why Connie? What are you doing to me? I thought we were...special?"

"Why? Because you betrayed me. And that must never happen. What am I doing? I am using you as my medical experiment. You survived the first round. And no, *we* are not special anymore. I hope you like it here Lucy – whatever your name is – because this is where your life will end among the brambles and scrubland of a derelict factory, a fitting end for someone who is also living in the past. I have to go, I have things to do, but I will be back later. See you after work. Ciao."

He pulled a strip of tape from a roll and placed it tightly over her mouth. He was sick of hearing her voice and did not see why his team needed to listen to her endless cackle.

The way he left was beyond bizarre, almost as if they were in a relationship. She turned to Bell and spoke with her eyes.

"You OK?"

Bell could only nod gently.

. . .

Roberts arrived at work, parked and walked to the stairs. Old habits die hard. He got to his office to be met by McGee.

"Morning boss. Cracking out there. Love mornings like this, cold but blue sky – I ran alongside the river this morning just as the sun came up. Ready for another day?"

She was pretty and really bloody annoying. So upbeat. Her eyes were the window to a soul that he admired.

Roberts looked up through his own rather hooded eyes and the veil of a pounding headache.

She knew straight away. "Long black. No milk, some sugar and a bacon sandwich, right?"

"Nice. But make mine a croissant, I'm vegetarian. Grab one for yourself though and get the team together in twenty. And Bridie."

"Boss?"

"Thanks."

A cardboard box sat on his desk, covered in bright yellow labels. It was dominating his workspace, so he pulled it towards him; he was too tired to read the labels or even shake it in a reckless manner. He slit open the tape with a packing knife and opened the box. It contained a hundred small polystyrene shapes and a candle with a pre-printed note.

'Thank you for your order which has been sent by a friend. We hope this product soothes your mind and aids your recovery. In each is a unique message that will change your day.'

"Can't get any bloody worse can it?" He laughed. "I'm talking to a candle. I need some sleep." He looked up. Nick Fisher was at the door.

"Guv. You look like shit. And if it hasn't dawned on you, you are having a conversation with a candle. Coffee?"

"I was waxing lyrical, detective sergeant." He knew it was awful but comedically he was spent.

"Anyway Nick, you are too late. Your gorgeous nemesis has already gone for one, and a bacon sandwich too. Text her. She'll bring you one. My treat."

Fisher produced his phone and started texting. "Do you want a light for that boss?" He pointed to the candle.

"You know, seeing as though you've become a fucking raging hippy overnight. What next, tantric massage and quinoa at the briefings?" He smiled.

"I didn't know you cared Fish. And I didn't know you smoked?"

"I don't boss. Stopped after I was an undercover officer at a *Rockbitch* concert."

"Rock?"

"Bitch. It's a rather long story. But a good detective always carries a lighter."

He allowed the blue flame to ignite the white wick. Roberts watched it dance and flicker until the cord lit and the flame became yellow.

"I can't smell fuck all boss? I'd ask for your money back from the Tibetan monks or wherever it was you got it from."

"It was a gift. No idea where from, I threw the packaging away. You're right. It doesn't smell at all. Come on, let's go and get this briefing done."

The flame teased the wax, heating it and causing it to liquefy. Its maker had no idea how long it would last, all he cared about was getting the message delivered in a way that was memorable and ideally it would reveal itself before its recipient in a way that made his day memorable.

. . .

"Right. You all know the history of the team that calls itself the Seventh Wave. You know about its hierarchy and how in the past they have targeted the main banks in this country? You know about the key players, where we think they are and why we think they have risen again as a tangible threat to the UK?"

Everyone nodded. There were no questions.

"Good. So why eleven years later?" Roberts left the question to hang in the air. He believed in the continuing questions methodology. Keep asking why and eventually you got to the answer. But for now, he didn't want to do all the talking.

"They've been banged up in the big house, guv?" It was Fisher.

"Or they escaped...?" McGee.

"Some escaped and re-formed, waiting for Stefanescu to get back to the helm?" Fisher.

"Something else boss." McGee.

It was like a rally at Wimbledon. Centre Court, match point.

Then another voice chipped into the conversation, female, assured.

"Because they failed to get what they wanted last time."

The team turned in unison. Fisher spoke first in tones that were meant to be hushed.

"Fuck me where did she come from?"

Stood in the doorway was Sassy Lane the former Secretary of State for Foreign and Commonwealth Affairs and now Home Secretary.

"Well to be precise, Detective Sergeant Fisher, my Jaguar, before that the Houses of Parliament, but originally, I was born in a small village in the very tip of Leicestershire. Need I carry on?"

"No ma'am, apologies. I tend to use expletives when I'm excited."

"Don't we all? Apology accepted. I'm glad I excite someone."

Fisher had no idea how she knew his name. It was a party piece. Gather photographs of teams that she worked with and memorise them one by one.

"And you DS McGee. Good to see you sparring with your colleagues. Great to see a woman in a position of authority too." She winked.

Lane's hair had shortened over the years and she had aged – government work did that to you but she still looked good, arguably the most attractive member of what was known as the Great Offices of State.

As attractive as she was – and she was – Lane had a bite worse than a piranha if anyone crossed her – or worse still, picked on the weak. Roberts remembered that about her from 2004 and he liked it at the time and still did. It seemed like a few months since he had first met her. The fact that she had remained in government, at the highest possible level meant she was either damned good at what she did or she was a favourite of the Prime Minister James Cole.

For eleven years Cole had maintained a stable and rational Conservative government and had promoted those that he trusted. Secretly he also favoured those that he liked – and in Lane's case loved. It was perhaps the best or worst kept secret in parliament. Somehow the gutter press had missed it altogether. Hiding in plain sight had never been more relevant.

She slipped off her goatskin gloves. They had become her trademark. Folding them she placed them on the table and took a seat next to McGee.

"Mind if I join you?"

"Not at all ma'am. You're the boss." And she was. Policing, national security and control of MI5. Her last portfolio was impressive, but this one meant more to her and she saw it as the next step to leading the country. Either that or become pregnant to Cole and live in the Home Counties and leave it all behind her. Two kids, nice home, Range Rover, a few ducks and a black Lab. Some chance.

She spoke. "DCI Roberts has outlined the core aspects of the operation – one which you refer to as Op Niko. You may be asking why the government is interested in a criminal syndicate. Well, the truth is I am interested in all crime that impacts upon the UK – but I don't expect you to buy that as a reason for deploying resources." She looked around the room, engaging with everyone in there including her protection officer who had taken a place at the back of the room.

"Here's the deal. Alex Stefanescu and his band of merry men took something that did not belong to them. Something very valuable, and we managed to get a copy back. We believe he has another and..." She paused and looked at the ceiling before forming her words carefully. "And there is another copy somewhere in existence. We feel it is due to surface any day now."

"Minister with respect." It was Fisher again.

"Do go on. And please don't use that term, we all know what it really means."

"No, but I really do respect you. However, you have told us something and nothing." He could feel the team's combined eyes boring into him and a few even gasped.

"Look, come on you lot, let's cut to the proverbial here. The door is locked and we are knee deep in this. We've historically lost team members to this shower of...shit. And now we've got another one missing. Personally I see that as more important than any document."

He knew he'd overstepped the mark.

"DS Fisher I admire your courage but let me make it quite clear, if I get the documents back then I'll be happy. If I have to expose people to managed risk I will. DCI Roberts when were you going to tell us about your missing team member?"

"In my office in ten, ma'am?"

She smiled. "There appears to be little point. Let's talk about it now."

Roberts outlined his concerns about Bell – bringing her absence to the attention of his whole team, some of whom had not been party to her disappearance.

"OK, what can we do to help?" Lane was genuinely concerned.

"Resources ma'am. Frankly, she could be anywhere."

"Then you will have your resources. Dear God if the woman who controls the UK Police can't get you resources then who can? I could draft the entire Suffolk force in if I chose to." She laughed, but it was uncomfortable given her audience.

"Minister?" It was McGee this time. "Forgive me Ma'am but you said documents – plural?"

"Well spotted. You are indeed eagle-eared. Is that right? Anyway, yes I did."

The team were discovering the frustrations of dealing with members of parliament who were the true veterans of avoiding the question.

"And?" McGee wasn't in the mood to give in with an audience that may never happen again.

Lane sighed. Spoke quickly, indicating a slight frustration.

"And eleven years ago, I thought this had been put to bed once and for all. Thought it would die a death. Do you want to hear the whole thing from the start?" She looked at her beloved Raymond Weil wristwatch and then at her

Personal Protection Officer, Dan Bradley, who nodded and held up his hands to show ten minutes.

"My PPO says it's OK, so I'll crack on! The team we are all hunting came into possession of documents that were stolen in a raid on a Hatton Garden diamond brokers. You may recall the job. We thought they were conventional thieves, they certainly took some of the jewels, but what they left behind was worth a fortune and you and your regional police colleagues recovered a lot more." She sipped some water from a nearby glass.

"It made no sense. Members of your squad, including Mr Roberts and Mr Cade were already investigating the team – the raid just happened to occur at the same time. Your team caught up with the group as they fractured and headed to British ports to head back to Europe and Romania."

Even though most knew the story every member of the Niko squad was looking at her, intent on hearing the whole thing.

"We were on the back foot from the get go. It was only when one of my team divulged that the cases that were missing contained a set of documents that were so damaging to the government and the British monarchy that we knew..." She stopped and looked at Nick Fisher.

"To use your vernacular...we knew we were knee deep in shit."

"And the other document boss?" Fisher held her gaze.

"Ah that little...diamond...was the one that related to Britain, or rather the United Kingdom leaving the European Union. The 'people' wanted a referendum, they had done for years. But we knew it would be a potential disaster. What with leaving the Union and destabilising the bloody monarchy too it could have spelled disaster for us on so many fronts. Financially it could have put us on a level with Greece. The Commonwealth is still a big thing and we could have seen it dissolve at a time when some of its members were looking towards independence. The pink parts on the map were diminishing..."

"But I don't get it ma'am." Roberts was now in the chair. "Surely we would just deny all knowledge, say that the documents were false and hope it washed away downstream?"

"Ideal worlds are just that, Jason. In this day and age when the media are so bloody ruthless, the left wing news media would have slaughtered us if they had so much as got a sniff of this. They would have served official information requests on us and demanded we had the documents examined independently."

"And the right?"

"And the right, particularly the far right would have leapt on it like a dog to a bloody bone. That is why we paid him to keep quiet."

A pin would have been deafening.

CHAPTER FOURTEEN

"You *paid* him?"

"Yes. We *paid* him. It was a calculated decision following a higher level meeting with your bosses and mine. Look for Christ's sake, none of this must leave this room. Do I make myself clear? You are the team appointed to sweep up the dog mess from the parliamentary garden." She rubbed her hands over her eyes and looked at the wall clock. Was it only that time?

"You've got four minutes left. Then I have to go. But I will be back. Any questions?"

There were far too many to complete in the time allotted. Roberts pursued the only angle he thought viable in the time.

"OK ma'am, so what we are saying is that he's back on the scene because he has escaped from prison – or was conveniently released, and is now blackmailing an entire *country*?" The last few words failed to hide the enormity of the situation.

"Look, I know this bastard, and he's too quiet for my liking."

"We've got GCHQ listening, we've got field sources gathering intel. Interpol, Europol, the whole nine yards. We are *onto* this DCI Roberts."

"Well, with respect Home Secretary you did not answer my question. And I for one am sick of being lied to." He knew it could be a career-altering statement, at worst, career-ending.

"Yes, Jason. He is too quiet. Paying ten million to a man who cannot spend it was deemed to be good value compared to the billions we would lose if this got out."

"Ten?"

She nodded.

"Million?"

Again.

"Surely we have ways of tracking this money?"

She shook her head, probably involuntarily. "No. Not yet. It was all based on cryptocurrencies and the dark net – all too much even for my understanding. You will need to find someone to act as an advisor on that. Pick a young person. Understand one thing. This bastard that calls himself Jackdaw may be an evil and at times savage thug but he's no fool. Pay the man and let him live a life of forever looking over his shoulder I say. He's got enemies from and of the state now. And when we have finished our campaign, he'll feel he's got enemies within too."

"OK, so we pay him and he doesn't go away. Can't you see he is playing with you? What is he after now? This is not about money."

"More. They always want more. If he gets the whole set of documents, he has the Royal Flush so to speak. And..."

A feather colliding with the floor would have been cacophonous.

"There's an 'and'? After all that ma'am? There's actually an 'and'?"

She stood, causing the whole team to follow suit. She shepherded them back down into their seats.

"The psych teams are doing their thing. They feel they are getting to know him. How he thinks. How his team think. How they work and what motivates them. Each component of the team is being drawn up at the headquarters of our new group that has been set up to hunt him down. The team is called Orion, I'm sure I don't need to tell you that it is named after the Greek legend, although most of the team that has been established so far refer to it colloquially as Hunter. And you will be their bow. Start gathering your team together. We expect some form of coordinated and targeted attack upon us soon. The two targets being the original documents and..." She couldn't bring herself to say it.

Roberts slammed his hand down onto the desk causing papers to rise and a cup of cold coffee to spill, which in turn caused the protection officer to place a discreet hand inside his jacket.

"You have not answered my bloody question Minister!"

Bradley stepped forward. "Sir – please."

Lane ushered him away. "It's OK, Dan. Mr Roberts has a valid point and if I can't trust him we are pretty buggered. Besides you could always shoot him."

He noted the thinly veiled threat and the use of Mr rather than his rank, perhaps it was a subtle and timely warning.

"They are hunting you, Jason." She let the words hang in the cool office air. "You, everyone connected to you and everyone in this room."

"Then they are very brave ma'am."

"No Jason, they are imbalanced, irrational, greedy and dangerous. I recommend you get your houses in order, surround yourselves by people you trust and get some of the old members of your team back here – and soon. Remember, this is bigger than *Ben-Hur*. Much bigger."

"When were you going to tell us this?"

"When the time was right."

Roberts escorted Lane to the lift, thanked her for her time, promised her his total support then shook her hand and nodded to Bradley. "Look after her."

He walked back to his office, calling to McGee and Fisher as he walked past the briefing room. "My office and now, please."

He sat on the edge of the desk and was joined by his two DSs.

"Well?"

"Boss this is not what I expected when I was running alongside the Thames this morning."

"No, me neither and I drove."

"So we are the arrowhead then?"

"Nice. Seems that way, Bridie. No disrespect but I need Cade and Daniel back here. I'll sort that out. And we need to recruit a few more too. Find a crypto-whatever she bloody called it specialist will you? And order some tea and coffee in, and Bridie..."

"Boss?"

"Biscuits. I need some of those nice ones with the chocolate on, no sprinkles, they stick in my teeth. No figs either, can't stand the seeds. And no..."

"Ginger nuts, boss?"

"You've got it. OK, you two have got enough to be going on with, I've got to make some calls. Seems money is no object, so let's do what she said, surround yourselves in kit and people you trust. And decent motors. And biscuits."

"She didn't mention kit, boss?" Fisher was already working out what to buy.

"Didn't she, Nick? Oh well, must be my hearing. We'll deal with that when the overweight opera singer has stopped her wailing."

"Very PC, guv. Are we considering safe houses?" McGee was experienced and capable, nevertheless the briefing had given her plenty to think about.

"Fair point. But do we really feel threatened yet?"

The three sat there pondering the situation when Fisher leant forward and looked at Roberts' desk. He was transfixed by the candle. The flame had changed and there was a hint of burning in the room,

He looked again then stood and bent over it. Roberts moved away as the smell was worsening.

"Nick?" Roberts felt he was talking to a wall.

Fisher looked again. "What the hell is in that bloody thing?"

McGee was starting to retch.

"Jesus Christ boss look."

"Put it out, put it out, Nick."

Fisher rubbed his fingers in the wick and found them pressing up against two more and a thumb. The wax had melted quicker than anticipated. Constantin had envisaged a slow reveal.

The detached limbs were clinging to a piece of paper.

"Get SOCO in here now. Can you read it?" Roberts was visibly distressed, angry and already forming an opinion about the note – that it might be a threat. He had no idea where the candle had come from but his inbuilt fear told him he knew who the hand belonged to.

"Boss, we won't get prints off it. We need to find the packaging."

"No, Nick, we need to find the bloody owner of that..."

He pointed to the hand, feeling more nauseous by the second. "What is wrong with these people?"

The team elevated the need for forensic support – and ensured that the new information was passed to Lane. She asked to be kept in touch, now was a chance to test her. She responded within twenty minutes with a simple phone call.

The on-call SOCO was in Roberts' office within half an hour.

"Well?"

"Give me chance boss. I need to get a lift off the note, it's one hell of a long shot. Seriously, this is all but impossible. This could be career-defining."

"This could be life-ending if you don't get your finger out."

"No pun intended, boss?"

"None, Peter, none whatsoever."

"Can you give me a clue as to who I am looking for? Might just narrow down the search if we can nominate a few people?"

Roberts grimaced as he spoke. "One is an Eastern European offender called Constantin Nicolescu."

"Will we have his prints on file boss?"

"One hundred percent."

"And the other?"

"Closer to home. As in those prints right there, embedded in that bloody candle. I think they belong to one of my team."

"Nasty. OK, but I still need to find the prints."

"Forgive me Pete but aren't they on the end of those bloody fingers?"

"Roger that, boss. Crossed wires. No more daft questions, no more puns."

The SOCO knew that the chance of gaining any forensic value from the note was beyond limited. Normal paper, yes, he could use a number of methods to extract the magical points of value. He needed ten at least, any less would render his evidence to be 'questionable'. The more, in this case, despite the subject matter, the merrier.

It all stemmed back to the late eighteen hundreds. A time when Sir Francis Galton had first discussed loops, whorls and arches and how they were found to be unique, like the markings on a zebra's backside. He wrote a book about fingerprints and came up against great resistance, however, the forensic seed had been sown.

It wasn't until the next century that the first successful conviction was allowed using the fingerprints of one Harry Jackson.

Jackson had stolen a billiard ball in a burglary in Denmark Hill, London. It was June 27th 1902 to be precise and only fifteen minutes away from where Roberts now stood in his office. A detective sergeant called Charles Collins had observed a perfect thumb print on a ball, its surface ideal material for fingerprint analysis. He took a photograph of it and later compared it to Jackson's prints. He was convicted and served seven years. It was a triumph of modern policing and led the way to many developments in a system that went on to safely convict thousands.

If only this case were so easy.

"Boss I need to photograph the candle. Then remove the hand, clean it up, preserve it, print it. This is a first for me. I may talk to the path' people, they could have more experience with this type of crime scene than me – but I doubt it."

"You thinking of this as a murder enquiry Pete?"

"Aren't you?"

"I wasn't." he dropped his head back and stared at the ceiling.

. . .

If Constantin Nicolescu was paranoid, then his leader was the opposite. He hadn't felt as free in years. He had money; he had girls; he had friends, old and new. He had cars that he couldn't drive but he had a home he could hide away in, in his beloved Craiova, the city in Romania that he called home and one which hid him with a passion that went far deeper than loyalty.

Alex Stefanescu was their criminal success story, and he was still feared. But they didn't hunt him anymore. The authorities of many countries, including his own. They knew better.

A year perhaps. That is all he felt he needed to stay off the radar. The British had actually paid him a fortune to stay quiet. But they failed to see it was not about the money. He had money already. He had assets that even the most powerful courts in Europe had failed to seize. That would teach them for tying him to that vile bed with chords so tight that his wrists bled.

He sipped on his favourite drink and admired the festival of flesh paraded before him. Dutch, Swedish, Moroccan and an Australian. The latter disinterested him. The last one he had from the southern hemisphere was good. But she had let him down badly, so he killed her and her lover in a rage that even awakened his own already low standards of depravity. He'd never had a Moroccan before although he had often wondered why some of the most beautiful women in the world chose to cover themselves up.

He could make this one do that, perhaps? Have her in her national dress? It added something. He wasn't sure what. But he was able to relax, finally, and she would help.

The local authorities were content to leave him alone and so he could live a life, of sorts, until one day with his ill-gotten gains he could buy the island or even a nation that occupied his mind all those years ago. He had dreamed of the day, night after sordid night in Pazardzhik.

'Aim high Alex' his mother had told him. He killed her too.

He lay back on the sofa and looked up at the ceiling as the almond-skinned girl revealed herself, dropping her burqa to the floor and stepping out of it. She was indeed beautiful. Such a pitiful waste. He needed to share her around his friends but something prevented him from pursuing this idea – morals?

Where had this notion come from? Morals? He'd lost those when he plunged the knife into his dear mother.

He was far from selfish with material things, just his love. That trait he saved for the very few women in his life. To date there had been two. His wife and his daughter.

The girl in front of him, standing awkwardly, trying to cover herself up whilst the drugs eased her shame was just another conquest from another country. Someone else to while away the minutes. A pin on a map.

"Put it back on. I want to remove it."

She followed his instructions. The other girls had warned her not to disappoint him. "You are so beautiful – don't tell me your name, I have no wish to get too close to you. Now come here and entertain me in ways your mother would have been ashamed of."

She approached him as if she were on an indiscernible lead. Pavlov's dog. He clapped his hands, she walked towards his bed. Addiction did that to a person. But not to Alex – his only addiction was notoriety.

She was sat with her legs astride him, staring at the ceiling, making all the right noises and knowing he wouldn't last much longer. Her mother had actually taught her well. In her homeland, disappointing a man could have cost her life.

He marvelled at her body, the way it moved, toned as if she spent day after day in a gym. She didn't, she was born that way and had starved herself regularly, as she felt, wrongly, that men only found thin girls attractive. Covering that form was like pulling a dustcover over a Bugatti and Alex knew this, for he had one, somewhere. It was blue he remembered that. He couldn't recall the last time it had ever even been started.

Procured from the proceeds of his crimes, ordered whilst he was in prison and put somewhere safe. Because he could.

Just like he could have her. When. Wherever and how.

CHAPTER FIFTEEN

TWENTY THREE MILES SOUTH OF THE CITY OF AUCKLAND, in the historical home of the New Zealand Special Air Service, Scott McCall waited to see the 'OC'.

His boss was also a long-term friend, however, he always called him boss, or in certain circles, sir.

He had run a parallel career with the officer in charge; McCall, a foot soldier and his boss, always an officer. Despite many tests their friendship endured and in Scott McCall the OC saw a true warrior. He knew McCall better than anyone. They had dug in once, no more than a foot deep scrape on the scorched surface of a remote plain in Afghanistan, and they had waited to be rescued from what McCall later described as the arsehole on the arsehole of the world.

'You learn a great deal about yourself – and the men you fight with in situations such as those.' Lieutenant Colonel Michael Steel had once said at a Rotary Club lunch.

Steel had the sort of spirit, attitude and importantly surname to ensure he was always going to make it. Mike to his friends, he was a leader and a gentleman. What he didn't know about the gallant art of soldiering was simply not worth knowing. And he had the same in-depth understanding of the man that was walking across the parade square – heading his way, back straight, eyes front, bang on time.

Steel watched him as he entered his office on what had already been a long day, but he knew McCall would look as fresh as a daisy. If he had just completed the fabled log run he would turn around and do it again – and again. Carrying the lion's share of the weight. And smile as he did so.

But the McCall that Steel looked at today was not the man he knew.

"Sit down, Scottie. What's troubling you?" It was a rare event for the boss to call him by his real name. He was Mack on any given day. Everyone had a nickname. Even the boss. Some had sported them for so long that no one knew what they were actually called.

McCall hesitated – enough that his boss spotted the delay. He leant forward in the chair, hands on his knees.

"Sir." He scratched at his neck – it was his 'tell'. He swallowed hard then continued.

"Mike, I just need a break. Some time away. You said it might happen one day. On a day when everything seems alright, far from the spoils of war and all that. Well, it's happened a while ago but I've fought the bastard black dog ever since." He had delivered the request in a single extended sentence and every word was hurting him. Both men knew it.

The black dog McCall was referring to didn't want to chase a ball.

"OK. No problem. How long do you need and where are you planning on going?" Steel looked at him, in the eyes, waiting, clicking the end of his silver Parker pen. Click. Click. "You know I need to ask this?"

"Two weeks at most, boss. England. There's a girl…"

It rocked Steel. "A girl? Jesus, Mack, we were beginning to wonder if you were batting for the other side! Not that that's an issue in the modern army."

"It's not, boss. You know my opinion. If you can stand shoulder to shoulder with me in a firefight, then I don't give a fat rat's shit what your gender, persuasion or creed is. But thank you for your vote of confidence."

"England eh? Good man. You'll enjoy it. I was based there for a while as you know. Good people. Grey skinned and they all live in back-to-back houses like in Coronation Street and their accents vary every second mile, but you'll take to them, some of the most dependable people you will ever meet. You should try to go to Hereford, meet up with the regiment there. You are bound to know a few of the boys and they can put you up, save a few dollars."

"Do you think I'm broke, boss?"

"No not at all, Mack. I was just trying to help." He waited just long enough before asking, "You sure you are OK mate?"

McCall did not hesitate. "Cast iron, boss. One hundred percent. Just need some space. That girl in the car last year…" He stopped himself, realising that the impromptu mission to save Elena Petrova's life had been just that, unplanned and secret. A year ago. He could still see her face, wondered if she survived. He had tried to find out but failed. Couldn't even establish her name. That hurt professionally. No one eluded the regiment. And now he was using her as an excuse.

"What about her? That was last year wasn't it? It's OK, I know all about your unscheduled touchdown. I know everything. A certain fly boy is dating my daughter don't forget." He smiled a warm smile as he sipped on a still-hot cup of tea; dark brown, two sugars just as God and the army had intended.

"Putting it bluntly, it upset me. She had an effect upon me that I've never experienced before."

"It was a while ago, Mack. So it's her you are going to see?"

"I wish, boss! She was stunning. I often dream about her. No such luck. I met this one online. She seems nice. Lives in London."

"Online, Mack? Are you sure she's a girl?"

"One hundred percent."

"Has she asked you for money – you know for an operation for her sick sister?"

"No, Mike, she hasn't. Look can I have this fucking leave or not?"

Steel tapped the keyboard on his desk, looked up and down the screen, sucked air through his teeth, then signed off the application. There and then, he knew there was no point in delaying.

Handing it over the desk he said, "Signed, sealed and delivered. Make sure you come back though, sergeant, or I'll be knee-deep – you have negative leave already. I'll put it down as a welfare visit to some long lost auntie. Now bugger off and don't forget to send me a postcard."

Pointing to his mug, emblazoned with his own nickname he said, "And bring me some decent tea bags back from Blighty. If there is one thing the Poms do well…it's tea."

McCall stood, saluted and walked quickly out of the office, through the secure gate, across the car park to his battered old Honda and then drove the short journey to his home. It was the first time he had ever lied to a man he respected hugely. He hoped it would be the last.

He had his girls to farewell. He knew they would understand.

Steel closed the desk drawer. Clicked the pen, shut down the computer. It was the first time Mack had ever lied to him. Christ, he hoped he was OK.

In the winter months, before his leave request was granted, McCall had used every conceivable method of tracing the girl from the Porsche and importantly the person – if indeed it was a person – called Jackdaw. The computer systems they had at his barracks were standalone, capable of great things and he had spent hours searching for her without leaving a footprint.

He had given a plausible reason for using the systems and the place being what it was, no one challenged him.

No reports of any activity in the Coromandel Peninsula on that exquisite day even existed, in a country that reported on most car crashes. He saw the air ambulance, saw the police. Nothing. She had simply vanished off the best radar in the country.

He had more luck with the name Jackdaw. At least he did when a subtle ping on his phone brought him to an article featured in the Bulgarian media and naming the man that stared out of the computer screen at him as Alex Stefanescu. He knew the Google alert would pay dividends in the end.

He had met some bad bastards in his time – killed a few of them too, one up close and very personal. But this man had the coldest stare he had ever witnessed. His eyes were comparable to black marble. Not shark-like. More like granite. He decided that he had mortuary slab eyes. And he disliked them and their owner. The problem was he knew he needed to work with him in the short term.

He now had his name, his location and a contact

number. All he needed to do was find him and make him an offer he would find impossible to refuse.

He dialled the number, prefixed with two zeroes, a four and another zero. He was never nervous at work, but then he was never doing anything illegal – even shooting people in a war zone had its risks of prosecution and he knew the risks, this was different.

He was lowering the steel into the forge – his plan to create a sword as strong as possible and one he could use to finally sever the debts that had dragged his family into the pit of despair. The problem for McCall was this sword, unlike the dagger on his sandy-coloured beret was double-edged in its metaphorical sense.

The dial tone changed to a ringing tone. He considered hanging up.

'Who Dares Wins'. It said so on the door that he walked through every day. He let it ring. And ring.

"Hello?" The voice was instantly recognisable as Eastern European. McCall was probably closer than he had ever been. Ever would be.

"Hello. Who is that?" An American accent.

The voice recognised an English speaker and changed accordingly.

"You don't ring here and ask who this is my friend. Either you know who you want to speak to or you don't." The ambient noise in the background told McCall that he had reached a pub or club.

"So can I help you? If not, I am a busy man."

McCall sensed this was a lieutenant not the general. His instinct had never betrayed him.

"I'd like to speak to Mr Jack Daw. Now is that possible please?"

The faceless voice laughed. "Man, you have some massive balls. No one rings this number and demands to speak to the boss – for that is his correct name. No one. Do you understand?" There was menace in the voice now. "And no one calls him Jackdaw anymore."

McCall now had two more pieces of information. He was content that for now he was dealing with the right person and he knew that his boss that he was clearly afraid of, probably owned the club.

"I understand. Completely. I must apologise. You sound like you are in charge there my friend. I have a parcel to deliver see? Sent to the owner – a Mr Stefan some time ago. We have been trying to deliver it. We were told he might have come out of prison...and...from what you tell me Mr Jackdaw, well he doesn't like being called that? Ain't that interesting? So what should I call him?"

"And you are?" Cold. Calculated. Tinged with a caveat that said 'I do not trust you.'

"Mike Brown from Federal Express. I'm the complaints manager."

"My boss does not make complaints. My boss does not buy things online. And my boss will not wish to speak to you."

"But the parcel?" McCall was clinging to anything now.

"Give it to someone else, the boss does not need anything. He has everything."

McCall was banking on someone else listening.

"OK, then I'm sorry to have bothered you. I'll return the parcel back to New Zealand where it was posted from over a year ago. Sorry to bother you my friend..."

The line went quiet but McCall knew there was still someone there. The tone had changed, the background noise was different. He could still hear human voices but things had changed. He waited. He had cast his bait out into the water, waiting for the float to slide under. For ten seconds he waited and then heard a new voice.

"Sir. I am sorry that my Pitbull Terrier was so unkind to you. Had you have been at my door he would have torn your legs off bit by bit! So perhaps you should consider yourself lucky eh?" The new voice laughed. It was also Eastern European, more polished, more assured.

McCall took the bait deliberately. "Hello, sir. Look, no problem at all. Glad you got your friend there on a tight lead!" Sounding more American by the second he continued. "We have a parcel that was sent from New Zealand to your address in Romania but it was returned and now sits in a pile of other unloved mail right here in my office in Memphis, Tennessee. See, thing is, I'm destroying them by the hour..."

The voice nodded to a laptop at his side. 'Check his credentials'.

"I'm sorry, your name was?"

"Mike Brown sir, Customer Experience Manager." He winced at the slight change in detail, hoping the voice did not detect it.

The lieutenant nodded. The data was correct.

"I have no wish to complain about anything. Send what you have to my post office box Mr Brown I have things to do."

"And you are?"

"The recipient."

McCall was losing the advantage. "But...I'm sorry, it needs signing for. Shall I just dispose of it? It's been a long time now. It just interested me...you know, with your background."

"How did you know I had been in prison?"

McCall knew he had him close to the hook so pursued things whilst he could.

"The media sir, a fine and powerful tool!" He laughed. "It

said you were Romanian, and it matched the name on this package, trouble is we can't read the full address." He was drifting headlong into a southern drawl now, praying it was convincing, turning one-syllable words into two.

"My club is called Byzantin, Mr Brown, look it up on the internet if you are that bothered about one old parcel. I have to go." He stalled, then added, slightly curious, "Tell me, can you see who it is from? And what it contains?"

"I can see it contains documents, sir. But the writing is all smudged, if I were to put money on it I'd say a girl and a right pretty one too!"

"You can tell that from a simple piece of handwriting? I am impressed. Mr Brown."

"Parcels are my life sir. I know a man's writing from a girl's any day. I'll be sure to send this one over tonight once I dig out that address from the internet. Been a pleasure speaking to you, Mr?"

"My name is Alex. Just put that and the name of my club and Romania. Trust me, it will get here, once the authorities have ripped it open and examined every inch of it."

Hook. In.

"Well sir, they look like important documents to me. Says so on the package. Perhaps we could arrange for them to be delivered by hand, you know...for a small management fee?" McCall had no idea where this was heading, it was so far off script he was in danger of forgetting his aim.

"And how much would this small fee be?"

"As I say, they look important and you seem to want them, so let's say two fifty American."

"That is very reasonable Mr Brown. Two hundred and fifty dollars it is."

McCall's voice hardened. "No sir. I meant a little more."

Alex yelled down the phone. "I know what you *meant!*

Do you have any idea who you are talking to? Who you are trying to negotiate with? Do you? Cowboy?"

"I ain't no cowboy son. Like I told you earlier, Mr Alex. Two hundred and fifty thousand dollars. It seems reasonable, you know, given how important they might be." As ice cold as Alex.

Stefanescu knew where the conversation was heading. He was dealing with a man whose standards were as questionable as his own so he was hardly holding the moral high ground.

He was calm, too. Either a professional, or reckless and a fool.

"Mr Brown. Can I assume that you have opened this package?"

Now or never.

"Well yes sir, you can, and I have seen the value of its contents – they were like manna from heaven. But Mr Alex, I am an honourable man, and working for Fed Ex you have to understand that I am not paid particularly well, but one thing we always do is deliver the goods. So, do we have a deal?"

"How much again?" He was gesticulating to his body-guard – a man he had found to be useful since his escape from Pazardzhik.

'Do we know any more about this caller?'

The guard just shrugged. He seemed to be genuine.

"You know, I reckon two hundred and fifty American is a fair price for what is in that package. I reckon I could get more..." McCall knew it equated to a hundred more in his home country, and that meant financial freedom.

"Mr Brown that is a very specific amount. Why not ask for a million? From my experience only those in debt give an exact amount. It rules their lives you see. Unlike mine which is secure beyond your wildest dreams. I may be a common thief but I am a rich one." He laughed a genuine laugh. "OK, here is my deal. Are you listening?"

"Yessir, I am."

"I will give you three hundred, that way you will be debt free and have some left over. That way you will not betray me. But I need you to deliver it in person. Come to the club and ask for me. I will take the package and give you the money, in whatever currency you want. Then we will say goodbye and never see each other again. But if you tell anyone, even your overweight American wife, who probably spends too much on shoes and doughnuts, well then I will slit her throat and the throats of everyone in your home that is dear to you, whilst they sleep – and you will watch. Do we have a deal?"

Scott McCall, a genuine veteran in a world where the word was overused was about to commit himself to his most dangerous ever mission. Against an enemy he didn't know, one who he had no tangible intelligence about and importantly one who he was going to meet. Alone.

Alex's lieutenant waved frantically. He had something. Turning the laptop around, he pointed to some new information. It seemed that Mr Brown, from Memphis was ringing on a computer line – and he had just made a potentially fatal mistake.

Jackdaw smiled. This would be enjoyable.

"Mr Brown. I believe in honesty. This may surprise you, given my recent release from prison. I am innocent of all charges by the way, that is why the Bulgarian government actually released me. They said I had escaped to save their reputation. You may be speculating why I am telling you this. It's simple, when I negotiate with people I expect integrity. From some simple checks made by my people I sense you are not who you say you are. I asked for honesty. One chance. One chance only."

He waited.

"So who are you? And what do you want?"

McCall knew he had made what appeared to be a mistake. It was a game of chess. He held the queen in his fingertips, pausing long enough for Alex to make his own move. He was confident, strong, physically and mentally, but this was different. When he faced an enemy, he always had his team alongside him, the backing of technology and intelligence and a belief that the mission would be a success.

One chance only.

"My name is immaterial. As irrelevant as the name Jackdaw is to you. If you use a nickname, then so shall I. You can call me the Bushman. And if we work well together, I will take what I need and disappear. You must respect that. I have not been greedy, you know I could ask for more, from elsewhere, from the media particularly, but your name is on the document, so in my world – a world enshrined in honesty – that means you own it."

"OK Mr Bushman, then bring it to me. You can have your money, and then yes we will both free of debt. Before you go, I have to ask one last question of my own." He did not wait for permission to continue.

"Just where did you find this document?"

"In the hands of a girl. In a car that crashed, a long way from where you are now."

Alex Stefanescu, the big game fish, the Striped Marlin, was running now, a foot or so under the surface, ripping line off the reel and diving deep.

"This girl you speak of. Was she beautiful?"

"Yes. She was."

"And alive?" McCall sensed that this was the absolutely critical question.

"No."

"And you know this how?"

He had to be careful not to play his hand. He heard Alex exhale deeply.

"A friend told me."

He expected one but there was no reaction. "Let me know when you are here. If I like you, I may even employ you. If you fail to arrive, I will hunt you down. You are committed. We have a deal."

The phone was dead before McCall realised it.

"You trust him boss?"

He laughed. "No, not at all. I trust no one, not even you. But he has what I want and I like his confidence. He's a brave man – how the American's say, 'pissing on my parade'. Killing him may be a waste. Only the Bushman himself will dictate his future."

McCall couldn't afford to implicate the people he trusted and respected so he took a cheap taxi to Auckland Airport – less of a start point for any investigation. In a black backpack, he had his essential travel items; noise cancelling headphones, bottled water and sleeping tablets. He queued with everyone else, tapped the side of his luggage and prayed it would make it safely through the hold stow system, then headed through departure screening, towards a China Southern Airlines 787 Dreamliner to Guangzhou and eventually, Frankfurt. It was the cheapest and quickest flight he could find at short notice.

His dark hair was collar length, slightly wavy and his beard neat and trimmed in a way that added a sense of ruggedness, seemed to emphasise his bitter chocolate eyes – eyes that drew in women and made men look away. His attire said man about town, or rather a New Zealand man from a tough background who had spent wisely on well-fitting clothes that allowed him to move easily, but also offered a sense of played-down style. They told a tale of what lay beneath – years of training, a physique that had been forged from years of hard labour, injuries and sheer physical resilience.

His coat was made by Barbour. Green, waxed, three-quarter length. Boots, brown and handmade by R. M. Williams were a luxury he could afford after his last over-seas deployment. He'd hardly worn them but they felt good.

Politic chinos and a Working Style navy checked shirt did the rest.

His theory was simple. He might not return to the Land of the Long White Cloud. So he may as well look good on his departure photo.

The cherished size eleven boots guided him through screening and towards duty free. He was in scanning mode. The black Labrador caught his eye first. He was a good-looking dog. He just hoped the handler kept him busy, hunting for whatever it was he had been tasked to look for. It had to be drugs. It always was.

'Please keep away.'

He continued at a pace that avoided attention whilst allowing him to get through and away from the crowds.

The dog followed.

"Excuse me, sir." He stopped. Disciplined. He'd been polite. His English voice had called him sir.

He turned and fixed his eyes on a white male, same height, slighter build. He had an inquisitive but kind face. However, his eyes remained steadfastly on their target.

"Yes sir. How can I help?" Equally respectful. It always helped. He had a job to do. And McCall had no issue with that.

"My dog here is trained to find drugs and cash. He has indicated on you. I must ask, are you carrying either?"

Two choices.

"I would never carry drugs."

The dog handler was now holding the New Zealand passport in his right hand. "I'm pleased to hear it. Cash then?"

"Do I look like a man who would carry cash? I'm married." He laughed. The handler followed suit. "I can recommend a great lawyer. Look, I'll cut to the chase, Ajax here knows you have something. I have the power to detain you, you could miss your flight, but you seem like a reasonable man..."

"I had cash a while ago."

"How long ago?"

"A few weeks..."

"Look mate he's good but not that good..."

"Fair call. I've got a thousand. Cash. Euros. I thought that was OK? It's for my kid sister. She's in trouble. I'm heading to Europe to bail her out. It's yours if you want it..."

The handler checked the amount, opened the backpack and satisfied himself that there was nothing else of interest.

There was something about the man who stood confidently before him – but there was also a sense of urgency and to a trained customs officer that meant something. Smoke or fire? Or just a decent Kiwi bloke heading overseas to bail out his sister?

"What is your final destination today?"

"It'll be tomorrow probably, but to answer your question, Frankfurt." They would know in seconds, anyway.

"And what do you do for a living, sir?"

"I'm what they call a Bushman. I look after forests – sustainable ones – I work the land for the future of our children. Not as interesting as your job, but it pays me a wage and keeps me fit."

The clothing, the physique. The vocabulary. It all fitted.

There was nothing else to hold him on. He was polite and had been honest. His case could have been full of Class A for all he knew, but it was too late to drag the luggage off and delay the flight. And besides who took drugs out of the country? Damned if he did.

McCall knew the luggage contained a stripped down Glock pistol with its parts distributed and concealed and his favoured knife. He had packed them in such a way that even the best aviation officer wouldn't detect them, unless the young Englishman in front of him, with the inquisitive black dog decided to take things to the next level.

The wait was worse than being told he had to do administrative work, whilst his team jumped from a helicopter into unfamiliar and unforgiving scrubland in a foreign land far away.

"Well, Mr McKee you are the best-dressed Bushman I've ever met. Whatever trouble your sibling is in, I hope you resolve it. Look after her, yeah? We need to protect our sisters. And don't forget, this dog is the best in the country. Remember that when you come home – he has a superb memory. Have a safe journey."

McCall shook his hand and exhaled. "Thanks brother. I owe you one."

You have no idea.

The handler and his partner continued their work. The faithful hound was focused on someone else already. His handler couldn't shake the thought that in the Bushman there was something he had missed.

Something bad? Or the alternative. Stay in law enforcement a while and you develop a sixth sense, you also risk becoming cynical.

He liked what he saw in the Bushman's eyes.

The passport had passed its test. Having aroused no

suspicion at the Customs' primary line – where the majority of passengers first interacted with border staff. The falsified document was as good as any in the world. His military colleagues were exceptionally skilled in that area; creating a false identity to allow their people to move around the globe quickly and discreetly.

And that is what he intended to do. Quickly. And ideally, discreetly.

McCall stopped at the first bar. Ordered a beer and a bowl of fries and sat in a corner away from the point-tilt-zoom camera system that now sat above his head – unable to fix its remote gaze upon him.

He laid his waxy coat over the adjoining chair and crossed his legs, sitting back into the red casual lounger he pretended to watch the rugby. It was what good looking Kiwi men did. The difference between McCall and his fellow countrymen was that he was on the way to make a new life for what was left of his family. He had already decided that if anyone got in his way, he would use the skills and knowledge acquired on faraway streets and jungles and deserts to deal with them.

That, or die trying.

He took a lone, last look at the passport, with its dark blue cover and his image, staring back at him from behind the laminated green bio page.

'Scott McKee' – it suited him and so far the document had worked. He knew he might not need it again, but it was worth the risk of removing it from his locker. He closed it, slipped it into the backpack and walked a hundred metres to gate ten where his aircraft waited to take him a step closer to his target.

CHAPTER SIXTEEN

Four hours north, an A320 Airbus was dropping, almost skimming over the blue-green ocean, skirting alongside pristine atolls and over the Hamilton Island harbour. Beneath it, yachts of varied sizes and much larger motor cruisers flitted from berth to ocean and back.

The small airliner landed with a familiar protest from its six wheels and taxied to the end of the single runway.

Clear skies, white beaches and a classic Australian accent welcomed the holiday makers to their dream destination.

"G'day this is your pilot Donald Sawyer welcoming you all to the glorious Whitsunday Islands. The weather outside is a reasonable thirty degrees with a cooling easterly. Please wait until we come to a stop before enjoying your holiday. On behalf of Virgin Airlines thank you for travelling with us and we look forward to seeing you again soon. Crew disarm doors."

He was there. On time. The note was still in his pocket. The easy part was done, he looked out of the aircraft window at a catamaran leaving the harbour and wished he was on board, lying on the rope deck and watching the dolphins play beneath him. One day. Perhaps.

"Right let's go Cade. We've got a job to do. First things first let's dump the luggage at the apartment. We'll look ridiculous riding around the island with all this lot in a golf buggy!"

"What?"

"You didn't know? Priceless mate. The only mode of transport for visitors is a golf buggy."

"But what if we get involved in a pursuit?" It was supposed to be amusing.

"I guess we'll have to use a compact version of the Stinger."

The notion of spiking a golf buggy at ten kilometres an hour was ridiculous. But equally funny.

They arrived at the apartment, left the luggage in the hallway and jumped into the buggy that was parked outside. Every apartment had one.

"To Catseye Lodge, Jack?" Helston was keen to get this done.

"No. Not yet. I'm hungry. Let's grab a bite to eat and a cold drink. It's warm, and it's been a busy day."

"You going soft in your old age, Cade?"

"Is that a euphemism, Miss Helston?"

"It's Mrs, and no, it wasn't."

They ate a light lunch, next to the harbour, sheltering from the summer sun under an avenue of white umbrellas and avoiding the gaze of the resident cockatoos that had done their best to beat the gulls in a lucrative turf war.

"So tell me about this girl, Jack." Helston gazed at him as she sipped on her G&T.

"More than I told you back in Sydney?"

"Yes, please. I want to know what I'm letting myself in for. Fair? You know there aren't many men who would travel halfway around the world to meet a girl. Unless they wanted to get inside her knickers of course."

She smiled, took a mouthful of the fish of the day and waited.

"Past tense, Kim. That happened. Oh boy did it happen. It seemed too good to be true. Caveat emptor and all that. Hashtag gullible, or whatever they would say these days." His sentences were clipped, guarded, but he knew she'd drag it out of him so he relented. She always did that, back in the day, back in France when they operated in the hedonistic world of organised crime.

"Jeez, you didn't tell me you'd fucked her, Jack?"

"Ever the eloquent Aussie!"

"Well, excuse me for missing that part. Perhaps I was pissed. That puts a whole different spin on things. Are you coming here for Round Two – whilst I watch?"

"Sadly not. I'm here to ask her a few questions and then go. If indeed it's her. Kim, I got to the point last year where I didn't trust anyone beyond probably three or four people. I trusted her, but then Stefanescu's group unleashed merry bloody hell on me and mine." He reflected back to the road-side once more.

"I was probably love drunk. A foolish, older male with a pulse and an oh-so-pretty girl laying herself bare to me. I should have known."

He went over the whole story whilst they ate.

"Tell me, Jack. Would you do it all over again?"

"Elena?"

"Yep." She swilled a fresh Pinot Gris around her mouth, washing the fish down, allowing its fresh flavours to cleanse her palate.

He smiled. "Yep, probably – in a heartbeat. But I would need a thorough briefing first, Kim. I'll go and pay for this." He stood and walked across the road narrowly missing two golf buggies that whispered along the main harbour thoroughfare, paid the bill and returned.

"You can drive. You know the territory better than me!"

They whipped into the convoy of identical buggies that took them up and away from the harbour. It was pristine, warm and spoke of its natural beauty at every turn. Minutes later they were on top of the island. Catseye Bay to their right and the main harbour to the left.

One of the most beautiful places on earth.

"Just there." Cade pointed to a white gate, bordered by two impressive stone pillars that led to landscaped grounds, filled with palms and the endless call of the local bird life. Helston stopped the buggy twenty metres short of the gate and stepped out onto the immaculate lawn. All that stood between them and the answers they needed was a stone wall.

"Shall we?"

CHAPTER SEVENTEEN

CADE PRESSED THE INTERCOM AND WAITED. NOTHING. HE pulled the slip of paper from his pocket:

'Catseye Lodge – Whitsunday Islands – 17th January 2015.'

He looked at his partner. They'd done this a hundred times, but they normally had some level of back-up. He looked up and down the street and checked for obvious cameras. A few seconds later they were both over the wall, landing in amongst the palms and native Hibiscus.

They took their time, checking for obvious trips, traps and surveillance equipment. Cade had no idea who owned the property, assumed it had been rented and convinced himself that it wasn't Jackdaw or any of his team. He saw the sea sparkling to his left and thought that it was a fine place to end his days. He held up his hand. Stop!

They both listened. Water. Still – not running, but disturbed.

They continued through the garden – its size surprised them both and then they saw the pool, one of those horizon pools that just demanded a camera and a drink and few days to relax in and around it, better still time with the girl that swam up to the edge and stared out to sea.

Helston looked at Cade. Without words she said incredulously 'That her?'

He nodded. She replied, again in a mime, 'You are punching way above your weight, Cade!'

It was her. Of that he had no doubt. He watched as she lowered her head back into the blue pool then ran her hands over her head, squeezing the excess water away before walking through the shallower end towards the steps.

Cade watched as the familiar figure climbed the alloy steps. She wore an orange bikini that barely covered her. It was reminiscent of the first time he saw her in swimwear, on board the *Black Marlin* as they had sailed to an island in the ocean off the east coast of New Zealand.

She took him by surprise.

"Aren't you going to join us, Jack?" She turned and looked up and into the trees, straight into his eyes. Then at Helston's.

"Both of you. Come. We have drinks ready."

Cade's senses were on overdrive, so much so that he heard the ice cubes first before the footsteps. A male was carrying a tray of drinks towards the decked area, in the shaded area of the pool, away from the ferocity of the Pacific sun.

"Well?"

They left the protection of the trees and emerged, like a pair of naughty school children, their pockets full of apples.

Cade's mind was a vortex. Shoot her – he didn't have a gun. Drown her. Didn't have the heart after what happened to her mother.

Hug her. Kiss her. Run away?

He stepped forward and walked towards her. She was wrapping a sarong around her waist and slipped a pair of gold-rimmed Ray-Bans onto her head. Jesus she looked good. But for the scars. No, she looked good full stop.

But he looked at them anyway and knew he should never have left her to die. They were still red, one was vivid, the other, smaller but evident, above her eye. Her legs looked amazing, but again a few reminders of that high-speed crash remained. How she had recovered in the time that had elapsed was one thing. How she had recovered at all was another story.

He was transfixed. Her hair looked darker – it was damp – but darker nonetheless. Was she taller? Had she lost weight? He could still see her hip bones.

'Just kiss her for God's sake.'

Their eyes were still adjusting to the light. The sunlight in the region was so intense that it took a while.

Helston was desperate to say something. But it was Cade who took a pace forward and held out his hand. He had spent days conjuring up a power-sentence, a way of saying 'you owe me an explanation' – all the while knowing he was equally expected to provide some answers.

"Hello Elena. How are you?" Was that it? Pathetic.

She smiled. Failed to shake his hand but lifted her sunglasses and allowed him to see those damned green eyes once more. They offered everything in one glance: an apology, a look of disappointment and a sense of complete covetousness.

"I'm OK. Thank you. You should really introduce me to your girlfriend." She looked at Helston and offered a warm smile but it was obvious why she was so guarded.

Kim laughed and broke the ice. "Christ no, I'm not his girlfriend love. I'm his ex-partner – from his past. You know, work partner? I came to back him up in case you tried to kill him, but I guess that would have happened by now? I'm Kim Helston." She held out her hand and

Petrova shook it, her own hands still damp from the earlier swim.

"I'm Elena. Would you like a drink? It is warm, and you have come a long way."

It took a woman's sensibility to move the meeting along.

Cade had been so focused on the girl he knew as Elena Petrova that he had failed to look at the male – taking him for a butler, stood there in the shadows with a tray of glasses and a bottle of chilled, fashionable mineral water, the brim of his hat shielding his eyes.

"Drink, Jack?" The voice was instantly recognisable. The face appeared from the relative darkness and into the half-light that the veranda provided.

"What the hell are you doing here?"

The equally British accent was clear and concise. "Yes Jack, it's me and before you say another word or try to throw me in the pool, or worse, there's something or things you need to know."

"Oh, trust me I am all ears."

Helston was half-standing, half-sitting and now contemplating the pair of strutting peacocks in front of her.

"Jack, this can wait. You haven't seen this dear girl for a while. From what I know she's had a rough time of it and you disappeared off the face of the earth...without an explanation..." It was evident that Helston was reverting to police negotiator mode and she was doing well.

"And, it's only fair that Elena finds someone new in her life."

"Oh my God, no! Stop. Please." Petrova was almost laughing. "No, you could not be more wrong. This man is not my lover."

"Then what is he?" Cade was filling with adrenaline. He could feel it, taste it – he knew the signs. He looked for somewhere to throw him that would hurt more than the pool.

"Jack. Please sit down. I have something to tell you. But first, I would really like that hug that you are so desperate to give me. It's OK. We are good you and I. Promise. Trust me?" She held her arms out in front of her as he hesitated, then stepped into her embrace.

He exhaled and felt the coolness of her hair on his face, then pulled her towards him. She stepped up onto her toes to reach his kiss.

"Forgiven." They said it at the same time.

"Come on, Miss Helston, I'll show you the garden and we can have a chat whilst these two put the world to rights. The Hibiscus is glorious at this time of the year."

As they wended their way up the flag-stone pathway to the upper garden area Helston turned and looked out across the harbour.

"It's a beautiful place. Must cost a fair bit to rent?"

"I have no idea Miss Helston."

"Call me Kim. Please. Australians are less formal than you Brits."

"Then I have no idea how much it would cost to rent Kim. You see, as far as Catseye Lodge is concerned, I own it. All you see is mine."

"'Curiouser and curiouser,' said Alice, as she stared down the rabbit hole."

"Ah, the classics. Never fail do they, Kim?"

She was impressed. It was a truly beautiful home. "So it's all yours? Then you are a very lucky man indeed Mr?"

"Of course. Sorry. How thoroughly un-British of me. That Mexican stand-off back there robbed me of my manners. As for my name, 'I know who I was when I got up this morning, but I think I must have changed several times since then...'"

"I'm not with you."

"You were quoting from *Alice in Wonderland*, I thought I would join you." He held his fair-skinned hand out to meet hers.

"Michael Blake. British Foreign Office and nowhere near the bastard that your friend Jack will tell you I am. Fancy a drink down at the yacht club? I suspect those two have some serious making up to do." He winked and offered her his arm. The old charmer was soon walking her towards his own rather grander buggy and pressing a remote to open the gates.

"So you are genuinely not an item, you and that red-hot supermodel back there?"

"Good God no. Some might say sadly not but not me. No, nothing could be further from the truth."

"Are you gay?"

"Good old forthright Aussie questioning techniques. One has to love them." He doffed his hat. "No. Categorically not."

"Fair enough."

He picked up the pace. "Come on girl, the sun will be over the yardarm soon. Mojito?"

"Rude not to. But you are buying."

"I have an account dear. You Australians are so uncouth at times."

He sent the red-hot supermodel a text. 'Back in a while. Sort it out.'

She strutted alongside the pool. Turned, looked at him, then looked away. "You have some explaining to do, Jack Cade."

"And so do you, Elena Petrova." He was looking straight at her. Wishing she would dress so he could at least stand a chance of having an undistracted argument.

Ever the British gentleman. "OK. You go first. I'm keen to hear this. You take the first punch."

She did.

"What the...?" It was painful, but more so, unexpected.

"Christ, El. I didn't mean literally."

"You deserved that for leaving me there. I could hear you, Jack. Every word. And don't call me El."

"But you told me to go. Have you any idea how hard it was...to just walk away. Elena I had fallen for you. You must have known that?"

"And yet you still just walked away." She slapped him hard across the face.

"Do that again lady and I'll drown you in that bloody pool." The blood vessels had reddened the skin around his left cheek, enhancing the ocean-blue eye that poured uncontrollably.

"I mean it Elena."

Slap. Harder than the punch.

He grabbed her by both arms but she was quick. Training did that to you, made you react without thinking about the act itself.

Her balled fists pushed up and through his arms and then the sides of both collided with his temples in a shock wave.

"Shit. Christ almighty. What is wrong with you?" He staggered around the deck area, looking for an escape route or a weapon. All he saw was a small earthenware pot. 'Great. I travel all this way to kill the girl of my dreams with that. Classy Jack, really classy.'

She was up on her toes now, in a fighting stance.

"Pretty Bulgarian girl shocked you did she Jack? Well, there is more where that came from."

"Can you not just behave like a bloody woman for once?"

She dropped her centre of gravity and lunged out with

her bare foot, towards his groin. This was going to really hurt. He had plans for that region. Clearly she didn't. She was enjoying this.

But this time it was Cade that was quicker. He surprised himself with his reactions. He slapped her, quickly, to the side of the head, gripped hold of her shin and pulled her towards him. Her face rushed at his as he jammed his elbow across her throat.

"There. Hurts doesn't it? Now, are we going to play nicely?"

She stared at him. Green eyes versus blue. A younger, fitter girl against an older, stronger man.

She kissed him. Fully on the lips.

"Whoa! Where did that come from?" She tasted great. Some things hadn't changed. Her response to his counter-attack was pure and sexy. He relaxed his grip.

She punched him again, a distraction strike with her right hand against his shoulder, then dropped to one knee and as she did so she drove her left palm into his liver. Cade dropped instantly. The blow was fast enough to cause him rapid harm but not powerful enough to kill him. She knew what she was doing and aimed her blow and the amount of force perfectly.

Cade's autonomic nervous system and the pressure wave that hit the liver capsule were his undoing. The blow compressed the liver, like a balloon, signals raced through his body, causing the longest nerve in the ANS, the Vagus nerve, to decrease his heart rate and blood pressure. His brain was now in survival mode.

This in turn create an involuntarily reaction and forced him into a horizontal position, lying on the ground. She could have hit any of his major organs, but she knew, from months of training, that the liver, being the largest organ was likely to provide the most effective reaction.

Cade was down and in agony.

"Now, will you apologise?" Elena Petrova, daughter of Nikolina stood over him; pretty, educated and downright bloody lethal.

It was finished.

He couldn't talk. For a while he was concentrating on breathing through the pain and praying that she hadn't ruptured something. As he began to recover he watched her pacing around the wooden decking, her lithe legs carrying her back and forth.

He decided that next time he fought with someone it would be like this, against a far prettier foe in a woefully small and startlingly orange bikini. It was sensual. It was surreal. And it was God-bloody-awful painful.

Look at her: perfectly cut hair, those eyes, those hip bones, that asymmetrically perfect arse. Breasts that were best described, by men and those that were on the fringes of bi-curiosity as flawless.

She bent to pick up her sarong which had come away during the melee. She had her back to him. He was up now and rushing at her, wrapping his arms around hers, and across her chest. He pulled her back, and then further, heading towards the pool. Praying he got it right he lunged backwards taking her with him, not releasing his hold. They hit the water and sank, as a pair to the bottom.

She was writhing like a demented catfish, twisting, screaming under water. Her words were indistinct, but the message was clear.

'I will kill you, Jack Cade. I will seriously, honestly kill you.'

He held her, as tight as he could. His own oxygen levels were plummeting as the pain started to emanate from his liver once more. But this was a fight he had to win. At that moment, on the bottom of the blue-glazed pool he needed her to know that she had brought hell to his doorstep, years after he had closed the door on it; closed, bolted and never to be opened.

He knew that she had travelled to New Zealand to deliver a message, and importantly, a package. Her mother had told her to trust only one man – the British man called Cade. There were others, close to him, but she had said that whilst one might provide her sanctuary, the other would save her life. No questions.

Things had gone to plan. She met him, chose to trust him, was about to hand over the remaining package of three documents – the missing link. She had been told that instinctively he would know what to do with them; where to secrete them from harm, prevent them from initiating the wealth of one man and the potential destabilisation of a nation.

Things had gone to plan: Meet. Hand over the documents. Leave.

That is until she fell in love with him. In a few days. On a beach, an island and latterly in his bedroom. Infatuation? Lust? Professional intelligence gathering? Or love?

Yes, things had gone to plan. He was just the bonus.

Until they had followed her, thousands of miles across continents, their mission to shut down the chain of evidence – kill those that were associated to Nikolina Petrov and her family, and whenever the chance arose, to harm the reputation of the Bulgarian Secret Service and above all, execute, torment and terrorise anyone who stopped their quest for financial supremacy and notoriety in Europe.

He had his legs wrapped around her waist and his arms across her chest. He was the breadth of a cigarette paper from ending her life. She fought no more.

Her skin was tanned, the colour of autumn leaves, her hair flowed in the tepid blue water in a luxury home on an island in an ocean far larger. And she spoke no more.

"I love you." Cade's words were distorted by the water, clear, at least clear enough for her to understand.

And then the dream returned to haunt him. The groping hands, the call of the Sirens, luring him towards the rocks once more. Bodies, drifting downwards into the river bed, through the dark green forest of weeds and dark black silt.

'Let her go....Jack. Let. Her. Go.' A voice from the past, from the depths. He knew who it was. The Old Man was visiting him once more. He released his hold on her.

She nodded and yelled something back, again the water disturbed the words but their rawness meant something to him. It was either an apology or a promise to end his life at the first opportunity.

He burst through the surface of the water, up and into the air. The heat of the day hit him first, followed by another autonomous reaction to breathe, then find her.

She was surfacing too; he hooked his arm under hers and propelled her up and away from death's grasp. She took in a massive amount of air, trying to shout at him at the same time and choking.

"I hate you. I hate you. I..."

"Love me?"

"You *bastard*."

She collapsed into his embrace and held him, breathing slower now but realising that he could have killed her. Just another few seconds. Like her mother. Her poor defenceless mother.

But she knew he had loved her too and could never blame him for her actual death – perhaps allowing it to happen, but not death itself.

He winced as she held him tighter, recalling the wildcat

blow she had delivered to his right side. What was she thinking?

She tried to slap him again. Then stopped.

Cade just stared at her until she looked away.

"Jack. I'm sorry. I understand why you were angry. My mother was right to trust you. I just never knew I would end up sleeping with her boyfriend. That wasn't supposed to happen."

He was controlling his own breathing.

"You think your mother and I...slept together?"

"Of course."

"No. That is not true. Not true at all. Elena, if you believe nothing else you need to know that. They killed her before..."

She didn't raise a red flag – just slapped him again.

"Do you want to go back down there?" He pointed to the bottom of the pool.

She shook her head. "Only with you." She exhaled deeply. "I'm sorry I hurt you." She drew more air into her lungs. "Tell me one more thing?"

"You must promise not to try to kill me."

"Did you sleep with Carrie O'Shea?"

What was the point of lying, this girl was better-trained than him.

"Yes. I did. But it was long before we met."

She wiped the remaining water from her face and did that thing with her hair once more. "I forgive you. Is that why you had her photographs in your house? To remind you of her?"

"No. I liked what she saw through the lens. She saw things differently to me."

"But now? You are still together?"

He shook his head. "No, we are not and we never will be.

It's just one of those things that life throws at you. They say things happen for a reason, or a season, or forever."

"So what am I?"

'Think carefully here Jack. You only have one liver.'

"All three."

An hour later, she lay with her head on his chest, listening to his still-rapid heartbeat and smiling. She had forgiven him in the best way she knew how, and he her. He was initially angry at himself for giving in so quickly. His plan was to make her wait at least a few hours.

It wasn't Olympic sex, gymnastic in its positions or even daring like it was the first time at his home in New Zealand. Just physical, visceral, entwined and close enough that their vision blurred when they tried to look at one another.

Laying his head on the cool pillows whilst the over-sized ceiling fan did its job he could have easily slipped into a deep sleep. He could hear and feel her breathing as he watched the wooden blades revolving. He tried to focus on just one blade, trying to stop time, right at that moment. A softly spoken sea breeze and a naked girl, in the afternoon, in an idyllic location, far removed from reality. It genuinely didn't get any better.

She waited for his heart to slow and his breathing to indicate that he was resting, then slipped her head beneath the sheets, heading lower, kissing him, licking his skin then blowing gently onto it. She knew it wouldn't be long before he responded.

"No, I'm not ready yet Elena."

"Jack. You were always ready."

"I need to ask you a question first." He had his serious face on. She frowned.

"OK, ask me. I will try to tell you the answer you are looking for."

"You survived."

She laughed. "Yes. I did. You seem not pleased?"

"Oh, I'm very pleased right at this moment. But Elena when I left you..."

"You thought I was dead?"

He could only nod.

"Me too. You did what you could. But it would not have been enough. Then, when I felt that I was going to die." She stopped. It was obvious that she was back there.

"I heard a helicopter."

"I saw it as I left. I knew they would help. The air ambulance teams are great."

"No Jack. This wasn't a rescue team. I opened my eyes for a second, when he spoke. He had a beautiful voice, a soft accent, softer than Australian. He was a Kiwi man."

"OK, and what did this covert Kiwi do?"

"He smiled. He apologised. Then I guess he saved my life."

"Why do you say that?"

"He was wearing green. Camouflaged clothing. He was confident Jack. He knew what to do. He said he would help me. That he was like a doctor."

"Army? Medic?"

"I don't know. Probably. He had longer hair. Handsome. When I woke up at the hospital...JD was there. I don't know how he knew, or how he got there, or..."

"It's OK. Take your time." This was new information.

"He didn't tell me his name, but I will never forget his voice. He even apologised for undressing me which is more than you ever do." She sniggered.

"Then whoever the mystery man is I will find him and thank him. Perhaps JD knows. I will ask him when I next speak. Thank you for telling me this. It sounds like you had great care in hospital."

"I was lucky Jack. That is all. Lucky. There was something else."

"Enlighten me."

She frowned.

"Tell me. Enlighten means let me know."

"He leaned across me, pulled something from the wreckage. I remember he said something then left. I won't forget what he said."

Cade nodded encouragingly.

"For the girls. No other reason, Scottie."

"Well, that helps. And what do you think he took?"

"The other set of papers. He has no idea of their value. At least I don't think he did. But why did he take them?"

She changed the subject. "Anyway, what has changed with us, you used to like me being exciting with you?"

"The thought of Blake coming back early."

"He'll be gone for hours. He told me he would."

"You planned this all along? You knew I would respond to your message?"

"One hundred percent."

"You knew I would come?"

She giggled. "In that area, yes. Two hundred percent."

"You are incorrigible Petrova. Then don't let me stop you. But just be gentle."

"Of course, always, Jack. And please, call me El. My very best friends do."

"And did the gallant man in green have a name for you?"

"He didn't. But he said he was sorry. Truly."

"Tell me about JD another time?"

"Of course. But not now. Are you ready now?"

His smile said it all.

. . .

Blake checked his watch, a black-strapped Longines Flagship, gifted by a nation that he couldn't recall – probably China after a trade visit some years before.

"It's been delightful meeting you Kim. But I think we need to return to the ranch."

"I'm in your hands, Sir Michael." She giggled, the mojitos and dehydration had taken their toll.

"I doubt I'll ever get a knighthood. But I can at least drive you back to your old partner. He's a good man you know. Shame he doesn't trust me."

"Jack doesn't trust many people. He always says six is the limit, any more than six degrees is suspicious."

"I'm inclined to agree with him."

They pulled through the gates and came to a halt on the gravel driveway. As they walked along the noisy footpath their feet crushed the lavender and rosemary, filling the air with scent.

They were met by Cade and his recently re-acquainted leading lady – both trying a little too hard not to look suspicious.

"Been for a swim, Jack?"

"No. Chance would be a fine thing. We've been discussing international security matters."

"Oh, how exciting. Does that normally entail leaving your shorts over the sunbed?" She pointed, mockingly at the garment that hung, in situ where they had been left, in a hurry.

"Ah, those. Yes, I was pushed into the pool after a disagreement. Hence the towel."

"Hence indeed. Anyway, Michael and I had a lovely time, and now he's going to fire up the barbie. They should be dry now. I'll turn my back so you can get dressed."

Elena walked inside and spoke to Blake.

Cade looked at Helston. "You know I hate you don't you?"

She smiled into the reflection as she watched her former partner slip out of the pool towel and regain what was left of his dignity. He still looked good. She remembered when she had stolen the first glimpse; he hadn't changed that much.

'Lucky girl'.

CHAPTER EIGHTEEN

Roberts' phone rang. Late at night or early in the morning there was always an expectation that he would answer.

It was early on a bitterly cold day and one that Roberts wished would allow him to do the decent thing and stay under the duvet, wrapped around his wife – any wife for that matter as long as she was attractive and warm. He put a hand out and grabbed hold of the phone and answered it under the sheets.

"Yes."

"Morning Boss. Pete from SOCO."

Roberts had never remembered his surname, but he knew he was arguably the best scenes of crime officer in the force.

"You always this fucking chirpy? Go on." He shivered. Partly from the cold, more in fear at what he was about to hear.

"Sorry, guv, no better way of saying this. The prints match Cynthia Bell. No doubt. I'll sort out the paperwork. Shout if you need me. You there, boss?"

He was. He just couldn't find any suitable words for a moment.

"Yes. Thanks, Pete. I owe you next time you are near the Sanctuary I'll get you a shandy."

He turned over and kissed his wife. "I have to go, babe. Sorry."

She murmured something from under the covers and went back to sleep. Roberts ate as he drove and rang the team leaders in turn. The crux of his en route briefing was simple. 'We need to find Cynthia Bell.'

What Roberts didn't know yet was that they also needed to find one of the best human sources he had ever managed, the eccentric and escort Lucy Thomas, who had been turned into an unwitting blood donor, and was now lying in a frigid room in a desolate and bramble-covered industrial cemetery. Alongside her and clinging to life was Bell.

They were both existing.

The life that had flowed from Thomas' into Bell's veins had somehow sustained her overnight, in spite of the glacial conditions. Despite not being able to move far she was able to turn her head from side to side, just far enough to see that her left hand had gone. All that remained was a dark red, stained but professionally applied dressing. They must be pumping her full of drugs as she couldn't feel any pain.

They were. Or rather he was. Fentanyl was extremely difficult to come by – unless you knew how. Its opiate effects were legendary, fifty times, some said a hundred times more powerful than morphine.

To her right was Thomas, or at least what she thought was a woman – she had a deep voice and was animated – like an off-duty drag artist. Bell remembered laughing at the notion of being held captive in a disused workshop next to someone who used more make-up than she did. Must be the drugs – as his situation was far from amusing.

To her left a newly arrived and identical table, with straps and the same rudimentary hole, beneath which lay a cheap plastic bucket. This was a red one. She had no idea what colour hers was, only that it must be filling. She hoped it was blue. She liked blue.

The new table was empty. Waiting.

Constantin tapped the clear plastic tube, locked off the IV and flushed Thomas' vein. He did the same to Bell. He really should have been a doctor, rather than a self-taught butcher with a fascination for human destruction.

"I need to go. You will be fine. Shout for help from all of your friends from the government. Oh no, they can't hear you. Such a shame. But this is good, because I have many plans for you both. You, my nightclub dancer and you the government analyst who will find typing a little harder now."

Thomas was writhing, trying to speak. Constantin tore the tape from her mouth.

"Yes. You have something to say you slut?"

"Please. You don't have to do this. I have money..." The voice was definitely deeper. Lower in tone than it ever was when he had been entertained by her for money.

The tape was soon drawn across her face and pushed back into place.

He bent slightly and whispered, "Do you really think this is about money? There is only one whore on display here." He squeezed her cheeks with his thumb and forefinger, leaving a deep white imprint on her cold skin.

He looked at the doorway.

"Don't just stand there staring boy, come in, and if either of these two cause you any problems, just hold their noses and watch them turn blue. Are the others ready?"

The young male – twenty to twenty-five at a guess – nodded and said something that neither captive understood.

"OK. But stand them up, strapped to the tables. Do not

release them. Expect that they will want to kill you and escape if you give them a chance, that way you will be safe. I agree, feed them, give them water, but do it as I have instructed. Clear? Or do you wish to ring the boss to ask him?" His sentences were deliberately in English.

Constantin – the evident leader of the group – walked outside, breathing in the cold air and stretching his tired limbs. It felt wonderful to be alive; not to have to depend on that evil that had for so long clogged up his veins, mind and body.

"Come, we have a job to do. You remember what I showed you?"

No questions, just a few nervous nods of the head.

They walked away from the set of buildings, along a rough track, breaking the thin ice on the overnight puddles before getting into a grey van and heading west.

It was bitterly cold. He was surprised his two prisoners had lived through the night. Getting up at three may have seemed like a humanitarian gesture but he had covered them up in old blankets to save their lives. They were valuable and a dead commodity was of no use to him.

Cause a distraction the boss had said. Do it how you like. He knew the police, and whoever else they decided to enrol would soon be asking questions. Selecting the old factory from an internet map was resourceful. Picking a warmer one would have been ingenious.

As the driver navigated through the streets of Erith and joined the commuter traffic, Constantin checked his watch. Their early rise was necessary. They needed to make the journey in under an hour and any later would have almost doubled the journey. Staying in the city overnight was not an option; with so many surveillance systems in the region Constantin knew how intrusive they could be. They had almost caught him last time as he hid in the shadows of their city. But it was only almost. And what a mistake that would prove to be.

False plates one way. Another set for the return journey. You really couldn't be too careful.

'Have fun. But be no more than a distraction.' The words of the Jackdaw replayed through his mind as he rubbed his hands over the weak warm air emitting from the vents.

Their arrival required one drive-by. There was no room for error and there had been no opportunity for a dry run. It was now, or never. But the recent days had seen him grow in stature. It was now, actually.

She was up at the normal time. Early. A creature of habit. More so these days as sleep often eluded her. Nespresso machine switched on, Ristretto coffee selected. It was her favourite. Bitter but fruity, and how she summed herself up sometimes. In the past, with him she had been full bodied and steaming hot.

She knew the machine gave her time to dress, grab some pre-prepared food from the fridge and walk to the machine in time to grab the cup and take a sip of its warming, aromatic brew.

Her hair was a little longer than it used to be. She liked it that way. Her make-up said subtle, but sophisticated. Her underwear spoke of seduction. Somethings never changed. Navy blue, trimmed with cream lace. Her father had always said wear clean ones in case you got run over. Her mother disagreed. Wear pretty ones in case you meet the man of your dreams. Worst case, her father added, make sure it's him that runs you over.

The pencil skirt accentuated her newly slimmed figure, and the shoes picked out the definition of her calf muscles. The cream blouse concealed what she considered to be her most important assets. Time in the gym was definitely paying dividends – she left a reminder on her calendar to renew the membership before the end of the month then placed the stiletto-pointed pencil back in the holder along-side three others.

Looking in the mirror, she smiled. Yes, she looked just fine. She despised the government for even thinking of bringing in a law to forbid builders from wolf-whistling at girls. Long may it continue!

Picking up her shoulder bag and phone she turned, three sixty, checked everything like he had taught her – once bitten – then set the alarm and walked down the stairs. As she entered the hallway she shivered. Was it that she should she have put on something more sensible for the short walk to work? Or more a case of this is where it once happened, in a semi-lit hallway, all those years ago – with him?

She opened the main door, looked left, right and straight ahead. It was still dark but the sodium street lighting lifted the ambience, making it bearable, navigable and somehow less intimidating. She was much more confident now – but still bore the hallmarks of someone who had been the victim of an attack in her own home many years prior.

This morning she shivered again as she turned her back to the street to shut the old and heavy black painted door, waiting for its familiar sound.

Thud.

There she was. Bang on time. Creature of habit.

There she was, outside the door, to the minute.

The van was alongside her, cargo door to the kerbside.

Must be a courier.

Up onto the kerb.

He is early today. Must be busy.

The larger male was out and matching his speed with the

rushing pavement. It could all go wrong. His team mate was leaning out of the door to grab hold of her.

They were after her handbag. She had read about this only the day before. Bastards. No way. This is *not* happening.

She turned to look at the male, taking her eyes off the bigger picture.

In ten seconds flat. That's all the one witness would later estimate it took. Twelve at the most.

'Did you get a number?'

'No. I didn't think anything of it. We have vans in the street all the time. Poor girl.'

'Was there any signwriting on the van?' Pressure.

'Well, now you come to mention it. There might have been. Perhaps a plumber. Yes. I think it might have been a plumber. Sorry I can't help more.'

Never lead the witness.

Twelve seconds. Count it. It's not very long at all. Not a sound, not a scrap of evidence. Door shut, locked, engine pushed, turning left, towards the bridge, heading south.

She was gone.

Roberts was at work early. He found it to be easier to get up and dive into the hot shower than lay in a now cold bed. He cleared the desk phone of overnight voicemails, did the same to his emails and then went for a walk into the main office.

In a matter of days Operation Orion had established itself as a viable and well-equipped counter to the threat of financial terrorism that they knew would start any day if the human intelligence sources were to be believed. But when?

"Bridie, Fish. You got a moment? And bring a tea would you. Strong. Three sugars."

"But you don't drink tea, guv?" It was Fish, wearing an up and at 'em purple shirt and matching tie.

"I do today, Nick. Nice tie. And can someone grab me a croissant or something from across the road? Preferably hot, with jam. Strawberry. No, wait. Make that apricot."

He sat down in his office, spun halfway in his leather chair and back again. Tapped his thumb and fingers on the desktop, used them to grab at his lower lip then spoke.

"Guys we've got a real problem developing and I don't know whether it's aimed at me and Jack or the police in general, or, a massive distraction for something that has yet to happen."

Both detective sergeants looked at him. Waiting.

"Cynthia is missing. It's official. It was her hand in that bloody candle." He swallowed hard. "I knew I was a vegetarian for a reason."

"There you go, guv. On me." One of the younger members of the team slid a paper bag across the desk which contained two croissants and enough stolen jam to sink a destroyer.

"Cheers pal." He opened the bag and offered the remaining one to Bridie, then Fish. He took a bite but couldn't help replaying the video in his mind. The candle. The wax. The hand. The note.

He swallowed hard.

"Actually, you can have this one too."

He needed to ring Cade.

It was still a summer evening in Hamilton Island, in the Great Barrier Reef when Cade's phone buzzed, danced and slid its way across the glass-topped table at Blake's impressive retreat.

He looked down at the display and considered killing it there and then. He was having a good time. He was almost relaxed. Another month…

"Do you need to get that?" It was Petrova, who had dressed for dinner in a simple summer dress, bare feet and a splash of Elie Saab – Cade loved the hint of orange blossom and frangipani. It made her smell good enough to eat.

He smiled to himself. She could have covered herself in manure and he would have found her attractive.

He blew air across his lips. "It's Jason. I guess I do."

"Jason. I hope this is important – you are interrupting a good old-fashioned Aussie barbie on a quite spectacular evening. You should see the colours in the sky – quite simply beautiful!"

He was on hands-free in the office at the Orion HQ.

"Glad you are having a good time mate."

"OK, you emphasised the word 'you' – what's happening Jas. I only want good news."

"Cynthia is definitely missing. Presumed dead. Her hand was delivered to my office yesterday. Inside a fucking candle Jack. You know, a candle, which I would light. So the wax would melt and reveal a note. A note to you."

"Christ, that's terrible Jason." He took a breath. "What did the note say?"

"You won't like this. It said, 'Jack. He will not spare when he takes revenge.' And it was signed with the letters A and S."

"OK. Sounds biblical to me. That's all we need a religious nut job sending us random warning notes. Look, she could still be alive. You've got the resources now. Use them to find her. Get the guys out on the streets, old-fashioned policing. You've got the skills."

"Oh, I've got resources to burn Jack. But I need a start point. I have a feeling the shit hasn't even started to approach the fan yet."

"I agree. You know who this is from don't you? Even if it's not his handy work. Sorry. Absolutely not funny or intentional. Jason, this is them. 'AS' is..."

"Yes, I'm fully aware who A bloody S is Jack! Right now I just need to find him. I think this is Constantin Nicolescu's work. I looked into that bastard's eyes that day on the train and I saw the devil."

Cade went to take a sip of the wine that Elena had poured him but placed it back on the table. Now wasn't the time.

"I was once told that the devil doesn't come dressed in a red cape and pointy horns Jason. He comes disguised as everything you've ever wished for."

"And your point, Jack?"

"Jason. You have always wanted to command the best team in the Metropolitan Police. And you have my complete backing. But at what cost? We've lost too many staff to this group already..."

He paused. "Jason, am I on hands-free? If so, take it off a second."

He did, "Go on."

"Carrie at work yet?"

"Why do you ask? Should be here any moment. You know what she's like for timing – ever the OCD analyst. Anyway, I thought she was in your past."

"She is. She was. But she worries me still. I just have a nasty feeling about today. Ring me if she doesn't show. And Jason, if I were you I'd be rounding up the people you trust. Those dark clouds to the east are bringing a storm with them."

CHAPTER NINETEEN

HE STARED DOWN AT HER. THE PLASTIC CABLE TIES HAD been applied so quickly she never stood a chance. Hooded to disorient her she had little idea of where they were heading. She knew it was a grey van, possibly a Ford Transit. The cargo door rattled on its hinges. An air freshener did its level best to bring a hint of vanilla to the damp interior.

Music. Radio 2. The Cranberries. *Linger*.

The words were so familiar and poignant.

She knew the date and time and she had counted three males.

Instinct told her they were heading south. Or east. Or maybe south east. God alone knew.

Perhaps the woman to her right – the one who turned, in the street, startled by the man running towards her. Gripping onto her handbag. She had read about it too. Perhaps she would ring, or tell someone?

Do something.

Please.

. . .

The voices were Eastern European; her educated and time-served guess was Romanian. She had listened to enough voice recordings back in the day.

One of the voices was somehow familiar – and yet they had never met.

The tape recordings that the former Romanian Intelligence Officer Valentin Iliescu had sent her – back in 2004 – they were flooding her mind now, filling the one small space that remained, the rest crowded out by her fight-or-flight mechanism, somewhere in the brain things were happening. The adrenal medulla – it was a trivia question. She couldn't recall exactly what it did, but she knew why. Muscles tensed, her digestive system all but shut down, she was now focusing on one thing only.

Her survival.

The hood made the interior of the van even darker, helped her to panic even more. She could count the microscopic holes? Yes, that was a fine idea. She started at one and ran out at forty-six.

Then started again.

Her breathing was rapid, she knew her blood pressure had increased. She needed to calm down. She needed to calm down now.

Talk to them. Don't reason with them. Just talk.

"What do you want with me?"

There was no response.

"Where are you taking me?"

Again, nothing.

"I don't have anything worth stealing." She paused, aware that her next sentence could provide an idea. "Please don't hurt me."

A hand moved the hood up and over her mouth, then another applied a strip of duct tape, pressing down the edges. She began to focus on the one source of oxygen and forced herself to breathe through her nose.

But it was unnatural.

Breathe.

Panic.

Breathe.

Silence would have been a better sound than the drone of the diesel engine, slowing, then accelerating.

South. They were heading south. She tried to listen for familiar sounds – that's what they did in the crime fiction world wasn't it? Listen for a train or a piece of music or a bird calling.

'Jesus a bird could be calling to its mate any bloody where you stupid cow.'

Calm. Down.

Face down, head slightly sideways, lying in the back of a sterile van. She could smell nothing but diesel and body odour.

Half an hour later by her reckoning, they slowed and turned left. The surface changed, it was a track, not the smooth road that they had driven along. The van lurched from side to side, there were potholes – and water; puddles, breaking. They were icy. Icy puddles. On a track – heading away from the main road and civilisation. This was anything but good.

"Jack? It's me." Cade could see who it was, but he accepted the introduction, allowing some space to take another sip of the Mt Difficulty Pinot Gris.

"It's Jason everyone." He was relaxed, and it was clear to Roberts that Cade was not alone.

The delicate tastes of peach and nectarine were dissipating. There was another flavour. White blossom apparently, but unlike its maker Cade was nowhere near qualified enough to detect it. Nor was he concentrating on his taste buds.

"Stunning evening, almost gone now but nice nonetheless. How are things there?"

"You've got an audience haven't you?"

"Yes, a few now."

"She hasn't arrived Jack."

He placed the glass onto the outdoor table, lined up the crest so it was facing him, looked at his fellow diners then spoke.

"I'll be on the first plane out of Sydney tomorrow. Suggest you round up the old team – from what you said when we last spoke, the budget is fluid."

"Thanks, Jack. I owe you."

"Good man, and can you book a few rooms at the nearest decent hotel? We'll need to rest when we can. This has been a fast turnaround on such a long journey." It was an understatement – the journey to the bottom of the world was never short.

"How many nights?"

"No idea, push for as many as you can until it becomes obvious and we end up in some barrack room somewhere!"

"How many rooms?"

He looked at Kim Helston. She shook her head.

Elena was also listening. She could hear every word, and Cade wanted it that way. She smiled gently then held up her index finger.

Blake looked sideways at Helston who did her best not to grin.

Cade raised an eyebrow at Helston then said, "Two rooms please." The younger of the two women looked disappointed.

"One for me and one for John Daniel."

She was happy again. She mouthed 'With a deep bath!'

"You want JD back? After all this time?" Roberts had an inquisitive tone.

"Don't you? He knows as much about this group as we do – and he can support you without stepping on any toes. Can speak his mind...and he'll be cheap. And Jason he knows more than either of us, actually. He was one of the original degrees of separation."

"That's settled then. I guess it will be impossible to keep him away. Especially with the less than subtle budget increase. I'll ring him next. And what will your role be Jack?" It was a fair question from the man in charge of the operation.

"Whatever you want it to be. I don't have rank anymore."

"It would be rude to ask you to be my second in command – after all you led this operation from the front last time. How about my tactical advisor?"

"Sounds good. Do I get a free pen? Or a jacket with it emblazoned on the back?"

"Respectfully...Mr Cade..."

"No need to finish the sentence Jason. See you in twenty-four. Stay in touch and for Christ's sake, be careful."

"Yes, you too. I'll arrange for a pickup at Terminal Three."

Roberts cleared down and looked at his two most senior colleagues. Two detective sergeants amounted to a massive amount of experience, many commanders had said that the sergeant was the foundation of any police team. He hoped they proved them all right.

"She's failed to show. Gather round, five minutes, no tea.

No biscuits. This just got very personal, and I have lost my appetite."

Cade drained his glass. It seemed a shame to do it so rapidly; it was a summer favourite, awkward in Helston's company, her being a winemaker too. But he knew she'd forgive him. She always had. He raised the glass to her.

"Thank you, Kim. I wish you were coming, but I know you have a new life here. If ever you need someone to crush a few grapes, just give me a call."

She smiled, winked subtly. "You can bloody count on it."

He turned to Michael Blake.

"And you sir – will you be remaining here?"

"Absolutely not, Jack. I have work to return to – I will leave in a few days. Catseye is just my escape from it all place. A shrewd investment you could say. A long way, but she is here for me when I need her."

"Just like Elena it seems."

Blake tipped his head to one side, it was an acknowledgement and a pause.

"Yes, of course. Miss Petrova and I go back a long way. I knew her mother – but I guess you know that? Anyway, I must begin to think about packing up the old girl until next time, close a few shutters, lock her down. It has been a pleasure to have you all here. Normally my guests are quite tedious."

"It must be a rare chance – to come here to this idyllic spot?"

"No, I travel to this part of the world whenever I can, and wherever possible I allow Her Majesty to fund it."

"You have a family? Do they come with you? Surely you must bring them too?" Cade was pushing now.

"Of course Jack. Do you think I use this place as some

sort of quixotic pied-à-terre? A romantic hideaway?" He laughed confidently. "Nothing illicit ever happens at Catseye Lodge. Well, not until today." Touché.

They took off the following morning, Cade, Petrova and Helston. Over the harbour, banking across Whitehaven Beach – quite simply the most beautiful spot on earth. Cade made a promise to bring Elena back one day, to allow them both to feel the satin touch of the silica sand beneath their feet.

"Next stop Sydney. Then London. Are you ready to head back into the wolf's den, Elena?"

CHAPTER TWENTY

THE HEAVILY ACCENTED VOICE ANNOUNCED THE ARRIVAL of the China Southern flight into Frankfurt International.

It had been a smooth journey, across China, over Kazakhstan, flirting with southern Russia, the Caspian Sea then into Europe. Beneath them, for a short while, Poland and finally Frankfurt, with its chaos-organised international airport, a major hub for European flights and still a day's travel from his real destination.

He picked up his hand luggage, left the plane with everyone else and again moved smartly through the control points until he reached the Lufthansa gate lounge, next stop Budapest, Hungary.

He had studied the airport layout from online imagery. It helped in many ways.

So far, so very easy.

The onward Lufthansa flight had been pre-booked using a credit card.

'Thank you, Scott McKee.'

A hundred and five New Zealand dollars and an hour and twenty-five minutes on a Boeing 737. That is all he would need to get him to Budapest, where he would overnight in a sterile motel, then travel by car, across the border and into Romania.

He slid the backpack beneath the chair in front, his feet either side. Precious cargo. Looking out of the window he could see the mountains of Austria in the distance. Snow. He missed the winter. Loved the training in his homeland, the colder the better. He had once dug into a snow cave for four days and waited for his hunters to try to find him.

Four days. They had to blow the whistle in the end.

'Sergeant McCall – will you please reveal your location?'

He smiled now as he looked down at the expanse of green unravelling beneath him, a small town, he had no idea what it was – or who lived there.

Forty minutes to go. Refreshments had been served. Fresh, strong coffee and a strange croissant with ham – he'd eaten worse, a lot worse and often not for a bet but because he was hungry.

Fifteen minutes, seat backs up, tray tables folded. Down, beneath the clouds, banking, people preparing for landing.

Five. Three. One. Down.

It was a perfect landing by an efficient crew. Taxiing, he looked out at the new airport – Ferenc Liszt International.

Like its German equivalent it was efficient, warm and welcoming, but he knew he couldn't stay. Passport control was a breeze.

"Welcome to Hungary, Mr McKee. The purpose of your visit?"

"Sadly, I am only passing through your beautiful country today – leaving after a short stop." It was true, and it paid to flatter.

The passport was handed over by the disarming woman who pointed to the baggage hall with a smile. He returned it, with a wink.

Another time perhaps? But she was already dealing with the next passenger.

Twenty minutes later the credit card had been charged. A small two door Hyundai was now his only companion as he left the airport road and joined the M5 motorway heading south east. Ahead lay a seven-hour journey – if he obeyed the limits – which training and common sense told him to. The last thing he wanted was attention.

At a motorway service station, in a car park furthest away from the retail outlets, tucked beneath the skeletal canopy of winter trees, McCall met an old colleague who was still serving with the Hungarian equivalent of the SAS. A soldier from his past.

A tall, slim man from Debrecen with an inquiring mind and a wiry, strong body. They had trained together and had vowed to stay in touch. They hadn't managed that part, but when McCall had rung the KMZ member and asked for a few pieces of equipment, his old sparring partner said he would do his best – even if their conversation was at best broken, it was long overdue and good to talk.

Three magazines. Three flashbangs, an incendiary device and an M18 smoke grenade, together with a set of ITT Exilis night vision goggles, as he intended to go in when it was dark – get up close and personal with his audience, convince him to hand over the money without any incident then bugger off quick.

He had everything else he needed.

The Renault backed into a space, quickly, efficiently. Close enough to throw the items across. Both men nodded to one another. The Magyar to the Kiwi. No time to sit around and chat. He didn't need to know.

"Sok szerencset Mack." *Good luck.*

And he was gone.

McCall's plans allowed for an overnight stop in the city of Arad, in the western region of Romania. It was half way. He arrived at the Hotel Maxim after lunch – it was an affordable hotel with a surprisingly-comfortable bed. Rest had eluded him for twenty-four hours. What followed was the sleep of kings and a chance to plan.

The following morning, three hours south east of his room, two men drank the distilled plum liquor called Tuica and toasted their successes in the luxury apartment above the biggest nightclub in the city called Byzantin.

The club had no opposition, despite there being five other similar clubs in the city. He owned them all.

In the beautifully presented and discreetly secure apartment the once-prized and genuine polar bear rug, scorched by a stray cinder, had been adapted so that the head now sat forlornly on the fireplace hearth.

The battle flags of the Romanian people, tattered, torn and faded still hung in the open plan lounge and kitchen. Not much had changed – but the place was immaculate. Its owner, having spent so many years living in a concrete room without a view, insisted upon it.

Obsessive. Compulsive. Methodical.

That was Alex Stefanescu.

Sociopathic. Disempathetic, dyssocial – deadly. That was him too.

The club, the people that frequented it, and the reputation of its owner were legendary in the city. The police never raided it, once a year a senior commander would visit – ideally to speak to Alex – or in his absence, as was more often the case, his senior security advisor who was only known as Gheorghiu. They would agree to disagree and a contract – of sorts – was formed over a shot of the commander's chosen spirit.

The second he left the building, lifting his collar to shield from the cold, any adherence to the agreed plans was aborted. It was how it was, and both sides knew.

There was a familiarity about the two men sat holding shot glasses; fraternal, close-bond. One was the epitome of his nickname – dark haired, which shone with hints of blues and greys; dark, black eyes – olive pock-marked skin. Slim but a sense of power. Confident, arrogant, supremely condescending. His was a persona that welcomed conflict. And crushed it.

The other, younger, with green eyes and fairer skin was solidly built, the result of endless hours in a gym. Not one drop of steroid had entered his body.

He had inherited his mother's looks and compassion. More naturally, one of his irises was brown, the other hazel. His heterochromic state had become a problem – too many potential witnesses describing it first, above all else.

He fished around with his index finger. "I have to get these damned lenses out brother. They irritate me so."

"Yes. Such an irritant. But now you are home again you can walk freely among our people. No one will betray you. You know how I feel about that subject – do you not my brother?"

"Of course." Stefan Stefanescu had recently been held at 'her Majesty's pleasure' – in England. For the sake of credibility, to the outside world, and the inmates at Belmarsh Prison, he was locked down in a cell, alone.

"Why do you ask Alex?" He looked at his older, smaller yet more intimidating brother. Holding his gaze as long as he could without appearing confrontational.

Alex – the Jackdaw – ushered his three staff away. "Go, we need to talk in private." The heavy door closed, none of the three would be listening on the other side, they had seen what happened to people that did that.

"I ask because we have been adrift you and I. Where have you been since last year? I gave you money, gave you things. Sent you to a land of plenty, in a very nice car. Did I not do this, brother?"

"Yes, Alex you did. You also sent me to that land to kill your daughter. And to recover the document. I did this."

"Did you?" He locked onto the bi-coloured irises, his own coal-black ones staring back. Someone, a victim most probably, had once remarked that they resembled a shark's eyes. Emotionless. Predatory.

"Well?"

"Alex, unlike me, I feel that prison has made you slightly paranoid. You know I did. Why do you challenge me?"

"You killed her? Left her to die?"

"Yes. Again, you know this. It was your instruction. I didn't agree but you asked me to and our relationship meant I had no choice."

"Because I killed our parents – back then – you feel afraid of me?" He was becoming aroused by the very thought of it.

"No, because you are my brother. It is as simple as that. In our community honour comes first. Are you afraid of that?"

Alex laughed, filled up the glasses and threw the cork into the open fire. It was never too early to be drinking Tuica.

He was relentless with his questions, brother or not.

"And you recovered all of the documents in the car?"

Stefan paused, took a sip of the Tuica, let it burn his

throat then replied. "I believe, in the time we had, that yes, I recovered them."

"OK. Then I believe you." Change of subject. "And you have been in prison in Britain since last year. What for?"

It felt more like a job interview than a reunion of blood brothers.

"Good. I am so glad you believe me." Chance to think. "Prison? You know why. They arrested me Alex – with guns – for evading Cade and his team – all those years ago. I had a warrant with my name on it. Who would have known? I always felt that someone close by had told the authorities about me. The moment I crossed back into Britain I knew they were watching me. They could have grabbed me at the border – but no, they wanted to do it with guns, in the streets, to show how brave they are! To make a statement!"

His brother did indeed know why. He just enjoyed asking the question. The British authorities had caught Stefan Stefanescu, at gunpoint on a bitterly cold Friday morning. People had posted the imagery on social media, almost before he had arrived into a secure custodial facility.

It suited them both. Alex felt that his younger brother would learn from a stay in prison and his younger brother had lived a life of relative luxury – 'locked down in solitary confinement' but essentially elsewhere – genuinely at her majesty's pleasure and working with the British authorities.

Stefan's time in custody was a false flag. He had maintained a low profile for many years, being well paid and occasionally revelling in the chance to work illegally, under the very noses of the people that now technically employed him.

He had laid very low, until he had cropped up on the radar in New Zealand. The local authorities had no idea he was there, or even remotely connected to the crash that had supposedly claimed the life of Elena Petrova. They had no reason to consider the crash anything other than a moment of recklessness.

Young girl. Fast car. Newspaper headline.

For ten years he had supported the British efforts to thwart Eastern European criminal syndicates. In doing so he risked becoming the most hated man in the region. It was a long, drawn out game of chess. Each move carefully thought out. Britain knew it had a cut-off, knew when it needed to act or react. That time was now. But for Stefan, the long game, the divinely timed checkmate had to wait.

That time was soon.

He had made a promise to his father as he lay dying, back in the hard-fought for family home.

'Support your brother. Please.' His lungs hissed through an opening in his chest, blood pulsing from his gaping head, revealing a light yellow mass, dark red blood and brain matter. That he had survived this long was a miracle.

'He is not a monster like you think. He just needs help Stefan. See to it that one day he is sent to prison, where they can help him. Do that for me? Do not hate him. Pity him. It is not Alex that has done this to us, but the devil that inhabits his soul.'

Stefan had held his father close to his chest until he heard him sigh, exhaling his last. He was soon as cold as his mother, who was sat upright, in a favourite chair, four feet away, her back to a wall, eyes open, shocked, the stiletto knife through her throat, pinning her to the cream-coloured plasterboard – the ultimate death notice.

At her feet were two pools of darkening blood where Alex had ripped what he considered to be repugnant varicose veins from her legs. That alone would have killed her.

She was beyond help. He had been unable to speak to her, to hear her last wishes, her dying declaration. But he felt that if she had lived, she would have asked him to seek revenge, for unlike her husband she had grown to hate her son. Rather, she hated what he had become – beyond the age of about ten.

As the years had untwined so had Stefan's memory of what had happened. Time and a supremely calculating older sibling did that to a younger boy. Alex had manipulated him, again and again until he had convinced him that his parents had been to blame.

'But why did you do that to them Alex?'

'I didn't Stefan. You have to understand and one day you will. Now help me clean up.'

Convinced him that his parents were to blame.

It happened – especially to a young and frangible mind.

What they said about blood and water was true. It took him hours to remove the glutinous mush from his fingertips.

Blood. Thicker than water? Of course it was, but in the familial, literal meaning perhaps it made sense. Would his commitment and love of his brother outrank everything else?

Stefan had made a mistake many years later. Two actually.

He had failed to see his brother for what he was and had failed to find the full set of documents in the wreckage of the once-pristine sports car.

The more he considered the event he realised it was three errors of judgement. He had carried out what was technically an assassination upon his own niece. A devastatingly pretty girl, the apple of her mother's eye. He was thinking now; how could he have been so callous?

He wished she had had died instantly, not slowly fading on a roadside far from home.

However, for Alex a debt was a debt, and in their community it needed to be paid. Prison had expunged the debt. And he could send him back there any time. He had friends in low places.

His sibling had made a mistake by not searching the crashed car on that secluded New Zealand road, had not pushed the dying girl to one side to extract the second set of documents. It wasn't the end of the world, for as providence would decree, the missing piece of the puzzle was potentially about to turn up – in his own nightclub, his home, and delivered by the hand of a fool.

It simply did not get any better.

What was that saying the Western people had? A fool and his money...

"There is one thing that troubles me Stefan." His voice was beginning to slur gently.

"And that is?"

"Why didn't you just kill Elena?"

"You mean slit her throat whilst she slept?"

"Well yes. That is one way. I can think of many more."

"You asked me to make it look like an accident. It was well planned, you could not have done better."

"Oh but I could." He looked into the nearby hearth. "I would have set fire to the car. Watched her burn, lingered a while to inhale the smell of her burning body, then, and only then would I have walked away." He laughed his signature laugh, a guttural cackle.

Narcissistic Personality Disorder. It said so on his prison notes.

And he was so very proud of that title. It was about time he started living up to his reputation: Pure Malicious Intent. Anyone who wanted to work with him had to adopt the same ethos. Either that or walk away, with a knife in their back. Twisted. Turned, cleaned and lovingly put away.

"We should put on our best clothes Stefan. The night is ahead of us. Pretty girls, drink and our own people, flocking to meet us. Come on cheer up. You look like your world is ending. Who knows, we may even meet someone who might change our lives."

The male who called himself the Bushman arrived into the city of Bucharest.

He had never been there before, nor Romania. In fact, for a man with so many contacts, such worldly-wise demeanour, he wasn't that well-travelled: Solomon Islands, East Timor, Afghanistan, twice. And a month-long training course in Germany.

He liked what he saw. In his mind Bucharest was a run-down place, surrounded by poverty and the ruins of a communist state. In fact, it was beautiful. The Carpathian Mountains to the north and the Danube to the south. A trading centre that had refused to be destroyed by an earth-quake, or war or at the hand of Nicolae Ceausescu the tyrant leader, the dictator or conversely, its hero; it depended upon which side of the divide you sat, with whom you dined or served.

Ceausescu got his own just deserts. Executed at the hands of a firing squad and succeeded by a man who led Romania out of the relative dark ages into comparative wealth and freedom.

McCall marvelled at the eleven hundred room Palace of the Parliament – Ceausescu's monument to himself. It was, he decided, impossible not to see it. Whilst its immense size and impressive architecture fascinated him he soon found it also made him nauseous, the thought of the power of one man and how he could make the lives of so many, so miserable.

He started to draw similarities with his target – the Jack-daw. If you sat on his side of the fence you were guaranteed a charmed life. If not, then you weren't. Black and white. Never grey.

He continued his tourist drive, observed the obvious growth, the modern-day phoenix, spiralling from the ashes; saw the evidence of new companies, of investment and improved infrastructure. He admired the country and its people for their resilience. He liked that in a race. He was partly glad he had made the journey, but unhappy that he had to leave it in such a negative way – for he felt that whatever the outcome, somehow his life would never be the same again.

One day. One decision. The girl, in the car, dying. If he hadn't been such a knight in shining bloody armour.

'No turning back now Scottie.'

He shook his head, bringing him back on track, returning to the mission. The capital, his research had told him was named after Bucur, a prince and some said, an outlaw. Bucharest had a relatively low crime rate, lower than most European cities. Equally, it also had pockets of highly organised crime – and he knew he was heading into just such a place later that day.

The Bulevardul Ion Mihalache. It was part of the older town and where Alex and his brother had first decided to put down roots, to make money and live a comparatively debauched lifestyle.

Towards the city lay the club that was the centre of it all – his mission, his target, Byzantin.

It was more upmarket than he expected. A gleaming jewel set amongst a crown that needed polishing and yet had an old-world charm. People appeared to flock to the area, making it easier to blend but harder to surveil.

The first drive-by allowed him to conduct a scan. Old building, in keeping with the surrounding properties, large hardwood doors, ten feet high at a guess. They opened inwards. Shuttered windows. Lighting. Cameras. He knew he had two chances, three at best, to drive along the road, posing as a tourist, hopelessly lost. There was no way he could just park up outside, or even opposite. The building and the sterile area around it was somehow revered. Parked outside were two cars; a white Mercedes E63 AMG and a grey Bentley Continental GT.

'Clearly money in nightclubs eh boys?' McCall chatted to himself, working out the tactics. He was used to doing this with a team, with their knowledge, individual skills and of course, their backing.

He knew that he needed to get inside the shark's mouth. In principle it was a great idea, but one which actually could be his last if he didn't formulate a plan to deal with those teeth. Two of the largest, who McCall christened The Incisors, stood outside the club; pacing, bored, but aware of their surroundings. Alpha male predators. Powerfully-built, dark-suited, cheap aftershave, wearing overly-gilt and gaudy wristwatches and earpieces. Standard stuff for any club – especially one not designed for dancing.

'Could do with my sisters to get into that place. Pretty girls my kid sisters.'

He expected to find The Molars – the next line of defence, beyond those doors and the sharpest teeth right outside Stefanescu's living quarters. They were the ones that were honed, angled backwards to cause the most damage to his precious flesh.

For the first time – ever – he shuddered. It wasn't the cold, although the temperature had noticeably dropped and there was a threat of snow. It was fear. And fear was good.

He knew that adrenaline and fear would keep him alive. What he really needed to do now was imagine that this was a regimental operation.

He had the Grounds clear in his mind – or rather the

layout of the building and its surroundings. The Situation was clear, but fluid. The Mission was what he deemed a multi-phase component.

Phase One. He entered the shark's mouth, exchanged the documents, for a return that far outweighed his investment – and left alive.

Phase Two he stormed in there, shot everyone and escaped with a lot more than he bargained for. Death was a distinct possibility.

He chose the first option. And the more he looked, the more he saw that there was only one way to carry out the last part of the operation – which he called Hammerhead.

The final aspect of the operation, the Execution component – the how – was last but importantly so, and it needed to be at the forefront of his mind.

He drove further, left, then again, tried to find a rear door but failed. A side street just returned to him to where he had started with no view into the building through the many trees that lined the streets. There was only one thing for it. One more drive along the main road, then park up and go in on foot.

As his feet stepped onto Romanian soil he sensed a feeling of excitement. This was what he did – how he operated. His cossetted R. M. Williams boots carried him along the boulevard, on the opposite side of the road to his target. He pulled the collar of his coat up slightly and ruched the body of his jacket, aware of emphasising any tell-tale signs that he was armed.

He shuddered again. Another layer for tonight. Or was it the general feeling that he was being watched?

He was. But the person who watched him was there for an entirely different reason.

. . .

"We have a new player."

A description was passed over the covert radio. The accent was strong enough to cut through stone.

"Any of you recognise him?" An authority voice.

"Negative sir."

"Get some images."

"Already done."

"How long have you been there?"

"Thirty minutes."

"Move out."

CHAPTER TWENTY-ONE

"I GUESS ALL WE CAN DO IS SLEEP, WATCH A FEW FILMS AND eat. Then do it all again. Twice. Then once we have crossed Australia, we can do it all again."

It summed up long haul travel. Whoever it was that said the world was getting smaller had clearly not embarked on a flight of such magnitude for a while.

She looked across from her own business class seat.

"I feel like a movie star. This is so nice. Just a shame the bed is only big enough for one."

Cade looked at the girl, sprawled in the aisle seat, upstairs in the Emirates A380. Younger. Far lovelier and ever-playful. Only a matter of months before he had considered her dead. Out of his life as quickly as she had entered it, she was now back once more and captivating him with sideways glances and raised eyebrows – but with too many questions left unanswered he was still cautious.

"This plane does have a shower though. You know Jack, for the sake of old time as you say in England."

"It does. But if you check the door, it clearly states maximum one occupant." He smiled, wishing it said two.

"When did you become boring Jack?"

He leant across and kissed her. "I didn't. I just had my life turned upside down by a devastatingly pretty girl, and honestly, I'm still coming to terms with her being alive. Just bear with me?"

"Of course." She pulled a sad face. "Sorry. I have a lot to tell you I guess?"

"You do. But we've got plenty of time. We won't get to London for a day, so relax, have some champagne or whatever, eat, sleep, shower, do what you want. However, yes, before we arrive, I'd like a few answers."

"You deserve them Jack." She held his hand awkwardly over the divider that separated the two comfortable seats. "And thank you for giving me such a wonderful way to travel."

"Hong Kong. Six thundering horses, drink and a reckless friend see to it that I can afford it."

She tilted her head. It was new information. The days they had spent together at his home in New Zealand had been more focused on love than life. She had found out what she needed to know, established that he was the man her mother had told her about – the one to trust. But she had never learned more than that. It had been a genuine regret. She had been sent to extract data from him, to elicit his help, not bloody well fall for him.

She raised a glass of champagne and chinked his glass which held a generous amount of Lagavulin malt whiskey and three crystal clear ice cubes.

"Then here's a toast to those reckless drunken horses."

Her glass was empty. "OK, let's talk. Where shall I start?"

He took another sip of his, spotted the crew member approaching her with a top up, waited a second for the bubbles to settle then continued.

"How about the moment you walked into The Ocean-side restaurant in Whitianga, my restaurant – and my life? And we'll take it from there. That should see us heading towards Darwin, you can plan to be finished by the time we reach Dubai. From there we can talk about anything. Even what you plan to do with me once we get to London."

It was an opening. A small one, but a chance. She was on his side. Always had been. Always would be. She just needed to rebuild the trust and make sure he never fell for Carrie O'Shea again. She had only been jealous once in her life – her looks helped in that department – but when he spoke about her, something happened to him. She sensed a change though. As if someone had covered the flame and watched it slowly die out.

They spoke. Covered old ground, opened up new lines of discussion. Ate. Drank coffee and then talked some more. They were over Indonesia when Cade ended the chat.

"So what you are telling me is that you went to New Zealand specifically to find me. That I was the one who would somehow protect you? It doesn't make sense. There are plenty of people who can do that. Plenty of agencies. People, better equipped than me. Aren't there?"

"Not according to the letter my mother sent me. The documents she gave me – the ones she said would provide me with a bright future – they were..."

She scanned through her mind for the right word. "A magnet. Yes, they were the magnet that attracted Alex and his men. He saw it as a chance to make more money than he ever could. All of his other crimes were training for his men, a distraction, a game. He knew that he needed to time his attack and the rewards would follow. His reward is to be feared by people and government agencies. He is a dangerous man Jack. He will not stop until he has that standing in Europe and amongst his own people."

Cade felt a little nauseous. Long day. Needed to eat. Uncertain future.

"A man that wants a reputation before he wants money, is a dangerous man indeed Elena."

She was asleep. He needed to follow suit and did so as soon as he laid his head on the pillow. The dreams were no longer what they were in the past; haunting, with darkened corners, vignettes of his deepest thoughts.

This one was of dark-coloured fish, swimming in random patterns, disappearing from sight, into voids beneath the surface. Freud, the eminent psychoanalyst would state his pension on this being an indicator, a sense of sheer frustration, of something out of his control.

Cade the Fisherman. Alex Stefanescu the elusive catch.

Slumber came once more. Unusually, he slept well and for hours. So much so that he was woken by a crew member.

"We are approaching Dubai, Mr Cade if you could prepare for landing, please."

The cabin became busy. Economy passengers moving around below, stretching legs and rubbing raw eyes, trying to look through the roof panels to business class above them with envy and hatred.

In two hours they would be airborne again, final leg.

Cade had no idea about what had happened in his adopted home whilst he circumnavigated the globe. When he found out, he would decide quickly that he would rather be back on that idyllic island, away from it all. Leave the past where it belongs.

He was heading back to help, to support, to offer a quiet and reassuring level of tactical diplomacy, allowing Roberts to do what he now did best – lead an ever-changing team, all the while knowing that his role was already defined by the British. Cade wasn't there as a member of the Operation Orion team. Neither was Elena Petrova.

They were being prepared for a carefully sharpened hook.

CHAPTER TWENTY-TWO

The Emirates aircraft was now on finals. The crew reduced height and began the approach to London Heathrow, over the English Channel, following a path towards the Thames, to their north a swathe of windmills, generating electricity offshore, tall, majestic, bleached white and standing sentinel at the approach to the mainland.

Theirs was one of a number of long haul aircraft coming into London after flying through the previous night, across northern Europe, guided into the iconic airport by the equally famous river. Come to London – all are welcome.

Below them in a desolate part of north Kent, just south of the Thames, three people, captives, were waking. It was early. They had no idea of the time, but one of them, Carrie O'Shea, knew that it was about six. She always woke at this time, she recognised the light levels, as a photographer it meant a time of great hope. Golden light. The dawn of a new day.

She speculated how this one would end.

She was freezing. Her skin tacky. Damp and cold. Her

clothes...were gone. She was lying on a rudimentary table, covered in an old blanket, desperate to get comfortable but failing. In a derelict building within half a mile of civilisation but essentially forgotten. They could have been in the middle of the arctic tundra, not within striking range of one of the world's busiest cities.

She heard the aircraft, its pilot busy adjusting whatever it was they adjusted, reducing speed down to around one hundred and sixty miles an hour. Her hearing was acute, attuned to everything now. She heard birds, a Thrush, no, it was a blackbird, an oystercatcher heading out towards the marshland protested about something.

Distant traffic caused a constant thrum of rubber on concrete. That was the motorway that crossed the bridge, which in turn spanned the Thames, joining Kent to Essex. She could hear smaller aircraft now. A helicopter somewhere.

She could hear her own heartbeat.

And she could hear gentle sobbing.

The room was light enough now, enabling her to strain her eyes to the side. To her right was the body of a larger person, clothed but indistinguishable as either a man or a woman. Her instinct told her that despite the clothing it was a male.

She tried once more to relax, going against all of her inbuilt human instincts. 'Relax for Christ's sake, Carrie.'

The nausea was coming back. She fought off the inner demons that encouraged her to vomit, knowing that if she did, she would choke to death, strapped to the table, duct tape across her forehead and her arms and legs also restrained.

She had spent the last hour, half awake, pushing her head into the tape, stretching it, slowly allowing another few valuable degrees of vision.

As a result, she was able to scan and that helped her to feel a little more in control. Who was she kidding?

'Don't panic. Stay calm, Carrie.' Her own voice managed to bring her back down to a level that meant of the two people in the room, she was the most stable.

Her left eye was sore, swollen. She must have hit it when they took her, dragging her into the van and forcing the dark hood over her head. Surely by now someone would have reported it? Surely.

Yes, by now her workmates would have been worried. She worked for the police; they were the protectors; they swore an oath they would come.

'Keep this up, Carrie. Stay focused. Do not give in to these bastards.'

"They will come soon." She spoke these words out aloud. They were the first she had uttered since being manacled to the table. She was unsure who the words were meant for, but they elicited a reply.

"Hello." It was the person to her right. A dry, lip-tearing sound.

"Hello." Was all she could think of saying in reply. Pathetic. She was so cold, hungry and afraid. However, she had been through worse.

She laughed, fear sometimes did that to people. She had been through worse? Worse than being strapped to a table with a hole to piss through. No food, no warmth, naked, no idea of where she was and why, and with who. And for how long? Things could not get any worse.

"For fuck's sake, Carrie." She chastised her spirit of hope. But it instantly led to a short conversation that would change her life. She tried to swallow, forcing saliva to gather, allowing her to speak.

"Carrie? Jack's girl?"

The voice was definitely male, an unknown person, but

the words were draped over her like a warm duvet, a log fire and a wholesome meal. And fresh, cool water to revive her parched mouth and throat. They were better than anything she had right now.

"Who are you?" She could hear herself swallowing.

"Are you Jack's girl, Carrie? I need to know." Equally arid.

She replied with nothing to lose. "Yes. And who are you?"

"The boys call me Lucy." The covert intelligence source christened Lucy Thomas – codename Harrier was hissing the words through chattering teeth, cold and terrified of being heard.

"Dear God, of all the places to meet." O'Shea felt a sense of control. She whispered each of her own words. Aware of the echo of the empty room and the chance of being overheard.

"OK, where are we?"

"No idea. They brought me here in a van. About an hour from home."

"Me too. Who?"

"I don't know." It sounded like a lie.

"Are you sure?"

"No. No, I'm not sure about anything anymore Carrie." Redemption came. "Look. You need to go easy on me. One of them is called Constantin. He was a...friend."

Great. Just fucking wonderful. She was isolated and alone; she was starving, naked, her skin so raw from urine burns that she could barely move without feeling pain. That was bad enough. Adding that name to the equation – Constantin Nicolescu, the moon-howling psychopath and then Thomas, a cross-dressing prostitute of dubious morals, it was more than fair to say that her morning just couldn't get any better.

She had a foul taste in her mouth too. Chemical, acrid, and it scorched her throat when she tried to swallow. They had used something to knock her out otherwise her injuries would be sky high as there was no way she was going to go down without a fight. Give her a sharpened pencil and she would have blinded at least one of them.

"He was a client more like Lucy – if that's even your name?"

"Oh, hark at the Queen of Morals. Anyway, don't judge me until you've walked a mile in my shoes." Thomas swallowed in a laboured fashion.

"So why *are* you here? Jason Roberts told me that this man loved you? If that's even possible."

"He said he did. But he was always a well-paying client, nothing more. He says I betrayed him to the police..." He stopped, listened. He could hear a few people moving around, heard footsteps disappearing, then continued. "Says I betrayed him to your team. Cade and Roberts. That he would have escaped if I'd looked the other way."

"That bastard tried to kill me. I'll be damned if he gets the chance to do it again. We have to try to escape if we can. How are your straps?"

"Covered in blood, probably. I've been rubbing my wrists against them for hours. I've lost track of time. I'm so cold. Why are they doing this to us, Carrie?" He started to sob again.

"Pack it in. I need you to be strong."

To the left she heard a new sound. Drawn back into life by the pitiful gasps from Lucy Thomas.

"Who's there?" O'Shea couldn't see. Despite trying her best to force her eye to focus, all she could see was a blurred outline, her lashes concealing the person from her.

Nothing, no words. And then it came again, a deep,

guttural moan, the type that indicated a person was close to death.

Who were these evil people? And why had they taken them to this place?

Constantin stood up slowly, his bed, of sorts, was low to the ground. He shook the cold night air from his pain-riddled body. He stretched out, pushing his body back away from the rotten wooden window frame that offered a foggy view through ancient glass, out across the marshland that bordered the river, down below the mighty bridge that spanned it and took thousands of people into and out of the capital.

His teeth hurt today. They were as rotten as the window frame that powdered between his fingertips.

Some days they were sore, today they hurt. His gums bled. The legacy of ill-health and drug taking.

He spat a mouthful of blood onto the floor and rubbed it into the concrete with his shoe until it formed a paste and eventually flaked and blended with years of manmade commercial activity.

"Another beautiful day in paradise." He missed the drugs. He knew if he ever returned to them – his mistress as he called it – it would kill him. And now, with the end in sight, he also knew that the money he made working for the Jackdaw would more than pay for new teeth.

He laughed as he drew a smiley face in the condensation – "I could buy a whole new head!"

"What's that boss?"

The voice was one of the younger members of his team, also trying to warm up, desperate to regain some level of human comfort.

"I was talking to myself. You shouldn't listen to my

thoughts, they might upset you. Go and get some coffee made. I have work to do. Bring it to me in the main room." He looked at the male. He was young, just like he was, and hopeful, looking to a brighter future.

"Would you like any food?"

"No thank you. I rarely eat, my system cannot deal with food."

"Just coffee then?"

"Please?"

The smiley face was crying as he walked out of his room towards what he called the main area – for all intents, a prison cell.

"Good morning, ladies. What a beautiful day outside. Birds are singing, people going about their business, free, free of the restraints of life, of misery and the taut feeling of tape across their bodies, holding them against their will."

He took the offered mug of coffee. "Thank you. Smells good. Stay here. I need some help. And you may learn something from me. One day someone will need to replace me. May as well be you."

The male did as he was told. Constantin's reputation preceded him.

He blew the steam away from the dark brown liquid, let the scent fill his nostrils, then sipped, swilling the remains of the night away.

None of the three captives spoke.

"You must be cold? It was a cold night, no? I know I was cold. I only had four blankets to keep me from freezing to death. God only knows how it must have been for you. Anyway, I have some good news. There will be a period of physical activity commencing in ten or so minutes. I need fresh air first, another coffee and perhaps something to eat."

He looked at the young male with raised eyebrows as if

he was responsible for his sudden hunger. He hadn't eaten in days.

"Such activity gives me an appetite."

Cynthia Bell let out another deep and visceral moan. It was the beginning of the end for her.

"Sadly, you cannot join me. I don't feed you, better that way, less messy. You understand?"

He turned and walked away. The stench was overpowering. The misery pervasive.

"Any news? Anything?" It was Roberts, at work early and asking the obvious questions of his team.

Heads shook everywhere. "Nothing, guv. Not a dickie bird." Nick Fisher was also at work early. They all were. About time, they moved in.

"I can tell you that Carrie is officially late boss if that helps in some small way?" Bridie McGee, Detective Sergeant and one of Roberts' favourites. He relied upon her to speak the truth. He knew that Fisher would do the same, but laced with expletives so rich a hooker would blush.

"Are we all prepped for the briefing at eleven?"

"As best as we can be boss. I feel we can't really add much. No new intel. No new chatter. It's all quiet on the western. We need to get out Jason, need to start shaking a few trees. OK with you?"

Fisher was old school and all the better for it. He would literally shake a giant oak if it meant getting a result.

"Do what you are paid to do, Nick. You too Bridie. Just get me some answers, ASAP." Roberts was tired, and it was beginning to show.

"I'm off to Heathrow. Got a pickup to make. Two old friends coming home to roost. Got to dash or I'll be late."

"Can't you send someone else?"

"I could. Privilege of rank. But I need some space – a chance to breathe – and think. Besides, I also need to learn the route for when I get sacked by the Home Secretary at five past eleven and end up becoming a cabbie!"

He threw his keys to Fisher. "Don't bend it. I'll take yours, it's got a bigger boot."

He was in the blue Mondeo moments later, his sat-nav pointlessly telling him the route to London Heathrow. He recalled the last time he had picked Cade up from the terminal and how they had laughed, mocked one another and then swept up the chaos that subsequently unravelled on the streets and in their lives.

She looked directly at the forty-something male stood in front of her. Immaculately cut hair, blond, suspiciously so, tanned, naturally, a good physique for a man of his age and workload and green eyes that glinted with hints of hazel behind the platinum-framed Police tinted glasses that he favoured. Pinstriped suit, blue, white shirt, blue tie and probably blue underpants and socks. He was a true Tory and enjoyed crushing anything or anyone that disagreed with him.

He had many friends, but some said he had more enemies. In Sassy Lane he had a colleague, and one in whose shadow he felt he lived every day.

"Are you ready for this morning, Minister?"

"I am, Home Secretary. Do you think the police are?"

"Good question. I really want as many of their people on board as possible. The problem is we need to keep this low key. So far off the radar that our normal thin blue line cannot be aware. How we've kept this under wraps so far frankly amazes me. This stays within our inner circles and the four walls of Operation Orion."

"You trust them?"

"I trust them. I actually have more faith in that team than I do some of my own cabinet colleagues when it comes to integrity."

"And this man Cade?"

"With my life."

"I meant, what about him, Home Secretary? He's a former inspector, bit of a blue flame, then petered out like a cheap Chinese fire cracker. Hardly a stellar performer in such exalted company."

"Interesting that you consider yourself exalted? Careful. You have no idea what he is able to do for us. It was actually Jack Cade that spoke first about this group. Had we have listened to him back then, we might have been better prepared now."

"Hindsight..."

"Bullshit. Do not give me the old hindsight is a wonderful thing speech, Harry. Not now. Not ever." She held his gaze. He knew better.

"OK, Sassy, I hear you. Forgive me if I lack confidence in one man making everything better for the entire human race." He pushed a cup and saucer out of reach. "We had better go. Your audience awaits."

His voice was always measured, some thought it cold. At times he had a minor stammer, almost indistinguishable, a hint of an accent, again, vague.

She smiled at her Minister for Policing – Harold 'Harry' Halford was a genuine blue flame if ever there was one. He had already been tipped for Lane's role by a junior ministerial colleague, who suggested in a quiet hallway that Lane would 'soon be overlooked by the Prime Minister' – pity he had been overheard by Lane and had been licking his wounds ever since.

"Finish your tea, you old drama queen. We've got plenty of time."

"Only you could get away with that, Sassy."

"Absolutely. And don't you ever forget it, Harry. We have a long journey ahead if Britain stands a chance of survival on the world stage. You arrived onto the scene late, but you are a fast learner. It's all down to trust, and luck. And people."

CHAPTER TWENTY-THREE

"OK, SO WHERE WERE WE PEOPLE?" CONSTANTIN WAS back in the room, entering without a sound. He had stood and watched his three prisoners. Two of whom were breathing quietly, the third quietly dying.

"Tip them over and then turn them onto their sides. Face the freak towards the windows." He pointed towards Thomas.

"And wash them down with some water, they stink. Make it warm, I want them to be willing, not cold and resistant."

O'Shea took the words literally. She did that. It was a trait that sometimes backfired. Like the time she had allowed Cade to walk away from her for good, instead of making her intentions clear. Men were from Mars and all that.

She listened for her jailer's next words. Why was he turning Thomas onto his side?

"That's it. Now rinse him off. Then her, but turn her to face the other woman." He gestured to O'Shea. "Let her see who her fellow guest is."

The three men that had entered the room did as they were told. They hadn't signed up for this, rather they had responded to a call to arms from their leader Alex. 'Head to Britain, have fun, make yourselves rich.' This was definitely not in the brochure. They were as cold and miserable as their hostages.

A bucket of water arrived. The youngest male, who was nineteen at the most, poured it over Thomas, leaving her wet through, and soon colder than the morning air that was clawing at the young man's clothing, pulling at his skin and chilling him to the bone.

"Better? Good. I'll come back to you in a moment." Nicolescu sneered.

Thomas spoke. "Thank you. Connie. Please. There is no need for revenge. I did what anyone would do when threatened by a government official. Please."

He stepped past Thomas, refusing to acknowledge him as a woman anymore, just 'the freak'.

O'Shea had been tipped to her left, the tape straining to hold her. She looked into the eyes of her teammate and friend and retched, leaving a small pool of yellow bile on the stone-cold floor.

"Wash it away. I cannot stand the smell of vomit in the mornings."

Cynthia Bell, a woman who would literally not frighten a goose, lay there, restrained, removed of all dignity, almost ivory-skinned, her normal bright eyes just pockets of desolation. Her lips bleeding and blue, the tips of her ears were blue as well. It did not bode well for the shy and retiring analyst. Her hair, normally immaculate, was matted to her head and face. What O'Shea looked at was the body of her friend.

Until she saw a tear.

O'Shea smiled at her. Willing her to stay alive another

day. She mouthed the words 'love you' – it was odd for a co-worker – but equally it made so much sense. Then she slowly said, 'Be strong. They will come.'

Water rushed over O'Shea bringing her back to reality. She was the coldest of the trio. The youngest, too. And the strongest willed by far. She needed to be. Her skin was alive with goose bumps. The last time this had happened was with the blue-eyed man she had fallen in love with. That was pure arousal. This was icy and driven by fear.

She was unsure how long she could last, but she knew it would be longer than Bell. She scanned up and down her body, saw the bleak and forlorn circles around her eyes and stale, dark brown bandaging wrapped around her left fore-arm. An avenue of congealed blood ran from the stump towards her shoulder as the warm water trickled across her body, breaking up the tracks of blackened blood and swilling away days of human expulsion.

Her torso was stripped bare but for a white bra. Constantin found no reason to punish her more than he had. He had needed her, that was all. She was important to the men that employed her and she was important to him too, albeit as nothing more than a conduit. No point in humiliating her more than he needed to.

Her skirt was soaked and stuck to her legs. Her tights torn and dirty, shoes long since discarded.

O'Shea studied the man that leant against the pale-coloured wall, his mind flooded with thoughts.

'If I get out of here alive, I will personally carve your face off with a blunt carving knife, so dull that I will have to saw at it, you evil piece of shit.' She couldn't say it out loud, but it felt good to rebel.

She watched the water, blood and tears wash away, down a hole in the floor. The ground stank of stale urine and the remnants of home-grown surgery. She retched again.

"OK, bath time is over everyone. Back up, into your places, please."

He clapped his hands, not dissimilar to a film director. He was losing it and rapidly. And that meant time was not on their side.

"First on today's list is you Lucy – what is your real name again?"

He tapped Thomas on the face. "Smile, my dear. It might never happen." He pulled a chair up to the table and then beckoned to a man in his thirties with shoulder length black hair and an expression that said he wanted to be somewhere else.

"My equipment, please. And the light. Start the generator."

He pulled a lamp towards him, switched it on and bathed Thomas' face in bright white light.

"Matthew Five."

"What? I don't understand." She was beyond panic. Crying now.

"I don't expect you too. Just learn. I had to whilst I was in prison. I learned a great deal. It was good for my soul and my mind. For example, I discovered that if you mix certain chemicals, you create a deadly gas." He waved at O'Shea. "Hi, yes, it was me, of course. You should not have survived. Sorry. I failed you."

He walked around, pacing, as if trying to recall something from his past.

"Yes, that was it. I still have your underwear somewhere, felt nice against my skin. Anyway, I'd love to talk, but I have work to do."

Thomas was writhing against the straps. "Please. What-ever you do, not my face. It provides me with a living. You know that. Remember our times together? Remember the games we played?"

Constantin was clearly embarrassed and pushed his fingers up to Thomas' lips. "Shh."

He pressed some new grey tape across her mouth and squeezed her nostrils together. "I remember how you used to like that game too? This time I will hold it until the blood vessels in your eyeballs burst. Perhaps you might want to keep quiet."

Thomas nodded, trying to regain composure.

"Now, imagine I am a doctor. I know, difficult, but please try, all of you." He looked around at the three male accomplices in the room who were unsure what was going to happen next, pondering how they would explain away their roles if the police should come crashing through the door.

"It's OK boys. Trust me. I learned a lot in my time away, just didn't get much chance to practice. But this is so exciting."

He picked up the battery powered drill, screwed a metal bit into the chuck, tightened it and selected the hammer. It had a light on the front which Constantin liked very much, all the better to see his work up close.

He cut Thomas' hideous, black, skin-tight leggings away and threw the material onto the floor, saving a length to roughly bind around her head, covering her eyes, shielding her, but also removing an essential sense and adding to her state of alarm.

The drill bit rested on Thomas' shin and then began to whirl, the motor making a high-pitched noise as it painstakingly propelled the clinically sharp tip into her hairless skin and begun to dig beneath the surface.

It took a few seconds of slow rotation for the nerves to start to react.

The bright LED light allowed the man they had once deferentially called The Chemist to enjoy the spectacle of flesh and blood spiralling up and around the drill bit, its operator doing his best to ignore the hideous stifled screams from his patient.

As the first flecks of ivory appeared on the drill, he announced that from this day he would really prefer to be known as The Surgeon. There really was nothing to it. Surgery and medicine were his new drug. He liked his new self-imposed title very much.

He took a moment to examine how bright the bone was among the blood. Then drilled deeper. Pushing on the back of the tool with the palm of his hand. He removed the bit and found a new site. Again, and again. In five minutes Constantin had perforated the tibia with a dozen or so holes and had allowed them to rapidly fill with the pain and despair of all the world.

The shin bled profusely. He wiped it away initially, then stopped, knowing he was fighting a losing battle. The holes were only a few millimetres in diameter, but very effective.

"That should slow you down – should you decide to run away."

He slapped Thomas' right cheek again.

"You asked about revenge? An eye for an eye and a tooth for a tooth. Is that not what it says in Matthew, Chapter Five? Or do you not know this?" He began to yell. "Am I the only one here with an education?"

He moved the chair up towards Thomas' head, noting that she had passed out. The pain was so intense. Constantin slapped her again until she came around. He was exasperated.

"You need to be awake to see this. This is special. What I did to your leg? That was simple butchery. Try and run on that and it will collapse. It is just a matter of mechanics. However, what is about to happen is biblical indeed."

O'Shea couldn't see the scene but had a cinematographic sense of it. The sound of the drill, the bone resisting the metal bit, and Thomas trying to scream through a thick band of tape.

"Why didn't you just break his leg?"

Constantin turned from his duties, picking pieces of bone marrow from the drill and flicking them across the room. "I beg your pardon?"

"Oh, you heard me, Nicolescu. Why not break her leg, if the only reason you just did that to her was to stop her from running away?"

It was a fair point. He liked her spirit. Suddenly delighted that he hadn't killed her the first time.

"Because my dear, now, if she runs, I will have a chance of catching her. I left her other leg alone for that reason. I may even release her tonight, see how long she lasts out there in the marshes that surround us. I am so glad you have not lost your sense of fight." He leant down, wiped the remaining blood off the bit and onto her face, pausing next to her mouth.

"Clean it."

"Fuck off."

"Nasty, no need to be impolite." He slipped the drill between her tightening lips. "Clean. It. Now."

She allowed the cold metal to enter her mouth, then closed her lips around it. Closed her eyes, too. She could smell the metallic tang of the fresh blood.

"Get on with it, will you? You are just making me more willing to cause you serious harm when it is my turn."

"Ah yes, your turn, my dear Carrie. Well, you see, I wanted to wait until later for that. Give you chance to cool off a bit. Perhaps outside, under a full moon. No one can see us and the cold would help me, would excite your skin a little more. I may even remove the gag. Scream all you like out there." He carefully wiped a trace of blood from her lips.

"See you later. Have a beautiful day. We have places to go and havoc to cause. Don't run away now." He ran the drill bit along the length of her upper torso, watching her stomach churn as he wandered lower. Then stopped and gently squeezed the trigger.

He watched her eyes widen.

"Carrie. Do you think I am some sort of animal? Please. I would never hurt you for the sake of it." His voice went up an octave. "There always has to be a reason."

He spun around and walked out of the room, followed by the three young men. They stopped outside and spoke. O'Shea closed her eyes, concentrating all of her senses into one.

"Give the older woman about an hour. Then get her out of here. There are plenty of rooms to store her in. Tonight, we will take her to the river and get rid of her. It is a full moon so we need to be careful, but the tide will be strong. By the morning she will hopefully be out at sea, or miles away or at the bottom of the river, in the mud."

She heard it all and began to cry. How could they leave a defenceless woman to die in such a derelict place, when all she had done was her job? And all they appeared to want was monetary reward?

They had killed her friend.

She started to think about her own mortality. What plans did he have for her? Here in this wretched hole. Or later, under the moonlight?

Constantin Nicolescu could well have been a doctor. He was erudite and patient. His infinite knowledge of the human body, learned during countless hours, pouring over books in prison libraries had served him well. When he announced that Cynthia Bell would last about another hour, he was accurate to within twenty minutes. He wasn't there when she did finally go, but his simple action of amputation, to send a message, was what had finally killed her. Or rather, the shock of it.

She knew too.

She found some resolve. From deep in her soul she rose up, pushing against the straps, turned towards Carrie and spoke through her tears.

"Carrie. I'm going. There is no light." She laughed. "But I hope there are forty virgin men awaiting me beyond the pearly gates."

"It's OK. Conserve your energy, Cynthia. We will get you out of here."

"No. I have lost too much blood. I know about these things. Tell everyone that I miss them, tell them I'm sorry for creating paperwork..."

"Cynthia shut up and listen. They know we are missing by now. They will come soon."

"They have no idea where we are, Carrie."

"You just keep talking to me. Talk about whatever you want."

"Hugh Jackman?"

"If that's what lights your candle." It couldn't have been a crueller statement.

Bell was quiet. O'Shea called out to her. "Cynthia!"

She shuddered back into life for the penultimate time.

"If you get out of here, make sure he goes down for a very long time."

"Oh, I'll do better than that, mate. You will be there to help me."

"That's nice." Her voice was trailing now.

"And the others, too. Alex Stefanescu is the reason for this. I'll make sure he gets treated terribly too."

Bell made only sounds. Her breathing laboured, clutching for a last breath, desperate to say a few more words.

"Take care, Carrie. Give 'em hell girl." Then a sigh. And she was gone.

CHAPTER TWENTY-FOUR

Cade and Petrova were through into the baggage hall picking up their luggage quickly, orange tags saw to it that their bags were first off. With typical Emirates efficiency, they were soon going to be together with Daniel, who had flown from Auckland to London, almost mirroring their journey.

All three got through passport control quickly and without encumbrance. Even Petrova.

She smiled curiously at Cade. "I always get stopped at international borders, Jack."

"That's because you are an attractive woman, and in my experience..." He stopped, realising that it was just such a situation that had led him to this point – he had met her mother, back in 2004 at a smaller airport and both of their lives had permanently changed.

"...And in my experience that means that men will find an excuse to detain you and ask lots of searching questions."

"But not today?"

"Clearly, El. Not today." Cade had no idea why she had not been stopped. He'd allowed an extra hour for just such an event. The discreet alert on her passport, viewed on a screen in the glasshouse of the UK Border Force control room, had seen to it that she was not stopped.

Someone, somewhere, liked her.

A Bulgarian female travelling on recently issued tickets was a certainty for a referral to the search area. But not today.

"Welcome back to England, Elena."

"Jack, this is my first time in your country."

He'd done it again. Confusing her with her mother, equally radiant and life changing.

"Sorry. Let's go, Elena." He pointed to the exit, dragging his suitcase and allowing her to catch up from the carousel. He had seen a distinguished-looking man walking towards them from Carousel Five, also pulling a quality suitcase behind him, his raincoat over his arm, well dressed, fit for his age. Who were they kidding? He was fit and well and as always had a less-than-subtle twinkle in his eye.

They stopped before they exited the airside area of Heathrow.

"Shake hands outside, JD?"

"Sounds like a plan." John Daniel, Cade's friend, former colleague and mentor smiled broadly, then almost got bowled over by Elena who ran and jumped up and into his arms, oblivious to the enhanced security measures at Heathrow and the myriad cameras that instantly swung in their direction.

"Wow, and I've missed you too!" He lowered her to the floor, allowing her feet to touchdown with the skill of a dancer. He held the hug just a little too long, kissing her on both cheeks and winking at Cade over her shoulder.

"I never thought I'd see you again, John Daniel. I am so happy." She turned to Cade. "You don't want to hug JD?"

"Not yet, El."

They walked through the frosted automatic doors and were landside in London. England's green and pleasant land.

Roberts was leaning against a polished steel barrier, with a handmade sign held up for all to see.

CROSS DRESSING ANNUAL CONFERENCE 2015

Cade spotted it first. "Seen that?"

JD could only smile. "You have to agree, it's good to be back, Jack. Fancy that hug now?"

The two men embraced, with Daniel whispering, "sorry" into the younger man's ear.

Cade replied, "I've got a few questions, but I'm sure I can forgive you John. How's Lynne?"

"She's fine, says to kick your arse. Been too long since you were back home in New Zealand, Jack. By the way, I think your Samoan friend emptied your drinks cupboard over Christmas."

"I told him too. Did he bend the Audi?"

"No. Said it was a hairdresser's car."

Elena laughed. "See? I told you. Girlie car for girl!" She was so attractive when she was being mischievous. Thank God it was winter, forcing her to dress for the occasion, covering that enchanting body.

They reached Roberts, who had carefully folded the sign in half and then again and put it into a nearby bin.

"Team! How are we all?" He smiled and emphasised the word all.

"I didn't know you were coming back, Elena. Jack didn't say anything."

"I thought Michael would have told someone?"

"Michael?" Roberts had a puzzled expression.

Cade replied, "It's a rather long story, Jason. I'll fill you in on the way."

They took it in turns to hug and shake hands.

"Do we have time for a coffee?"

"Sadly not, Jack. Grab some for the journey?"

"Indeed. What are you two having?" He took their orders and diverted to a café. "I'll see you at the car park Jason?"

"You think Jason Roberts, Detective Chief Inspector and local hero is going to pay to park on his own patch?"

"Fair point well made. Where then?"

"Rental car spaces, fifty feet away. And I'll have a long black with a Kit Kat. A chunky one. Don't be too long I don't want to get towed."

JD and Elena walked together. "I never thought we would see each other again, JD. That day..."

He held her hand, a true English gent. "No, me neither. I sent help, you know. But I understand that help arrived in the guise of a guardian angel."

"You know about that?"

"Well, put it this way: I made a career out of gathering intelligence. It took a few calls until I got to speak to the Westpac Rescue team. They told me that another helicopter landed nearby, a military one, deployed a few of their medics and the rest, as they say, is history."

"Military? So he was a soldier?"

"Yes. Did you see him?"

"For a brief moment. He spoke to me John, calmed me down. I watched him through my eyelashes, for a few seconds, then I was gone. He had a beautiful voice. So kind. Like you."

"Thank you. You mean like Jack?"

"Yes, him too!"

"I'll tell him."

"He knows. But you can. I am not afraid of him. We had a fight in Australia. I punched him, then kicked him. He tried to drown me."

"My goodness, it must be love."

"Yes. I think so. I couldn't let him win though, so I punched him in the liver. I could have killed him."

"I can see what he sees in you. Such charm." He smiled at her, causing her to slap him across the backside. "You are a naughty man, JD."

"And old enough to be your father. Come on, let's get to the city and find out what has been happening."

"Do you think Alex is going to cause more harm to us? To the team? To Jack?"

"I have no idea but the word is that something is building, a storm, ready to cause chaos to Britain, and apparently we are part of the team that the government of this delightful country has appointed to stop who or whatever that is."

They met at the car, loaded the luggage into the boot and took their places. JD up front with Roberts – deliberately, and Cade and Petrova in the back.

"To London, Jason and do not spare the horses!"

"Yes, my lady. Would be my honour. Now, talking of ladies, when we get to Scotland Yard we have a meeting with some pretty powerful people. Having met a few of them already, my advice is watch and learn, say nothing, nod at the right time and worst case, laugh at their jokes."

"But what if they are not funny?" Elena's question was naïve but fair.

"Laugh anyway." Cade replied. "If they are men, smile at them, but don't raise the hem of your dress like you did with me when we first met."

"It worked with you, Jack."

The two front seat occupants stifled a laugh, sipped at

their coffee and considered what the meeting would bring, who would make the cut and who ultimately might survive. The heat had been turned up, fingers and reputations were preparing to be burned.

"Shits just got real team. Our government is pouring resources into this that frankly they don't have. The potential loss of reputation, harm to the economy, and even loss of life is tangible. I'm leading the operation with a direct line to an assistant commissioner and the Home Secretary, Jack is my tactical advisor. JD, I need you to be my liaison please, it's what you do best. I need to know what is happening up, down and sideways. If we get this wrong..."

"All points noted I'm sure Jason." JD was thoughtful but as ever, able to juggle his thoughts. "Timescale?"

"Now that's the billion dollar question."

"Billion?" Elena was quick to pick up on the amount.

"Minimum Elena. Minimum."

"Do we have anything new to support all of this?" Cade wanted answers, he also knew the difficult question about Roberts' staff had to come soon.

"GCHQ. The Service. Special Branch. Interpol. Doesn't get much more interesting, Jack."

"And?"

"And in the words of the Prophet − we've got sweet Fanny Adams."

"Great. We are happy that is all still linked to a few pieces of lousy paper?"

"Ecstatic Jack." He wasn't. He was so far removed from ecstasy it wasn't funny.

"Pieces of paper? It seems that Alex is risking a lot for a few pieces of paper." She knew the answer.

"Elena. Somebody is coming to my city to remove its heart, its lifeblood, drop by drop. I cannot allow that to happen. And I won't. And if anyone gets in my way, they will be dealt with."

It was a newly fired up Roberts. Sick and tired of his beloved streets being claimed by malicious intent.

"We are losing control, Jack. You've got a hell of a job on your hands."

Cade was pensive, he knew that she knew. They both understood that what she carried with her, when they had first met, was worth more than any jewel – it had a currency that was unique.

He was calculating the cost in terms of financial and political fallout. She was looking at it from an entirely different angle.

If she had just given him the bloody thing when they first met instead of flirting, and falling for him, then perhaps the entire episode would have been filed away in the corner of a discreet office in Whitehall, or wherever it was that the British kept their secrets and lies.

"Do I get paid?" Cade asked, optimistically.

Roberts laughed. "Bloody good question. I guess you do if the Home Secretary requested your pleasure. Goes for you too John."

"And me, Jason?" Petrova looked at him in the rear-view mirror, causing him to look away. Those eyes.

"Oh, fear not fair lady. I have plans for you too."

"I'm sure you do. But what do I get for helping you?"

"Have you tried my world famous tea in the morning?"

"No. And I won't be doing. You love your wife too much."

A flustered Roberts replied, "I meant..."

She smiled, pulled a face that was somewhere between amusing and mocking.

"So what's the ultimate goal Jason?" Cade interrupted.

He was pushing for some answers, ground-movingly tired from jetlag.

"Find them all. Lock them all up. Shut down their op. Save a few red faces, home in time for tea and the proverbial medal. End of."

"By fair means only I assume?"

"Another good question, my friend. I guess for the police officers involved, yes."

"And for those that are no longer bound by the rules?"

"There are always rules, Jack. We both know that."

"Then I will be seeking some parliamentary approval to overlook them. Starting today."

They had covered only a mile in the endless traffic, JD nodding against the passenger window when Cade spoke.

"Did you find us a decent hotel?"

Roberts replied, "Did I?"

Cade followed with, "Well, did you?"

"Did I!"

"You've done it again. Did you or didn't you?"

"Yes, I said did I? Didn't I?"

Petrova joined in.

"Do you answer all of his questions with a question?"

"Do I?" Roberts was having fun now.

"Does he?" Cade was also having fun at her expense.

A slurred response came from the front passenger.

"Do you two ever shut up?"

"Do we?"

It was a moment of levity ahead of a tense and life-altering day.

Roberts indicated right, veered across the road and then left, left again and into the car park. Ten minutes to go.

Cade pulled his old team mate to one side whilst Daniel and Petrova were signed in, security had taken a marked step upwards after the UK threat level had once more risen from

Substantial to Severe – the Prime Minister holding back from initiating Operation Temperer – the presence of military personnel on the streets of London – but he was close.

"I said I would tell you about Michael Blake."

"You did." Roberts' eyebrows raised. "Good or bad. You know I don't trust that bastard, don't you?"

"I do. But seriously Jas, there was something about him last week that said we have both misjudged him. Can't put my finger on it yet but he cares for Elena, looks out for her, for that reason alone he gets my vote."

"OK. And Elena? Did you manage to get that finger put on her at all?"

"You know I hate you, don't you?"

"One hundred and one percent Jack. Look, mate, before we head upstairs to the briefing." He cleared his throat, genuine concern.

"Cynthia is missing."

"I know, you told me. No news?"

"Nothing. Sorry to sound callous, if it was just her I would still be worried, but Harrier has also failed to answer any of my calls."

"You telling me you are worried about a bi-curious prostitute? You going soft in your old age, DCI Roberts?"

"Was that an unintentional pun?"

"No. But now you mention it." Cade couldn't help smiling, recalling the fight during which part of Thomas' anatomy had been seen, smelt and almost tasted by Roberts. Happy days indeed.

"Off the radar. We've been to the address. Nothing. Not even a false eyelash out of place. Local bloke said Thomas left with two men."

"Fair enough, he, she can look after him herself."

"That was the comparatively good news, Jack."

Cade could almost sense what was coming.

"Carrie has failed to show for work too. No replies, flat's all quiet. No one has a clue where, or why. She's gone. And that worries us all."

"Worries me too. Can we get all local units in the city and north and south of the river to be on the lookout? We cannot allow her to come to harm. Not again, Jason. It cannot happen. Clear?"

"Crystal. I'm with you. Two steps ahead, I've already circulated her."

"Good man. Seriously, this is no longer mildly worrying – I have a horrible feeling about this." His knuckles were tense and his temples pulsed. It was a bad sign.

The fact that Roberts hadn't circulated O'Shea as missing would have worried Cade even more.

CHAPTER TWENTY-FIVE

THE TEMPERATURE HAD RISEN SLIGHTLY AND THE STREETS surrounding the Medical District of Bucharest had been thankfully quiet during the night, both positive elements in the few precious hours that Scott McCall had grabbed, in his bland rental car, in a side street half a mile from Byzantin.

He unwrapped three high protein muesli bars and ate them in succession, washing them down with a bottle of water.

He pulled the mirror down a notch and stared back at the drawn, unshaven face. He looked tired, but the spark in his eyes said otherwise.

He ran through his own op once more, checked his weapon and equipment, switched off his phone.

"Time to get your game face on Scottie boy. Who fucking dares and all that."

Alex Stefanescu woke with a start, his heart beating so fast it surprised him.

He couldn't stand for a second. He looked around the lounge of his substantial apartment, above the epicentre of his considerable business world – or at least the front for it. He owned mainly commercial properties, cars of all types, so many he'd forgotten the total. His money was elsewhere. And as far as he was concerned, he owned the government of Britain, or soon would do.

For now, he was just like any other man who had consumed a little too much alcohol the night before. A heavy head with hair that hurt, dry mouth and a bank account that had lessened overnight. He had lost money on a bet, on something irrelevant. He'd get the money back tenfold. One day.

He looked across the room. His brother was already awake, drinking coffee and feeling great. Smug bastard was better off financially too.

"Ah, look at you. To the victor, the spoils. Where have you been since you failed me brother? Be honest. One chance." Straight for the throat. There was an edge to him this morning. Worse than normal. The pretty girls had been dismissed before the night had even begun. He was slipping into his favoured darkened state: Unstable.

"We discussed this last night. Why can't you let it go Alex?"

"Trust. That is why. A simple word, Stefan. You have betrayed me and our people. And that dear brother is against all of our laws. I hoped that some drinks last night might remind you of your loyalty and honour."

"This is not true, my brother. Not true at all. I have been more than loyal. I put my life on the line for you, time and time again. And yet you challenge me. How dare you?"

"How dare I?" He was shouting now. Probably still drunk. No one spoke to him in this way, not even his sibling. "How dare I speak to my little brother? How dare I tell him that I no longer trust him? For letting me down, for letting the team and his people down? Should I continue?"

"Oh, please do Alex. I can't wait to hear where I went wrong." He was clenching his jaw, his mismatched eyes starting to narrow, fists balling, stomach tightening. They were chalk and chalk in that respect.

Alex continued, he felt that he had his brother on the ropes. "Apart from being born?" That hurt. "You went wrong when you lied for the first time. I gave you everything."

"Alex, we have been through this so many times. It is becoming boring. Can we please move on and finish this thing that we started? The thing that you obsess over? Remember, I am as guilty of trying to kill people to achieve our aim as you — you just get to gain so much more than any of us in the group."

His brother threw a glass at the wall, sending fragments ricocheting across the room.

"I *am* the group. Alex, the Jackdaw, is the group. I am *everything*. I am the Lord of all I surveill."

For the first time since childhood, Stefan saw something in his brother that concerned him. Frightened him. He knew of all the harm he had caused before, how he had brutally harmed people, some for no obvious reason — for practice. For fun. And now he was closing avenues quickly, destroying evidence in his mind, shredding, shredding, shredding.

If his brother ever discovered just how disloyal he had been his retribution would be vicious and sustained. Unless Stefan struck first.

Alex walked across the room, stepping over the glass fragments — someone else could pick that up — then pushed his way past his brother.

"Move!"

"Or what?"

Things were escalating.

"You will keep for another time, baby brother. You can leave whenever you like. I need to shower. One of us stinks."

He hated him. Hated his older brother. Hated what he stood for, but despised himself even more for being associated with him.

"OK. I will move. Just calm down. Let us drink and talk through what is troubling you brother."

Alex appeared to calm – on queue. "True, my little baby brother. We should be working together, not against each other. We have enough enemies, what with our rivals in this country and across Europe and in London, the Russians and Albanians.

He looked sleepy.

"Another drink to our mother country. And our dear parents. May they always rest in peace!"

He poured two more drinks. It was not the time. Yet.

The drinks remained untouched. Alex slept on the sofa, leaving his younger brother to pace for a while, until he too decided to get some much needed sleep. When the time came, he needed to be alert. He just hoped he'd be alert enough to recognise that the time was now.

McCall walked the half mile route from his car to the club. He took a zig-zag approach, using all of his field craft, shielding himself from surveillance, hugging building lines, pacing vehicles and blending with people until he got so close he could smell the aftershave. It was even cheaper in the flesh. He smiled.

Waiting for five minutes allowed him to listen, observe and absorb. Bird song, traffic, cycles, footfall. Five minutes invested now was time well spent, an investment in the future – if indeed he had one. All successful surveillance operations did this. Becoming one with the grounds was a must, and McCall was an expert.

Training had taught him so much about how to blend into the theatre of operations. Familiarity had given him the edge. Now it was just a numbers game, but mornings, from his experience, were the best time to hit somewhere like this. All recent military battles had been fought at night. It made sense. But these people were not soldiers and therefore did not play by the rules.

For now, he too had to wait for the right moment.

The eleventh floor briefing room at Scotland Room was standing room only. People who thought they had a need to know, didn't. A few that did had nowhere to sit. There hadn't been a crowd of this size since the Commissioner had bought in his wife's carrot cake.

Mike Collins – the new assistant commissioner operations waited a second for the room to settle then spoke. Crisply ironed white shirt, black tie, name badge. Black hair, greying at the temples, trendy Boss Orange glasses and as goal driven as they came. He had a three-year plan to be the next Commissioner and didn't hide the fact.

"All here? Door closed, please. Anyone without the right clearance needs to leave now. The following people can stay. John Cade, John Daniel and Elena Petrova."

Roberts was stood, due to the level of brass in the room and spoke first.

"Sir. Two of my team, DSs McGee and Fisher, are not cleared to this level – but I need them to be here. They are my eyes on the ground."

The two assistant commissioners looked at their boss, who nodded.

"Granted. Let's move on. Prime Minister, Home Secretary, Police Minister Halford and our friends from Defence, welcome and thank you for finding the time to attend. It is my intention to keep this briefing true to its nature – brief. However, we cannot overlook the importance of this. I will assume you are all, at the very least, familiar with the history of this operation?"

He looked around the room. No one was prepared to admit a lack of preparation – not in this audience.

"Good. You all have the operational order in front of you. Note the classification, leave them in this room at the end of the briefing please. OK. The primary purpose of this operation is to prevent harm to the reputation of this country. By that I mean financially, its reputation in Europe and on the world stage." He paused, not for effect, but to simply let the facts of the matter sink in.

"The people in the photographs in front of you are members of the criminal syndicate that call themselves the Seventh Wave. Their leader Alex Stefanescu is well known throughout Europe as a..." He stopped himself. "As a member of the Romany community made good. A common thief who garnered a huge following in prison and within his own country. He dabbled in mid-level organised crime, then, his luck turned."

The people in the room read the next two paragraphs which outlined the series of events that had embroiled the Metropolitan Police – and other law enforcement agencies – and had seen the loss of two of Roberts' team and one notable other that they had once been charged with protecting.

"This has taken us by surprise in one respect, yet in another we have known this was a storm brewing out at sea. But we all know that we have had other priorities over the last few years; knife crime, burglaries and latterly, direct threats upon our city – our country by terrorists." Collins was trying to avoid a theatrical performance.

"Questions?"

A few came, mainly operational questions from the mid ranks. Collins answered them all skilfully.

The Prime Minister had listened and now spoke. He was a natural and warm orator, liked by most people he met.

"Thanks, Mike. Two things we need to keep at the forefront of our minds. The first is simple. If this goes wrong, everyone in Britain and that means everyone that has families in this room will suffer in some way. Therefore, I want us all to own this. This is about teamwork, not elitist behaviour. Need to know can take a back seat to need to share. The first prima donna I hear of is gone, no appeals. Do I make myself clear?"

"Crystal sir." Collins was still chairing and knew when he was outranked.

"Second point. Now this is important. As important as the first point, actually. In a world in which a reputation can be undone in a single tweet, or post or whatever the other one is, we must, I repeat must be aware of what we say and equally, don't say. I do not want people filling in the gaps. If we have gaps, they stay as such. We do not speculate. And that means all of us. If the media ask a question, we don't know the answer to, we say so and we tell them we will get back to them. Making it up to look good is not an option."

A look at the leaders in the room cleared up any ambiguities.

"Lastly, in the current climate, I do not want this group to be associated with Roma."

There were puzzled looks. Had the briefing not started with a hint to this people group being connected?

James Cole had a personal issue with people groups. He couldn't afford any more mass migration into his country –

but equally he knew he could not be part of a xenophobic backlash. The streets of Britain were changing rapidly and Cole wanted to lead the party that settled nerves, not inflamed them. Besides, it would finish his otherwise unblemished career and in the world of modern politics that was a reputation worth cherishing.

"Assistant Commissioner Collins referred to the connection between the Seventh Wave syndicate and the Romany community. Careful. If we cast a veil across the entire community, we can set back relations seventy years – longer. The Roma community lost countless people during the Second World War, some would argue more than the entire Jewish population. Let that sink in for a moment."

A few people were uncomfortable with this.

"Roma families had been responsible for a significant rise in street crime too," said a grey suited man in his forties.

Finding a balance was going to be difficult.

"All I ask is that you work with us to get on top of this quickly – and quietly. Any questions?"

Petrova stood, then leant forward, palms on the table.

"Hello, Prime Minister. Nice to meet you. I know these people better than any of you. I can add so much. Your report said Alex escaped from prison. This is not true. The authorities released him. Why? Because he was causing chaos among the prison and staff populations. He has a... what is the word, Jack?"

"Charisma?"

"Yes, charisma. He has a way with people that makes them want to work with him – and he manipulates people who don't. Please be careful."

"And what makes you think you know him better than our intelligence people, Miss Petrova?" asked an anonymous forty-something with ginger hair, a slim-fitting suit, pointed chin and officious eyes. He was revolving an expensive pen between his fingers, smiling confidently and working the room.

"I don't know who you are, but I guess someone likes you enough to allow you into the room. I also guess that you are an intelligence officer. I am one too, trained by my government to be the best in the world. How do I know? That is easy. I come from the same region as him, I know how he operates, I talk his language and I have an agenda."

"Oh, I can't wait to hear," said the male redhead to his far more attractive female equivalent.

"Oh, I'm so glad." Cade smothered a smile – she was on a roll, God help you ginger.

"I know because Alex Stefanescu ordered my mother's death." Her voice was raised now, but measured. "And this happened, eleven years ago, in your fucking city. So read your briefing notes, don't sit there with your false hair colour and pull that face at me or I will take your cheap pen and…"

"Thank you, Miss Petrova." Collins, ever the professional MC stepped in, avoiding a he-said, she-said argument and from the quick scan of her bio, potential damage to his manhood and feelings.

"But I haven't finished."

It was Sassy Lane that chose to speak. "So I see. Do go on Miss Petrova."

"Call me Elena." Quieter now. "You see, Alex is a sociopath – loves little puppies, but happily slits the throat of an enemy, or drags a girl to a frozen lake and pushes her under – then bets on how long she will keep breathing. I wasn't there, but believe it to be true. Alex is also very clever, and he knows he has you by the balls, lady. He has what you want, and you want, what he has. I cannot say it any simpler than that, even for our orange-haired friend here."

"I understand. And for the record, whilst it happened a

long time ago, I am truly sorry about your mother. But we have laboured the point about Stefanescu and his mental state, his ability to manipulate etcetera. What I need to know is what is he going to do in order to convince us to hand over the sort of obscene amount of money he thinks the documents are worth?"

"Please know, with Alex, it is not always about the money." She had spoken her last for today.

Cade looked at Petrova, visually asking her for permission to speak. She smiled and nodded.

"Jack Cade. Former inspector and now tac advisor to DCI Roberts and Assistant Commissioner Collins. I am also the Operation Orion Liaison Officer between police and the government from today. Now, the man who calls himself the Jackdaw – for the record, he gets the name due to his distinctive laughter which cackles like his namesake – I know because I have heard it." He looked around the room, memorising new faces and acknowledging those from the past.

"My gut feeling is that he will look to hold the government to ransom. He will use the British media to great effect, if you give him chance. You need to get to them first, get them on side, offer the story before it goes global. You need to shore up your borders, not easy, but you need a blanket border alert on all Romanian nationals. The good ones, and trust me on this, there are millions of them, will understand. To a point they are used to it."

He remembered how far they had come as a team from the very first attack through to the more audacious gas attacks on the bank machines that invariably caused more damage to the buildings than the cash that the teams got away with.

"ATM bank attacks around the world carried out by a small percentage of their own people have seen an upturn in border agency operations targeting the nation. Unfair perhaps, but that's the harsh reality. I suggest what he will look to do is use new teams, bringing them into the country as individuals and then regrouping with already-domiciled individuals, like iron filings to a magnet. Then he will start a series of distractions, a few subtle messages, building in confidence until he hits us with a grander plan – the ultimate extortion attempt."

"And that will be what, Mr Cade?" It was the secretive redhead once more.

"Sorry, I didn't catch your name, sir?"

"I didn't give it. And you don't need to know."

John Daniel had heard enough. "May I refer you to the Prime Minister's heartfelt introduction during which he discussed prima Donnas?" The ball hit the back of the proverbial net.

Slim-fit, pointy chin knew he was beaten. "Donald Donaldson."

"Nice. Such inventive parents. So I assume you work on the other side of the bridge with a load of other insipidly named staff? To answer your question Don, I doubt Jack knows. I'm guessing he's relying on you and yours to help us. But from my experience, once the Jackdaw gets his feathers ruffled, he doesn't stop. Expect something spectacular. And expect it any day now."

"Terrorism?" Mike Collins beat the Home Secretary to the question.

Cade answered quickly. "No. He once told me he despised terrorists."

Donaldson was leaning back in his chair, fingers steepled, laughing. "And *you* believed him?"

"Yes, *I* did."

"And what qualifications do you have to lead you to this summation ex-Inspector Cade?"

"There is no such rank, Donald. But for the record, three tablespoons of policing, mixed with a pound of common sense and placed in the oven on gas mark seven. It's called a common sense cake. I'll save you a slice. Unless you are intolerant?"

"Time gentlemen, please." James Cole stood, causing everyone else to follow suit. "Can we get this written up please Mike? Copy to me by this afternoon? Thank you all. Jack, John, Jason, I'd like you to stay behind with Mike, Sassy and Harry. A few things to iron out. Thank you for hosting. Do not be strangers, between now and whenever, this is our priority."

CHAPTER TWENTY-SIX

THE MAJORITY OF THE ATTENDEES HAD LEFT VIA THE LIFTS and staircases that were the arteries of Scotland Yard. Experienced cops knew it paid to leave quickly, better that than end up with a job you didn't want or one you pretended you did.

Cade hadn't finished with Donaldson, however.

"Donald, to answer your earlier question, which I feel warrants a response. I have spoken to this man on a number of occasions. I know when I can trust someone and alternatively when face to face would happily kill them. I can assure you that in Mr Stefanescu's case the latter would be an honour. It's a long story, but his actions led to one of Jason's best staff taking his own life." He deliberately allowed that to drift around the room like an unpleasant smell.

"A member of Stefanescu's unit, I call them a unit because they are well trained, poisoned our best criminal analyst and she happens to be a good friend. Poisoned her in her own home. His name is Constantin Nicolescu. Close your eyes and think of what a disturbed and certifiable man might look like and you will have him perfectly painted in your mind's eye."

He had Donaldson's attention completely.

"Prior to that, to make a point, he ordered the death of my covert intelligence source." That piece of information would have been sufficient, but Cade knew he had to drill home. "He drowned her in the Thames, roped to a wooden frame, crucified at high tide opposite Battersea Power Station. And do you know who she was?"

He shook his head, feeling that a conversation wasn't required.

"It was his wife. He drowned the woman he was betrothed to – married as far as he was concerned. Not that she had any choice in the matter. And, importantly, the woman in question, Nikolina Petrov, was Elena's mother. The one she mentioned earlier. So please do not challenge any of my team on this again."

"All points noted, I'm sure." It was laced with sarcasm.

"Listen, mate. I am tired, but I make no excuses for this. Either get on board with this or fuck off. I have flown halfway around the world to learn that people I hold dear to my professional heart are either dead or missing, presumed dead." He counted his friends – it was an old method of forcing you to take a moment, to breathe, before you said something that would hang you out to dry.

"So you want to go toe to toe with someone and be a smart arse, then let's just crack on." He was visibly shaking, adrenaline hijacking his veins and causing him to shudder, but he was more than ready for a fight.

"Well? No, I thought not. All talk and no balls."

"Jack." It was Daniel.

"No, John. I'm not rolling over. The government knows what is happening here and from my angle, is doing sweet..."

"Mr Cade." James Cole brought the argument to an

abrupt halt. Cade was no longer a police officer, but he recognised authority when it stood up and took control of a meeting.

"I think we all appreciate how much this is hurting your team. Frankly, I'm impressed that you've kept quiet as long as you have. But please calm down and take a breath. I think we all need to. We are one team. One goal and all that. You start falling out with one another and it will soon be a game of Jenga where the only remaining piece is likely to see the whole bloody thing topple. One team. Are we not Donald?"

Donaldson looked around the room. "My apologies for being an arsehole. It's in our training package – Day One."

"Apology accepted. Jet lag and I don't make good bedfellows." Cade smiled, holding out his right hand.

It raised a smile from Donaldson and a handshake that smacked of surety. "I accept your acceptance. Ring me if you need anything, Jack. That goes for your squad too. Anything."

The Home Secretary spoke. "Moving swiftly along. We can carry on in this room, Jason?"

"Of course ma'am, mi casa su casa and all that."

They entered a side room, big enough for who was left from the earlier meeting. "Donald join us, please." Sassy Lane was in control now, and the PM was happy for her to take the lead. It was her domain.

"Elena, before we continue. What we discuss in here, in the briefings, it goes no further."

"I understand, I am very familiar with keeping a secret. In my country they are the foundation of everything we do. We have been keeping them for a long time, longer than you." Her smile was disarming. Lane saw what men saw in her.

"Good. It is good to have you on board. We will not be involving the Bulgarian government, however, the Romanian authorities are already working with us. They want this group off their radar as much as we do. They have been simply outstanding with their help so far. Now Jack, a wee history lesson if you are up for it?"

"My favourite subject at school Home Secretary."

"Oh wonderful, then you will enjoy this. You are a man of Kent according to our records?"

"I'm impressed. I am indeed – anything you don't know about me?"

"Not much. You have a penchant for actresses beginning with the letter K, prefer raspberries to strawberries, find redheads attractive and at one time, earlier in your life tried to join the military. Your namesake, Jack Cade was from the same place as you. The government rebel of the fourteen hundreds?"

"So I'm led to believe. It was a story told to me by my old history teacher, Jim Seal. Great man, brought the subject to life, ex-copper, inspired me to join up. But I don't see the connection?"

"Your teacher would have done. In 1450 Cade led a rebellion against what the people saw as the corrupt government of Henry VI. Cade entered the city and struck his sword against what was known as the London Stone. When he did so he declared himself to be Lord of this city. Shakespeare wrote a few lines about it."

"And?" He was intrigued.

"And this inconspicuous lump of limestone, which has been semi-concealed behind a cage, open to the elements on Cannon Street, is surrounded by mystery, ley line theories, magic spells and even witchcraft. More than that legend decrees that it can choose the next King and so long as the Stone of Brutus is safe, the city of London will flourish."

It was interesting, but neither Cade nor his colleagues saw the connection.

She pursued the point. "They say all roads lead from the stone, that it had origins dating back to the Trojan or Roman era. In all that time, the city has never been truly taken by a foreign invader."

"Forgive me?" It was John Daniel. "I've worked this city all my life. Started as a constable. Out on the beat, I covered Cannon Street. I know the history of the stone. However, I don't see the relevance, interesting though it is. Can you expand at all?" He spoke candidly for everyone.

"And that is a fair request, chief inspector. The point is Alex Stefanescu has set a challenge among his people to steal the stone. It has survived countless invasions, even the Blitz. Not even the Luftwaffe could destroy the bloody thing. If Stefanescu gets hold of it we could argue the stone might be worth fifty quid in scrap value or about twenty trillion if you take the current worth of the City of London."

"But it's a stone." Daniel could feel the ground moving, jet lag was playing havoc with his inner ear, flirting with his balance organs and creating a sense of drunkenness. If only.

"It's not about the stone, John. It's about making a point. Donald's team are listening to this and that, and it was either a this or a that conversation they heard a few days ago that suggested that someone is going to have a go at something iconic in London. try to steal it, or at least have a damned good go. One could go further and say he is looking to strike his own sword on the stone."

Roberts chipped in. "One of my sources has heard the same – told me that the Tower – or a tower is involved. I took that as the obvious one – and the jewels, but they've been safe since before John here was born."

"Distractions DCI Roberts. All distractions. They are planning something else, I can feel it in my water – as my grandmother used to say."

"So, what do you suggest we do?" Cade was also in need

of a decent night's sleep. "Put an armed guard on every monument this side of Nelson's Column?"

"Hardly Jack. No, what I suggest is you ramp up your human source collections out on the streets, link up with our Romanian colleagues. Let's see what they have on Stefanescu's team, shall we? Might be a good place to start. If we can come up with at least a theory on what this pain in the arse is planning I would rest easier. Either that or we need someone to put a bullet right through the Jackdaw's eye. And soon."

His sigh was audible. "I can offer you a theory." It was Cade's turn at conjecture. "He plays us off against the British media – the world media at that. Blackmails the British government for a sum so audacious that it makes him rich and notorious, but a figure that we see as being worth paying – and frankly that could be many millions. You have said yourself this needs to remain close to our chests. I'd suggest it is already out there. These places leak like sieves. And if money is being bandied around, then that is even worse. It's just a matter of time."

"Interesting theory. Blackmailed by a blackbird." Her own smile was used to great effect. "You've forgotten the impact on this country, Jack." Lane looked at the group, once again discreetly checking her watch – places to go, people to see.

"Remember the Poll Tax riots back in the nineties? When cars were set alight, fridges dropped onto police from ten stories above? When Churchill's statue was desecrated?" All three police staff recalled them with a mixture of dread and financial fondness. Daniel could still hear the fridge hitting their shields as they formed up under a roof made of polycarbonate, ready to storm into the tower block.

Harry Halford had been quiet but cleared his throat a few times, coughing into the back of his hand. "The halcyon days that the Minister refers to will be like a walk in the proverbial park if this hits the streets. It will start with a gentle flow, then become a torrent. The divided will form sides – there will be those that are pro-leaving Europe, the passionate and the misguided and anti. Then, as if we don't have enough to worry about, there's the Pro-monarchy and anti-royal protests. Pro this, anti that. If this waits until the summer then we could be in for a long hot campaign of civil disorder. As the Minister responsible for policing, with the reduced police forces that we are now having to work with..." he let the sentence end, deliberately allowing it to hang like a week-old corpse.

"Or if it's anything like a normal British summer a few weeks of torrential rain Minister." It was an opportunity to lessen the impact but failed and Mike Collins, who had also been suspiciously quite up until that moment, knew it had backfired.

Cole took over a political tag team if ever one existed. "Thank you, gents. In the midst of it all we may well see a resurgence of political posturing – right-wing movements hell-bent on creating a new Britain, a Britain without immigrants – fuelled by the media, pounced upon by the opposition who will cite integrity and honesty and core values and anything else they lack and can latch onto for a win here and there. What some of these people wish for is a country not unlike the one that existed around the time that the London Stone appeared."

"You mean where the locals threw piss out of their windows and cattle strolled around the streets, Prime Minister?" Roberts couldn't help but smile. "Really?"

"No, Jason, I mean a country that is devoutly British. And for many that means white, working and middle-class people, without, and I quote, a funny accent."

"Do you think it will come that, sir?" Cade was convinced it could.

"Yes, Jack. Honestly, I do. If it goes wrong, we will lose credibility and confidence. Look at what Black Monday did to our funds. Need I remind you we lost billions? This could trigger a wave of sentiment like we haven't seen since we buried Diana, Princess of Wales."

All three police officers remembered that day too with a mixture of emotions.

"Donald. Ramp up everything you have on the current migrant population that could fit into this group. I want Immigration involved, but tell them it is a stats thing. I need numbers, and if we don't know how many are in country, then a bloody good guess." Lane was known for not taking prisoners or suffering fools.

"Ma'am, you are casting your net too wide." Cade was unintentionally rubbing his eyes, trying to wipe away ten thousand miles of air travel.

"Go on." She liked Cade and was prepared to give him some air time.

"This is a group that has two aspects. The first is that they are almost entirely of Romany descent. That means they come from a long line of people who have been treated badly by the rest of the world."

Roberts interjected, "You afraid of being cursed, mate?"

"See? However, Jason is right in one respect, he's battled with the itinerant traveller as much as the next copper, I'm sure. We've all locked one up at some stage in our career, one who tells you his surname is Lee and that he is twelve years old and so is his father and that anything that is not bolted down is fair game. But you miss the point."

James Cole had stopped checking his own watch. They could wait. This stimulated his interest.

"The second is that this group may be able to cast their

DNA back a few thousand years to a proud heritage of travellers, but in the case of Alex and his entourage, they are different, a modern version of a proud and stubborn people. They use skill, and cunning, guile and fear to attract their members. And they are very, very good at it. A simple team of women and children working the underground can make thousands. You've read the papers? Another hitting ATM, like was seen in the city a few years ago, can make much more. At its heart is a group of managers, the logistics people, organising the worker bees, allowing them to have a sip of the nectar, but always providing the royal jelly to the queen."

He waited for a sign that he could continue. A simple nod from the Prime Minister was all he needed.

"I once worked with a man called Valentin Iliescu. He came from a background of working for the Romanian Intelligence Service, the SRI. He was once an enemy of mine until I realised that like most of us he had an agenda. He saved one of our staff and I owe him. At the time, he said something most poignant. When we were last looking for the Seventh Wave team, he uttered a sentence that has remained with me. He said, 'Jack, you are looking for the copper wire when you should be looking for the electricity.'"

Cole and Lane began to nod. Cole spoke initially, "So you are saying we are looking in the wrong place?"

"I am sir, yes. Sorry, but I think you need to look within your own house first. Alex is the ultimate distraction – the conduit if you like. There is mischief afoot, Prime Minister, and it is far from amusing. If you want to see rivers of blood in London, you will decide to do nothing at all. With your blessing I want to round a few people up and prevent that from happening."

"What do you need?"

"Who, sir. Not what. I need the team that is here now

and the rest of the Operation Orion squad. A good crypto-currency specialist, too. None of us have a bloody clue about it – I doubt even your own advisors do. Secondly, I want Valentin on our team. And you may want to track down a certain Johnnie Hewett. The Foreign Office played a part in the last operation, so it's only right they are involved this time around, sooner rather than later with your concerns about chaos on the streets of Britain."

"And their role?"

"Find the team before they achieve their goal. Couldn't be easier." Roberts answered for Cade, who acknowledged his synopsis. It was his op after all, and Cade became suddenly aware that he was in danger of taking over.

"I agree with DCI Roberts, sir – one hundred percent. We'll find the copper wire – you find the electricity."

Harry Halford spoke. "I suspect that the gypsies you refer to have already taken all the copper wire gentlemen."

Cade shook his head discreetly.

There was a knock on the door.

"Come in."

"Good morning Prime Minister." He looked quickly around the small room. "Home Secretary. Harry, Mike, DCI Roberts. How are we all?"

The man that entered was upbeat and immediately recognisable to Cade and Petrova. Dark blue pinstriped suit, white shirt, matching handkerchief, a silk tie with a motif and leather-soled brogues.

He walked towards Cade, fixing his gaze onto the eyes that stared back. "Mr Cade, Michael Blake, British Foreign Office – we haven't met, but it's fair to say I have heard a lot about you." He shook his hand firmly. He was doing well. It had only been days.

"And you must be Miss Petrova?" He didn't kiss her

hand, but he exuded a classic sense of Britishness that said he might, almost.

Cade was quick to recognise that he was acting. Petrova, too. Neither challenged him nor looked at one another.

"And you too, sir. I have heard only good things."

"Nice to meet you, Mr Blake." She smiled, head tilted to one side.

"Forgive me Prime Minister, Home Secretary, but I was party to what our police minister was saying as I entered the room."

Halford knew immediately that this meant 'I was stood at the door listening for a while.'

"And I couldn't help overhear the statement about gypsies."

A few people had confused expressions, some a look that said 'I distance myself from the earlier comment.'

"You see ladies and gents, we are not dealing with gypsies in the sense in which you make the statement. These are people no doubt descended from Roma – but do not fool yourselves. This is not a band of merry men cavorting around our homeland stealing our women, selling clothes pegs and offering to tarmac our driveways."

Halford had heard enough. "Isn't it Michael? I think you need to get out more." He laughed, but it was far from sincere.

"It is you sir who needs to leave his office once in a while. I have studied these people most of my adult life. What we are dealing with here is a well-organised, highly effective and goal-driven group. Well led too – and funded, and they are in town and ready to play. Now you can mock them all your like, but you need to know your enemy. Sun Tzu and all that." He took a breath.

"This is not a bunch of wandering nomads in a fleet of caravans plugging their cables into street lights and stealing anything that is not nailed down. Get that idea out of your head. They associate strongly with their ancestry, have a resilience borne out of sacrifice and xenophobia, but they are not harmless 'tinkers' as I heard them referred to recently."

"Right, thank you, Mr Blake. Good stuff, I'm sure we all agree about our targets and their capabilities. We all know each other, now let's get to work, shall we? Or to use a Cade analogy – we find the lock, you find the key." Lane announced that both and Cole were already late for a meeting.

"Lord of the city team. Don't forget who that needs to be. Must go. Keep in touch," she said, hurriedly walking towards the lifts.

They were both being individually met by their respective Diplomatic Protection Group staff. Lifts were already being held and cars were waiting. They would travel separately. Different routes. Twice the cost. Half the risk.

Michael Blake pressed the light blue lift button. "Fancy coffee, you lot? My shout." It was what was best described as a stage whisper. Deliberate.

Cade, Petrova, Roberts and Daniel followed him into the lift, which arrived with a gentle rush of air. Their presence was obviously mandatory. They could tell by the tone.

The door closed. Blake hovered over the ground floor button. He wished they had been on the twentieth floor. More time.

The five people were all in the wood-panelled lift, three on one side, two on the other. It started to drop and Blake began to talk.

"Team, we have as long as it takes for this thing to hit the ground floor. In that time you are going to have to decide whether to trust me or not. I don't intend to do that sports team thing where we all put our hands in the middle and roar our allegiance. Are you on board with this?"

They all looked at one another. Floor Seven.

Cade spoke first. "Go on, Minister. I am all ears."

"Firstly, thank you for playing along with me up there. We need to maintain that façade. You said mischief, Jack. It goes way beyond that."

Floor Five.

"There is a leak, as you suggested. I'd call him a mole. Others might say a treacherous bastard. Either way, I need you to know that you must not trust him. He is in bed with the wrong people. My man has managed to find this out. Best not ask how." His eyebrows flicked upwards.

Floor Three.

"Hewett sir?" Roberts had already made the decision.

"No. Far from it. I trust that smooth bastard with all of our lives. Harry Halford is our traitor. He is working with Alex Stefanescu. It's all about money. Isn't it bloody always?"

"Our *police* minister?" Daniel was incredulous.

"Yes, John. The very same. I think there are others too. Can't say, won't say. Not until I know. Have you ever questioned why he only has one Protection Officer? He plays those cards very close to his chest. Damned good politician, mind you, came from nowhere. But I distrust him." He looked at the lift progress. The neon lights were changing quickly.

"But you lot, I trust. Either that or I misjudged you all. Ground floor coming up. We meet in person, no emails, no calls. This wave you keep referring to Jack? It's coming and for the life of me I don't know where from or how."

The lift arrived, the door opened and Blake was already walking. "You can buy your own bloody coffee!" Fifteen seconds later he was in the back of a government car heading to his office.

Cade stood in the foyer. "Well, I fancy one. Anyone want to join me? My treat. I need something to get over the eleven floor debrief we've just had."

"I'll have a soy latte. And can we have one of those cake fancies? The orange gluten-free ones?" Roberts was hopeful.

"Is there anything you *can* eat, Jason?"

"Two slices of humble pie, twice a week."

They laughed. Petrova too, although she had no idea why.

Daniel opened the main door to Scotland Yard – ever the gent. "It's good to be back on the old patch." He allowed Elena through first, a chance to discreetly admire the view. Why should Cade have all the fun?

"If it's any consolation, it's good to have you all here. Blake was right, we've got some fun times ahead. At least now we have staff and a budget. That's more than can be said for the rest of the thin blue line."

Roberts turned to Cade. "You OK?"

"No, Jason, I'm not. But I learned a long time ago that attitude to an operation like this can change everything, call it a viral response. If the team see me lose it then slowly their morale will collapse too."

"But you have every reason to lose it mate."

"And that is the reason why I can't. It doesn't mean I'm not volcanic below the surface."

CHAPTER TWENTY-SEVEN

IN TWO DIFFERENT COUNTRIES, THREE DIFFERENT MEN were about to carry out activities that could at best be described as precarious, at worst, plain reckless. Two of the men led a group, one acted alone.

In England, Constantin Nicolescu was in charge, leading three of the team from the disused fireworks factory. They were en route to their three target destinations.

One team, three towns, two banks and a preliminary reconnaissance mission. Their role was simple. Create a diversion. It would be the first of many. Money was not the goal, but it helped shore up their living expenses, Jackdaw had assured them they could keep every penny.

Get caught? Don't come crying to me. He made it quite clear.

Constantin had left enough men behind at the old site to ensure the two remaining captives would not escape. They all knew the risks, and their brief was simple. If people came to the site asking questions, escape. Do not engage with them. Burn the place down if given the opportunity. Leave no trace. They have succeeded in doing just that so far. Hiding in plain sight was working.

The team of four would be gone all day. They needed to swap their van for another, no point in burning the current one out as the bastards in blue would only get their forensic people onto it. And he respected them – and their ability to find a clue in a single fibre.

In Bucharest, on the Bulevardul Ion Mihalache, Scott McCall walked confidently along the street. He needed a caffeine fix. That was his cover anyway. The coffee stall diagonally opposite the nightclub answered his plea and provided him with a perfect, unobstructed view across the road. Close enough. Far enough away.

"Can I get an Americano to take away? Extra hot. You have a beautiful city. Great weather!" He had banked on the long-haired white male speaking English.

The young guy behind the counter wiped his hands on a towel and spoke. "I love your Australian's and your sense of humour. So sarcastic. It is freezing today!"

"Good call, mate. It is pretty cold, I'll give you that." He shuddered to reinforce the temperature. "You been to Aussie?"

"Yes, mate, I have. I got to Sydney, then walked across country to Perth. Took me months. I love to travel."

"Marvellous effort!" He was extending the drawl now, hoping that the young man would only recall him as Australian and not a Kiwi. He was also hoping he didn't get pinned down on where he lived. Always talk about what you know or steer the conversation back. Quickly.

"You like to travel then?" Scott was leaning against the counter, watching across the road. "Must be expensive to get to my country from here, young guy like you?"

"That is why I have three jobs. I do modelling in the evening, I work here and I am a barman across the road at Byzantin." He pointed with his head whilst he handed over the coffee.

'You've just struck gold Scottie.' His mind was flooded with the potential to work this new source. But he didn't have long.

"Oh wow, good on you, mate. Can't be easy? I'm back-packing my way across Europe. I was thinking of looking for work too. Is it good across the road? I can throw a cocktail shaker around a bit if it helps?"

"The team is OK. They pay in cash. I don't ask questions. No one does."

"Looks like someone is doing well out of it. Nice Rolls Royce."

"It is a Bentley. A GT. Belongs to the owner."

"Lucky man, should I ask for him? You know, about getting a job?"

The young man smiled and looked awkward, started serving a new customer. "No, I wouldn't say that would be a good idea."

"Does he not like Aussies?" McCall was laughing, acting at his very best.

"Mr Stefanescu doesn't really like anyone. He has an apartment over the top of the club, the whole floor. He's probably looking out at us now. They say it is filled with beautiful things. So yes, he is doing very well. He has a brother too, Stefan, big guy, strange eyes. The girls like him. That's his white Mercedes. They say they are millionaires, many times over."

"Any other criminals in this area?"

"No one challenges them – not even the police."

"They don't sell drugs, do they? I'm not going if they do. Killed my cousin. Filthy stuff."

"I've been offered them by customers. But I have never seen the customers again."

He served the business woman and then shook Scott's hand. "Alex does not allow drugs in his clubs, nor does he sell them. Brother, I should stop talking, the security guys are watching. Alex owns this place too, in fact he owns everything around here except the hospitals. His men keep them quite busy with patients that disagree with their boss!"

"Hey brother, I really appreciate your help. Can I say you sent me, you know, give you chance for a bonus for finding a good bloke like me?" McCall was overt in his hand gestures. He had his reasons.

"No. Please don't sir." He meant it. The boy had genuine fear in his pale brown eyes. "Just stay away if I were you. If criminals aren't watching the place, the police are. People say they are desperate to lock up the boss. They are possibly watching right now. I feel like I am in a bowl with the goldfish sometimes!"

"Is that right?"

"Yes. It is. Look man, I have to get on, I like you, you remind me of my older brother. He is a soldier. Good luck yeah. You'll need it if you upset the Jackdaw."

McCall feigned a look of confusion.

"That's his nickname. Like the bird. The one that steals pretty things." He was barely whispering, covering his mouth in case someone was watching that could lip read. Paranoia did that to a person.

"You will know it is him by the way he laughs."

"Nice. I'll do my best to avoid him then. Keep the change." McCall walked away with his coffee and operational knowledge that was priceless.

. . .

"Vasile to Andre." The comms hissed a little, but they were clear enough. Using first names only, on a secure digital network, they could never be too careful. Accept nothing. Believe no one. Challenge everything. It was the same the world over in their job.

"Go ahead."

"Two outside the door. Both vehicles in place. Usual foot traffic. No new visitors for nearly half an hour now."

"Received."

"Stand by. The male we saw the other day. He's back. Stood at the coffee stall across the road from the target."

"One hundred percent sure?"

"Yes, sir. One hundred percent."

"OK. Who is he? Why is he there? Is he a tourist?"

"No idea, boss. Right now all we know is that he's a European male, with black hair, well built, drinking coffee. He's just shaken hands with the coffee guy, but they look like strangers. A lot of hand gestures, as if they are not speaking the same language."

"Received. Confirm he's the only repeat target this week?"

"Yes, sir. Images coming through to you now." Vasile hit send, and the image appeared on his commander's screen.

It appeared a second later. The man was a new player and did not look like a local.

"We shall call him Tourist One."

Andre Grigorescu – son of Grigor was known as Grig by his colleagues in the Special Intervention Brigade, an arm of the Romanian Gendarmerie, the military branch of the national police. Their role was normally counter-terrorism, hostage rescue and riot policing, however, someone, some-where with more stars than Capitan Grigorescu had earned in his eighteen years, had made the decision that their number one target was Alex Stefanescu.

'Find something on him and make it stick. He must be arrested and kept in prison for a long time. He is destroying our reputation as a good country with good people. Get rid of him, or convince him to leave this country and never come back.'

The briefing was as covert as their operation. Deniable, too. No one knew quite how well their target was connected. He had apparently walked free from a Bulgarian prison without being challenged. At least that's how the story went.

"Can we deploy someone to talk to this male?" It was a call that wouldn't normally be made, but Grig's team were ready to hit the club. The warrant had been prepared weeks before, pending a judge's signature.

'I want you to watch the premises for a week. If there are no obvious risks to the public, then yes, you may enter by force.'

The warrant was explained away as being necessary to search for drugs. However, they intended to search for one commodity only.

"We go in thirty minutes. Repeat three zero. All units."

They started calling in. The covert vehicles parked around the corner. The observation team, across the road in a telecommunication company maintenance tent and a further surveillance team opposite the club. All were ready.

They watched for five more minutes.

"Stand by all units. Male target – Tourist One – is moving towards the club."

Twenty minutes later, the radio chatter started again.

"He's gone, sir. Tourist One has disappeared."

"No one disappears. Did he enter the club?"

"Cannot confirm."

"You have no idea? Could he be there?" It was a tactical question. The last thing he wanted was a bloody tourist, if he was a tourist, standing in the way when his team went through the door.

"No, sir. Sorry. He just vanished."

"Then we wait to see if he shows." Grig punched the desk and swore.

In the apartment overlooking the street, Alex had risen from a drunken coma. He needed to learn how to drink again; the legal potion they had consumed most of the previous night was smoother, sweeter and easier to swallow than the foul, but highly alcoholic prison cocktail that he had overseen the manufacture of in Pazardzhik Prison in that brutal regime that called itself Bulgaria. The problem with it being sweeter was that he drank more. And now his head was reminding him why he needed to stop drinking. He was losing interest in its effects, in the endless stream of girls too.

He had never abused drugs, so the only thing left was instilling fear or gaining respect. He smiled as he watched a good-looking stranger shaking hands with his coffee boy across the street.

He knew that McCall would show soon. His sort always did. Such greed, they should learn to earn it by crawling on their knees, like he had. Again and again until they bled so much that only bone was visible. It taught a man a great deal about sacrifice and greed. He still had the scars.

"Time for the next wave."

Stefan was also moving about the apartment, slowly, deliberately, and actually nowhere near as drunk as his brother.

"What's that brother?"

"Nothing, my dear. Just watching the world pass me by. We should eat something and then plan tonight."

"Tonight? What is happening?" He was genuinely surprised.

"It's Byzantin night, Stefan! Every night is party night. Have you forgotten? Let's open the doors, get the drink flowing, the pretty girls will be everywhere, get the place buzzing like it used to, when we were the kings of this city. Make some calls today. Come on. Do it. Yes?"

He was smiling for the first time since he had walked out of prison and turned left onto the highway, heading home.

Stefan knew it was a fait accompli. "Of course, brother. Yes."

Two thousand kilometres to the north west, Alex's men were approaching their first target. In broad daylight, the first operator approached the ATM of a busy local bank. As the van he had arrived in screeched theatrically to a halt nearby, and everybody turned to see what had happened, he pushed the false aperture onto the machine.

Technology had changed at a real pace since the last time the team had hit London. New data gathering equipment, slimmer phones, all helped to capture the evidence and information they needed to exploit the bank accounts. They chose busy branches as they were the most lucrative. Not without risk, but lucrative just the same.

One device could gather enough card data in two to three days to convert to tens of thousands of the local currency. In a few days they would return and removed the device, leaving nothing but a slightly tacky change in the surface of the host machine. Detectable to those that knew what they were looking for. Those people made up a few small teams of detectives. In Kent, where this machine was, there was no one looking at this type of crime. They were too busy fighting more international matters and what was known as volume crime – burglaries, theft and occasional street robberies. In other words, things that caught the media attention and lost votes for the politicians.

Across the county boundary into Greater London there had been a team – once. The Dedicated Cheque and Plastic Crime Unit had become famous for its arrest rate, targeting Eastern European, Baltic, and smaller groups from Malaysia and Singapore. They had achieved greatness under the leadership of Jason Roberts. Just as the team began to really perform, to win cases without challenges from the defence, they were shut down.

It happened. Teams were cyclical, often changing at the whim of a new commander. Sometimes they went full circle.

Roberts had harboured a professional grudge ever since as he saw the crime as damaging. Most saw it as victimless – 'oh the banks will refund the money so no one loses out.' What the public failed to grasp was how their data was exploited in the world of the dark net – where parcels of data sold for thousands and the new owners could then continue to exploit the accounts. In turn damaging reputations and increasing bank costs and charges. Victimless indeed.

Banking was changing rapidly. Branches were closing, the rate at which online banking was escalating was considered by many to be the reason. Why get wet trudging to a bank when you could sit in the bath and carry out the transactions? For Roberts, that meant potentially fewer crimes. For the Seventh Wave teams, it meant fewer potential victims. As a result, their focus was shifting rapidly, onto online attacks.

But this whole thing, this entire component of the operation was a Trojan Horse and as per the fabled attack on Troy, only one side knew.

The ATM attacks had been relatively quiet, even Roberts had released his iron grip on the problem, now forced to target a rolling set of criminal problems in the biggest city in Britain. Roberts, like Cade, could never truly let go though and ran a private spreadsheet of bank related crime in the area. He considered it a professional distraction from knife crime.

"We'll keep a weather eye on these cases, Nick." He had said only a week ago. "Until something new comes along."

"You mean like hordes of villains using mopeds to target vulnerable people in broad daylight boss?"

"Jesus, don't even mention that outside this place. Can you imagine?" he trembled at the logistical nightmare that would bring to his favourite place in the world.

Whilst Roberts sat in his office, reading the stats and working out which way he was going to write them up this week, the first victim approached the HSBC branch, slid her card into the mouth of the ATM, tapped in her PIN and selected mini statement.

The understated machinery in the false housing was reading everything it needed to, her personal identity number and the card data. There was nothing to gain in inserting a device to grab a twenty here or a ten there. Those days were long gone. The Lebanese Loop had become a museum piece, laughable when compared to its modern equivalent.

The customer selected fifty. She needed a treat, had been working hard, nothing like retail therapy. The operator who had placed the device in place only minutes before couldn't agree more. In twenty-four hours, what she had in her account would be gone. Her and a few hundred others.

The first aspect of their operation was under way. They would carry out similar attacks on banks in north Kent throughout the day. Disturbed at one branch, they ripped the device from the wall and ran. Winter provided sufficient clothing and headgear to make their detection challenging. Gloves and forensic awareness made it almost impossible.

Ten thousand pounds a day. Not bad for men who didn't pay tax – anywhere.

Constantin smiled a fractured and painful smile – the taste of blood ever-present.

"Get the little mice scuttling and the rats will surely follow."

Sat in the front passenger seat of the van with the heater on, he was enjoying the freedom of being able to function without being discovered and more so, the freedom from his mistress – heroin. Resembling any busy man that worked in the city he was looking forward to getting home – in his case back to the old factory, with its brambles and flaking beige walls, puddled floors and a long-forgotten sense of industry – and where he had plans that excited him.

On the way back, mirroring the Thames, he had one more job to plan. This would involve another element of his team – three men who had been living in a cheap rental for the last few weeks, waiting for the call. Until now, they had never met. Their task was simple. Carrying it out without being identified and caught was another thing altogether. Constantin had used the same caveat with them as Alex had used with him. Get caught, you are on your own.

He met the three men in a lay-by on the road outside the town of Bexley. One was older, ex-military but disillusioned and looking for greater financial reward, the other two, easily led.

They swapped vehicles. Constantin left the Ford behind and headed back towards the factory in the white Mercedes Sprinter van. Now they were just another courier, another delivery driver or trades team. Now they were anonymous.

. . .

At Scotland Yard, a red motorcycle started at the touch of a button. Its rider carried out a few pre-ride checks and accelerated away, heading home. He always enjoyed the ride home.

CHAPTER TWENTY-EIGHT

It got dark early in England in January. It started dark; it ended dark, by four, four thirty at the latest, it felt as if the light had faded for the day. Street lights self-started, their timers breathing life into the sodium bulbs that cast a sulphurous glow across the highways. Curtains drew, fires were lit and doors locked. Here and there a car would be covered to prevent the penetrative frost from delaying the next commute. The world closed itself off from its neighbours and the weather and shuffled about trying to get warm.

As Constantin and his small team made their way north east to their temporary home, gathering food from a cheap supermarket where security looked to be a secondary concern, he knew that in ten or fifteen minutes his new team would strike. Later they would abandon their vehicle and be picked up by yet more associates.

They were becoming viral. And he liked that very much.

. . .

It was now dark. A red motorcycle negotiated traffic on the faster stretches of the road south, out of London. Its rider was at one with the machine.

Detective Constable Steve 'Church' Hall had joined the police as a cadet. He'd lost count of how many years he had served, and unlike many of his colleagues, he was dreading the day he had to retire – he was counting how many pay packets he could prise out of his employer rather than how many were left.

Married to the job and a stream of girlfriends that never became a wife, he had fashioned a life that was a mixture of singles holidays and a great social network, where he was always invited as the plus one and habitually the life of the party.

He had a love of great wine. His favourite was a beautiful red, a Pinot Noir, the vineyard in the stunning southern reaches of New Zealand that crafted it was called Mt Difficulty – it was a great name, after a mountain, near a bluff and a stream that made going tough, back in the pioneer days when men were men and women, were glad of it, or so the tales went.

He as good as worshipped it as a wine, better than its French counterparts, and please, don't even mention the others. He set a plan to visit one day and sip slowly on a glass, or two, by an open fire, watching the tantalising streams of liquid rouge clinging to the glass.

His personal favourite in their range was called Roaring Meg. His old and short-term boss, Jack Cade had told him a tale or two about it and even ordered a bottle to be delivered to Hall's cottage, for a job well done but long forgotten. If Cade was the sommelier and Meg was the drug, then as a dealer he had got Hall hooked.

Roaring Meg. His mind often deliberated. He liked the name as much as he liked the contents, had no idea whether it was named after a girl or a waterfall. He chose the former and wanted to meet this petite girl one day, this Meg, he imagined her to have caramel coloured hair and spirited eyes, green probably, and with a sense of adventure – fantasised that she'd like nothing more than storming down an alpine road on the back of his bike, her perfect, powerful legs wrapped around his, feeling the power of the bike beneath her.

If Meg was his lover, then motorbikes – of which he had four, were his real mistress. He hated cars; they were for people that had never tasted the thrill of speed upon the tip of their tongues, had never smelt the anaesthesia that foretold an imminent crash on a blind bend, the shiver on the neckline, the twitch of the machine as it fought, hand in hand with its rider to prevent the latter from crossing the bridge and entering the kingdom of the born again biker.

He had bought a rundown cottage on the edge of Bexley, a commuter town in the upper reaches of Kent, and within striking range of his work for the Metropolitan Police.

Six foot two, broad shoulders, grey-blue eyes and as he called it, matching hair, he was a good-looking man who should have found a mate by now. Even his mother asked if he was gay – not that it mattered, of course.

Hall had joined the police, carried out his two years' probation, then joined the Traffic Department, where, within a few months he was fortunate enough to get a place on the motorcycle course. He had fallen for the temptation of speed and independence and never looked back. Actually, that part was untrue, Steve always looked back, and sideways. As such, his record was one hundred percent safe.

He was always thinking about safety. As he swerved to avoid a white van that pulled into his path, in the dark on that weekday evening it was at the forefront of his acute mind. He hit the brakes hard, balancing them expertly, no time to sound the horn, yelling a muffled 'wanker' and raising a left hand in defiance was all he could do.

He could stop and remonstrate, but what was the point? The driver looked foreign. Probably didn't have insurance either. Bastard. He should, but he couldn't be bothered. Tomorrow was another day, and he was tired. Operation Orion was taking it out of him.

Orion, a computer generated name from the police system, was perfect for their task of hunting down criminals, however its long hours and little success had begun to take their toll. Working for Jason Roberts was always fun though, and getting to his stage in his police career and still having fun was worth celebrating.

'Wanker' he said again, subdued by the insulation of his Shoei helmet. He indicated and turned right onto Stable Lane, towards a small hamlet, out into the countryside that joined it to the town. He was gently winding down, thinking about work, watching the road.

The new operation was at least interesting. They had some new people arriving each day, and Roberts had enthused about Cade and Daniel arriving back in the city. Things were looking up and with the Home Secretary herself signing the cheques it rarely got better.

Catching the team before they struck was their goal, and Hall wanted to be at the forefront. His boss DS Bridie McGee was a saint. A naturally lovely person – the only woman he had actually fancied, probably truly loved in years – she allowed Hall a sense of leeway that few others achieved. But then few others worked the hours he did, or showed the level of commitment he did. She loved him too. But not in that way.

His new focus of affection was a Honda Fireblade or CBR1000RR, to be precise. Bright red. He wanted the black but knew he was better off visible than dead.

As road bikes went, and he'd had a few, it was his favourite. Ultra-responsive, super reliable and those brakes, as responsive as a high-class hooker on cocaine. He always said they could stop him before he started. And they just had back in the town where he only ever went for a few groceries and an occasional pint of beer.

He accelerated, loved to hear the sound of the bike, exhaust sounds ricocheting off the trees that stood guard either side of the road.

They were ready. The wire was tied around one tree. Rigid. The other end was loose enough to manipulate, waiting for the sound of the bike – just as they had on two previous nights. Their target was a creature of habit, started early, worked late. Died, middle-aged.

Bright lights. Fiercely bright. 'Turn them off, you arsehole!'

He shook his head twice, and that was the last thing he ever did.

The blackened wire had come up, quick, well-rehearsed. At sixty-five miles an hour Hall was hardly breaking the sound barrier, but when the wire collided with his collar bones it was enough, it catapulted him backwards, in a vicious decelerative move causing him to resemble a rag doll, thrown around by its owner, the Pitbull.

Instead of thinking about Bridie McGee or Roaring Meg, or even his dear old mum, or his new bike, or England's green and pleasant land, his last word was arsehole. What a bloody awful ending. He would find the bastard that did this and if he somehow ever defrauded his way into heaven, he'd break his bloody neck too.

The worker looked up, then along the road. She left the van, running, called his name, panicked, unsure whether to remove his helmet, felt for a pulse, scrabbled for a sign of life, looked around, pointlessly, fumbled in her pocket for a phone that wasn't there, then ran back to the stables, leaving her van in situ, hoping that it would act as a beacon.

As she ran back up the dark lane, the only sign of life was the rhythmic flash of amber from her hazard lights.

He'd have spent hours recounting the story, how his bike was so well balanced. The glistening red machine had continued upright for almost eighty metres. Then it began its own descent into chaos, drifting side to side, swaying, slowing and then pulling left into the hedgerow, through it and out the other side, crashing into saplings and finally coming to rest next to a larger tree, one that was always going to win the battle.

The Honda fared well with minor frontal damage. Its back wheel was still rotating moments later, long after its rider had left this world. For 'Church' it wasn't a case of by the time he hit the road he was dead. He was dead whilst still in the air.

Steve Hall ended his days on his left side, head down onto the road, almost perversely in the recovery position. There was no exhalation, no final resistance, no blood contusions around his neck and shoulders, but no blood. His leathers and gloves bore the hallmarks of a short-lived fight with nature, and his ending was equally brief.

The sorrow at his loss would be much more sustained.

Leather against the road surface, hands grazing tarmac. Machine versus tree. Neither the victor, nor the spoils.

'And I never passed a cry for help.
Though at times I shook with fear.'

The initial investigation would struggle to find a reason for the crash. The three-man team had done their job and done it well. Their payment was continuing employment with Alex Stefanescu and respect among their peers.

Within five minutes they had removed the wire, rubbed soil into the wound that told the tale of a blunt and brutal trauma, a cable that had dug half an inch into the fresh bark and provided the only possible clue to his demise.

It would take an extensive daylight search by an accident investigation unit to find it. But they would. They were the best, no stone or leaf would remain unturned. Each tree, each bush, every mark on the road surface, plotted, mapped, marked. Their search was wide, expanding in eccentric circles. They figured out how. Now they needed to know why.

Before long they found the track that led to an adjacent lane, through the woods, tyre marks that eventually aligned to a mid-1990s' Ford van were located and casts taken – evidence of a vehicle that they would never find.

It had been ten minutes before 'Church' was found by Liz Stevenson, an apprentice from the nearby stables.

Having left work early she had been sat in the work van, headlights on full beam, engine ticking over as she swept left and right trying to find a mate for the night. So engrossed in her potential choices, she hadn't even heard the collision.

'Church' was a just watchman now, guarding his spirit, ensuring it made it to where it belonged. His body lay in black and white leathers, an angel face down on the road with only the feint glow of headlights in the woods marking the last resting place of his bike, his beloved red machine – that he also called Roaring Meg.

He never heard the quietly spoken words of the stable girl, the pleas for him to live, or the sound of sirens, not even the random patter of raindrops around him.

He was no longer there.

CHAPTER TWENTY-NINE

S{\scriptsize TEVE} H{\scriptsize ALL} {\scriptsize HAD SPENT THE NIGHT ON A COLD METAL} shelf along with every other body in the local morgue. That was the only thing they had in common. His spirit was very much alive. He joked that he didn't care much for his body anyway, broken as it was.

'What was that smell?'

'Why am I here?'

'Who is that next to me? Do I even know you?'

It had been a quiet night, no conversation. No one seemed interested, so he counted the holes in the slab above him until he slept.

He woke moments later. It was a dream. People grabbing him from the side, below, above.

'Please, just leave me. Leave me alone.'

He had them, often. He'd be fine by the morning, coffee, a quick bowl of something that was probably bad for him, then a chilly ride back into work where he knew he still made a difference.

'But you are dead, Steve. It's how it is. You need to

realise this, and the sooner you do, the sooner you will learn to cope. You can then enjoy life again.'

His crime was being part of a team that had poked the bear, shaken the tree or whatever the phrase was. His punishment was an instant and violent death, one that that the doctors told his few relatives had been quick, and painless. But how did they really know?

It was a punishment that did not fit the crime.

Steve's issue, like so many, was that he was far from ready to leave, and that caused a few problems for those that managed the spirit world. He'd just have to learn to live with it.

DS Bridie McGee had taken the call late that night – Steve Hall's next of kin was 'Scotland Yard' and a phone number. He had done this deliberately to avoid upsetting his elderly mother, who he adored.

"Boss, it's Trev. Sorry to wake you." He wasn't. It was just something that police staff said as an icebreaker.

"Just had a call from Kent Police. There's been an RTA."

She tried to figure out why a road traffic accident would warrant a phone call, late at night, to her.

"Who?" McGee was rubbing her eyes, switching on a bedside light.

"Church." One word. He didn't need to add anything.

She exhaled, sat up now, swinging her legs out of bed, already unbuttoning her pyjama top – never wore the bottoms.

"I'm on my way."

"Where to, boss?"

It was a rational question. She laughed – it was a release.

"Good point, sorry Trev, I've just woken up. Give me a second."

He waited.

She blew away the metaphorical cobwebs, stood up and spoke normally as there was no one to disturb in her flat. It was at times like this that she wished there was.

"OK, let's start again. Where did this happen? How? Injuries? Anyone with him?"

Trev Meakin was old school, and sometimes old school said it how it was, bluntly. It didn't make him a lesser person; it was just how his generation of police officers coped.

"Boss the injuries were fatal." The sentence hung in the air until it slowly entangled her and started to crush the air from her lungs. She sensed an immediate change, almost a panic. All she could say was, "Where is he?"

Meakin filled in the gaps and apologised again.

"It's OK, Trev. Thanks for the call. I'm heading there now. Can you let DCI Roberts know? In fact, no, I'll do that. Can you get a message out to the team? With the exception of late shift, I want everyone in the office tomorrow morning. No excuses."

"Absolutely boss. You take care." Meakin, like everyone else on the team, knew that McGee and Hall were close. No one knew how close, but they had often added two to itself and come up with the wrong answer.

Less than ten minutes later – despite the fact there was no rush – McGee was dressed and heading south east. Her black de-striped Mini Cooper moved quickly and efficiently across country. She parked in a police bay at the hospital, threw a business card in the dash and made her way to the most sterile looking part of the building. Beige walls, white interior, bright lights, subtle smell of something she couldn't quite identify. Find that building in a hospital you've found the morgue.

She held her warrant card up against a camera and was allowed in. Half an hour later she was back in her car, sitting silently, window down, wishing she smoked, or drank, or had a vice of some kind.

His face was perfect. She wanted a look at those eyes once more, but they were closed – thank God. So instead she lowered herself down to him and gently kissed his cheek. His skin was icy, but somehow he looked peaceful. The dichotomy with how he had died did not escape her.

"He's far too quiet," she said, but the mortician was busy doing something else. She went to pull the cover back across his face but couldn't. She'd leave that for someone else to do. It was incredibly final.

The Mortician had heard her. He had just learned over the years to let loved ones and visitors do what they needed to do, say what they needed to say, even if it was nonsense, a special phrase or a private joke – he'd even heard confessions.

"Will there be a postmortem?"

"Oh, I suspect so, given his age, job and how it happened."

"It *was* a road accident, wasn't it?"

"Well, he was riding a motorcycle when he had an accident. That much is true, my dear. But coming off the machine is not what killed him. In my humblest of opinions, you understand?"

"I do. Go on. Is there something I'm missing?"

"One hundred percent."

He rolled down the sheet to reveal the massive bruising and linear cut which ran from shoulder to shoulder.

"I'm no doctor but I suspect what had happened here is your friend has hit something that was more rigid than him, in doing so it has caused him to dismount from the machine at a great rate of knots and has left this mark just here."

"A weapon? Was he hit first? Or after he came off?"

"No. I believe not. Simpler than that. Unpleasant and no

doubt planned, but simpler nonetheless. There are no other significant marks, a bruise here and slight contusion there. You are welcome to look."

"No. Thank you that won't be necessary."

"My diagnosis is a broken neck. The weapon? If you want to class it as one was a wire, across the carriageway. He has hit it and it has struck here, ridden up, and the helmet has taken some of the blow. I suspect you will see the marks on the helmet just as I did. It's in that bag over there."

"Thank you." She didn't mean it, but it helped.

"If you ask me the helmet kind of saved him."

"I don't understand. My colleague is dead."

"But he still has his head, my dear. And that makes our job a whole lot easier."

Like most police officers, she had seen her fair share of bodies. Too many, perhaps. Her first was a hanging. She found him in the summer months, putrid, his blackened skin rotting onto the wooden hall floor of a quiet house in a pleasant street in suburbia. Literally walked into him, her face colliding with his lower body in the half light of the hallway.

She had clawed at her face, trying to rid him from her as one would with a spider's web.

He didn't even leave a note. She had never forgotten her first. Could even remember his name and date of birth. He visited her now and then, in her dreams, so vivid that when she woke she couldn't tell, for a second, whether it was real – or just a nightmare.

It took her a year to recover. At least that's what she told the force psychiatrist.

She sat, inhaled and said mid-sigh, "Oh Steve...tell me what happened."

She couldn't say anything else. Nothing else seemed even remotely appropriate.

A blackbird sang out somewhere in the grounds of the hospital, confused into thinking it was daytime by the bright lighting that illuminated the grounds. It was a pleasant song; it reminded her of her childhood when she used to stand and listen to one in her bedroom, window open, she could clearly hear it calling to a mate. She would often look down to the end of the garden to see her father, whistling back at just such a bird, oblivious to his audience. It always made her smile. It did now. She missed him terribly, too.

McGee came from a strong family with respectable values and one that expected her to teach, so she studied English, ironically not far from where she now sat alone in her car crying.

She hadn't disappointed her parents – more a case of a surprise. But she had done well, and that was all that mattered. They were always proud to show her course photograph to anyone that would spare a moment to look. But they noticed how much she had changed. The 'job' made you tough, gritty, cynical – able to cope.

She'd only learned to swear when she joined the police and at times she could match an irate fishwife. Or as her colleague Nick Fisher had once said, 'She's a lovely lass, as pure as the driven...but at times she's like a nun with Tourette's.'

She gripped the leather wheel of her beloved Mini. Gripped it so tight the blood retreated and revealed pure ivory.

"You absolute bastards." She almost spat the word out, punching the rim of the wheel, slipping and sounding the horn. The blackbird stopped, then flew away.

Bridie turned the ignition key, ramped up the heater then hit dial on her phone which connected to the hands free system. It was even later than when she had received the similar call, but the boss needed to know, regardless of the time – 'That's why they get the big bucks'.

It's how it was, up the chain, down the chain.

"Jason Roberts."

"Guv. It's Bridie."

He allowed her to vent, to cry for about a minute, then asked the question.

"It's OK, DS McGee, tell me, tell me what's troubling you?" He chose the formal approach to solicit the information he needed. He could sense that good news was not going to be forthcoming.

She spoke quickly. "Church had a crash, was in a crash, crashed his bike. He's dead." It was the best she could offer.

"OK." He took a moment to clear his own head, started counting his staff, working out who he had lost.

"Was this an accident Bridie?"

"No boss. It wasn't. How did you know? Someone, some..."

"Say it. It will do you good."

"No. If I start I may never stop Jason. Somebody pulled a wire up across the road, waiting for Church...for Steve, to pass by, then almost decapitated him. Whatever the agenda, there was no need to do that." She fought back the tears once more. "We've got a problem, boss, and it's getting worse."

She was right. This was no time for management buzz words – or Mingo, as the staff called it and often played, waiting for a well-worn phrase to complete a line or the whole grid.

"I'm completely with you Bridie. Right now if I could get my hands on them, in a dark lane, or a quiet corner of an industrial estate – I'd happily shoot them."

"That's the thing though, boss. You say them. But who are we dealing with? Do you know? Because if you do, it's long overdue for a briefing to the troops. We need to push this out beyond our team. That's Steve gone, probably Cynthia and Carrie is missing too. Are we even safe?"

"I honestly don't know. I'll be raising this up the food chain first thing in the morning. We've got an enemy and need to locate him. The cavalry is coming. My problem is I'm told we have to keep the lid on this, so how do I throw it open to every man and his bloody dog, but still maintain an air of covertness?"

"Bugger being covert boss – this is way beyond that now, surely. We've got people dead, people missing, God only knows what might be happening to them. Isn't a hand-filled candle enough to alert you to the fact that what's going on is far from normal?"

"Bridie. Please. I need you to understand that this is bigger than our team. Greater than the Metropolitan Police, even. You were at the briefing."

"But the briefing told me two-fifths of fuck all boss!" She was getting angrier by the second.

"It told you that there are players at another level. It told you that documents are missing, that those very items could see the United Kingdom as we know it fall to its knees. We are talking billions Bridie."

"So this is just about money? Money over people?"

"I am afraid so. Right now we need to focus on that. Not our colleagues, who may or may not be missing, presumed dead."

"Permission to disagree?"

"Granted. Try to get some sleep. You'll be fine."

"Thanks, boss. Keep your enemies close and all that. You sleep well too." Neither would.

The final call of the night was made by Roberts to Cade.

"It's me. How's the hotel?"

"Strange time of night to ask? Do you work for Trivago now?"

"Funny. I am officially allowing you to release the dogs of war, Jack. You are unchained. No longer a copper, not bound by our rules. I know you will resist for a while, but I need you to follow what the Home Secretary said to us just before she left."

"I thought she was saying it with her tongue firmly in her rather lovely cheeks, Jason?"

"So what if she was? I took her at her word. And that, let me remind you was this, and I quote. 'Do what you need to do to rid us of this evil. I will back you, completely.'"

"Fair enough, she did. So why the change Mr Company Man? You've always played by the rules, been the nice guy."

"And you haven't Jack? Come on, tell me you haven't once wanted to bend the rules and I'll apologise."

"Not once, Jason. It made me who I am. So come on, what's changed?"

"They've killed one of my best detectives earlier tonight."

"They?"

"It's them. Has to be. Too brutal to be a common thief."

"You saying they are not common thieves?"

"Forget that, Jack. It was Church. They almost beheaded him, wire across a road, hit him, on his motorbike. Filthy bastards, I mean it..."

Cade thought before he replied. Anything he did say was at risk of being a platitude, and they both knew they were clichéd beyond the norm.

His cheeks puffed air out until he continued with what he hoped would be the right thing to say. "It's OK, my friend. Be angry. I'm very sorry, Jason, he was a really good bloke. I understand. I really do."

"Really?"

"Really. Don't forget I helped your boys fish Nikolina out of the Thames once, brushed the mud from her lips so I could kiss her goodbye. Shed a tear onto her face, tried to wipe it off, but just made more of a mess. I understand. But as you say, I don't have to be quite so rigid in my adherence to the rules now. However, there's still the matter of the law..."

"There are no laws from here on in. None at all. If it means the end of my career, then so be it, but let's start taking the fight back to them instead of being so bloody British."

"Then so be it. I'd say let's have a cup of tea in the morning, but a scotch may be preferable?"

"Possibly. I'd be pissed though, Jack. Can't handle the stuff, late at night or over breakfast, and I'm more Scottish than English."

"Since when?"

"Since I slipped from my mother's womb – as an ocean liner slides down those slippery planks into the sea, after being belted around the face with a champagne bottle."

"Jesus, you had a rough start in life, DCI Roberts."

"It was a metaphor ex-Inspector Cade. And yes, I'm Scottish, more Jockney than Cockney my son."

"Well, you learn something every decade. As metaphors go it's one which may never allow me to sleep again. I was going to mention how many men went down on that ship, but at this time of the night it could be misconstrued – and after all, it's your mother we are talking about."

"Goodnight, Jack. See you in a few hours. And thanks."

"Pleasure mate. What for?"

"I'm not entirely sure."

He laid back down and asked his mind to switch off. Each time he told it to stop thinking, it did, twice as fast and then the tune started. The same bloody tune that starts, and creates a self-imposed loop, over and over again, until half an hour before the next melody is the alarm.

"I hate you, Cade."

He lay for at least an hour, thinking of Steve Hall, and Cynthia Bell, of Clive Wood, the first of his team to lose his life, and then he turned his mind to Carrie. He knew somehow that Bell was dead. O'Shea was a different proposition. If anyone could survive it was that girl. She had caused him some real issues over the years; common assault, not so common assault, stabbings, allegations, counter allegations, and more. It was the night she had been poisoned and left for dead in her apartment that he saw her true spirit, realised what a thoroughly stubborn cow she was. Wherever she was he hoped she was OK, prayed she was, and he hardly prayed anymore.

CHAPTER THIRTY

She was also wide awake, had no idea of the time, she had been counting the hours the best she could, watching the light change in the dimly lit room, working out approximately where they were in the scheme of things. It got dark early, and it got cold too. She began to question whether she could make it through another night – the sense that she had heard her friend and colleague breathe her last hit her again, and she began to cry. It was a quiet expression of sorrow, for she wanted no one to know about her weakness for her fellow human.

What have you done with Cynthia? Her family needs to mourn her. To lay her to rest. You cold-hearted thugs.

It was so cold. She now wanted to die. Would be quite happy to.

Next to her, Lucy Thomas was in the same state of mind.

"Why can't they just kill us?" She whispered.

"I don't know, but they can bloody well start with you. You are the reason we are here. The reason Cynthia is dead." O'Shea was doing nothing to disguise her anger.

"Hey sweetheart, this has nothing to do with me."

"Anyone who is or has been connected to these arseholes needs reminding that when they had the chance to kill them, they should have done. I mean, what do you see in him, anyway? He's hardly Mr Romania 1987, is he?"

"He was loving. He treated me well."

"Oh please." O'Shea would have spat in her eye if she had been able to reach. "It was for money. There was no love between you. An impotent psycho and an overweight tranny."

"How dare you? I am so not overweight."

It would have been funny if they were somewhere else other than captives in a rundown factory, miles from anywhere and yet, ironically, only miles from somewhere.

"You are so. I can't believe that people even refer to you as a female. You're a bloody insult to female kind."

"There's no such word, Carrie."

"Well, there bloody well is now Derrick, or whatever you're really called. I mean, how can you be classed as a woman? If I really force my eyes to look I can see that you aren't. It stands out a mile."

"Why thank you for the compliment, honey. Considering how cold it is I'll take that."

"You're a bloody freak. You should have been around when PT Barnum was recruiting. A woman with stubble on her stomach? Whatever next? Christ, what a mess. It's official, I bloody hate you, and if that toothless bastard of a boyfriend of yours doesn't kill you, trust me, I will. With my bare bloody..."

She stopped. Thomas had hissed at her. It wasn't a 'I've heard enough from you love' type hiss, more a 'Please, stop, they are coming back' noise.

She remained quiet for a moment.

Nothing.

The problem with the buildings was their disconnected

nature, footsteps were difficult to detect, and it was easy for anyone to quietly walk up to their room and listen or act without warning.

Both Thomas and O'Shea had adapted well to their surroundings. Both knew that their time was limited. It felt like weeks since they had been brought to this desolate place, when in fact, it was only days.

Dehydrated, hungry, cold and afraid. Four elements that colluded to make their hosts fear for their lives, but equally plead for their deaths.

"I'm sorry, Carrie." He was sobbing again.

"Yeah. I'm sure you are. Look, I may need you to be strong. If we have any chance of getting out of here alive, we need to work together. Agreed?"

"Of course. What is your plan?"

O'Shea stared at the dark outline of the magnolia-painted ceiling and tried to come up with something that resembled sensible.

"Honestly, mate. I haven't got a clue. Slowly edge out of the room, down that rough track and then hitchhike back to the office? Might do it in six months, maybe a year. Leave it with me. After all, I've got fuck all else to do."

"You swear, like a trooper girl, should have been in my game."

It brought a bizarre sense of relief, strapped to a rigid table, freezing cold and raw from their own urine burns.

"I get it from my old man. True Londoner. I reckon we are no more than an hour from the city. Put me down on the ground and I find my way back, like a homing pigeon. We are away from built-up areas, and traffic, but I can hear vehicles somewhere in the distance – busy too, almost never stops. I think it's a motorway. Or a bridge, there's a noise I can't put my finger on."

"I can't put my finger on anything right now, sweetheart.

God, I'm hungry. My head is splitting. Can you hear my stomach? Can you?"

"Lucy."

"Yes?"

"Shut up."

The footsteps increased in volume until both captives were aware of people in the doorway. They were back.

Satisfied that his remaining prisoners were still in situ, and beyond reach, Constantin ate with his men. They had gathered in a room and feasted on Indian takeaway. It was the finest thing they had ever eaten. They were so hungry that every spice could be tasted. Paid for in cash, they chose the place that looked like it needed the trade. No cameras and staff that were willing to lie if necessary.

The scents drifted across from the room to O'Shea and Thomas. They were even hungrier – genuinely starving. O'Shea could differentiate between the chicken and lamb dishes, smell the coriander, the turmeric, garlic and ginger. She would willingly murder someone for a spoonful, she'd even stoop so low to eat it off a homeless drunk's fingertips.

Constantin had earned the admiration of his team in a matter of days. Despite his physical appearance, he had an aura about him that the younger men appeared to acknowledge and respect.

They knew he had a reputation as a cruel man, however, he also had a gift – killing people in inventive ways. They had watched as he expertly removed the woman's hand and sent it as a message to the policeman. It was inventive. Cruel, but creative. Whether he had intended for her to bleed to death was unknown.

To a man they had decided it was better the devil you know and on the subject of malevolent behaviour, four of them knew they had an unsavoury job to do as soon as they had finished eating.

The men walked to another part of the building, leaving the remaining men to rest. They would have their own duties to attend to the next day.

"Carry her to the place I told you about. No torches. Do it as I showed you and she will be gone. I need her to leave now. She has overstayed her welcome. Take as long as you need. I have things to do."

The four young men divided their labour, two picked up Cynthia Bell, the other two carried what items they needed. It was a walk of about half a mile, beyond reach of the van, marshy in places, but if they stuck to the footpath, they would be fine. All the way to the river.

In Bucharest McCall was ready. He had been an accomplished actor since his schooldays and playing a drunk was second nature to him, partly due to his skills and mainly due to his experience. Service life had taught him how to fight and how to drink. Everything else was a close second.

His slightly dishevelled appearance, staggered walk and distant look was familiar to the other footpath dwellers that shuffled home later on a frigid January night in the Medical District. Three steps forward and two back.

Byzantin was noisier than normal – must be the cold, driving everyone in, or free drinks. The posters said free drinks, with admission. The sound told him that there must be at least a hundred customers beyond the main doors. The party that the Jackdaw had planned was yet to flourish, but it was building in tempo. Time yet, the city was just coming to life. When Alex Stefanescu threw a party, people came, people even paid to enter.

It had been a long time since they had been turned away

in their hundreds. And he knew it. Those days needed to return, or soon, there would be another king to wear the crown.

Tweedledee and his counterpart Tweedledum, or to give them their operational names, The Incisors, were pacing around on the pavement, theatrically pressing their ears and checking their watches, like they knew what they were doing in their cheap Armani replicas. Amateurs.

In the observation post across the road, Vasile was awake and pressing buttons – one on his camera, the other on the radio. Kicking his mate awake with his left foot.

"Vasile to Andre!" This was more urgent than the last time he had called in. The words came through with an aura of excitement draped around them. He repeated the message.

"Vasile to Andre."

"Go ahead." Grig had been about to stand his men down after days of fruitless activity.

"Boss. Tourist One is back!"

"OK. Give me a sitrep. All units stand by to strike."

"Boss Tourist One is in the club. The staff entrance door. He looked drunk, but the two local targets have gone in after him and haven't exited. Do you receive?"

He received. Loud and clear and the bastard tourist wasn't, was he? It was his stance. The way he held himself. His confidence. Even the way he dressed. He should have gone with his instinct and had him taken out on the street. But why was he in his city, who was he and critically, was he a friend or a foe?

As experienced as he was Capitan Andre Grigorescu was regretting the decision to halve his manpower for the night.

"Vasile, you are the closest team. Break cover and get to the club. We are on the way."

. . .

McCall took the first two steps, bumped into Tweedledee, apologised in a broad Australasian accent, laughed, smiled inanely, then apologised again, before spinning him around and staggering towards the side door of the club, trying to shake his hand.

"No boys, seriously, she'll be right. It's all sweet. Trust me, I'm a doctor. No, really, I am. I saved a pretty girl once. You should have seen her. Stunning..."

Tweedledum, the larger of the two tried to grab hold of McCall's arm but he was quick, quicker than his foe. To an onlooker he was yet another drunken tourist, staggering, trying to get into the club, to meet other tourists or pick up one of the pretty local escorts.

"Oh, do me a favour boys. Can't a man just get a bloody beer when he wants in this..." He laughed, waving his arms around like an enthusiastic tour guide, "...beautiful city of Budapest?"

"It's Bucharest, and you are not welcome cowboy. Go before we hurt you."

"Fair dinkum. Just let me go for a piss and I'll be on my way. Don't want to get on the wrong side of the law or you fellas do we?"

He started to unzip his fly.

Then took two more steps and was through the door, falling forwards and into the main hallway. His hope was that team two, The Molars, as he had labelled them, were having a break. He spun around, as a drunk would. It gave him seconds to scan his new environs, up, down and sideways. He was in.

It was his lucky night – The Molars were elsewhere.

Target Dee, as he was now known in McCall's electric mind, was through the door in seconds, panicking that the boss might be watching on the closed circuit system that safeguarded every corner of the business. Target Dum was metres behind.

In the main club a remix of a popular euro track was pulsing, causing the fittings to vibrate lightly. A girl in a dress that really didn't qualify as such walked into the hallway, letting the sound drift in behind her, looking for the bathrooms. She took one look at the doormen and turned, giggling, her miniscule silver-spangled dress enough to draw their attention for a second. That was all he needed.

The first strike was a straight arm into the right upper quarter of Dum's slightly overweight frame. The pressure wave was immense. It was the same blow that had felled Cade only days before in the altogether more peaceful Whitsunday Islands, but the effect was the same. In Dum's case, calculated to be a whole lot worse. His organs had collided, smashing into one another. It was a dense, animal, biological collision, absorbing the shock but reacting as only a human body can. Before he had even slumped to his knees, he was bleeding internally. He wouldn't get up again in a hurry. For all his size, bulging sleeves and snarling expression, he had lasted only long enough to be a nuisance.

McCall turned, light on his feet, balletic, cracking the back of Dee's right knee with his foot, causing him to buckle, lower now, target in sight. He drove his balled fist onto the top of his collarbone. The electric shock that ran through his stocky but overweight body was impressive. It was one of McCall's party pieces.

A hundredth of a second later, he had wrapped his arm around Dee's throat and was applying pressure to the carotid artery. McCall's face was so close to Dee's that he could smell what he had eaten an hour earlier. Dee thrashed about, an ocean predator jigging for his life on board a charter boat, down among the heady mix of blood and seawater, gasping for air.

He was down. McCall drove his foot through the side of Dee's kneecap, immobilising him with a ligament-snapping crunch, then turned to follow up on Dum. It was pointless; he was also immobile, and out cold. The decision not to kill both men was premeditated.

They were not soldiers. This was not a battlefield.

It was pointless trying to drag them to a store cupboard or secrete them in some way. If the cameras that he had observed were working, then someone was watching, it was just a matter of time. He had made the leap of faith.

He checked his watch. Two minutes. Time flew when you were having fun. He ran his hand over his cargo pocket. Documents still there. Time to move on.

Vasile and his partner Tomas, both in their twenties and fit and fast were bailing out of the OP as quickly as they could, but they needed to secure it first, then get down a fire escape, out of the grounds and over a wall before running across the street. Their dark-coloured jackets were doing their best to hide the body armour which was slowing them down, standing out like a beacon under their plain clothes.

It was the sight of the men running that caught the Jackdaw's keen eye. He missed nothing. A man on the run and with that many enemies never missed a beat. You needed eyes, in the eyes in the back of your head if you played in the same sandpit as Europe's finest criminals. If you didn't, you died.

Police or a fierce competitor? He went for the former. His competitors walked to a fight.

This was the moment the fortune teller had warned him about, many years ago. If you believed such things. He did. He had been sent to see the Drabadi – the fortune teller, when he was a young man. She hoped for luck and good health and the benchmark things that those that future-gazed hoped for, and skilfully blended the truth to suit her agenda, which was to keep the young man in front of her happy.

However, with the boy they had started to call the Jackdaw, she knew she had to be truthful. He had once been rumoured to be the next Gypsy King. He had an air about him that concerned her, even frightened her and that meant she had to respect him or end up somewhere in an unpleasant situation and cast out.

"Beware." Her first words made him smile. He feared no one. Foolish old woman. Less of the drama and more of the facts. However, he listened, for equally he feared what she might say next.

Divination, or fortune telling, is as old as Roma themselves. More than an art form, it is woven into their way of life, practiced by most Roma, but almost entirely frequented by the females of the group and only ever for profit when practiced with non-Roma – or Gadje as they were called.

The middle-aged woman ran her eyes over the tarot cards. It was an unconventional method of fortune telling for her – however; she was far from conventional. Moved on by her own, she had travelled across Europe before eventually finding a home near Craiova.

"You have drawn the Seven of Swords." She shuddered theatrically, looking around, gathering momentum and hoping for a greater reward in the form of her social standing. Jackdaw was young, but he was already wealthy and influential and with any luck he would be charitable in some way.

"Beware the Seven of Swords, Alex. In the picture we see a man carrying five swords, running from a place, a place where he should not be. You are this man." She fixed her gaze upon his and did not yield until he looked away.

"He enjoys the feeling of getting away with this, of not being caught. But look, on the horizon, a soldier waits, he too has a sword, and somewhere, another man, also armed."

"You have my attention, my dear. But I am scared of no one. Only God."

"There will come a day." She gazed soulfully into the future. "A day when you will need to face your enemies. You cannot run away from the truth anymore. You will become a victim."

"Of what?" His arrogance was building.

"Of deception. Of betrayal. And of treachery. Someone has an agenda Alex. Someone you thought you could trust. Trust no one. The Seven of Swords is not a card to ignore. You need to be vigilant."

"For how long?"

"Until the day comes."

Something triggered this memory as he had stood at the full height window – the observation post at the epicentre of his business empire where he often stood and watched the world go by. Perhaps the old woman was right after all.

Grig and his team were also out of their buildings. Two were running, four in a car. Another car was en route, ploughing through night time traffic and avoiding the drunks. This was not how it was planned.

CHAPTER THIRTY-ONE

ALEX MOVED AWAY FROM THE TINTED WINDOW. HIS SPEED caught his younger brother by surprise. He was making for the kitchen.

"Something I need to know, brother?" He was rapid now, pacing as a caged animal would, paranoia setting in. Stefan recognised the symptoms. They had been here so many times before, always on the run, a crick in the neck from looking over his shoulder. When would it ever end?

For Stefan, it had all been a lie. The past decade, longer, since his bastard of a brother had killed their parents. Always doing what his brother wanted, when he said, without question, yes Alex, no Alex.

He had lived a very nice lifestyle – but he was living a lie. He had waited for the day, allowing the business empire to expand, to stink of money and allow its very name to have such a viral reputation that no one would ever challenge him. He could live that sort of a life, couldn't he?

However, he also had his other master to appease – the British. The life of a double agent. Sounded glamourous. In his words, it was utter horse shit. A puppet with two sets of strings, and occasionally they tangled. It was dangerous beyond your wildest dreams. People wondered if it was glamourous. 'Please, do not insult me' he would say to the limited number of people he trusted. It was a game and one which ultimately he knew he would never win, slashed across the throat by his big brother or stabbed in the back by the British government. But it seemed that they were his only ally for they wanted Alex dead as much as he did.

"What is it to be Stefan?"

He paused. The words sinking in, through the mental haze that had quickly descended.

Alex was looking at him, a razor-sharp kitchen knife in his hand. He always preferred the knife. Firearms were too quick. He liked to hear the wound he was inflicting.

He was looking into his little brother's eyes now. People were fascinated by them, each a different shade. He'd like to cut them out one by one and force them down his throat. How could he betray him, to the Bulgarians was one thing, but to the British of all people, why them? They both had a chance to put hundreds of millions into their bank and the British wouldn't even ask for it back as long as they had kept their side of the bargain – keep quiet, tell no one. For what Alex was asking, it was a deal worth striking and all he had to do was hand over some scraps of paper.

But no, Stefan had to be honourable.

Alex turned his back on him, making towards the panelled wall where he knew he could begin his escape. The police were coming for him, on a charge that had no substance, but Alex held no sway over the judges anymore. There was a time, when he had all of the local judges in his back pocket in one way or another, but those days had long gone. Now, it seemed that judges had integrity. He spun and mid-turn launched the knife at his brother, then began to sprint towards him.

The knife hit him in the upper left bicep and flapped around like a harpoon in the back of a whale. He had missed.

It was a sign that the Jackdaw was still hung over. As the upright wooden beam in his grand apartment, with its myriad entry wounds could testify, Alex never missed. He was a master with the knife. Now he had to get it back or twist it where it remained, trying to tear open the brachial artery.

He leapt onto Stefan, who had fought the urge to pull the blade from his arm. They collapsed backwards, his head almost striking the hearth that surrounded the impressive log fire which spluttered now, flames of green and yellow, fiery tendrils desperate for more fuel.

On one side of the hearth were a few weapons of opportunity; a fork and a poker, forged from iron, hanging on a hook. On the other side the forlorn polar bear's head, sat with its black eyes mirroring Alex's – deep holes of coal-black that spoke only one word – predator.

The Jackdaw was crowing. Grabbing at the knife, he pulled it swiftly from the wound, which now began to bleed more profusely. He raised it up, ready to strike again. His brother was quicker and stronger, pushing him backwards, knocking the bear, or what was left of him, to one side. Droplets of glass scattered from within the head, across the hearth. Fifty or a hundred, maybe more, it was difficult to tell. To an experienced eye they were more than glass beads, they were diamonds and beautiful ones too. Stolen years before from Hatton Garden in London during an operation that was supposed to be a roaring success but had ended like the spluttering fire in Alex's apartment, warm but no inferno.

That night had been the start of his demise. The night he learned who to trust and who not to. Who to hate and who to kill. It left him with few friends and fewer family members. He had lived underground, in isolation or in prison ever since.

Stefan couldn't help being distracted by the cascade of sparkling colours, blue and green and red, silver and white, attracting light and answering a question he had long harboured.

"So that's where you have been hiding them."

Stefan glanced down. "Those were half mine you thief!"

Alex laughed. "Me, a thief?" He looked genuinely shocked. "No, nothing is half yours. Everything is all mine. You should know I don't do things by halves, my dear." He was smiling, actually enjoying the moment. The sociopath versus the traitor.

Stefan picked up the poker and walked towards his brother, who was rubbing the back of his head. Fresh blood, but not enough to worry about. "Now we are even."

A patch of bright red blood was forming on Stefan's shirt, but the wound was not bleeding enough to worry him. He had experienced a lot worse. They both had, from their childhood days when they fought like cat and dog and more latterly, when they fought like pack animals, often together for what appeared to be a common cause.

"The police will be here any second, brother. Let me run. If you love me you would."

"But you see, I don't. They can take you for all I care. You are no brother to me. I will happily turn the key on you. You murdered our parents, for God's sake. What are you?"

Alex stepped backwards towards the kitchen – an arsenal of opportunities.

"All this time? You have born a grudge all this time. You

have had many opportunities to kill me, smother me whilst I was drunk, slit my throat as I slept."

"I should have done."

"I am the Jackdaw – King of the Gypsies. People look up to me, worship me, women throw themselves at me, men cower at my feet. There is nothing or no one I cannot have. And you are jealous."

The first knife left the wooden block and struck against the poker as Stefan swiftly raised it in defence, sparks flew. Another was drawn from the block, longer, less accurate, but thrown nonetheless. And another. It seemed that Stefan was riding his luck. The next was a broad-bladed carving knife. Too big to throw. He needed to be closer.

"And you even killed your daughter. What sort of animal does that?"

"No Stefan, you did that, remember? And you killed Nikolina too."

Even mentioning her name caused his stomach to knot. He wished now that she was here, in his bed. Such a sweet girl, such an exciting lover, but she had betrayed him, Bulgarian whore. Even she had grown to love him. He had proved to everyone that he was capable of loving at least one person. In the end it was a simple case of if I cannot have you, as I want you, then no one can. He had sent a message that day too, etched onto her naked corpse.

Stefan had made the decision that he could not allow his brother to leave alive. He ran at him, throwing the poker. Rather than using it as a weapon, it hit the target in the chest, but caused no immediate injury. Grabbing Alex around the midriff and propelling him backwards, he knew he needed to use his superior strength. Alex countered by thrashing around with the carving knife, but now he was too close. They clattered into a stainless steel pedal bin, knocking its contents across the marbled floor. Now the fight was feral. Two street kids, rolling around in the mud, blood, tears, mucus, all mixing into a heady cocktail of unbridled violence.

Alex sank his teeth into his brother's neck, clamping down, biting as hard as he could, tearing a chunk of flesh away and spitting it out. Stefan responded by driving a thumb into Alex's eye, so hard that he could feel the eyeball moving backwards, slipping under his thumb, ready to pop at any second.

"I will push your eyeballs out you bastard."

"You haven't got the guts to kill me. Mummy's little boy."

Stefan leant back and punched Alex in the face, and again and again. Somehow he rode the storm. This wasn't his first outing after all.

Alex lifted his knee up and into Stefan's groin. It was the standard way to stop any man in his tracks.

Both men were quickly up, on their feet, bleeding, hurting, almost dancing, weaving left and right, trying to read the other man's thoughts. Stefan was struggling. Alex jinked with the knife, getting closer. He was nimble on his feet – years of street fighting and gaining a reputation in some of the harshest prisons, backed into a corner and knowing the guards were turning a blind eye. Stefan picked up the bin and used it as a shield. He was slower but stronger.

"Just let me go, Stefan!"

"No. Not this time. It's over."

Alex threw the first of the kitchen appliances at his younger sibling, a small coffee machine, followed by a toaster, then a stone rolling pin. It gave him enough time to fumble in a cupboard. He produced a pistol – he had run out knives, so option two it had to be. He'd parked the weapon there years before, loaded and ready, near to his intended escape path.

The first shot was wildly inaccurate. The second drilled into the plaster walls as Stefan sought cover. Alex needed to leave, but he wasn't going without a fight.

Outside the door to Alex's apartment, McCall had stopped and was listening. What he heard said 'conflict' – muffled voices, angry voices and noises of urgent activity, and now gunshots. This was not ideal, especially as one of the protagonists was called Alex. And it was Alex he had come to have tea with, chat a while, hand over a few lousy pieces of paper and Foxtrot Oscar as they said on the team, return to the ranch a few hundred thousand richer and back to work on Monday morning. No questions asked.

'Great, so now I arrive to a fight already underway. Now what?'

Gunshots. Chaos. Heightened activity. Yes, it was time to do what he did best.

He looked over the balcony down into the main hall. Dumb and Dumber were still out cold, although one was making a pitiful noise – one that sounded to McCall like it equated to months of physiotherapy for the victim but in a note a few octaves up from his normal pitch.

McCall pressed gently against the door. It was open. OK, unexpected bonus. 'What's it to be Mack?' He carefully looked inside and could see two engaged in a fight. It was a fight that seemed to be lacking fairness, with one man holding a gun and the other using anything he could to avoid getting shot. One man was taller, stockier with blond hair, the other smaller, wiry with gloss-black hair. But which was the infamous Jackdaw. If he had to choose it had to be the smaller one with the shiny hair. Made sense. He already hated him.

Then the Jackdaw laughed. "Is that the best you have, brother?"

Well, that confirmed that. Target very much acquired, and it looked like the other man might be an ally of sorts, but this was all very unfamiliar territory.

He checked off the possible issues that might face him if he burst through the door and then took a second to recall why he was there in the first place – stick to the mission.

He dearly wished his team were alongside him. This would be so much easier. Done by now, and as his British counterparts liked to say, 'Home in time for tea and medals.'

All this activity and he hadn't even begun to barter with this bloody foreigner, all this way with a few documents for a few hundred thousand. There was no going back now. The price had just gone up too.

He eased the Glock out of its holster. Didn't need to check the safety, there wasn't one. You just needed to know it had one up the spout and it did, little point in carrying an unloaded weapon. He patted the knife too. Lastly, he reached into the pocket of his jacket and fished out the smoke grenade. Through the door or down the stairs?

Decisions, decisions. And then he saw something that made his mind up quickly.

'Christ, the bloody feds are here.' Two men had appeared at speed down below and had now stopped short, in the doorway, confronted by the sight of the two doormen, one unconscious, the other now stirring and complaining that a freight train had run over his leg.

The police had their weapons drawn. They were speaking rapidly into their radios and McCall knew that in any language it wasn't good. He was outgunned if they called for back-up and genuinely didn't want to start a firefight anyway – not against the good guys. 'Geez Scottie, this is really not going to plan at all. Time to re-evaluate.'

His options were simple. Jettison the weapons and revert back to being a shameless drunken tourist, who was lost in the big city; found himself in this lovely building and was just looking for the bathroom when all hell had broken loose. Good, but flawed. What if they had seen him enter? What if the coffee boy was right and the police were watching?

Option Two was crash through the door and hope the police followed. If he lived, he could always produce the amnesia card. Again, flawed.

Option Three came to him on a plate, edged in gold.

Artur Gheorghiu, Alex's trusted lieutenant, had seen the commotion on the TV screen at the back of the nightclub. He had pushed back from his comfortable leather chair and calmly walked through the dance floor to a side door, carrying a pistol, followed by two younger men with stereotypical haircuts and miserable expressions. What Gheorghiu had seen was the result of McCall's handiwork, not the cause. Right now his two primary doormen were down on the ground, and that concerned him enough to draw a weapon. He favoured a heavy calibre pistol and fired it correctly, not side on, gangster style, which was about as accurate as the local weather forecast.

As he arrived into the hall, his two men fanning out behind him, he was confronted by the sight of his two doormen on the ground, two men standing in the doorway, both armed and a commotion upstairs in the boss's flat. He too had three options. Surrender. Make a few enquiries or start shooting. He chose the latter. As his pistol came upwards, into the firing position the two police staff responded.

McCall chose that moment to toss the grenade into the

void. A second later it detonated with a massive bang which caused a chain of events to occur. The nightclub came to a halt, patrons already streaming towards the main door and fire escape panicked. The remixed track on the speakers would normally have made McCall smile, perhaps one day it would.

Ballroom Blitz by Sweet was blearing out of the huge sound system.

Their lead singer referred to a man in black and how he was encouraging an attack.

As the song ended, the words ballroom blitz reverberated.'

The M18 grenade was pumping purple smoke into the hallway. It rapidly filled the room. Gheorghiu started firing. The police responded. Cars slammed to a halt nearby and disgorged more police staff, weapons drawn. Grig ran towards the impressive old façade of the city's leading nightclub, saw the purple smoke billowing from the door, a slumbering dragon coming to life in Little Paris – as his city was often referred – and wondered when his life would ever be normal again.

'Shots fired.' 'Urgent backup'. All he needed was 'Officer down' and his day would be just perfect. But it wasn't like a US drama. Real life rarely was. Shots were fired but randomly into the acrid smoke curtain, and now both parties retreated. And when shots hit you, they hurt. They thudded into your skin and muscles and tendons and bone. They whistled sub-sonically into their target; screaming hot, reeking of black powder, cutting their way through anything they could or diverting up, down or sideways if they met something harder than themselves.

You rarely got up and carried on. But adrenaline did strange things to people.

The police had backed out of the doorway, onto the

street to a place of safety, and Gheorghiu and his men were back through the door, mixing with the nightclub guests who heard an explosion, saw smoke, heard gunshots and feared for the worst.

'It was electric. So perfectly hectic.' Sang the British band to no one in particular. An empty nightclub, plastic cups, two abandoned high-heels and the remnants of dry ice were all that remained of Alex's great comeback. He hadn't even made it to his own party.

For Sergeant Scottie McCall 1NZSAS it was good to back in the saddle. Hectic, Electric. Words he simply adored.

"Should have had them tattooed on your arse, Mack!"

The first flashbang went down into the void to keep both parties at bay – he hoped the police had no idea he had started it all. McCall uncovered his ears. The second went through the gap in the door, which McCall hastily pulled shut, covering his ears again. It was of limited use, but he knew it would at least stop the percussion effect.

Half a second afterwards he was through the door to Alex's apartment, the room still ringing with the effects of the flashbang. His weapon was up in the ready position, scanning the room and identifying just two targets. Shoot one? Shoot both? Shoot neither?

Alex saw him first. Stefan had his back to the door, still fighting and with the feeling that blood was cascading from their ears.

Police? It had to be. That explained the commotion downstairs. But this man didn't look like a police officer. He was quite scruffy, with a few days' growth and longer hair. Undercover perhaps? Or an assassin sent by his primary enemy from across the border – the Bulgarian government.

Alex pulled away from his brother hurriedly and pushed his hands up to the ceiling.

"Please. I am unarmed," he yelled in Romanian. Shouting overly loud due to the recent detonation in a confined space.

And he raises his hands to the sky.'

That was the last line of the song any of them heard, downstairs in the abandoned nightclub, the rest was just a muffled and disorderly set of words, somewhere in the distance, as the police hurled more flashbangs into the hall-way, hoping to disorientate their enemy, waiting for the smoke to diminish and praying for a fast arrival from their tactical colleagues.

McCall saw the pistol on the breakfast bar and then the arms move. 'Better to ask for forgiveness than permission, Mack.'

He had already squeezed the trigger twice, bang, smooth and fast, trigger reset, bang, hitting Alex in the chest knocking him backwards. Two 9mm rounds struck him like house bricks fired from a cannon, but the vest he wore, always, took the lethality out of the ordinarily deadly rounds. The third shot, to the head never came. Alex was lucky.

For Scott McCall, it was now about the money. He had risked everything and for all he knew the New Zealand authorities could already be hunting for him, along with the locals and God knows who else.

All McCall had wanted was a target incapacitated long enough to tell him where the money was. He knew this option only gave Alex a few minutes, but he felt little compassion towards him. If he had caused that beautiful girl to suffer on that quiet New Zealand road that day, back when McCall still had a moral compass, then Alex's days were numbered. The more he looked him in the eye, the more he despised him.

And besides, it served him right for being so damned arrogant on the phone. McCall had decided to keep the documents for himself too. Could come in handy.

He'd made the decision on the flight over that he trusted this Jackdaw bloke about as far as he could kick him.

If he had known what was going to happen next, he would have taken the third shot.

CHAPTER THIRTY-TWO

McCall was having serious doubts about the veracity of the whole operation, realising that he really should have stayed back in New Zealand and found a legitimate way to deal with the debts. It would have been so much easier than engaging an enemy in his own backyard.

He'd done it before, in some weird and wonderful places, places that never offered to stamp his passport and ones which when asked, the New Zealand government would politely decline to answer.

'We were there in an advisory capacity only.'

Mike Steel would have helped him. He wished Steel was alongside now; a moral and fatherly lighthouse in a raging shitstorm.

If nothing else he might be able to figure out where the greasy little bastard had gone – Mike was good at that, when all else was breaking down he could be found on a nearby hilltop with a cup of tea, figuring it all out, before arriving on a white charger and clearing everyone else's mess up. It was why they sent him to places in conflict. That said, his last post had been London whereas a Defence Liaison

Officer he had won many friends for his gentle humour, integrity and candour.

McCall walked carefully towards the island, with its white marble benchtops and matching sink. Glock in the favoured SUL position, close to his chest and under control, ready to punch out into the aim in a fraction of a second – it became an extension of his own body and up to about twenty metres his grouping was measured by the size of a human eye socket.

Three LED lights bathed the area in an arctic-white light.

Left, right. Up, then down.

He was gone. And McCall was distracted. 'Never take your eye off the ball, Scottie.'

Stefan's reactions were lighting fast. He grabbed the last of the knives from the woodblock and threw it sideways, across the worktops, slicing through the air and hitting McCall in the leg.

"Fuck me!" He almost shot him, a reaction and mark of his sheer and unbridled anger. If he had been able to see his feet he would have drilled a round through each one. Then stamped on them.

He strutted for a second, trying to reduce the pain. "By the looks of it, I'm here to bloody save you, bro'. What the hell did you do that for? Where is he?" McCall was furious.

"You are English?" The sudden realisation that McCall had been sent to help struck home, albeit it was entirely wrong.

"I'm sorry. OK? Don't shoot me. He's gone, through here. I thought you were one of his men." He was looking down towards his feet. Perhaps he had read McCall's thoughts about putting a hole in each.

Stefan pointed to a panel in the bottom of the kitchen island area.

"It's called a priest hole. They used..."

"I know what they are, mate. And your man, there is no priest. So where does it go?"

"He's my brother and no mate of mine. It heads into a set of tunnels. They were built during the Second World War. He built the kitchen around it. Said it would come in handy one day. He's used it a lot since then to escape various people."

"Such as?"

"Police. The taxman. Competitors. Criminals. Angry girlfriends..."

"Funny guy. So I have no chance of finding him?"

"None. Not once he gets into the city. It is not safe. But we are not safe either. We need to go. Do you have transport?"

"I do."

"I need to get out of here. To get to London. I need to see someone in the city – someone very important. They need to know what Alex is planning, and I can only do that in person. I trust no one in Bucharest anymore. Alex has seen to that. This is of national level importance to Britain. You are British services, yes? Military?"

"Shut up. Just belt up will you before I shoot you, anyway."

Stefan was the bigger of the two, but knew when he was outclassed by a man who exuded training and skill.

"You really expect me to believe that you are connected to the British government?"

"I do." His eyes fixed on McCall. There was no telltale sideways glance. His non-verbals were spot on.

McCall scratched his head, "Mate, I was just coming here to sell a document for a few hundred thousand dollars. That was the plan anyway. Gone now. A lot of hard work and risk down the gurgler."

Stefan's mind began to engage on what this man had just said. The way he had handled himself was impressive. If he wasn't police, he was definitely ex-military. Men like that always had a bearing, a sense of assuredness.

"I think I could be on your side. But I need something from you to show me I'm not deluded." McCall continued, pointing the Glock at Stefan with one hand and checking the wound with the other. He would live.

"Truce?" Stefan put the last of the weapons down, a short-handled paring knife. He raised his hands slowly. "OK partner, don't shoot. Seriously." He spoke in English with a heavy and affected American accent.

"I think we might be on the same side too. But I need to know who you are before I make that decision. You haven't shot me yet, so this is good – if you were one of my brother's men, I would be dead. Police, possibly. Bulgarian Intelligence..." He threw his hands up in the air.

"I don't know anymore. But I know we need to go soon. Those police down there, they'll start searching the building soon and they know where Alex's apartment is. Right now, I reckon we have minutes."

"Trust me, I bloody well feel like shooting you. I've got fifteen left and I can change a magazine and start firing quicker than you can tell me your name and date of birth. So tell me who the hell are you?"

"I am Stefan Stefanescu. I am not armed. I give you my word. I am Alex's brother. The man you foolishly thought you could negotiate with. He would have killed you as soon as you had the money."

"You think? He didn't do a very good job of defending himself here. I could have shot him if I was a contract killer. His thugs outside lasted seconds."

"So, are you British, come to rescue me from my brother?"

"Kind of depends. British, no, British trained, yes. Did you need rescuing?"

"As it happens yes. So I will guess that you are on my side. If anyone asks, you did a great job. But you are alone? That is not normal."

"I am. Don't ask. I'm not normal by any normal yardstick. It's a longer story than yours. And right now with a gaping hole in my leg, no prisoner to interrogate and an empty bank balance, I'm feeling a long way from home, far from normal and very much out of pocket."

"So how can I help you?"

"Work out our next move and find a first aid kit."

Hobbling around the lounge, McCall headed back to the main door and dragged a chair into place, hoping it would give him time to think. He was right. They would be searching the building anytime soon.

Stefanescu smiled. "You barricade the door. I'll work out our escape route." He was already opening the priest's hole. "Tell me, do you have a name?"

"You can call me Mack."

"And you know my name, of course. One last question."

"Go ahead."

"Do you still have the documents?"

How did he know? Of course, he had mentioned it earlier, so no point in lying. Rookie mistake.

"I do. Do you want them? If as you say you are important to the British government? From what I have read, they may as well go to a good home. I want to get rid of the damned things. They are a poisoned chalice."

"More than you could ever imagine, Mack. So much more. Their value lies not in their content, but the damage that they could achieve as a whole set. My brother has a set, the British government has a set, and you hold the Royal Flush."

"Quite literally, from what I read in there. Literally down the pan."

"Quite. Do you trust me to take them from you? I can deliver them. You can't just walk up the British Home Office and say 'hello, anybody want these?' But I will help you, make sure you can return to wherever it is you came from on your conquest – and hopefully a little better off. Deal?"

It was his one and only integrity test. "No questions..."

"You've got yourself a deal. Ready?" The main door was well barricaded, giving them a few extra minutes. He tossed a field dressing and a bandage, it spun through the air, caught in his left hand.

He dropped his trousers. More vulnerable than ever. He pushed the pad into the small hole and wrapped the bandage around his upper leg. It would suffice until he could have a proper look or get to a friendly hospital where he could make up a story.

"Ready?"

"As I'll ever be Stefan."

"Before we go, there is something on the fireplace that you might wish to take with you. I saw nothing." He put his hands up to his eyes.

McCall looked around. Was this the trap? He had to trust him at some point. He considered it his next test. Now he and the man he could have easily shot were about to exist on what Mike Steel referred to as the level playing field. He fully expected to turn back and find the multi-coloured eyes of Stefan Stefanescu no longer staring at him, but gone, down the priest hole along with their host. It was like Alice in Wonderland, but without the fairy tale ending.

"Mate, I have some weird shit in my house, but I think even I draw the line at a polar bear's head. Besides, where I come from, the biosecurity guys are red hot. I'd never get that over the border."

"Look closer." Stefan was discreetly looking out of the window.

"Coal? Come on mate, we haven't got time for this?"

"Well, similar, coal is compressed carbon. Look to the right of the bear, there, in the carpet. Grab as many as you can. We leave in one minute. They will be here very soon."

With the Glock holstered, McCall was able to move more freely. He lowered himself down on his decent leg. "Holy Mother of God. Where did these come from?"

"Precisely, or literally?"

"Either."

"Best you don't ask. But he stored them inside the bear's head. They came out during the fight you so rudely interrupted."

"They real?"

"As real as they come. On that, I do not need challenging. Thirty seconds to go."

McCall had the gift horse saying flying around his head. But it was theft. But stealing from a thief, to give to the poor. Even Robin Hood would approve. And he could donate some to charity. The kid's hospital, back home. Decision made.

"Fifteen seconds." There were footsteps approaching, fast.

He had picked up twelve from within the deep pile of the carpet when the first thump of the door rang out. The Big Red Key was being used, and he knew they'd be through in no time at all.

Twelve diamonds? Couple of hundred thousand dollars. That was all he wanted. Called it quits at fourteen. Pushed them into his deepest pocket. Then one more, a pretty blue one, calling out to him; one for luck.

"I'm coming." He ran to the hatch, scanning rapidly, ensuring he'd left nothing behind.

He climbed into the hatch and stopped.

"Will they follow us? If we go I need to know I can get away and never be caught."

"I cannot guarantee it, but if we go now, we may have a chance. Come on! Unless you have a way to slow them down?"

"As it happens, brother, I just might."

He smiled, thought of his sisters, patted his pocket to make sure his future was financially secure, and then produced the pink TH3 incendiary grenade from his jacket. His Hungarian friend had been wise indeed. It was his last offensive weapon, and he knew it gave him at least thirty seconds of cover. Now or never.

If it performed like all the others he had used Alex's beloved apartment would soon be engulfed in flames; the jewels, cash, animal heads, flags and all of the secrets that lined the walls, the tales of greed and cruelty. Gone.

There was a risk that any subsequent investigation found the grenade, but they were plentiful and any forensic evidence would be destroyed in the first few seconds as the device burned to its peak at around four thousand degrees Fahrenheit.

Stefan looked at the pink canister. "Will it keep them away for a while? We need a few minutes."

He actioned the grenade then tossed it towards the door. Hopefully the small explosion and smoke would give the police a clue that evacuating would be their best plan.

"This little beauty will burn through steel, underwater. So yep, I reckon it will. Say bye to the flat. Hope you've left nothing behind of value?"

"Well, I..." It was far too late.

It hit the floor, tink, tink, tink, bang.

The grenade erupted, discharging screaming hot chemicals which ignited everything in their path. It was highly impressive. An arsonists dream.

"Oh Jesus, that felt good. Come on Lone Ranger, Tonto wants to head back to the ranch."

He lowered himself into the small doorway and down four steps, which opened out into a narrow passageway. Stefan was sealing the door behind them, locking it from inside.

"Let's go Mack." They shook hands.

"Last chance for your share of the diamonds, mate. I can go back."

He smiled. "No, I have exactly what I want."

He led the way along the carved tunnel, following the dimly lit bulbs that had served as a guide since the war.

"When we get the end, I will need you to check for any traps. I trust my brother about as far as I could kick that polar bear's head."

"Yep, copy that. You just lead the way. I will be right behind you. I'm parked two streets away. Where does this tunnel exit?"

"Into a park. There is an old gate. Don't worry, I have the key. When we get to the car, we need to head north."

"To the airport?"

"No, that cannot be our way back. We need to drive. I am on every watch list there is in this country. Alex, too. But I think he is already heading to a private airstrip. He has a woman that flies him anywhere. No questions asked."

"Can we get to the airstrip before him? Cut out the middleman?"

It was an idea. He remembered the last time he had travelled in her aircraft. She did a good job, but there was something about her that he didn't trust.

"The pilot is a woman. Called Maria Anghel. I haven't

seen her for a while, many years in fact. She is like an iceberg."

"What do you mean? To look at?" It was an unusual description. To McCall an iceberg was thirty: seventy in its ratio. So he could only assume one thing.

"Maria's got small tits and a massive arse then?"

"No." He laughed as they made their way along the tunnel. "She is cool, very calm, calculating. Best pilot I have ever met. There was a time when she landed a plane on a runway that was way too short. Anyway, she has four planes now. Makes a living above the radar, but keeps one of her aircraft for special stuff."

"You mean like helping your brother escape?"

"Exactly like that. And she charges, like the wounded buffalo."

"Then how else do we get to London?"

"We drive."

"I've got a rental car. At some point it needs to go back."

"Did you hire it on your credit card?"

"Not my credit card exactly, no..."

"So you are a thief too?"

"Hardly. I'm one of the good guys. Look, we can exchange notes on the way, if as you say we've got to drive then we have at least a day to get to know each other."

"We will be at the end of this tunnel in a hundred metres. Quiet now."

The light was changing. As they got closer to the entrance to the tunnel the bulbs extinguished, now they felt their way to the old grid that sat across the gateway to what the local kids had long said was a secret Nazi underground bunker.

Stefan approached cautiously, the gate was open, left ajar, clearly his brother was in a hurry. They could both hear sirens approaching, closer now. Fire and ambulance, red lights, blue lights, strobes, ricocheting off the walls and into the night sky.

McCall drew his weapon and held it in front of him, did a sweep behind, checking they weren't being followed, then carried on, up on his toes now. Nice and quiet.

They got to the gateway and squeezed through the gap, closing the gate behind them. Stefan pushed the sizeable padlock back through the opening and clicked it shut.

"Which way?"

The club was to their left, McCall was completely disorientated now. He got his bearings and pointed right. "Up there, on the left, the Hyundai. Christ, look at that."

He pointed back to the club, which was engulfed in flames. The innocent-looking pink canister had a set of teeth after all.

Both men tried to blend into the foot traffic, some of which resembled nightclub patrons, fleeing the scene. Others were heading to the fire to see what the commotion was. The whole neighbourhood had turned out to watch the demise of a man they quietly hated.

The chaos suited the two men who walked at a pace to the boring looking car.

Within hours, the club would be all but destroyed. Investigators would say, days later, that the seat of the fire was in the owner's apartment, however they had found no evidence of foul play – or a body. Alex Stefanescu was reported as being missing, which surprised no one, least of all the man that had been sent to hunt him down.

"Well, now what boss?"

Grig scratched what was left of his hair, flicked a cigarette into the smouldering wreck that was once Byzantin and said, "Two options. We do nothing and get new instructions for a different operation or we convince the bosses that the Jackdaw is worth putting into a cage – forever."

"Where do we start?"

"I have an idea. Anyone fancy a coffee?"

It seemed an odd invitation – until their boss walked up to the counter, ordered four Americano and started asking questions.

"Australian? How do you know that?"

"He told me."

"And you believe him?"

The boy laughed. "No, sir. He was from New Zealand."

This was new information, call it intelligence. Whatever it was, it was a start and long overdue. They had missed an opportunity, and he knew it. Best keep that one to the team. What goes on tour...

He sipped the hot black liquid, which gave him an instant lift.

"So tell me, why would you think that?" He was smiling, for this was not an interrogation.

"Because he had a piece of greenstone around his neck, on a leather strap."

Grig looked at the boy, blowing on his coffee to cool it a little, watching the last of the flames being doused, across the road at was left of the once iconic club.

"You have lost me."

"The Aussies don't wear it, greenstone, it's a New Zealand thing. It is a very special stone to them. You don't buy it for yourself, has to be a gift. Has real meaning to the people."

"Maori?"

"Yes, sir."

"And do you think he was a Maori?"

"Sir I don't know, but I think he was a soldier. My

brother is, so something told me he was too. Did he die in the fire? I didn't see him coming out."

"I Sir,don't think so no. But you could identify him?"

"Yes, of course. I have a very good memory for faces. Your colleague there, the one with the beard. I've seen him four times this week going into the house over there. I don't miss anything."

"You don't do you." He held up his cell phone, showing him the face of a man, captured by a telephoto lens, grainy but easily identified.

"That him?"

"Yes. One hundred percent. He has a good man."

"Why do you say that?"

"Just the way he spoke to me. I know the difference. When you work for the Jackdaw, you know."

"I'm sure you do. Well done, my friend. Here, you keep the change. If I need to find you, you will be here?"

"I have no idea, sir. With the club gone and the boss too, who will pay my wages now? I will probably move on."

Grig turned to Vasile, his most junior officer. "Hey, he spotted you four times. You can stay behind and get a statement off him. I want everything in there, especially the part about the Kiwi soldier boy."

Grig shook the young man's hand. "Thank you. You have been most helpful. Any questions?"

"Only one. Who gets to drive that?" He pointed across at the Bentley.

"Actually, I do. We will be seizing it, along with whatever is left behind. Pity the keys are somewhere in that lot!" He pointed to the club.

"Can I have his brother's car then? It's an AMG. With the right tools, I can start it."

As he had finished the sentence, the first floor of the nightclub moaned and creaked, then groaned and collapsed, sending a dust cloud across the street and debris onto the late model German saloon. The Mercedes alarm began to fill the street with its high decibel chant as the street disappeared in a blanket of dust and debris.

"Be my guest. If you have the keys, take it!" It was at that point that Grig stopped in his tracks.

"Dear God." He ground his knuckles until they whitened. "Stupid idiot. Where is his brother?" He dropped his empty polystyrene cup into the bin, thinking on his feet. Moving backwards and forwards like an expectant father. He turned to his second in command.

"Speak to the Fire Brigade. I want to know the minute they find anything. A body. Bodies. Firearms. Anything. In the meantime, get onto the control room and have Alex and Stefan circulated as wanted. I want Artur Gheorghiu found too. Bring him in as quickly as you can. And any other thugs that hang around with him."

His phone rang. He tucked it under his jaw and started a monosyllabic conversation. He picked the cup out of the bin and gestured to the coffee boy for a refill. He cleared the call and pocketed the phone.

"I want to find this mystery man. Very soon."

"You assume he's a bad guy, boss?" It was a fair question from Tomas.

"It seems a little too convenient that he arrives and the gates of hell are opened. Do you not agree?"

"Your call, sir. Anything else?"

"Do we have a friend in New Zealand?"

"I doubt it, sir. It's so far away."

"Then make one. Tonight. They must have an ops centre over there, or an Interpol office. We have to start somewhere."

"I will make it happen, boss. I need to head back to the office."

"Go. And get the image of the New Zealander out there, too. I want to know who he is and why he was in my city. If he's a soldier, then that changes things. Ex-soldier is different. Send his image to the Kiwis. I hear they have a successful team over there. Small population, easier to find the bad guy. Worst case, he's a good guy who has got involved in something. Equally, I need to know."

An hour later, Vasile Dumitru was speaking to an officer at Interpol Wellington. It was a warm and harbour-sparkling day in the New Zealand capital. The man that answered the phone wished he had that view, instead he looked out at a grey concrete car park wall and prayed that his team would soon move to the top floor.

"Hello John Ashton, how can I help?"

The Romanian officer outlined what he wanted and agreed to email the request from Interpol's Bucharest office. It was how the organisation worked.

"Sounds interesting. Unfortunately, we only ever hear about your people when they come here to steal from banks."

"Yes, and for that I apologise. There are an awful lot of people in my country sir, please do not think that they are all bad. The group you refer to is but a tiny part of our population."

"Of course, just seems that the awful ones ruin your reputation. Look, what you've told me is interesting, kind of borders onto military police territory. But we'll do our level best to help you. We know a lot of people in the Land of the Long White Cloud."

"Thank you, sir. Oh, one last question. Does the name Alex Stefanescu mean anything to you?"

"No, not me personally. Should it?"

"I don't know, but can you look at your system, see if he ever entered New Zealand, either him or his brother Stefan."

"Of course, that's easy. Get that request sent and I'll deal with it personally."

Grig was now back at the office in central Bucharest. His desk phone chirped into life.

"Sir. Fire Investigators have found two bodies in the hallway. Badly burned, but both neither have gunshot wounds. Looks like it was the two doormen. I guess the pathologist will tell us how they died. Possibly smoke inhalation."

"Anything else?"

"The apartment fire was caused by a fierce heat. The source is by the main entrance door."

"No other bodies? Nothing?"

"No, sir. Our targets are not in the building. We think Gheorghiu escaped with the crowd. As for Alex and his brother and our Tourist One target. No idea. Sorry."

"OK, thanks. I need you to be creative. This tourist, this Kiwi, had balls of steel to walk into the lion's den and start demanding. I want to know what he wanted. He was clever in the way he got information from our coffee boy, so he's a pro. Keep asking. Someone will talk now the Jackdaw has flown his nest. If it takes money, offer it."

CHAPTER THIRTY-THREE

THE HYUNDAI JOINED THE MOTORWAY AND STARTED ITS journey north. McCall wished he had rented a more powerful car – seeing as though he wasn't intending to return it. He offered his newfound partner a stale muesli bar. It was all he'd eaten in days, so why should he be the only one to suffer?

"Are they nice?"

"No. Fucking awful brother, has the texture of damp sand and the taste of rotten apples. But I've eaten a lot worse and it will keep you going until we reach France – or at least somewhere friendly."

"Where is friendly?"

"My guess is northern Europe, but right now we could be in the top three most wanted for all I bloody know. I should have just taken on an overdraft. Would have been easier."

Stefan knew that ahead lay Hungary, Austria, Germany and Belgium. They had a long haul before they reached Calais.

"It's two and half thousand klicks to London mate. Can we not just fly? In fact, why do I even need to come with you?" McCall asked the obvious questions in a no-nonsense style which appealed to Stefanescu.

"I know how far it is. And the answer is no. The minute I try to get on a plane, I will attract the wrong attention. As for you, well, you are involved now. The Brits will want to talk to you."

"But I could do that over the phone. I need to head home."

"Look, new friend of mine, you cannot head home. I need you to help us hunt down my brother. I've seen you operate. It's a long and boring story, but it starts with a pretty girl in a faraway country, in a fast car, on a quiet road. And I think it ends with you, Mr Bushman."

"What makes you say that?"

"Because there was no other way you could have got those documents before I did, unless you spent more time in the car with her?"

"I have no idea what you are on about mate."

"Oh, but you do. You are one of the good guys, Mack. I think you saved her. And then temptation got the better of you. The first and only time. However, you saved her and for that I owe you."

"Say I did. Why was this girl so important to you?"

"This girl? Her name is Elena. She is my niece."

"Was your niece?"

"Still is."

"She's alive?" McCall braked instinctively, veering slightly to the side of the road. He was now very much alert, awake, back in that upturned sports car, feeling for a pulse, admiring the view and willing her to wake.

"Yes. She is. And this is where it gets difficult. She doesn't know that I know. But I suspect she knows that I tried to kill her."

"Jesus mate, what sort of animal does that?"

"This type of animal, Mack. It is what the Americans call the long game. And between you and me, I wish I had never started playing it. I blame that weasel that ran down the tunnel before we did. You should have shot him in the head. Shame you can't shoot."

He spent the next hour talking through his life over the previous ten years, summarising where necessary, developing, but never embellishing.

"So you trust me? You understand why I did what I did. Now you know a bit more about Elena, perhaps it will help. If you had been minutes earlier the day of the crash, we would have met on your soil and things might have worked out differently. My people believe in fortune and perhaps it will be good for both of us in the end."

"Of course. The only problem is, I told myself I would find her one day. Hold her hand again and ask her if she was OK."

"I wouldn't advise you to do that. Elena is the prettiest girl I have ever seen, but she comes with..." He gazed through the windscreen at a few spots of rain. "She comes with baggage. And she is dangerous if you don't know how to handle her."

"I wouldn't mind trying."

"Plenty of men before you have thought the same. She is spoken for. A British man. She was sent to get information from him, and important to give him something. She did the first part beautifully. That was until she fell in love with him."

"Not in the plan?" McCall had her in his mind's eye as he tried to concentrate on heading north at a speed that would reduce the twenty-six hour drive but not attract attention.

"No. Not at all. You see Nikolina, the woman I told you about? She was sent on a covert operation, at a young age. That mission was to kill my brother. A government in a foreign country sent a girl to do a man's job. Then she went to England to seek out a person, a friend she trusted, and to gain asylum. But that didn't work either. It all changed when Alex tracked her down and decided to drown her in the Thames. It was more about a statement than the act itself His men took her from under the noses of the British, who swore an oath to protect her. I am ashamed to say I was there for that too. I organised it." He rubbed his eyes, blinked a few times. There was a tear there.

"This whole mess has nothing to do with a couple of women, a career criminal and the British government. It all started years ago. The Bulgarians, the Russians and my people, even some of the conventional Western nations. Everyone wanted to get their hands on a set of papers that had been stolen. You would say a hot potato. We have our own phrase. Only the originals were worth anything, like a work of art. We are talking blackmail at international level, Mack."

Mack was nodding enthusiastically "Worth millions I guess?

"Not millions, not billions. Their value was in the power and influence that they provided. You have no idea of the possibilities. Power over a nation and the potential to divide Europe."

"Like the stuff of spy novels?" McCall unwrapped another muesli bar with one hand and ate it in two bites.

"But real. Imagine you are a former Soviet-ruled country and you need to move people around, divide up wealth and create strongholds in other countries. You can either do it illegally over twenty years or legally in a week. The plan was to allow countries such as Romania, Bulgaria and a few others to join the European Union. It would give them overnight visa free status across most Western nations. The ability to move their people around, further too, Canada,

Australia, even your country. In doing so, it would free up jobs and houses and remove the burden on our crumbling welfare states. Get Britain to pay for that, too. It also opened up the borders to opportunists like my big brother."

"Why didn't the Brits just put a team together and hunt down the perpetrators? Seems easy."

"You tell me. Perhaps they didn't want to advertise the fact that the politicians that ran the country were so corrupt that they were prepared to sell their people down the river. So, you see, it is not as easy as you might think. The monarchy in Britain had no idea, still don't. The people, again, not a clue or there would be riots against immigrants and capitalism, and the industrial chiefs – the ones who keep the United Kingdom profitable? No, not them either."

"That's a real mess. Makes my problems seem miniscule."

"You have problems?"

"I did." He tapped his pocket. "Now all I have to figure out how to convert these to cash and why I need to come to London with you."

Stefanescu smiled, he was as tired as McCall and knew he should take over the driving soon. "That's just it, Mack. You don't. We stop at the next service station, I drive onto Calais. You say you were robbed and the local police will help you. Then you can head home. But something tells me you came on this journey for another reason. And she has red hair."

He had a point.

"By the way. I chose not to shoot your brother in the head. For tactical reasons. I could have emptied the magazine into him in a few seconds. I needed to speak to him. Now, I wish I had shot him between the eyes."

"Me too." Stefan crumpled the muesli wrapper and dropped it into the footwell. "You are right about one thing, Mack. These muesli bars are horrible."

"So ungrateful! You can buy breakfast."

"OK, it's a deal. I will, I don't think you should offer to buy two breakfasts with a blue diamond." He smiled. "Wake me when you've had enough of the driving."

"Roger that." He wished he had taken the car with cruise control too. All he had to do now was stay awake. He hadn't slept properly in three days. The signs weren't good.

As the Hyundai sped north McCall got comfortable, propping his right shoulder into the door pillar. He'd taken a knock somewhere in the previous few hours. Scanning ahead, watching behind. Deliberating, trying to understand what the hell he had got himself involved in.

The car behind caught his eye. A silver, older model BMW, 5 series at a guess. Kidney-shaped grill, mid-2000s. Amateurs living in a big boy's world.

McCall accelerated gently, up to one hundred and ten kilometres an hour. The BMW matched his speed. He slowed to seventy again, subtly. Once more the silver car slowed. There was only one thing to do. It was late, and they were still a long way from the Hungarian border crossing area. Stefan had been very specific. Turn left well before for the town of Nadiac. 'We must avoid the border.'

He was programmed to always follow instructions and wished he was now about to navigate through the quiet streets of the border town. For him border meant guards and that in turn meant guns. But they were a long way from that level of civilisation. The next built-up area was a small city called Pitesti, and it was where, according to the map that McCall squinted to read, they had a chance to take control of the situation. He came off the main highway and started to circumvent the small city.

With the street lighting now more prominent, he could see the BMW had followed and could easily make out four occupants. Far from ideal.

He slowed, indicated, and then pulled onto a petrol station forecourt.

Stefan woke. "We need petrol already? Or more muesli bars?"

"Neither." The calm way McCall answered actually concerned his passenger more than him having a concerned tone to his voice.

"What's wrong?"

"We may have company. Been with us most of the way. On and off, slowing when I do, accelerating as I accelerate. Let's just see if they need petrol, shall we? Give 'em the benefit of the doubt. Perhaps they were just avoiding the border post too."

"OK. Doesn't look like cops. Do you have a plan?"

"I do. But not in a town of this size. Too many eyes, even at this time of night. Cameras, too. We want to make it to Calais unscathed."

He pulled to a stop, checked the fuel gauge and knew that with half a tank they had enough to get to the next stop. "Ready?"

"Yes, but I still don't know the plan."

"It's called Operation See How She Goes." He smiled, checked the whereabouts of his Glock in the door compartment and wished Stefan had one too.

As soon as he had stopped, he accelerated again, off the forecourt in front of a small delivery truck, and began to head north west again. Within thirty seconds, the BMW was behind them.

"It's official. We have some admirers. Not even Lewis Hamilton can re-fill that quickly."

"OK, so now what?"

"You tell me, they are either Alex's men or the police. I suspect the police would have stopped us a hundred klicks nearer to their home. So my plan is to get to a rural location, then we go for what I call an up close and personal introduction, or as it's called in the manual of guidance, The Hard Stop. Either that or we hightail it to the Hungarian border and claim asylum!"

"If only. The border post may not be manned. We are outnumbered."

"Never. Not my motto, mate. Who dares and all that."

Stefan had no idea what he was talking about, but agreed to go along for the ride.

"Fifteen minutes ought to do it according to my map."

"What do I do?"

"When we stop, I need you to do exactly as I say. That way it will look more convincing."

CHAPTER THIRTY-FOUR

On the north Kent coastline, Carrie and Lucy Thomas also had company. He had been there for a while, loitering in the doorway, watching, deciding who should go first.

He pushed a makeshift stool along the floor. It screeched across the old concrete. That and nails down the face of a blackboard was enough to get her really on edge.

"Hello you two. It's been a while. Have you had a good day? You must be hungry?"

He spooned cold curry up to O'Shea's lips. She was so hungry she ate it. She knew if she had any chance of survival, let along escape, she needed to keep her energy levels up.

He switched on a portable spot lamp.

"There, that's better, now I can see you both."

He ignored Thomas completely. Constantin had decided that his old lover needed to die in a way that humiliated her, he just didn't know how. In order to do that, he needed to keep her alive too.

"Here." He pushed a tablespoon of the dark red curry

into Thomas' mouth, then another, and one more. Then turned to O'Shea and offered another spoonful, with some congealed rice. It tasted like nectar.

She took the water he offered, in gulps, voraciously consuming it. Thomas, too. They were both dehydrated and were beginning to smell worse than the gelatinous curry.

"I think it is bath time for you two lovely people. I'll be back in five."

O'Shea managed to crane her neck towards Thomas.

"You OK?"

"No, not really. I'm bloody terrified. He's lost it. What is he doing? Why doesn't he just get rid of us? I am of no value to him. You are, but not me. He's just playing games."

"Just be strong. People will be looking for us. I know they will. We've been missing too long now."

"But how will they find us? I have no idea where we are let alone the police. This really isn't good. Shh he's coming back."

It was a fair point. Carrie could only guess where they were. As it happened, her guess was incredibly accurate.

Constantin was back with a bucket of water. He cupped his hands into the warm liquid and scooped it onto O'Shea's body, washing her down, almost worshipfully, taking time to cleanse every part of her, slowly, deliberately. It was far from arousing. She actually wanted to retch. He had always been bi-curious, and her body was a thing of beauty. She wasn't a supermodel, but she had a figure that he could best describe as a study by the famous artist Titian. Probably a little more voluptuous.

He could also find beauty in the male physique – if backed into a corner it would be the latter he found more arousing. But Carrie was attractive and he could admire her for a while. She was his to admire, after all.

He placed two bricks under the feet of the table, tilting it slightly, allowing the water to run off and down the drain.

More soap, again, gently rubbed into her naked torso, up and over her breasts and into her neck, gently washing away the stench of days of neglect.

Then he rinsed her hair, added soap, massaged her scalp, quietly humming a tune to himself which neither prisoner recognised. Then he scooped more of the warm water onto her head, cleaning out every last remnant of soap until her hair squeaked under his fingertips.

O'Shea couldn't help thinking that as a psychopathic kidnapper he would have also made a great hairdresser. She could have almost relaxed.

"There. How is that Caroline?" He used her full name to great effect.

She said nothing.

"I said, how is that?"

"Fine."

"Fine, what? Did your parents not teach you nothing?"

"It's did your parents not teach you anything." Defiant as always.

"Whatever, English is not my first language, Caroline."

"And only my mother calls me Caroline."

"Called. Past tense. She is dead. So, how was dinner tonight?"

"It was divine. Best curry I have ever eaten. A bit cool for my liking but scrumptious nonetheless."

"Good. Then there is dessert for you."

He produced a can of what looked like whipped cream.

"It's OK I have had enough thank you."

"Oh, but this is not what you think it is. Do you think I am weird?"

"No comment, Constantin Nicolescu." Anything you can do...

"No, this is shaving foam. It's time to tidy you up for the cameras."

Her mind was whirring. A hundred miles an hour in one direction, two hundred in the other. 'No, No. No!'

"Look, whatever you want with us, just do it quickly. Please."

"But dear Caroline, no one knows where you are. Not even you, with all your analytical training. So there really is no rush. Shout. Scream. Call for Cynthia. No, wait, she is probably floating down the river as we speak, on the night tide, unless she sinks and gets trapped beneath a log or something."

"I cannot cry any more tears. So just do your worst."

"I suspect you can. Anyway, I must get on, time is money. I just need to finish a little message that was started many years ago. A little love letter to Mr Cade."

She stared at him blankly. "You've lost me."

"Me too," said Thomas, earning a slap full across the face, then a punch, driven deep into the groin. It would keep her quiet for a while.

"Remember when Alex sent a man into your home all those years ago? He cut a line into your neck and a curl from your pretty hair and mailed it to your lover boy?"

"How could I forget?"

"Well, I would have done a better job."

"You mean like the one you did when you tried to poison me, you sick bastard."

"That would have worked, but for the knight in his shining armour. I watched him arrive, you know. Watched him run to be by your side. I just got the mixture wrong."

She said nothing.

"No, you see, I need to send a message to the men in your life once more. Alex told me I could play with you for a while, but he was very specific. He wants to distract your team, so he can get on with his final operation in your beautiful, overcrowded city. That is why you are here."

He inhaled slowly. "It is not personal. If the team are looking for you, and putting out our fires, they will have no time to see what is going on, under their pretty little noses." He held the tip of his nose up with his index finger.

As he laughed, he ran the scissors down her body, removed a patch of lustrous hair and placed it into the bag. He laid the scissors onto the table then sprayed the first of the white foam onto her stomach, drawing a smiley face before massaging it with his fingers until it covered her stomach and down into her hips before finally spreading it into and over the dark brown pubic patch.

"Bear with me, I have never done this before." He smirked, producing a gleaming cut-throat razor, turning it into the path of the bright light, admiring the clinical edge as the reflection lit the darkest corners of the room.

He gently ran his finger against the grain.

"Ouch. So sharp."

The first scrape was clean. He teased the hair up and allowed the blade to do its job. He flicked his hand at the end of the stroke, deftly, almost as a concert pianist finishes a note. The first cut left a smooth track of skin between the dark brown margins. Again he slid the blade against her flesh. She laid completely still. Now, she was quietly panicking.

Thomas spoke. "Please Constantin, there is no need for this. For any of this. Just let her go. Do what you like with me."

"Oh, but I intend to. She is part of my strategy. You are a plaything for my amusement. Shut up now, you have said enough, unless you wish me to slip?"

He had removed three strips of hair now, dropping them onto the concrete. He was, to be fair, adept with the blade.

In minutes she was cleanly shaven. He rinsed her off, with real empathy, as if he knew it was a highly personal thing to do to her. Then, just as gently, he patted her down with a towel. Then ran his nose along her torso, inhaling.

"Lovely. Now you look and smell so much sweeter." He took a photo. "Smile."

He then ran a length of tape across her neck and under the table, wrapping it until it stuck to itself. She was going nowhere.

He cut the tape from her head and pulled it quickly, causing her to yelp as it clutched at smaller hairs but allowed him access to her head.

"Now, for the best part." He walked around the table and produced a set of scissors. He held them expertly, lifting the first strand of her precious hair up and between his middle fingers, cutting as if he did it for a living. She could hear the blades sliding against each other, rhythmically removing sections of her hair, which was being carefully collected.

Ten minutes later he had removed all of her lustrous curls. She now had a basic military-style cut. It was the ultimate insult as far as she was concerned. How did he know she prized it so much?

He put the hair into a plastic zip-lock bag and sealed it.

"A present for Jack and Jason. They will be so thrilled. DNA will show it is you and they will know you are alive. Or rather, you were when I removed it. Can they tell how long a person has been dead from their hair?" He thought for a while. "Interesting subject. Something to read about next time I am in a prison library."

"You could have taken one hair and sent it, you sadist twat."

"Well, that is hardly very kind, Miss O'Shea. A haircut like this in London would cost you hundreds and I haven't finished yet."

He wet her scalp and squirted more of the soap onto it, rubbing it vigorously with his fingertips.

"Dear God, no." O'Shea began to cry. He wiped the tears away, licking one. "Salty, we must be by the sea!"

The blade slid across her scalp, inch by perfect inch until she was bald, almost shiny. It was strangely rather attractive. It was as if he had removed the last of her strength, her dignity and her fight.

Two small cuts were tended to until they stopped bleeding.

He took another photo.

"OK, last time. Smile."

He took one from above her. The flash lit up the room. Then one up between her legs, capturing her breasts and chin in the same shot. Then he swapped to the other end of the table and obtained one from her head to her toes.

He ran his hand over her head, down her cheek, across her neck, held his hand against her windpipe, watched her eyes bulge, then pinched her nostrils shut with his spare hand. Waited. Then smiled as she hauled air into her lungs.

His hands continued to explore her, up and over her breasts. He drew a line across her stomach, walked his fingers down towards the newly smooth part of her body, circled around her, then down her thighs to her feet.

Lastly, he licked the sole of her foot, marvelling at how it tightened under his touch. Just in the middle, curling the toes.

"Isn't the human being a wonderful thing, Caroline?"

She didn't answer.

"I asked you a question." He placed the cut throat blade on her stomach, handle pointing up to her face.

"Yes. It is. Now, have you finished your sick game?"

"I am simply shocked that you think this was a game. This was to make you feel better. You were dirty and I know how compulsive you are. Your bathroom was a thing of beauty, all the bottles lined up in a row. The mirror. Oh, so clean. The towels, straight, not a stray hair in the shower tray or that lovely deep bath. And your underwear drawer, lined with paper and a sprig of fresh lilac. So pretty. You see, I know what my customer wants. You will feel *so* much better."

He pulled a sad face. "Or, if you are unhappy with the service, then please complain to the manager."

"No. It's fine."

"Good. You do understand what I have just done, don't you, my dear girl?"

"Given me a great haircut?"

He smiled a splintered smile.

"No. I have deliberately and expertly humiliated you." He tapped her below the right knee, watching her reflexes remonstrate. "Marvellous. Simply marvellous. You can relax now. It's your turn, Lucy."

He gave a look that said he hadn't slept well in days and had bottled up years of hatred that he now needed an outlet for. And she was it.

"Lucy, Lucy, Lucy. Such a lovely name. For a *woman*. But you are something else entirely. I mean, look, there it is. We can all see it. Small and insignificant though it is. Cold, are you?"

"Yes, I am freezing. Please, we were such friends. Be kind to us."

"Again, past tense. In the past. And now very tense!" His knowledge of English shocked his audience, but they forgot he had spent a lot of time reading, and alone.

He rubbed his fingers along the soles of Thomas' feet too, gaining the same reaction.

"Aren't feet strange, Carrie? I am not a foot person, but they are a remarkable contraption. Hideous things, but we are lost without them. Unable to run away. Would you agree?"

"Yes, feet are strange."

"Have you heard of Bastinado?"

"Other than when people refer to you? No."

"Such wittiness. Then watch as I educate you." He picked up a cane. Ran the tip over Lucy's feet, making them squirm. She was obviously ticklish. Then Constantin struck the soles with a vicious blow.

"*That* is bastinado!" The sound was similar to a high velocity rifle shot, cracking in the air. Then he did it again. "Practiced in many prisons as a form of discipline." He walked around as if presenting a lecture to a group of eager students.

"Very painful, isn't it?"

"Yes." Thomas could hardly speak. And then it came again. And again.

"Happened to me as a child, then in prison. My feet are like granite now. How would you..."

He whipped the soles of Lucy's feet again.

"...describe the pain? Burning? Throbbing? Piercing? I used to find it piercing. Painful, oh yes, very painful. The guards in my first prison used to whip me until I was almost bleeding. Then they would barely touch me and the pain was worse. It has something..." Thwack, he hit her again, harder, right in the middle of the foot. "...to do with the nerves."

He stepped forward and snapped the cane through the air. The tip hit Thomas' genitals, almost tearing a hole in the skin.

"But they say that that is even more painful. Or here..." The cane rushed through the air as he struck Thomas across the nipples.

"Nice, eh? A good feeling. So good to be alive!"

He dropped the cane and grabbed hold of a roll of flesh

above the pubic bone and ripped the hair by the roots. Thomas screamed.

"Please. Can't you do it like you did it to her?"

It was exactly the request he wanted.

"With the razor? Yes, my dear, it would be a privilege. The only problem is..." He yawned as if he were in front of an intimate theatre audience. "The problem is I am so tired and I could slip...at any moment."

He lowered the blade towards the greying-brown hairs and took the first cut. "Et voila! It means there you go."

He threw the hair to the floor, knowing it would be washed away soon. The police would probably empty the drains when they finally found the place, but by then Constantin knew he'd either be a long way away, or dead.

"And another careful cut..." He handled the blade very well, cutting, turning, wiping it on a towel. Then he ran the blade across Lucy's stomach, in a curving, free-form line, creating a scarlet wave.

"That is beautiful. A wave, like the one I have on my wrist. Yours is red, whereas mine is blue. You should see this Carrie, a work of art. I need to get a mirror next time I go shopping."

He then ran the back of the blade up Lucy's body, pausing at her neck, knowing that one cut would end her life. He ran the handle over the Adam's apple just to see the reaction. He raised his eyebrows, indicating a sense of irony. "Such a shame it ended this way."

"No, please Constantin, no, think. Think what you are doing. Please." Lucy was most certainly a male now, no more show business, cross dressing fantasy or roleplaying. He was a naked male, strapped to a makeshift platform in a derelict factory. Nothing more. And he was potentially minutes from death.

"Oh, I am not going to kill you. When you make love to

someone beautiful, the best part is the foreplay. This is the foreplay."

He checked the tightness of duct tape that held his head in place, a tight band across the forehead, wound a few times around the bed. It was simple but effective.

The blade started to cut into the left eyebrow, Thomas felt a combination of nausea and fear, then heat, then cold. He was sweating. His pulse raised. Then he blacked out.

Constantin cut diagonally, downwards, skirting the eye socket and missing the nose, slicing through his lip, which bled profusely, bright red, dripping down and around his neck. Then the lower lip and across his chin.

He carefully placed the blade next to Lucy's right eyebrow and repeated the action. His work was done, for now. Thomas' face was covered in blood, but when it stopped, as it would, he would be left with a perfect red cross on his face.

"I'm done with you. I have crossed you off my list! OK? Time for bed. Let me cover you both up, you look frozen. Imagine how it must feel to live like this for weeks, months, longer? My family members died in the Nazi prison camps... gassed and tortured because they were Romani. Did you know our people were the second largest group to be exterminated because of our ethnicity?"

Carrie knew she needed to engage with him.

"Yes. What they did to your people was terrible. But what you are doing to us, for revenge or whatever your agenda is, it is just as bad. Constantin, I just need you to stop and think. It is just as bad." She had hoped this would somehow plant a seed of doubt in his shattered mind.

He walked around for a while, composing himself.

"Just as bad?" His voice raised, his mouth filling with bile. "My family were at Dachau, Caroline. I was told of one little girl who leaned forward to catch a raindrop in her mouth. She was shot where she stood and left there for days. They took our people's names and replaced them with a number etched into their skin. My uncle told me of a time he saw a door opened by soldiers and a wall of pregnant women and children fell onto the floor. He had no idea how many there were. He was a little boy. He lied about his age so they would put him to work rather than kill him."

"I despise what they did to your people. But you mark yourself now, with that wave tattoo." What she was about to say wasn't without risk. "Isn't that similar?"

"Similar? Forced to stand for days, without food or water, then eventually, thankfully, killed? No. The wave shows I belong to a better group, one that rewards me for who I am, and where I am from."

He picked some old damp blankets from the floor and lovingly tucked both of his prisoners in, kissing them both on the foreheads.

"Goodnight. I am off for a stroll by the river." Then he walked out and switched the portable light off.

O'Shea waited a second, blinking to try to regain her night vision. "You alright?"

There was no reply, just the gentle sound of a broken man sobbing, his tears washing the blood away from his face. Sticky, drying, congealed.

O'Shea continued. "He's lost the plot, Lucy. We have to get out of here soon. I don't know if it's the heroin or just psychosis, but we have to leave. Tonight."

Half a mile away, Constantin's younger team had edged down a bank and lowered Cynthia into the Thames. They couldn't do it quick enough. Touching a body is considered taboo by Romani, connecting to the supernatural, something that is to be avoided.

They turned, but one, the youngest, couldn't take his eyes off the body as it began its last journey, face down along the impressive river; covered in a veil of mist and drifting silently towards the sea.

Cynthia moved gently with the tidal flow before getting stuck in an eddy, which caused her to slowly turn. The men watched, transfixed, as she appeared to come back towards them.

Romani believe that the dead might come back to wreak havoc on the living. Their rituals are massively different to other ethnic groups. They distance themselves from the dead, burning their possessions, asking for forgiveness and concern themselves that should they not make a good impression on the dying or dead, that the spirit will return as a Mulo – what gypsies refer to as the undead.

Their greatest fear is that the spirit may reappear to resolve unpaid debts.

"That woman has a debt to settle. Come on, let's go. Please. We need to go now." The boy's voice was breaking, stammering. It wasn't the cold.

Watching Bell's corpse change direction caused the men to retreat up the bank, one falling, sliding into the river, grabbed by a friend.

"Get me out. Get me out!"

Bell turned over in the frigid river, her face now visible in the partial moonlight. She was staring at the men; her face illuminated, cold eyes open. The water began to cover her face, but they could still see her, just beneath the blackened water. They were unable to look away. Mesmerised.

She began to slide into the depths, her grotesque arm the last thing to disappear below the surface.

And she was gone. For now.

CHAPTER THIRTY-FIVE

THE HYUNDAI TOOK THE NEXT CORNER AT EIGHTY, THE narrow front tyres screaming in protest. Stefan grabbed at the door handle, trying to turn, to look back, fighting against the G-force. They had been driving like this for a few kilometres since McCall had lost them in the town of Pitesti. The BMW was a distant threat for now.

"Where did you learn to drive?"

"New Zealand mate. You can start at fifteen there."

"You can start at that age in Romania."

"But I'm talking legally. I first drove on the old man's farm, everywhere sideways. Then later, I got a licence and when I joined up, they taught me how to drive properly."

"So you are military?"

"Yes, mate. I thought we had established that?"

"By the way you caused havoc back at the nightclub…"

"That was nothing. If my team had been with me…boom!"

Stefan found a moment to smile. He felt that if he had a chance to escape, then it was better to do it alongside this man. For once he pitied his brother, if anyone knew how to outsmart him it might be this mysterious man that had called himself the Bushman.

"So now what?"

"Do as I say, remember? Ready?"

"As I will ever be."

McCall decelerated then eased the handbrake on, causing the little car to skew across the road in an inch-perfect J turn. No brake lights. No other traffic either. It was late, and this was a quiet road. It looked that way on the online map and it was very accurate.

The car came to a halt across the road, facing the way it had just come from, straddling the white centreline, lights on full beam.

"Get out and lie down on the road, by the driver's door. Facedown. And don't move, even if they shoot you." Stefan did as he was told, but he was not sure he would ever appreciate the Kiwi soldier's humour.

"OK, I think they are coming. A little way off, but that's a car travelling at speed. Stand by."

Stefan called back but McCall was gone, into the trees, running as fast as he could, avoiding hazards and gaining ground. If Stefan was to trust him, then it would be in the next ten minutes.

McCall could see the lights approaching, hear the six cylinder German engine screaming.

Stefan laid perfectly still, feeling intensely vulnerable. He could also hear the car approaching, swear he could feel it through the coarse road surface, where he lay, face down, as instructed.

The BMW took the corner fast, its driver fighting to correct the understeer, knowing that if he went off the road at this speed, into a wall of trees, the car and its occupants would come a distant second.

The forest canopy was dense, almost midnight black,

row after row of five-year-old fir trees, green at the front, under the partial, cloud-covered moon, then dark brown, fading to black; a deep, dark mass without an apparent ending.

The BMW came to an abrupt halt, about a hundred metres from the Hyundai.

"Wait. It could be a trap." The front seat passenger lifted his pistol out of his lap. "That looks like Stefan. Do you think he has been killed?"

"We should see if he is alive. The Jackdaw will want to know. It is his brother…"

"He told us to bring him back alive. What if he is dead?"

"Questions, questions. Enough! We need to focus!" The older member of the team took control. "I will go. Nicolae, you come with me. You two stay with the car but be ready to help. You have your guns?"

All four were armed. Two favoured Glocks, one a Sig Sauer, the leader, a long-barrelled Colt that had been gifted to him by its deceased victim. It had stopping power, and that appealed to him.

He knew it was secluded. So desolate in fact that he had never been anywhere near there before. The chances of anyone being out here at this time of the night were less than remote.

The response by local police to gunshots, somewhere in the forest even less likely.

He raised his arm and fired a round through the grill, shattering the plastic moulding, splintering the silver H logo and drilling into the radiator. The noise was immense in such a quiet place. It was enough to wake the dead. It stopped somewhere in the engine block. The damage was done. That was fine by McCall, who watched and waited.

Colt stepped forward. "See, that is why I carry a

powerful handgun. Now they cannot leave." His grin was supercilious, his eyes narrow.

"But where is the other man?"

"He has run off through the woods, like the coward that he is." Colt yelled the word coward, allowing it to echo through the dense timber.

"You think he killed Stefan, then ran away?"

"Yes, I do. Come, let's go and have a look." He kept his weapon pointing at the inert figure on the ground. "Be careful."

"Should we shoot him?" Sig Sauer was trigger-happy and wanted to fire at least one round from the P226, which he had convinced a young student to part with only a week before.

"No, fool. If he is injured we take him back to Bucharest, then we ring the Jackdaw. He will reward us well for this. He is only in the city for a few more days. Then, he will leave – and we may never see him again."

"Where will he go?" Glock One was the most excitable of the quartet. "Where to?"

"Shut up, and wait here, and do not shoot. I don't trust you with that."

Glock One waited, shuffling from his left foot to his right, like a drug addict waiting for a fix.

Colt gradually edged forward, mirroring the footage he had watched online, sweeping the road and the surrounding trees with his gun. But never actually looking. He waved to Glock Two.

Glock Two followed him, doing the same, turning around now and then to check the other two men were still there, not whisked up and into the trees. He'd watched too many films.

McCall waited patiently. All he could hear was the amateur soundtrack and the purring of the BMW.

All four were out of the car now. First mistake. The group had separated, second. At least two of them looked uncomfortable with their weapons and surroundings. It just got better.

The Bushman blended quickly and skilfully with the scenery, bracken stuffed down his collar, face smeared in mud, hands too. The Seven Ss were never more at the forefront of his mind: Shape, shine, shadow, silhouette, sound, speed and surroundings.

He used vegetation to break up the familiar shape of the human form. The only thing that he had that shone was stuffed tightly into the cargo pocket of his trousers. He cast no shadow. Silhouette wasn't a problem, his background was blacker than a coalmine.

He made no sound, moving slowly and carefully. As a deer walks through a forest, so does the Bushman. Last, but by no means least, he had become one with his surroundings. There was a saying in the regiment that when Scott McCall walked into a forest, he became it; the wildlife approached him; the trees enveloped him. He could disappear in seconds and not be seen or found for days. He killed only when he needed to eat and concealed his tracks with such skill that the best military trackers couldn't find him.

His escape and evasion course had caused chaos when he refused to surrender. He was one of the few to avoid capture, therefore his interrogation phase took even longer. Naked, hooded, exposed to interminable white noise and stress positions – all the while smiling.

They isolated him and mentioned his kid sisters. Over and over again.

They broke him eventually. They always do.

And now he was in his element, his natural environs. It had taken moments, and he was only twenty metres into the forest. He could smell the forest floor, the terpenes, chemicals in the conifers that gave them their distinctive sweet, sharp smell and he could hear everything, eyes closed briefly. A scan of the sky had told him where in the world he was right now. He had done all of this without moving an inch.

Colt was halfway. Stefan had been good to his word, not moving, barely breathing. Hoping he was doing it right. He had spent so long being the hunter that this was foreign territory. He quietly longed to know that McCall was still there.

Glock Two was on edge. He started talking again.

"Where's the second guy?" He earned a swift rebuke.

"I told you. He has run away. Wouldn't you if you saw me coming? Go forward and check on Stefan. Do you know how to check for a pulse?"

"Of course. Do I look stupid?" Colt didn't answer.

McCall was now in the middle of the two groups. To his right, the Hyundai, Stefan and the two pursuers. To his left, the BMW and the two younger men.

He reckoned on about forty metres each way. A tall order for an average shot. But the humble Glock was a remarkable weapon. With it loaded the way it was, seventeen rounds and a couple of replacement magazines, he felt confident. It was all down to the first shot.

Glock Two was a few metres away from the inert body now and felt very uneasy. If Stefan was dead, he didn't want to touch him. If he was alive and it was a trap, then it could be even worse. He stepped quietly, one small stride at a time. Could hear his shoes rasping on the road surface, every crackle of every leaf, every heartbeat.

He could hear his own breathing, swear he heard something in the trees. It was different out here. He yearned for the city. Where it was light and he felt safe. The hunter preyed upon.

At the BMW both men had switched off, had started

looking around, up at the stars that begun to reveal themselves from beneath the cloud cover. Next error.

McCall breathed in, let the air out quietly. The Glock fired. That was how it supposed to work, anticipate the shot and you would probably miss at that range. Trigger reset. The second round was away.

The targets were perfectly lit.

The first round hit Glock Two in the neck. The second ploughed into Colt's chest as he turned instinctively to see what was happening.

McCall now had a tactical choice. Fire another round at each, or arc left. He chose the latter and hoped that Colt wouldn't shoot Stefan, who had remained on task with the utmost professionalism, but was now understandably moving for cover.

Two shots rang out. Then two more. Two seconds. Two down. The rear guard was out of the game before it had the chance to react. The whole incident had taken moments. McCall was out of the woods and moving through the smaller trees towards the road.

"Let's move!" Stefan responded, not waiting for another instruction. He knew not to compare his own experiences with that of a professional soldier. In his shadow he considered himself nothing more than a street thug – with style. McCall had impressed him completely. If ever he had needed a bodyguard, it was now and here in the darkened rural setting he realised he had just found one. He knew little about the man, but he trusted him.

He heard his shouts, breaking through his uncharacteristic sense of anxiety.

"To the Beemer. Now!"

Stefan ran towards the BMW, past the two bodies. Glock Two was dead, or at least very unwell. Colt was still alive. Stefan covered the eighty metres in an impressive time. As he got to the German car, he stopped and looked at the younger two. Both had a single wound in their heads and another in the torso. The car was undamaged. Not a scratch.

McCall was approaching tactically, listening for traffic. Nothing. God bless rural Europe.

Colt turned. His gun was nowhere near him. The 9mm round had hit him in the rib cage and had entered one of his lungs.

For McCall, it was head over heart. Leave him to tell the tale and enhance the reputation of the enemy, save his life, or put him out of his misery?

He was looking into the eyes of a man who had never experienced mercy – least of all believed in it.

He stared down at him, watching his laboured breathing, air sucking in through the dark red hole in his chest. "Let me guess. A little birdie sent you?" It meant nothing to the twenty something who looked like he had lived a hard life. Tacky gold watch and matching tooth aside.

"I'll try again. I take it you work for the Jackdaw?"

Nothing, but the eyes told him all he needed to know.

"Mate, I'm going to shoot you anyway, so it's your call. You want ruthless? I can do ruthless. Your amateur circus has no idea what it is dealing with. Now, I asked you a question, friend. Three seconds. There will be no four. One…"

"Yes. I work for the Jackdaw and who are you to ask?"

"That's better. My name is irrelevant. You speak English which helps, I am really not sure how this little chat would go if you only spoke in your own language. Pleasing to see your education wasn't entirely wasted."

McCall could see a blue tattoo on the man's right wrist.

"What's that?" He pointed with his left boot, pinning the arm to the road.

"Again, who is asking?"

"Friend, I've told you once. Don't push things. Need I

remind you that you are no longer running things here? You say the Jackdaw. Does he have a real name, or did his parents hate him?"

Colt reflected on his situation. "It is the mark of the Seventh Wave. It is who I belong to. Alex is our leader. Alex Stefanescu. We all belong to him. You will never know what it is like to belong. You are just the bastard who happens to be holding the gun." More confident, defiant almost.

"Pretty sad that you can't make your own way in life. Big fella like you."

Colt responded, breathing shallowly, struggling to push the words out between breaths.

"And you...you have never been part of a group...that you feel loyal to?" It was an arduous but great question. Given his circumstances, he did well to talk.

"I have. But my group operates on a different level to yours. And by the book. I have a tattoo as well, different to yours. Mine has a dagger on it, but I guess in our way we all follow a leader."

"Good, so at least you will let me live. Brothers in arms, and all that..." There was now a sense of desperation in the question.

McCall lifted him onto his side with his stronger foot.

"My friend, that round is going to kill you soon. I am a decent person. I can either let you bleed out here in a desolate forest, alone, where trust me, the chances of anyone coming to help you are average to poor, or I can do the decent thing. It's what I would do to an animal if I'd just run it over."

"Shoot me. I don't care. I am better off dead here than facing the boss – he sent me to follow his brother. I won't be the last, they will keep coming, for him, and now you."

He looked down the road at Stefanescu, not for an endorsement but to make sure he was ready to go. Stefan nodded, as if to say 'Yes, I am ready. Do what you need to do.'

McCall looked at the overweight male lying on the road.

"Oh, aren't you just a little ray of sleet, you are depressing me now. What's it to be? Your call."

The male nodded and entirely against the flow of the conversation smiled and said, "Do it. If you ever meet Alex tell him I was a brave soldier."

"Soldier? Is that what you consider yourself to be?"

"Yes. I am a soldier of the people."

McCall shook his head. It seemed that Walter Mitty was alive, and well, and living in Eastern Europe. He pitied him.

"You haven't earned the right to call yourself a soldier."

The gun went off and had reloaded before McCall turned to the second male. Glock Two was already dead, but he fired a round through him too, back of the head. He walked the hundred metres, listening to the forest settling down after the last shot. Approaching the two remaining men, he noticed both were also dead. He repeated the act, one shot each.

"Why are you doing that? They are dead already." Stefan was supposed to be a higher-echelon criminal, his question surprised McCall.

"Why? So that when they are found the police will assume they have been targeted by their opposition, not a soldier and his new escapee partner. I doubt the authorities will carry out a postmortem on this band of merry men, so the head shot is designed to make a statement. Come on, we need to move."

They got into the BMW, which had been ticking over faithfully.

"Heated leather seats, nice. Should make for a more comfortable journey to France. You drive, I've got some thinking to do."

Stefan got behind the wheel, put the lever into drive and moved off. They drove by the four men and the woeful Hyundai, turned right in a kilometre and re-joined the main road.

"Aren't you worried this will be reported stolen?"

"No. Because I doubt your old crew ever reported anything legal. I'm going to close my eyes, mate, need some thinking time. Wake me when you've had enough." He closed his eyes but spoke again. "Oh, and if you are thinking of abandoning me, make sure it is in a picturesque French village filled with grateful and willing maidens."

CHAPTER THIRTY-SIX

IN A CENTRAL LONDON HOTEL, A NETTLE-STREWN factory within walking distance of the mist-laden River Thames and a car heading to northern France, three people woke, similar time, different places.

It was a sudden awakening, hearts pounding. The type of awakening that shocks the system, makes it demand to know where it is. And then the chest beats, fast, furious until normality returns.

The first person recovered the quickest, looked around, checked his bearings, let out a sigh of relief, then lowered his head back onto the pillow. The second wished her heart would stop – permanently. The third opened and closed his eyes repeatedly, trying to free them of sleep, then extended his arms, clicked his knee joints, the pop audible from half a mile away and finally ran his hand over the condensation, watching it run down the green-tinted glass of the stolen BMW. He looked out at the beginning of a new day, in a new country. They were almost there – well, to be accurate they were a long way from home but closer than they were when they started. It was still dark. In their wake, at least six bodies, a smouldering shell of a nightclub, an abandoned rental car and potentially, on their tail, a varying group of people, some law-abiding, some not.

"Where are we? How much longer?" McCall had slept for hours, a deep sleep too, which was unlike him. He felt a little vulnerable.

"Still in Germany. Forty minutes, fifty possibly we will stop. We are not going through the tunnel."

"Ferry?"

"Neither, we can't risk it. The police will know by now that I am not in the nightclub – and they probably want me as much as they want my brother. I'm still a big name on the Interpol website." He was almost proud of the claim. "And you, who knows, they may even be after you. So we stay away from ports. OK?"

"Fine by me. So what's it to be? Boat or a refreshing swim across the channel, I reckon if we leave now, on the early tide we could be there in fifteen hours." He smiled.

"Are you always this sarcastic, Mack?"

"Always brother, always."

"I've arranged for us to be met. Up ahead. You could say I've cashed in a favour with an old friend."

"Wouldn't it have been easier to get to your contact called Maria? Jump on her plane and hightail it to England, tea with the Queen, maybe a knighthood?"

"I changed my mind. I do not trust Maria Anghel, and she does not trust me. We make our own way from here."

"I'm intrigued. Can we at least stop and get something to eat?"

"Why not? What's the worst that can happen? I've never felt safer than around you. I meant to ask Mack, back there, in the forest..."

"Best you don't my friend. Let's just agree that it never happened."

"Your call. It seemed that you knew exactly what you were doing, very professional. You tracked my brother down, that takes some doing. Takes balls of steel. You know he intended to kill you once you arrived?"

"Of course. I've made a career out of being shot at. It's what gets me out of bed in the morning. Anyway, we have the documents, I have something of value and you are alive. I'd call that a success. Wouldn't you?"

"In a way. I was once told that if you grab a shark by the tail, then you'd better have a plan to deal with his teeth."

"Tiger."

"Sorry?"

"It was a tiger. It was in a Tom Clancy novel and it's very true."

"My brother is the tiger. He won't forget you, he won't forgive you. Once he's done what he plans to do, then he'll come after you. This year, maybe next."

"Do you think he's in that plane with Maria?"

"Most likely. You know he won't rest until you are dead? Either it's him or you."

"Good. Then I have an option. We'll be fine. I guess for now I'm along for the ride, nothing else to do, and as far as work are concerned I'm touring Europe, finding myself."

"Makes a change from Afghanistan?"

"What makes you say that?"

"It's written on the lines on your face. Any man who sleeps with his hand on a weapon has a story to tell."

"Perhaps. Read my autobiography when I finally settle down. It's called *He dared*."

"OK, then I will. How many chapters?"

"So far I've written the acknowledgements."

"Do I get a mention?"

"Perhaps. For now, what's the plan?"

"We fly to London, meet up with a few people and

between us work out what Alex has in mind. Whatever it is, it will involve money – that, and harming people along the way. When he left the club, he had a look in his eyes that I last saw when I was a kid."

"He harmed you?"

"No, he was wiping my mother's blood from his hands. Told me that they were dangerous people, that he was protecting me. I eventually came to believe him. When I was old enough to know the truth it was almost too late. But I had a chance to change paths. It involved a long journey, Mack, but as they say the long game is the one to win."

"And now?"

"And now, the final chapter is beginning. The story is set in stone. I know his plans. Well, almost all of them. And that makes me vulnerable but also equally valuable to the British government, probably my own too. I need to be able to walk through any city in the world and know that I am not being watched. There is only one way I can do that. And that's where you come in."

"Sounds like a long story." McCall was genuinely interested to hear it too. "*And their blood shall be on their own heads*."

"Sorry?"

"It's a quote from the bible. One of the few I remember, carry it about in the back of my mind."

"I'm ashamed to say that I only know one. 'He destroyed all living things that were on the face of the ground,' Genesis."

"Your brother?"

"Yes, unless we stop him. And that journey starts there." He pointed to a helicopter. "Come on, let's dump this old thing and head to London."

He pulled into a small airfield, drove beyond the barrier, parked the BMW and left the key in the ignition.

"Free to a good home?" McCall was sure someone would make use of it. "As long as they don't go on holiday to Bucharest! Should we check the boot for bodies, drugs and guns?"

McCall was joking.

"Good idea," said his new associate. He lifted the boot and was relieved to see a spare wheel and a jack.

"Let's go, Mack. I've got people I need to speak to and some of them still don't trust me."

The silver Augusta 109 lifted off the ground, turned to the left and gained height, its Turbomeca engine soon propelling it northwards at one hundred and seventy miles an hour. They would cruise just below ten thousand feet and with luck have enough fuel in the tank to get them to London.

"Sit back and relax, gentlemen. We've got a fair journey ahead and no cabin service, but there are drinks, sandwiches and snacks in the back. I aim to have you in the city before too long."

McCall enjoyed feeling the torque beneath him, the rotation of the blades above him and the static buzz from the headphones. It felt like he was home, albeit whose home he had no idea. He chose not to ask. He'd been in situations far worse.

He sat back and closed his eyes. God knows where he was going next. More importantly, God himself knew what Mike Steel would say.

He looked across at the blond with miss-matched eyes. He was already asleep, mouth slightly ajar, head slumped into the seat, jammed against the window, as beneath them Germany slowly became Belgium.

· · ·

The light aircraft was wheeled up quickly. A light payload and a full tank meant it got up to speed quickly and was soon cruising towards Britain.

Maria Anghel was an experienced pilot, and importantly, her passenger trusted her with his life. The feeling was mutual. Her bank account had just grown too, by more than she had ever earned. She set a course for Kent, on the south coast of England and would soon join the criss-cross pattern of aircraft, light and heavy that plied their trade across the channel. Beneath her the ships, small boats and ferries, above the long-haul aircraft heading further afield.

Her headphones hissed. "It's good to see you again, Maria."

She raised a thumb. "You too. It's been a while. I thought you had forgotten me."

He smiled and rested his hand on her thigh, despite knowing that he was barking up the wrong tree.

"Never. I never forget my friends and never forget my enemies. So how long before we land?"

"A while yet. Close your eyes. Nothing to do now. The weather ahead is OK, a few patches of cloud, so it may get a bit bumpy as we approach England. I'm landing at Rochester Airport, it's a small place about forty minutes from London. It's discreet. Perhaps you can send a message to be collected?"

It was a sensible idea. So sensible he had done it hours ago.

Sleep was the next sensible plan. He also rested his weary head against the door, a jacket folded to create a pillow. Sleep was what he needed. And it came quickly.

It seemed all roads led to London.

CHAPTER THIRTY-SEVEN

In London, nightshift workers went about their business. Security staff patrolled their given locations, cleaners cleaned, maintenance workers repaired, airports prepared for the onslaught and milkmen arrived, stocking their vehicles for delivery. Meanwhile, everyone else slept, oblivious to the world that existed in their slumber.

To the south east of the capital a small aircraft was approaching the runway at Rochester Airport. It was a rare landing at night, illegal and bound to attract the wrath of the local residents. The pilot had said it was discreet, what she meant was completely illegal.

A landing at night, with limited vision and lighting. To some, it was suicide.

She landed proficiently and as quietly as she could, taxiing, dropping off her passenger, who travelled light. She was skilled at using grass airfields, a skill learned over many years of covert flying. Hence the price she charged and the price people willingly paid.

She waved. He waved. He was already running across the unlit outer margins of the airfield.

She checked her instruments, looked out at the night sky and watched the breath from her passenger fill the space around him. There was a light frost, the longer grass surrounding the manicured runway was rigid, spider webs glistened. The air was quiet, distant traffic on a motorway, somewhere.

Her cockpit was warmer, her fuel gauge was one the low side of half. But she needed to leave, and quickly. If she was found it would mean the end to her business.

Within ten minutes she had landed, said goodbye and left, heading back across the channel to a friendly location that would provide fuel and a bed for the night, probably in the back of her cherished aircraft.

Her passenger shrugged off the cold. Jogged five hundred metres through a parking area for light aircraft and climbed the fence as if he were on the run. He hit the inner fencing, gaining a foothold and rolling skilfully over the top of the angled wire, catching his shin on the wire. He had escaped from far worse. He would heal.

The airport was closed for business, so he needed to avoid any further attention. He chose a spot as near to the emergency gate but out of sight of the nearby Holiday Inn. The last thing he wanted was to be seen by a late-night smoker or an amorous couple, up against the window, abandoned and careless.

The locals would say a plane had landed during the night. But they had no proof. Its sole passenger was already gone. CCTV would indeed show an aircraft arriving and a passenger leaving. But that was all. No markers, no clear facial imagery. No trace.

Alex Stefanescu, the Jackdaw, was back in Britain. And only his closest people knew.

. . .

He was heading to see a small team, one that was linked to other teams and those in turn to others. He had created a pyramid system that rivalled direct-sales companies across the world – each cell was connected by one person only, and each had no idea who was in charge. A honeycomb of criminality.

They heard rumours, and some members of the cells purported to be its absolute leader, the frontrunner and iconic talisman of the Seventh Wave. Each now had the familiar blue tattoo, except one. His was black, created by infusing the molten rubber from a prison shoe, many years before. And that rode roughly over any deceitful stories. He was the leader. Everyone else followed.

He laid down in the back seat of the old car, could smell the damp carpets, hear the tyres thrumming across the concrete road beneath. He needed to stop running. For years now he had either been incarcerated or on the run. The time was right. He had money; he had the trappings of a highly organised, much-followed leader. What he didn't have was the space and freedom in which to enjoy the wealth he had accrued. The time was right indeed.

The old grey Nissan Primera drove past the entrance to the considerably older fireworks factory, parked up in a layby, and waited. Waited for the few cars out at that time to pass by. Then it sped back along the road and turned left, switched onto side lights and slowly navigated its way along the rutted track, never braking, reached the outbuildings, then parked. The driver used a small torch to light the path and held the door open.

Alex walked in and saw Constantin standing in the hallway. He came out of the dim light and held out his arms.

"Salut prietene vechi." Hello old friend.

"Salut." They embraced, each hugging the other harder until Constantin yielded.

"Good journey?" The older man asked.

"It was compact and personal. The airport facilities were limited, no time for duty free, and it is the first time I have had to jump over a fence after arriving into a foreign country." He laughed, causing the growing group of men in the hallway to join in. They were captivated by his persona. A smiling façade that barely covered the sociopath that lay beneath the weather-beaten, stress-laden skin.

"Coffee? Something to eat?"

"Yes, that would be good. You have made the place so homely." Alex had not lost his sense of humour.

"You told me to be discreet." Constantin almost bristled at the comment.

"Relax, brother, you have done well. I asked for somewhere remote but near enough to strike out. And you have done well. How are the men doing?"

"They are learning quickly, but their test is yet to come. That starts tomorrow. They need better food."

"Yes, of course. Send them out to get what they need. Cash only. And our guests? How are they finding the hospitality?" Alex smiled – his eyes narrow.

"I think the word the girl used was inhospitable."

"It can be arranged."

Constantin stared back.

"Oh! You said inhospitable, not in hospital!"

He laughed again, slapping Constantin across the back.

"Come brother, lighten up. I am here now. Shall we eat? Then I will go and introduce myself." He lowered himself onto an old chair, its red PVC cushion torn at the sides, a leg slightly rickety.

"Tell me more about the last few days."

Alex ate with the men, listened to their stories of the

British banks that they had targeted. A small group openly conveyed their delight as they recounted the story about how they had almost beheaded the police officer on his motorbike. Alex clapped his hands together warmly.

"I love your passion for work. Do you know what Confucius once said?"

Many did not know who he was, let alone what he had once said.

"Then I will tell you. He said, 'Find a job you love – and you will never work a day in your life.' Isn't that so true of here, and now?"

They all murmured, clapped and nodded enthusiastically. They had no other option. Many of them had never met this man, but his reputation preceded him.

Alex finished his food, wiped the corners of his mouth and stood. Everyone stood too. He ushered them back down. "Please, I am not God, nor his son, but I am probably in third place. No?" He had a serious face.

One young man cheered – the rest backed away as if the very noise was enough to render him dead, at the hands of an expert killer.

Alex looked at him through coal-black eyes.

"You cheer because I am number three?"

The man hesitated, swallowing audibly. "No, sir. I cheer because I am proud to serve with a man who is only two steps behind God."

Silence.

Alex stared at him as if he was something noxious on the sole of his shoe. Then slowly a smile developed, then laughter.

"You, boy, will go a long way in my organisation. A long way indeed."

Constantin edged up to his leader's ear and whispered.

"Oh, I hear you disposed of the British woman earlier on. Well done. I hope she has gone?"

"Yes, sir. We watched her sink."

"Good, then you have nothing to fear from me. Constantin, show me to our guests please, then we must sleep. And bring me an apple, I have not had fresh fruit in weeks. And a knife. And your phone."

"Did you hear that?" O'Shea was leaning to her side, further than she had done for days. She was cold, and damp, her skin was raw where the urine had pooled against her. Her stomach growled – like a wildcat in a forest.

"Yes. Someone new has arrived." Thomas hissed his reply. He was also covered in an old and wet blanket that did little to maintain a healthy body temperature. "Who do you think it is?"

"I have no idea. But I know we need to leave here soon. If necessary I will go and bring help."

"No. Do not leave me. They will be like pack dogs if they find you have left. They will beat me, torture me and humiliate me."

"More than they already have. Look at you." O'Shea moved her head towards the table that he lay on, careful not show how far she had stretched the duct tape. "And anyway, don't you like that sort of thing?"

Thomas could barely open his eyes. The blood had dried into a crust, sealing the right eye completely, blurring the left. He could taste the dried fluid when he parted his lips, which were raw, the nerve endings singing a song of torment and pain.

"Shh. They are coming." O'Shea laid still, waiting. Barely breathing.

Two men walked in. She knew that much by their footfall.

The lights were switched on. Dazzling. Thomas tried unsuccessfully to pretend he was asleep.

"They stink. Have you showered them?" Romanian. Authoritative.

"No. There is no shower. But I bathed them earlier. Washed her hair."

"No shower? That explains why you all stink then. We need to do something about that if I am to stay here more than a night. But I have to agree, her hair is beautiful." He held the clear bag up to the light, displaying large pieces of it as if he were holding a trophy aloft. He smiled at O'Shea as he emerged from the glaring light that surrounded him, an aura, a silhouette, as dark as his eyes.

Alex stepped into the light, and for the first time became real.

Now she couldn't breathe. Fear. Anxiety. Sheer terror. But somehow she needed to show strength.

"Did he use product on you Madame? Bring out your natural highlights?" He mockingly showed her the bag.

O'Shea did nothing. Did not engage him in eye contact, but kept her eyes open.

'So, that's what you look like, you evil piece of shit. Get me off this table and I will break every bone in your face.'

"It's been a long time, Carrie. I know we have never met, and yet, somehow it feels as if I have known you all of my life." He inhaled sharply, then exhaled, slowly before smiling. He was in control and it aroused him, as did the sight of her lying there – even with a totally shaved head. She was still attractive. Yet part of him pitied her, wanted to let her go.

His inner voice began to recover his thought processes.

'No, you must not do that, Alex. She is your ace. Without her it will be so much harder.'

He then spun sixty degrees, looking at Thomas.

He peeled the apple and ran the skin over Thomas' lips. Despite the pain, he snapped at the peel and savoured its sweetness. The skin cracked around his mouth and a fresh stream of red ran down his cheek, across his neck and onto the table.

"Awake now I see."

He walked around the table and lifted the soiled blanket from O'Shea. "So we meet at last. You look different to how I imagine. Naked for a start. Pretty, in a girl in a cheap motel kind of way. Talking of hotels, I hope you have enjoyed the facilities? That you will go online and give us a glowing review, five stars at least..." He grinned, eating the apple off the tip of the knife.

Nothing. He tried the same approach. Lowering a piece of the fruit onto her lips, leaving it there. She resisted. It smelled delicious. He pressed with the blade, forcing her to part her parched lips and allow the apple to drop into her mouth, causing her to choke. She used every ounce of her resilience not to lean upwards and reveal how she had created some space. She flicked the apple with her tongue, then savoured it, breaking down, releasing water and sugar into her mouth and down her throat. She could hardly swallow.

It was almost sensual. Rather, it would have been if the Jackdaw had not been running the blade across her naked body, playfully but with a look that said, "Pick a spot, any spot, this is where the knife slips beneath your skin my dear."

He scratched his name into the area around her navel, emphasising the X, allowing it to weep with blood.

He cut another piece of apple and put it between his own teeth, then lowered his head down to her body, squeezing the juice across her breasts, then crunching the fruit with his teeth. It was the loudest noise in the room.

Another piece, this time held between his lips. He lowered once more and gently sealed his lips around hers, forcing the apple into her mouth with his tongue. Her breath was far from sweet, but he enjoyed the moment.

"You really are very pretty. It would be such a shame to kill you just to send a message to our friend Jack. But, as you know, being his very best analyst, I am not..." He hunted for the word. "...averse to sending a message in a cruel and unforgiving way, just like my men did with your friend."

She tried desperately to look away.

"Look at me! Remember Nikolina? What I did to her?" He ran his fingers across O'Shea's neck. "Of course you do, my dear." He kissed her gently on the neck, then licked her skin, lower, stopping near her sternum. He was so close he could hear her heart beating.

"No. For now, you are far too valuable. You will be my ultimate bargaining tool when the time comes. I will need the very best distraction to lure him away from the scent. I have to agree he is a smart man. A good detective. He dresses well but like me has demons. He too is a gypsy, drifting from place to place. A nomad. And above all he is a man, so he is led by his loins. I'm sure he longs to be back there soon." He gently placed what was left of the apple between her legs, let the nectar seep down her thighs, then smiled, which at any other time could have been mistaken for compassion.

"And you are rather lovely."

He ran his hand over her stomach, wiping the blood from the X and rubbing it between his fingers, then gently tracing a heart with it, around her belly button before allowing his hand to rest against her lower stomach, watching her body pulse beneath his hand, he spoke.

"Very pretty."

He picked up the apple and took a final bite, then dropped the core to the ground.

He spun around and tutted, clicking his tongue against his teeth.

"Whereas this *freak* next to you." He turned, pointing with the knife, emphasising the word freak. "He, she, whatever it is, can offer so many opportunities to alleviate boredom." He looked down at Thomas' forlorn face.

"I see someone has already begun to play with you. How heartless. Look at you, that must really hurt?" He prodded the scabs with the tip of the blade, lifting one away, allowing it to bleed. "Worry not, dear Lucy." He turned to look at Constantin.

"Did you really call him Lucy? Isn't that a little bit strange? Can you imagine anyone paying a person like this for sex?" He shuddered melodramatically. He knew everything about their relationship. Knew that his esteemed torturer was gay – but no one ever mentioned it. It was best that way.

He did not despise those that chose to be gay. He had met some men in prison who were. He liked them, actually. Articulate, bright, strong and potentially the toughest men in the building. He avoided them and they kept their distance too.

Alex knew to treat the older man with respect, too. He looked at him now. Constantin Nicolescu had a hair trigger and few people trusted him. Alex was one who did.

"Miss O'Shea. I suspect you are an educated woman. Now bear with me. Remember, if you will, the day you watched them recover my dear Niko's body from the river. Up she came, cold, muddy, blue lips. Dead. Then they lowered her to the pavement, behind a barrier to prevent others from seeing her. Typically British. So thoroughly polite." He feigned a British accent.

She chose not to acknowledge him in any way.

"I'll take that as a yes. I know everything you see. You may not know that I chose to kill my wife to pay Jack Cade back for his greed. For stealing her from me. I know she was heading to London to find him."

O'Shea knew it was untrue. Chose to ignore him. She had been heading somewhere else.

"And I know she wanted to betray me as soon as she could. The spiteful whore tried to kill me with a poison. I mean, who would do that to their husband? Terrible." He looked at Constantin for assurance. Who smiled and said, "Terrible indeed."

"See? Even this man who has killed more people than I have slept with, and that is a large number, even he agrees. It is all about revenge. Not money, as nice as money is, not love – for I have only ever found love once, but revenge. He was pacing like the defence counsel during a televised summing up.

"What was it that the bible said about revenge Carrie?" He waited. Rested the blade against her thigh.

She knew he would do it. So she licked her lips, allowing them to form the words. "That every wrong should be equally penalised."

"Yes! Well done. And the book, please?"

"Book?"

"From the bible. Oh do tell me you have read it. Or, do you suggest that a man who has lived so many of his months and years in prison has not? That he is an ill-educated dog."

"I don't know."

"Exodus. Twenty-One. An eye for an eye, a tooth for a tooth. Simple words but very powerful."

"And how does that have anything to do with us?" O'Shea was gaining in strength, temper did that to her.

"Well, you see…" He sat on the edge of the table, rested his hand on her stomach, thumb facing up to her head, his little finger marvelling at how smooth she was. He teased her as he spoke.

"…Mr Cade deprived me of my wife. That is worth an eye. Then, he took my daughter away. Let us call that a tooth. So far? You understand me?"

"So get on with it." She bared her teeth. Defiant.

He laughed. "It also says a hand for a hand. But Constantin beat me to it. I would have given anything to be a fly on the wall of Detective Inspector Roberts' office when the candle burned down. Genius."

"Chief inspector."

"Oh, I *am* sorry." His reply was dripping in sarcasm.

"No dear, you see, I wouldn't want to harm you. The bible goes onto to say, 'And if a man smite the eye of his servant, or the eye of his maid, that it perish; he shall let him go free…'"

"I don't understand."

"Well, let us pretend that you are my maid. Then this thing next to you is my servant. I need to send another message to your team. These messages are such fun. One thing in return for another."

"I have no idea. OK? I have no fucking idea what you are rambling on about, perhaps it's time for more heroin or whatever shit you lot take to give you these ideas. There is no point anymore. Wherever you go Jack and the team will find you. You cannot hide anymore. Unless you head to a mountain range and live in a cave." She went to turn away but resisted.

"Have you heard the term hiding in plain sight?"

"No."

"Well, it means to be closer to your enemy than your enemy realises. Like us. Here we are, almost under the noses of the British authorities but as far as they know we are at home in our mother country, or, as you suggest, in a cave."

She was at least able to confirm her suspicion that they were closer to London than made sense. It gave her hope. At last.

"We are so close we can send little messages, parcels of joy and goodwill, but never be suspected of being so close to where we actually want to be. Your city. Your home and what makes it famous."

At the Op Orion base Nick Fisher placed a mug of tea – a mug with the cross of St Andrew emblazoned on it. Its owner picked it up, inhaled the Yorkshire Tea.

"Superb Nick." He took a sip, sensed that his DS wanted to ask something. "Alright Nick? Something troubling you?"

"It troubles me that no one seems to give a flying fuck about Carrie or Cynthia, guv. We are sat here with our fingers up our arses..."

"Did you use it to squeeze my tea bag out?"

"Respectfully boss..."

"Fair point." He stood, leant on the side of his desk, eye to eye with Fisher. "The best answer and tell everyone this Nick is that yes, I give a flying fuck or any other expression that sums up how much I am worried. I think about it every day and most of the night until sleep finally allows me to have a few hours. I've got frontline staff in three counties looking, airports on standby, border alerts in place, bulletins, dogs, detectives."

"What about the media?"

"Again, fair. But we both know Nick, the second they

start pontificating about their whereabouts we can start writing an obituary for *The Times*."

"I think Carrie is a *Guardian* reader." He tried to smile.

"Thanks, Nick. I appreciate your passion for this. Know that I am more than a hundred percent behind you and my maths teacher would kill me for saying that."

"Do whatever you need to do. Bring them home. If you overstep the mark doing it, I'll be here, alongside you. You have my word."

"But what if..."

"There will be no what ifs or buts or maybes, Nick."

"Guv." Fisher left the office, strong shoulders swept back just a little further than they had been when he had found an excuse to enter the boss's office.

CHAPTER THIRTY-EIGHT

Alex turned to Constantin. "Tape him down, securely. He must not move. Not one inch."

It happened, quickly, the aluminium tape left the roll and bound Thomas to the table, across his chest and around his neck and then back onto itself, sealing, fast.

"Good. Shall we begin our journey towards redemption? You are free to watch Carrie. In fact, that is a wonderful idea. I think you would say, inclusive? Yes? Completely. A night to remember."

O'Shea remained quiet as Constantin slid the table with his legs, butting it up against Thomas'.

"Best view in the house. Can you see or do you want to look away? Your choice."

She tried to stare up at the ceiling, but something drew her back to the scene and she watched Stefanescu remove a pair of pliers from the clear plastic packaging.

"Cheap, but cheerful, and they will do the job."

He prized upon Thomas' lips but he wrestled against him. As sore as the earlier cuts were he had discovered a newfound strength.

'No way you bastard.'

"OK, so you have decided to make this so much worse. Constantin, come and hold his nose will you?"

Thomas' eyes bulged, but he relented.

"There, isn't that so much better?" He parted the arid lips and gripped onto the left eye tooth, the one with the longest root. And started to pull.

Thomas tried to scream, his throat was so dry. It was a hoarse, desperate bid. 'Please, no.'

The fresh blood provided a hint of lubricant as the tooth slowly gave way. Thomas could hear it leaving his head; a deep, rasping, cracking sound and then, it was in front of him. Blood-soaked Ivory.

"Well done, you were a good boy. My assistant will clean you up and give you a sticker. So brave. You should put it under your pillow tonight. One fairy for another." He dropped the tooth into a new polythene bag and sealed the plastic strip.

O'Shea hated him more every second. Oh, that she had a gun, or a hammer, or just a phone.

"OK. That's the tooth." He smiled at O'Shea. "So exciting. And you get to watch."

She closed her eyes, sealed them shut. She knew what was coming but feared that her co-prisoner did not. It was the biblical quote in all its reality.

"OK, do we have the phone ready? This will be a first, for all of us. At least the pain of the tooth coming out will mask what happens next."

He looked at Constantin. "Well, shall we toss a coin?"

Constantin shook his head. "It depends on whether you want this person to survive. You do it, he dies. I do it, he dies in a few days, having suffered a great deal of pain."

"You make a compelling case. Over to you. I will help.

This is fascinating Carrie. Isn't it?" She forced her eyes to look away.

Constantin put his hand out, waiting for the first tool. The Surgeon.

A cheap scalpel touched his palm. He placed it against the right eye, lifted the lid and started to cut. As he did so Alex filmed, capturing the surgery in the half-light of the cold room.

Constantin skilfully cut into the cornea, slowly releasing the eyeball which fought against the point of the blade. A circular, clinical motion allowed the coloured orb to emerge, leaving him free to cut through the muscles that surrounded the eye, allowed it to move, held it in place.

He had once known their names, but years of abuse, drug, alcohol and mental had robbed him of his long-term memory. What he did know was what each one did and as a surgeon would he cut through each, slowly releasing the ball. He snipped with scissors, cut with the scalpel.

Alex watched, in awe. Partly amazed, partly nauseous. It was one bet he was glad to have lost. Not many things made him squeamish. Every part of this operation did.

He looked though – via the small phone screen.

O'Shea could only listen.

Thomas whimpered in pain. Fear had paralysed him.

Constantin sawed through the last muscle – the superior oblique – he remembered something after all.

In true optical surgery the surgeon would have created a harness, held the eyeball in place, then deftly removed it, cleaning the wound, applying sutures and then stitching up the void. After care would follow, then rehabilitation.

Constantin had no such concerns. All that remained was the optical nerve. He stared at Thomas, knowing that the image of his face would be the last thing this particular eye would see. Then snipped the nerve with the razor-sharp scissors.

Blackness. Horror. Bleeding. Panic. An end in sight.

He dropped the eyeball into a new plastic bag, leaving it coated in fresh blood. He laid it on the table where it remained, watching him.

He pushed a gauze pad into the wound and stepped back, away from his patient.

Thomas' tear ducts still worked and now they filled both of his eye sockets with fluid. And it hurt. More than anything ever had or ever would.

O'Shea could feel herself retching. Her top lip moist, bile surging up into her throat.

Alex pushed the tables apart. "Revenge Carrie is a cruel mistress. As we said, an eye for an eye. If only we were there to watch when your friends received it. Sleep well."

He stroked her face, then slowly removed his hand, allowing his fingertips to linger on her cheek where he knew it would be more sensitive.

He then dropped the instruments into a separate plastic bag, the scissors only half concealed. They would need to be disposed of for perpetuity.

He began to walk out of the room, a silhouette once more, then stopped, waited a moment in the shadows.

"Oh by the way." His voice carried through the sparse corridor into her room. "I have so enjoyed our reunion – if that is what we can call it. When this is all over I will have you cleaned up. Then we can see just what it is that Mr Cade finds so captivating about you. For now, we all need our beauty sleep."

And with that final sentence he was gone, walking towards the light of the communal room, a corridor away, followed by his smiling surgeon. Another procedure to add to his list.

O'Shea knew that her next words were likely to be futile, but she spoke them anyway.

"Look Lucy I don't know what your real name is but trust me, when they are asleep, we go. Tonight."

"You go on your own Carrie. Please. They cannot do anything else to me. Save yourself girl. Save yourself."

O'Shea was a belligerent soul at the best of times and there was no way she was leaving the building without him. She had one last question.

"No, we are going tonight, whether you bloody well like it or not. But before we do, I need to know your real name."

He laughed, more a snort, the smile cracking the drying blood on his cheeks.

"Does it really matter that much to you, darling?"

"It does."

"Then you will be the first since my dear old mum to call me John."

O'Shea snorted now. "You have got to be kidding me?"

"No. It's true. Possibly why I chose Lucy."

O'Shea had a newfound respect for her cross-dressing, call-girl cellmate. And she was more determined than ever to get them both to safety. She strained to hear the conversation next door. They talked of a team, heading into the city. Something about a stone. Then banks. Then the river. Three words. Stone, bank, river. Then another. Tower.

She could only hear these words. Somehow she was able to tune in, erase the white noise of her heartbeat and the ever-present distant flow of motorway traffic. Four words now. Bank was obvious, it was their signature to attack

ATMs; adding devices to steal data and in some cases even blowing the safes to pieces with oxyacetylene.

Three words then.

Stone. River. Tower. If she could remember nothing else.

Twenty minutes later the first team left the building. Then another. And one more. She tried to calculate how many had gone, how many were left. The problem was she had no idea how many they had started with. Ten? Twenty? Two?

She recalled that the teams that had attacked London in the past worked in threes. So that could be nine. Who had they left behind? Him? And that other bastard that had so cruelly deprived Thomas of his sight and her of her much-admired hair? She could forgive many things, but not her hair.

In a few hours they would begin their escape. And when the time was right, she would exact her own revenge. A dish that she would enjoy, cold or otherwise. She spent the next hour considering ways to carry out her hideous retribution and whilst she did so she slowly stretched the grey metallic tape, easing her head up further, her arms too. It was now just her legs that were tightly bound.

The three vehicles left the old factory, split up and drove off towards their chosen targets – all grey vans, all sign written with company names and phone numbers adding to their assumed identities; builders, couriers and telecom companies.

One headed north. The second west and the third stayed south of the river. Worst case they would get home and regroup.

Their team consisted of twelve people now. And ten more were on the way – due in two hours at the old factory.

The first van, a Ford, traversed the invisible boundary that marked the change between the County of Kent and the Royal Borough of Greenwich. They followed the A200 road as it skirted its way north west and south of the River Thames. Eventually the A200 became Tooley Street which in turn led to London Bridge.

They crossed the Thames. As they left the bridge, the road name changed and became King William Street. In a hundred metres they stopped, eased the van to a halt, waiting for the traffic lights to turn from red to green. In front of them the House of Fraser department store, its window displays creatively set out to lure passing shoppers. Below it the Monument tube station, identifiable by its red circular sign with a blue horizontal stripe running through it. They turned left onto Cannon Street.

They kept to the speed limits. Pedestrian numbers were low. A few black taxi cabs plied their trade and a late night bus headed back to the depot. It was quiet. For one of the busiest cities on the planet it was almost abandoned. A few hours and it would come to life once more.

They drove along Cannon Street. 107, 109 and there it was. The only signs of life were near to and within the Cannon Street railway station, which luck would have it was directly opposite their target.

111 Cannon Street, London, EC4N 5AR to give it its correct title. And there in the wall surrounded by a decorative but easily missed Portland stone fascia, behind an iron grate, was their quarry.

The London Stone.

"Is that it?" One of the younger members of the team said, almost deflated. "We have come here, into the city, to risk ourselves, for *that*?"

"Shut up. And get ready. If the Jackdaw says it is important, then it is. Or do you want to go back and tell him we failed, let him cut your eyes out too?"

He didn't.

Two of the men got out and started to erect a workman's tent over the site. The driver swung the van around and reversed it up to the tent, pulled out an amber beacon and stuck it on the roof. Switched it on. Opened the back doors and sealed them to the tent.

Late at night, in the city, underneath a temporary structure, telecom workers doing something to something else. They were just another team of nightshift workers anonymously keeping the city alive.

The tent was up quick and the team went to work, a large pallet truck was lowered into place and power tools began screaming in protest against the metal grid.

It took minutes to run the heavy chain from the back of the van and wrap it around the stone. Then three more to remove the large piece of limestone from its long-term home; a lump of old stone that had been in the area, some said for at least a thousand years.

The stone was linked to the Romans, to Druids and had once been built into the front of St Swithin's Church, a place of worship that had survived the Great Fire of London, and was then rebuilt by Sir Christopher Wren, only to fall into disrepair and be demolished in the 1960s. They built a church *around* it.

Throughout the transition period and over the course of hundreds of years, before and after, the Stone had remained, defiant. It had survived countless attempts to have it relocated, and had mocked the Luftwaffe, who never managed to destroy it during their ceaseless raids.

Moved once, from one side of the street to the other. Worshipped. Revered. Even the legendary historical figure

Jack Cade has struck his sword against it and declared himself Lord of the city.

And now, many hundreds of years later Alex Stefanescu was caught in a battle of wits with his namesake. And, like it or not, the stone had to go. Tonight.

It resisted, screamed in protest, then slowly began to leave its place of rest, digging into the pavement, gouging a broad mark as it slid towards the van. The winch was doing its job. It's one and only job in fact. Stolen and due to be burnt out, along with the van.

The London Stone rumbled, then rolled up and onto the pallet.

By the morning the gouge marks, a brass plaque and the empty chamber from whence it came, would be the only sign that the fabled rock had ever existed.

It seemed that all roads now led to the Jackdaw.

CHAPTER THIRTY-NINE

Two of the teams had already completed their tasks. In the West, one had deployed its men at a dozen bank ATMs. They had nonchalantly approached the machines, knowing they were being filmed and placed false fascia plates onto the host machines. They looked up at the cameras and smiled. At least they did behind the scarves that covered their faces.

This was now old school stuff. Teams like theirs had made their mark around the world, mainly targeting Western banks. But the banks were fighting back with new technology and counter measures. They reported the attacks very quickly, and unlike the past, the banks now talked to their counterparts, sharing intelligence. It made sense.

What they missed was that the devices were thrown away items. Of no use, monetarily. They were Trojan Horses without a team of soldiers secreted within. They were a distraction. Nothing more.

The next team approached an ATM south of the river. They waited, patiently, then fed the hoses into the mouth of the machine, pumped it full of gas, then, as Constantin had shown them, using chalk, picked from the local soil and written on the old concrete floor of the factory that was their home, they introduced a spark.

Gas, meet your new friend spark.

The explosion was incredible and woke everyone for at least half a mile.

'Take what you can, but do not get caught.'

The hole that the explosion tore into the machine was unexpected. The amount of money that sat there, that floated back to earth, all around them was nothing short of wondrous. Each one fluttered to the ground like a valuable snowflake. They grabbed at the cash, whilst one checked his watch, a cheap copy of a Rolex.

'You have less than ten minutes once the explosion has happened. Do not be greedy. Take what you need. Leave the rest behind. Wear gloves. If someone approaches run, get back to your vehicle and leave. If you are spotted, dump the cash, dump the van, set light to it, split up and do not come back here. Understood?'

They understood.

'But look at all of that money.' Thought the middle one of the group who had travelled to the United Kingdom to seek his fortune. He had been told the streets were paved with opportunities. Now he stood, laughing, looking at those pavements strewn with bank notes.

They heard a siren in the distance. Someone had reported an explosion. Constantin said this would happen. The Fire Brigade would tell the police and they would both tell the Ambulance control. And soon the circus started. The nearest fire station was a five-minute drive away. They had timed it.

The police were thin on the ground in the area. They had checked.

Ambulances didn't matter, for they had no desire to get hurt.

They had loaded the cash and the evidence of their nefarious hobby into the back of the Ford. Closed the doors.

"OK, let us go now, whilst we still can."

He secured his two team members into the back, locked the door then jumped into the driver's seat. He illuminated his own amber beacon and drove off into the night. They were all buzzing with adrenaline.

The first responder on scene reported into his portable radio that there had been an explosion, that there were no casualties. That the ambulances weren't needed. And a glazier was probably pointless. But let the police continue, it was over to them now. And for the first time in years, the control room of the Metropolitan Police had recorded a gas attack on a bank safe. The Operator feverishly typed into the system and then sent a copy to a team at Scotland Yard. As per the brief.

'Any attempts on any banks, send to:'

As the van navigated along the south London streets, the driver couldn't help but laugh. Candy from a baby. They were right. Tomorrow would be another day. Same shit, different bank. He turned the radio on, got comfortable, watching the door mirror for company. The only patrol car in the area screamed by, going somewhere, its sirens competing for priority with Supertramp's Roger Hodgson who was in turn was waiting to follow the haunting harmonica as they both considered the *Long Way Home.*

Hodgson began to sing. The driver joined in, although he didn't know the words.

By the next morning, Detective Sergeant Bridie McGee would strut into her boss's office and slap the stats onto his desk.

'They are back, guv.' Staff members on the floor below would hear his head hit the desk.

The first two vans were heading back to the ranch. But they had been told to wait an hour, then approach, individually, checking for traffic, then adopting the favoured lights-off approach.

The third van was waiting for its team to hoist the stone into the back of the Transit. It sighed as the famous bolder dropped onto the floor and announced its presence on the chassis and suspension.

It sat there, illuminated under the solitary interior light. A lump of bloody rock. It had better be worth it. The back doors were closed and two of the men sat either side of their ill-gotten haul and hoped it stayed in place. Their amber beacon pulsed and ricocheted off the walls of Cannon Street station, then retail outlets, and offices and then with no more walls to rebound off it was switched off as they retraced their steps, back across London Bridge.

They left the tent behind. It was stolen anyway. And a few days later someone might think to look inside, see what they were doing there, a passing cop or a nosy business owner, annoyed at the inconvenience of the whole damned thing.

The team adopted the same approach. It would be an hour before they reached their temporary home.

To the south a silver Augusta helicopter, navigation lights flickering, blades cutting through the night air slowed and descended as if it were landing in the Thames. On board were three people, the pilot and two passengers.

Waiting on the ground, at the London Heliport was a

solitary male, dark blue suit trousers, white shirt, no tie – it was late, leather-soled black brogues and a substantial woollen coat. He checked his watch, his favourite. Stainless steel, clinical, cold, with a coal-black face and sweeping second hand and a trademark cyclops lens over the date. He had one proviso. It had to feel as if it were hewn from a solid ingot of steel.

They were three minutes early. He paced, from left to right.

"Good, it's bloody cold." The man pushed his un-gloved hands under his armpits. He could have sat in the silver BMW, enjoyed heated seats, but he liked the smell of a winter night, the hint of snow, the smell of the river, only fifty metres away.

They had opened the facility for him, pushed the boundaries a little. When a minister or even a minister's aide rang and asked, nicely, you did. London was, after all, a small place.

He turned his back to the aircraft, inhaled the avgas, listened the birds fluttering, protesting, then turned back, waited a few minutes then approached the Augusta. The pilot was out and nodding, opening the door.

The two men climbed out, one looked more at ease with the rotation of the blades than the other but both looked exhausted, as if they had spent the last few days on the run.

The pilot walked around, checked for foreign objects, strapped himself back in and commenced his take off procedures. On the concrete helipad next to the River Thames overlooking Chelsea Harbour, the three men shook hands, shouting against the noise of the helo.

"Good to be back."

"It's good to have you back."

The two men walked with their host, got in and headed for a hotel, a shower and some room service – the kind where you left the remnants outside the door on a tray.

O'Shea pushed now with all her strength, up and against the tape. 'Come on you can do this. No gain without pain and all that nonsense.'

She shuffled down, trying to be as quiet as possible. Somewhere, possibly the next room she could hear a deep, relaxed snoring sound. She hoped it was the person tasked with guarding them. She sensed that Alex and the gap-toothed assassin were elsewhere in the building, their voices had trailed away as they walked. The further the better.

'Come...on. Better to be mocked for being bald than celebrated as a life force at your funeral, girl. Push.'

Her head was free. It somehow gave her new strength. She wiggled her arms until the tendons screamed 'Stop!'

She had one arm free. She reached across and shook Thomas who struggled to focus, but knew straight away that this was an ally, not a torturer.

"Stay quiet John." She ripped at the tape, piece by piece as it slowly relented and tore the first layer of skin from her wrists. She was buoyed by her success and leaned forwards, timing the shuffling of the table with the snoring. He snored, slapped his lips together, she moved. Again and again, until she was able to stretch out and reach for the blood-stained scissors.

The snoring stopped.

She paused. Waited for it to start, then began to cut through the tape as Constantin had sawn through Thomas' optic nerve.

She was free. Tears began to flow.

'Control yourself you stupid cow.'

She sat for a moment, probably two, waiting for the

equilibrium to return. She had been laid down, motionless for so long it now felt like she was on an ocean-going yacht.

'Steady. Don't rush.'

'What do you mean don't rush, what the f...'

She listened to her other self and pushed on, lowering herself onto the cold concrete floor. It was freezing. She now realised just how cold she was, had been, and knew she needed to find clothes, for both of them. And there they were, thrown in a heap in the corner. She probed with her hand, feeling through the damp clothing, working out what was what.

She had decided that worst case, she would dress and make a run for it. Get to the road and wave down the first car and hope they bloody well stopped. She remained silent, stationary, listening. The noise was her own heartbeat. She wished it would do her a favour and bugger off.

"John, we have to go." As she spoke she cut through his own bonds.

"I'm in no fit state Carrie. Go and get help."

"They will kill you. With me gone there is nothing left. Trust me."

She handed him some clothes, hoping they were his and eased him from the table. She couldn't see his face but knew he would look hideous. It was a good job it was dark.

"Steady."

The clothes were wet, and stank, but they were no longer naked and that felt like a victory. She pocketed the scissors. 'Come anywhere near me and I'll ram these into your face.'

"Stay here. I'll be back." With her heart beating louder than ever she left the room, stepped quietly into the corridor and found the first room that had been converted to a dormitory. Their guard was propped up in an old battered armchair. Alex would no doubt kill him later.

For now, he slept, in another room, close by. Close enough that she could have surprised him, slitting his throat as he dreamed of a successful future. But she knew she would be unable to kill them both. Which one of them was better to kill first? Alex? Or his psychotic sidekick?

For now, they both had to survive. Their time would come.

She allowed herself a brief and rare smile, then decided to walk no further. To her left was the door, or what was left of it. Most of the panes of glass had been smashed by countless kids, throwing stones and firing catapults. The wind blew through the voids and chilled her even more. There was no moon, or if there was it was hidden under an eiderdown of clouds.

She gently opened the door, expecting it to creak, but instead it dropped, hanging on one hinge. She cursed, silently, then held it, not knowing what to do next. Let it go and make a noise, or stand there all night like a frigid, pathetic concierge?

She let it go and in turn it repaid her confidence by hanging by a thread. She stepped though the corridor. The soles of her feet separated from the cool concrete with a barely audible noise as she edged back to what she considered to be their tomb.

In one of the rooms a loud snore woke its host. They waited until the rhythmic sound returned.

"Come on. We are getting out of this fucking chamber of horrors." She led him to the door, and they stepped into the fresh, cold night. And it felt magnificent.

They both inhaled the clean air, allowing the cold to burn their lungs. Thomas frantically tried to focus with his remaining eye, trying to see out through the dried blood. He wiped at it but it made little difference.

"You'll have to guide me Carrie. I'm sorry." He almost hissed his words.

"No time for niceties. This way."

They turned right, towards the noise of the motorway and with ever-improving night vision walked along the track, staying to the edge, ready to dive into the overgrown hedgerow. Ahead and to their right she could see the traffic, it seemed to float in the night sky. She shook her head. It was her mind playing tricks. They needed to get there and fast. If it came to it she had decided that she would climb over the barrier and walk out onto one of the busiest motorways in England and start waving her arms like a woman possessed.

She'd either be run over, which would annoy her immensely or attract somebody, either in a car, or a heavy goods vehicle or on the network of cameras that scanned the area. She wasn't choosy.

In five minutes they were five hundred metres away. Nothing. No alarms. No shouting. No frantic activity. Ten more and they were closer to the traffic noise. It was to their right, but the track went straight ahead.

Cross the fields, with their uneven surfaces or stick to the track?

The wind whipped across the open landscape and wrapped itself around them, cooling their body temperatures, dragging them down.

O'Shea recognised the signs. "Come on John we need to keep moving. If we stop, we die. Here, in a freezing field. OK?"

"OK." It was all he could find in his otherwise normally flamboyant vocabulary. It was enough for her.

"This way, come on."

It was getting damp underfoot, their strides became laboured. They were on the track now and they sensed that their environs had changed. The moon peered out from under the covers and for a short time offered them a view. Of the River Thames. They had gone the wrong way.

She steepled her hands up, against her lips then drummed her fingers against her knuckles. It was how she thought in times of stress, done it since she was a troubled teenager.

"Where are you, Jack?"

"I'm behind you."

"No, sorry, I said Jack. God I wish he was here now." She took stock of the situation, looked around. The motorway was there, to their right, but to get to it they had to navigate along a riverbank in the dark and Old Father Thames was an unforgiving soul at the best of times.

They could go back. No, that wasn't an option. Sooner or later someone would raise the alarm. She knew where they were, roughly. North Kent, at this time of night, half an hour from London and yet there wasn't a single bloody house for miles. Cars, hundreds of them snaked back and forth across the Queen Elizabeth Bridge. Aircraft, overhead, heading for Heathrow and the smaller airport in the heart of London. And the river, flowing from their left to their right, wending its way out of the capital, past the marshes and banks, and mudflats and the estuary and the place where fresh became salty and then the North Sea.

So they had to turn left. A sound stopped them both. A haunting call. A female screaming for help.

'Help...help...'

The sound was one of solitude, visceral.

"It's OK. It's a vixen. We need to move."

Thomas nodded. Living in a city, he had seen foxes in an urban environment, but had never heard the call. He shuddered.

"John. This way, we walk slowly, they won't find us out

here, we've made some ground on them. We just need to get to a house with a phone, then we are safe. Do you hear me John?"

She knew she was losing him.

"John? We have to go." She grabbed his arm and led him into the undergrowth.

"Stop!" It was Thomas this time. "There's a car coming."

"OK. You stay here and I'll flag them down."

"No. It's them Carrie. I know it is."

A swathe of bright light lit his face, red, dried and weeping sores and a dark crimson hole where his eye had once been.

The driver was concentrating on the task and had looked down to turn the radio off. They were passing the old factory and making their way to the river.

The face could have been a barn owl, silently drifting around the night sky, hunting. Or an optical illusion, a reflection off the surface of the river. It mattered not; he had turned the lights off now, hadn't seen a thing, and that provided O'Shea with the one chance she needed to drag Thomas into the undergrowth.

"Stay down. And don't move." Her words seemed to echo across the field and beyond. She could hear both of their hearts pounding.

They half crouched into a ragged hawthorn bush and waited, prayed that they would remain unseen.

The van slowed, changing down instead of braking, then rolled to a stop. No brake lights. Smart.

They were all within feet of the river. Three men got out, two from the back, one, the driver shone a small torch into the load area.

She could hear them now. Their accents were heavily laced, foreign to an English-speaking girl and her cripple of an associate.

She couldn't understand what they were saying, yet she was able to gather from their tone that one was in charge and what he said, went.

"Come on, we need to hurry, Jackdaw told us to do this and be back..." He checked his watch. "In ten minutes."

The three of them climbed into the van and rolled the rock out and onto the pallet truck. It clattered down, snapping the weak timbers and remained where it had dropped. Now they pushed and pulled and moaned and wheezed and sighed. Mopped their brows, looked at their watches.

"I will push it with the van."

Who were they to argue? It seemed like the only idea they had left. He turned the vehicle around, tyres slipping on the wet mud, then lined it up, turned on the sidelights so he could see. The last thing he wanted was to end up in the river too.

He released the hand brake and began to accelerate in second gear, hoping to get more traction. The two men stood back, but the driver called out to them. "Push me, we need to do everything we can. If we fail we will end up like that woman. Come on!"

He drove, they pushed. The London Stone was resolute.

O'Shea and Thomas watched, motionless from the sanctuary of the hedgerow, amazed that they hadn't been seen, feeling that they stood out like the Shard on the London skyline.

The men were focused on their task.

The driver pushed the accelerator harder, trying not to spin the wheels. Nothing.

"Stop brother," said the youngest. "I have an idea."

He began to break the pallet into pieces, creating a roadway of his own. "Try now."

The stone began to move. It wasn't rolling, more a case of sliding in the cold mud. Slowly it edged towards the river.

"We need more light."

He knew it was not without risk but turned the lights onto main beam. The river lit up, a slight mist rolled across the surface. The water was cold, and dark and deep.

He pushed more, eager to complete the task. They had come all this way for this. This apparently famous stone had been stolen, torn from its roots after a thousand years just to make a point. And now, they were tipping it into the river? It made no sense. But he knew it made less sense to challenge his leader.

And then it rolled, and kept rolling. Momentum was a wonderful thing. A gentle, steady pace, gathering speed until it began its journey down the bank and entered the water with a tremendous dull thud. A few ducks, startled by the noise, cackled and took flight.

The men stood and watched it sink, away from the bank, a few muddy bubbles rising to the surface.

Beneath the misty river the rock continued to roll, down, deeper towards the river bed, colliding with a long-submerged tree. It struck it hard, pushed it at least a foot and then came to rest.

The London Stone was gone and its theft would send shockwaves through the city and across the internet.

'Famous city landmark stolen!'

The men shook hands quietly. One produced a packet of cigarettes. Offered them around. The youngest declined. "I don't smoke."

"You do tonight brother. Come on, let's finish these and go and get some sleep, see what the other team did, see if they have brought us some money. Yes? A good idea?"

The younger one coughed, trying to clear his lungs. He flicked the cigarette into the river, its arc followed by the red embers until it hissed defeat into the cold water. He watched it circle in a small tidal eddy, then sink. He was transfixed, stood, swallowing hard, shaking and pointing.

The two older men looked at where he was pointing, ten feet off the bank, in the water, illuminated by the headlights.

O'Shea saw her too. Pushed her right hand up to her mouth to stop the scream, took it away, then back, silently retched. Thomas said nothing but stared. He could see now.

All five living were staring at the dead.

The rock had dislodged her.

Cynthia Bell had surfaced, her bloated, bleached body bobbed up, face first. O'Shea could swear she was smiling as she drifted downstream, towards the sea.

The men turned, got back in the van and headed back to the factory. Terrified. The dead had come back for them. The woman had looked at them. They made a pact. Tell no one. In fact, keep driving, to the port, head home. Forget the money, forget the fame. Forget it all.

Take the long way home.

O'Shea stood for a minute, maybe two, trying to compose herself. She had known her friend had died. Yet somehow hoped they had just buried her. Not tipped her body into the river to join the floating debris, cleansed by the outgoing tide.

"Bastards."

"Not now Carrie. We need to get to safety. Come on." For the first time Thomas had taken control, peering out through his good eye he took her hand and made towards a partially lit house about half a mile away.

He broke her trance again. "Come on. When they get back to that place they will wake the others and then we will be hunted. Right now we have the advantage, a head start. But not for long."

· · ·

The Transit van was about to drive by the old fireworks factory, turn left and head to the motorway and the port of Dover. Home was calling. The driver stopped and turned to his colleagues.

"We can't go. We have to tell Jackdaw. If we leave, he will have us tracked across Europe. Before we even get home, they will find us and we will be treated like animals. Or if we are lucky, he might just shoot us. I cannot live a life looking over my shoulder. Think about what he did to those people. That was for fun."

He had made the decision. He reversed back down the track and parked. They walked in, through the unsteady door, the noise woke the guard, who jumped up, flashed his torch at them, then realised he had been asleep. He stared at them. "Please do not tell anyone. I beg you."

He handed over his own cheap watch and some cigarettes. It was the currency of shame and he was easily bought. He walked quickly to the room that had been a cell, stepped through blood-tainted rags, slipped on a pool of stale urine, tried not to inhale, then turned on the light.

He put his hands up to his head. Balled his grubby fists. He may as well kill himself right now. He called out. Weak at first, then louder. "Help. Help"

They came running.

Jackdaw lifted himself off of his make-shift bed and walked. He knew.

"I will deal with you another day. Go. Get out there and find them. On foot, no cars. No lights, do I make myself clear? And when you come back, I need to speak to you, man to man."

The second and third van arrived. Constantin went to them, up to the driver's door.

"We have cash boss. Lots of it."

"I don't care. Go back out, onto the road, you go left, you right, they have escaped. Find them, but bring them back alive. If you have to, kill the man, but bring the woman back in one piece. Now go."

Men ran into the night, trying to find their footing on an unforgiving landscape which the moon chose not to illuminate. It was on O'Shea's side. Someone had to be.

She was moving at a pace now but suddenly found herself pushed down in the long and cold and wet grass that had a cool crispness to it. If they made it to the next morning, she knew they would see a heavy frost.

"Stay still. They are coming."

"I can't hear them."

"I can. I have the advantage Carrie. My ears are working better than they ever did. They are close. Stay down."

They waited. "OK, let's go, make for the house. Split up if we have to. Good luck."

She stopped him. "John. Thank you."

He smiled, focusing with what was left of his favoured sense and nodded. "No sweetheart, thank you."

CHAPTER FORTY

It took an hour of crawling through the deep grass before they had reached the outer-edge of a garden. A solitary detached house, inland from the Thames, shrouded in mist and now frost. Bordered by a tall hedge, chickens safely tucked up for the night, away from the inquisitive eyes of the vixen.

There was a horse somewhere, disturbed by their presence but loyal to their cause.

O'Shea moved slightly, causing the clothes she wore to creak and crack, their damp seams now frozen. She was right. If they hadn't been in such an abysmal situation, it would have been magical. The frost was beginning to appear, around them, on them, crystals linked together plunging the surroundings into an arctic pallor.

"Christ, it's cold..." She was too exhausted to lift her hands to her mouth and blow what warm air she had left across them.

How they had made it this far was beyond her. Human endurance and all that. A headline that would never appear.

'You are a belligerent soul Miss O'Shea...' The words of

her deputy head, long ago. He was right. She was. 'I can only hope your stubbornness rewards you one day.'

"You stay here John, I'll go and get help. There is a light on, looks like the kitchen. John? John?"

She pushed him but all he could do was roll over onto his back, mouth open, eye socket oozing blood, thinned by the night air, matting his face and hair and mixing with the last remains of eye liner and foundation. A grotesque carapace, on a forlorn face, in a lonely corner of England, only metres from salvation.

They were so close.

O'Shea began to sob. Each inward breath hurt her lungs. She tried to stand but had little in the way of energy. She lay down, her eyes close to the tundra-like soil, bitterly cold. Only a small insect was moving. It stepped cautiously across the ground, picking its way beyond her line of sight, stopping, she was sure, to gaze at her and smile, before slipping between the cracks and heading for somewhere less hostile.

She was hearing voices now. A rolling series of words, cascading through her mind. None of them made sense, but they carried on regardless.

Jackdaw had called off his attack dogs a few hours before. She had lain in the undergrowth, watching tail lights; some turning left, the others right. Hour after hour, waiting for the all clear and a chance to move.

The group had left the old fireworks factory, also leaving one of their own behind, forced to step off an old wooden box into the next life or die another day. Either way, it would be at his own hand, whilst Alex Stefanescu watched.

'Your choice.'

A rope. A knife or a cooling drink of battery acid. Laid out like a recipe challenge on a television programme.

'All fun and games my dear boy.' He had smiled as he watched the young man grabbing at the rope, legs spinning, eyes bulging, his feet frantically trying to get back to the box, which Constantin pushed with his foot, teasing, each time, an inch too far. His body swung and kicked and writhed, desperate, worse, dying. He had seconds left. He could hear his young girlfriend calling him. Then a violent, pulsing heartbeat.

"This is what happens when you fall asleep on duty gentlemen. Do I need to say anything else?"

Whilst he waited for anyone brave enough to answer he looked at the young male, who was now slowly swinging to a halt. Arms at his side, palms facing the group in a hopeless, almost inquisitive gesture.

'Why me?'

There was no time for tears. That function had been shut down. Eyes open. Tongue sticking out of the corner of his mouth. A pendulum of death, saved onto Alex's cell phone as a movie file. Short and sweet and unsavoury. Another one for the holiday snap album.

'No sir. Nothing.'

"Good. Then clear this place up, put him in one of the vans and find somewhere to dump him. But please...do it where no one will find him!" He almost danced as he paced around the floor, partly fuelled by adrenaline, mainly to fight off the cold.

"So now what?" Constantin asked his boss, impassive as it was possible to be. He had seen hangings before. Preferred to drown his victims.

"Now? We execute something more worthwhile. Phase Two. Send home those that have had enough, with the usual warning. Select the better ones and contact the new teams. I want to start very soon. And find me somewhere better to stay than this shithole."

"It is all organised. We will pick up a car soon. A local friend will help us. Someone from the travelling community.

He asked no questions. Then yes you and perhaps I can sleep in a far better place, whilst your workers earn their corn."

Alex smiled a lopsided smile. He did need to sleep. But not just yet. He needed to run a few things through his mind. Once or twice.

Their vehicle had stopped. He could hear Constantin talking, somewhere nearby. He opened one eye. People looking at him, wrapped up against the cold, almost bowing, willingly handing over a new mode of transport, one that would not attract attention. A reputation was worth its weight in gold.

When his head clashed against the tinted side window of the Audi A7 for the third time, he knew he needed to sleep. "Did you send those postcards and packages?"

"I arranged it, yes."

"Good. Wake me when we are there?"

He didn't hear the answer.

In the fields, close enough to smell the early crucifixion of some wholemeal bread O'Shea shuffled further on. She had laid alongside Thomas, all night, hoping he would still be alive, and praying she would survive long enough to call for help through her frost-parched lips.

She knew he was dead. But hope cost nothing. She raised an arm, a desperate attempt to attract the right attention, tried to focus through chilled lashes that tore at her sensitive skin each time she opened them. She looked at the bloodied fingertips, raw from crawling along the frigid ground, then let her arm drop back down beside her and closed her eyes.

It had been the longest night of her life.

· · ·

Half an hour north west, at the Home Office the mail was being delivered. Bright and early as it always had been. A simple yet effective system ensured the In mail was dealt with first, then the Out when things had calmed. Another brutally cold day in London had seen staff arriving, some on buses, some on the tube. A few had cycled, some hardier souls had walked. All were cold, wrapped in heavy coats and scarves. Stamping their feet at bus stops to stay warm. Talking to no one.

Frost clung to skeletal trees, bringing them to life with a sparkling cloak, windscreens and aerials of cars that had been left out in the streets were twice there normal size, again laden in ice crystals.

He breezed in with his usual savoir faire attitude to life. If there was a mail problem, he had a fix for it. Blue trousers, brown shoes, white shirt, red bow tie. Hair, just so. Trademark and he dared anyone to copy it.

"Morning, sir. Just an overnight folder from Brussels today sir." Official. No theatre.

"Morning. Nothing for you sir." Professional.

"Morning Alana just a couple of cards." Playful.

"Morning, sir. Yes, freezing. Nothing for you." Warm. Familiar. Perhaps too familiar.

Two members of the Prime Minister's department eyed the postcards, addressed to the PM, read them twice in fact.

One, the more senior, put down his tea and recited the words, slowly.

"Looking for something?" He then said it again. He placed the card back onto the desk. Lined it up with the edge of the blotter pad.

"Try Cannon Street. It rocks!" This one was read twice too, then lined up next to the first card.

He then reversed the sentences. Made the decision that the first way made more sense – that is what the writer would have intended. If indeed there was any sense to be made.

He looked up, finally. "Good morning Alana. Any idea what this is all about?" He pointed to the postcard – a scene of London's skyline, franked with a local postmark.

Sharply dressed. Black skirt, cream blouse, black shoes, medium-sized heel. Nice legs. No point in flaunting them. Not here.

"None at all boss. Same handwriting. The ramblings of yet another mad man? Not worth retaining?"

He agreed, then tossed them in the bin along with two-thirds of the other mail items received overnight.

His phone rang. As he listened, he looked down at the much-used waste bin. It contained a coffee cup, an apple core from the day before, brown, no longer pristine. But as rambling and senseless as they appeared, he lifted the cards back out of the bin and put them next to his diary. He had a friend at the Metropolitan Police and he knew he would find help if he asked. 'If ever you need me...'

Cade's hotel door resonated from a brisk knock. A police knock if ever he had heard one. He was ready, finishing off the knot on the navy striped tie and rubbing the caps of his shoes against the back of his well-pressed trousers as he peered through the spyhole. Old habits die hard. The face he saw was not its normal beaming morning vision but familiar nonetheless.

"You ready?" Roberts smiled at him, but Cade knew it was a troubled smile. Dressed in grey with a light grey shirt and red tie. Brown belt, brown shoes, brown watch strap. It didn't work for Cade but Roberts was content with his own expression of style.

"Too brown?"

"Possibly."

"So, you ready then?"

"Almost."

Cade nodded backwards over his shoulder towards the bathroom, smiling. The door was open wide enough for Roberts to see Elena, still in the process of dressing; dark blue bra, trimmed, perfect and lacy, hipster knickers. Her breasts were on the smaller side, but to most men, pretty, and perfect. She was tying her hair into a simple ponytail. It was still on the short side. And that suited Cade. As she bent forward to flick her hair backwards her obliques and abdominals were visible. Defined without being too much.

She stepped out into the bedroom, into a navy Milly Kalie dress, pulling it up and over her shoulders. Completely unfazed by the presence of two men.

Roberts tried to look elsewhere, fixing his gaze on the hotel artwork which smiled back in the form of a classically nude woman.

She peeked over her right shoulder, trapping his eyes with hers.

Men. Mars. Women, some other planet, one where they ruled – every day, regardless.

"Will you zip me up...Jason?" Playful as ever. The accent really worked on the darker corners of his very-male mind. His was a table for one, other people were in the room but he didn't even take a second to allow the other part of his brain to suggest, just for a moment, that his thoughts were understandable, but wrong.

Cade just gave him a discreet smile. 'You've zipped her

up mate. I've unzipped her, slid those dark blue knickers slowly down those incredible, smooth thighs...'

A thought best kept to himself. 'After you. Be my guest.'

What would Mrs Roberts say?

'What goes on tour, chief inspector?'

"Indeed." Roberts responded outwardly, causing Cade to lock eyes and frown, try to shield a half-smile.

But Roberts couldn't avoid looking. It was what most honest men did. Many women too, although they were more reluctant to admit it except in a group, a pack of them feasting on the body of a helpless firefighter or construction worker in some female-only club, somewhere, living out their girlish fantasies.

Roberts was back there. Feeling the need to take too long with the zip. Trying to get a discreet look at the tattoo. Perhaps pretending the zip was stuck, pushing it to clear her bra strap. It was pathetic. 'Stop it Jason. You are old enough to be...'

'Why not just unclip it, reach around and hold them mate?' Again, Cade knew when to verbalise and when to smile.

The tattoo was real. Small, between her shoulder blades, a black scorpion. No extra colours, no red poisoned tip or scrolled writing declaring the owner or anyone who viewed the artwork should 'live the dream', 'seize the day' or the words to a favoured song.

Just a jet black scorpion.

Roberts cleared his throat and the short-lived daydream.

"Anyway, it's been a long night for all of us I'm sure." He looked awkwardly at the unmade, king-sized bed. "And a lot has been happening. We can talk on the way. It seems that every man, his dog and his dog has been called in. Ready?"

Cade held the door for Elena who reeked of her

favourite perfume and a smile that said 'I know what you did last night Mr Cade.'

"Ready."

Along the corridor, John Daniel was also ready. He stepped out into the hallway, buttoning up his navy Aquascutum Bogart trench coat. He was carrying his trademark leather folder, a legacy of a conference, somewhere. Creased from many years of command-level battles, it contained his favoured pen and a few things he needed to get through the day.

"Morning Team. Time for a coffee and some breakfast?" Big smile. Earning well. Not many cares in the world.

"Morning JD. No sorry, we will be fed at the Home Office. My car is outside on double yellows. There have been some developments."

"Fair enough. Coffee with the government it is."

They all made their way to the car and five minutes later Roberts edged out into the traffic, lit the blue lights and forged his way through the snaking commuter chaos, in turn causing just a little more.

Very little was said for none of them had an idea of where things were heading.

"Did you sleep?"

"Yes. You?"

"Of course. A large bed with fine Egyptian cotton beats a squalid camp bed in a freezing piss-soaked concrete shelter any day. Or night."

Constantin smiled the vacant smile he was known for, allowing the steaming coffee to penetrate to the roots of his crumpled teeth, making them bleed just enough that blood overtook coffee in the taste challenge.

"I have always admired the feel of such bedding. When I become richer, it will feature in all my homes. I may even invite *Horse & Hound* to come an do an interview with me!"

They laughed. Although the older man had never heard of the magazine.

"So how long before they step up their patrols, their intelligence gathering?"

"More importantly Constantin how long before their little parcel arrives?"

"The men told me it would be there this morning. I paid extra for an urgent delivery."

Alex laughed, genuinely. He would give almost anything to see the reaction. It had been worth the ten thousand he gave to the traveller in exchange for the newer car and the services of one of their own people, disguised as a motor-cycle courier, moving with speed, among his apparent peers, in a city awash with such people. People to see, places to go.

"OK. Have we got everything? This meeting needs to be secure and go well. No hitches. No outstanding issues or questions. I want everyone to be fully briefed, completely aware of the rules of engagement. Any last minute 'stuff'? We can walk and talk." Sassy Lane looked intently at her PA – a male, in his fifties who knew more about politicians than almost anyone he knew.

"Nothing major, ma'am. A few mail items." He turned. A junior was hurrying with two courier parcels, sealed and bearing the familiar yellow logos of a very familiar delivery company.

"These just came, sir. I know you are going into a meeting, but they need signing for."

He looked at the labels. The first was addressed to Sassy Lane. The second the Prime Minister.

"You've done the usual with this?"

She tried not to reply with a 'do I look stupid' glance.

"Yes, of course. No trace, clear on the ION scanner, all good to go."

He looked at the declaration. 'Sporting goods.'

He showed it Lane. "X-ray image looks like a golf ball. The other is small, indistinct, but not large enough to cause concern. Nothing sinister. Any idea, boss? Shall we open them?"

"No. It's fine. Golf? I have no idea. None at all. Haven't played in years. Someone obviously has my name on a mailing list. Come on, let's go, we can open it later. If you have put them both through the system, then Jim can do what he likes with his. I don't feel like opening presents."

She walked towards the major incident room and was met en route by one of her colleagues.

"Ah Minister, glad I caught you."

"You haven't, I'm busy."

"Appreciate that Minister, but I have intercepted these. They made no sense until I put in a call to a police colleague."

He showed Lane the postcards. "Turns out the clue was Cannon Street. There was a crime committed there overnight."

"Oh, don't tell me Karen Millen has closed down?"

"Hardly ma'am. Actually, it would appear that your stone has been stolen."

CHAPTER FORTY-ONE

Her jaw lowered, her eyes closed. Knuckles whitened. There were days in politics. This was going to be one of them.

"Jesus...no. Cade was right. They have made their statement. Find out how the bloody hell our people allowed this to happen? Ask questions, Charlie and ask them now. It's been there a thousand years!" She punched the wall, not hurting herself in the slightest but leaving a fist-sized impression in the plasterwork.

She turned and walked at a pace to the incident room. People moved out of her way. They knew the signs.

"I might not play golf anymore, Charlie. But so help me, I will *swing* for these bastards." They moved through the corridor at a pace now. Minutes later they would be at the most secure briefing room in the building.

As a house name *Riverview* was a misnomer – you had to be sat on the roof to actually see the Thames, but her dear old dad had a sense of humour. And as was often the way at this time of the year the detached property looked almost desolate, shrouded in a fine veil of mist that sat a few feet off the surrounding arable land and only ever immediately around her home.

The local kids said the place was haunted and stayed away. And that suited the owner.

As the crow, or Jackdaw flew, about half an hour away from central London, the remote house had a remote garden and a faded black front door, black peeling paintwork and pebbled-dashed walls.

The owner was walking down the hallway, back to the kitchen, when she heard the bread pop out of the time-served toaster which sat to the left of the well-polished Aga that provided both cooking and warmth.

Wholemeal. None of that bleached rubbish they sold to people who didn't know better. She scooped it out with a fork, and contrary to what people told her, she had yet to be electrocuted.

She needed another mug of tea, because in her words it was 'bloody well cold enough to freeze the nipples off a nun'. It was actually a saying of her dad's and one she never quite understood.

She lived alone so spoke to herself, a lot. To be completely accurate, she lived with her canine pal, a Golden Retriever called Nick.

"Looks cold enough out there, Nick…" She pulled the curtains back, rubbed the condensation away, drew a smiley face and continued to create a breakfast of sorts; a hard-boiled egg, toast and marmalade, an over-ripe banana and a mug of what she referred to as 'builder's' tea; dark, strong and hot – like she would choose her ideal man, if she ever met him.

"I wonder what today will bring?"

She finished the meal, put the mug into the sink and called for Nick.

"Walkies!" He was alongside her in seconds, unnecessary lead in his soft mouth, running for the back door where once opened he would almost bowl her over, spin around in circles, his paws crushing the frost-covered grass, head down, bottom up and then back to Marlene Bradley, his equally dutiful owner. It was the highlight of his day.

She didn't bother to lock up, slipped her hands into grey woollen gloves, pulled the collar up to meet the scarf and set off on what would be the first of four walks across the fields towards the river.

She glanced up into the blue but bitterly cold sky which was its usual criss-cross of contrails, vapour marks of where aircraft had been. She often stood and admired them, trying to guess where they were heading. A blue and white plane was cruising from her right, lower all the time, no doubt heading towards Heathrow. She waved. She always did. It made her smile.

Nick pranced across the paddocks towards the old fireworks factory, his head visible now and then as he leapt up to look for his mistress. Make sure she was still there. That made her smile too.

It had been minutes since he had done it. He'd come back, he always did. But she could hear him, making a noise. It wasn't a growl – or playful, inquisitive bark. In fact, she had never heard it before. She walked towards where she had last seen him, through the cold, frosty grass, among the mist and weeds and taller native grasses that had grown during the autumn. She could hear her own footsteps, and her cold breaths, that and the call of a rising Skylark. Well, that and the airliner and the distant traffic. And the low-level moaning of a human voice.

"Help...me..."

· · ·

The Boeing 777 was turning south before the Thames Estuary, leaving yet another white trail in a crisp winter sky. Wherever the pilot looked there were planes, short haul, long haul and small, private commuter aircraft. The Thomson Holidays jet had flown north over London Heathrow and was now lining up on finals, picking its slot in the jigsaw that was the London sky.

Below, in the English Channel, somewhere near Thanet a battalion of white windmills rotated with the wind, generating electricity for the people of the city, their tall, solid towers in a constant battle with the sea and the elements.

The chartered flight was full, and its semi-bronze passengers were preparing themselves for the sharp drop in temperature, having spent the previous ten days in Florida. It looked cold, down there on the streets of Kent.

One passenger, thirteen-year-old Abigail Gripton, was doing what she did every time she was lucky enough to fly, staring out of the window, intently watching, looking at the cars and minute people, imagining who they were and where they were going. Her imagination ran riot.

There, to her right, was the River Thames. It looked cold. She decided that she didn't want to go for a swim today and instead counted the small boats that were littering the river. Her eyesight was as exceptional as that of any other thirteen-year-old, but Abigail had already developed a sixth sense for the unusual.

And then she saw it. Sat up, lifting herself against the pressure of the seat belt, trying to gain a better view. She had seconds.

"Daddy, there is a person swimming – down there, in the river."

"I doubt it love. It's far too cold." Her father Steve, a retired police officer, smiled, tapped his daughter on the head. "Not long now."

"No, Daddy, look. A person, floating."

Gripton was a former tactical observer with the north Midlands Helicopter Support Unit. He had spent years looking down on the world below and was proud of his success rate – they said he could spot a stolen car without the high-powered lens – had a nose for trouble.

He lifted himself up in the middle seat. Straining to see. Surely not? Two seconds. He focused as best as he could. Trying to see through pockets of mist.

"Where?"

"There! The lady doesn't have any clothes on. Look!"

One second.

"Jesus." He pressed the call button on his seat back. Pressed it again. Stood up.

The crew member could see that something was happening. Told him to sit down. Gripton shouted down to the rear galley area.

"Get the pilot to mark the area. Do it. Now!"

He knew it was probably futile. The crew member just shrugged, mimed 'I can't hear you.'

"There is a body in the river, north side, somewhere near the bridge!"

She heard that.

Marlene Bradley stood for a second, lowered herself down through the covering of mist, trying to process the sight before her. A man, at least she thought it was, lying on his back, a fresh and vivid and bloody diagonal cross over his face and make-up. Yes, he was wearing make-up. It was then she realised that the blood-soaked cloth that was protruding from his face was where his eye used to be. Dark red blood. White cloth. And make-up.

She looked, then looked away. And then she vomited

into the long grass, and then again, bringing up the breakfast in spasmodic waves of which she had no control, the heat of her stomach contents causing the grass to steam.

She fished around in her pockets, hunting for the cell phone that her brother had bought her. 'You'll need that one day, girl!'

"Bugger, it's in the house. Come on, Nick."

As she turned to run, she heard the voice again.

She stepped back around the body, moving slowly towards the sound, as slowly as she dared. Looking around her, above the layer of cool moist air, now frantic. Her head and upper torso were all the distant motorists would have seen. It looked surreal. What was beneath the shroud? Was she next?

She took a breath. A cold, biting breeze collided with her windpipe. Tried to calm herself down. She had been in situations like this before. 'Calm down.'

Her eyes narrowed against the wind, teeth chattered, lips raw.

A hand grabbed hold of her foot, gripped onto her as if its owner's life had been determined by her arrival. It had.

"Oh my God!" she shrieked, kicking out. No one heard her. If she slipped beneath the surface, what then?

She dropped to her knee and immediately faced another person. Curled in the foetal position. Whispering. Then nothing.

She was transfixed. "It's a woman, isn't it? Oh God, please tell me that wasn't her last act? Do something. I have to do something." Her mind churned with thoughts. This was far from normal, Very, far from normal.

She spoke to Nick, who was pushing the body with his paw, still playful.

"Good boy, Nick. Stay with mummy. Stay."

Something told Bradley that this was a friend before her,

not a foe. A victim, not an offender. Impassive, eyes fixed shut, bald, she was bald. But she was a she. Her coat gaped, two buttons missing, revealing a shapely breast. Her features were definitely female. And she needed Marlene's help. Now.

"My love, are you OK? Talk to me." She lowered herself down, still wary of the other body, then prodded the frozen form with her boot, slipped her glove from her hand, placed two fingers against her carotid, just as she had been taught, all those years ago, as a student nurse at Guy's Hospital. A pulse. Shallow at best. This was a hypothermic woman clinging to life.

She wracked her brain. What was the important temperature? Come on. Thirty-five, that was it, any lower, and you were heading the wrong way and it happened rapidly. This woman was almost frozen. Her core temperature was probably in the twenties.

It all depended upon how used to the conditions a person was. She had read about humans who had drifted into a state of hibernation and survived. She was thinking about it now, mesmerized by the situation that was unfolding, walking distance from her warm and inviting home. She needed to get help.

"Come on, Marlene. Stop messing about. Get help."

And then it happened again, but this time the eyes were open, startled, trying to scream, desperately trying to swallow away the cold and fear, her lips peeling apart, leaving skin torn and bleeding.

"Jack. Jack. Jack. Cade."

"OK, my love, I'll get Jack…you just relax."

"Jack…"

"Stay here. Stay here." It seemed a ludicrous thing to say to a young woman who was as near to death as she could be. "I'll get help, dear."

She ran now, but Nick stayed, lying alongside Carrie

O'Shea and willing her to stay alive.

"...daw. Jackdaw..." She closed her eyes again. Slept for five minutes, woke with a start, her heart pounding. She could feel something warm in her hand.

She broke a smile and whispered, "A rescue dog. I don't suppose you have any brandy do you?" She laughed a weakened laugh, then laid her head down once more. She was safe, but was she alive?

In the house Bradley dialled and spoke. "Ambulance. And Police. I need an air ambulance or she won't make it. Look for a mad woman waving like someone's life depends on it. The house with the Union Jack. We need to save one of them." She outlined the situation as best as she could.

"You can't miss me, I'm the only house here. Not far from the old firework factory."

"There is more than one casualty?"

"Yes, but one hasn't made it. I need to go back to the girl."

Bradley put the phone down, grabbed a pile of blankets and a first aid kit and ran. It was the first time she had run in fifty years.

The ambulance operator shared the information with her police colleague, who in turn did the same with his boss.

"Possible murder scene ma'am just off the A206 – male deceased. One seriously injured female, up near the old Wells Fireworks Factory. Ambulance en route." She hit enter and started the incident log, unaware that it had just shared with the larger Metropolitan Police command system.

In the Essex control room, northeast of London, another operator was entering a job into their own system.

"Boss. Report from Heathrow Air Traffic Control. Crew of a Triple Seven say a passenger sighted a body in the Thames, somewhere near the QE2 Bridge. Could be anything, but we've got a maritime unit on the way."

"I want all jobs within thirty miles of us to be read, re-read, and then analysed by our intelligence people. No exceptions." These were the original words of AC Mike Collins at the initial briefing for Operation Orion.

"Knowledge is power, and I want every bit you can find. I don't want to be two steps behind this lot. One, at the very worst. I want them to feel us breathing down their necks. Clear?"

The system worked. It was amazing what could be done with the correct funding. The Met Police were already crunching the data and hitting send to the Op Orion team before the air ambulance had even left its base in Kent.

She heard it before she saw it. Bradley did too. The blades chopping through the cold winter air that whipped off the Thames Estuary.

"They're here, girl. They're here. Just hang on a little longer." She laid alongside her, under the blankets, giving as much of her bodily warmth as she could.

The MD902 circled, the crew decided on the best landing place, and in under fifteen minutes were calling their own control room.

"Helimed Two One – Helimed Two One. On scene, please."

CHAPTER FORTY-TWO

LANE CLOSED THE DOOR BEHIND HER, ENTERED, EVERYONE made to stand. She ushered them down. It was what they always did.

"Good morning." She looked around the room. All were present. The Prime Minister, the police minister, various police commanders including Acting Deputy Commissioner Mike Collins and the key members of the Operation Orion team, led by Jason Roberts and supported by Cade and Daniel. Elena had been accepted and acknowledged as the Subject Matter Expert on Eastern Europe but more notably the SME on Alex Stefanescu.

"Good morning, Prime Minister. I'll begin if I may?"

James Cole nodded and smiled. He had a coolness that had little to do with the weather outside, weather that clung in various forms to the tinted windows and aluminium cladding of the Terry Farrell designed building and wouldn't let go of its grip for a few more days.

"You may."

She moved straight into the latest news.

"I find swearing only helps in certain situations. This is

one of them. Overnight...some bastard or bastards have removed the London Stone."

Silence.

"It's been there for a thousand years Minister."

"Oh thank you for telling me something I didn't know."

"Thank you Home Secretary." Cole could sense the chill. "I think the point of Minister Lane's anger is simple. The stone is just an ordinary lump of sandstone or granite or whatever it is. Its position in the city is what counts. It is an icon. Ignored by countless commuters yet cherished. Like one would cherish a weatherman or newsreader. Take them for granted until they are gone. And now, the stone has gone. Under our noses, with surveillance and yet we had no one to respond."

He turned and looked at Mike Collins.

"Sir. I can only apologise. We were busy last night. In fact we are permanently busy. But last night was off the scale. Calls all over the city to bank alarms, traffic light signalling issues, even a few explosions at ATMs. This is not the time to discuss cuts to our service and how that impacts upon our ability to..."

Cole cut him off. "No, Mike, it isn't. But I get your point. I need this thing, this beloved lump of sandstone back, in situ or somewhere safer, today, or sooner. They have sent a message, now we, the people of London must reply – as we always have done – in acts not words. Keep this out of the press please."

Lane took the hint and moved on.

Collins stared down at the list of priority jobs that had distracted his staff. Two more stood out. He ran a yellow highlighter through them.

Lane continued. "New intelligence indicates that our targets are aiming to attack a property within the 'walls of London' – makes no sense to me, after all we are not Paris are we?" It raised a small, much needed and unexpected cheer. And a smile from Lane.

"As it stands our counter terrorist intelligence teams tell us that whilst an attack is considered likely as yet nothing has happened. This I'm sure you will all agree is a blessing." All nodded. She had their attention.

"So, whilst the streets are free of the rivers of blood my father waxed lyrical about we need to focus on this team – this Seventh Wave. We are stepping up surveillance, increasing covert patrols, targeting human sources, listening. If it comes to pass that we are doing anything illegal then only my head will roll. You have my word." She meant it. They knew.

"But for now, I am hereby unleashing the Operation Orion team. DCI Roberts, I need you to allow a number of your squad to become a little bit more...feral than they have been. Do we understand each other?"

He cleared his throat, unintentionally straightened his tie. Stood.

"Absolutely Minister. Unleashed they are. Now what?"

"Well I would have thought that was pretty obvious. Your boys and girls need to start shaking the tree. All of them. Give them a bloody shake and see what falls out. Need I remind you that this is not about a lump of sandstone but the potential reputation of the United Kingdom on the European – no, on the world map. Leaving Europe is one thing, admitting it had been planned for years will be an unmitigated disaster."

Cade's phone buzzed in his pocket. He discreetly looked – as a schoolboy tries to discreetly unwrap a year-old toffee.

"Something more pressing Mr Cade?" It was Halford peering over the brim of his glasses as a cat would at a mouse it was about to tease.

"As it happens, yes. If you will all forgive me?"

"Do we have any choice?" Halford pressed, enjoying the game.

"No." Cade's reply unsettled him. There were few people that had the courage to go beyond the first round with Halford.

Cade nodded to the Prime Minister and discreetly left the room, dialling as he walked.

"Cade here. Talk to me please. This had better be important or I have just sacrificed what is left of my tattered reputation at the altar of the police minister."

He nodded, made the right noises then stopped in his tracks.

"And David how is this anything to do with me?"

"Well Jack I appreciate a murder may not be within your current remit, but we were told to identify any jobs of interest within thirty miles that might relate to Op Orion."

"And this does?"

"We don't exactly know yet sir, but I can tell you the survivor is a woman, and she has asked for you by name."

"Did you get her name?"

"No. Not yet."

"Well ring me again when you do."

"Of course."

"Oh, and Dave."

"Yes."

"Well done. Get stuck into it and keep me in touch. Anything. And I mean anything, I want to know. We've just been given the green light by the Home Secretary, we are officially, in her words, feral, and that means you too."

Dave Francis smiled. He was back in the game. All he needed to do was stay off the drink and focus. He could start by scanning the systems and finding as much information about the two latest jobs and the two overnight jobs that stood out on his list. He also ran a highlighter through them but his was green.

Cade returned to the briefing, edging by the guard who recognised him immediately.

"Going back in boss?"

"I am. All quiet on the western front?"

"So far yes."

Cade walked quietly back in.

"So, let's sum this up. We are all busy people. Intelligence Units will feed into the analysts working on Orion. Frontline units will be told that there is a heightened risk of an event, targeting London. DCI Roberts will form a break-away team who will report to myself and Mr Halford. That is the reporting line. Clear?"

Heads nodded.

"Jack. Nice of you to join us again. Nothing serious I hope?"

"No ma'am, not yet."

"OK. One last thing I would like you all to do. Please stand and join me in the time honoured tradition of singing happy birthday – and on this occasion I know the recipient won't object to you inserting James instead of Prime Minister."

Cole smiled and feigned embarrassment. "Oh no really Home Secretary. Do we have to?"

Halford started the singing, a chance to gain an advantage over Lane, a deeper than expected tone that caused a chill to run along Lane's spine.

As the group sang, some with gusto, some awkwardly, some respectfully, Cole opened his parcel. He pulled at the contents, a white linen handkerchief embroidered with his initials. Classy. He unwrapped it and the tooth fell onto the desk, ivory encrusted with aging blood.

"Bloody hell!" The song was on its third line.

"Happy birthday dear James..."

A few people stopped, some gathered around Cole. Some continued, unsure what the protocols were in such circumstances.

Roberts assumed the lead role. "Sir. Leave it. Don't touch it. Or the packaging. DS McGee get someone down here with a camera and an exhibit kit now please."

Sassy Lane was tearing the security strip from her own parcel. She looked at Roberts and without words asked, "What Jason? Can it really get any worse?"

"Boss, don't open it. Please. Let me. Move away."

She did as she was told. Roberts picked up the package and tried to gently tease the seams apart – to have a look inside. He knew he was breaching something in a security report, somewhere deep in the vaults of the Home Office. But he had gone this far and the package has met all of the security standard operating procedures.

As the final line of the song finished, the parcel's seam gave way and the partially-deflated eyeball left the package and shot across the table, rolling a little further, then stopping at the edge, as a golf ball would on the edge of the hole, pausing, teasing the crowd, the lens staring up at Halford.

"Happy birthday...to you."

CHAPTER FORTY-THREE

Halford stared at Roberts – ice cold, impassive, as a Tiger shark examines its prey before it rips it in two. His own eyes as lifeless as the one that sat, awkwardly staring back at him.

Unusually he stammered slightly then spoke.

"W-what the bloody hell kind of circus are you running here Roberts?" He thumped his fist down onto the table, causing pens, cups and the eye to bounce and then return to the table.

Roberts was still reeling from the shock of seeing the eye, as a staunch vegetarian he began to have bizarre thoughts, trying to focus on the Minister for Police he found himself almost able to feel his teeth crunching into it, an amuse bouche before the main meal.

It made him nauseous to the point of retching.

Then he responded – and it was career limiting.

"Us? Sir, respectfully, this is *your* domain, your staff checked these packages, please do not blame me and my team. Need I remind you...?"

"No, you bloody well need not, chief inspector, you

damn well know your place or I'll call the taxi for the... bloody labour exchange. Do you hear me?"

Roberts was caught by an uppercut but had had enough. He was happy to walk, leave it all behind and find a role somewhere else. There was always work for someone like Jason Roberts.

"Yes, I hear you Minister but again, as these people present are my witnesses..."

James Cole held his hand aloft – it meant stop in any language.

But Roberts was far from done.

"As these people are my witnesses and that includes you Prime Minister..." He let the words hang like the smell of a freshly-opened airliner door. "My team are not responsible for this appalling act. My men have worked their bollocks off..." He gritted his teeth and nodded at Bridie McGee acknowledging that she was one of the last women left on the team.

"...Day and night. None of it claimed as overtime. Sir, need I further remind you that in recent times I have lost one of my best Detectives, no, make that two. One hung himself because of this, the other was decapitated. My analyst was kidnapped and her body had yet to be recovered. All doing what they did best. But you..."

"Enough!" said Halford, trying to regain ground.

"I have not fucking finished Halford!" Career. Limited.

"You think an eyeball is bad? Try having your analyst's hand posted back to inside a candle. It sat on my desk, slowly revealing itself when I lit the bloody thing. They cut her hand off to make a point! She was harmless. But they have got her somewhere right now and for all I know she may be lying in a gutter somewhere."

James Cole interrupted a clearly impassioned Roberts.

"Thank you, chief inspector, I think we all need a break. We'll get some tea…"

"Tea? I'm the first to love a cup of tea boss but this is no time for tea. I will not and cannot stand by and be criticised by a man who has had his own hand involved – in this case in slashing police numbers." Now it had become political.

"To cap it all my senior analyst is also missing – along with one of the main Operation Orion intelligence sources. Gone. Without a trace. This is not a team of amateurs here Minister. They are hunting in packs." He was calming now.

"This is a group that have targeted this city over and over again and each time, they get away with it. And everything I see tells me that this is the beginning. The worst is yet to come. They are organised. Practically no signals or electronics. Using Blackberries. Face-to-face meetings that we never see. They hold a few aces, they want them all. And it's going to cost the United Kingdom dearly. You lose face. I've lost three possibly four staff. They have families. And so do the rest of my team. And sir, so do I, and I want to return home safely."

Mike Collins leant forward, the eyeball was still there watching the ongoing debate but it had turned to face him, twisted, the only thing it didn't do was blink.

"I have to back my DCI, Prime Minister. The Orion squad have invested countless hours and resources to prevent the UK's potentially darkest hour since the Second World War. You owe them at least a debt of gratitude. As he pointed out eloquently he has lost staff, and that means the Met Police family has too. Two and two unconfirmed is too many."

Cade stood. Watching hawk-like for the opening.

"Prime Minister, Home Secretary, Mr Halford. If I may?"

"Ah the inevitable police tag team!" Halford grinned at anyone who would reciprocate.

"Well the way I see it someone has to look after us – because you as our minister appear to be doing sweet Fanny Adams about the situation."

Cade had nothing to lose. Financially secure. Independent. Carefree – except for the fact that he was a hated man, hated by a sociopath who was also secure in both financial and physical support. And he was on the prowl for Cade and anyone else who associated with him.

Cole gestured with his hands, palm outwards. 'Be my guest. Why not, everyone else has.' Cole actually liked Cade and he knew his Home Secretary did too. He was a case of what you saw you got, wrapped into a sophisticated package that was grounded in reality. Certainly wasn't spy material – he was a well-trained and instinctive cop at heart and they were a rare commodity. Roberts and Daniel were cut from the same cloth and Roberts' two DSs were their equal.

"Thank you. I left the room as I needed to take a call from my Field Intelligence Officer."

"The drunk you employed to crunch data because you daren't let him out onto the streets Cade?"

"Need I remind you minister that I choose to be here. Unlike you, I don't need to work. However, yes Mr Halford, that's correct. David Francis. A man who is five times better drunk than most sober people. He's far too dangerous to let him off the leash, never know what he might get up to – or who he might visit – better still, what he might find. Now, if you don't mind I'd like to encourage a few people in this room to take their collective heads out of the sand, before they turn to dust." The Tiger shark had just met the Great White.

"As I was saying, I took a call. The Maritime Unit responded to a job about a body in the Thames. Turns out a little girl on a plane spotted her. She'd make a good cop one day. The body has been recovered and is being examined at the scene. It is female and has a hand missing."

He looked across at Roberts. "Sorry Jason. Truly."

Roberts heard what he feared the most. Stared at Cade, then Halford. He would and could happily break the man's neck.

"The second bit of news, and call me pedantic is that the London Stone is made from limestone."

Halford, the Tiger was cruising in the shadows, away from the sunlight, his stripes disguising him well, a fearsome predator. Laced with sarcasm, a slowly dripping tap of disdain.

"Well, thank you Jack for your enlightening lesson in geology." He clapped sarcastically, emphasising each sound. Holding the hands together just long enough, but he was clapping alone.

Lane caught Halford's eye and in in own inimitable style mouthed an expletive that no one else saw.

"No, Police Minister, it was actually a lesson in how to differentiate fact from supposition." The Great White nudged him back into the dark, tore a few deep gashes into his flanks.

"The London Stone is limestone not sandstone. It's a fact, I deal in them, they are really very rewarding – perhaps, if I may, you should try it sometime." He looked at his fingernails, needlessly examining them but deliberately stalling. "And I know where the stone is."

Halford was bitten in two and sinking.

Sassy Lane looked, almost pleaded with her eyes. "What? Talk to me."

"It's in the river ma'am – as it happens across the water from where they have found the body of Cynthia Bell earlier today. Call it her last act of defiance. A naked and cold middle finger up at Mr Stefanescu and his cohorts."

"I'm not with you, how do you know this? If as you say Miss Bell is sadly dead?"

"Sadly I have to agree, for I am certain Cynthia is no longer with us. But she left a legacy. Her demise was the catalyst for Carrie O'Shea to escape. They had been held at a disused factory on the Kent side of the River Thames. Desolate and off the radar. That is where the Seventh Wave team have been operating from. Thirty minutes from this office. Hiding, in plain sight. I have taken the liberty of sending armed units from Kent into the area to sweep the place."

Lane was delighted, saddened, but delighted nonetheless. "Sorry Jack, call me docile. "How do we know all of this?"

"Because I have just had word that Miss O'Shea is in an air ambulance on her way to hospital."

Roberts clenched his fists, wanting to punch the air. "Yes. Oh this is outstanding news." He needed some and cared not for protocols. It would take a cold man to divert his new-found energy.

"She was found by a member of the public. Hypothermic, close to death, injured but alive. It transpires that the body of a male was found at the scene, alongside her. Kent Police are dealing with that too. We will send DSs McGee and Fisher to the scene now. I will head to the hospital with your blessing. May I venture to suggest that the time for British nicety has ended Prime Minister? We need, as my dear father once said 'To put our boot up someone's arse' and like Cinderella the boot fits my foot just fine."

"I hear you Mr Cade, but proceed with caution. The lion's den is a dangerous place. But moving on, this is good news. Good news indeed. The male, can we, dare we assume that this is the body of Stefanescu?"

"Sadly not. The body is mutilated and missing an eye. I may be wrong ma'am, but if I were a betting man, which I was on one occasion, it will be the one that was staring at your police minister. Its owner was a colourful character who had provided lifesaving intelligence to both Mr Roberts and I, often at great personal risk. The very least you can do is organise some form of acknowledgement for his family, if indeed he had one. His codename was Harrier. We will raise a glass at the Sanctuary at some point, you are welcome to join us."

"Thank you but I must decline. Do send our best wishes to Miss O'Shea." She turned to a practically silent Elena Petrova.

"And you Miss Petrova, you must be delighted that Miss O'Shea is alive?"

"Delighted. Of course." She pushed her chair back, crossed her legs.

She wasn't delighted and three men in the room knew why.

And so did Lane. She was a women after all.

"All you have to do now is find the men that did this. Before I do."

Cole wrapped up the meeting, handed responsibility back to ADC Mike Collins then stood causing everyone to follow suit.

"Not since the Falklands War has there been such a threat to the British reputation. This is no longer about money. This is about that reputation, a reputation built over hundreds of years, when the Union Jack flew proudly across the world, and being British meant something. I will not stand by and watch that standard torn to shreds by some nomadic thieves. We do not negotiate with terrorists, and in my book these people are next in line."

He slipped the cool blue glasses from his face, laid them

down, lenses up, on the overly-large and immaculate table and looked, slowly and deliberately at each person in the room.

"They want to play the game of an eye for an eye and a tooth for a tooth then so be it. Gloves off. No media. Chatham House Rules. The first person to discuss this beyond the teams represented in this room deals with me and me alone. Need I remind you the Commissioner and his Deputy are out of the country but looking to return within days? With that in mind, there is something else you all need to know."

It was clear that something else was concerning him. He looked across at his most senior intelligence advisor, waited for the nod.

"Some new information came to light last night, via an electronic interception. The threat to London has been increased. Tenfold. We now sit at the next level team. By March something is going to happen that will cause chaos. And right now, we haven't got a clue."

Cole exhaled slowly, allowing him time to think, to compose himself. "Eight weeks. And that troubles me, keeps me awake at night. I will never say 'on my watch' – that's reserved for our colonial cousins."

He looked down at the table, picked up the tooth, examined it.

"But what I will say is this, you heard the Home Secretary. Let's go and remind a few people that the British lion has these."

He held the tooth up between his thumb and forefinger.

"But much, much larger. The meeting is over. Take care of each other."

The room was empty in minutes. Two staff arrived and exhibited the body parts and the caterers wheeled away the tea and coffee that was never served.

Roberts grabbed a handful of biscuits off the trolley and walked to his car with Daniel. Cade hung back.

"Elena. You OK?"

"Yes. Of course."

"You seem tense."

"Wouldn't you be if you knew the man you were related to was the greatest threat to a country since a war that happened before I was even born?"

She had a point.

"Fair enough. But you are safe. With me."

"I can look after myself Jack. You know that. I don't need any one to act as a body guard." She smiled but it was false. She knew, he knew and at that point something had changed. "Least of all you."

He walked her to the car. Opened the door, let her sit down, avoiding the flash of thighs, then closed it and walked around to John Daniel who was stood on the pavement leaning into the stiffening northerly.

"She OK Jack?" Daniel was hunched own against the biting wind.

"No. And I don't know why." Cade shivered, but he was far from cold.

As they drove back to their office through thickening snow flurries none of the four spoke. Daniel's phone vibrating brought an end to the silence.

"John Daniel."

"John, good to hear your voice. Johnnie Hewett."

"Well, hello. I thought you had headed off into the sunset? Last time I saw you, you were wearing a paper suit and the kind of half-smile of someone that had stood in cat shit and come out smelling of frangipani."

"Hardly. You can't put a good man down. You know that

better than most. Talking of sweet smelling tropical flowers how is the lovely Elena?"

"She's fine. Sends her regards."

"Yes, she looks it." A less than delicate hint that Hewett was watching them.

"We need to meet JD."

"OK. Any reason?"

"Ever the cop. JD I have two members that need to join your team."

"Won't the Home Secretary have to authorise that?"

"Oh come along John, a minor issue. Yes, of course, she signed this one off days ago. Where can we meet? This evening. Late."

"Overt or covert?"

"Somewhere that our friend Alex won't easily stumble across us but not a police station of government building. We will be involved in history making, why not surprise me with the location. And bring Jack."

"What about the other members of the team?" He looked at Roberts, eyebrows raised.

"Just Jack. For now. And JD, take me off hands-free for a moment."

"OK. Go ahead."

"John, you need to trust me. I'm wearing a new suit these days. What you saw last time was a carapace. We fly the same colours, you just need to accept that and convince your protégé too."

"Alright." He thought for a moment. He had a friend that had always promised to help. Now was the time to make the call.

"I'll ring you back in an hour."

He did. It was arranged.

CHAPTER FORTY-FOUR

Arriving back at the unit the four people went their separate ways. Before that happened Daniel had stopped Cade in the car park.

"Jack. I know you are heading to see Carrie. I need you back here for nine, nine thirty latest – we've got a date. Send her my love."

"See you later Jack. Say hello to her for me." Elena's words were sincere but her look said otherwise. It had nothing to do with the temperature outside. She let the door close behind her without looking back.

It was warmer in the main secure office where she was formally introduced to David Francis, she pulled a typist's chair alongside Francis, smiled and said, "Thanks Jason. Hello David. I am here to help. What do you need?"

Francis rubbed his eyes which were sore from scanning the myriad systems employed by the Met Police and a few others that he now had access to – she was a sight for his sore eyes that's for sure. Cade was a lucky man, but there appeared to be a growing gap between him and the vixen that leaned into his personal space, sweetly smiling, smelling even better. Roberts has summed it up best. 'Jack's got the keys to the sports car Dave, but it's locked firmly in the garage.'

Francis owed Cade more than a debt, financial or otherwise. He owed him his life from a time they would both rather forget.

"I'd love another set of eyes to look at what I'm finding. I also need your knowledge of how this man thinks. Do you know what I'd like most of all though Miss Elena? Coffee. Strong and plenty of it."

"Are you allowed out?"

"Absolutely just don't take me to any bars."

"It's a date but please call me El."

Roberts gathered the team together for an impromptu brief – told them what the various ministers had told him. Updated them on the situation with their colleagues Cynthia and Carrie. He needed sustenance too.

"Richard, do the team a favour, go and fetch some coffee from across the road, cake too. Lots of it. My shout."

He walked back to his office and leaned back in the furrowed leather chair. Thinking. Trying to work out the next event.

"Penny for them? I used to do just that. Lean back in that very chair, close my eyes and hope the answer would land in my lap." JD leant against the door frame smiling. "You look tired mate, why don't you kick the door shut for half an hour?"

"I'll rest when this is done JD. Or when I'm dead. We should have crushed this group when we had the chance."

"The gloves were on, we both know that. Last time they marauded around this great city we treated them like amateurs. That was a mistake. Jack was right. Still too many questions left unanswered."

"Such as?" Roberts was doodling, filling in boxes on his desk jotter.

"Where do I start? Alex – as much as I hate personalising him. He's a clever man. But he hasn't got this far without having people in his back pocket. He's swanned around Europe, ignored by police units, practically allowed to walk free from prison, and trained his men using our banking system as a proving ground. Yes, they've made money, but it's not enough to sustain their lifestyle. He's successful in his own right in his home city."

"He should bloody well stay there!"

"Agreed. You could say he wants to send them global, bring in the money. But he craves something else. He's got money, even when the authorities take it from him he has more stashed here, there and offshore. What he has is a cold heart, but what he lacks is deep confidence – often the case with a sociopathic type."

"He'd make a good friend of Harry Bloody Halford."

"Well, given what our friend Michael Blake told us, that ship may have already sailed."

"I don't get it. Not at all."

"I do. Got a minute?"

"For you ten. But let's make sure the cake doesn't all go. Those greedy buggers out there are like a pack of dogs where a Swiss roll is concerned."

"My theory, which is based upon years of experience as a police officer, personal gut feeling and a long and happy marriage where second guessing has been my saviour, is this, it all started with Nikolina. She turns up here in the UK. Or, rather, she leaves Spain, not her home, having tried to kill her unintentional husband and leaves her daughter behind in Europe, for all intents, to look after herself. Makes no sense. Why not head somewhere else? Take her daughter with her?"

"Agreed." Roberts had drawn a scale replica of the Houses of Parliament. He nodded, gesturing for JD to continue.

"She came here for a reason. The original notes that Jack took at East Midlands Airport, all those years ago, state she was coming to London to meet someone. Find him, you find the start point to this maze." Daniel took a second to recharge.

"Or her?"asked Roberts, showing he was still engaged with the conversation, whilst sketching the Thames and the Embankment.

"Indeed. But no, it's a him. Mrs Daniel always says the way to a man's heart is via his stomach, whereas the way into a woman's bed is directly linked to the size of the man's... credit card."

"No good looking at mine. Mrs Roberts had hers stolen a month ago, I've not reported it as the thief is spending less than she is!" He made a drum roll sound, miming it with his Mont Blanc pen – a gift from the aforementioned upon his latest promotion.

"Do you have any other jokes Jason?"

He smiled. "Actually I do. Why does Dr. Pepper come in a bottle?"

"I don't know."

"Because his wife left him."

"Incredible. Do you have a filter? No, I didn't think so. Jason, I need to make a call. Catch up later but for now think about this. She came here for a reason. Her daughter tracked Jack down in New Zealand. It was no coincidence and he knew it, just couldn't put two together with itself. He was fooled, like any man, by her looks. But there was, and possibly still is a chemistry between them. I saw it, with my own eyes, in my own home. Alex sent people to hunt for her – her uncle as it happens and he all but killed the girl. He states he didn't mean to and that we should believe him." He took a second to compute it all in his head.

"We know that documents went missing, but despite there being indications about their apparent value no one seems to have been that bothered until another copy surfaced. Or rather until that copy surfaced in New Zealand in the hands of Elena Petrova."

"Who, need I remind you is sitting in the next office?"

"I am aware of that." He pushed the door to wish his heel. "Elena is a not just a pretty face. She's trained Jason, could probably hospitalise both of us. She was sent by the Bulgarian government to find a man and ask him to do a job, a job that her mother was never able to finish."

"And?"

"Christ I don't know. Let's throw theories into the wind. Bulgaria and a few other Eastern Bloc countries are coming out of the comparative dark ages. They know that the only way to make a success in the post-Soviet era is to join the new kids on the block – Europe, or rather the European Union. Get in there and their world opens up just a little. Trade, travel, security. But it also allows those nations to export their more troublesome members. They want to rid them from their country too."

Roberts had abandoned the drawing and was now creating his own organisation chart on a clean sheet of A4.

"So Jack was the man?"

"No. I don't think so. I think he was the conduit. She flew to East Midlands Airport as it was the only flight that day that she could get onto. She needed to get out of town. If it had been Birmingham or London Gatwick, then Jack

Cade would still be a street copper in Nottingham and someone else would have had to sleep with a beautiful Bulgarian intelligence officer. Her aim was to get to London. Her aim was to meet someone. She met Jack. But he was the catalyst."

"I was on secondment at Heathrow at the time. Typical. Could have been me!" Roberts knew his wife would have just loved that. "But you know Jack always maintained that he and Nikolina didn't, cement the European Union, so to speak."

"I believe him. Her daughter is another story altogether and I think he kicks himself, as a professional that he didn't see through her act."

"If it was? Who knows?"

"She had the means to find the document. But there should never have been copies. One document. No copies."

"Or so they thought."

"The document is the key to the lock. The lock opens the office. The office is Europe. Simple. We need to find the lock." He repeated the word twice.

"Who is the lock, and why are they important? And what do they gain from this? Wealth? Migration? Power? The document talked about the United Kingdom leaving Europe behind and in turn sealing up its borders. It's the border Jason. Migration. Worth more than any bank has in its vaults." He scratched his head.

"One person wanted to open the floodgates, another wanted to keep them firmly closed... Who and why?"

"Well, JD, thanks, I started with one question and ended with twenty. What about an underground society?"

"You mean one that takes the tube to its meetings?"

"Respectfully, former chief inspector..."

"Point taken, current chief inspector."

"Detective chief inspector."

"Then detect. Go out and find the answer. You heard the lady – gloves off – feral – teeth – lions!"

"I'm trying but it's such a frigging mess JD. This time we've got backing and an iron fist finally out of the velvety glove. But it's still a mess. I feel like I've got the cherry and the icing, but no bloody cake."

"You are obsessed with cake! Look, I agree this is a nest of vipers. Stroke one, get poisoned by another. In each camp there are venomous and non-venomous snakes Jason. To a point this is about money, not reputation. Someone, an organisation or a government is set to lose a lot. My suspicion all along is that Alex Stefanescu is in this for money and the notoriety that it provides him with. Someone else stands to lose more than both combined."

"Or gain?"

Daniel nodded. "Or gain."

"You know that Jack struggled with who to trust at one point don't you John?"

"I do." He rolled his lower lip over the top one creating a popping sound. It gave him a second to think. "Jason, one day I will tell Jack this." He locked the office door, walked towards Roberts and sat as close to him as was possible before things became uncomfortable."

"A number of years ago I was on a unit. Based in the city. Long before my overt days of patrol inspector and manager of the Communication Centre." He saw Roberts' face alter.

"What are you trying to tell me John?"

"That the unit was covert. Back then, I was a detective sergeant. I worked with the current commissioner. We were good friends. Still are. The government of the time was heavily embroiled in Europe and was looking further afield, trying to see how we could make Britain great again. Heads rolled, enemies were made and secrets were taken to the grave."

"Can you elaborate without garrotting me in my own office?"

He laughed, quietly "Hardly. Besides, I checked, under my old desk there used to be a long piece of wire but it's gone!"

"So? What do I need to know?"

"The unit operated under the title of Griffin. Op Griffin was chosen as it signifies courage, strength, intelligence and leadership. Ancient folklore told of the Griffin's feathers being able to give sight to the blind. The long story short is that Griffin and its team was designed to protect British interests – almost at any cost. There were military units attached, and a select group of diplomats – including the parents of our Mr Hewett."

Roberts' face dropped. "John Hewett? The bad boy made bloody good? Mr Teflon?"

"The same. Explain now why he was given a cloak of protection?"

"No, not really."

"Griffin still exists Jason. I am still a member. Op Orion is unwittingly a part of it. Protect the city. Protect its people. But protect its interests first and foremost, and that means preventing the flood of immigrants, tying up business deals, arms supplies, strategic networking. And the core to all of that lies in that one document."

Roberts lifted his head off the desk, stared at the ceiling. "Three documents John. Three. Now I start to see how this is important. What I don't understand is how some Bulgarian girl ends up with the damned thing. What's the connection?"

"Griffin is made up of five units. Us, that is Britain, Germany, France, the Netherlands, and everyone's favourite neutrals, the Swiss. Everyone else was going to be persona non grata. The richest in Europe forming their own union, espousing the rest, leaving them to fend for themselves. The leaders wanted it, however, there was one proviso. It would be a republic; no monarchies."

Roberts was chewing the end of his Mont Blanc. "This is the stuff of SPECTRE..."

"No. It's not. It's real. You couldn't make this up. It's as real as the pen in your mouth, and the plan was to tell the world as one harmonious and future-proofed unit 'We are the new order in Europe an exclusive brotherhood of the best performing nations in the EU.' But not just yet. Seems like the cat was let out of the bag – and the cat burglar in this case, the ones who were just beginning to the evolve and could see light at the end of a long dark tunnel, and how this could benefit them in so many ways?"

"Bulgaria by any chance?"

"Bingo! Their intelligence officers are among the best. Somehow one of them managed to embed themselves into the UK – spoke the language, had an impressive C.V. – even sounded British. It was whilst they were here they found the document, headed home to a hero's welcome, albeit one that would never be publicly heralded. They banked it for their own future. And all was fine, until one cold and blustery night."

"It's OK, I'm sitting comfortably."

"Good, then I shall begin."

Daniel spent the next seven minutes outlining what he knew, the old days and how he had met and worked with some Eastern European teams, some he owed his life to. This was not a world that Roberts had equated Daniel to, not at all. When he had returned to normal policing Daniel was offered any role he wanted within the Metropolitan Police – a secondment here, an attachment there, even overseas posts. He turned them all down. He joined the police to make a difference – to protect life and property.

And that is what he did. And he did it well. Spent years in the Criminal Investigation Department, a brief spell running a traffic unit, some quality time at Bramshill, the school of excellence and then a commission. He could have been a Commissioner with what he knew. His friend chose that path instead.

"So that's why you came to head our unit, after the night of the bus crash?"

Daniel was nodding, wishing he had his own pen to dine on. "Yes, that and a few other reasons. Wheels within wheels. I policed the city for years but three times a year I attended a conference." He did that thing with two fingers of each hand to emphasise the last word.

"The conference was a briefing, a chance to ensure that Griffin and what it stood for was on track."

"And the blustery evening?"

"One Alex Stefanescu entered the hallowed grounds of the Durzhavna Sigurnost."

"The Bulgarian State Security place?"

"The very same. He turned a photograph of the Director upside down, just to prove a point. I'm told that he left it so perfectly square that a spirit level would have failed to find fault."

"And that was all he left with, a wry smile?"

"No, of course not. He left with a very nice document; the cat burglar had entered the lion's den, clawed the curtains, pissed on the carpet and left through the metaphorical cat flap. They knew, he knew and that my friend is how our man Alex has led a charmed life ever since. Locked up here, released there. Allowed to roam, to exploit, but every now and then pulled to heal on the choke chain."

"By Nikolina?"

"That was the plan. We were in on it too. Provided intelligence, and a few deniable resources."

"SAS?"

"Need to know."

"So what happened with Niko then?"

"Stockholm Syndrome. She fell for her captor. As brutal as he was she couldn't leave, kept telling her bosses that the time wasn't right, that she just needed a little more, and each day and week that passed by she became more infatuated with him and the lifestyle. She became pregnant, and that is when things changed. They gave her one more week, or they would find her themselves – and she knew they would. She needed to protect her own life and that of her unborn child."

"Not nice."

"No. And she knew they would always look – making her glance in shop windows, scanning, never relaxing. One day they would get her."

"Poor girl."

"So, the tough question. Where do we fit into all of this?" Fair question.

"You, me, many others – we are pawns. You and I are the small fry and the government the big game fishermen. We have ended up working with the live bait."

"Jack?"

"Jack. If it wasn't him, then someone else, it's how it is. Sacrifices they call them."

"Funny how the word expendable is only used when we win."

"Indeed. It's all about timing and luck. Britain, or rather the United Kingdom had hoped to keep this whole thing tightly sealed under the floorboards. The bus crash, believe it or not, was the first time I got that feeling that the mouse trap had been primed."

"So what about the likes of Elena?"

"Ah, she's the honey trap – again, no one expected her to fall for Jack."

"It's understandable I guess. Good looking guy."

Daniel smiled. "Yes. But right now we need to wrap a cordon around him and everyone else connected to Griffin and that includes Elena – treat her as one of us until we find out differently. Carrie too. You need to start, if you haven't already, planning for the next phase. It's not coming Jason. It's here."

"Noted. I've got this you know JD."

"Oh I know you have my friend. Don't take anything I say over the next few weeks as a criticism. They brought me back from my peaceful place. Have you never questioned why I chose to head so far away to live what is left of my life?"

"I just thought it was the combination of great food, beautiful beaches and stunning women?"

"Talking of stunning places. Tomorrow I'll take you for a stroll along the Embankment, show you a few things you may have missed, things that most Londoners do, subtle, but there – understand where they fit in, you'll understand everything else. It's like the moment you figure out how to do the Rubik's Cube."

Roberts laughed. "I took mine to bits."

"Me too. It's how we conquered the world. I've got a meeting tonight but I'll be on deck in the morning. May be worth ringing Jack, see how they are doing?"

"Will do. And JD?"

"Yes."

"Thanks for coming back."

CHAPTER FORTY-FIVE

CADE TOOK A POOL CAR AND DROVE TO THE HOSPITAL nearest to the old factory. He arrived at the Princess Royal near Orpington, Kent. It was the best facility to deal with a trauma case such as O'Shea. Helimed Two One had landed long before Cade had even started to negotiate traffic heading south out of the city. His discreet blue lights and less discreet wailers helped him negotiate his way to her bedside in forty minutes.

He parked wherever he could, and walked at a pace – Englishmen should walk and never run and all that. The walk helped him to warm up; it was getting colder by the hour.

"A and E please?"

"That way, but you won't be able to get in without..."

He unbuttoned his jacket and flashed an ID at the pursuing security guard.

"You're doing your job, commendable, just back away or I'll bring all hell down on you. No hard feelings." Cade smiled.

The guard wasn't content. "You need to move your car

and I need to see that ID."

"Yes, you do. Here." He held it up. It displayed his photo and a name on a watermarked background that simply stated, in red capitals, UK Government. On the back were letters, each one denoting levels of security clearance. Cade's resembled a Scrabble board.

"OK. Happy? Good man."

"Well, it's not that simple, I need to..."

Cade's infamously blue eyes were ringed with red lids, raw from the freezing wind. Weeks of travelling around the world, stress and a desire to end this, whatever this was. He held his hand out, encouraging the guard to do the same.

"Jack Cade. Love that you love your work." He checked the opposing ID. "Malcolm. I've been awake for days and I'm trying to resolve a situation that might one day save your grandchildren from a life of poverty, if indeed you are ever lucky enough to meet that special person. I make one phone call and you will disappear from here by..." He checked his Tissot Seastar, its face as blue as Cade's eyes, "... Four o'clock. By six you'll be guarding the main door at Tesco in Wolverhampton, retiring early with a pension the size of your manhood after you walk miserably around the car park in a snowstorm hunting for that one elusive trolley."

"It's that way, Mr Cade."

"Thank you. Now let go of my hand, please."

"Jack. I've always wanted to be a police officer..."

"Fuck off, Malcolm."

"OK. Ring me if you get chance."

"Dear God. Do you want to find a bed next to the patient I'm in a hurry to go and see?"

He begrudgingly took the hint and walked off, checking doors, pressing his earpiece.

As Cade marched towards the ICU, his hip pulsed – a

call. He pulled the phone up to his eye line without pausing.

"Cade."

"Jack. Long-time no. Mac Woods here from Kent Police."

It was a genuine distraction. Woods had worked with Cade in the early days of Operation Breaker and had made a great impression.

"Well, bugger me Mac. How are you?" Cade was smiling for the first time in days.

"I'm OK. Still on the squad, same crew actually, now that they've stopped blowing themselves to bits we are doing well." He sucked busily on a trademark roll-up. "We are at the old fireworks factory, Jack. Little birdie from the CID tells me you have an active interest."

"I do. My two sergeants with you?"

"Yes, DS McGee is charming – if only I were five years younger."

"Ten more like."

Woods laughed down the cell phone. "And Sergeant Fisher is cut from the same cloth as me. Swears when it's necessary. Which is all the time. Look I'll cut to the chase as I know this is a fluid op. Nothing here, mate. We put the full team onto it. Dogs, air support, voice appeal. No answer. We went in and the place was abandoned. Couldn't even toss in a flash bang."

"Nothing?"

"Oh no old son, I didn't say nothing, just abandoned. A few rooms were being used as dorms, twenty beds at least, possibly hot bunking, catering kit, generator, black out blinds and what looks like an operating theatre. Bloody 'orrible. Old shitty bandages on the floor and a stench like the gates of Hades had been left open. I've got a cast-iron stomach, Jack, but Christ...this was very nasty. God alone knows what's been happening here."

"OK, thanks. I suspect the body that was lying in the field to the west of you was their last patient."

"You know they've recovered another body across the water?"

"I do. Bit of a mess, Mac. Appreciate the call."

"Hold on, my old mate. I'm not done."

There was a sinister tone to Sergeant Mac Woods' voice. Cade waited.

"In what I can only describe as their briefing room were some photographs – call it an organisation chart."

A shiver ran along Cade's shoulders and down his back.

"Where do I feature?"

"In the middle, actually. Did you expect to be at the top, you vain sod?" There was almost a bit of light-heartedness in the question.

"No. I'm not that important."

"The PM is at the top, his team below him. Pyramid, very pretty. You, Jason and a John Daniel are next, then three females."

"Carrie? Cynthia?"

"Yep. And a rather pretty lass called Elena."

"Thanks Mac. Get my crew to photograph everything. Are you putting a SOCO through or do you want me to send a team?"

"Being done as we speak. The Kent Police don't wait around for orders, Jack. You know that. Hey look after yourself and that team. If they were mine I'd be thinking about safe houses. The shit hasn't hit the fan yet, but it's mid air, somewhere over London, and looking for a place to land."

"Eloquent as ever, Mac. Great to talk and thank you. Say hello to the team. Is either DS McGee or Fisher there?"

Woods handed his phone over. "Your boss would like a word."

"Boss."

"Bridie. Photograph everything. I'm expecting loads of prints. They aren't worried about forensics. Check bins, check hiding places, check the perimeter. They left in a hurry. Nearest CCTV, petrol stations, you name it, you know the drill. And get that org chart taken down, bagged up and brought back. I'm at the hospital. Ring me or Jason if you need anything."

He pressed the red icon and opened the door to the ICU. A series of five beds met his gaze. He looked from bed to bed, feeling intrusive. She was here somewhere.

"Can I help you, sir? Visiting is..." She stopped when she saw the ID. Cade smiled, "I'm on your side. You have one of my team. Was medevacked earlier today."

"Ah yes, the young lady in bed four. She's unwell. It was a cold night, and she was in a bad way when she arrived. We've stabilised her, but she is still very groggy."

"Drugs?"

"No, toxicology was clear. Just hypothermia. It's not nice. Can ruin the body. Take your time, stay as long as you need to. She could do with a warm hand to hold. Don't be surprised if she doesn't respond."

He turned the volume down on his phone and quietly sat beside her. The rhythmic noises from the other beds told their own story. People in varying degrees of survival. Belligerence and medical expertise were all that lay between them and a gathering of people in black suits singing hymns they didn't want to sing.

"Hello Carrie. It's been a while. I love what you have done with your hair."

He held her hand as instructed, actually; it felt like he should. It was cold. He exhaled. It had been a long week. It had been a long bloody decade. He craved peace, the hiss of the Pacific Ocean on the white sand of the Coromandel Peninsula. As he looked at her, her head savagely shaved, eyes drawn, skin white, sunken veins trying to drag blood around her body, he knew, there, at her bedside that he had let her down. The girl with the fancy taste in knickers and under-the-table humour. He laughed quietly, sat in the half-light of the Intensive Care Unit.

Intensive. Care. He'd failed on both fronts. He had allowed her to be poisoned. She survived that, left her in a bad way, so much so that she sent the wrong signals. Or, in his defence, Cade read had them badly. Women. Venus. Men. Mars. And she was definitely a girl.

The girl with the view of the Queen's private quarters, a bright and shining light in a world of darkness and depravity.

The girl he had dragged to safety. The girl who had told him, repeatedly, to fuck off in a style reminiscent of an upmarket fish wife. The one he had shared vintage whisky with, and a smile, and expensive coffee and a bed. Once.

She squeezed his hand. He squeezed back. It said it all.

He had to make a choice and Elena, as pretty as she was, as sexy as she was and as captivating as she could be, there was something about her that said red rag/bull. And yet he went back, moth to her flame. The world was screaming no, avoid her, she is trouble.

But oh God, she was pretty, sassy, sultry, athletic and clever. No one wore his shirts like she did. No one, no girl, looked over her shoulder as she entered a bedroom and dragged him along on an unseen lead.

But then there was Carrie O'Shea.

He checked the Tissot. Time yet. A few hours. Allowing a drive north against the traffic. Blue lights if he needed to. Hours. She was worth it. He held her hand.

"Can I get you a tea?" It was the same nurse. Whispering.

He replied in a similar tone, "Actually, that would be really good."

Speak to her, she had said. They can hear you. He'd been here before. Nothing to lose.

"So, Jason sends his love. Still has an awful taste in ties. JD is doing his level best not to run the squad. The Home Secretary sends her best too. Quite a following you have there..."

He was running out of things to say. They were platitudes.

"Carrie. I'm sorry. First day I ever met you. Well, to be accurate, heard you, I thought 'now there's a girl with some fight in her.'"

Her eyelids flickered. She could hear him. Just couldn't open the damned things.

"We've been through a few things, you and me. Some fun, some not. Some naughty. Some nice. I bet you wish you had never met me, eh?"

His phone buzzed deep in his pocket. He ignored it. They could wait.

Outside a Kent armed response unit had arrived, dark clothing, baseball caps, Magnum boots, Glocks in leg holsters, the whole works. Overtime probably, paid for by the Met. Cade could see them talking to the Ward Manager. They took up their places. Sent a message. About time, Cade could have been anyone. But they were all on the same side. Competing priorities, it was called. For the next few hours, O'Shea was his.

He'd met a few women since Penny. One or two were just moments in time – Elizabeth Delaney, for example, those perfect green Irish eyes and that velvet-smooth skin, against the moonlight. He often wondered how she was. But it was one night. And neither of them regretted it. He would go back one day, but she would have moved on. They always did.

Elena was different. More confident. Tangible. And

bloody dangerous. The blow she had delivered to Cade's ribs in the Whitsundays could have easily killed him. Pretty girl indeed.

He'd travelled all that way for what? A place in the sun, white beaches, blue waters, and her – a chance to experience her once more. But there was something different. She was carrying a secret, and he had needed to make the journey to look into her eyes. He still wanted her. Who wouldn't? That island off the coast of New Zealand, just them on a boat, alone, wild. It was incredible. They were incredible.

And yet a voice said, 'You are a fool Jack. Call yourself experienced? She is playing you.' Or was she?

His hand twitched again. It was her – O'Shea, communicating, trying to break his chain of thoughts. She was mentally screaming, 'Hey Cade – over here!'

He nodded and pushed back, gently increasing the pressure. It was her and no one else. He'd speak to Elena Petrova another day. Tomorrow.

He needed a rest, a break from the insidious chaos that had surrounded him. It had made him unwise in the way he made decisions – he knew he had let people down. His career growth had been stellar – possibly too much. Right place, right time, his old boss had said.

Tomorrow. He'd tell her tomorrow.

O'Shea jolted. Cade hung onto her. Leaned in and gave her a hug, whispered into her right ear. "It's OK, mate. I'm here."

Whether he would be in a few weeks, he didn't know. He yearned for the good old days of policing, haring around from A to B via Z, drowning in work, backed into a corner, pushing the panic alarm on the radio, chasing someone you should be running away from.

'I'm two minutes away!' When everyone knew, that meant ten.

He was back on that platform, Nottingham train station, in an unwanted embrace with a fiery drunk, rolling onto the lines, in front of that train. He could smell the tracks – mixture of steel and diesel.

And he craved it.

O'Shea broke the spell once more, not with a grip or jolt but a slurred word or two.

"Good. When I'm better."

"What? When you are better what?"

"I'm going to kick your bloody arse." She had no energy to smile, but he knew she was.

"Well, I come all this way to rescue the damsel in distress, wrap some cotton wool around her and that is all the thanks I get?"

"Funniest..."

He nodded encouragingly.

"...Looking knight I've ever met." She was struggling. But he loved the fact that she was as sarcastic as ever.

"Well, hello. Welcome to earth. We are peaceful people."

"Go fuck yourself." She emphasised every word, made it sound sexy.

"Wow. What have they given you?"

"Hope," she smiled, "I heard every word. Just couldn't speak. We'll be OK, won't we?" Her words trailed. He needed to leave soon, hand over care to the nurses and the two staff with G36s and a three-hundred-and-sixty-degree awareness.

"We will be absolutely fine. Thank God you are safe. You really need to stop bringing attention to yourself. Bridie and Nick are down at the scene." He stopped himself.

"It's OK. I escaped. John didn't."

"John?"

"You knew him as Lucy. He was a brave man Jack. Very." She was drifting again.

"I have to go. I'll be back as soon as I can. We will move you nearer to home as soon as we can. You are safe. We are stepping up a gear, even the PM is involved."

"What the hell have we stumbled across Jack?"

"Between you and me, Carrie? I have no idea." He leant forward, kissed her on the forehead, ran the back of his fingers across her cheek.

"We'll be just fine." He stood, waved, and didn't look back. A tear had formed, and he knew that was the indication he needed to change tack. Feral was the word she had used. She wants feral? She'll get it, in bucket loads.

As he left, he shook hands with the Kent Police staff.

"Do whatever you need to do to keep her safe."

"Anything boss?" One of them smiled. He was missing the tip of his finger, which Cade thought was strange for a marksman and also somehow familiar.

"Have we met?"

"Rochester, boss. I understand your targets are still on the run. About time we turned up the heat." He winked. "Blew the tip off my trigger finger at that job."

"Sharkey!" They shook hands warmly. "It's been a while. Nice stripes. How's your tea making?"

"Thanks. Someone needs to look at lessening Mac Woods' workload! Tea is still shit boss. But I have learned to shoot again. Your girl is a hundred percent safe with me on deck."

"Good man. Here is my number. I'll take yours. Anything you need, and I mean from government level down – you ask."

As Cade walked back to this pool car one thing resonated. 'Your girl'.

CHAPTER FORTY-SIX

HE LEANT AGAINST THE IMMACULATE WHITE-PAINTED balustrade that separated him from a reasonable height and the Wellington Court, Kensington address where a contact had acquired him a six-bedroomed penthouse with five receptions, a lift and a gym.

He looked down onto the street, hidden by the height and the perfectly manicured hedging that ran around the rooftop, hiding them from all but eyes in the sky. He could walk around naked if he chose. He might do later. Stand on the rooftop garden and gaze down at Harvey Nichols or across to Hyde Park. He laughed. Raised his hands skywards and blew a kiss into the evening sky.

"More coffee? It's the very best. Made from beans that weasels vomit up in the jungle."

He pulled a pained face. "Do you have normal coffee?"

"Blue Mountain good enough?"

He smiled. Raised the mug to the air. "Yes, of course. Isn't this place incredible?"

"It is – and for the price it should be. Eighty thousand a month."

They laughed. It was the first time Alex had genuinely relaxed and felt the chemical infusion that laughter provided. The first time since Pazardzhik.

"Did you see how many cushions were on the bed in my room? Ten. Ten, my friend." For a sociopath he had taste. "Ten more than I had in prison where all I had to lay my head on was a damp concrete plinth. Bastards." He took a moment to allow the bitter taste to drift back down his throat.

"There is a bath that I will never use, bigger than my cell. This balcony, ten times bigger than the exercise yard that we were never allowed to visit. The marble in that bathroom there? Worth more than my first ever squalid home in Romania. But look at us now."

"We have come a long way, Alexandra. Your grandfather would be proud. Your parents too..." He stumbled, cautious.

"It's OK. Theirs was a short life. But they were happy. Anyway, we must eat. I am hungry. Mexican. I want Mexican."

"Shall I call someone?"

"No. Are we forever to be looking over our shoulders, Constantin? Afraid?"

"In a city with half a million cameras? Is that wise?"

"They remember us from our prison photos. Not looking like this – and besides, our friend has created new identities that will fool anyone, anywhere. Come on. I am hungry."

Constantin pressed a button on his phone – one of a series that was destroyed daily. He left footprints, but Alex told him not to worry. Their friend assured them they were all but invisible.

It was dark when the Uber car pulled up outside the address moments later. A dark blue Jaguar. It was understated, like the clothes the two men wore and pulled away smoothly into traffic, the driver asking to confirm where they were heading then indicating that he would only speak if they wished. They didn't, so he headed north east.

The immaculately shaved dark head and blue eyes that reflected in the blackened glass stared back at their host. He nodded, confidently, almost a smile as they wended their way through the inevitable traffic towards Covent Garden.

Practically invisible.

The driver sensed the need to be discreet, so he turned onto Constitution Hill, the familiar barbed wire, brick wall to the left, St. James' Park to their right. Arguably one of the most surveilled areas of the city and here they were in their understated car, expensive but understated clothing, in a city overflowing with similar, understated people.

They arrived thirty-five minutes later. The fare had been pre-paid, the driver did not expect a tip, not even a goodbye, but he got one anyway.

"Be safe, my friend. You never know who is around the city these days. I can get you a lot of work, work that requires discretion. Do I make myself clear?"

The driver held his hand and nodded – chose not to match the steel grip. He understood entirely. He would, for they spoke the same language.

They walked ten feet at most, and were met at the large wooden door by a good-looking man in his early thirties. Twenty pounds found its way into his hand – he declined.

"Sir, thank you, but I am sure we can find a table. Welcome to Cantina Laredo."

"Hola. Tienes algun lugar privado?"

It wasn't perfect, but the manager knew that they required somewhere private. He had just the place.

"Por supuesto." Of course. It suited the manager too, tuck them out of the way. They had a look that embraced his belief that they were to be treated well, but not at any cost. There were plenty of places where their type could eat.

Criminals or cops, these days they all looked the same. He was in London now though, not Mexico City. He needed to learn to unwind.

"A drink for your gentlemen?"

Alex replied in Spanish, it was passable anywhere the language was spoken. At least he tried.

"Patron silver. Two. And bring us some of your best food. We are hungry, my friend – guacamole to start, your best and steak, cooked in the true Mexican style! Bring it all at once. And please, allow us some privacy. My friend here has just arrived from Bangkok. He is sick of the food there. Loves Mexican. Just doesn't speak Spanish, or even English!"

It was a lie that none of them believed.

He'd seen their type before. Faces that spoke volumes about their past. But they had money, a hint here, a clue there. Money. It was the younger man's eyes. Blue over black. They disturbed him, but he valued the reputation of the restaurant far more than kowtowing to criminals. He could ask the owner to ask them to leave – but whilst they behaved he would accommodate them. Be nice. Be professional. But if the police ever asked, yes, he thought he would recognise them again. He was good at it; you had to be where he had lived.

He looked down at Alex's bald head. It was gleaming with a dark sub-layer, freshly cut but without a blemish, the only scars were faded and plentiful, a scrape here, a slice there, rudimentary stitch marks.

The manager handed them over to his best waiter, a young guy with a tan and a dazzling smile who told them with pride that he was from the Dominican Republic – as he deftly cut avocados in two, scooping the flesh, mixing it at the table with skill and speed; sweet onion, apples, coriander, serranos, pineapple and pomegranate seeds.

"Bravo. We shall eat well. Gracias." Alex slid ten pounds across the wooden tabletop.

His time in Spain was not wasted. He missed it, especially the Sierra Nevadas. As he stared at the young waiter he vowed to return there one day soon, then found himself thinking about the last time he was there, bound, hand and foot and dragged away from his exquisite mountain home by the elite armed police unit.

Some good they were. Once again, he had walked away from incarceration. They couldn't hold him for long, anywhere.

The waiter stood up, carrying the empty dishes and spoke, "I will look after you personally from now on, gentlemen. And where are you from, sir?"

Alex took a split second. Decided to answer truthfully, in a cosmopolitan city such as London he could have been dealing with his own people – he chose to remain slightly vague.

"Eastern Europe."

"Beautiful. Thank you for choosing to dine with us this evening. You are lucky to get a table. We are the busiest restaurant in the area. If you come again, ask for me." He handed a light grey card across the table, noting Alex's wrist as he accepted it – a black tattoo. A wave.

Best say nothing. He didn't recognise it. Chose not to search for it on the internet. Perhaps he should have done? Perhaps.

Instead he nodded, smiled and walked back to the bar – back to business.

Seconds later their tequila was on their table. Handmade, from the best blue agave.

"Noroc!" Cheers.

The glasses were emptied as a waiter arrived with their meals.

"Ah yes, this looks good. Mucho gracias."

"Filete de res con Chimichurri de Cilantro for your sir. And Rib Eye con Mantequilla de Habanero for you, sir. Enjoy. Can I get you some more drinks?"

"Yes Ambar – two, in fact no, leave the bottle."

"Excellent choice, sir." He needed to be pleasant and professional, not fawning. These men would tip him well.

Alex knew his wines, and he loved his spirits. He had chosen the extra-aged Tequila. He had some in his abandoned Spanish home, left on the kitchen island, the half empty bottle reflecting in the black granite surface. An empty home that he would never return to.

The highland red clay soils and a higher altitude, therefore more rain, and cooler nights meant the Tequila suited his palate. Under those conditions he knew the blue agaves grew larger, sweeter, and fruitier in flavour. He knew Constantin would enjoy it too. He needed to focus his mind on the finer things – lure him slowly away from his mistress, heroin.

And he knew the waiter would expect a significant tip from a man who had just spent three hundred and eighty pounds on a bottle.

Why not? He could choose whatever he wanted from behind the bar – when the British people were paying it would be positively rude not to treat yourself?

Alex waited until they were alone. The booth at the rear of the restaurant was exactly what he had hoped for. He looked into the main dining area; it was packed, buzzing with an atmosphere that was alive with the spirit of a very modern city. He raised a glass to the manager, found himself, for a moment, wishing he could eat and relax at any of the thousands of cafes and restaurants that joined the dots in a place that he was hellbent on causing misery to.

"So, we are here. Under their upturned noses. The next phase. The final one. You deal with the teams, get them to cause chaos, Gheorghiu is on his way, he can support the other team, if they are as good as you say they will cause their own havoc. Then I can sit back and plan what to do with Cade and his band of brothers, and talking brothers, if I can find him, I will feed him to the pigs and whoever his friend was that turned up to ruin my last party in Craiova. They messed up a perfectly good party Constantin." He examined the empty glass.

"Can a man not celebrate freedom without the damned police crashing through the door?" He shook his head, picked up the bottle and studied the label.

"In a few weeks' time we will be able to bathe in this stuff. Noroc Constantin. Let us toast the night that the foxes were finally allowed to enter the chicken coup."

They finished their meal, left cash and a tip, and walked back towards the blue Jaguar that purred outside. As Alex walked past a table of four, three attractive women and a hopeful-looking businessman, he placed the bottle, three quarters full on the place mat, next to the prettiest girl – the one he decided he would have. Could have. He could have anything he wanted – soon. In just a matter of weeks. That's all it would be. Just a few weeks.

"Noroc. This is going to be so much fun." He didn't look back.

CHAPTER FORTY-SEVEN

CADE PULLED INTO THE SMALL PARKING AREA ON GREAT Peter Street and walked in. He was speaking on the phone as he walked.

"Five minutes JD. Better be good."

They met in the shadows of Westminster Abbey. The security officer Liam Evans saw Daniel first, smiled, opened a side gate and ushered the two men through. Discreet. It was dark, but the area was well lit. It needed to be. As one of the city's most iconic buildings it looked good day or night.

"Strange choice? Was there nowhere more discreet?"

"You'll see. Thanks, Liam. I owe you. Been a long time. Down here?"

They walked into the eastern end of the building, then allowed Evans to press a button, taking them up to the new feature of the Abbey – the Triforium.

"Over to you, John. Ring me when you are ready to come back down."

Daniel and Cade walked into the void that had sat in the roof space of the Abbey for over seven hundred years – used as a storage area and unseen by the public. The views across to the Houses of Parliament, the Thames and through a stone arch, down into the nave were truly breath-taking. But both men knew they were there for a meeting. And the two men that stood, waiting, next to an ancient painting – the Westminster Retable – were probably having the same thoughts, in that they would rather have an access all areas tour in an empty abbey where one literally stepped onto kings and queens and became wrapped in British history than be here, at night trying to justify their existence.

Cade smiled an ironic smile. "Well, Stefan, we meet again. I guess John's choice of a place of worship was two-fold."

Stefan Stefanescu held out his hand. "Allies?"

"I guess so."

Daniel shook his hand too. He knew he had taken a risk in coming, a greater one of supporting the Griffin team.

"And you, sir? Who are you?" Daniel was leading the conversation, allowing Cade to observe. Once a chief inspector, always.

"Scott McCall. And before you ask I am not entirely sure why I am here either sir."

The New Zealander shook Daniel's hand, turned slightly, and held his hand out to Cade.

"Kiwi?"

"Yes, sir. Nice not to be called an Aussie."

"I have a business interest over there. Huge difference to my ear."

Cade looked around him, effigies of kings and queens and dukes and paintings waiting to be presented in a better light and that view, the one that the people saw when the royals exchanged vows.

He was running his hand across the stone arch, not really looking at McCall.

"Long way from home?" He was looking at him now, studying him. Long hair, tanned beard, stocky, confident in a non-arrogant way.

"It is sir, yes."

Daniel walked and talked. "The items you see form just a part of the history of this building. Look at the walls, that's graffiti, but hundreds of years old, stonemasons leaving their mark, chipping out their initials. Not some hooded shit with a spray can. The place is alive with history. Down there, knights, over there bishops, everywhere, you are breathing in history. That is why I chose this place. It sums up what we are going to start fighting for."

As they walked, the long-haired man stayed quiet, was aware of the burning questions, but waited, disciplined as ever. And then Daniel moved onto the million dollar question.

"You asked why Scott was here Jack. It turns out you have something, or someone in common."

He took five minutes to outline the links and how Stefan had ended up escaping from Romania, running from his brother but chasing him at the same time.

Stefan spoke.

"This man saved my life. He was coming to do business with my brother – but I knew he was coming to be killed. But Alex failed to take into account Scott's training and he left without what he had bartered for. More importantly, Mr McCall now has something of his. And knowing my brother, he will not stop until he gets the final document – the final card in the suit. Scott can keep the rest. However, this man also chose to betray everything he stood for, and has since that day lived in regret. I know how this feels. That is why I have brought him to you. He is seeking redemption, Jack. Listen to his story, then understand why he is the ace in our pack."

"More like the King of Hearts – the Suicide King." Cade wanted to push McCall a little, there was something he was holding back.

McCall answered, measured, assured. "It's actually the result of poor copying over the years, Mr Cade. The King of Hearts once carried an axe. Now, a trick of dimensions shows the sword apparently going into his head. Two dimensions. Nothing more."

"Do you believe in tarot Scott?"

"No sir, I don't. One God and all that and to be fair to the fella upstairs it's been a long time. There was a time in Afghanistan but as they say that's in the past."

"Me neither. But the last card that was turned for me was the Seven of Swords. Any idea what that signifies?" Both Daniel and Stefanescu were tuned in now too.

"Probably that someone is about to stab you in the back?"

"Not far off. Betrayal Scott. It signifies betrayal."

"Then I had better watch my back."

"We all had. So Scott, what is your second dimension?"

"I broke the law. My own. I betrayed my family, my parents, my siblings, but above all the unit I work for."

"Special Air Service?" Cade almost whispered the words that drifted among the stonework, their masons hiding behind pillars, listening, gasping at such revelations, and then vapourising back into the seventeenth century.

"That obvious?"

"No, an educated guess. But the other dimension, what is that?"

"Elena." It was Daniel who beat Stefan to it. It caused Cade to turn and face McCall.

"He arrived shortly after you left. A military unit. Call it luck. Long story, but he saved her life, Jack. Then, just as his white knight persona was guaranteed to go down in New

Zealand folklore, like some of the people buried here, he was betrayed."

"By?"

"Greed." McCall was looking down the nave, running his thumbnail in the initials of a craftsman. "And I'm sorry. But I am here to make amends."

Stefan outlined the moment McCall had crashed into his brother's apartment. "He was a very smart operator. But my brother left during the gunfight, call it luck. It was chaos downstairs, police here, our people there, and in the middle, this man. Alex left in a hurry and didn't get the document he craved. He knows Scott still has it – or had it. It's safe now."

"So you know how to handle yourself?" Cade knew the answer.

"Yes, sir. Prefer to be with my team if I'm honest, but beggars can't be choosers."

"We need to speak to your boss. I'm guessing you are AWOL?"

"I guess I am."

"Then I have just the job for you." He began to outline the proposal as long-dead monarchs held their hand to their ears, listening in the hushed tones of the cold stone building – some said the abbey was alive at night, they said it was alive with the souls of the dead and the chronicles of the courts of kings and queens. This place defined history.

"One other thing."

"Sir?"

"Stop calling me sir and thank you for saving Elena's life. She's a great girl, just misunderstood. But trying to kill her for the sins of her father was taking it too far." He looked at Stefan and winked.

"It was my pleasure boss, it's kind of what we do, when we are not killing people. She was a lovely girl, eh?" McCall was as humble as ever.

"Is a lovely girl, Scott. And tomorrow you can get to say hello in person."

"I would like that very much. Is she single?"

"Sort of Scott. Time will tell." For the first time since he had met her, Cade felt a tang of jealousy.

The handshake was as firm as he had ever experienced. He liked Scott McCall, expensive boots and all.

Daniel began to walk back to the lift. "Gents, I chose this place for two reasons, one it was discreet, no microphones in here, centuries of secrets have remained here never to be told – and what we are dealing with will easily match the greatest of those."

Stefan was nodding, encouragingly. "And the other?"

"This new extension opens to the public in a few years. It's a wonderful example of what we have and what we should protect. Plus, it will cost five pounds to enter and will be busy, and I'm as tight as a duck's arse and hate queueing."

It broke the ice. They walked back out towards The Sanctuary, an aptly named road, and were about to go their separate ways when Stefan turned to face Daniel.

"But what if this fails?"

Daniel drew the cold evening air into his lungs, coughed a little, cleared his throat and spoke.

"See that building over there?" He pointed to the Houses of Parliament. Stefanescu nodded. "Of course."

"On June 4th 1940 Winston Churchill made a speech that is feted for turning the British politicians and people around, giving them strength and unity at a time of great suffering and worry. He made many speeches but my favourite quote is this, 'Success is not final, failure is not fatal; it is the courage to continue that counts.'"

"And what does that mean seventy-five years later, Mr Daniel?" McCall was looking at him – expecting an answer.

"It means my friend that we have nothing to lose by bloody well trying. If we all give into a modern form of tyranny, then my ancestors – and yours..." He pointed his index finger firmly in McCall's direction, paused, then said, "Will have given their lives in vain."

The four split up, Stefan and McCall heading south, Cade to the west, leaving Daniel to look around the hallowed streets and buildings that helped to define his city.

Daniel rang Cade moments later. "So?"

"So I think it will work. He seems like a good man."

"The Home Secretary has already put things in place to erase any evidence of McCall's wrong doing. He's a definite asset. I just need to get his leave extended. I'm going to be late in tomorrow. I suggest you take Elena for coffee and break the news."

"I'll sort that out. It's not a priority. You know we've probably only got one chance at this, don't you?"

"I do, Jack, but she is also one of our pack of cards. She can make or break this. We play the daddy-daughter card when we have to and not before."

"Seems to be a card-filled night."

"It does. Anyway, since when did you believe in tarot cards?"

"I don't. Read it in a book somewhere. Some thriller about a group of people fighting an evil henchman."

"Shouts like a load of crap. See you tomorrow." Daniel cleared the line.

As Cade walked back to his car, he couldn't help finding himself back at the roadside, the deserted country road, the upturned Porsche, watching the life drain from her bright red blood fusing with the dust and debris of the lonely highway.

He did everything he could, but he left her to die.

He was as guilty as Stefan and as naïve as McCall.

He peeled the parking ticket off of his windscreen, got in, dropped it into the centre console with three others, started the car and drove towards what he called his very temporary home.

Daniel dialled the overseas number provided by McCall. It rang for a while. He expected it to go to answerphone, but then it was snapped up and a smiling voice answered.

"Good morning, Mike Steel."

"Sir." Daniel introduced himself. "We need to chat about one of your team."

"So the nomad has surfaced." Steel was relieved, like a father who had been frantically searching for a missing son, not sure whether to slap him or hug him.

"He has. Look Mike, it's late here, and it's a long story that Scott is best to outline with you over a beer in the officers' mess when he gets back. Needless to say, he's now considered a great asset by the British government – as he's the only independent person to have looked Alex Stefanescu in the eye."

"And what do you plan to do with Sergeant McCall?"

"He's the fresh cheese on the trap."

"Great. Do him some good to get his neck stretched a little – bastard has caused me no end of paperwork that I'll now have to shred. Send my best and tell him it'll be more than a beer he owes me. I'll go and see his family, tell them he's overseas, they'll believe me. It happens all the time. Anything else you need? I've got a particularly troublesome corporal in need of a boot up the backside?"

"Send him over, Mike. Good to talk. I won't follow this up with an email. It's very much need to know."

"Pleasure. We've never had this chat. Regards to London, I was there a few years ago. Lost an umbrella on the tube. Do you know if they ever found it?"

Daniel decided he and Steel would get along famously.

"They did, it's here waiting for when you next come."

Daniel opened the car door and was about to get in when he heard a voice. His muscles locked and his fists balled. It sounded threatening, at best it had a menacing undertone.

"Chief Inspector Daniel. Late for a stroll isn't it? Anything could happen out here, cold night, deep, dark river. So easy to fall. Dangerous place, London. All those years as a police officer, that reputation as a thief catcher extraordinaire. Would be so easy to erase that memory..." He clicked his thumb and second finger, the echo resounded off the nearby walls. "Like that!"

"It's Mr Daniel. And one could say the same about you minister. You have a lot more to lose." He was looking at Harry Halford, stood in the shadows, collar up to prevent the cold air penetrating.

"Somehow I think we both know that is not the case, John. As besides once a copper always a copper. Look, I've read your file. Remarkable copper you were too. Plenty of good inside that manila folder. But it's the bits that exist in another vault. He stepped slightly into the light, steam emitting from his mouth as he slipped the brown leather gloves back onto his hands.

"Cold, isn't it? Shall we walk, here amongst the history of our beloved country?" It wasn't a suggestion.

Daniel knew how to play the game. "As you wish." The term beloved stood out, the way he said it.

"How's Lynne?" It was laced with toxin.

"I have no idea. I'll ask when I next speak to her. We hardly talk these days since the separation."

Halford stopped. Clapped his hands together quietly. As he had done at the briefing, it was his signature. "John. Come on. You need to do better than that. I could tell you what's on the menu at your delightful little café down under. Or we could piss about out here in the cold until you get the hint that I'm not here for the good of my health."

"Threatening me and my family? I could take you right here and now, Halford – and you know it. Let's step back into the shadows where you came from."

"Possibly. I wrestled for Durham Uni. If we end up on the floor, down in the gutter, you are mine. No holds barred and all that bullshit. And besides, it's hardly even." He gestured to his right. Halford's Protection Officer was shadowing them. As far as he was concerned it was a late night favour to the boss. Best not to ask why.

"OK. Another time. What do you want that can't wait until the morning?"

"I want to know who you were speaking to a moment ago. I want to know who you met. And, I want to know now." He smiled his assassin's smile. This was really enjoyable. Chess, but with only one winner.

Daniel felt in his pocket for a while until his fingertips touched on the Queen.

"I asked you a question, John. Do not make an enemy of me."

"I'm not. I do question why the Minister of Police is out and about at this time, loitering never used to be part of the job."

"Very good. Once a cop...Look John, pack up, go home, whilst you still can, make the most of your pension, whilst you can."

"That sounds suspiciously like a threat to me Minister."

"As we both know John, any criminal offence reported in this beautiful country will be investigated to the nth degree. From my humble law training may I suggest Section Five of the Public Order Act. I suggest you report it in the morning."

"Harassment? I'd say it was more a case of Section Four, the fear or provocation of violence." He said it loudly enough for the Protection Officer to hear.

"You are wasting your time, John. He hears what I want him to hear. Will go far that boy, promotion is in the offing."

He stared at Daniel, allowing a few late night revellers to cross over and away from them.

"I'll ask you again."

"That's very much a need to know Minister. Now, if you will, I have an early start tomorrow."

PART FIVE

7

Success is not final, failure is not fatal; it is the courage to continue that counts.

Winston Churchill
Prime Minister
London 1940

CHAPTER 48

London Embankment, 06:20 hrs

DANIEL WAS A CREATURE OF HABIT. YEARS OF WORKING shifts meant that he rarely slept beyond five. He had been online with his wife Lynne for ten minutes, assured her all was well, shaved, with a blade, ensuring every errant hair was removed. A generous dousing of Burberry Brit, a crisply laundered white shirt, red and blue tie, navy pinstriped suit. Aquascutum overcoat. Shoes, shined.

He caught a cab that weaved through almost stagnant traffic.

"Foggy this morning chief. Off somewhere nice?" London cab drivers were the best. Full stop. You wanted to get somewhere in a hurry, they knew the shortcuts. Wanted to know a secret about London, they were the people. Daniel spoke through the Perspex safety screen.

"Just my morning stroll along the river."

"Call it a fiver chief and have a nice one. Stay safe yeah, looks like it's in for the day."

The London black cab, the epitome of a taxi, slipped off into the cloak and was gone.

Daniel walked a few paces, tried to look out across the river and realised he was fighting a losing battle. He had chosen to meet Roberts and not Cade for a reason. It was nothing personal. He just knew that one day soon Cade would be gone, moving on, back to his new home in New Zealand – or anywhere he could find peace.

Equally, he knew Roberts had up to ten more years at the coalface. If he knew the inner workings of Griffin so much the better. Better still, if he understood what held London together – mythically or otherwise that might help as well. There was an assumption that Londoners knew London, every inch of it. But it was often far from the truth.

His phone chirped. "Hello, good morning. Smashing isn't it?"

"It would be if I could see beyond the end of my fucking nose JD. Jesus you pick your days for a fact-finding mission."

"I'm probably a hundred feet away. Keep heading towards Cleopatra's Needle. I'll meet you there." He peered back across the road towards the Shell Mex building, which housed the largest clock in London. Five minutes to go. He adored promptness.

Roberts emerged from the fog, walking as quickly as he could. They shook hands. Roberts checked his black-faced Police wristwatch. Bang on time JD." He smiled. He knew.

"Come on, down here." They walked down into the recessed area that looked out across the Thames and back, towards the familiar needle-shaped landmark, a gift from the Egyptians.

"So what's this all about then John? You drag me out of bed at oh my God o'clock for what? A walk along the bloody Embankment. In freezing bloody fog." He shivered, pulled the black Berghaus coat up to meet the tartan scarf. "Well?

I've had to travel a lot further than you. There had better be coffee at the end of this. A nice long black, with an extra pot of hot water and one of those gluten-free lemon cake fancies?"

"Yes. If you are a good boy. Come on, I've got something to show you down here in the mist."

"Sounds dodgy."

Not surprisingly, apart from a few cars, buses and cabs there was little else moving. A boat, or two, chugged along on the river, commercial stuff, with skippers that literally knew their way in the dark.

A jogger eased her way along the Embankment praying she wouldn't get run over by a bike.

"I love this time of the year. This time of the day. Look, just there." Daniel leaned over the wall slightly and pointed to a row of bronze lion heads. The familiar patina sat across the heads making them green, a chemical reaction between the atmosphere and the oxidation of the copper.

"Yep. I see them. Great, now we've minced around beneath the hieroglyphics of Cleopatra's Needle and a few lion heads, can we have that coffee?"

"Look again. See the rings in their mouths? They are there for boats to tie up to. The locals have a saying Jason. 'When the lions drink, London will sink. When it's up to their manes, we'll go down the drains.'"

"Marvellous. Enlightened of London. I feel I couldn't go on another day without knowing this."

"Jason." He spoke like Roberts' old history teach Mr Seal. Authoritative but passionate. "We are surrounded by history. Listen to the words. They are saying that the heads are linked to river levels. I think I know what he is going to do."

Roberts looked down the row of heads. They slowly cleared, revealed by the drifting river mist, one after the other until he could count six. The water was well down, even though the tide was high. He wasn't cold anymore. He understood.

"Me too."

"Good, then this was worth it. I need to meet someone. I'll see you in the office, coffee on me. May even throw in a pain au chocolat. Seven thirty at the latest."

They parted, one heading north east the other south west. The fog soon wrapped its arms around them and in seconds they were subsumed, walking with others on a cold and damp winter's morning.

Cade was in the office. Checking his phone, checking his emails. Asking for an update, a briefing, a sit rep, a sign that they knew what they were doing, who their targets were and importantly the sheer scale of the operation.

They had formed a sub-room, locked to the outside world. A strict need to know, even within the team. Maps, photos, operational orders, i2 charts, all took their place. Op Griffin subtly sat within Op Orion. As far as ninety percent of the team were concerned there was only one operation.

Cade walked from the kitchen to the main office and lowered a cup of green tea onto Elena's desk.

"Penny for them?"

"What? I do not understand."

"It means tell me your thoughts and I'll pay you."

She shrugged her shoulders. "I have no thoughts. I feel I am wasting my time here. David and I spent hours yesterday trying to plot what they were going to do next."

"And?"

"Nothing. I'm bored Jack. Not even you interest me anymore." Francis cringed, pretended not to have heard.

It was blunt. Cade had thick skin, but that one hurt a little.

"Thanks." He feigned a wounded face.

"No, I mean the work. You always make me feel OK. We are just...drifting a little." She pulled a sad face too.

Cade walked away. She stopped him, pulling his arm back slightly. He turned and looked at her. She was looked good enough to pour maple syrup onto and lick it off. Sticky, sweet and hedonistic.

"Can we go out tonight? Please? It's been so long. This thing is eating us up. I never have time with you anymore. You are worried about Carrie I know, but, we have something that is worth fighting for. Don't we?"

"We do. Let's just accept that we need to get the next month out of the way. Hope that your man does something stupid to give his location away, then we can swoop and lock him up."

"He's not my man Jack. Do not say that again. You are... my man."

The understated, minute pause was enough for Cade. It had changed. The sight of her perfectly moulded arse in that navy shift dress was worth fighting for, if only the girl at its heart was the same one he had fallen for in New Zealand. He was confused, that was one thing he did know.

"So what are you plans today?" He was her boss, at least for a while.

"David talked about us heading out somewhere."

"Random isn't it? Do you have a plan?"

"No, we thought we would go and have a look at all the locations where banks have reported attacks. He thinks it would be good to physically see them."

"Fine. Just keep him away from bars."

Fisher and McGee were in early too. It seemed that no one could sleep these days.

"Piss the bed again boss?" Fisher was at his merciless best in the mornings and wished McGee was too. He had figured she was a night-time girl, away from work, away from the carapace that being a detective created, a few drinks, relax, slip off the blouse, kick off that grey pencil skirt, find it the next morning; smile.

He wanted her so much. Would have been happy to just lay and look at her for hours. He couldn't resist a sideways glance here, an innuendo there. She smiled her way through them, quietly asking herself if he would ever be enough. She had a few specks of grey forming in her short hair but her blue eyes sparkled just as they did the first time he ever saw her. She was enough.

One day.

Cade retorted. "No, Nicholas I did not. But nice to see you too. Any chance of an update? Any closer to figuring out what we are chasing, rather than who?"

"Fair point, guv. As you say we are certain we know at least three of the players. Alex Stefanescu, Constantin Nicolescu and a third party called Gheorghiu."

Cade was quick to butt in. "I know Gheorghiu. Nearly shot him once. A boat on the Thames, they were escaping from me having just put the boot in to your DCI."

Fisher continued. "They all feature in the sporadic chatter we have heard from among the traveling community. Bridie has cultivated a close source too. I think he fancies her, but despite her name she's not into Irishmen."

"I'm sure he will be gutted. What did he say?"

"Same as normal, guv." Fisher was right, her eyes did sparkle, tired though she was. "But the link we are picking up over and over again is that they have an inside man."

"Inside of what and what for?"

"The British Government – but what for we have limited knowledge."

"Money?"

"Fame more like. The Kardashians were unheard of, now,

they are famous for being famous. They want notoriety. At least that's what my source says."

"Then keep going but stay safe. Throw some money at it if you need to. Put me down as the authorising officer, forge my signature if you have to. I have to head out. I'll be about an hour, more if this fog doesn't park up somewhere else."

Elena ran her eyes over the screen in front of her. Dave Francis has created a map of the offending – links to possible associated crime and a timeline. The recent surge had been seen over months, but there were years between when it started and now, but things were increasing at a rate that concerned everyone involved. ATM attacks were on the rise, fifty a week now. Crimestoppers information talked of jewellery raids, bank raids and kidnapping. This was a case of ignore the crying wolf at your peril.

"Looks pretty. All those stars." She gave him a great smile. She smelt nice too. He had no idea what it was. Didn't care. Nicest thing he had smelled in years.

"I think you know a bit more about the science of crime than most people in here Elena. Come on, with your knowledge, where is he going to hit next?"

She looked, stood, hands on slender hips. Then flipped things on their heads. "OK, where would *you* hit?"

"Me? Bank of England. Run away with all that cash."

"I was being serious."

"So was I!"

"No come on. Think."

Francis scanned the screens. She was right. The Poacher needed to turn Gamekeeper and all that.

"OK. I'd hit the communications. No, the power. I'd find a way of knocking out the power."

She turned to one of the squad. "Charlie. Can you get

onto the power companies? Ask them what it would take to knock out their networks. Ask them to be honest. No lies. Tell them it is of national importance, because it is. And Charlie."

"Yes." He didn't see her as a boss, but knew she came with some real credibility and rumour had it she was capable of flooring most men. "What else do you need?"

"Can we have it in an hour?"

"You can but Jack asked me to go and fetch Carrie from the hospital."

"OK. Where is Jack?"

"No one knows."

"Does he know she needs collecting?"

"No, I took the message from her."

Petrova was engaged with the operation. Her skills lay in a mix of analysis and field work and first-hand knowledge of the target. She was enjoying work again, getting well paid too.

She put her hand on Francis' shoulder. "I know you have a reason to be here. I want to help you. Jack told me your story. Sounds like you are good friends. He was a good man back then no?"

"He still is, miss. Always will be. Cade is a good police officer, but a better man, he's not perfect and sometimes lets the job interfere with everything else. But he always puts David above Goliath. And he saved me."

"What from?"

"Myself."

"That's good to hear. Right, I need to go and get Carrie." She walked across the office and out into the corridor to find Roberts. He was in the office, pacing, trying to clear something from his mind.

"Penny for them?" she asked in her broad Bulgarian accent.

He turned and smiled, took the pen from his mouth and said, "Well hello. And how are things going? Anything exciting to tell me? I need something to inspire me Elena. Or sooner or later we are all going to be out of work."

"I have run a few ideas around out there. The team are trying but they are too busy looking at bank machines and money. This is about Alex. How many times do I have to say?"

He scratched his head with the tip of the pen. "I get that. So what?"

"So what?"

"Yes, so what, it's the classic question. Keep asking it and you get the answer, unless it's about women of course, they remain a mystery. The so what here is if it's not money then what is it and why?"

"He is determined to make the news. He steals the stone you all care about but he throws it in the river. He kills people you care about. He takes money – the money is to help them live whilst they are here. I think I know what his plan is."

"Would you like to enlighten me Miss Petrova because in a few weeks I'm going to have the Commissioner breathing down my neck?"

"That will be nice."

"No, it won't, trust me."

"I need a day to think this through Jason. Is anyone going to collect Carrie?"

"Oh God, is that today? I thought she was staying in. Isn't Jack collecting her?"

"He could be. I'll go. I would like to drive. Will be good to spend some time with her. I'll get her to Jack's apartment. I'll ring you when we are leaving the hospital."

"Sounds good. Do you want to take someone with you? Or one of our radios?" He was pushing the organisational security boundaries, but if she was good enough for the Home Secretary then frankly, she was good enough for him.

"Will it reach here from the hospital?"

"No."

"Then I won't!" Smiling, grabbing the keys to his car, she left. Roberts carried on dining on the pen, trying to merge some thoughts and work out a way of appeasing his wife and the Commissioner, both of them questioning why he was doing so much overtime.

Cade was at his own rendezvous. Eating a take away breakfast thing in a polystyrene container. It was the sign. And he was waiting.

Three days earlier and unbeknown to anyone except Roberts and Daniel he had put a message on the Interpol website.

It read simply:

Romanian man wanted for his part in a major operation targeting an organised crime syndicate.

The article outlined that the Operation Orion team were searching for the man and that he could help them with their extensive enquiries. They named him but didn't add a photograph. The truth was, they didn't have one.

There was a phone number, in bold, at the foot of the article.

Two days passed before it had been dialled, from a payphone in west Holland, a village called Kuilenrode, where some of the properties had thatched roofs, it seemed everyone had a bicycle and the place was friendly and discreet enough that it was easy to hide.

He had settled there, somewhere new, as he had settled

every year, or as often as he needed to stay a step ahead. It was how he worked. He had made his money, didn't invest it, kept a lot of it in a basic current bank account that was accessed by a secure link, which in turn was activated with the details of his wife, deceased.

He was a professional. A company man who had turned against the company when they had killed his darling wife. And they had been paying for it, every year or so.

Until he met Cade. It was then that his crimes of intent became crimes of passion, where the memory of his wife drove him, not to carry out the killing, but to stop it. He had had enough. He'd 'turned'. And Cade was the man to convince him where others had failed. He was a true intelligence officer – and that meant integrity above all else. It was in both of their DNA strands.

From that day on he had become a 'consultant' – in other words, a well-paid operator who could guarantee money from a number of government sources in Europe. Especially the British, and especially when their backs were up against the wall.

He knew enough to be both helpful and dangerous. Cade was tasked with managing him, but knew he never truly would. He helped them, they ensured he could move on, across Europe or even enter Britain uninhibited. It was a quid pro quo situation borne out of necessity.

Cade outlined what had happened since they last met. How things had altered, for the worst, and, importantly what he wanted him to do. He would be well paid, but he acknowledged that there were some things he didn't do for financial reward.

They would meet soon.

'It is long overdue Jack.'

· · ·

The next day, at London Victoria train station Cade had watched as his target did what he did best – interacted with the public, made them look up from their head down commute, briefly, long enough to humiliate them, made them look away, made them feel selfish. And then he struck. They pitied him. Good. It was meant to be that way. A copper coin here, perhaps a gold one there. Some food, that would be quite acceptable. He wished more people would think about the truly homeless.

At the end of each session of overt begging he would sit or stoop, leaning against a modern, upmarket retail window and watch his fellow beggar. The real ones, not those with expensive football tops under their scruffy outer garments, the ones whose hands were worn, whose faces told a story. They were the benefactors.

Cade walked up to him, dropped a banknote into his scruffy woollen hat and walked off with the rest of care-less commuters and waited.

He was still waiting three days later. The target knew that they needed to meet again, same place, or as near as possible to not arouse suspicion. Same drill: Banknote. Hat. Phone call. Task.

But he had failed to show. Cade found a bin for his fast food wrapper, watched it land in amongst the other rubbish then walked off along Victoria Street, back towards his office, tossing half of the breakfast onto the floor, leaving a horde of pigeons to fight over the bread.

He checked his phone. A few missed calls, nothing new there.

'Where are you?'

· · ·

He was where he felt he needed to be. He had done his homework. Been watching, blending in, gathering intelligence, identifying the most feasible targets of a team that consisted of people he knew and despised, and others who he knew were just out of his reach. He needed them to make a mistake – on his terms, in a place and at a time that he could exploit.

He watched them. Hour after hour. Brushed past them, was pushed aside by them, dropped tasty morsels into their pockets then retreated, back to his temporary home, for all intents just another resident of London. His ability to morph from street dweller to city slicker was world class.

CHAPTER 49

ON VICTORIA EMBANKMENT A FEW PEOPLE WALKED, HEAD down, shielding themselves against the cold. Hats on, scarves wrapped, headphones in, listening, for company and warmth. A few walked alongside each other, oblivious. Even more, they were deliberately oblivious to the homeless man; old clothes, tattered carrier bags and a crudely-fashioned walking stick which he leant onto, as he kept himself in the shadows, away from the dawning day on the streets where no one knew his name nor cared.

He carried an old Starbucks paper coffee cup and pushed it towards anyone that would allow their barrier down for a second, just long enough to drop a copper coin into it. As slow as he was, as crippled as he was, he had covered enough ground to show he was as determined as the next Londoner to get somewhere.

Shuffle. Grimace. Stop. Shuffle...

John Daniel knew London as well as most cab drivers. He also knew that a walk in the fog was likely to get him to

Scotland Yard as quick as a journey in the back of one of the familiar black vehicles. He reckoned twenty minutes should cover it.

Brisk. Along the Embankment, avoid a few pretty joggers, up onto Westminster Bridge, around the back of Parliament Square Garden, Broad Sanctuary and a few more left and right turns and he'd be there, fresh, revitalised and feeling smug about saving ten pounds.

He had placed a seed into Roberts' mind and hoped it would germinate. Now, the more people that knew and agreed with Daniel, the better.

Within a hundred paces he had decided a cab would have been the better option, the light was a dense grey with morning valiantly trying to introduce the day to the night. He approached the Hungerford Bridge, spotted some flashing amber beacons and prepared to divert across the road to avoid the construction site and its inch-deep concrete dust.

'Don't want to get those shoes dirty JD.'

As he walked under the bridge, alongside the hoardings, the first sense that something was untoward arrived via a sudden and brutal blow to the torso.

He wasn't down, but he was winded. He grabbed for his phone, hoped to hit a hot key that dialled for the emergency services. The best he could hope for was that the operator would listen, hear him shout his location and send help. But they were too quick for him. Another blow, then one to the head. He picked his hands up quickly, placed them at the side of his head – training – muscle memory. Protect the head.

He needed to get a strike in. A punch, a kick, a knee, a slap, a claw of the fingernails across the face. Gouge an eye. This was not a Home Office approved fight, the type they always trained for. This was a street fight.

Thunk…Slap. Two or more blows, this time from his left. There were two of them and he was going down to the ground. If they got him into the builder's hoardings, away from prying eyes, he was dead. Was it a robbery? A revenge gone wrong? Blatant violence with no reason?

These were sharply dressed men.

He lashed out, tried to get a look at them. He saw a partial face, saw the eyes. He caught one of them across the temple. Heard him moan. He struck again. Kicked out with his immaculate-shoed foot, raked it down his assailant's shin, the metal Segs grinding into the shallow skin, instantly blackening the surface before the blood flowed. That one always hurt. And again. Then a stamp and an elbow strike. He was fighting for his life now.

'John Daniel. Chief Inspector. Retired. Died after an altercation near Victoria Embankment January 2015.'

No way. He pushed. Struck out. But the counter-blows were getting faster. They had stepped up a gear. In the shroud, under the bridge, traffic passing by without a care or any intention to stop and help. No one phoned. No one saw them. At least no one that in the eyes of the commuting public was deemed to be worthy.

The old homeless man dropped his bags and shouted 'Hey!'

It was enough to cause a distraction. Daniel was down, on the ground, smothered in fog, battling for breath, scrabbling for weapons of opportunity. He was down and all he could do was hope. His head hit the pavement and the last thing he saw was a shoe.

Dark tan. The toe cap was fashioned by hand, darker tones indicating the shoemaker had taken time to finish the product with pride. It had a rubber sole. More comfortable, longer lasting. A man after his own heart. Daniel had always spent wisely on clothing and shoes. He had said it spoke volumes about a man.

That shoe. He'd seen it before.

The eyes. He'd seen those too.

"Go away you old bastard before you join him." The smiling face was clearer now. The fog shifted, just a second, swirled, allowing more than a glimpse. The old man looking into the eyes of the younger, suited man with overly blond hair. He would remember him again, anywhere.

In the background, the second attacker was kicking Daniel. And still no one stopped a car or even glanced.

"Go away and annoy someone else, somewhere else. This is not your fight." He wafted his hand as he would if he were in a restaurant, skilfully guiding a bluebottle from his crème brûlée. "Shoo."

In terms of that fight, the old man clearly had nothing. And he had nothing to lose. He walked towards the blond who looked down at him, mocking.

The darker-haired male stopped kicking Daniel and also walked towards the vagrant, taking control, perhaps protecting the blond.

Speaking through a twice-broken nose he punched out his words. "Do you not listen? Fuck off before you end up dead." He pushed the man backwards, daring not to touch him too much, pleased with his decision to wear gloves.

Not nice.

Show some respect.

The older of the two, superior in tone as well as demeanour then followed up with a well-spoken, "Go on, you heard the man."

He did. They made it quite clear, and for the old, bag-carrying itinerant that was the signal.

'You have just over-stepped the mark gentlemen.'

His stick arced upwards, fast, faster than the target expected. It struck him under the jaw and sent a crashing blow, upwards, driving his lower jaw into the top. He heard the teeth breaking, tasted fresh blood, his ears rang and the bridge that they were sheltered under only helped to make the pitch higher, enhancing the sense of pain. The old vagrant liked that, a lot.

His target tried to shake the shock of the counter-attack but failed. The second strike was equally swift. The old man spun ninety degrees and drove the mid-section of the cane into his throat shattering the hyoid, snapping his neck backwards with such force that deep inside his head he heard the third vertebrae grinding against the next.

The blond was on the move. Not towards the vagrant but away, as fast as he could, across the road and towards the Embankment tube station, his rubber-soled shoes making hardly any sound as he navigated through the mounting vehicle traffic. A businessman in a smart coat, with a tartan, Merino wool scarf across his lower face. On a winter morning.

Nothing unusual there.

The old man let him run. His day would come.

He walked back towards the younger, dark-haired man, lifted the seam of his black casual jacket to one side, felt for a wallet, pushed with his stick, searching him for weapons.

When the younger man moved, trying to offer resistance, the tramp just held him in place with his stick. He lowered himself down onto one knee and then picked up his attacker, raising him up just far enough to talk to him.

There was an unexpected strength in the way he lifted him, and the way he spoke.

The young man was struggling to reply. His tongue was

starting to swell, in four hours, maybe five he would be unable to swallow, without medical aid he might die.

"This is what happens when you pick on older men." He placed his own hand behind the man's head and turned it towards Daniel who was lying on his side, trying to get up. He was regaining his breath, nursing his wounds and fumbling for his cell phone.

The old man ran his hands over the younger one's body, searching, he found a wallet, gave the contents a cursory glance and then put it back, safely in the jacket pocket, just as he'd found it. Intact.

The tramp smiled from under hooded eyes and spoke, this time to Daniel.

"Perhaps leave the call for a while, sir. This man needs time to consider his future." He lay his head down onto the pavement and tapped his cheek twice. The look he gave him was without doubt one that said 'stand up and I will finish what I started.'

The fog had once again shrouded the street.

He stood, walked to Daniel and offered a hand. Daniel studied it through swelling eyes. Unlike his clothing and general appearance the hand was well-cared-for, not that of a homeless person who had given up on himself. The nails were trimmed, the skin softer than that of someone who lived on the streets.

Beneath the dark circles, the eyes were alive; active, eagle-like, experienced.

"Do I know you, sir?"

"Sir. It has been a long time since I was called sir." The accent was tinged, foreign. "But no, you do not know me." As he raised Daniel back onto his feet, allowing him a moment to compose himself, he put his mouth next to his ear and in a heartbeat, whispered, "But I know you. Sir."

He picked up his bags, grabbed the stick, bent forward

slightly and walked off into the fog. Daniel had a choice. Follow him, stay with the attacker or leave.

He left, blending in as quickly as he could. He called for an ambulance from the nearest payphone. The last thing he needed was to be investigated for a murder.

"Yes, looks like he has fallen over. I have to go."

No, he didn't want to leave his name.

It was five minutes later, six possibly, that Cade took the first of two calls. The first was from Roberts. JD has been attacked. A car was on the way, he'd refused an ambulance, said he'd be OK, bruised and a possible fractured rib. His coat was ruined. More angry than hurt. That coat was a no-longer-available classic.

"I'm on the way to meet him. This just gets worse by the day, Jack. Apparently some old dosser stepped in to help him. Gave the attackers a right going over. One legged it. We've already got local police looking. CCTV coverage is appalling down by the river. I was there earlier, really foggy. I should have stayed."

"Why were you there?"

"Do you know I'm not entirely sure. JD wanted to show me something. Said it was important."

"And was it?"

He trusted Cade better than he trusted anyone on the team.

"If you like lion heads, yes."

"OK. A real shame I wasn't there. Must have lost something in translation."

"Possibly. Listen, I'm going to go and sort this pile of shite out and let's meet up soon. Hey talking of translation. JD said his saviour had an Eastern European accent."

"And? Sadly a huge percentage of homeless and beggars

in the city do Jason. The fact that they are down on their luck doesn't make them bad people. You know that."

He did.

"I do. But he said there was a familiarity, a sense of awareness. Like the old boy was trained."

"Perhaps he was?" Cade began to smile.

"Anyway, no time for blame Jason. And the other one? You said there was more than one?"

"Yes two. JD thought it was a robbery. Business man in the fog, early morning, nice suit, you know the drill Jack."

"And?"

"And he's not sure." It was obvious Roberts wanted to return to his earlier conversation.

"But the old tramp that stepped in, he said there was something about him. Something that said he was not just an old man wandering around London with his life wrapped up in a few third-hand Tesco bags."

Cade smiled. "Then he was right."

"I'll be back at the station in minutes, I need to get a few things done before I head down to pick up Carrie then we can have a proper tea-fuelled debrief, like we used to, when policing was a noble art, frequented by a broader blue line."

"You are going to pick up Carrie?"

"Of course, why wouldn't I? Everything alright Jason?"

"Yes. Fine. All things considered. Look mate Elena took my car, said she thought we were all busy. She's gone to get Carrie. I've been left with the shitty old Vauxhall that no one ever fuels up and the carpets smell like somehow has pissed on them. I'm the boss for Christ's sake!"

"Great. Are you serious?"

"Yes. It says so on my bloody door!"

"I meant that Elena has gone to get Carrie."

"You OK with that Jack? She's on our side you know."

"I'm no longer sure who is on whose side my friend. Send

another car south. Quick as you can. I need to stay in the city, I've got three hats to wear and only one head."

"What can I do?"

"You need to stay there, run the show. It's about to start."

"What is?" Roberts was smart, no fool, liked to mess around on a Friday afternoon with the best of them, a quick game of office cricket, that sort of thing, but he was one of the most switched on coppers that Cade had ever met.

"If I knew that I'd stop it. Prepare for a few losses, and headlines. We need to round up our people too Jason. We've got folk scattered across the city, let's make sure they are all in pairs." He stopped, took a quick glance at himself in a shop window. "Sorry mate. This is your show, I need to back off."

"No you don't. Just try to find out what you can, whilst you can yeah?"

"Sounds ominous. Know something I don't?"

Roberts snorted down the phone. "Like I would keep that to myself you old slag!"

"Takes one DCI Roberts. It takes one. Oh, and sorry about the carpets."

CHAPTER 50

CADE DIVERTED FROM SCOTLAND YARD. DIALLED A number and waited at the side of the road, oblivious to the exclamations from his fellow commuter.

"Dave, Jack. I need you to stop whatever you are doing and run some searches for me."

"Go on."

"Find what you can on Harry Halford. Do it without leaving a footprint. Leave the building if you need to. You talk only to me."

"Anything particular?"

"Anything that will hang the bastard out to dry."

"And why do you ask?"

"Just do it Dave and trust me."

"As you say sir, but before you hang up on me John." Francis was one of the few people that called Cade by his real name. The other was his mother.

"I may have unwittingly got a hit on our human source system."

Cade waited at the side of the road, ignoring the two-fingered gestures and silent expletives from myriad road users. "Do tell. But make it quick David I have people to see, places to go."

"Don't you always? Just a word to the wise, you need to find time to watch over your young ladies. They are vulnerable. We've got staff here, there and everywhere John, we are at full stretch. I'll burn the midnight oil to support you, but you know you can't afford another loss. John?"

The silence ended. "Yes, of course, but this is bigger than just me."

"Tell that to Mr Daniel. He's just walked in. Doesn't look well. And Cynthia. And your man Lucy."

"Your point?"

"Is a clear one. I am worried about you. You might crave a quiet night; brush your teeth, comb your hair, slip into bed with one of those lovely young ladies...but until this is done there is no time for normal. Normal is a slice of life we take for granted. You know you are the target here don't you?"

"And how do you work that out?"

"Oh, come on, man. Because he's making his way through the ranks, picking us off, one by one, by one. I'll be on that list too so forgive me if I feel like hitting the bottle again. Ask yourself this, how does your man Alex know who is on your team?"

"Insider?"

"Insider threat John. And yes, I too feel that Mr Halford is at the top of that food chain. But we don't know why. He's a senior minister for God's sake. Add to the fact we don't know what your bloody Jackdaw is planning and you exacerbate things way beyond our control."

"Have we established anything from Elena, or McCall or his brother Stefan?"

"No. Well, I say no, what I really mean is yes. We know that Alex's teams are almost certainly behind the London Stone, the bank jobs and some random cyber stuff."

"Cyber?"

"Yes. Our team are picking up some interesting chatter, takes some translating as it's in Romanian and in code but it seems that your Interpol search for a star worked. He's a real asset. Pity we will never meet."

"I'm glad he's on board. How do you communicate?"

"Blackberry."

"OK, good. What type of cyber stuff?"

"The type where we think someone took control of the traffic light system a few nights ago. No issues, just a test, but it wasn't anyone on our side. Our cyber geeks have recommended it be locked down – could cause public unrest, especially with the weather as it is."

"OK. I need to know this sort of stuff David."

"Apparently not. If you ask me, there's a few too many chiefs in this team, top heavy, we need to spread the love, share the experience a bit more."

Cade had always admired his candour.

"Trust me John you'll be told what I think you need to know. The other stuff, I'll let slip for the price of a decent coffee."

"Fair trade."

"It's all I drink since I watched a BBC documentary." It made Cade smile. Francis still had a sense of humour. He had an agenda too, he wanted to find the men responsible to vapourising his dear old uncle in a house explosion not so far away.

"David, was there any good news this morning?"

He laughed. "I remember the first day we ever met. You a wet behind the ears constable and me a washed-up ex-soldier. But we needed each other, you promised me you'd always be on hand to help and you've never once let me down. You always used to ask me if I had received any good news. It was our code for local intelligence. I told you what was happening in the area, you acted and locked up the bad bastards but always kept my name out of it all. Nothing has changed – now it's just on a far grander scale with less chance of an arrest."

"Dave I need to go. Cut to the chase as they say."

"Wait a second."

Francis walked into a side office and shut the door.

"Your insider threat is John Daniel." It was abrupt to say the least.

Cade shuddered, turned the heater up to thirty.

"What? No."

"Yes John. Yes. His name has come up on some checks, old-fashioned ones, where I ask a few pertinent questions, ran a few searches, deep in the systems the Home Secretary herself gave us access to. There's an operation that is so locked down so tight only a few know it ever existed."

"Called?"

"Griffin."

"And John Daniel was a part of that?"

"Yes. I'm afraid so."

"Its theme?"

"Not for the phones John. Later."

"Fair enough. But you make out it's a negative. Could it be positive?"

"It could. It started years ago. JD was recruited to gather intelligence, his knowledge of Eastern Europe is up there with the best...as I say, the rest needs to be discussed face to face."

Cade nodded, sat in the car, wiping a hole in the condensation with the back of his glove.

"He certainly knows a bit of the language." His mind drifted back to 2014 when Daniel had talked to Elena, at his restaurant in New Zealand. At the time Cade put it down to a rapid self-taught desire to impress a pretty girl, a

Google search and twenty minutes practice in front of a mirror.

He had cursed his naivety ever since. Years had somehow dumbed down his ability to see the wood for its humble cousin, the trees. Cade had met Nikolina Petrov, had listened and nurtured her as an intelligence source. He had learned a lot about Eastern Europe too, but he always felt like he was a pawn, a conduit to something bigger. The day she had run away from him, across a golden cornfield, dropping to the ground and waiting to have two nine millimetre rounds drilled through her head.

The way she had looked up at him.

The way her daughter did the same on a desolate road, many years later. Call yourself a detective Jack?

Niko had died a death that was cruel and indicative of the way her estranged husband thought. Elena would have too, if luck and some pinpoint calculation had not played their part.

He should have known. But the thing was, he never was a detective. He was just a straightforward, down to earth copper, who had unwittingly met the girl who had the pieces of a jigsaw. Sadly, he had no idea which picture they came from.

Two women, two countries and one enemy.

He should have seen it. He wouldn't be the first and without a doubt wouldn't be the last. Women. They were after all the best intelligence operators in the business for they had one weapon that men didn't. And she had used that weapon on him. She had walked into that bar, sprinkled moon dust in his eyes then walked away. Hook. Line. Sinker.

She was the best. Grooming him from the moment she walked in, the sunlight shining through her simple cotton dress.

Not the first. Possibly, not the last.

And now she was back in his life. Alive. Trusted, possibly, and on her way to pick up the one woman who had offered him compassion, love and the other side of female thinking. And he had repeatedly pushed her away since the day they wheeled her out of the pub – her wish, her in control, her regretting it too.

But now, sat on a side road, surrounded by busy traffic and angry people he knew he had more enemies than friends. At least, that is how he felt.

He started to count his friends. Marking them off on the tinted glass, wiping the figure with his index finger. He knew that if he were to be the main bait that he would need everyone he believed in to be there to back him up. The government needed to find a scapegoat, worse still a human sacrifice.

Yes, normal, was most agreeable.

He had drawn a picture of the London skyline in some detail, the Tower of London seeping down the lightly coloured coloured glass, into the door trim. The London Eye, the Gherkin, Big Ben, the Thames Barrier.

He flicked the window switch and watched his artwork disappearing by the second. He was back in the conversation.

"I trust JD as much as I trust you Dave."

"I'm glad. I'm not saying he's a threat to *you*. I'm saying he's a threat to the other members of the team. And according to my feather light searches he's one of the few remaining people that can still be brought forward to give evidence."

"About what exactly?"

"What is in those documents and who had the most to gain. This morning's little meeting down on the Embankment was a less than subtle hint that he should pack up and head back to his adopted new home. Whilst he is still alive."

"I'll ask again, evidence about what?"

"About the decision by a select few to carry out an act so atrocious that it would meet and exceed the conspiracy theories of what led to the horrors of 9/11."

"But why? And for what? And who? Government intervention?"

Francis repeated Cade's last words.

The last part of the drawing was disappearing, cleaned off, never, in that guise, to be seen again. And then he stopped the window.

It was there. And he saw it. And he smiled. Perhaps he was a detective after all?

"Dave. Tell JD I was asking about him. Get him some ice."

"For the bruising?"

"No, for the bottle of Talisker *Dark Storm* that he keeps hidden in his drawer."

"You know you shouldn't have told me that John?"

"Of course I should. Those days are behind us now David."

He indicated, lights on, back into the enduring fog. As he drove, he spoke into the hands-free.

"Call Scott McCall."

McCall answered within three rings. He had stayed at the flat with Stefanescu.

"Scott I need you to go to a restaurant in Covent Garden. Take Stefan with you. Tell them you need to see their CCTV."

"OK, but don't you have detectives for that type of thing?"

It was a reasonable question.

"Yes, I do, but I want to put you out there, if he's watching, let him see we are overt, nibbling at his cheese."

"Do we need to be armed?"

Another reasonable request.

"Probably, but no, you can't. Anyway, I've had some intelligence from one of my best analysts, he's constantly scanning the environment, looking for clues. Someone connected to the restaurant I need you to go to has made a call to Crimestoppers. Said they thought they had had two guests in there that were criminals."

"Hardly a revelation in a huge city like London."

He liked McCall. They'd get along well, despite their Elena Petrova mutual appreciation society issues.

"Again, you are right, but the caller works there, so we should be able to narrow it down. That should have been taken out of the message really, ties him to the job, but that is our gain. I'm guessing it's the manager. Go and see him, find out what he knows about the two men, the men with the wave tattoos on their wrists, get to see the CCTV, tell him we want to seize it, and hopefully you can start your journey towards redemption."

"OK, roger that. I'll brief Stefan on the way, if anyone will recognise them he will."

"Oh, I'm counting on it."

Daniel drained the glass.

"For medicinal purposes you understand?"

Francis smiled. "The boss said you might appreciate it." He turned to look at a distinguished man who had stopped at the office door.

"Jesus JD you look awful. Can we assume that the other man looks worse?" There was a smile, but also a genuine sense of concern.

"David, this is Johnathan Hewett. He works for the Foreign Office. That's all you need to know."

Hewett held out his hand. "Heard a lot about you." Hewett had a way with people, made them believe he knew all about them, was able to throw a line here, a few pieces of information there. He was very good at it. Even Francis believed him.

"Look guys I need a favour." He outlined his request which mirrored Cade's. It made for an awkward few minutes.

"Just between us – oh, and Roberts and Cade. But no one else. And I mean no one." He was gone in seconds after a positive thumbs up, dialling on his phone as he walked to another meeting somewhere else.

Francis looked at Daniel. He face said it all, and he prided himself on being the army's best poker player.

"What is it David?"

"Jack will shoot me."

"You want a scotch?"

"Yes. Hell no. He'll shoot me if I tell you, but I feel we are past that now. Jack asked me to carry out the same checks."

"Then do it and leave Jack to me. Same hymn sheet Dave. Same hymn sheet."

Forty minutes south east Elena Petrova had parked up and walked into the side ward, finding O'Shea's police guard in situ. Her looks had got her a long way in her relatively short life but she didn't rely upon them now.

"Hello officers. I am Elena Petrova." She held her ID aloft. "I am here to collect Miss O'Shea, to take her back to our office. Thank you for your help. You can go home now."

The younger of the two physically held her ID card, looked her in the eyes. Yep, she was beautiful, but he was equally professional.

"I'll need to speak to Miss O'Shea first."

"Of course. I will wait." Proficient. No attitude. Confident.

O'Shea had been discharged by the On-call registrar. She said she had had a very lucky escape. It seemed like months ago she was lying in her own urine, strapped to a table, waiting to die. A long shower and food had helped, but nothing would ever rid her of her dreams. She feared they would come for her again, and now, outside was this girl, the pretty Bulgarian that Cade adored and she trusted about as far as she could kick.

'Onwards and upwards Carrie.'

"Miss O'Shea said it's fine to go in. We will wait right here. Outside." He nodded to the Glock on his hip and the G36 across his chest. Subtle he was not. PC Simon Wright was determined that if anyone was going to balls things up it wouldn't be him. He made a call to his boss and he in turn to the Met Police.

Bases and arses covered.

She stepped into the half-light. "Hello Carrie. How are you?"

"I'm fine, no thanks to your lot. What is wrong with those people Elena?"

"My lot? What do you mean my lot?" Slightly edgy.

It was a mistake. O'Shea knew she needed to backtrack quickly.

"I'm sorry. I'm tired. Can we just go? I assume you have come to take me home?"

"Not home, but somewhere safe."

"And you think you can keep me safe? Shouldn't those two officers outside be coming along with us?"

"Yes, I guess so. But why attract more attention? You are safe with me. I taught myself to drive on the left on the way down." She beamed.

"Fair enough Elena, but seriously, I just need to get back in one piece." She picked up a plastic bag full of hospital detritus and thanked the police staff, shuffling inelegantly past them in her borrowed, baggy clothes.

"We will take it from here gentlemen." Petrova flashed a smile at the younger of the two. That would allow him a few stories back at the station.

O'Shea lowered herself into the BMW and waited until Petrova was in and the doors were locked before she put the seat belt on.

"Trust me?" Petrova asked as she did the same.

"No, not really." O'Shea tried an unconvincing smile.

"Well, you should." She started the car and was quickly heading north west, scanning her mirrors. "Here, ring Jack." She handed over an already unlocked phone.

It was what O'Shea needed to do, to settle her nerves.

"Hi, we are on our way back. Yes, she is driving. No, nothing so far. How are you? Team OK?" It was staccato conversation but hearing his voice helped.

"I will, as soon as we get back. And Jack?"

"Yes."

"We will be OK you know. There's more of us than them."

"Always. Be safe. Catch up soon. And Carrie?" She had already gone. He cleared down, happy that she was en route and that as his dear old dad had often said 'the bastards hadn't ground her down just yet.'

Petrova was a skilled driver. She had learned young, and fast, been taught how to react to the contours of a road, the accelerative and decelerative effects, understeer, oversteer, throttle response. She had been involved in one crash in her life and she blamed herself for that.

Stunning day, stunning place, great roads, music, something to live for. Too much clouding her mind. Then it happened. And all her training meant nothing – at that speed. It wasn't the speed that killed people. It was the stopping.

Today there was no music. Just two women, attractive in their own right, sat side by side in an anonymous silver German car. Blending with the traffic, she merged, indicated, accelerated and stopped. Then again, until she was on the open road.

Through Crystal Palace and north to Gipsy Hill. Doing well. She looked at O'Shea who was struggling to stay awake. The warm air and heated seats didn't help and the sheer exhaustion was still taking its toll.

As she entered Dulwich she saw a change in the housing, Victorian, double-fronted, with gardens. The sort of place she would like. Tree-lined streets, nice cars, healthy kids.

The polished satnav voice told her to turn left onto Alleyn Road and continue towards the A2199. The houses were even more attractive now, bigger cars, large gardens, even the trees were more substantial. She imagined attractive women, working out in their home gyms, keeping their swimsuit bodies in great shape for the summer and their city-dwelling husbands.

She looked in her rear-view mirror, then ahead. Reading the road, suddenly alert, switched on. Trying not to wake O'Shea.

An Audi Q7 had joined them. Gunmetal grey, new model, LED lights, three on board. Coming in fast. Towards O'Shea, straight at Petrova.

Threat.

Initial action.

Accelerate.

The owner of the white Mini Cooper was as innocent as they were but there had to be a victim here. O'Shea woke with a start, saw the Mini approaching, its driver's door flailing in the breeze, a perfect target.

"Elena!"

She hit it hard, tearing the door from the solid hinges, fishtailing her car along the normally quiet street, leaving the buckled door in her wake and into the path of the Audi.

Now she was alive again in a high-powered car that didn't belong to her. She looked, saw the driver swerve. It was a great effort; she gave it a seven. But he was too slow. The door caught the underside and began to grind along the road surface, slowing them, then stopping the car a hundred metres behind.

She kicked the BMW down a gear and ignored the hazards. It was them. She knew the signs and felt it deep within her sixth sense that had served her so well, and besides, people in Victorian, double-fronted streets with six-pack nannies did not drive like that.

"Carrie, ring Jack. Press redial."

She was already doing it.

CHAPTER 51

"Jack. It's me. We've been compromised. An Audi. Grey. Dulwich, we are somewhere in Dulwich. We need help."

She looked in her door mirror; the Audi was moving again. The passenger was talking on a cell phone. The bald-headed man on the other end of the line laughed. A cackle, mid-range, visceral – haunting.

"Wonderful. Go and get them. Drive it like you stole it. Force them off the road. Kill the passenger with your bare hands, watch her gasp as you choke her to death. This is war and no one will even notice in a city where neighbours don't speak to each other. But leave the driver for me. We have some things that we need to talk about."

They were expendable. Three young men in a nice car, living what for them was an upmarket and unexpected life-style, and one with a promise of money and continued employment. But they were expendable. They wanted the money, but what they really craved was the tattoo and the sense of brotherhood that it provided to a group of other-wise lonely and isolated men.

Petrova braked hard, locked up slightly, off the brakes then left, and a right, trying to stay calm, looking for the Audi. Shuffling the leather-clad steering wheel expertly through her hands. It was then she saw the blue BMW 535. Same ardent faces. Two this time, but she knew they were from the same region. She gestured to Carrie.

"Yep, seen them." She shifted in her seat, trying to get a better view of what lay ahead and what might be screaming up behind them. She'd been here before, years before, in a police vehicle, lights flickering, sirens wailing, people pointing, moving out of their way, but he was going too fast. Should have known better. They all said so at the inquiry. At least it wasn't an inquest.

Her heart was racing, her mouth dry, tainted with a hint of aluminium and her skin was clammy, cold. She was back there, a passenger, helpless, young and desperate to escape. The difference this time was that she was older and wiser and she trusted the driver.

"Jack we've got more company. Any chance of some help?" She sounded calm and that was a good thing.

"On its way." He dropped the phone into his lap and keyed the microphone, calling for air priority. They all heard it. Out on the ground, in the stations, on radios attached to body armour, and in the hub of Op Orion Dave Francis spun round in his office chair. It was good to be back in action.

"Hear that boss?" He had, and he was already heading to the car park with two others.

Daniel called after Roberts. "I'll come with you."

"No JD you stay here, run things for me, you've had enough fun for one day."

They ran down the stairs; it was quicker than waiting for the lift. He called up on the force radio and asked for any available unit to head south. Then listened as each one failed to respond.

"Cutbacks. I hope the bloody PM is listening to this. Come on boys, the three of us can make a difference, let's go and kick some Eastern European arse."

"Jack we are on..." She looked for a road sign. "We are approaching a crossroads. Stand by." It was typical of a high-speed vehicle-borne conversation where the speaker got frustrated with a lack of information as much as the listener.

She was also back in the saddle, saying the right things. Adrenaline-fuelled but back and it felt good.

"Jack we are heading north, satnav says Croxted Road." She repeated it. Cade did the same.

"Carrie. Get onto force radio! I'll monitor. Help is on the way."

It was so obvious she could have kicked herself. In the main glovebox was the handset, already dialled into the Met Police VHF channel. She keyed the mike and started talking.

"Air priority. O'Shea. Op Orion staff. I have no idea of our call sign. This is an urgent call for back-up." She repeated their location. "Under a railway bridge, Shell petrol station, right-hand side. Speed six zero."

She opened the central glovebox. A small black box had all the bells and whistles she needed. It seemed bizarre, but why not? She switched on the sirens.

Elena's face lit up. "This is so much fun. I have always wanted this moment!"

"O'Shea from MP – we have units trying to get to you. What is the registration of the vehicle you are pursuing?"

"MP. We are the ones being pursued!"

The Dispatcher looked at her nearest colleague, raised an eyebrow and then spoke. "So, whose are the sirens?"

"Ours MP. Trying to warn others. We are in an unmarked silver BMW."

"Received. All units heading to Croxted Road be on the lookout for a silver BMW and a blue BMW. The blue is the target vehicle. Repeat blue is the target. Proceed with caution."

Petrova looked into her mirror, gunned the throttle, overtook a bus that was pulling out from a stop, then shouted at O'Shea.

"Find a police station on the GPS."

"Carrie you still there?" It was Cade.

"Yes, trying to juggle Jack." She had at least four plates spinning precariously on their canes.

"OK. I'll hang up, just keep heading north, lure them in towards us. I've got at least two Kent Police cars bearing down from the south and our boys are heading towards you from every other direction including above."

In the blue BMW, similar conversations were being held. They were coordinating too. On the phone, looking at online maps.

The old brown van waited at the side of Norwood Road. Two up front, two in the back. Stolen quite easily the evening before, its owner ever-grateful that it had finally gone. Old, but it would serve a purpose.

The Audi was on the move again. The BMW a hundred metres behind the girls. To the casual onlooker both BMWs were police vehicles. It wasn't unusual to see such events, and so everyone ignored them, got out of their way and carried on with their business.

"MP we are going to turn right onto Norwood Road, our aim is to get to Brixton police station. Received?"

"Received. Speed and road conditions and class of driver please?"

"MP I don't quite think you understand the nature of this job." She pulled a face at the microphone. "As fast as conditions will allow. Traffic is heavy, and the driver doesn't have a licence. But she's doing really well."

The control room inspector stood up from his desk and walked towards his staff member. "What?" He strutted towards the screen, looking at the even unfolding in the screen. He could see the headlines now.

"Abort this now!"

"O'Shea you are to abort. I repeat abort."

"MP from Cade. Air priority."

"Go ahead."

"They abort, they get harmed. Your call."

The inspector was young in service; he did everything by the book. He picked up the desk phone.

"Yes sir. Unmarked car. Being pursued. Not a police driver. Some operation called Orion which frankly you have as much of a clue as I do and be advised I will be asking some stern questions about this when..."

The voice cut him off. "Get armed units to that vehicle as soon and as safely as you can, inspector. Do it now."

"But..."

"No buts. Put my name to the job if you have to. Have we got the air support team up?"

"Yes sir Nine Eight are en route as we speak."

The silver car was navigating traffic at speed, the sirens helped, but they also allowed the blue vehicle to slip through the chaos. Sooner or later something had to change.

"Norwood Road. We are approaching Norwood Road. Jesus...no!" The urgency in her voice changed. The observer in the helicopter saw it. Watched it happen in real time; there was none of the usual myth that 'everything slowed down' – that didn't happen in the real world, in real-time.

Cade heard it. The office heard it. The Control Room too.

The brown van was driving straight at them, through the red lights, at speed, from their right. The driver was actually smiling.

The BMW was approaching fast from the rear. Their mission had been pointed out in simple terms: Finish them off. The ante had been upped and Alex Stefanescu considered that he held the winning hand. 'Me, cause chaos? You have no idea. I haven't even started!'

"Carrie hold on tight." Petrova didn't look at her, gripped the wheel and stamped on the brakes. Ahead was an old wrought-iron fence and two long-established trees. To the right, the van. Behind the BMW.

"Go left! Go left!" O'Shea screamed.

"We won't make it at this speed. Hold on!"

Above, circling in a Eurocopter, the rear observer looking down through geo-stationary binoculars and his colleague in the front seat recording live, linking back to the Control Room, zooming in on the action from a thousand feet, the pilot ever-watchful over London skies.

"India Nine Eight we are overhead. Standby! Crash, crash, crash! Junction of Norwood and Croxted Roads. Two vehicles, fire and ambulance to scene – plus ground units please."

They all heard it but only four people saw it.

The brown van disintegrated, its rusting front end crumpling pathetically, built long before airbags, it stood no chance against the Might of Munich. What it did manage to do before its final journey was stove the driver's door in and deploy the airbag, forcing the driver back and into the seat, unrestrained, his neck broke instantly. His passenger heard the snap of ligaments and bone, and somehow managed to live.

Petrova swung the silver car in an arc, scrubbing the speed off as quickly as she could. She came to a halt, hard up against the kerb, against the flow of the London-bound traffic.

She buried her right foot, causing the rear wheels to yelp in protest and the back end of the car to judder as it gained a hold on the cold tarmac.

"Nine Eight the silver car is making off along Norwood. One out and running from the blue BMW, front seat passenger, blue fleece top, jeans, over the fence and into Brockwell Park. Can we have a ground unit to that location please? It's a large expanse of parkland, he won't get far."

The only patrolling dog unit was the first to respond. Zeus his devoted land shark was already at fever pitch in the back of the blue and yellow Skoda estate car.

His handler picked him up and hoisted him over the railings. Called for the male to stop. Checked the surroundings. Then made the call to deploy the dog.

"Go get him Zeus!"

It was quite the most perfect location to deploy a dog – open ground and only one other person present, and he was running as if his lower leg muscles depended on it. They did, and soon, if he didn't stop they would be flapping around the tibia in a gory, ruined mess, like the scene from an amateur barbeque, undercooked and bloody.

The streets were brought to life now. Sirens approaching from every angle. Engines being thrashed. Overhead the EC135's blades were cutting through the freezing winter air. And all the while calm voices spoke on the radio, guiding, controlling and making sense of what for some was a two-dimensional landscape.

"Nine Eight we have another vehicle, grey Audi Q7, at speed, behind our vehicle. Norwood heading south. Any ground units heading north on that road?"

Silence.

"I have had enough of this Carrie. Trust me?" Petrova was busy multi-tasking but her training was evident. She had been here before, some other place no doubt, but she knew how to handle a car.

"Yes. Just get us somewhere safe."

"No, no. This ends now. Either we do or they will. I know these people. These are not common thieves Carrie. These are Alex's best men."

"MP from O'Shea."

"Go ahead."

"Where is our backup?"

"Five minutes over." It meant ten in the current urban traffic, the winter sun trying its best to finally burn off one or two stubborn patches of mist.

"We can't wait that long. My driver is about to take control here."

"Received. You are to continue at a speed that is safe until we can get support to you." She turned to the inspector who had aged at least five years.

"What or who are they running from exactly boss?"

"That is the best question I have heard so far." He picked up the desk phone again and began an animated conversation where he tried to take charge but lost.

Petrova had lost her trademark smile. "Hang on. We are going to take control. Or as Jack says, we are going tactical!"

O'Shea turned in her seat, grabbing the seat belt. "You are going to do *what?*"

She dialled Cade who was also busy forcing his way through traffic. Roberts too, although he knew he was quite a way from the action. God, he missed the old days and the thrill of the chase, that sense that you were literally living on the edge, that any moment now could be your last.

Red Mist they called it.

CHAPTER 52

THE AUDI WAS FEET AWAY NOW. THEY WERE READY, seatbelts off and willing to carry out their explicit instructions. Kill the passenger, grab the driver and try to make it to a safe location.

For them, whatever it was called the red mist had settled, and now, regardless of the consequences they were going to finish this off, in a busy street, in front of school kids and their mums and the watching world on CCTV, cell phones and the fractured memories of countless witnesses who would soon swear they saw six men, all armed, one with an eye patch, and yes, they all had beards.

The men they were witnessing were the new wave. Paid more, respected more. Worth more.

These were Alex's foot soldiers. Well trained in the style of the military but only one had actually served and he was their leader, had spent time with the Jackdaw at Pazardzhik Prison. The others had just watched him – and learned. They were strong, fast and independently capable.

. . .

In the nearby park retired dog handler Andy Pickers was strolling with his new charge, a seven-month-old German Shepherd called Sultan, named after his beloved canine friend who had served him so well in his incredible days as a frontline police dog.

Pickers saw the male running. He knew the difference between a jogger and a runner. As in a runner from a car, or a burglary.

And the familiar thrum of rotor blades overhead and cacophony of sirens, squawking tyres and organised mayhem also told him the party was about to start all over again. God he missed it.

He held onto Sultan, tight at the lead, watching a jet black missile hurtling across the parkland, low, sleek and on target. The poor bastard didn't stand a chance. Until he stopped, turned and produced a pistol.

Aiming it high, trying to steady his arm, his own veins pulsing with adrenaline. He pulled the trigger and missed.

A solitary puff of grey smoke on a greyer day in a leafless inner-city park.

India Nine Eight saw it. The handler saw it, heard it too, knew immediately that the only thing stopping someone getting harmed was Zeus' instinct as a firearms dog.

The male fired again. And again. Now it was reckless. Firing round after round, and trying to run, instinct was also playing a huge part.

All the while Nine Eight hovered like a watchful mother and relayed.

For Andrew Pickers, a veteran of more chases than he could shake a stick at this was unfair. He wished he could deploy Sultan, but he was a pup, and too precious.

"Take him for me, love?" He pushed the lead into a passing jogger's hand, then ran, as fast as his slightly-heavier than-when-he-was-a-copper body would allow. It was risky, foolhardy almost.

"Nine Eight we have a member of the public assisting. Dog on the ground too." He spun left in the seat. "Our car is braking." He didn't know where to look next.

Pickers hit the male in the midriff, hard, as hard as he could. He knew this was a one-stop-shop. The handler saw it too and screamed at his dog who was now committed in his own crimson-misted mayhem.

The three collided. Pickers took down the male with a tackle that an England rugby forward would happily celebrate, Zeus hit the male with everything he had, thirty kilos of lean muscle and a set of teeth so white and polished that they easily glided through any limb that they met.

Biting at anything that moved, including Pickers. Pain first. Then bleeding, made worse by the coldest day in years. Retired Police Constable Pickers held onto him with a grip so tight the other male could barely breathe. Face down in the grass, the smell of damp and cold soil and rotting leaves striking his olfactory system. It was surreal. He'd remember that later when they stitched him up. That, and the sight of the black pistol lying in the cold, well-kept grass.

Pickers was joined by his modern human equivalent who wrestled Zeus from his prey. All was as quiet as a pile of badly mauled men could be.

Two hundred metres away the silver BMW had slowed. There and then, in the high street where people were suddenly sitting up and paying attention. Some lifted their cell phones like clones and just filmed.

Who were these people?

There were two waves in town. The Seventh and the bluer one.

The Q7 was racing towards them now. Petrova accelerated, so fiercely the rear tyres smoked. It was a lighter car and with fewer people on board had the edge. She was a hundred metres ahead now. And then she braked. Hard.

O'Shea did as she was told and gripped the door and her seat.

"Here they come. Hold on."

She brought the car to a halt, changed gear, into reverse and powered the car back along the road.

O'Shea bellowed, "No!"

The Q7 driver was ready, he knew the greater weight of his car would give them the advantage.

"Go faster!" The passenger yelled. "Hit them!"

They were now nose to tail, at speed, as the London-bound traffic queuing in the opposing lane could only watch and try to film, social media feeds buzzing with the amateur footage within moments.

The traffic stopped, creating a gap, occupants watching, open-mouthed.

What they saw next shocked them.

The police vehicle was accelerating violently. Petrova twisted in her seat, one hand on the leather-rimmed wheel the other on O'Shea's seat, looking backwards and steering the car expertly. Thirty metres away from the Audi she swung her car in a pendulous curve, ramming into the door pillar between the driver and rear passenger with pinpoint accuracy.

The Audi airbags inflated in milliseconds as the men inside were trying to get out. The driver was incapacitated and bleeding, his head having struck the green-tinted auto-glass and coloured it bright red.

Petrova shoved the gear lever into first, drove forward, fifty metres, slammed the brakes on then back into reverse.

The rear bumper was gouging the road surface. But only one thing mattered now.

O'Shea's cell rang. She ignored it. Praying for the whole episode to end.

They careered back along Norwood Road, this time aiming for the passenger side. The front seat passenger was half out of his door, pistol in hand and deciding which of his three options to take. Stay in the car, shoot or run.

He chose the latter. At twenty-nine he was fit, and wearing street gear and trainers he thought he would easily outpace the lumbering silver car.

Petrova drove at the door, pushing the accelerator deep into the carpet just as her instructor had taught her when she was young.

"If you commit my dear, then commit. There is no place for half-hearted attacks upon your enemy."

He would have adored this one.

The already-battered rear of the five series BMW struck the solid grey door of the Q7 and smashed it against the male's upper legs and chest. Her aim was not as honed this time, allowing one of the rear occupants to scramble from the car, falling to his knees and only able to watch as she repeated the move, forward, back. The rear of the car hit him as he tried to stand, upper body and head, forcing him into the bodywork of the Audi. He heard his own bones and ligaments breaking – a sound like a deep bass-like popping candy going off in his head.

He was now on the floor, lying on the cold tarmac and breathing his last. The sheer power of the collision had caused his sternum to collapse. They called it blunt anterior trauma. If you survived.

For the black-haired thirty something it was later written as his cause of death.

It had taken a minute; maybe two. She had taken

control. On the busy urban road lay men in various forms of decay, crushed, battered and bruised. One had run, over the fence and was being feasted upon by a large black dog. One remained.

Petrova had pulled forward. Stopped. Got out.

Cold and calm. Now her training was coming to the fore.

"Nine Eight the female driver is out of the silver BMW. Occupants of the Audi are trying to decamp. We need more units to the scene. Female passenger is also out of our car. Repeat two out."

"They are doing *what?*" Cade yelled at the speaker on his dash, changed to third and accelerated as hard as the conditions and traffic would allow. He was now doing what police called making progress. Basically weaving in and out of standing traffic, balletic, highly organised and technically very illegal as he was no longer a police officer.

Kids waved. Mothers sheltered their kids. Cars, and buses and lorries moved or stayed put, depending on what Cade indicated he was going to do next.

Ten minutes behind him Roberts and the team were doing the same. There was truly nothing like haring through standing traffic – every metre or so avoiding a collision.

Behind them two more patrol cars, weaving snakelike through one of the most built-up cities in the world.

Cade checked his watch. Ten minutes away. Ten, long minutes. Go faster.

Use the pavements, wrong side of the road, force people out of the way. Dominate. Take control. Part the waves.

God, he missed the thrill.

. . .

O'Shea was out of the car. She'd heard gunshots. The throb of the helicopter. The screech of tyres. The dull, metal-on-metal collision. Then her heartbeat. Then nothing at all. Her hearing was the first sense to evade her. It was common in high-stress situations.

This was all way too soon. She'd been in a hospital bed less than an hour ago. And now she was standing on a freezing busy urban road trying to decide what to do next. She looked and saw Petrova walking towards the Audi. There was a real purpose to her walk.

She decided that behind her was probably the safest place to be. She knew the helicopter was watching, relaying live imagery back to the control room. Surely the frontline would be here soon?

She walked. Gently at first, then feeling exposed by the distance between the two cars she got quicker, shaking off the last hints of her recent experience on that table in that hell-hole that was to have been her morgue.

She froze. Unable to go any further. All she could do was watch and learn and admire.

Petrova was so much quicker. Running, stopping, picking up the pistol, kicking the passenger door hard against the man who had tried his best to recover. Her sole aim to find the fourth and put him out of his misery.

On board India Nine Eight, the former Army Air Corps pilot had seen enough. He knew they were relaying the live feed back to the people that made decisions – that gathered and gave evidence.

He had seen enough in his time to know that what he did next was for the right reasons; he was sick of protecting the guilty. With a less than subtle shift of the cyclic and the collective, he had turned the aircraft on a sixpence.

"Just need to reposition. Winds are stronger than they look."

Petrova was firm up against the bodywork of the Audi, waiting to be shot at. She could hear the one remaining occupant preparing to leave, racking his own weapon. He had been far too slow. She stepped into the doorway and fired. Not for her an arduous risk assessment or verbal challenge. Step, aim, fire.

Two shots. Finger on the trigger, push, don't anticipate, let the round go – and there she goes, thwack, and again, reset the trigger, one harmonious action, a slight jolt of the front end, the master hand doing its thing. And a second round, same place, drilling through his outer body and into his lungs.

She hit him in the central mass just as she and most tactical shooters had been taught. Tempting as it was to follow up the serial with one to the head, she wanted him alive. His own weapon dropped onto the deep black carpet as he slumped back into the buckled driver's side passenger door.

Now gripping his stomach and lower chest, he tried to breathe. She looked at him through lifeless eyes.

"Stay."

O'Shea saw it all.

"Elena!" she yelled.

"It's OK. We are safe. Stay here. Police will come soon. You will be OK." She walked away, back down the road, looking at the blue BMW and the brown van. Led with the weapon, watching for signs of life. What a mess. And she had caused most of it. She smiled. She allowed herself to relax for a second.

The forty-two-year-old front passenger of the old brown

van had played dead. Now, he was out of the vehicle and moving towards Petrova, unseen.

Cade was a minute away. Two local traffic units were even closer, approaching from different angles both were being advised by their colleagues in India Nine Eight. Three ambulances were closer. Holding back until Nine Eight could confirm the ground was safe.

As Cade sped along Norwood Road, away from the city he looked at his speedo: Ninety. Fast enough to get there, slow enough to allow people to die.

He saw the gun before he saw the man. A short-barrelled shotgun was suspended from the van passenger's hand and with no attempt to cover its presence the male deliberately walked towards Petrova. He knew who she was, he'd seen her picture on his phone. It was how he had been briefed. Jackdaw has said bring her in alive. But he had watched how she had systematically killed his colleagues, and he would risk the wrath of his boss to wipe the smile off her face.

Up on his toes, oblivious to the cacophony of the sirens approaching from all angles, grey clothes, grey hat, dark grey weapon, he blended well. Now, raising the weapon up into the aim he moved along the road and between the cars.

"India Nine Eight for the information of all ground units, we have a male carrying a firearm. All grey clothing. Has left the brown Bedford van over."

The first local area car stopped on the next road to Norwood and allowed the armed response car to pass, it was far better to yield to their firepower and experience and go home that night.

Cade was five hundred metres away, slowing, sirens off, blue lights still flickering. He looked along Norwood, heard the broadcast, could see the carnage and saw O'Shea standing in the middle of the carriageway as if she had been struck down with fear. He saw Petrova, stepping away from an Audi, unarmed. And then he saw the ultimate grey man.

Risk assessed. Decision made. He looked to the left as he shot through the wide junction, saw the marked armed response vehicle, swerved and then drove straight at the male.

The man knew the difference between the steady background noise that accompanied them and the different, high pitched scream of the car engine. He turned slightly, keeping an eye on the female, but it was too late. Stepping right, he walked into Cade's path and as his knees buckled he was scooped up and over the windscreen, hitting his head on the solid, dense glass. To a bystander it sounded like a ripe watermelon hitting concrete from a second-storey window.

At that speed he cleared the roof, collided with the rear boot and then collapsed in a pile of broken bones twenty metres further down the road. His body faced the wrong way to his head, his arms twisted and his left lower leg distorted.

The weapon skidded across the road surface and stopped under a small modern white hatchback, its driver holding her cell phone in shock.

Cade stopped. He was unarmed. He held his hands aloft as he heard the scream of a firearms officer, tucked behind the wing of his Volvo, pointing the G36 rifle straight at him.

"Stop armed police! Down on the ground. Do it. Do it now!"

He did.

The officer's partner did the same, pointing a weapon at Petrova and O'Shea. Scanning the scene, sweeping his weapon in an arc, checking, covering down, scanning, finger off the trigger, safety off and weapon loaded, ready to fire.

"Female next to the Audi. Show me your hands!"

They repeated the drill until all had been considered safe. Cade yelled back. "Police. We are police."

Roberts' car pulled up into the junction. Engine hot, brake discs crackling. He was out in seconds. His two staff too.

"DCI Roberts. Operation Orion. The two females are with us."

"Sir. We need to clear the vehicles."

"Yes, of course. Go ahead. But for Christ's sake don't shoot my people."

The blue BMW, the old brown van and the Audi were cleared. The two surviving occupants of the Audi were cuffed, for safety's sake, allowing the paramedics to approach.

Cade was allowed to stand. He held his hands in a position that said, 'I'm on your side.' He walked towards Petrova.

"You OK?" He smiled the best he could.

"Fine. Absolutely fine. It was good fun." She shrugged her shoulders. Not a sign of stress. He actually believed her.

"Looks like you have done their job for them." He nodded back to the uniformed armed staff.

"It was what I was trained to do, Jack. I guess there will be paperwork now?"

Now he smiled more. "I guess. Well done, Elena." He paused. "Your mother would have been proud of you."

"She is proud of me, Jack. Every day. I am just not proud of me."

"Well, you should be."

"You don't know me. What we had was brief, and wonderful. You thought I was dead, me too. And anyway, talking of dead, did you see where I led that lot?" She pointed over her shoulder with her right thumb.

"Away from any cameras. I have looked. No one was

filming either."

"You're certain?"

"I am. Now go to Carrie. She needs you more than I do." Dismissive.

She looked at him through bright green eyes, wiped her hands through her hair, allowed the adrenaline to dissipate through her body, let herself breathe, paced from foot to foot, then leaned against the Audi, looking at the two dead men and the ambulance staff working on the others, scissors clipping clothing away, bloodied pressure pads being placed and dropped onto the road. Bright red liquid trickling down the road and into the gutter. CPR being performed. Moans of the living, pitiful cries of the dying, the silence of the dead.

"Go on, Jack. Go. Our time is done." Dismissed.

He wasn't sure what she meant, but a suburban road was not the place for in-depth discussions.

He walked over to O'Shea who was squatting against the silver car; her back to the prying eyes of the now moving traffic and an arriving film crew.

"Hello Miss O'Shea. You did well. Better sort your mascara out, looks like the BBC is here to film it all for posterity. You OK?"

"Do I look OK? A balding, shattered wreck?"

"You look good enough to me. And besides, I like short hair."

"Then take me home, Jack, before I wake up from this bloody nightmare." She looked up, enormous tears about the burst their banks, swallowing hard, breathing shallow.

"Come on, you." He pulled her into his chest as he stood her up, steadied her for a second and then led her to his car. "Best you don't look, Elena is pretty ruthless."

"Attractive and ruthless. What more could any man want?"

"I'll settle for attractive."

"Well, you had your chance."

"I did. And I apologise. I'm here for you whenever you decide to give chance a second go."

She sniffed a sound that was meant to show her disinterest but it failed. She wanted to hug him, felt lighter, lifted, almost normal.

"Jack?"

"Carrie?"

"The Home Secretary did say the cuffs were off, didn't she? She said we needed to reclaim the streets, didn't she?"

Cade offered a bemused look. "She did. Why do you ask?"

"Oh, just something I need to do. Open that door would you?"

He clicked the large handle that sat among the bright red and yellow striped rear end of an ambulance. He opened the door and saw a paramedic busy finishing off the primary care of the first of two survivors.

Cade winked at the woman who was in her thirties and filled out her one-piece uniform nicely.

"Can we have a minute yet?"

"You can. Don't be long, we need to get going soon." She walked, stepped down and out onto the street. "Be my guest."

Cade entered the ambulance, staring through the tinted glass back out onto the scenes of carnage. O'Shea followed.

"Over to you. I'm looking forward to hearing this."

She leaned into the bed and spoke. "I know you understand English. So listen carefully. This is my city. I was born here, my mother too, and hers before her. Hitler failed to take it from us and I'll be damned if you think you can stroll into town in your stolen car, with your cheap gold watch and sneering grin, stripping the city like a plague of locusts."

He was doing a great job of ignoring her. Lying there, staring at the bright lights and anticipating his future.

"Fine. But I know you heard." She removed his oxygen mask. "And for the record, whilst I can't prove it, I know you were back there at the shit hole that you and that gap-toothed clown Constantin kept me in. So here's some summary justice."

Her actions caught Cade off guard. He had seen her balled fist as a measure of her anger, not a preparatory act. She pulled her arm back and followed through with one single punch – not a slap – straight into his mouth, splitting the top lip and shattering the enamel on his front tooth.

Then she just stared at him as he lay on the stretcher, cuffed and unable to react.

"Not nice, is it. Anyway, have a nice life." She stood upright and walked to the door. "I'll see you outside. I'll wait in case you need a chat too." She had left the mask off.

Cade clicked the door shut, then locked it. Took three steps back to the end of the stretcher where the man's head was laid on a basic foam cushion. Blood oozed out of his lip and ran down his cheek, onto the pillow. He replaced the mask.

"She's right. Not nice is it?" He looked into the man's eyes. They were like all the rest of the team, shark-like.

"You see, that young lady has a mean right hook, whereas I know other ways of causing you real discomfort. The type that your boss, the Jackdaw, decides is acceptable to dish out, to a captive audience."

He pulled the clear mask up and onto the man's head and left it there, waiting for the lack of oxygen to start to take effect. Checked his favourite watch, admired the sweep of the second hand. Waited a minute. Watched as the young man's eyes started to change and his skin started to subtly change colour.

He tied to resist but this was a battle of wills he would lose.

Next came the increase in blood pressure, then the dizziness.

Cade checked his watch.

"Are we ready to be sensible yet?"

There was a knock on the door. "Can I come in yet?"

"Another few minutes should be all I need – thanks. He's doing well."

He looked down at him, then up at the drip, flicked his eyebrows up and down and smiled.

The PM himself had said the team needed to become feral.

"Listen, pal where I come from, we respect the police. We acknowledge the hard work of the authorities and we certainly would never do that to a lady." He gestured out of the ambulance, looking at O'Shea stood on the street.

"No, you see, in Britain we do things by the book. Now, the problem for you is I've never read this particular book, so it's kind of ad-lib from here. But I have seen plenty of films. I think this might have been in one."

He reached up and turned the screw on the intravenous drip. Slowly at first, watching the trickle of pain-reducing fluids come to a stop. Blood started to run backward now, up the clear tube.

"The thing is I have no idea what this is doing to you. But I'm guessing it hurts?" One minute left. He watched as his prisoner's pupils began to dilate. The fentanyl in his bloodstream had reduced his pain levels to bearable, now they were back and worse. Seventy times stronger than the morphine he had been given at first, he needed it, desperately.

"You've got one minute and then I leave. And no one comes back. If the pain doesn't kill you, the heart failure will. Start thinking about what it is you really need to tell me about the Seventh Wave."

He let the combination of air and drugs, or rather the lack of it, take effect.

"You have everything to lose." Fifty seconds.

"Nothing." The word was spat out, blood-laced.

"Oh, dear." He turned the screw fully now.

"Think of your dear mother back there in Bucharest. She is waiting for you to return home. So proud...her special son..."

"The Jackdaw will kill me." Good, he was seeing sense. Thirty seconds.

"No. You will kill yourself within minutes. Feel that chest starting to hurt? A sense of panic? Breathing getting laboured now? I can hear you from here. Talk!" Cade held his cheeks between his thumb and forefinger and squeezed until it felt as if his gums were going to collapse.

"I can't."

"You can."

"I can't" It was a like the men's singles at Wimbledon and Cade was Federer, masterful across the court, slicing, spinning, finishing off the unseeded folk hero with a powerful volley until he relented.

"OK. Please."

"Please?" Cade's raised eyebrows emphasised the question.

"Give me air." Wherever the air was escaping from Cade could only guess, but knew he needed to replace it. He slipped the mask back over the man's face. "Ten, nine..."

"There are two teams. One is going to hit the banks and get cash. They are splitting it fifty-fifty with Jackdaw." He looked as if he had just plunged a knife into his boss's heart.

"And the other?"

"The other is...the vault." He struggled to push the word out, but Cade heard it clearly.

"The vault? The Tower of London?" It was the intelligence they had heard, the chatter, the source of information. Perhaps it was true. But no one targeted the Tower. A few had tried, but it was beyond impregnable. It made no sense.

"The Tower of London?"

"No. That would be impossible. The vault...where the money is kept. That is what Jackdaw wants."

Cade felt he had nothing to lose. The door was being banged again. He ignored it.

"Keep talking my friend and you have my word that I will protect you from further pain."

"No one can. He is everywhere. They say he is the Gypsy King." He was drifting now. Perhaps time to increase the opiates? He teased the dial back, watching the blood flush and the fentanyl re-enter his bloodstream. Once more he held him in abeyance.

"Well, I'll tell you that the man you clearly fear is nothing more than a man with money and power. He's as invincible as you, or he is until someone shuts down his air." He held onto the mask.

"No! I will tell you."

"Then hurry because our friend outside in the green jumpsuit is getting impatient. The vault?"

"Where they keep the gold. There are seven vaults in London."

"Seems to be his lucky number." Cade twisted the man's wrist, looking at the blue tattoo. It was fresh, the blue tinged with a black border around which the skin was a vivid red.

"Is this all worth it, just for that?"

"I have nothing else to...value."

"Why is he going after the seven vaults?" It was a question designed to trap.

"He isn't." He breathed deeply, inhaling the elixir of life. "There is one within the city. Not the biggest. But it still has gold. He is going for the three at the airport. Now please, go, let me live. I need to learn how to lie to his face." He looked genuinely afraid.

"Mr Cade. I am coming in in one minute." That was fine. It gave him a minute more.

The male looked up, over the misted-up mask. "I will tell Jackdaw I met Mr Cade. The man he hates more than anyone."

"Impressive street skills there, but you heard her shout out, and that is cheating in my book." He stood up, stretched his back and made for the door.

"Jack. Mr Jack Cade. She is Carrie O'Shea, the girl who punched me. The one who tried to kill me is Alex's daughter. There is a price on her head."

"OK, so you listen well."

"I was a soldier, Mr Cade. I know what to remember and who to forget. If you threatened to stop those drugs again, I could name most of your team. Pick them out from photographs. You are all targets. He's coming for you one by one, by one."

"So that's it. You all know my name, and the names of my team and one of your groups is going to try to break into a bank vault and steal gold. Sounds great in theory."

"Trust me, it will happen. He has an ace card in his pocket." His smile creased the cut in his lip and allowed the bright red blood to flow into the mask.

"Don't tell me? Mr Jackdaw has a secret government document that will bring down the British government, and he intends to use it to blackmail them for more than is in that vault?"

The man shrugged as best he could. "Maybe."

"Then maybe we already know that. So your value is limited." He removed the mask and turned the dial.

"The document is of no value. It has always been a smokescreen."

"Seems you know a lot more than a humble foot soldier should."

"Then it seems you are right, Jack. I am one of Alex's best men. He calls me his lieutenant – I'm just happy to be called Gheorghiu."

Cade smiled. It was ironic, but a smile nonetheless.

"Well, we meet at last. I almost shot you a while ago, on the Thames. I recognise you now."

"You did shoot me. Luckily, you are a very bad shot."

He hissed as he gasped for air.

"We can make a deal together Jack." His skin was changing from tanned to blue once more.

"Only if you reveal the ace. You have one turn of the cards left Gheorghiu."

"Then turn it for me."

"You people have no scruples, do you?"

"I do not understand."

"You have no honour. Alex would betray his own mother."

"I honour one man and one woman. Me, and my mother. And I need to tell you I forgive you for shooting me in the boat that day." He even smiled. "And as for Alex's mother... he killed her. And his father, too. He is beyond evil."

"But you choose to stay with him?"

"Consider it like a bad marriage."

Cade moved closer, put his ear as close as he could. Then listened. He had at last made a deal with someone other than the devil.

"Now please, give me the drugs. The pain in my ribs is unbearable."

"Happily." He looked at the tray of controlled drugs. Fentanyl. He knew that they would have given him fentanyl.

He leant on his rib cage, causing him to recoil in pain.

"Not nice, is it? I bet it hurts, just there." He poked the wound, causing another instant reaction. "Talking about the Thames. A long time ago I went to the aid of a lovely young lady, lying in the cold river, dying. Tied to a metal grid and left to choke on river water. Not nice."

"I am sorry to hear that, Jack."

"I'm sure you are. Another friend of mine drowned there. In the same river. Seems to be a trend. She was a good person. A beautiful person, whose only crime was one of passion. Tied to a wooden platform." He watched Gheorghiu's eyes shrink. Got you, you little bastard.

"Pegged her out in the mud, let the river consume her. She would have drowned really slowly. She was deprived of her dignity too, naked, disrespected. What sort of man would do that? Her name was..."

He nodded a weak confirmation. "Nikolina. I know. And I am truly sorry. He made me do it. You need to understand he is a dangerous man."

"And so am I, Gheorghiu."

He slipped the needle into the vial, drew out the drug and inserted it into the injection port on the intravenous bag. Then pushed the plunger until it all blended seamlessly.

"That should help."

"Thank you, sir." His eyes began to close.

"Sleep well."

It was only murder if you could prove malice. As far as Cade was concerned the intent and the act would be subtly separated. And besides they had to prove it.

"Forty-Fifteen."

He pocketed the vial, slipped the mask back onto Gheorghiu's face, put a thumb up and smiled.

"That's for Niko and her daughter."

Match point.

Outside he thanked the paramedic, then lowered O'Shea into the passenger seat, leant across her as he clipped the seat belt into place and gently kissed her on the cheek, then walked to speak to Roberts.

"So, all is well in the world. I see you and the boys turned up as it was all over!"

"Cheeky bastard Cade. I'll have you know we've driven a long way and set off at least three red light cameras." He held out his hand, which Cade took. "You OK, buddy? You look like you could do with a long black?"

Cade exhaled. "I need more than coffee, pal. It's fair to say I've had better years."

"Well need I remind you it's only January?"

"Thanks, Jason. Helps enormously. This is a cluster of the highest order. How the hell are we going to write this one up?"

"*We* are not. *I* am. And we'll take the Home Secretary at her word shall we? What was it she said? 'Do what you need to do my boys, to protect the city from this scum.'"

Cade's eyebrows raised. "I don't think that was verbatim Jason."

"Well, it's good enough for me. Look, you do what you need to do to get Carrie and Elena back to the ranch. I'll send one of the lads with you. I need to stay here and control things, make sure we come out of this on top. Word will soon get back to Stefanescu. This is personal now, Jack. Oh, and it's a crime scene so watch where you bloody walk."

He put his hand on Cade's shoulder. "Not good, my friend. So, you learn anything from the OK Corral here?"

"More than you could ever imagine." He outlined what

he had heard, then threw in some hypothesis.

"And you think they'll be brazen enough to go for the vaults?"

"Absolutely. The mad leading the blind. You forget he was allowed to walk out of a top security prison because doing so was easier than him staying behind and running the bloody place."

"It's war, Jack. And having been literally bitten, you and I are in no place to be gentlemen any longer."

"I couldn't agree more. See you later." He walked towards the pool car and as he did so he checked the surroundings, then quickly flicked the vial up onto the roof of a Chinese takeaway.

'They'll never look there.' His internal dialogue was calm and guilt-free. They never did.

He got into the car, buckled his seatbelt, looked at O'Shea who was still fighting the adrenaline rush and then looked in the mirror at Elena.

"Thank you."

"This is the beginning, Jack. You need to end it. You didn't fly all the way to Australia just to see me in a beautiful swimsuit."

He blushed slightly. "I'm not with you."

"You obviously believed I could help you – that's why you went. And I can. Remember what I told you that night. But also know that it is going to get very..." She hunted for the word. "Messy." She smiled her smile and once again Cade was torn between the daughters of the Devil and the deep blue sea.

O'Shea closed her eyes. Tried not to think of them, on an island, blue seas, white beaches, warm evenings, the scent of Hibiscus flowers, wine, alone.

She could tell her own mind all she wanted. But she still wanted him more.

CHAPTER 53

ALEX STOOD ON THE BALCONY OF HIS RENTED APARTMENT. Rented in another man's name, using his account in fact. It mattered not. He was long dead anyway, lying in the third mortuary stretcher from the right, waiting for the day that someone was finally able to identify him. Somebody may as well benefit from his demise.

The man they called the Jackdaw looked out across London. It was a beautiful city. Not like so many he had visited, with their lines of tall, faceless buildings. London had its skyscrapers, but most were cleverly designed; distinctive, glassy and caught the eye.

And he liked London.

Decided he loved being there.

He missed the attention of the opposite sex. In his heyday, when he ruled the city of Craiova, he could summon two or three to his bedside. Whores, in many ways just like him, willing to do almost anything for money. But London was different. At this level a high-class escort was needed or they would talk, and even then would he really trust a woman, who when it all came down to it was a prostitute just like the rest?

For now, he was relishing the freedom.

He loved being there alright. Absolutely.

Better still, he adored being able to walk the streets, watch the skyline and cause chaos, all from the lap of luxury. They would never find him. He was one of many. Too many.

"There should be a club for people like us, Constantin. A place where men like us can go, here in the city."

The voice responded from inside the cavernous Kensington apartment, sitting on the top floor of an already prestigious block.

"If there was a gentleman's club in London for top-flight criminals, it would have a waiting list a mile long." He smiled as he filled two simple, crystal glasses with single malt, straight from the cupboard, then threw the cork into the bin.

Taking the glass out to Alex, he too admired the skyline. An eclectic mix of new and old, and older still. They had such a wonderful view.

"Are you ready to teach them a lesson?"

"I was born ready, Constantin. Bring the laptop."

The older Romanian man walked back into the kitchen, picked up the laptop, checked the connection to the dark net then opened up the dialogue box and typed Romulus Six.

He hit enter and waited. For the sake of the interchange, he was Remus Seven.

Romulus and Remus, suckled by the she-wolf. Mythical beings of Roman folklore. It made sense to both of them. They had both been betrayed before.

Constantin had asked the question on the dark web – where could he find a specialist in crypto currencies, and where would he find another that could manipulate systems?

In Romulus Six he had found both – in one person. They assumed it was a man.

Trust was nothing more than a five letter word. Do the job, you get rewarded, paid in whatever currency you care to name. Betray us, we will find you. Dark net or not. That was the extent of their contract.

The pursuit through the streets of South London had attracted media and public attention. Two days at best, then the newspapers became chip wrappers, Will-o'-the-Wisps that littered the street corners for a day or two before joining a pile of other no longer relevant things.

Four days passed.

Ninety-six hours.

And the team had counted every one of them. Some of them had even started to place bets on things happening at chosen moments on the clock face, a phone ringing, a church bell ringing, which a few of the tired ones had failed to grasp seemed to happen on the hour. Anything that could alleviate the boredom. They were bored, and bored cops were like underemployed puppies.

How many red buses in a minute?

Bored.

Cade, O'Shea and Petrova had moved into a new apartment, courtesy of the government. Three bedrooms, two bathrooms, a flat screen TV that could be seen from space. Roberts too, sharing with Daniel. Their wives had been moved to places of safety, one in the UK, the other twelve thousand miles away. Safe.

O'Shea had tapped on Cade's door that night. Asked to enter.

He was stood in a shirt and boxer shorts. She couldn't help admire his legs, still good for a forty something.

"Of course. You OK?"

"No, Jack. I need a hug, actually. Nothing more so you can take that look off your face." She smiled for the first time in weeks.

"Does the lady consider me that shallow?"

"Yes, she bloody well doth."

"You really should sort that lisp out, you know. But then again, it can be quite endearing...I guess."

It earned him a pillow around the side of the head.

"What's troubling you?"

"Jack. Why *did* you go all the way to Australia just to see her in her bikini?"

"Well, I didn't *know* it was her Carrie. Remember, the last time I saw her, she was at death's door, quietly knocking?"

"So you went not knowing it was her?" She seemed lifted by this.

"Yes. But as I say, I needed to check. And what she told me, well, it made a few things clear."

"And can you tell me?"

"No. Not yet. I've been accused of letting people down Carrie. It won't happen again, not until Alex and his team are either behind British bars or dead. Then, if you are a good girl, maybe..."

"You know I can be." She flicked her eyebrows up and down. Playful again. First time since she had been poisoned in her own flat. It was the last passionate gesture from a lover to another. The last eye contact at the time was made the night her colleagues had wheeled her out of the local pub and out of Cade's life.

"I do know. And one day, who knows? I might just let

you. But right now, I need to focus Carrie. Focus on what is important, and that includes you."

The rest of the team had done what police officers and the military do best, adapt. They had converted a briefing room into a bunkhouse, installed a TV that they had 'found' in the building, stocked the kitchen with every conceivable snack and had built beds as comfortable as they could be.

Black kit bags lined the walls, each lying next to a sleeping bag. Cell phone chargers hung from wall sockets. Men and women together.

"I suppose you lot watched me undress last night?" It was a playful DS Bridie McGee.

"Yes." The whole room answered. Except DS Nick Fisher who looked at his phone, but actually stared over the top of it, longingly into her blue eyes, waiting for a sideways glance or a gentle flicker of those eyelashes.

"We've all seen it before anyway, Bridie." Came the collective response.

"Not this body you haven't. It is a temple, and trust me it is firmly locked to lecherous old bastards like you!" There was a cheer and one of her detectives threw a pair of his underpants at her. She caught them deftly in one hand, stretched them out.

"As I thought Rob, size, small..." She put them in a bowl, added water and put them in the nearby microwave to a roar of approval from the team. "About as hot as you'll ever get in that department."

Cade was stood watching. "Morning. Got a moment DS McGee?"

"Yes, boss. Absolutely." She liked him. Always had. It was the eyes.

"Sorry about that."

"Not at all Bridie. Work hard, play harder. How's the team holding up?"

"Honestly, guv, they are bored shitless." She rarely swore and when she did, she got away with it. Her mix of northern tones and a southern education gave her a soft and suggestive voice. The more passionate she became, the more northern.

"Intel tell us nothing is happening. Our Human Source Unit has nothing to offer. Frontline staff are seeing nothing. It's like a city of bloody ghosts. We need some action."

She was joined by Fisher. "Guv. How's it?"

"Nick. Fine, thanks. Look both of you, I had an interesting chat the other day with one of Stefanescu's top men. He told me a lot. I've got some of our intelligence staff looking at that. It takes time."

"This wouldn't be the same top man that died on the way to hospital? Rumour has it you might have had a chat with him before he shuffled off."

"And what if I did?"

"Then I for one like your style boss."

Cade briefed them. Let it sink in. Then answered his cell and gestured five minutes to the two DSs. He was glad he had told them what he knew. So far, only the staff with rank were told, in a sliding scale. Need to know.

"Yes, hello..." A pause to allow the voice to compute. "Well, if the devil should cast his net."

"Hello Jack. How are you?"

"I'm fine. Really. But I've got a team here that are champing at the bit."

"I have no idea what that means, but it sounds painful. We need to meet. St. James' Park tube station. Soon as you can." He was gone. His calls never lasted longer than they needed to.

"Bridie. Nick. Come with me, I need you to be my

backup if something goes wrong." On the way he told them to wait around the corner out of sight, warned them not to approach, that they were dealing with a professional.

"Will there be a sign if things do go pear-shaped?"

"I'll think of something."

Sancus logged onto the dark net. And waited.

Sancus, the Roman god of trust.

Sat in his office, with its solid walls, thick, double-glazed windows and a view that many cherished, he managed a wry smile as he watched the screen come to life. He always faced the door of his office, didn't like anyone walking in and disturbing him, or looking at what he found to be of importance that day. The screen was angled away from the window too, same reason. Trust no one.

He waited, drew a circle in the fine layer of dust in his spare office, the one where few people ever visited. Then scraped a diagonal line through it. No entry.

Viduus also logged onto the net. Safe and secure, his own internet traffic bouncing between so many levels and layers that the authorities would never trace him. The Onion Router – TOR – the safe haven of criminals and law enforcement teams.

Viduus. The Roman god who separated the soul and body after death.

Romulus, Remus, Sancus and Viduus. Four of the most powerful Roman gods. Three of the most powerful men in London and one entity who remained an unknown. But they all ended in 'us' and that meant, for now, they were a team.

They started to talk, typing as quickly as they could. Encrypted. Locked down, confident but far from arrogant.

Yes, a great idea. Soon. Weather? The worst it could be

would be the best they could hope for. Times and dates were exchanged. Pre-arranged passwords used, challenges met.

Trust.

John Daniel tapped quietly on Jason Roberts' office door, his old office door.

"Any sign of any action? Seen Jack? How are you holding up?"

"No. No, and as well as can be expected John."

"Fancy a walk?"

"Anywhere particular?"

"Close."

"Risky, isn't it?"

"We are coppers Jason, not bloody girl guides. I will not abide by this current no-go policy. Come on, grab your coat, and bring your wallet."

Ten minutes later, they were in the Sanctuary, their favoured drinking hole, pushing the wintry gales out of the door and back onto the street as they keenly offered hints of snow.

"Bit early?"

"Never. Scotch?"

"Christ JD, you drying out or something, have you seen the time?"

"I have, and when I tell you this, you'll want another."

Cade was also wrapped up against the worst that winter was throwing at the city. The wind seemed to funnel up the Thames, from the estuary and the North Sea beyond.

He waited and watched, and there, among the crowds of commuters and beggars and the rich alike, was his source. Minutes passed, became fifteen, then twenty. Now.

He walked towards the homeless man, pushed by him, then held him at arm's length with a look of revulsion. It was done.

"It was something that she said to me, when we first met at my place in New Zealand, Jason. Possibly a throwaway line or a deliberate hook, either way I let it sink deep into my cheek and I've struggled to get it out ever since."

"I'm intrigued."

"It was about her father." He spoke for half an hour, outlined his feelings, thoughts and theories.

"Never?" Roberts drained the glass.

"Another?"

"Yes, and make it a double."

Alex drained his own glass, shuddered a little as the last drop slipped down his throat. A chill in the air made his neck tingle, the hairs standing up. The saying, someone has walked over your grave came to mind.

For the first time in his adult life he paused long enough to think about who he had killed, harmed, maimed and tormented.

Was this the turning point? The road to recovery, or the last chapter en route to retribution?

He held the glass out over the edge of the balcony, watched his finger and thumb create a line in the condensation, slipping, slipping, gone. It dropped silently to the ground, landing in a hedge, the last drop spilling out onto the floor.

Recovery? Never. Recovery was for people with a soul.

He looked at the reflection of Constantin in the main patio door. He was a deep and interesting man, twisted in many ways, bitter, tormented, intense. Constantin the two-headed coin. On one side the brilliant chemist, self-taught in prisons across Europe. He had spent days learning recipes for poisons, compounds and explosives. He knew as much as many commercial chemists and was a borderline genius. On the other side of the coin, a cold, ruthless and unpleasant killer for whom the word evil did not begin to describe.

Alex picked up the bottle and drank from it.

"Noroc uncle. And thank you for always being there for me." He wiped the bottle and poured another shot into Constantin's glass.

He replied, "It has been a long time since you called me that. Why the sudden change, nephew?"

"What is it that they say? Blood is thicker than water?"

CHAPTER 54

Another day had passed. Same old, same old.

On the next day, one of the analysts was at work early. Coffee was his new addiction. It kept him awake, and alive. He had arrived with three more in a cardboard carrying tray. Free to a good home. He was enjoying being back in the saddle, glad that someone had found a use for him. When Cade had slipped the small USB drive into his hand the day before he had hoped he could do something with it. Then immediately questioned why he doubted his own abilities. He was well trained, disciplined, and had once saved Cade's career. They owed each other.

And now he sat at his desk with Cade, Roberts and Daniel stood around him. The rest of the team were already out, or logging into their own systems. A few of the night shift were making the most of a chance to sleep, pulling pillows over their heads and trying to block out the noise. Their sleep would be the sleep of kings until someone woke them.

The voice in the next room kept them awake for a while

anyway. It belonged to ex-Army Intelligence Corps legend David Francis.

"Romulus, Remus, Sancus and Viduus."

Roberts was quick. "A firm of Roman lawyers?"

"Hardly boss."

"Front four for Inter Milan?"

"Nope, not that either."

"Have to be roman gods then. So what's the deal?"

"Well, the drive that Jack gave me contained a file. Probably caused the IT department to have a meltdown, but I slipped it into the slot, got it wrong, two tries, then back to the first one, you know how these little things are."

The screen started to come to life.

"And hey, and some presto too."

"What is it?" Daniel had leaned further forward.

"The dark net, John. The place where criminals go to play. And Mr Cade has been given the key to the front door. All I need to do now is decipher what they are rambling on about."

"Code?"

"Absolutely. This is a professional setup. We don't know who Viduus is. Nor Sancus. Not yet anyway. We can make an educated guess about Romulus and Remus."

"Can we? Honestly?" Roberts was interested but sceptical.

"One hundred percent. Romulus is our man, sir."

"Valentin." Cade spoke at a decent volume. Walls were trusted in this team. "I met him yesterday. He's on side."

There were nods of approval. Both Roberts and Daniel remembered his role, poacher turned gamekeeper, coming in from the cold and a lifetime of hatred towards his old employer, the Romanian government. And now he had a chance to make amends for almost ending the life of one of Cade's team.

"The device that Dave is using came from Valentin. Remus is Constantin – or Alex – they use the same sentence structure. Could be either."

"And the other two?" Roberts was already getting tired.

"No idea. The speech is broken, code, almost street talk. But it is someone who has an education, of sorts. And that someone is knowledgeable – has the inside line. Read that part just there." He pointed to a paragraph in an earlier chat line.

"Does it support what Gheorghiu told you?" Roberts again.

"Partly, yes. Looks like Alex has deployed a few teams already. How long do we give them before we strike?"

"Tonight. We go tonight."

"May I suggest tomorrow?" It was Daniel.

"Reason?"

"Gives them just long enough to make a mild mess, but time to provide us with evidence of what their intentions were. If we are quick, then perhaps we can even be waiting for them."

"JD, they will never get into those vaults." Cade was adamant.

"Agreed. And I know this for a fact, because I helped design the perimeter security. Seems like yesterday too."

"But this talk is of tunnels. I reckon they are tunnelling into the city system, via the old tube network and the airport locations will be out and out, old-fashioned blaggings." Roberts was animated again, his lime green double Windsor-knotted tie as vibrant as his manner.

"Shooters?" Francis. Equally upbeat.

"The whole nine yards, my son." Roberts was actually enjoying the thrill of the pre-chase.

"Can I come?"

"No Dave, sorry, no place for an ex-soldier with a Glock and a grudge." Roberts tried his best to be empathetic.

"What if I used my bare hands?"

The day became the evening, which gave way to a colder night. Minus four the weatherman had predicted, and a heavy frost.

The old Mazda 6 was tucked up for the night. Two on board. A Toyota van a few hundred metres away. It had been parked among other vehicles in a place where cars parked overnight and as such was hardly anything to write home about.

In the back, and carefully moving around, was a man and a woman. Dressed for the cold, but still feeling it.

"Minus four. Fuck me, Bridie, it's going to be a long night."

"Was that a weather forecast or a chat up line Detective Sergeant Fisher? I'm not sure where the full stop was or should have been." She held his gaze, then looked back through the Canon SLR, perched skilfully on a ledge, its telephoto lens extending just far enough into the van's cockpit to get a shot of the scene.

"I'm not with you."

"Nick. How long have we known each other?" Her voice appeared even sultrier, this close, in confines that were borderline intimate.

"Since training school actually."

"So, it's fair to say I know what is going on in that head of yours. It's been bloody years, man. Your innuendos, my seemingly apparent willingness to agree to whatever it was that was whirring around up top, in what you call a brain. Just relax and stop trying so hard. Just ask the question and

I'll say yes. That's all you need to do." Her smile lit up the dimly lit surveillance van, their home for the night.

Years. He'd waited years and all he needed to do was ask.

"I hardly think a van that's rocking as if it's in a bloody earthquake is what Jack and the team would call discreet. Would you?"

"No. Perhaps not. But my bed is more than big enough for two. Imagine slipping into it in the morning when everyone else is heading out to work, miserably scraping the ice off their windscreens with a credit card?"

"But I'm married."

"So am I."

"Actually, you are not, technically."

"So you've been stalking me, DS Fisher? I should have you hauled over the coals for this."

"And I should have you by the coals of a roaring fire, DS bloody McGee. And technically, for the record, I'm no longer married either."

There it was, the green light. He leaned over and kissed her. Gently, on the lips. They were sweet-tasting, honey-like, smooth like satin. She swallowed hard, eyes open, then closed. He could feel the heat radiating from her skin.

He smiled with his eyes, let her go, knew it was wrong.

She had her right eye back on the cup, looking at the enhanced image, biting her lip, trying not to scream in delight that he had finally made the move.

He was about to ask. And she was about to say yes.

"Wait one." McGee held her hand up. Consummate professional once more.

"Activity?"

Fisher logged the time.

"Two vehicles. Vehicle One. Grey VW, Vehicle Two, a blue Ford." She read the number plates back to him, allowing him to check them with a colleague back at the Orion HQ.

"Both in trade."

Vehicles that were somewhere in the ether between a car trader and a new owner.

"There's a surprise."

"Vehicle tyre pressures look normal." Obviously not carrying anything overly-heavy.

"Three exiting Vehicle One. Two from Vehicle Two. All males, stand by for descriptions."

Fisher noted and relayed her words to the letter.

In the Orion HQ, a buzz of activity commenced. Traffic units were put on standby. Armed. Plain cars, three of various makes, and two marked BMWs.

To the south of the building, another van of armed staff waited for the signal to strike.

Dave Francis was up and climbing out of his sleeping bag. Northern Ireland had conditioned him to not sleeping, that, and years of alcohol.

"India One receiving."

Fisher was pleased to hear his voice. Liked Francis a lot.

"India One, we have no activity at this time. The three have moved to the side of the building. We'll leave them to it as per the brief."

The first two men waited, received a text, then walked nonchalantly past the CCTV system, bags in hand.

"They may as well be whistling the theme to bloody Snow White." McGee couldn't understand how the team could be so arrogant.

In his cheap but clean hostel room, Valentin manipulated the camera system on the outer layer of security on one of the premier bullion vaults in the city. He'd been there the night before, added and replaced, removed and camou-flaged, all in a matter of moments. Poor baby, having its candy ripped out of its little adorable fingers so easily.

As Mr Cade had told his trusted colleagues, 'Valentin is a true professional.'

The text message lit up on the throwaway Nokia, which was held by the more thick-set of the trio. In Romanian it simply said *Intra acum*.

Enter now.

And that was the first hurdle leapt.

Valentin sipped on another black coffee. Entered a few words into the dark net site. Miles away, but not many. Two men read the script as it unravelled on their larger screen.

Further north west another man did the same, on his tablet, tucked up in his deeply cushioned sofa, as his attractive wife watched a British drama, about a politician and his mistress. She was sat on the next sofa, knees tucked up and under her bottom, allowing her black kimono dressing gown to gape at the thigh. Bluest eyes, dyed blonde hair. Athletic, an ex-tennis player with a voracious appetite for one man only.

She'd have to wait until the weekend. He performed best at the weekend. Their games, that Chanel perfume, his dominance, her look of submission. Their contract that said she would never kiss and tell.

Intra acum indeed.

The fourth member of the syndicate that would never meet sat in his own office, working late, gently brushing his fingertips over the keys of his laptop. Click, click. Fast typing, make no mistakes. He really should go home.

Twelve paces away, seven metres, seven and a half yards,

it mattered not what the conversion was. Another male was also reading and typing as quickly as his well-manicured fingers would allow.

'Trial run tonight. By courier to the restaurant.'

'Will it work?'

'Of course. I do not deal in failures.'

'Neither do I.' Typed another member.

And the messaging ended.

In the office, twelve paces away, the man smiled, steepled his fingers and leant back in his brown, cracked-leather office chair, each line of which told a war story.

"Come to papa."

Valentin checked the package, wiped it clean. A new iPhone 5S was carefully wrapped and lowered into it. The bag was sealed and verbal instructions given to the courier. Sixteen minutes later he was met outside the Mexican restaurant, hadn't even entered before the anonymous male took the package from him and pushed a fifty-pound note into his gloved hand. The rider nodded at the man and walked away. It took seconds.

'If you have a memory for faces, make sure it stops working today.'

They meant what they said. And besides fifty pounds, tax free, was fifty pounds. He was told there would be no more business. It was how it was. An hour later, the device was sat on Alex's lap.

Five minutes after that, the last swirl of his index finger created a failsafe entry into the device. He placed it on the floor of the safe, tapped in four digits, closed the wardrobe door, turned off the light.

Two and a half hours later, the electric blue digital read-out on Jason Roberts' bedside clock shifted from 11:59 to midnight. He knew because he lay awake, curtains open, watching out across the full-length glassy view of the Thames, the London Eye and into north Kent. The government had been generous with his accommodation.

There was a knock on the door. It was Daniel.

"Can't sleep?"

"No, you neither I guess?"

"No. I confess to having a rather full mind. I've just been watching the world go by and trying to figure out what it is Alex is going to do next. We agree all of the other stuff is a sideshow?"

"Absolutely. That said, there were three ATMs literally blown out of their wall mountings last night. Two west, one down south. One in Bedfordshire but apparently that was members of the travelling community who ripped what was left of the bloody thing out of the wall and dragged it down the street on the back of a tow truck, pursued by three patrol cars and a rabid police dog."

"Quiet night then?"

"Unless you also factor in what we've got going on at the vaults."

"How's that going?"

"Slowly, by all accounts. Can you seriously believe the government is allowing this to happen? Literally sitting back and waiting?"

"Honestly, yes. I'd do the same. We need Alex to believe he is in control."

"He is, isn't he?"

"He thinks he is. Slowly, slowly catchee monkey Jason. Fancy a brew? Looks cold out there."

"Yep, sounds like a plan. Any biscuits?"

The two men stood in their boxer shorts and stared out of the large patio door, sipping their tea, looking down onto the Thames with its twisted reflections and a murky blanket of green-grey mist that fought to cover the muddy riverbank and the centuries of history that it retained.

Roberts remembered hunting for treasure along it with his uncle, knee deep in chaos and loving every minute. Some things never changed.

"We will get him, won't we, John?"

"Is the Pope a Catholic?"

"Is that a rhetorical question JD, or do you actually not know the answer to that ecclesiastical conundrum?

John Daniel smiled as he sipped his police-standard tea; milk, no sugar, then nodded wisely. He knew the answer to many things.

CHAPTER 55

ONE OF THE THINGS THAT JOHN DANIELS KNEW WAS THAT you didn't send out your best people without back up. Jason Roberts knew that too. He had insisted on two armed staff supporting two of the best DSs he had ever worked with, Nicholas John Fisher and Bridie Anne McGee. It made sense. But who would look after them?

Fisher was getting agitated. Sat in a van with a bladder screaming at him to let go of its contents, he refused to piss into the bottle that was supplied for just such an occasion. Not in front of a lady. And certainly not in front of one called Bridie. No. No way. Not happening.

"You shy Nicholas?" Eyebrow raised.

"Me? No. I'm just a gentleman. Call me old-fashioned, but I respect you."

"You know, sometimes I wish you didn't." There was that look again. Wise beyond her years, eyes that burst with life and knee-deep sensuality.

"Stop it. Not here."

"Oh, so you are willing to at least try to take advantage of me?"

"Not with a full bladder, I'm not!"

"Then let it go, then try…"

She raised her hand. 'Quiet.'

"Movement. A new pedestrian. Showing interest in the doorway." She checked her watch, called out the time.

"I wish these bastards would hurry up and do something. I am now officially desperate for a piss." The more he tried to ignore it the worse it got.

She slipped her arms out of her sweater.

"Bridie, seriously, we'll get sacked."

"It's for you to piss into you fool, I saw it done on a training course once."

"What?"

"Use it to soak it up, go and kneel in the corner, close to the door as you can so it runs out of the bottom, but the steam doesn't give away our position. I promise I won't look."

"Turn off the light." He had never been so terrified. Fisher had been there, done that, got so many T-shirts he needed a separate drawer. Slowly he knelt down and produced what for him was without a doubt an above-average and much-prized possession, and pushing it into her sweater he began to finally let go. The feeling was exquisite. If not a little odd. Hours he had waited and yet it was so now so surreal. Erotic? No. Surreal yes, urinating quietly into the still-warm clothing of the girl he had become besotted with was nothing if not bizarre. There was probably a word for people like him.

It was just wrong. But it felt so incredible. He almost let out a sigh of relief. Then midstream she called out.

"Stand by! Stand by!"

"No! Not now!"

"Nick, we need to move. Now! Get that thing away." She found a second to smile.

. . .

Up the street, the two armed and plain clothes staff had deployed to something. No comms. Not ideal. But McGee could see everything. She called it in. Nothing. No transmission, no response. Dead.

In his room Valentin was fighting with technology too, overriding, trying to relay a signal, to steal one from anywhere, racing through a series of close circuit cameras that he should never have been able to access. Three were near, fixed lenses, no use to anyone. He found himself wishing he was working from a modern operations centre not ambiguous bedsit in central London where no one knew his name, and better still didn't care. He needed and wanted to remain anonymous.

There had to be a link somewhere on the London network. Government, negative. Large-scale commercial, nothing.

There. A standalone, some sort of wi-fi set up routed through an iPhone. Cheap but effective and it came with a pan, tilt and zoom camera. He was in. He hit record and then saw the activity. Three men running from the vault. A van entering the frame, at speed. The men were running as fast as they could with bags, but they looked empty. One had a pistol. The van came to a halt, side door open. Shots fired.

The first officer was hit. The second took evasive action, returned fire, ripping through half of his magazine, feeling for the spare and seeking cover. Where was their back up?

Valentin hit speed dial three. Cade answered.

"Your team needs urgent armed support. Shots fired. Officer down." He added the location, then repeated his message and added, "Someone is using a powerful jammer Jack. They mean business. This is high-end stuff."

He cleared the line. Rang the Metropolitan Police via the operator. Repeated the message again. No, he didn't wish to leave his details. Instead, he sat and watched, and wished he was closer. He knew his place. Had to adhere to the briefing. Stay put, add value. Fight another day. It was what all of the world's best field operators did. He was a professional, able to think on more than one plane, whilst peeling an apple with a knife and solving a Rubik's Cube with his feet. That was what they paid him for.

The firearms that the van occupants were pinning down the surviving officer with were very effective. Valentin was zooming, capturing it all.

Soviet. GSh-18s with 9mm rounds. He'd fired them plenty of times. Rounds that ripped through body armour like a samurai sword through satin. Russian made and that meant simple, effective and guaranteed to cause mayhem.

Cade had raised his red flag a minute before the Met control room had keyed the microphone and deployed armed response units. His next call was to Roberts.

"Jason. Get dressed, mate. We've been hit. One officer unaccounted for. We've lost footage. Our man is trying to restore imagery, but someone has overruled him and it's not us. Units are travelling to the scene. I'm heading that way too." He hung up as Roberts and Daniel dressed and headed to their own car.

Cade was met by Elena. She was a light sleeper too and busy dressing in the hallway. Hooded top, track pants and trainers. He didn't have time to remember how beautiful she was.

"I'm coming with you."

"No, you are not El. Stay here and be prepared to defend

this place with Carrie. She knows where the weapons are. Hit the alarms if you need to. Go and wake her."

"But Jack…"

"No. No buts. No challenges to my authority, Elena. Please. Not now. I need your experience and training tonight, and I'll need it every day from here on in. Deal?"

"Deal." She shrugged her shoulders and relented but felt she should go with him. She knew she was a superior shot too, and if things got up close and personal, all the better. She liked up close – and personal, enjoyed the smell of bad breath and adrenaline.

O'Shea heard it all, opened the gun safe and racked a Glock. She wanted to have hers first. She'd only ever fired one once, over and over again. Three hours later she was accurate up to twenty metres. That was enough. She picked up the second of three pistols together with a magazine loaded with hollow point rounds and then walked out into the lounge.

"We might need these." It was ludicrous. "Worst case, I'll throw mine at someone!" She was an analyst. A trained bloody analyst from Scotland Yard with a reputation second to none. Why couldn't they bring in the entire might of the Met Police and deal with these bastards?

An analyst and a Glock. Her weapon of choice was a pencil.

Fisher was out of the van now, running, tucked tight into the building line, one weapon drawn, the other safely away. The patch on the front of his trousers would only embarrass him if he ended up in an ambulance, so he chose to stay in the shadows.

Of all the bloody times!

He covered the ground quickly, found a place to stay in the dark, and then rang McGee.

"Any update? I've got a fairly clear shot from here. Anyone else lurking around before I commit to this?"

"Nick. Stay down, help will be coming."

"Bridie, no one answered us. This is not good. Those lads need our help."

"Then I'm coming with you. The time for photographs is over." She pocketed the phone, slipped the Glock 17 into the leg holster, and left the van.

Fisher could literally sense that she was nearby – could hear the material on her cargo trousers swishing together. He could hear her, it was such a good sound. So could the steel-eyed gunman that raised his weapon and fired a burst of seven or eight rounds down the street towards her.

She actually heard herself say out aloud, 'Well, this is a first.'

Reaching a doorway she rammed her body in tight, could smell the dampness in the wall, feel the chill, rubbed the red powdery surface as the brick beneath her fingertips crumbled. She hoped it was strong enough to provide some cover.

Instinct versus recklessness. Time to put into practice all those hours on the range. She dropped down to one knee and leaned carefully out from the door, reducing her own target picture. Nothing.

Sweeping the street, she saw a shadow. Friend or foe?

Foe. The shadow fired another burst from his own weapon. On the move.

The van engine was also being gunned. They needed to leave, and soon. And this was her opportunity.

She fired a few rounds from the fabled Austrian weapon, two into the tyre, one into the cockpit. The trigger reset each time, smooth as silk.

'Don't anticipate the shot, McGee!'

Another exited the short barrel.

The time for health and safety had also long passed.

Two men on board the van heard the rounds hitting, striking steel, ripping into plastic, shattering the side glass with a dull crack, sending tiny cubes of it across the cockpit. For the driver, it was time to go.

He started the van, into first and away, leaving the trailing team members behind him. His passenger, straddling the side cargo door, cared not either. It was every man for himself. That was what Jackdaw had said in the briefing. And what Jackdaw said...

Fisher took the chance to fire off two bursts of two rounds, keeping the now abandoned burglars at bay. He looked down the street, blue lights, strobes of hope, approaching fast. He called out.

"Armed police! Put down your weapons."

Silence.

He could see a pair of feet at the side of a car. Immobile.

Injured? Dead? He swept the street, looking over the foresight, not distracted by the Tritium dot that surreptitiously guided his aim. He called out again.

Down the street, a 5 Series BMW came to a halt. At a safe distance but within tactical range, the three staff on board also announced their presence. The German Shepherd was on the prowl too; black body armour and a ferocious set of teeth. For this was the domain of the Land Shark.

It was time to take the fight back – even up the numbers.

Members of the original burglary team were now reduced, and what was left of the group was inept when it came to a firefight against armed and trained police. The military component of the small Eastern European team was gone, heading God knows where, but somewhere other than prison.

The men looked at one another, checked their weapons, realised they had been used as scapegoats and knew their choices were limited to surrender and an uncomfortable mattress, or a blaze of glory. It was what they had grown up on; American cop films, shooting from the hip, weapons, side on, no aim, just pure luck. And no one ever got injured.

Fisher was on the move again, with McGee sprinting up behind him, weapon at the low carry but ready.

As he reached another natural barricade, it happened.

The thirty-two-year-old former carpenter had left Cluj, the second largest city in Romania, looking for a better life, but now found himself an isolated and hunted man. He swung his weapon up and over the bonnet of a Renault Megane, narrowed his eyes and fired. Three randomly placed rounds screamed down the street and skidded off the road surface, changing the shape of one bullet, altering it just enough to create a larger entry wound. A straightforward shot may have been better – at least for the victim.

Fisher heard it first, a high-pitched yelp then a freight-train-collision, hitting him below the pelvis. The bullet remained intact but being misshapen it caused havoc. He began to bleed, then more, then violently. He carried on operating, squatting down, standing, firing.

'Bastard. I am not done yet!'

Fibres from his clothing were wrapped around the base of the round, showing that the ricochet had turned it in flight and hit him base-first. In a hunting accident it would have been a plausible defence to recklessness, in a quiet street in London it was murder, at best an attempt.

McGee got alongside her partner and knew even in the dismal orange street lighting that he was badly injured. His face spoke volumes. White, almost green, clammy, yet calm. He slumped down, onto his knee, then turned, tried to fire again, then dropped his weapon and tried to smile instead, tried to say something.

McGee ripped the phone from her pocket and dialled a number. It connected.

"Yes. Now!"

She pulled the belt through the loops of her trousers, wrapped it around his leg, pulled it as tight as she could, thought about ramming her fingers into the wound, but didn't know where to start. She pulled him towards her and kept his head down, legs raised. Was this right?

Where were those bloody paramedics?

"Nick. It's going to be OK. Promise. Just keep talking, mate."

He had a vacant smile and was moving his lips, trying to do as she asked.

"Mate..." It sounded good.

Then a word or two, no more. Neither made sense.

She leaned in. "It's OK, just rest."

"Don't tell them..."

"What?"

"That I pissed myself..."

She laughed. It was the other aspect about her that he adored. A playful, deeply attractive laugh. She wiped the blood from her hands, from the index finger, settled it over the secure locking system, waited an eternity for the system to register, then dialled again. Five minutes.

This couldn't wait. She dragged him by the feet, back along the shadows, away from the streetlights, running backwards as fast as she could. A shot was fired. It was all Kato the jet black dog needed. Darker than the night, the only thing that betrayed his presence was his impressive set of teeth, jewels of blisteringly white enamel, soon to be laced with highly oxygenated blood.

His bottom jaw ripped into the right arm of the first

shooter, locked down with its upper cousin, and then tore the sinew and tendons and ligaments from their natural places, never to be useful again. McGee heard the scream, knew what had caused it and felt not an ounce of pity. Bite the bastard again. She heard the screams of male voices too...Armed Police! Repeated, fast, dominant. A bean bag round hit one of the offenders in the chest, knocking him down. The dog did the rest. The handler left him in place for a second or two longer than he should. Call it a slight bending of the rules, call it karma.

DS McGee got Fisher to the van, ripped open the door, dragged him inside, leaving a darkening red trail along the pavement and up into the back of their surveillance post. He let out a deep sigh – a noise that she would remember forever.

"No, Nick. Not this way. Do you hear me?" She yelled at him, lifted his head up to hers, shouted into his face, pleaded. He was getting heavier. Sirens sounded, more blue lights, flickering, dancing, ricocheting too, along the road and into the cabin of the van, lighting them both up. Her face blue, then white, his just white.

She ripped open the material on his trousers, found the wound. It was a mass of darkened red, wet, a congealing gel of life-providing fluid. She spoke again, but there was no reply.

He was gone. And she knew it and she never had chance to say the three words he wanted to hear. She leaned down, all too late, and whispered them, held him, then started to shake involuntarily as he bled no more. His eyes stared back at hers. She willed the eyelids to move, to blink, for his chest to rise.

Cade, Roberts and Daniel walked the ground fifteen minutes later. Three dead, one injured, a van had been stopped by another armed unit ten minutes away from the vault. The van had nothing of value on board. The burglary team were experienced – they said – and had given up before they had really started. They felt that they had become victims too. Ten years in a local Category A prison should give them time to reflect.

"It just got really shitty Jack." Roberts was professionally inconsolable. "It just got really, very shitty." He kicked a Coke can down the street, watched it spin to a stop, next to a drain. Then it was silent again.

As pretty as McGee was, the bloody streaks across her face did nothing for her appearance, told their own story. She was leaning against a wall, not wishing to talk to anyone, regardless of rank. Then, out of the blue, she lifted her head and began to speak. Her soft and gentle northern tones were broken with emotion, but she managed to say what she needed to say.

"You know Nick had a theory? About what their plan was. I told him it was a load of bollocks, but he was pretty insistent. God love the man, the least we can do is listen now." A tear welled up on her right eyelid, balanced, defying nature before eventually bursting its banks. It was the tear, the one solitary human reaction that stopped Cade in his tracks.

"Bridie. Excuse me for a moment. John, Jason, over here."

They re-grouped. "He was right. JD, you *know* something and I think it's about time you cut us into this too. None of the need to know bullshit or I'll become really unpleasant. Feral, the Home Secretary said. Remember?"

"I do." He looked around, checked no one was listening.

"He plans to flood London. Every single one and every bloody thing."

Both men looked back at him. It wasn't possible.

"What? Not possible, JD." Roberts was confident. "Not in a million of our lifetimes."

"Remember our walk along the Embankment the other morning?"

"The one where you are adamant the police minister and his protection officer gave you a good kicking?"

"The same. Remember the lion's heads? They are our benchmark, Jason. If the water reaches them we are in serious trouble."

"But we've got the barrier?" Cade was also confident. "It cost half a billion quid. Tell me it's up the bloody job?"

"Normally, yes."

"I'm not liking this JD. Talk to me." Roberts was becoming anxious, angry, had a feeling that his high-level briefing had missed something out.

"Operation Griffin was raised to another level yesterday." He grimaced as he favoured his ribcage, still raw from the repeated kicks.

"Intelligence indicates that Alex has the key to unlocking London. There's a king tide coming boys and with no barrier in place we go under."

"How? Why? What?" Roberts.

"No idea. Money. Not sure." Cade.

"Someone has hacked the mainframe. Not money, power." Daniel.

"Now what." Roberts.

"Now we cash in all of our favours, around Europe, internationally if we need to. And we deploy a few expendable and hugely deniable resources."

"Anyone in mind, John?" Cade was staring straight at him, demanding an answer.

"Us. Scott McCall – no one even knows he's here. Alex's brother. His daughter. There's enough cheese to fill ten traps."

"And what if he doesn't like cheese?"

"Then we find a dairy-free option, Jack. Either way, this stays as close-hold as possible. The government is very quietly soiling itself, if this gets out there will be a mass exodus, riots, then more riots in response to the response to the first riots, then looting in all the familiar places, then more riots. Get my drift here?"

"One hundred percent, John. Do you get mine?"

"I do. Jack, Jason, you need to work with me. This has been a long time in the making. Alex is not the kingmaker here. He's a knight, or a rook, at best. He's been allowed to gravitate towards a persona of super-criminal. We've lured him in, he's played with our hearts and our minds, but he's as big a puppet as we are."

"So with the documents referring to our withdrawal from Europe, the abolition of the monarchy and now the bonus of eight-and-a-half million people getting their feet wet..."

"Gents. This remains a secret. Those in the Orion team and those aging dinosaurs like me from Griffin – and that includes the current ministers and former ones who swore a deathbed allegiance – it stays in-house. Anyone who chooses to walk or talk will end up in custody or dead."

"That serious?" Roberts.

"That serious. And some. The tide is due in two days. We won't be sleeping much between now and whenever."

"Surely we just man the barrier, move into the control room, armed to the teeth, shut it down?"

"Normally I'd agree Jason. But our intelligence tells us otherwise. They've got eyes on, possibly even people inside. We get this wrong we all suffer. This is unprecedented, and it's going to take some blue-sky thinking to get this back on a level playing field."

"I wish I was playing management bingo I'd have a full

house with that sentence." Cade feigned a smile. He checked his phone. No messages. No texts.

"JD. One question that has been haunting me, possibly Jason too."

"Fire away."

"Why would the Honourable Minister of Police be strolling along the Embankment and throwing his weight around? It makes no sense."

"Jack. It makes total sense, he's up to his nuts in this. I trust him as far as you could kick him. What I can't work out is why, or what, or how he stands to gain. Because if he isn't gaining, then why is he pushing his weight around, threatening people. And why did Blake give us that little high-speed briefing in the lift?" He made sense.

"Yep. It's been bothering me ever since. I get the impression he's got something on the PM too, possibly even the Home Secretary."

"Why do you say that?" Daniel knew the answer.

"Just a look I saw a while ago. Have they got something going on? Both single...call me old fashioned..."

"On the money, Jack. Blackmail?"

"In order to achieve what? Leadership? Money? Hell of a risk taking on the two most powerful members."

"You forgot the Deputy PM."

"Hardly. He's got enough shadows and skeletons and career-limiting things hanging over him it's just a matter of when he jumps. No, the link is Lane and Cole." They left Jason Roberts to try to pick up the pieces as more of his team became scattered to the four winds.

Roberts walked over to McGee. "Bridie, we need to go my love, need to let these folk do their jobs." He gestured to the medics and police backup teams that had arrived. "I'm sorry about Nick. He's a star. He won't die in vain. I won't allow it." It was heartfelt.

"Too late, governor. He already did. Tell me I'm still on the squad?" She rubbed the blood between her palms, watching the dried flakes flutter to the ground. It was all she had left of him now. "Don't stand me down, sir."

"If that's your wish. Get back to base and clean up. Between us, and I mean between you and me, things are about to get pretty hairy. Sleep, eat, but be prepared."

Less than three miles away Romulus logged back into the secure server and sent a simple message. 7:23:48.

Two days. Be ready. Thirty seconds later he received the reply.

Hewett turned in his office chair, smiled his usual confident smile and greeted the Home Secretary as he hit control, alt and delete, locking the screen.

"Ma'am, forgive me if I don't stand. Got to keep an eye in this bloody thing every second from here on in." He pointed to the desktop screen.

"Everything in place?"

"If you mean are we potentially going to witness mass flooding, looting, murder, mayhem and increased insurance premiums? Then yes, possibly. But between you and me, I'm happy the team can deal with this. Just keep them all on their toes. We will come out of this stinking of roses."

"What's in it for you, Johnnie?" Everyone had an agenda.

"Reputation. Nothing more. I've got money again, dabbled here, lost some there. Reputation, both mine and that of my family. This whole Griffin thing goes back to my parent's days you know, can you believe they've been planning this for so long?"

"An independent Britain?"

"That, and a country that is led by power brokers, bereft of any shame, or morals."

"You've done a few things you can't exactly be proud of Johnnie."

"Abso-bloody-lutely, but it was all for a great cause. Mother England and all that."

"We meet in twenty-four hours. The last briefing before D Day. I pray this works."

"You've entrusted your police minister himself to run this operation. What can go wrong?"

"That's what worries me, and I think you know that already. I'll see you tomorrow." She walked out of Hewett's office and into Blake's.

"Michael around?"

His secretary approached. "Oh, hello Home Secretary. If you are looking for Michael, I'm sorry, but he's not in yet. Most unusual, probably stuck in traffic." She didn't believe it either.

At The Orion HQ, Dave Francis was in grave danger of replacing alcohol with caffeine as an addictive commodity. He looked up through bloodshot eyes when he saw Cade.

"Boss. You look like you've lost a pound and found a penny."

"Call it lack of sleep. I take it you and the team are up to speed? Everyone gainfully employed? Busy? I need everyone who isn't, to be, and for at least the next forty-eight hours."

"This might help. Carrie was trawling through some stuff on the dark net. It was a fractured message, we think from Romulus. It just says 7:23:48. She's got her theories." He looked at her, her own eyes as red-rimmed as his. "Want to explain?"

She shuffled across the floor, expertly stopping her typist chair next to Francis'.

"Morning Jack." It was an upbeat effort, and he appreciated it. "It was a long night waiting for bugger all to happen. At least Elena and I got to know each other a little better."

Cade smiled.

"Not that way, you filthy old sod. Anyway, you pay me an appalling wage to be your lead analyst, however bitterness aside, here's my theory. Strap yourself in as it's a bit of a wild idea – you'll either thank me or have me sectioned under the Mental Health Act."

The red-tinged blue eyes of the former career cop scanned the nearby percolator. He poured a dark, over-brewed mug of coffee and leaned on the back of her chair, imperceptibly squeezing her arm. "Hit me with it, you bat-shit crazy thing you." It raised an equally subtle smile from Francis.

"I've run the sensible ideas and their not so sensible cousins – let's call them the stupid relations. It's a time? Maybe this time tomorrow, or the next day, or the next. It could be a date of birth. Or, using my infinite wisdom, it could be from the bible. Genesis Seven. It's the part that talks about Noah and the ark."

"Yep. You've got it pretty much covered off Carrie." He sipped as she stared incredulously.

"You know about this?" Her look was a composite of anger and shock.

"You *know* about *this*?" Her voice was raised now, it reminded him of the first time he had ever met her, well, to be accurate, heard her, prodding an eminent detective chief inspector or some other rank of great enormity in the chest and accusing him of some bestial act against her.

Other members of the team were stopping their work, looking, failing to disguise their interest in the fact that

O'Shea might be about to unleash one of her notorious outbursts.

"I knew. OK? A few of us do. But we weren't convinced. The reference could have been all of your theories. And I needed you and the team to be busy doing your analytical stuff, but above all I needed someone else to come up with the same theory."

Cade looked across the office, to the doorway where Daniel and Roberts were stood, holding a take-away coffee and munching through a bacon sandwich, eyebrows raised.

Daniel coughed, closed the door behind him and then whistled through his fingers. Everyone stopped. All of them, the whole team.

"Team, and that includes you, Carrie, time to listen in and no questions until the end. The briefing you had a few days ago was top secret. This one goes beyond that." He spoke, they listened. They made calls to their loved ones – brief, ambiguous, and as informative as 'I'll be home when I'm home' could be.

"Repeat that to anyone beyond these walls without the blessing of the bosses, the Home Secretary or the PM himself and you will find yourselves serving piss-poor coffee to your fellow, pasty-skinned inmates at Belmarsh Prison until the sun finally goes down on your scabies-laden five by five prison lifestyle. Any questions? Good. We go live now and we remain so until told otherwise."

He swept the room. They were all already exhausted, but they were good people, what the job called smart operators. Every man and woman of them.

In Roberts' office, four people finished off plans on a whiteboard. Then briefed the fifth, who had arrived with neither pomp nor ceremony. In fact, all were so shattered none of the four even stood.

When police commissioners didn't care about protocols nor had any questions, it was reasonable to assume that the team had done a first-class job. He thanked them, asked to be kept in touch at all hours, and they assured him that yes, they would.

"Be under no illusion at all on that score – day or night." He had said as he rushed to his next meeting, head down, reading the briefing notes, slipping brown leather gloves onto young hands as he prepared to engage with the worsening winter weather. Career-wise, he'd done well to get so far in such a short time. The next few days would outline his future reputation.

Live by the sword. Die by the keyboard.

PART SIX

And every living substance was destroyed which was upon the face of the ground, both man, and cattle, and the creeping things, and the fowl of the heaven.

The Bible
King James Version

CHAPTER 56

"READY?"

"Yes. But are you?"

"Of course. I have waited for this moment all of my adult life."

"Then let us go."

"And when it is done may we bathe in the glory of this for the rest of our lives my brother?"

They both had facial hair, had changed their eye colour, sported broad-strapped military-style watches on their right wrists, wore the requisite corporate clothing, and knew the drill – knew everything they needed to know for their part. They had spent days reading and readying for this.

The best part of the whole charade was that the most important people in the British government actually had the arrogance to think *they* were in control of their own future, not a small team who had grown up, in some cases, quite literally on the streets.

Gypsies they called them. How dare they?

They got into the latest of half a dozen throw away cars and drove east along the Thames until they reached the

North Woolwich Road, before turning onto a minor road where they parked in a staff car park and confidently walked into work with the others. IDs clipped on, orange hi-vis vests, safety hats, matter of fact faces, heads slightly bowed, another day at work.

It looked completely normal. It needed to and did. They had first arrived a few months before. Skilled migrant workers, just more of the same, over from mainland Europe with a dream to fill and pockets to line and families to feed. They worked hard and kept themselves to themselves. That suited the locals who tended to get the higher paid jobs – and so, everyone was happy.

Across the water, south of the river, another team mirrored those to the north. Two men, same dress, bearing falsely created but highly accurate IDs. Heads down against the wind that glanced off of the river.

God it was cold. Soon indoors.

Back at the northern side a coach party arrived. Old people. And a school bus. Younger. Both with the same goal, to quickly get inside the visitor centre and have a look at one of the new wonders of the world. Another twenty or so day visitors had also arrived, tourists and locals who checked in at the visitor centre and waited for their tour to start.

"The last great event was in January 1928." He had the group in the palm of his hand. In 1953 we almost witnessed another, of equal drama but it would be six years later that we learned just how much power nature has."

The tour guide was passionate and the old folk listened, stopped to read everything, kept warm, down below, watching in awe, nowhere else to go. The kids did what kids on school trips did – annoy the ones who were there to learn and try the patience of a saint. Or their teacher in this case.

One mixed-race boy from Shepherd's Bush had decided that he was bored and pulled away from his care worker.

ADHD they called it. Attention deficit. He seemed pretty switched on to the male who had grabbed his arm as he ran, full tilt towards a solid steel door.

The boy had never felt such strength from a man who was smaller than most men he had met, including his long-departed father.

Wiry arms, dense black hair, a smart watch, broad strapped, sitting below a cuff, knitted, black like his new growth of hair. He had blue eyes and dark hooded brows, looked like he hadn't slept in days.

He smelled of something. The boy had no idea. But it was nice.

He somehow felt that this was a battle he was going to lose.

The male lowered himself down onto one knee, watched by the teacher and the carer, then leaned into his personal space before whispering.

"If you go through that door you will drown in the river and trust me it is very, very cold today. Dark too. They might never find you. You will swirl around beneath the water, dinner for the fishes. Perhaps be a good boy instead?"

The look that followed said everything it needed to say. The man had a nice smile. The man with him didn't. He looked scary, the boy would later tell his mother, a hard-working white girl in her twenties with a heroin-shattered smile of her own.

"Thank you." The teacher smiled. "He's a handful. I don't know what you said, but it seemed to work."

"My pleasure." An accent.

"Polish?"

"Yes, how did you know?"

"Call it an educated guess." She smiled, thanked him again and returned to the group as the pensioners tutted and shook their heads.

The party walked down a narrowing corridor somewhere under or within the iconic structure. It was considered by many to be the most influential building in the city, up front and purposeful, but the actual heroes lay elsewhere, hidden from view.

The pinewood interiors added another unexpected smell to what was already a sensory overload; wood and metal and a feint mustiness that never quite left the air.

The tour took in the control room, then down into the tunnel. Borough engineers would willingly state for the records that there are twenty-three tunnels under the River Thames, conspiracy theorists suggest more and some even said there was at least one secret subterranean thoroughfare for government workers only.

Deeper into the tunnel they walked, beneath the river, out of sight. The guide stopped, raised a hand, waited. "Hear that?"

It was a small ship passing overhead. The throb of its propellers mixed with faraway voices, workers in inaccessible parts of the structure. The children were finally quiet. It was an amazing place to be.

The place was built to last. Anti-terror, anti-aging, anti-anything, they had thought of it all. Thick concrete and immensely heavy steel doors were everywhere, each back-up system had another. Each gate had its own motor and five spares. If the National Grid failed to provide power, three generators seamlessly stepped in. Bomb-proof, beyond failure.

The guide laughed poignantly as he recalled the time a three thousand tonne dredger had hit part of the superstructure. It sank, he said, with practically no damage to his beloved workplace. He was so engaged with the story that he never looked back and counted heads.

"The main tunnel components lie under the water. So

yes, ships can simply pass over the top. We close them now and then, when heavy weather is expected or for maintenance. Last September. Approximately three thousand seven hundred tonnes." He was fielding questions from all angles now. "With this wonderful machinery in place only a truly immense event could defeat us."

"Is security tight?" an old warhorse asked, his British Legion veteran badge proudly displayed on his collar as he leant onto his walking stick.

"Imagine a duck's bottom sir?" He was. "That tight." It raised a giggle from the pensioners.

"Right we need to move along folks. No gift shop but a really nice café with great views."

In the time that the questions had been asked two of the group had discreetly swapped places. Through a door marked P5.

It was as planned; in quick, behind the door and away from any surveillance, a rapid change of clothes, IDs exchanged, hands shaken, an embrace from the boss. Job done.

In the control room the operator swung the pan-tilt-zoom system near P5 back into place. The tour groups waved goodbye, the wind continued to whistle along the Thames corridor. Business as usual.

In the Atlantic Ocean, a low pressure system was rapidly building. Pushing a surge north of Scotland, down the coast, towards the southeast of England where the rising waters funnelled into the natural opening created by the Thames. A gaping, voracious mouth swallowing all nature could throw at her.

The Meteorological Office was monitoring the situation. The Environment Agency checked data and checked again. The UK National Tideguage Network ran tests, then repeated them. The Ports of London Authority began to issue a warning to small and larger craft in case a decision was made to ready the Thames Barrier for action.

Closing the system was not something the managers took lightly. They needed twelve hours to notify the many river users and to put safety measures in place.

The actual closure took ninety minutes. A slow, meticulous process.

"Mister Speaker, Prime Minister, colleagues, friends. I bring news of a meteorological system fast approaching the city of London." He let the words hang in the air. "A king tide, a surge driven by an Atlantic weather system. One, which need I remind you could have an effect upon our livelihoods, our security and the economy."

The Minister of the Environment spoke, calmly, and concisely, passionate but cautious.

He waited for a challenge.

"Shadow Minister Barnes." The Speaker controlled the house as eloquently as always, as an umpire controls a tennis match.

"And when is this great flood likely to hit us?" Barnes was standing as he spoke, smugly.

"I did not say flood Mister Speaker. I simply said a king tide and one which we simply must prepare for. We would all agree that today this is not a political podium but a platform of common sense. Assuming of course..." He looked at his opposition with a raised eyebrow and a cheer erupted. The Speaker frowned.

"Order. Order."

"We would be better prepared if this government had invested wisely in the past Mister Speaker!" A larger cheer emanated from the left of house. "Should this tide that the member for Thurrock refers to come to fruition then need I remind the house that the very House itself would be under threat…" He paused for effect causing Barnes to leap to his feet but he was ready to knock him back down.

"Mister Speaker not only would this venerable house be damaged but Canary Wharf, eighty-six rail and tube stations, sixteen hospitals and over half a million homes. And to allow us all to focus the news that the weather has worsened will change all predictions."

"So Mister Speaker when are we to expect this tidal surge?" Barnes was quieter. Battle lost.

"Tomorrow night. Now, perhaps I have the attention of the house?"

He did. The Speaker controlled the house, restoring order. All agreed that for now politics should take a back seat. The session ended.

As the Prime Minister exited the house he was approached by his opposition leader Jeff Cartledge.

"Prime Minister. Do you have a second?"

"For you Jeff, anytime."

They walked, Cartledge talked. Politics aside they admired one another.

"Rumours abound James. Let's forget policy for the next few minutes. I've got a source, they tell me that things are about to heat up. Need to know or not, what can you tell me?"

"What do you want to know?" It surprised the staunch Labour man.

"Is it true that there is a document in circulation? One that could undermine our position in Europe?" Straight to the point.

"Yes." Equally minimalistic.

"Does it concern you?"

"Would it concern you?" Spin.

"I imagine it would." Non-committal.

"Then it would concern me too Jeff, concern both of us. Can we at least work together on this?" It was unprecedented. He needed to establish Cartledge's agenda before he dared to release the more timely aspect of the next forty-eight hours – and God knows when he might discuss the potential end of the monarchy – something which he knew Cartledge would endorse without any fight.

He told him what he could. Swore him to secrecy. They shook hands and parted. James got back to his office, had calls made to his Home Secretary, Police Minister and Deputy. Michael Blake was still not answering.

"So we know the bank vaults were a major piss take. A chance to distract us?" Roberts was swirling a pen between his fingers, it helped him to concentrate.

"We do. But we had to chase that side of things. They've been hammering the banks lately but the front line have done well to rein it in. Damned if we do and all that. Worst case is we've lost Nick in the process. The team is devastated. They are quieter than I have ever seen them." Cade looked at Daniel. "Anything to add, seeing as though you seem to know more than most of us JD? How many more staff do we lose before this finally gets thrown open to the masses?"

"I detect a hint of anger Jack. We are too close for that to happen. You'll just have to accept I did things for a reason. No one likes losing a team member – least of all me. But we simply cannot go public on this. You have to understand that? And for the record, I'm sorry, to both of you. Deceit is not a word in my thesaurus."

"That I accept, and your apology too, however, any more

ambiguities to clear before we step into the minefield that is the next forty-eight hours?"

Daniel inhaled through his lower teeth. This one wouldn't be easy.

"When you met Elena for the first time...?" Cade nodded, he was back there at his restaurant in New Zealand the *Oceanside*, visualising the moment she had walked into the bar and his life.

"You told me you were cautious, yet threw that caution to the wind. She's a stunning girl, who can blame you after the problems you had had with your ex?"

Cade didn't want to dwell on the past. "Your point?"

"She was there to meet you Jack, but didn't plan to stay long, nor did she anticipate actually finding you as attractive as she did. Her goal was actually to find me. She knew I was in New Zealand. Someone had told her that if she found you, she would find me." He frowned, worried he had offended a man he considered a lifelong friend.

"So, in that case how did she know where to come looking for me?"

"Her mother. Nikolina sent her a letter, back in the day, when she was a younger girl, outlined it all, except for one small detail. She never provided her with the full story. Her dream was that having killed Alex she would get to London, meet her contact and then get Elena to the UK too. But as we all know that never happened."

"And?" Cade pressed on, Roberts sat back and listened.

"And the letter also told her how to pursue her one real question in life – one that troubled her - who her father was. It was something that troubled her greatly, something that was once said to her about her parents. But she maintained her stance. Perhaps a reason for her determination in seeking revenge against him when he tried to kill her too."

"Well, forgive me for appearing cocksure but that's easy JD. It doesn't take a detective to work that one out. You only have to read the intelligence files on Alex Stefanescu to work that little conundrum out. He loved his little girl, loved her mother at one point too. Problem was, he fell out with her dear old mum when she tried to make good on her promise to the Bulgarian government to kill him, so he drowned her. But he's a clever bugger is the Jackdaw – made it look like it was all Jack's fault and in turn mine, and in turn anyone else that worked on our operation to target him." He placed the pen onto his desk, straightening it so it ran parallel to the edge of the blotter.

"I rest my case."

"I get the impression that you know the answer to her conundrum John?"

"Sadly, I do."

"It's not you is it?"

"No! And her father is going to very unhappy." He let the initial bombshell settle, then there was a knock on the door stopping him in his tracks.

"Guv, the team is ready to move." It was a resilient McGee.

"You sure you are up to this Bridie?"

"Hundred percent boss. We leave in three."

Scott McCall had shaved his beard off, leaving a tanned face and curling dark hair. He shaved that too. Then dressed.

Stefan Stefanescu lowered a brown contact lens into his eye, creating a pair, then stepped back and admired his handiwork. His hair was darker, much, his facial hair was also darker, longer than it had been in years, the odd grey hair was appearing, which he had plucked from his chin. He checked the ID, it looked good. Tried on the hard hat, it fitted well.

"Do we have all we need Scott?"

"All the Ps are in order, mate. Let's go, who dares and all that."

It meant nothing to the Romanian brother of a notorious criminal. But he sort of understood McCall's passion.

"We've deployed three teams ma'am." Roberts was addressing the Home Secretary and doing his best to be professional with the Police Minister, a man he disliked intently, but one he had to kowtow to, just like all of his colleagues.

Harry Halford spoke. "Describe the make-up of these teams please DCI Roberts."

"Three teams, two in each, five men, one woman."

"And you really feel that six people is enough to counter what might be the greatest threat to the city of London in forty years?" He glared at Roberts, scanned the room like a ravenous barn owl, waiting to pick off the weakest mouse.

"Given the circumstances, the need for secrecy, we do, sir. Yes. Now if I may continue?"

"No, you may bloody well not Roberts. I asked you a question and once again you have been at best disrespectful." He slammed his palm onto the meeting table surface.

"And respectfully I answered it." Roberts could feel himself subtly shaking with rage. Wanting to slam his own fist into the furniture. Just one punch. He was itching to do it. Would happily break his hand doing it.

"I fail to see what more I can add Minister?" He looked at Sassy Lane, hoping for support.

She stepped in. "Harry, I think what the DCI is saying is that he has confidence in his squad and time is of the essence. So, can we move on?"

"Report on my desk within the hour. I want to know

who is one the teams, their background, skills etc. No errors, no omissions. Understood? If this goes tits up Roberts I will hold you personally to blame." He stood, bid Lane goodbye and left.

"Ma'am. I'm sorry but..."

"Not another word DCI Roberts." She smiled a half smile and also got up, this time causing the staff present to swiftly jump to their feet. Respect was earned.

"If I may Home Secretary?" Cade fixed her with his trademark gaze.

"Briefly Mr Cade, very briefly."

"No one knows who to trust anymore ma'am. You'll note the Commissioner himself is absent. It's how it needs to be. But people are getting a little tired, a touch fraught. Hence the scene you've just witnessed. I need you to support the team in a way that may cause you some consternation, possibly even risk your own reputation. I can explain why off record. In the meantime I will have our analyst knock out that report. It will be bullet points only. With your blessing I would like to redact the bio data of my staff."

She accepted, he outlined his concerns. She promised she would do her best. It was all anyone could ask. He trusted her. They trusted her.

Did she trust Halford?

As she was whisked through traffic she pondered this question, then made the decision to redact the names of the mission staff from the report, then made a call to James Cole.

"You really believe this is necessary?"

"One hundred and one percent."

CHAPTER 57

THE SQUADS HAD BEEN DEPLOYED AFTER A HECTIC twenty-four hours of planning, preparation, checks and rechecks. They would travel lightly, operate overtly as part of a viable team, or remain undercover, speak when spoken to, communicate via their standard operating procedures. No more, no less.

A Squad tore into buildings, executed warrants, arrested seven members of a bank targeting syndicate. All spoke the same language. All bore the tattoo. All hit the ground hard, face down, hands cuffed tightly behind their backs, shoulders screaming in agony.

B Squad sat on the ferries, the airports and tunnels. No one moved.

C and D united and were also working with two members of the Romanian Police, willingly provided by Andre Grigorescu the Capitan from the Special Intervention Brigade in Craiova. They had been provided via a mutual aid request which Interpol had organised. Having the two staff on the team, asking no questions about why, but spotting their own targets in a sea of faces proved to be priceless.

E Squad did what they did best. Monitor Electronics – voices; cell phones, landlines, whatever it took. They listened then provided recordings for translation. That would take weeks. They had hours, but evidentially it would prove to be valuable.

F were the firearms team, and they were wherever they needed to be. They had the training and kit to take the battle to the enemy. Holding a black leather tactical boot tightly on the neck of the man that had inadvertently killed Detective Sergeant Nick Fisher was a highlight. Speed-cuffing others, all at gunpoint was intended to send a message.

But still they were playing catch up.

McGee was sat, back against a metal wall, back in a surveillance vehicle with a new partner. It was too soon and far from ideal but they would make it work for Fisher's sake. The street outside had been dug up, providing a perfect opportunity to blend and watch in a utilities vehicle.

People were joining the site from the south. Two more at the northern side.

The online community was being monitored. Social media was a double-edged blade at the best of times, but sometimes, just once, or twice it gave up its secrets, created a lead.

Carrie O'Shea had sharpened her pencil – figuratively speaking.

David Francis had tuned into all of the Met Police systems and a few that the government had loaned to the department. He wanted to wreak his own revenge.

Remotely, from a sterile bedsit Valentin had also begun

to let the intelligence wash over him. Ready to pounce electronically on anything or anyone that provided a chance of success. He owed the British officer that had been gunned down that much. The money would be nice too, a final chance to head back to Europe and disappear once more.

He ran his finger over the mouse pad on one of three laptops. It came to life. Nothing from Remus – as expected. He knew where they were now and online chatter was not likely to happen.

Viduus was there waiting. He had never met Johnnie Hewett the man behind the alter ego, but what he was told made him relax a little. A smart man, savvy and able to adapt, a chameleon just like himself and one who had also been let down by his own people in the past. It seemed that a lot of people on the Op Orion team were trying to make amends or inflict pain.

The cursor was blinking.

Valentin typed. 'Romulus expects that everyman will do his duty.'

Viduus smiled behind his own screen. Hewett appreciated the reference to Admiral Horatio Nelson. He wanted to type 'Kiss me Hardy' but decided against it, instead writing 'Victory will be ours.'

Sancus appeared online. Watched by Valentin and Hewett and now Francis who had spent nights working out how to read and not be detected.

Sancus wrote 'Remember the Seven of Swords.' He outlined a few key components of their own operation, a few less than subtle reminders then finished with 'Message ends.'

He pushed the keyboard back across his desk, crushed the report that Roberts had supplied, then carefully unfurled it and shoved it into the cross-shredder.

"Bastards. You will all regret the fucking day you met

me." He deleted his search history with a pounding collision onto the enter key, then turned to another screen where a picture of Michael Blake was looking back, an old media shot of him in a pinstriped suit, red tie, smug little prick. Look at you now.

Harold Halford was a man not to be crossed. By anyone.

"Seven of Swords. Let's find out the relevance team." O'Shea was in charge now, loving being back in the saddle. Minutes later a voice called out, "It's about betrayal Carrie. Comes from the tarot deck. Basically, a lesson in trust."

"Thanks." It was a topic she considered herself an expert in.

McCall and Stefanescu were walking into their newly adopted workplace with six other workers. The Operations Manager Andy Darkin had been told a team of environmental engineers were attending, were there to monitor the site during the impending tidal surge and were allowed free access. He wasn't entirely happy but when an instruction was backed by an email from the government one tended to abide by the rules. Tell no one. Not even your wife.

For McCall it was a chance to pay back what he owed – minus a handful of diamonds that he had been convinced to retain, another chance, to give his siblings a brighter future. His partner was to be the man he had rescued from a burning nightclub and one who had yet to fully earn his trust, but, he had led him to safety and for that alone he had earned some credit.

McCall slipped his hand into his kit bag and gained immediate comfort when it met the plastic pistol grip of a Sig Sauer 9mm. Stefan had one too and a spare magazine.

Their overt role was to at least try to look as if they knew what they were doing. McCall had studied the floorplan until he dreamt about it. Ask me a question. No one did, they knew he knew the answer.

His frame was slightly bulkier than normal due to the presence of a SlashPRO full sleeve slash resistant shirt, the rest of his outfit was the same as everyone else's.

His knife was where it always was. Within reach.

He turned to Stefanescu. "Now I guess we wait."

The cloud bank had settled offshore, out in the Thames estuary. To the north, open water, to the south an island and then a shore that had defended against invaders since Roman times. A series of sea forts fought for attention against a swathe of windmills, all rotating silently out in the channel, up close, blades whipping through the air, creating much-needed power for the colossal city nearby.

McCall had found a small office within the structure, had sat down, feet on a table and was talking to Stefan.

"Nothing. Why we don't just walk up to him and shoot the bastard is beyond me."

"We were told not to. You being a soldier should know how to follow rules Scott?"

"What if I do have to shoot him? He's your brother after all."

"Only if I don't first. He was trying to kill me when you burst in onto our argument if you remember!"

And so they waited out of sight. Access all areas, except the one where the man himself was likely to be.

Why? It made no sense.

· · ·

Cole looked up, saw Lane entering his office. "Shut the door Sassy. Ken you can leave us now and thank you."

Once alone Cole switched his cell phone off, unplugged the desk phone, turned off the computer, drew the curtains, pulled up a chair as close to Lane as he could and spoke.

"Forgive the ludicrous paranoia?"

"Of course. You OK. This is all very romantic..."

"Another time Sass. Listen things have changed. I agree Halford is...worthy of attention. Something about him hasn't sat right with me for a while now. Call it my mother's intuition. The Orion team have joined forces with the remnants of Griffin as you know. A small team has deployed to the key assets. Another is still watching the bank vaults and one more is trying to locate Michael Blake." He shook his head. "He's disappeared off the proverbial face Sassy. No message, no sick leave. His family think he's at work, we need to enforce this." He was brooding.

"So where is he?"

"Michael Blake, our most senior man from the Foreign Office, and our talisman for any European deals if this bloody report gets aired – is missing. No phone traffic, no internet. He was picked up from home a day ago. No signs of a struggle. Next to you, or Harry or my Deputy vanishing, it's just about as bad as it gets. Christ almighty!"

"I'll get the Orion team onto this right away." Helpful.

"He's part of the old Griffin team Sassy. Have John Daniel briefed in person. I want him to lead that aspect, leave the others to concentrate on keeping my city from danger."

Twenty-four hours earlier a vehicle with blackened windows had arrived at the Surrey home of Michael Blake. It was as normal as any other day in the life of an intensely busy man.

Picked up here, dropped off there. He waved to his adoring wife and kids. They waved back.

Theirs had been a successful life thanks to their father and husband. His wife knew of his past, of a life in the Foreign Office and the endless raft of cocktail parties. There was talk of a girl too. Just one. She could ignore all the history in lieu of a rather beautiful six bedroomed place on the edge of London and a retreat on a beautiful island off the coast of Australia.

"Goodbye my darling." She waved, then closed the door on her husband for hopefully the last time. The offer had been made, backed up by photographs of him in compromising positions with two young and eager girls. Photoshop was a marvellous piece of software.

She was still waving as the Volkswagen minibus crackled across the shingle driveway. "Farewell you bastard."

"Mummy what's for tea?"

"Anything you like dear." She could afford it now.

The children would soon forget a father who was absent for at least half of the year, anyway. They hadn't seen the stun delivered from a pair of probes that were rammed into his arm. By the time he came too he was PlastiCuffed and gagged and had a solitary small hole in the top of his thigh.

"One down. One to go." The driver high fived the passenger who was busy calculating how to spend his wages. He made the call. "Yes sir, we have him. On our way now."

They joined the eastbound traffic and made for a rendezvous near the Thames.

"They have Blake." Constantin grinned. "I bet you will enjoy this part. Can I do as planned?" He was almost excited.

They had finished their shift for the day, left with everyone else, having pretended effectively that they were maintaining things that needed maintaining. They had chosen the deepest, darkest parts, where no one was in a hurry to go. Once again, it reminded Constantin of his demise in the Channel Tunnel. Not this time. This time would be different, he would emerge in more ways than one.

They made it to the next location.

McGee had called it in, "Targets on the move." A surveillance unit had followed them, desperate to take them out in an armed stop.

'Why won't they just give us the word?'

Then in a moment of madness the minivan lost their observers. Left, right, up a pavement, down an alley. Gone.

The VW Kombi pulled up alongside a solid steel door, its own side door perfectly positioned to extract Blake without attracting attention. Two men dragged him into the void followed by the third who helped manhandle him down a staircase that got mustier the deeper they descended. Paint was flaking from the walls and a noticeable sense of moisture filled their noses. They could hear trickling water too.

Their chosen place to hide Blake was alongside the Thames. Underground, beneath a concrete building that was as anonymous as it was abandoned. At one time it had been a pumping station, designed to support the nearby major construction phase. The men that headed into its depths had no idea how the system worked or why, but they knew it offered a solution to a problem.

Simply killing the Foreign Office guru and burying him somewhere was an option − if he had been just a government employee that needed to disappear. However, the instructions were clear. Make him suffer.

And so they had delivered him, bound and gagged to a large chamber that sat beneath the waterline and occasionally flooded. Especially during a high tide. And water eventually rotted a corpse, peeled the skin from the bones, and the foot or so of dank river water that was a permanent feature would hide the rest.

They pushed him down onto one of two old metal-framed chairs that appeared to float in the stagnant basement. The chair was welded to a beam, at the other end another identical one sat out of the water, higher by a few feet.

The large steel tube that they sat within stank of rust and mould. Every word they spoke echoed, but he already knew that shouting for help was futile. So he spoke quietly, tried to retain control, talking to the men that stood on the metal gantry halfway up the tube but hidden in the shadows.

"Whatever it is you want I will provide. Immunity? Money, I can get my hands on about a quarter of a million today. Is that what you want?"

Nothing. Silence. So he tried again.

"My name is Michael Blake but I guess you know that. I'm just making sure you have the right man. There are a lot of bad people in government." Humour failed too. His words just circulated around the massive tube and came back to their maker.

He looked around, there was a green line halfway up the chamber, which was about twenty-five feet across and three or four times deeper. Above the line was dry, rusty. He guessed that the line was a tidal mark. Twenty feet? Perhaps twenty five?

He tried to discreetly move the chair. It was fixed to the base and he in turn was fixed to it. No handcuffs or chains or fanciful contraptions. Just plastic cable ties; black, thick, single use. One around his right foot and one on his right arm, tightened at the wrist onto a steel hoop that was welded to the beam.

He was left handed. At least that helped.

The only light came from the gantry.

Between him and the second chair was an old oil drum, higher than the water, once green, now rusty and dull.

A bright green Cyalume glow stick was tossed down into the void. Then the door to the gantry closed. He was alone, cold and wet. But at least it wasn't dark. He watched the green glow for a second, drifting around in the water in a clockwise direction, indicating that whilst small there was a current of sorts.

He waited five minutes then tried to stand. He reached for the drum, managed to put his hand into it. He recoiled, pulled out his hand and saw droplets of blood.

It would be a long night.

"McCall will be fine Jason. Guys like that are harder than woodpecker lips. His biggest problem is making sure Stefan doesn't give the game away. Hence the decision to brief him to shoot Stefanescu if necessary – I don't think we trust him one hundred percent. I'm heading to my apartment. Been a long few days, I suggest we all need a rest before tomorrow. The night shift is on and active, all is quiet on the western front."

"That's what worries me pal. I'll be along in half an hour mate." Roberts needed to clear a few things and clear his mind of the frustrations – why couldn't they just get the helo up, lock down a street and conduct an armed stop, get him into custody, prevent chaos?

"I'll come with Jason. Sleep well. Check on the girls on the way?"

"Already done. Elena is asleep, Carrie is searching for evidence of something. I'll leave her to it. She's the best I've got. Well, her and Dave." He laughed to himself. "Never thought I'd end up with one of my oldest contacts actually working for me JD."

"Doesn't surprise me at all Jack. Was always going to happen." It was said in a matter-of-fact way that surprised Cade.

"Another bombshell pending here Jason. You may wish to stand by!"

"Don't be like that Jack. Look, it's simple. The way this team works is best summed up by saying they like to play with your heads. Kidnapping, torture, humiliation, power. The best way to do this is target a family member." Daniel knew the bait had been taken, and he was pleased.

"I'm all ears."

"Dave Francis' uncle Ted was his only family surviving family member. It was no surprise when Constantin set up shop directly opposite his home. Even less so when they killed him, poor bugger. No better way to unsettle your enemy than pick off members of his team."

"What? Explain."

"David was one of our team long before he was yours Jack, best Intelligence Officer Op Griffin ever had. Straight from Northern Ireland and 14 Intelligence Company. Highly trained, very capable. Just a bit of a drink problem since being captured by the opposition. All very political and way too much for here and now. All you need to know is that like the rest of us he ended up on a list..."

"So me meeting up with him in my old policing days was no surprise then?" He seemed slightly disappointed.

"Not at all like that Jack. Your friendship with Dave was genuine. You were there when he needed a contact. He probably helped you more than you realised. And you him. We were watching over him, not all the time, he's a big boy, but when he rang me to introduce you into the equation...

well let's say people sat up and listened. Drunk or not he made sense – and you were in the right place, wrong time."

Cade tried not appear flattered.

"So none of what followed was fate then?" He didn't expect an answer, but pressing on he asked, "This list. Who's on it nowadays?"

"Me, Hewett by virtue of his parents and the way he lured the Spanish towards Alex, Dave Francis, the deputy commissioner, and an old sailor called Tom Denby."

"Interesting mix. The last name is a new one on me."

"More interesting than you can imagine. Tom was my boss, back in the day, now sits in an anonymous old folk's home waiting for his next meal – he's got more need to know in that head than he can ever remember, but that's another story."

"Still doesn't explain why a group of Eastern European criminals is giving us the run-around. I've never understood the connection. I may be thick?"

"In that case join the club. Me neither. They came into this late in the game. Another distraction? Who knows, more pawns in this game than kings, but there is a king, just not sure anymore who that is. But one day it will all become clear. Right, go on bugger off, bright and early tomorrow?"

"I'll have the kettle on John – and thanks. Makes a few things clearer. I can relax. For a while."

He took the stairs, got into the pool car, exited, waved to the gatehouse, connected his phone via Bluetooth then turned left down past O'Shea's old apartment – one he doubted she'd ever return to, then headed towards the safe location that he was sharing with O'Shea and Petrova.

He hit search. Found Radio Caroline. Nic Perrins was on, a northern girl with a beautiful voice and an ear for eighties music that belied her comparative youth.

A song by *Yes* was introduced. He settled into the short

journey, found himself tapping the black leather-rimmed steering wheel. Perhaps the song was meant for him? He certainly felt like he had a lonely heart.

Relax. Red light. Come to a stop. Amber, prepare to go. Green.

He pulled away, first, second, turned left, amber glow, quiet streets, cold. He indicated, right, past the all night garage. Looked down, needed fuel. He was about to enter the forecourt when it happened. Discreet. A blue van came up behind him, then alongside him, edging him to the kerb. The grey vehicle in front stopped. Another came up behind the group and he was in a hurry.

No longer inconspicuous.

To an onlooker Cade's Ford was the target of a police tactical pursuit and containment manoeuvre. And all carried out without a scratch. To the onlooker it was perfect. To the occupant, it meant one thing.

He hit speed dial on his phone. Pressed One.

The phone began to dial. Six men were out of their vehicles, running to the doors, life hammers smashing glass as Cade hit the horn, tried to reach for the glove box, undo his seat belt, escape. He rammed the gear lever into reverse and accelerated back into the white car behind him, tyres burning onto the road surface. He was too close to cause damage, let alone escape.

JD answered the phone. "Jack?" He waited. Listened. All he could hear was a dynamic situation. Visceral sounds, effort, blows being exchanged.

"Jack?"

Cade grabbed hold of a canister of CS spray, fired it into the face of the first attacker. He was down. Evil stuff, minute crystalline hooks that clung to any and everything. He fired it at will but they kept coming. He hit himself with a foaming backlash of the noxious liquid, then started to choke, his eyes streaming.

He propelled the car forward, into the grey car, tearing the bumper off, pushing it slightly, making little ground, horn sounding continuously. Surely someone would ring the police?

But the two people that bothered to look saw the police, saw a familiar tactic of vehicle blocking, saw the crazy guy in the Ford lashing out, so closed the curtains and went back to their separate beds. Bloody racket, they'd make a complaint tomorrow, probably.

"Jack...?"

O'Shea listened to Cade's answerphone message then left her own.

"It's me. There's something about Elena you need to know. Speak when you get home. Wake me."

PART SEVEN

CHAPTER 58

"Job well done team. Grab a brew, we'll talk this through and see what's left to sweep up out there. Nice to show these buggers that we mean business."

The operation to round up and detain as many of the known targets of the Seventh Wave syndicate had gone better than expected – it had been planned for days but kept at a level of security so high that only a few knew. Executed on the day and not a moment before. Loose lips and all that.

Using the Orion staff and selected members of specialist squads who were already cleared to a high level was a masterstroke. The team knew the consequences of betrayal. They could also be forgiven for feeling quite smug, but that changed when the news broke that Michael Blake and former Inspector John 'Jack' Cade had failed to attend their places of work.

Blake had been reported absent by the Foreign Office. His wife said she thought he was away. Expected him back in a few weeks. Quite normal.

Cade was different. Cade was dependable. He'd made some mistakes, but then he'd been propelled into a senior position quickly. He was from a line of Johns in the Cade family and all, historically, had been nicknamed Jack.

Cade was indeed different. Put into a role, unwittingly, yet one he thrived in – the ultimate live bait for the bigger fish that lived just the other side of the reef.

"Where the hell is he, Jason? He's failed to answer my messages, didn't get home last night. His car was missing. I rang you, I rang the comms centre. I rang JD. Jason..." She was beginning to panic.

"Carrie. We'll find him. Grab a coffee. Take a moment."

"Don't tell me to take a moment, boss. I'll take a bloody moment when I'm dead. Either that man has been taken or he's done what he seems to be good at in times of stress. Walk away." She shook her head but repelled the urge to sob too. If ever there was a tightrope of emotion, this was it for the analyst who had never recovered from a near-death experience, that ironically Cade had saved her from.

Elena approached Roberts, walking between him and O'Shea. "They've got him, haven't they?" Matter of fact.

"You tell me. You seem confident." Defensive.

"Call it...a hunch. When people go missing I look at the facts. I normally start with Alex. It makes sense, no?"

Roberts nodded. Waited. The deputy commissioner joined them.

"This is it, people. The weather is atrocious, the tide's expected to be high, and the bad news is our main target hasn't come back to the location this morning..." His words hung like a toxic aroma.

"We've missed them, haven't we?" Daniel looked gutted.

"I'm afraid so. Perhaps we should have struck yesterday."

Alex Stefanescu and his long-term accomplice Constantin had done what they needed to do the day before. And now, they sat and watched.

· · ·

Cade shuddered awake. His heart was racing, he could actually feel it pulsing, pounding out of his chest, compressing his chest, making it difficult to breathe. He tried to stand but came to the same conclusion as the man who shared his cell.

He squinted, trying to use the last light of the glow stick which still clung to life, half submerged in the dank water. He looked up, then down, then sideways. Took a deep breath and then exhaled.

"Well, this is nice."

"Didn't want to wake you, Jack. How did you sleep?"

"Like a bear before the sore head." He looked around again as the natural light started to increase from above, illuminating the gantry. "Where are we?"

"I have no idea. Actually, that's not entirely true. I know we are semi-submerged in a massive steel tube, sat, on what can best be described as an adult see-saw." He laughed, but it wasn't funny.

It was at that point that Cade realised he was higher than Blake, who was fifteen to twenty kilos heavier. He felt ridiculous. Probably looked ridiculous.

"This is ridiculous, Michael." He struggled with his arm, which he realised was stuck fast. His leg, too. But for some reason, his captors had left two limbs free. He saw the drum in front, midway between them. Looking down, he could just about see the contents. He needed more light.

"That thing comes around about every twenty minutes. They last about ten hours. I figure it's been glowing most of the night. Feels like morning." Blake was obviously exhausted. He hadn't eaten in a while, was dehydrated and had long-since given up worrying about personal hygiene.

"And?"

"And it might provide a bit of light. If we are going to get out of here, we need light, then a plan, then..."

"I think a plan would be my first bet..."

They both laughed at the same time. But it still wasn't in the slightest bit funny. Tiredness and stress did that to you.

Cade reached out with his foot. "Try to be as light as you can. Come on, remember the old days in the playground?"

Blake tried to rock back and forth, pushed up with one leg, and Cade began to lower down into the water. He was right, it did look absurd.

"Yes, come on, you beauty." He grabbed the glow stick between his big toe and its neighbour, bending slightly he picked it up with his hand, grabbed hold, tight, never letting go. He held it up, had a look around. It was pretty much as he thought. Large steel tube, the bottom filled with water and a ladder up to a gantry. He had no idea what it was other than a foetid tomb.

"How long have I been here?"

"Hours. No idea what they did to you, but you were out of it when they brought you down here. How's the eye?"

He favoured the socket; it felt vast – it at least explained why he had a throbbing headache. His ribs and stomach were raw too. The longer he thought about it the greater the clarity. A driving punch to the head. Two kicks to the stomach. Then repeated punches to the ribs. Then dragged, cable tied and dumped onto the floor of a people mover.

Above them, the light changed. They heard a door opening. He slipped the glow stick into his pocket, tried to balance, waited.

Three voices could be heard. However, a familiar voice called down to them from the gantry.

"Sleep well, gentlemen?"

Neither replied.

"Hello Jack. Been a long time. Since our paths first crossed, we have both travelled a long way. You from New Zealand, then back to Australia, Hong Kong, Europe. I know every port you have visited. Every girl you have slept with, every dollar and pound you have spent. I know what coffee you like and how you love to sip Central Otago red wine from Elena's most intimate body parts. I know more. But that can wait."

Blake looked at Cade, twisted his mouth at the corners, indicating his sense of concern.

"Things were going well, my friend. You lived your life, and me, mine. C'est la vie. By the way, what you and Mr Blake are attached to is entirely Constantin's idea. He has what you might describe as a warped mind, some might say child-like. I would have just killed you, but he insisted on having some fun. He doesn't talk much, but when he does, he is a very smart man. Anyway, I have places to go and chaos to cause. If it's OK with you I'll just watch for a few minutes? Nothing like humiliation to take the wind out of a man's sails."

He cracked another glow stick and tossed it down into the water. As it left the gantry it partially illuminated his face.

"So that's what you look like. Handy to know." Cade spoke as clearly and confidently as he could.

"How marvellous for you, but our paths will not cross again Jack. I mean, look at you both. You remind me of a circus I went to as a boy. My delightful mother took me."

Constantin whispered something into Alex's ear, but Cade beat him to it.

"Was that the day you murdered your dear mother?" Two could play at the knowledge game.

"Yes, you are right, my friend. That was the day I came home and decided to kill them both, actually. Dear mother and my adoring father. I had such a wonderful day. When I got back mother was too busy to listen..." He mimed her racing around the house. "Always too damned busy. So I put a knife through her windpipe. Heard it slice through the cartilage. She didn't smile after that. Father looked so horrified. I think my thoughts were that he would be lonely. So, if memory serves me correctly, Jack, I hit him with a hammer. And again. And again until his skull could resist no more. When I touched it, it felt like pigs liver."

"And now you have us where you want us. Can't say I'm in any hurry to know what the plans are here, but at least it's better than a hammer blow."

Alex picked at and pulled a hair from his nostril, examined it in the half light, then flicked it down into the void. He checked his watch. He did disinterested rather well.

"In a few hours you will find out just how devious Constantin is. And seeing as though you, and me and him will never meet again, it may be time for some honesty. I dislike you immensely, John Cade. Immensely. But I admire your spirit. Hence not clubbing you to death with a hammer. This way is both entertaining and painful. The clock starts now. Look down, see the water, it's arriving. Soon time to see if you can work as a team. Take care of one another. Either way, see you in hell."

Cade and Blake looked down. The water was swirling in from a place in the tube. The tide must be on the way in. Cade knew he had about two hours, three at most, before the levels defeated them.

Blake whispered. "An hour at most." As he discreetly rubbed the plastic tie against the metal hoop, burning his wrist to the point of bleeding.

Cade frowned. Then realised Blake was working out high tide figures, about six metres, the rough height of the tube or at least near to the gantry.

"Gentlemen, you are not working as a *team!* Come on. If you want any chance of surviving, you must...work...as...a... team." He clapped his hands in glee. It was the first time he had smiled in days, possibly weeks. "Many hands make light work. Simple. Blake, you go first. Oh...did you want a clue?" He pulled a sad face, rubbing his fists at the sides of his eyes. "Try the barrel."

Cade moved, and then so did Blake. They balanced, allowing Cade to look into the green barrel. All he saw was as mass of broken glass. Cubes of it, brown, safety glass, neat little cubes with razor-sharp edges. Just beneath the surface he could see a package, simple, wrapped in white paper.

He pushed his hand into the glass and recoiled. Safety glass? Hardly, his fingertips bled, ten cuts or more, slicing the delicate skin.

The water was swirling around them now, noticeable, slightly deeper than it was when the day had started. Cade flicked bits of the glass away but for each piece he moved another tumbled to fill its place. It was like gold mining in a sand dune. Like playing Jenga with the devil.

He could hear Alex laughing. "Come on Jack, your life is at stake, dig deeper. There may be a sword in there, or a knife." The three men on the gantry all laughed in a sneering way – they were enjoying the moment.

Cade ripped a piece of his shirt, then using his teeth as a vice, wrapped it around his fingers, forming a barrier, then carried on digging until he reached the paper. He exhaled, feeling the fresh blood oozing into the cloth. He retrieved the package and unwrapped it. It contained a pen and nothing else.

The water rose.

At Scotland Yard the command team plus their senior and lead analysts sat around a microphone, knee-deep in a voice conference with the Home Secretary and the police minister.

Halford spoke first.

"So, to recap, you have everything in place and it's just a matter of time before you lock these people up. Correct?"

"Correct, sir." Roberts nodded at the microphone, steepling his fingers. He preferred it when he didn't have to look into those cold black eyes.

"However, in the mean time you have lost so many of your team..." He scanned a report in front of him. "...A senior detective, one of your best analysts, a detective sergeant, and now your main man Mr Cade has failed to turn up for work – along with the cream of the crop from the Foreign Office Mr Blake. Perhaps they are together somewhere having breakfast, Mr Roberts, eh? What do you think?"

'I think you can go and...yourself!' Was going through his frenetic mind.

"Yes, you are also correct on that score, sir. We have grave concerns for Mr Blake and Mr Cade, they are..." He was interrupted.

"Absent without leave, detective inspector. Absent. Without. Leave." He deliberately missed out the word Chief and then emphasised the next, almost spat them out into the microphone. And he enjoyed each more than the last.

"We need to move on. Execute the plan today. The weather forecast is appalling, we cannot delay. If Cade turns up, dead or alive, you can deal with him after the event. He's one man. Right, go about your duties. I have nothing more to add. Home Secretary?" He looked at her, boring holes through her eyes and out of the back of her head. He was infatuated with her, yet he knew she despised him in equally large amounts.

"Look after one another, DCI Roberts. We cannot afford to lose a single person more. Not one. Do I make myself clear?" It was obvious she was very much on their side.

"Crystal ma'am. Thanks, all for now, I'll update via the reporting lines as and when we get anything new."

They called the flow of intelligence into a cell an 'inject'. Any new piece of information was collated, then analysed – then, if the analyst didn't have a complete picture, a request to collect more intelligence was sent out. The people on the ground were the collectors, every man and woman in blue, and those in jeans and hoodies. They all had a part to play.

So far the only inject the team had was that Cade and Blake were missing – presumed dead.

"You think he'll show up, John?" Roberts was genuinely worried.

"What do you think? He's the recovering alcoholic at an all you can drink cocktail party. He'll surface Jason."

"Is he? First I've heard."

"Well no, actually I made it up. But you get the point. He'll be fine. Right now, wherever he is, he'll be figuring out his options."

Daniel looked across at O'Shea and winked.

She wanted to sob. Years they had known each other – they had come so close to being a couple – and yet one or other of them was destined to drift like a piece of wood on a tide, swirling around in an eddy, hoping for salvation before drifting out to sea.

"Where are you?" She sharpened a 6H pencil, then snapped it on her desk, then sharpened it again. "Jack, where the bloody hell are you? Talk to me."

Stefan Stefanescu and his new partner Scott McCall were in place. The back of the van they inhabited had one way glass in the tailgate. They both sat and watched, waited. For

McCall it was what he did, almost why he existed. Although why he was sat in a cold van, near a busy waterway in a foreign city with a foreigner was something he chose not to dwell on. He owed a debt to the British, and he was going to repay it – diamonds aside.

Francis was on his fifth cup. Dark, strong, made his heart race. Just how he liked it. Not since the notorious job on the Irish border had his heart been so ready to beat. He looked at O'Shea. She was tired, but a series of words activated her adrenal gland, got her firing on all four cylinders.

"Fancy kicking this into touch and going out and doing some real intel gathering?"

Of course she did. "We can't though Dave, Jason would string us up."

"He has to catch us first. There are plenty of analysts doing what they need to do, scanning here, adding value there. I don't know about you, but I'm feeling stagnant. Whatever happens today is not going to happen in the square mile of London. So we need to spread our wings."

"I disagree. If I was Alex, I'd hit a target right in the heart of the city, the tower, a bank. You name it, there's certainly enough of them. But I'm open to suggestions?"

"You've missed the markers, they are there if you look. He's not looking to steal anything. People need to clear that from their minds. He has enough jewels and bloody gold to last a lifetime." He picked up Carrie's pencil and pointed at the map on the screen.

"There. That's where we find our man, his team, and the answer. But we won't do so sat on our collective arses now, will we miss?"

She couldn't put it better herself. Looking around, she saw a set of keys on a hook. "Come on then, let's take the fight to the bastard blackbird – and when we find him, we can bake him in a pie."

He was called the Jackdaw. Francis was in no mood to correct the girl. He took the keys and headed for the car park and north of the river.

Remus logged on once more. Ran a couple of checks then began to type.

"Gentlemen, start your engines." It was the pre-planned statement indicating the team was ready to go.

Romulus acknowledged. "Received. Activating now." He sent a piece of coded data to Remus and crossing his fingers prayed it would do what he had planned.

Sancus watched the cursor flashing on his screen. Sat in the back of a silver Jaguar, cossetted by leather and walnut and darkened glass, he was whisked through the capital to his next meeting – a discussion with the Police Federation of England and Wales, and how they were predicting a nation-wide meltdown if the Minister didn't dip his hand in his pockets. They would tell him to do something to recover from the chaos that his predecessor had caused by cutting back so violently on frontline staff.

He'd listen, nod at the right time, tell the Federation they were doing a marvellous job, the frontline too – 'yes, do tell them how much they are appreciated.'

Then he'd get back into his Jaguar and return to his office, purging his mind of all of that nonsense. Pay rises, better working conditions, what next better pensions?

Police Minister Harold Halford was the least popular holder of that title in fifty years. In fact, the rank and file despised him and one or two would even be happy to push him into the path of a bullet.

But they were a housefly in a sink, swirling, and he held

control of the mixer tap. There they were, twisting, turning, on their backs, down, into the drain. He cared that much.

He checked his reflection in the tinted glass, swept his hair aside and grinned. 'Good looking bastard.'

Alex was on the move. He'd left the old building and posted one of his team to watch over the two captives. He was moving at a pace now, to his vehicle, then back into the corporate clothing and closer to the target. Constantin mirrored his every move.

Into the car park, space forty two was free. Parked. Exiting, they walked at a slower pace. He checked his right trouser pocket. Tapped the phone for reassurance. He resisted the urge to look around, for all he knew there could be a sniper on the roof, as far away as across the river. In his backpack, all he needed for his stay.

In their home city of Craiova they could walk the streets day or night and never even get approached by the police, they were untouchable. He missed that. Now, for the first time in years, he felt slightly on edge. But considered that a positive.

They flashed their IDs to the gate guard, then across the reader on the staff entrance door. They were inside once more, this time as staff. Alex checked his pocket again, trying not to appear paranoid. He'd mapped his way to the control room, fallen asleep with the map on his chest. Dreamt about it. Left, left again, up, along, left, door, straight ahead, door, in.

And that is what they did.

Behind them, by a minute, his brother and the kiwi soldier.

. . .

The radio operator called across to Roberts.

"Three clicks from McCall, sir. He's in and behind the target."

"Thank you."

Alex approached the first of two secure doors, picked up the pace and then tailgated the first with Constantin a pace behind him. They feigned swiping their cards and got away with it. The staff member in front of them picked up the pace now, started to pull away. Sixth sense.

Alex did the same, almost a jog. The male looked over his shoulder, and not liking what he saw, he began to run. Alex followed, but faster. One of them would reach the door first.

They approached the door to the control room. The male fumbled with his card, tried to be quicker than he had been at any time in the preceding year, then dropped his ID. It was all the encouragement Stefanescu needed.

They called him the Jackdaw because he had glossy hair that shone like the birds' feathers, eyes, soulless, dark and unforgiving, but many thought of him as the ultimate nest raider – just like the bird itself. He was here to raid the nest.

The Jackdaw was also known for its inquisitive nature and intelligence.

An Italian criminal group once trained one to steal from cash machines. Alex loved that story. It made him smile. Clever boy.

He wasn't smiling when he caught the forty-five-year-old Londoner. As he lifted his head back upwards from picking up his ID Alex hit him hard with his knee, driving it across his face and temple, knocking him out cold. It was a swift attack and seen by no one.

Constantin had covered the nearest lens with a cloth

held up by a telescopic handle. Two minutes later Alex had returned. The male was in a side room, where research showed no one would go. He might wake, but he wouldn't be able to move.

Constantin checked the remaining plasticuffs in his backpack. Then nodded at his boss. 'Time to go.'

CHAPTER 59

CADE LEANT FORWARD AGAIN, THE PEN NOW IN HIS
pocket. He had no idea of its value but secured it, anyway.
He picked the largest piece of glass he could see and held it
tight just as momentum saw Blake win the balancing act.

Even before Cade was up in the air again, he was sawing
at the plasticuffs. Gripping the cube of brown glass, he cut
and cut again. It would take a while, but he figured he had
nothing else to do.

"Reckon you can catch this if I throw it?"

"I played cricket for Surrey."

"I'll take that as a yes then." The whole conversation
took place at less than a whisper. The guard, if he could be
called that, illuminated his face in a side corridor, flicking
his finger across his smartphone. Left for no, right for yes.

He swiped right for all of them. Overweight, rarely
showered, a squint and poor skin wasn't the description he
had used in his profile picture. He found two matches,
wondered if they could form a threesome. He was
engrossed.

And so was Cade. Cutting had become his life, slowly

etching the plastic away, stroke by painful stroke. Piece by piece, tiny shards of the material falling into the water. His thumb and index finger bled. He gave up worrying about the blood when he noticed that the water was now lapping over his seat.

Elena had also found transport in the guise of a young detective who had spent days glancing sideways, then looking away whenever she looked back. She was beautiful, every man in the office thought so.

"So you're certain that the governor said this was OK miss?"

"Absolutely. Does this face look like it could lie?"

There was no way on earth he was going to disagree. He wanted her, couldn't stop thinking about her, had even started dreaming about her. The northern bloke Cade was a fool to have let her go. Lucky bastard. Perhaps, if he played his cards right, he might just have a chance.

"Not at all, miss. Now, where do you need to go?"

Alex was light on his feet. He reached the next secure door. It looked like it weighed a ton. Technically it was half that but either way it performed its role admirably. However, all the weight in the world was nothing when matched against a simple piece of plastic that activated the motor and allowed it to slide open.

Two of the control staff were wearing Peltor ear defenders that they had adapted to look like radio headsets. They had worked there for six months – and had done a very good job. Sleepers, and now covering their eyes and hoping that the plan worked.

The electronic ear defenders were rated to deflect the sound of most gunfire. At a 170dB, the flashbang that

Constantin casually tossed into the room was testing their effectiveness to the maximum. The light was blinding, a million candela at least causing immediate flash blindness. The bang part did the rest, temporary deafness, tinnitus and balance issues followed. They affected different people, differently.

The control room had seven staff in total, the duty manager, two radio operators and four staff that monitored everything else, and there was plenty to keep them occupied.

The two members of Alex's team were up, on their feet and cable-tying, as the group, all men except for one woman who was stumbling around as if she had been shot. Her ears rang, and she staggered into the Duty Manager who had the air of a drunk. The concussion had disturbed the fluid in his semi-circular canals – three delicate half-circles of tubular matter filled with saline. And then there were the microscopic hairs – those practically pointless things in the human body that allowed their owner to stand, sit, jump, walk or fall.

He fell, hitting his head on the corner of the nearby desk, and remained there until he came around, strapped up and angry.

The four-man team had done its job – as fluidly as the human ear, a precision team working to great effect. Alex stood, pistol in hand, watching the staff come to terms with their situation and minor injuries. He tapped into the keyboard nearest to him. He then turned and gazed out of the window of the control room, downstream towards the city centre, then upstream towards the sea.

"Lovely view, don't you think?"

. . .

O'Shea and Francis were making slow progress through the traffic. "Dave, is this the best you can do? I could walk faster!"

"Then walk. But where exactly are we supposed to be going?"

"The river, then just drive along the Embankment until I tell you to stop."

"Hardly scientific, my lady."

"More than you can imagine. Now, let's get through this traffic, shall we?" She flipped open the central glovebox and found the switch panel, turned the dial to yelp, decided that was too much like hard work then selected wail. And it did. And the sea parted. And Dave Francis smiled for the first time since his uncle Ted had been systematically blown to pieces by the very men they were now hunting.

"This is great Carrie, but she's a big city and I don't have the Knowledge." He was referring to the ultimate test of memory that London cab drivers studied for years.

"No, but I do. Left here, straight on, then right, at the T-junction stop. I need to think."

Sancus was back in his office, sipping on Earl Gray from a bone china cup, he had logged onto the 'net. He too smiled for the first time since the last time he had been particularly spiteful.

The Police Federation had approached him, cap in hand, grovelling.

'You should have seen them, grovelling little shits.' He said to no one in particular. Then he hit send.

'Well done. Next phase. One hour.'

He rang his executive assistant. "Caroline, I'll be out for the rest of the day. Hold all calls, except from anyone higher than me. Clear?"

"Completely boss." She knew that as far as Halford was concerned, there was no one higher.

Viduus watched the screen, as he had always done, quietly, discreetly and unseen. So that was his game. Time to tune in and announce his presence. He walked towards his car, plipped the remote, flashing the hazards twice, then slipped into the leather heated seats, started the Audi and moved into the commuter traffic. He didn't need sirens. His journey was relatively short.

Valentin had been watching too. He replied, "I have done as you asked. We are now equal. The birds have fled the nest. They have flown in every direction, but in yours. Good luck. We will never cross paths again. Our debt is settled. Romulus."

Alex – or as his alter ego in the cyber world was known Remus – leant back in the high back office chair, spun around a hundred and eighty degrees, then pointed his pistol at the duty manager.

"How's the head Andy?"

Andrew Darkin was in his fifties, a career man with more integrity than the Jackdaw had lustrous hairs on his head. He tried to stand, but soon realised his ankles were cable tied. He shook his head, trying to clear the remnants of concussion.

"It's just great. Like the time Arsenal beat Chelsea in the FA Cup – or rather the morning after."

"Oh, so you are a comedian as well as the Duty Manager? How nice, I look forward to your next joke with great eagerness." He pointed the pistol as Darkin's head and mimed a shot, recoiling, the round leaving the barrel and striking him with the sound of a motorcyclist's head hitting a concrete wall.

"It's that easy, Andy. Bang. You're dead. Or we could chat about your boy Samuel, the one at boarding school. He's fine, honestly, a little scared I'm sure, but he'll pull through. Your wife on the other hand is having the time of her life."

He turned the computer monitor around so the whole room could see. Two of Stefanescu's team were with her. Darkin could feel the bile rising in his throat.

"Why? She's done nothing to you. Let her bloody go or seriously I will..."

The shot left the gun. If Alex hadn't blinked, he would have seen it travel through the air, such a short distance. It hit Darkin in the left thigh, slicing through the thick flesh, superheating as it travelled through the limb, and instead of burrowing out of the back of his leg, dragging creamy-white strands of flesh with it, it stopped. It was no longer the shape that had left the brass casing, now the copper head was distorted, re-shaped by Darkin's femur.

"You should think yourself lucky I wasn't aiming. Now, let's try again, shall we. And for the record, my boys are very careful, such gentle lovers."

"You didn't ask for anything yet, you still shot me you twat."

"Oh, that's not nice. I don't even know what it means. It's not a word we have in my country."

"Then why don't you go back and learn to read." Darkin was looking away from the screen. His wife of thirty years was clearly not enjoying herself.

"Stop. Please. Just stop. You obviously want something or you wouldn't be here."

Alex clapped, sarcastically. "Give the man a round of applause."

No one clapped. He pointed the pistol at the woman, a plump, forty something with brown split-end hair in a pony-tail and oversized hooped earrings.

She clapped vigorously. Like a sea lion on death row.

"That's better. OK, Andy, my new best friend. How's the leg?"

"Superb thanks." He gasped each word. "Cut the small talk, I need medical help and you are obviously a terrorist so get it over with. Shoot us all...but do me a favour, make Sheila the first. You can see how afraid she is."

Alex looked genuinely hurt. "A terrorist? Andrew, that is a terrible thing to say. Why do people always think I am a damned terrorist? Does a man who shouts obscenities in a public library necessarily have Tourette's? No! They might not have the book he ordered."

"So what are you then Mister Bloody Perfect?"

Alex liked his courage. He was actually quite funny too. Pity. Another time, perhaps?

"I sir, am your worst nightmare. I've walked into your professional world and..." He searched for an analogy that worked. "Pissed all over your British roast dinner ad watered down your gravy."

It didn't work.

"That makes no sense. Possibly in the world of the nomadic people that you inhabit..."

"I thought it was funny." He paused as he rewound Dark-in's sentence. "Sorry, you said nomadic? What do you think I am Andrew?"

"I didn't like to use the G word."

"Gypsy? You think we are gypsies?" He looked at Constantin. "They think we are gypsies!"

Alex stepped towards the Londoner, pulled his head

into this waist, held it there, rubbing the back of his head, affectionately. Strangely it aroused him. That was a first. He pushed his head away.

"Did you know what the Nazis did? Actually, you probably did, you seem like an educated man. I haven't got time for a lecture. I need to finish what I started. But for the record Mr Darkin we are Roma – and very proud."

He looked at the screen where Mrs Darkin was frantically trying to evade the two men in her lounge. "Looks like the boys are ready for dessert." He had Darkin's attention again.

"Ask me anything."

"Which of the magic buttons do I press to operate the machinery here?"

"It's more complicated than just pressing a button."

"No, Andrew, it isn't. I'll ask again. Then I will command my two men to finish her off. She'll like that, right at the last minute, that feeling of euphoria mixed with the lack of oxygen. Some women really get a thrill out of it. Such a pity your wife won't be around long enough to ever ask you to try it."

"The three switches marked Master, Override, and Alarm. See the red, yellow and green illuminated switches on the main panel? Press them in sequence, then step back and admire the view."

"Is it really as simple as that?"

"As simple. As that."

"Thank you. You have earned my respect."

He looked at the computer screen. Rang the taller of the two eager males. "Enough. Secure her to something and leave. Ensure she is not harmed. And get rid of those hideous masks."

Darkin let out an audible sigh of relief as Alex

Stefanescu pressed the three buttons in sequence, and as instructed, stood up and admired the view.

Constantin held the microphone at the radio operator's lips.

"Speak. Say what you say to the little boats, and that big one over there. Tell them to go away. But do it professionally, just as you would if it was a normal day at work, Martin."

Using the young man's first name ensured a rabbit-in-the-headlights response. He did as he was told. Eloquently, calmly and with no obvious code words.

"All shipping Thames, all shipping Thames, east and west of Woolwich, be aware we are moving into the operational phase. This is not an exercise. All vessels to stop and report to Port of London Authority. Port of London received?"

The radio was silent for a second. Then a familiar voice responded.

"Received sir. Thank you. Please advise when you are fully activated."

"Will do PAL and thank you."

There was nothing in that sentence that attracted the suspicion of the two members of the Seventh Wave team, men who had worked with Martin Bradley for months. He wished there had been, wished he had been so brave. His face showed he was far removed from being a worthy poker player.

The machinery that raised the immense sections was an engineering work of art. The massive blades scooped water by the ton. A reservoir nearby began to flood. Lights flashed on panels, gauges monitored. All part of the awakening hydraulic monster.

And the water below was a part of the whole process. It surrounded the tunnel and swirled and snagged and clung onto any and everything.

To the north east another situation was developing. She was seamless and reliable too, but in addition, she was dark and brutal.

At the shores, north and south of the Thames and midstream, she began to change. Nature versus Man.

In the Houses of Parliament, he had said she was coming and they had done what? They had laughed and heckled and waved their papers in the air, jeering, sneering, and in the end, ignoring him.

In the North Sea the storm had added momentum and anger to the surge that now raced south, insidiously enveloping the shore line of Suffolk, then Essex, gushing into the massive estuary, beyond piers, boat moorings and bridges, relentless.

People saw it, some say they heard it. The older members of the riverside community had seen it before. The water slewed along, salt overcoming fresh, colours mixed from blue to brown and the darkest green. A green so dark it was practically black. It took on a persona rarely seen. Eddies became whirlpools, riverbanks were devoured, some washed away, wooden jetties, long past their prime creaked and moaned against the force of the water. Some gave in to its almost gravitational pull and collapsed.

Boats, old and new, swayed and bucked and twisted at their moorings. Those that were out on the water, under sail or driven began to feel the tug of the tide. Skippers, experienced or otherwise, began to make the call. Before long, the authorities were overwhelmed with calls.

To the north around Canvey Island and the south at Allhallows the water rushed into the natural funnel, rolled around, tried to head back out to sea but met itself in overwhelming odds.

The city was prepared, they had even discussed it in the House. MPs had jostled in a verbal debate not seen since Thatcher's days.

The party in power were confident. The authorities were good at this.

The opposition seized the moment – they were brilliant at it, such a shame those in power had made so many cutbacks, they said, to anyone who would listen.

She was there. She protected the city. Had done since 1984. Her iconic steel structure had stood firm, never crumpling under the strain. As the knights had sat in Westminster Abbey, holding court, centuries before, securing the city, so the shining pier heads had remained resolute, safeguarding one of the oldest cities in the world from the high tides and storm surges that threatened to flood the city of London.

She was there. Her piers were named in alphabetical order from south to north, starting with Alpha across the river, ending at Kilo.

The Thames Barrier.

She had no nickname. But for the team that manned her each and every day she was just simply referred to as her. She was their professional home. But on this day, the day that would be recorded in the annals of British history as one of the strongest tidal surges to approach the city in years, the team were locked down, strapped to chairs, concussed, bleeding and bloody helpless.

And the man they called the Jackdaw finally had what he needed to gain what he never truly had, respect.

CHAPTER 60

"You have to admire the British Constantin. This really is a feat of engineering to be proud of."

He looked upstream. It had taken a record seventy minutes to close the barrier.

"They built it here because the river bed is stable enough, over five hundred metres across, each section weighs over three thousand tons, they can raise them in minutes if they need to. I could go on, there is very little I don't know about this project. I like to learn. Prison does that to a man, makes him a little narrow-minded, obsessive perhaps..." He grinned at everyone in the room. "This must be a wonderful place to work. Such power."

He was squatting down, next to Andrew Darkin, the once-in-charge Ops Manager of the Barrier. He was looking unwell; pale, quieter than he had been before the barrier had hauled itself, pier by pier, up and out of the Thames. Sixty-one metres of sheer power.

"That leg looks nasty." He pulled a pocketknife out of the small shoulder bag that he had brought with him.

Darkin tried to shuffle away but was restrained by two sets of black cable ties that did nothing for his recovery.

"I'm fine. Just let me rest."

"You could die if I don't do this." He pushed the blade into his leg then pulled the skin apart with his fingers as if he were tearing satin. He pressed them deeper into the hole, through the outer layers of magnolia skin, darker, creamy red, the dermis, hair follicles, sweat glands and deeper connective tissue. As the deep red ended the whiter parts began, then the blood vessels appeared, scarlet upon the bleached sections, he marvelled as he separated the flesh from the bone.

The femur. A fresh leg of lamb. He couldn't tell the difference.

"Why are you doing this to him?" Bradley was now the spokesman of the group.

"Because I am bored, and that bullet is evidence. When we leave, we leave nothing behind." It explained the blue surgical gloves, they weren't just there for hygienic purposes.

"And as I said earlier, he might die if I don't remove the evidence. This way he lives with a scar to remind him of the day."

Darkin has passed out long before Alex found the spent round. It sat alongside the bone, had gouged it before skidding off and down his leg, towards his knee, avoiding the artery but rupturing everything else in its path. He'd be dead if it wasn't for Alex's prowess with a firearm. He smiled to himself. He was the only person he found amusing these days.

"And there we have it." He flicked the buckled bullet up with his fingers, pocketed it and wiped his hands on Darkin's white uniform shirt.

"Pass me that, would you? And the first aid kit." One of

his team turned away from his captives and handed the black object to his leader.

Alex pulled the flesh tight with his fingers, fruitlessly stapled it together, and then wrapped a field dressing around this thigh. "My work here is done, quite literally. Come on team, we need to be somewhere."

Hewett was parked, watching. Waiting. He had been here before. This time would be different – if anyone so much as asked to get into his car, he would shoot them. In the face. At point blank range. He made a call.

"It's me. This may be our only chance. Planetary alignment and all that."

He then rang Roberts.

"Jason. I'm in place. Seems like the world and his wife are focusing on the same place. But I see nothing untoward. In fact I see very little. What about you?"

Roberts lied. "Nothing."

He wasn't even remotely near to where Hewett had been sent. As unprofessional as it felt, both Roberts and Daniel had made a decision – use Johnnie Hewett's skills but divert him to another place entirely.

"Once bitten JD."

"But he came good, Jason. We need all the bodies we can muster here. Remember, this is as need to know as it gets. Become feral were her words. So let's not disappoint the lady."

"Fine, you ring him back. But what can he do? We are all sat here like surfers bobbing around in the ocean waiting for the biggest wave in history and only a few will get to ride it."

"Perhaps this one will be the seventh?"

"Perhaps." He tapped his chewed fingernails on the steering wheel. "Ring him. Get him to the safe forward point. Tell him to keep an eye out for Halford. I trust him less than I do Hewett. And Halford respects dear Johnnie – and that, is a rarity."

Hewett listened, then cleared down. He knew they didn't trust him. He understood. It was how it was. He had skin so thick a rhinoceros would look on from a distance, quietly envious.

He also needed to exact some revenge on a few people. Those that had made his parents lives a misery. He didn't need a satnav, he knew where to go and go he did, as fast as traffic would allow. He pressed CD on the audio system and *Frankie* sang once more.

Halford was already in a prime place. He was watching too. His protection officer was outside the secure door to his city apartment, overlooking the Thames. 'Deal with anyone that doesn't look like the milkman or the postman. Kill them if you have to – I have paid you more than generously.'

He stood on the balcony, binoculars in hand, smiling as he made the call. It had taken years to get to this point. It had all started when that stupid girl had tried to get into the United Kingdom, to see the man she said could change her life. She knew too much, way too much, and she was clever. Pretty, too. Very. But she had to die. Her daughter was supposed to as well. They had made a complete pigs ear of that operation – the only positive being that the girl they called Elena had tied up all of the loose ends, delicately weaving a web for someone else to take all the credit – and he was the spider at the centre.

He pressed the button on his Blackberry. "Make the call."

He called out to his protection officer.

"Be ready to leave in ten. I don't want to miss this."

"Will it be safe?"

"As houses."

Alex hit redial.

"Hello News Desk, how can I help?"

"It is the other way around. Listen, don't interrupt. Not once."

Four minutes later, the young journalist ran to his editor.

A minute after that, Alex pressed the pad of his index finger onto his iPhone. It started the sequence that had taken six months to programme. Valentin was a genius. Alex always knew he could trust him. He was a loner, but a great operator, and he too hated a government that had betrayed him. He was best described as a truly astute man. And as far as value for money was concerned, he was worth every penny.

The software processed the instruction. Alex had no understanding of its inner workings, he didn't need to, as long as it worked. And it did. Oh, it so did. He walked along a corridor, looked out of a window and watched for a second.

"Look, Constantin! We have control at last. Now we need to get what we came for and leave before we die with the rest of the rats."

"Alex, there is something I need to tell you."

"Later, when we sip our favourite liquor on a private jet, one that takes us home once more, where the people will carry us on their shoulders."

Constantin knew it was futile, he had lied to the Jackdaw, and that normally meant one thing, so he kept running, as fast as his withered legs would carry him. Right now, he wished for his eternal mistress, heroin.

They sprinted along the narrow walkway towards Kilo,

the northerly pier head. It was further than they thought, but the adrenaline propelled them and as they approached the door it opened seamlessly. The simplicity of having one if his team watch their every move on close circuit television.

"OK, are you ready?" He was genuinely smiling. Ear to crooked ear.

The case had been put there the last time they had tested the facility. It had seemed like the perfect place for it. At the time.

It would prove to be his greatest mistake.'

Alex told him to trust one of the Barrier team, and so he had met, handed it over and tried to forget about the black, waterproof Pelican case. But it woke him, whenever he was lucky enough to sleep. They visited him every night, the lucid dreams of the case, a girl holding it, as it slowly unclipped, the document and the transcripts, soaked, breaking up and useless, floating away in the water.

But how could he tell him? He was his friend, a brother in arms, they had experienced so much, had been tortured by the state, but that would mean nothing in the scheme of things, for the contents of that well-constructed case were his future and the future of his people.

To let down a family member was one thing, to let down and disappoint the Gypsy King was an entirely different proposition.

He needed to tell someone, and soon, but Alex was being carried along on the tide. The clock was ticking and the King had asked, quite specifically, for the documents in their original condition to be made available, and he had given a day and a time. They were to be the ultimate bartering weapon.

And for many months they had sat there, in the black polycarbonate box, dry as the proverbial bone. Accessible, within reach, if you knew where to reach.

What a fool. He could have chosen practically anywhere in the world, anywhere in the vast city, but paranoia had driven him to over think, to trust no one – except the young boy from Bucharest who had sworn he was doing the right thing with the well-constructed box that contained their future hopes.

They could hear the massive hydraulic pistons, pushing and pulling, easing the sector gates into place, one by one. They could hear engineering greatness too, and in the distance the less than subtle rumblings of a gathering storm.

"It's coming, Constantin. It's almost here. This is it!"

Scott McCall could almost smell his prey.

Equally Stefan could sense his brother, he didn't need to smell him. He closed his eyes and knew he was ahead of them. That is how they had been, since the days they had evaded the police in Craiova, on the run after a spree of shoplifting, then heading home to their thoroughly ashamed parents.

The psychologist had predicted a future for Alex that was either brilliant or riddled with cruelty, tainted by crime.

McCall considered any man that could order the death of his own wife and then his daughter to be the lowest creature in the animal kingdom, and he'd made a living out of hunting the filthiest of them all.

McCall held up a hand. Stefan stopped.

"Down this way, brother, it heads to the pier you were telling me about. We get there, we finish it, then all home for tea and medals."

He moved almost silently, pistol in hand and a back-up

magazine of seventeen, a well-practised four seconds away. He signalled Stefan to remain, whilst he forged ahead.

The first round took him by surprise. It came from behind, from behind cover and well-aimed. It missed. By the breadth of the hair on a bluebottle's arse.

It missed because McCall was always ready. Who Dares Lives. He was down on one knee, sweeping the corridor, up and sideways. The Glock was gripped by the hands of an experienced operator; balanced, thumbs interlocking, taking control. He glared over the top of the front sight.

Bastard.

He knew it. He suspected Cade knew it too.

He couldn't go forward and he couldn't return. Now he needed luck to support his field craft. He checked the cargo pocket on his trousers, tapped it reassuringly.

In the steel tomb Cade had made the final cut, he pulled his wrist free, leaned towards the drum and fished around again, deeper into the glass, cutting himself as he plunged deeper.

He couldn't help quoting to himself, 'The pen is mightier than the sword.' Why had the man he loathed put a pen in among the glass? Just a cruel trick? Or was it to allow Cade to write a note to his loved ones, before he drowned in the fetid water?

Deeper, his hand was now lacerated, but he felt no pain. He sifted through the debris, questioning the mentality of men that could just walk away from someone and allow them to choke to death in a watery grave. It seemed to be their forte.

Blake was willing Cade on now. With one breath he'd urge him on, then look up, checking for the guard. He coughed, the signal. Cade stopped and resumed his position. The see-saw tipped Blake back down into the water, which was now lapping at his shoulders and rising. The guard hated the sound of running water; it played havoc with his over-active bladder. He was bursting. There was nowhere to go either, except...

He unzipped himself and began to urinate down into the void, a stream of foul-smelling, dark yellow liquid dropped metres down into the tube, hitting the water and adding to its volume. He shook himself a little too vigourously, then zipped back up and went back to his website. Not once did he glance down into the eerie green space.

"Gone?" Cade hissed.

"Gone. How much longer, Jack?"

"Five, maybe ten."

"Look, if only one of us can get out of here, so be it. There's something I need you to know."

"Is it a long story Michael because I suspect we don't have much time?"

"You know when you flew to Australia? It was a hell of a long way just to make love to Elena. There must be other girls in your life – and besides, you could have just rung her." Blake looked at Cade in the half-light, waiting.

"It *was* a long flight, I'll give you that." He carried on shaving layers of plastic from the ankle strap. "But I needed to look her in the eyes and ask her the question."

"Which was?"

"Why she also made the equally arduous journey to New Zealand – why she came to find me. But I think I know the answer now."

"You spoke to John Daniel?"

"I did. And he explained that Elena was hunting for him, not me."

"That's right, but did she also say that it had become an affair of the heart? She fell for you, Jack, in every possible way. You know that. But look at you now, so much distrust, almost two different people. Why? She's a beautiful girl, Jack, with a wonderful soul. You could do a lot worse."

"She is. I met her mother once, she was equally beautiful. But I trusted her and she me, and I let her down enormously. I can't allow that to happen again. Letting people down is becoming a theme."

"I met her mother once too, Jack. And no, you didn't. She got to London because of you, and she met the person she needed to meet. Again, down to you. We've covered some distance since those early days Jack, but you need to know that Nikolina treasured what you gave her."

Blake continued to whisper, timing his story with Cade's frantic cutting. And the water edged upwards, and Blake began to push himself up, trying to maintain the balancing act. He admired the cunning of the man that had built the contraption, hated him too. What sort of mind dreamt these things up? This was evil beyond anywhere he could ever imagine. Perhaps the countless hours in a prison cell did that to a man?

He pushed, up and through the water, but it held him in place. Tired legs and a weight disadvantage locked him down in the pool. Cade looked down at him. He could see Blake was almost done. The water was now teasing his throat, passing the Adam's apple. He had minutes.

"You'll do what I asked, Jack? Please."

"I don't intend to leave you here, my friend." He moved suddenly, and the cable snapped. "I'm free. Stay there I'll cut you free too."

"No, go. You haven't got time. Go, but tell her..."

Cade looked up at the ladder. It was hanging by a thread. Deliberate? Part of the game? Another few minutes and he could reach up. It needed the ever-increasing volume of water to allow him to stretch the final few inches. They knew this. They had calculated it, to the last minute. Pure evil.

"I'll hold my breath as long as I can, Jack. But don't look back. Do what needs to be done. And Jack."

"Yes."

"Thank you." Blake's words were short. He kept his lips tight, forming a seal. It was time.

Cade knew he didn't have time to cut him free. The mythical knife never was in the drum, all it contained was glass and chunks of his fingers and a puddle of scarlet that washed around the tube with the churning water.

Francis did as he was told, switching the siren off but leaving the grill lights flickering.

"Where are we heading, Carrie?"

"Just bear with me, Dave. Along here."

"Do you actually have a plan?"

"I do, kind of, but it needs some help from above."

"Helicopter?"

"No, further up than that. If you believe in guardian angels Dave?"

"I didn't until your boyfriend appeared in my life, Carrie."

"He's not..."

"Come off it. We all know you are besotted."

"Fuck off, Dave." She said it with venom but she couldn't help but reveal a guilty smile.

"Here. Stop here."

"What?"

"Now." She pulled the handbrake on.

"What are you doing, woman." He fought to control the car and steered it safely into the kerb.

"Come on. This way." She was out and running.

Cade had once confided in Francis, told him his true feelings for the wild child Carrie O'Shea. He had also said she could find the needle without the haystack. 'Call it a sixth sense, David. Call it anything you like, but trust me that girl has a gift for finding stuff. I once heard her referred to as a shit magnet. And that is what we have in common.'

They ran, with O'Shea holding the pistol awkwardly. They reached the partly derelict concrete building with its authoritarian but faded signage.

"In here. And please take this off me." She handed him the pistol. It felt good to be holding one again after so long. The door opened with ease. As if the owners never expected anyone to simply walk up and enter.

Francis took over. Held a weather-worn palm up. It meant stop in any language. They waited and listened. Nothing.

But there was a faded light coming from the next corridor. Francis pointed and ran his hand across his throat. It must have meant something from his military days. He beckoned her closer. Then whispered.

"We need to see who is in there. You may have the wrong place."

"No. This is it."

They edged forward. The light flickered. A shadow flitted off the ceiling like a circling bat, hunting for its quarry. They reached the door and saw the outline of the male, too busy swiping the screen on his smartphone. Somewhere nearby they could hear water.

"We go on my count of three. I will lead. You follow. We'll deal with whatever we come across."

. . .

Elena had also arrived at a building. Hers was larger, more modern, and despite the many cars in the car park, apparently abandoned.

"You come with me or you stay here. Either way, it is going to get very noisy soon." She was pumped full of adrenaline.

"But why don't we wait miss?" It was a fair question from the detective who was beginning to doubt his decision-making skills.

"No, we go now."

"No miss, we stay. And that's an order."

"No, we go or I shoot you." She levelled the gun at him. God alone knew where she had produced it from.

"As you wish, miss."

She stuck to the perimeter wall like a shadow, moving quickly. The five-year cop was a pace behind her, hoping to hell that she knew what she was doing.

"In here. Come on, follow me."

Halford was being whipped through the traffic now, faster than everything else, with his devoted protection officer behind the wheel, bullying his way along the arterial route alongside the river.

"Remember, if this goes wrong, you are on your own. My reputation is worth more than yours. And I have paid you very well."

"Agreed boss. It's been a pleasure."

It seemed that all roads no longer led to Rome.

Cade was bleeding from every finger now but rising in the water, closer and closer to the ladder. He gripped hold of the bottom rung and quietly pulled against it. Above him, to his left, a drainage hole became visible. He realised that must be where the overflow ran to. He took a second to realise that even if the river water reached it, the tube would still not empty until the tide began to turn.

He tucked in close to the ladder, but it moved; the bolts giving way. He looked down. The view of Blake's face was all that remained. His hair moved in the circular current. He still looked alive. There was hope in his expression. If he was holding his breath Cade willed him to hold it just another minute or two. Just long enough to get him out of there and deliver the message himself.

Above him, the light flickered once more. Then a crack rang out. An ear piercing, head scrambling bang. It resonated, had nowhere to go and rang out, announcing a single gunshot. The male appeared at the gantry, holding onto his abdomen. He leant over, staring at Cade who was now propelling himself up the ladder to meet him.

The male tipped over the edge, hit Cade and fell into the water, which was a cocktail of misery, a mix of brown and green and red.

A hand appeared. Female, left, no wedding ring. Soft, cared for, but as strong as the right hand that joined it, male, older, time-worn skin, redder by the second as Cade's fingers covered them in his fresh blood.

He allowed himself to be pulled up the ladder, got to the top, saw a face, friendly, a deep smile, then one of concern as it looked down, past Cade to the floating body and the second, near-lifeless soul in the bottom of the darkening tube.

"So this is where you hang out, Inspector Cade?"

O'Shea hauled him up by his shirt, onto the level floor and allowed him a second to breathe.

"It's Blake, we need to get back down there now." He was pointing, exhausted.

Francis slipped a foot over the side, tested the ladder which creaked and then gave way, falling down, into the water, partly dragging the Eastern European guard down further to the floor of the tube. All that remained visible was his face as he slipped below the water, a realisation that if he wasn't dead yet he soon would be.

"I'm sorry, Jack. We can't get down there."

"Find some rope, a knife, do whatever you can. I need to get back down there."

Cade looked over the railing, down into what was to have been his tomb. Blake was staring back at him, his eyes were the last thing to fade. They spoke a thousand words.

"Tell her." Then he let go. Bubbles radiated around his mouth, then his nose, then they overwhelmed him. His eyes widened, water poured into his throat, he gagged, he coughed, and then having fought it with an intense resolution, he relented.

The river and the syndicate that called itself the Seventh Wave, both had claimed another victim.

CHAPTER 61

O'Shea held Cade by his shoulders, up against the wall, let him compose himself.

"See? I have my uses." She pulled him close. Hugged him at arm's length. He stank of stale air and putrid water. "Don't think much of your new aftershave, Mr C."

"Channel Number Five." He laughed. "Come on, get me out of here. Dave ring for back up, get a team to recover Blake, I want him treated with complete respect. Let the other fat bastard stay at the bottom of that bloody place. Let the rats feast on him."

He threw up, his body rejecting the dark water that had begun to fill his body.

"Better now?" O'Shea again.

"Enjoying this?"

"No, not at all. The team is descending on the Barrier. Jason has deployed the whole group – it stinks Jack, we've got the biggest police force in the country at our beck and call and we can't even bloody tell them what's happening."

"And we will never will." He wiped his mouth. "How far away are we?"

"Quarter of a mile."

"So what are we waiting for?"

"You, Jack. Just you." Francis patted him on the back and led the way back to their car.

Scott McCall tried to peer around the doorway, reducing his frame, just as he had been taught many years ago. It had saved his hide on more than one occasion. He could make out the leading edge of something in the next doorway along, about forty metres back, along the corridor. The shape was organic, human. He raised his weapon and knew when he committed to the shot there was a risk of being hit from either side of his place of safety.

Fortis Fortuna Adiuvat. It was written on his right shoulder, next to the tribal tattoo. And there was never a better time to test the theory.

He checked to his right, looking out quickly, to where he suspected Alex and his partner would be. Nothing. He'd head there next.

Another quick look to his left. He visualised the image. Worked out where the shot would fall, knew he had one, maybe two seconds to aim, and fire.

He emptied half of the rounds from his spare magazine, pushed them into his pocket. Tactically it was suicide. But he needed a distraction. This was a game of cat and mouse, and the cat was currently pinning him down. But cats were easily distracted. They liked shiny things.

With a prayer to his ancestors he resorted to his roots, a young Maori warrior, in the forest with an uncle, hunting deer.

'We use many things to distract our prey, boy. Watch this...'

He was back, in the woods, far from home. His favourite

uncle Amiri had spent days tracking the deer. He had shown him how to read the trails, what to eat, what to avoid, how to find water and how to build a shelter from the canopy and floor of the forest.

When McCall eventually trained to join the Special Air Service he was already halfway there. Amiri 'Scottie' McCall. Mack the knife to his friends.

His uncle's first name meant 'From the east wind.' He was a legendary hunter. Scott had taken his name when he had been born. His anglicised name was purely for the army. With his piece of treasured greenstone, tied to a dog-eared leather thong, nestling among the black chest hairs, and secured around his neck, a treasure, gifted by his uncle, he knew he would be safe. His whanau, his family, were watching over him.

The hunted became the hunter.

He fired. One handed. Better that way. Less of a target.

The round screamed out of the barrel, along the corridor, it missed, but the second, fired with autonomous reactions didn't. It struck the kneecap, shattering it, dispersing bone upwards and out, preventing it from ever being used again.

The scream that followed was immensely satisfying.

Stefan fired back in anger, but they were random, pain-induced shots and in doing so he exposed his hand and his weapon. McCall didn't need a second invitation. Firing a burst of three shots, he hit the target. Stefan's index and ring finger left the hand, spinning, spiralling, landing and coming to a halt down the corridor, pointing at the exit. A bloody sign if ever there was one.

The weapon clattered to the floor and McCall was up and running, on his toes, purely tactical now, a slave to his training. He was firing on the move, two shots left the weapon and struck his former partner in the chest. He was down, a crippled man with a devastated heart.

McCall got to the Romanian with the inequitable eyes before he could do anything to counter the attack.

He held his head, which had dropped, looking to the concrete floor.

"Look at me, you bastard. Why?"

Stefan let out a nonchalant exhalation. "You wouldn't understand."

"Try me, fucker. I put my life on the line for you."

"No, you didn't. You were a well-timed piece of luck. Nothing more. You got me here. And anyway..." His head dropped.

McCall snatched it back up. "Oh no buddy, you are not going anywhere until I allow it. Speak."

"You got the diamonds. You are as bad as us. Once my brother hears that you killed me you will never be able to live a normal life again. He is...as bad as they can ever get. Did you know he killed our parents in a fit of rage? No? Did you know he killed his own wife?" He was fading now.

"He's one amazing man, your brother. But trust me, he'll find out that I killed you, two seconds before I empty the rest of this magazine into him and then reload and slowly finish off his snivelling little friend. You lot have no idea what comradeship is."

"Fair enough. Kill me." There wasn't an ounce of fear. He knew he was dying, and that tended to remove the sense of dread.

"Before I do. What is this all about? You owe me that much."

Stefan coughed, his breath smelt of aerated red blood – a metallic odour his assassin had long become used to.

"We are just the disciples. There is always someone

further up the food chain, Scott. We live good lives, money, girls, cars, respect."

"Yep, I hear you buddy, keep talking."

"But we are just disciples…"

"You said…and who is the true Messiah?"

"The Gypsy King, of course. And no one betrays his true name."

McCall knew he didn't need to waste another bullet, but recovered the magazine he had thrown and the spare from Stefan's gun. He tapped Stefan on the left cheek.

"Been nice knowing you." He leant him forward so he would choke to death on his own blood. No reason why he should enter the gates of hell without some further suffering.

McCall was up and moving. Ahead of him, Alex and Constantin had heard the commotion. Constantin rang the Ops Room.

"What is happening?"

"Stefan has been killed. By the soldier."

"Then secure the room and the people. We don't need you there anymore. Go and find him and make sure you really hurt him."

"But the river…"

"Let the river do what it wants. Go!"

Roberts answered his phone without checking the screen.

"Mr Roberts, Tell your people to leave us alone. That way no one else will be harmed." An all too familiar voice.

"Funny Mr Stefanescu, but I really don't believe you. We are closing in, I suggest you give up now whilst you can. This will not end well for you. Prison is a very lonely place."

"Nice psychological games, Mr Roberts. But you see, prison does not scare me. Within a week, I would be in control of the wing. My reputation is greater than you would know. But what would you know about a reputation, Jason? You have achieved so little in your pathetic life. A slave to the government, earning a pittance, whilst I live like a king. Oh, I almost forgot, Constantin just asked me to send his best wishes. He asks how your arm is."

"Strong enough to punch him in the throat."

"Ah, that's better now we are on the same...singing sheet."

"It's a hymn. And in your case, Mr Bloody Jackdaw, it's a song for your funeral. And I'll be there, behind closed doors, where none of your beloved people can join in. I know that will hurt you more than anything else."

"Jason, I would love to talk more, I really would, but I have a job to finish. I do hope you and your loved ones can swim. Ciao."

Roberts looked at John Daniel.

"So the intelligence is correct, John? He's going to flood the bloody place."

"Makes no sense. He has nothing to gain. He's made no demands."

"Not yet, anyway. Any sign of Jack?"

"Negative. Nothing. We've got our people in as many places as we can put them. Hewett is on the way too. And I've rung the Commissioner. He seems happy to stay in the office and wait for the result."

"At least he won't drown on the eighth floor."

"Are you ready, my friend?"

"Do I look ready?"

"No. Not at all."

"Good, then neither do you. Let's go and kick some arse, shall we?"

· · ·

McGee held back, watching. Her new partner was driving. It gave her chance to think.

"If we get one opportunity to wipe that smile off his smug face, I want to do it. You can look the other way."

"Is that what Nick would have wanted, boss?"

"You bet he would. Tuck in tight, run the light, but don't be too obvious. I do not want to lose him."

The first of the two Barrier Ops Room team entered the corridor system. He could hear the hydraulic systems hissing, pushing tons of steel, pumping water from somewhere in the vast building. It spooked him. He kept moving. A lamb to the slaughter.

McCall had the T-shirt. It said, 'Been there. Done that.'

He also had the feeling that others would come for him or to recover Stefan. He had seen the cameras. So instead of moving, he waited. Hunkered down, put the Glock back into the holster on his belt.

They called him Mack for a reason.

The amateur boy they sent to do a man's job came around the corner, gun at full reach, just like he'd seen on the television. Fool.

McCall saw the gun before its owner, and that was all he needed to enable him to strike. He moved forward, grabbed the pistol, fingers around the breach and twisted it violently. The would-be killer's wrists snapped with a resounding crack. He was as good as useless now.

McCall led with the favoured knife in his left hand. The blade, which was always wickedly sharp, sliced through the man's neck, into his windpipe, then slit upwards and out. It took seconds.

One movement. One less pursuer. All as quiet as a barn owl hunting a terrified mouse in a darkened outbuilding.

The second man was close by, but did not hear a thing. In the time he needed to cover the distance between two of the main piers, McCall was ready once more.

"Come to papa."

In a dry, secure and warm office the Home Secretary dictated a letter. She was on the second paragraph when her desk phone rang. She held a hand up to the executive assistant.

"Hello."

"Madame Home Secretary. We do not know each other. But please, do not hang up. I am helping your people – at Orion. My name, for the benefit of this conversation, is Romulus. Can we speak?"

The voice was laced with a Russian accent. Perhaps further south. She couldn't quite pick it.

"We can." She was tactfully hesitant, but enough for Valentin to notice the change.

Lane waved to her EA. Then mouthed 'Record this!'

He continued. "Good. Thank you. Jack has been meeting me, he has been tasking me with work. Jack and I understand each other."

"OK, and how does this affect me?"

"Jack asked me to...look at one of your colleagues. Let us call him Judas."

Lane's shoulders rolled forwards. She sighed.

"Yes?"

"For the benefit of this conversation, he is called Sancus."

"Lots of Greek gods, I see."

"Roman. He was God of Trust. But that does not matter. You to stop doing what you are doing and read the email in your inbox. No need to contact me. Jack can do that. I owed your people a debt of gratitude. You keep your side of the bargain and finish off the people that have destroyed my country's reputation."

"OK, I will read the email but I cannot promise..." She paused. He had gone.

"Bastard hung up on me, Thomas!"

"Perhaps read the email Ma'am?" Succinct, edged with candour.

She did. And in seconds she was marching along a corridor, cell phone in hand.

"Prime Minister, we need to meet. Now."

"He's *what?*" James Cole was incredulous. "I can't stand the bloody man Sassy, you know that, but he's damned good at his job." He paced, matching the awful pattern on his red and yellow carpet. "No, I refuse to believe this. Get him here. Now."

"I tried, Jim. He's gone off the radar. Blake, too. And meanwhile the storm is causing havoc."

"Thank God for the barrier."

The river was rising fast; the surge was powering along the estuary, towards the city. All that stood between it and physical and financial chaos was the series of gates and a large helping of providence.

All the gates were closed.

The Port of London Authority was monitoring the flow and demanding to know why the barrier team was not answering their calls.

"Get someone down there." He slipped his coat on.

"Sir, something has been bothering me."

"Go on, but make it quick." Zipped it up.

"The radio operator at the barrier said 'thank you PAL.'"

"And?" Paused.

"He speaks to us every day, sir. He never gets it wrong."

"So what exactly are you saying?" Impatient.

"I think it was a distress signal. Something's very wrong down there. They have activated the system under urgency. The gates are in place, in fifteen minutes. It's unheard of."

"And so is this bloody storm."

"You are missing the point, boss. I think there is more to this."

"Then so do I, lad. Ring the police. I'm on my way."

Alex and Constantin were where they needed to be. They opened the solid door and stepped out into the freezing winter air. It took their breath away. The sheer scale of the barrier added to the moment. Above them a huge silver hood, watching over the river, supported by twin yellow hydraulic arms, leviathans, both there in case its twin failed. Electronic back-up systems were in place. Fail-safe.

They could hear the flooded river pounding against the gates. The noise surprised them both. In normal operations, the team would allow some of the flood to pass underneath the gates, reducing the impact. But the speed at which it was deployed had sent a rebound wave, back along the river, finishing off what damage had already been caused.

"Come on, this way." Constantin was now leading. They reached the spot. "In there."

"What? Why? You know I hate small spaces. Why there?" At last, something he feared.

"And I hate them too. More than you. But it seemed like the logical place to hide them."

"Logical? Logical is a bank vault and look how much time we wasted trying to get into that place! I forgave you

Constantin, but this is worse. Do you actually know they are still in there? Look at it. It is like a washing machine in there. If you have let me down..." He gestured to the entrance.

"Alex, I can't go in there. I will panic and die. You know what prison did to me."

"Fine. Then you are not the man I thought you were. Did I not spend time in prison, alone, strapped to a bed, lying in my own shit for days? Here, hold this." He handed the iPhone to his uncle. "We will talk about this later. Do not drop that."

He climbed into the void, through the steel railings. The sheer scale of the thing was breath-taking. The river water stank, poured out from the cavernous inner element of the gate, litre after litre. He was soaked in seconds. Inside, partially submerged, it was dark, on a winter's day when daylight was already scarce.

He waded through the receding waters, then yelled, "Where? Where is it?"

"Inside. That is all they told me. Tied to the gate. It's there, yes?"

"I need light. It's so dark in here."

"I only have the phone."

Alex's knuckles whitened. He needed to deal with Constantin, but that would wait. "Then pass it to me. Now!"

Constantin turned on the small yet powerful light, then reached into the cavern.

Alex waved the phone, looking for the case. He slipped, steadied himself, then searched again.

"Where is it?" he was beginning to panic. The Jackdaw was to use one of Roberts' favourite sayings, suddenly on a level playing field with everyone else in the City of London.

He reached out, trying to cover ground quickly. The gate

was immense. He felt like a Lilliputian, insignificant and suddenly very vulnerable.

Then he dropped the phone.

The silver Jaguar came to a halt. Across the river, south of the city. The wiper blades quietly swept the rain from the tinted windscreen, affording Halford a clear view. Better to be south of the action, away from the chaos and subsequent inquiry.

'Me, Prime Minister? I was visiting a police station, to see how the troops were holding up in the storm...when all hell broke loose...'

Keep your friends close.

"Great view. We are watching history today. When I give the signal, you need to head south, get away from the city, we won't have long."

He ran his hand across what for him was the Holy Grail. And he smiled. He had allowed himself to be corrupted. And that came at a cost.

Constantin shouted into the gate. "Are you OK?"

The noise was increasing around them. A roar. Sheer power and none of it manmade.

"No, I am not. I have dropped the damned phone. I need to find it. Get in here and help me or I will drown you with my own hands."

Constantin cautiously climbed through the grid and into the half-light.

"Alex. I need to tell you something."

· · ·

Halford needed to time his next move to perfection. He knew he had control. Getting it right meant he could put his feet up, retirement by the poolside on the French Riviera and entertain women and drink the finest champagne and enjoy the feeling of being untouchable.

He made the call.

The water had risen faster than in history. Calls from concerned locals had now reached the emergency services. Boat owners, apartment dwellers, they had all seen the surge, and many assumed the authorities would respond as they always did. Those with a view watched the barrier gates appear out of the river in record time. It was OK. No need to call after all.

Those that had called were assured by the call takers that everything was fine. But in truth, they hadn't got a clue.

CHAPTER 62

"WE NEED TO ALERT EVERYONE, SASSY. IF THOSE WATERS breach the barrier the city will come to a halt. The cost will be catastrophic."

"We can't. We'll lose more than that if we announce what we have known for weeks, Christ, we've technically known for longer. And to add insult to injury, if we release that we knew about the documents and their potential impact, then the party will go under with the city. I predict a riot at best. God only knows what the opposition will make of it."

"Bugger the party Sassy, bugger the bloody opposition too, think of the people. Christ, this is a bloody disaster. Get the key staff to Whitehall now, I want COBRA up and running in ten. No excuses."

The look said it all. Friend or no friend, Cole was a man on the back foot after years at the helm.

Politics was a cruel mistress at times.

The junior staffer at the newspaper took the call.

His screen showed Number Withheld.

"Listen, do not interrupt. You took a call earlier. Now I am going to add to it. This will sell more papers than you can print. Go live with this at two o'clock today. Not a minute before." The caller outlined what he wanted them to print. It was damning. It was unbelievable. It was sensational. And, if it was real, then the reality was worse than anything they could have dreamt up.

The caller hung up, removed the SIM card and dropped the phone into the river. He walked back to the car.

"It's done."

Cade and his two team members arrived at the barrier.

"Jesus, this is bigger than I realised. How are we going to search it?"

"We've got people inside already, Jack." Francis looked sheepish.

"OK, then that's fine. Who?"

"McCall and Stefanescu."

"Great, a soldier of fortune and a reformed bloody criminal. Any good news?"

"The boss is on the way here too – he's with JD."

"Right, so we all just sit here with our fingers up our arses and wait, do we?"

"We could do what she's doing, Jack." Francis pointed across the car park to where he could see Elena and a guilty-looking detective trying to climb the perimeter fence.

Cade smiled, shuddered as the cold wind wrapped itself around him like winter ivy. "Trust me, if she thinks there is a way in, then there is. Come on. She'll find her own way. She can handle herself."

A split second mental picture of her diving off the *Black Marlin* into the clear turquoise waters of the Pacific flashed through his mind. He'd give anything to be back there. With her.

The three ran across the car park and were met by a ruddy-faced Yorkshireman who was weeks from retirement. He had a PLA yellow jacket on and a look that said 'not today.'

"Who the hell are you? State your business here or I'll call the police."

"We *are* the bloody police. Let us into the building or things are going to get really messy." O'Shea was holding up her ID and a look that more than matched the man from Leeds.

"Messy? A bit bloody late for messy! 'Ave you seen the amount of water that's 'itting them gates lass? We need to think about reducing the impact. Someone 'as to get into the Ops Room and reduce the pressure. There's hundreds of thousands of tons of river 'itting that system and it won't survive long. I'll come with you. God only knows where the staff are."

"If our theory is correct, then they are being held."

"Fuck me backwards, that's all I need today. Terrorists?"

"Can't say. And if you do, you can watch your pension wash away with those flood waters."

"So it's terrorists then? Just bloody marvellous."

"Not as you would know them, no. Now move before I shoot you."

They got to the Ops Room without incident. Cade took one look and bore an expression that said 'I told you so.'

The team were released from their shackles, a few gave first aid to their colleagues whilst a groggy Andrew Darkin tried to offer advice. He spoke quickly and mainly to the

Yorkshireman, as he knew him and knew he'd understand the dilemma.

"They've done something to the controls. Not physical, a software add-on, I don't know, but I know we can't override. There were four of them. The leader had jet black hair, laughed like a..."

"Jackdaw?"

"Yeah, just like that. Who is he? I'd love to meet him in a dark alley."

"You and me both. He's a man who I have come to hate Mr Darkin. Look, can we raise and lower the gates any other way?"

"Yes, manually, but it's a tough job, especially in these conditions. But why do you want to lower them?"

"I don't but there is someone who might."

"That's madness. Suicide. The city..."

"Will drown. Get me to the place where I need to be."

"You don't understand, we need more people. There is a separate system to manually control each gate."

"Then we can only pray, my friend. Stay here. try to regain control."

Cade shook his hand and walked outside and looked along the building.

"Penny for them?"

"Carrie. This place is vast. He could be anywhere in here. With no CCTV and a lack of specially trained staff we are struggling. This needs to go public. I'm sick of the cloak of secrecy."

"You heard what the minister said. If we go public, there will be civil unrest, commotion, panic."

"And if we don't?"

"Answer D. All of the above."

. . .

Elena was over the fence. Having used her coat as a barrier against the razor wire she had dropped at least twice the height of her body, landed, rolled forward and was back up on her feet and moving quickly.

The detective stood on the legal side halfway up the fence, shaking his head. He rang Roberts.

"Guv, I'm not sure how to explain this, but Miss Elena has just scaled the security fence at the..."

"Thames Barrier. Yes, thanks, I can see for myself. Where was she going?"

"That's the weird bit, guv. She was rambling on about her old man."

"Her father?"

"Last time I looked, that's what it meant boss."

"And?"

"Said she needed to say something to him. Somehow she knows he's here." The young investigator hung up when he saw Roberts approaching him on foot.

"Do you know what she needed to say?"

"No, Sorry. But it was important. She said she could kill him. I took that as a casual, throwaway line. I say it about my missus all the time."

Roberts rubbed his eyes vigorously. He couldn't remember the last time he had actually slept. He could easily kill someone too.

And he could murder a cup of tea.

Cade was being escorted down into the corridor system. He flagged for the three people behind him to stop. The only noise they could hear was the constant straining of the tide against the building. It sounded like a hurricane, trying to suck the air out of the place, pushing, pounding, wilful.

"Where does this go?"

"Each pier is given a letter – A to K. Bigger than they look up top, aren't they?"

"Much. Where would you head – to cause the greatest damage?"

"The middle two, my friend. That's where the greatest pressure is."

"Come on, let's go. I'm right alongside you." He showed the Glock to the Nigerian immigrant who had learned to love his adopted city.

The very black man stopped in his tracks. He'd seen death before, but not for years and never in his place of work.

In a recess that housed myriad pipes and lights, a man was slumped against the wall. A pool of blood surrounded him, trailing back to where he had been killed. It was dark red, almost black, aging and no longer able to sustain life. He had at least three gunshot wounds.

Cade lowered himself down, lifted his head. He knew the face immediately. So did O'Shea.

"One down. All we need to know now is if he was a friend or a foe."

They moved on, passing two more bodies, both with their throats cut.

"Professional job Jack." Francis had seen plenty of bodies, and all in his place of work.

"Yep. And I suspect it is the work of a friend, not a foe."

The Nigerian shook his head. "I am not going any further. Over to you guys."

The newspaper headlines were set in place.

'STORM SURGE.'

'CITY UNDER SIEGE.'

But one journalist had a different headline ready to release.

'THE SECRET IS OUT.'

The demand finally arrived in the form of a sentence within a web page.

A COBRA analyst found it, tried to retrace the steps, but failed. The amount was ludicrous and the nature of the threat implausible.

'Transfer the money. Provide immunity to the following people.'

The analyst briefed those present.

Many of the names were lower-level criminals, but all had a common link. He continued to quote from the demand.

'Do this by fourteen hundred today.'

"High tide, sir. I can't think of any other reason."

'Do all of this without announcing a word to the outside world – or we will release the final part of the most damning media report in British history. It will make all other conspiracy theories appear feeble.'

"I'm not sure what that part means, sir."

So the secret wasn't entirely out.

'Failure to comply will see countless lives lost and the destruction of the reputation, economic stability and respect of the City of London.'

"This part is beyond question, sir."

Cole whispered to Lane. "Well? What are your bloody people doing to stop this?"

"Everything. Everything they can, sir. You have my word."

"And Halford?"

"As good as dead."

She stepped out of the room. Dialled a number.

"Do whatever it takes, DCI Roberts. You have my blessing and the backing of the government. I will personally brief your Commissioner that a higher-level security threat to the city is being dealt with, and that for now, that is all he needs to know. Either way, it won't go down well."

"Like a leaden fart, ma'am."

"I'm sure if I knew what you meant I'd laugh Mr Roberts. Now go and sort this out. Please. And if any of your team leak this to the press, I will re-open the Tower of London. No en-suite. No free paper. And absolutely no mini bar."

McGee was in place. She knew better than to let her heart rule her head. So wait it would be. She had all day. All night if necessary.

Hewett was close too. He had the rest of his life. What he knew kept him going, drove him. He had risked his own life once, twice actually and was most willing to try once more. Someone had once talked of a dish of revenge being best served cold. He liked his slightly warm; it tasted better that way.

He checked his watch. A new one, a Tudor Pelagos, another to add to the collection. Silver strap, black face, a dominant luminous 'snow flake' on the tip of the hour hand. Would be useful later, when the sun went down, which at this time of the year was soon.

He sat and watched the second hand sweep around the face. Lost himself for a minute. Wondered why he was sat, alongside the river waiting for a man he hardly knew to give him one opportunity to stamp him into the ground.

Another minute passed.

. . .

Cade moved forward. He wished O'Shea had stayed behind with the Nigerian. Nice and safe. But he also knew to ask her to do so was likely to be far more dangerous. Francis was an old hand at this game. His actions told Cade that something had clicked, that he had found himself once more.

Beneath the surface the noise was becoming unbearable, pounding water mixed with hydraulics, steel clashing against steel, unidentifiable hisses and deep bass sounds, echoes in some far-flung corner.

Cade imagined what it would be like to explore the place without light. He'd searched an old mental hospital as a junior police officer once. At first it was exciting, then, later, when the lights faded and finally went out, the place took on a different persona. Dark corridors, half-open doors, staircases. Old medical apparatus left in situ, waiting for an apparition to return to it. Scary shadows, arcane noises, voices.

This was different. This was the Industrial Giant versus Mother Nature.

He stopped. Dead. And so did his team. A door was opening ahead. They looked for cover; they were in No Man's Land. Cade held his pistol out, punched in front of him in a reactionary move. O'Shea had mirrored his every move, over his shoulder. Damn, it would get noisy if they started a gunfight.

Ahead, the barrel of a pistol appeared. Then arced, to the left. A hand followed. The body behind it spun, and the weapon was up and facing Cade. He called first.

"Armed Police. Put down your weapon. Do it now!" It was muscle memory.

"And if I don't?" A voice that displayed no fear at all. Foreign, with a double helping of sensual.

"Then you know what I will do."

"I think we all know you don't have the guts."

O'Shea interrupted. "Can we save the flirting till another time? Please."

Elena appeared. She looked cold, but as dynamic as ever. She lowered her weapon.

"So Cade, have you worked it out yet?"

"The meaning of life?"

"I have no idea what you are talking about. Have you worked out why Alex is here? Who he really is?"

"Well, I know he says he's your father. And I guess he's here because he wants to play the big scary international criminal who can do whatever he likes, piss the world off, then escape into the sunset without so much as a leaving party. Close?"

"Nowhere near close. But we don't have time. I need to find him. Will you help?"

"One team, one dream?"

"Again Cade, no idea what you are talking about." I think he is this way."

"Elena, two questions before we go."

"Shoot."

"Perhaps later. One, who do *you* think Alex is, really? And two, where is the nice young detective that was supposed to be looking after you?"

"OK, I answer. One I know who he is, I just need to talk to him one last time. Two, he was a boy. And as you know Jack, I only play with big boys." She tilted her head to one side and raised her eyebrows, in a move that instantly reminded Cade why he found her so attractive and pissed off O'Shea at the same time.

"Oh, please." O'Shea probably meant it to be heard.

"Carrie. He's yours. I was only a...summer plaything. Like a sand castle, beautiful, surrounded by seashells, then washed away on the next tide. I have the big fish to fry."

She turned, and soon a fast walk became a run. They reached the door to Pier K.

Roberts and Daniel were also making progress in another direction.

"This a good idea, John? We have so many specialists that are actually trained for this shit."

"Oh, come on, where's your sense of adventure?"

"JD, when was the actual last time you fired a weapon in anger?"

"1989."

"Exactly. And what was that all about?"

"I shot my partner. He was irritating me."

"After you, sir."

In the gate, strapped to a length of steel, Alex finally found what he was looking for. He held it aloft, up into the light as a new father might hold his son.

"I told you we would find it."

Constantin was the more relieved of the two men. They moved slowly towards the grey light that indicated their future.

"Is it all dry?"

"Uncle, they say these cases can float. Of course it is dry."

"Good. Do guns still fire if they are wet too, Alex?"

"Yes, of course, you could fire it under water if you wanted to. Why?"

"Because I feel we are not just going to walk out of here without a fight."

. . .

Across the Thames Halford adjusted his gaze, refocused, then watched again. His chosen observation point allowed a clear view of the pier and the men as they began their exit from the gate. He ran his finger over his phone, teasing the screen.

"Have you ever read a book, that takes ages to get going, then suddenly you find yourself there, at the end, shaking with adrenaline, hoping it doesn't end and wondering how you managed to read a hundred pages in ten minutes?"

"No boss, can't say I have. Do you recommend it?"

"No. But it reminds me of now. Talking of which you need to go. Fifteen minutes to go. Look after yourself out there."

The PPO walked a short distance to an anonymous saloon car, opened it with the key and drove off.

Alex and Constantin slipped, grabbed hold, waded and made their way to the opening. Alex held the Pelican as if their lives depended on it.

"What about the phone, Alex? We need the phone."

"Not now. Leave it. Now we have this, we wait five minutes, then we make our move. They will come soon."

He looked across the river, scanning the horizon. The sky was so dark the tower blocks had started to light up, one office after the other, street lamps followed and the safer drivers illuminated their headlights.

Only a few paces away, the main access door opened.

And there he was. The Bushman. Mack the knife. Call him what you will.

And he was in perfect range.

Alex pointed to him and hissed. "Shoot him!"

Constantin levelled the weapon and fired. Had he have

aimed, he would have hit the soldier. First mistake. He fired again, giving away their position. Second.

McCall fired back with relentless accuracy, on the move, five rounds straight at the gate. They heard it in the control room. They heard it in the corridors. They heard it across the river. They heard it over the roar of the river.

The bullets struck the huge metal structure, shattering and striking anything that got in their way. A piece of shrapnel hit Constantin in the hip, drove deeper into his muscles and tendons, detaching them from the bone. He let out a pitiful scream. Then dropped.

Alex dragged him to cover. He pointed his index finger at him, gained his attention.

"You will be OK. Keep shooting back, one shot every twenty seconds. Let me make a move. I will come back. I won't leave you here."

Constantin did as his nephew asked. McCall knew he was also pinned down. He heard a bang, quieter than a gunshot, but it was near.

Alex had thrown the case, out into the open and now it sat, waiting to be claimed. The single most important set of documents in living memory were now in a plastic case on a windswept deck next to an angry river.

The RIB appeared, skating across the flooded Thames. Black, with black superstructure, a cockpit, of sorts up front, the blisteringly white logo on the side. MP10, they called her. One of the Met Police's fast boats and used by its specialist units. Today it had one occupant.

It swung in a wide arc across the water, with no other river traffic it had a free reign. McCall heard it. Smiled to himself. 'The cavalry are here.'

Then he heard a noise behind him, purposeful, but friendly.

"Scott. Lower your weapon." Cade knew McCall was a threat if cornered or surprised.

"Boss. How's it going? Bit pinned down here, not used to working alone. By now my team would have ripped those bastards a new arsehole."

"Nicely put. You're the tactician, what do you suggest?"

"Can't smoke 'em out. No flashbangs. Plenty of bullets. They may have too. I've had a quick look. They are stuck in one of the gates, also pinned down. The Jackdaw is wanting to leave. He's got a case. And somewhere I can hear a RIB out on the water. We need to identify that. Should be one of yours?" He looked at the group.

"No idea. So we wait?" O'Shea didn't know the answer either.

While they planned their attack Alex was out, and running.

The RIB swung violently, the driver, dressed in a black one-piece was cutting across the wild water that churned and twisted, powering up and out of the base of the gates which had now been eased open, just enough to reduce the pressure.

The rain was hammering into his face, sideways, cutting through him, to the bone. He fought against the flow, powered into tempest, backed off, then waited, accelerated, then carried out the whole activity again.

He pointed to the river, making it clear that today, there was no other option. Alex waved wildly, the wind buffeting him, clawing at the case.

There was no way. He simply couldn't go into the water. Regardless of the weather, the flood, his reputation as a hardened and unpleasant criminal, Alex, the Jackdaw, could not swim. It may have explained his unrelenting fascination for drowning people.

He ran, back along the rails, back towards the gate, away

from where he needed to be. Like an indecisive and headless chicken.

He climbed back in as McCall fired again. He was safe. But for how long?

"Brother...my uncle...I need you to help me. I cannot go into that river. You can swim. You escaped from these people once before, remember?"

Constantin flashed back, beneath London, in an old river outlet not so far away, under water, unable to see, leaving behind that girl, tied to the fence, dead.

"And what must I do?"

"Get to the boat. He will take you away, to safety, they won't touch you. Take the case, give it to the man. This is bigger than both of us now. Go and don't look back. I will get away from here. You know I always do. A Jackdaw has more lives than a cat."

Seeing the RIB arrive on the water was the signal. The driver was struggling to get to them, not even close.

He nodded, exhaled deeply, then hovered his finger over the iPhone, then hesitated. He tapped the same finger onto the dashboard of the luxury car, waved it across the screen, adjusting his Bailey Nelson art deco glasses onto his nose, clarifying everything.

Then he chose his favoured track, which announced itself with gusto via the Meridian sound system.

The tenor sang his heart out, sheltering him from the rain and the wind and everything that threatened to ruin his day.

Leather seats, walnut dashboard, deep pile carpets. He leant back in the driver's seat and closed his eyes.

Of thunder and of brimstone should they perish,
Anyone who would flee the glorious place,
When our land or our mother, with a sorrowful heart,
Will ask us to cross through swords and blazing fire.

He thought of the men and women who had spurned him, the people that had talked behind his back, mocked him, despised him, and the country that had discreetly adopted him and the one that he called home.

Could he really do it to them?

Absolutely.

He ran his finger across the phone, allowed the device to read his index print, piece by precious piece, until the whole pattern had formed. He had arches on his fingerprints, rare, only about five percent of the population had them. He held it for one more second as the signal left the phone, went to a server, was processed, then returned to its recipient in a microsecond.

Should he?

Absolutely.

Cade gathered everyone around him. "Right, the way I see it the fewer people we expose to danger the better. Scott, you in?"

He nodded, smiling.

"Right, that's that sorted then."

"Whoa, hang on here, what gives you the right to charge off into the night like Butch and Sunset?"

"It's dance ma'am." McCall gave her his best smile,

tanned, five o'clock shadow, piercing eyes and a look of complete control. His clipped southern hemisphere accent was evident. "Look, the boss here makes total sense, reduce the odds. If we get taken out then by all means, you can follow us. I don't see the boys in the black pyjamas zip-lining down from helicopters. Do you?"

"And what about me?" Elena was defiant. "I have not come all this way to watch. I am here for a reason." She pushed herself forward, edging O'Shea out of the way.

"I have to take your place, Jack. I am trained. She is not. Look at your hands, they are ruined. You cannot shoot like that. I can."

He looked at both of his hands. She was right; they were ripped to shreds, still bleeding and way beyond being able to control a weapon, let alone fire it.

"I am the best for this. Not you. And not you." She looked at O'Shea pointedly, "I am not being bad Carrie, I know how to look after myself. You don't."

"Look lady, if you want to get killed that's fine by me. You saved my skin once and I am grateful, but I can't save yours, I am not skilled like you. But I do know how to work things out. And from where I sit, there's only one solution here."

"And what is that, Carrie?" Petrova was looking forward to her answer.

"Open the gates. Completely. The water is not as bad as they said it would be. Now is the time. We need to do it. Jack?"

"Carrie, it makes no sense. That river is like a torrent. If we get this wrong London will be inundated. No, we can't take that risk on behalf of a million people."

Francis was listening. He'd walked up to the next pier and back.

"Guys, I hate to say this, but I think someone has already made the decision."

Constantin ran for his life, the case under his arm. Blood flowed from the wound and he knew he needed some form of intervention – soon. Alex had told him what to do, to the second.

'I will escape. I will escape.' He said it to himself over and over. He reached the point where the RIB tucked into the pier. He threw the case, which floated in the wind, then dropped, hitting the boat before falling into the river. It floated, it could wait.

Constantin leapt into the water, hitting the surface, then disappearing beneath. He saw his mother. Holding him down once more. No, not again. He pushed, ripped her hands from his arms, twisted and turned, fought against the tide, against his own lungs that screamed for air. Then he emerged, panicked, drawing air and water into his mouth, swam, dipped beneath the surface, swam again, drifted, losing his battle.

The RIB driver was alongside him, a strong hand dropped down to him. "Come on, we need to go."

He hauled the older man onto the side where he was able to grab at a black rope, then went back to the controls and accelerated, dragging the Romanian along in the bitterly cold water, leaving him to climb in.

Was it all really worth it? He wished he had died in a heroin-fuelled haze under that whore in Germany all those years ago.

"What about Alex?" He yelled into the squall.

The driver shouted back. "You are not Alex?"

"No. He's back there. We need to go back."

The driver spotted the Pelican case drifting into an eddy

where it span like a fairground ride. He needed to get that before he did anything else. He made the decision – it was the case or nothing.

Turning the boat against the flow, he let it drift, bounding on waves that rarely formed on the inland waterway. "Grab it when I say!"

"I need to get in the boat, slow down, I will die in here."

"Grab the bloody case first."

"No. get me in."

"Nu-mi spune ce să fac!"

He understood the language immediately. 'Do not tell me what to do!'

Who was this man, this British police officer that spoke his language? It wasn't the river that made him shudder. And he now felt colder than he ever had when thrown into a wintery cell in his homeland, or made to stand outside in the rain by his mother, or here in the city of London, hiding in the shadows.

The driver grabbed at the Pelican but it jinked and moved and rode the wave. The RIB was bigger than it looked. He shouted again.

"Get the case! Last chance."

He turned, then powered forward, Constantin reached as far as he could, felt the handle on his numb fingertips and started dragging it through the water. They were fighting the tug of the tide and the cacophony of the flood water that battered them, and the dark that had descended upon the water. But he had the case.

"It's dark, Elena. We go on my signal. OK?" McCall was in charge. Paying his debt for the last time.

"I don't like your plan." She wanted to run the show. Cade shook his head.

McCall ran his tongue over his teeth, then spoke. "I'm sorry, miss. Truly." He began to walk towards the door.

She stopped him. Put an arm across his path.

"Wait!"

He gave her a searching look.

"It's you, isn't it?"

"I have no idea what you mean, miss. Now, if you don't mind..."

"It's you. Jack, it's him. The man who got into the Porsche with me. This is him. This is him. The voice..." She was almost crying, her voice packed full of emotion.

On that bend, lying on her side, her life ebbing – and then he came from the sky, administered drugs, spoke to her, held her just long enough. A guardian. That voice, she would know it anywhere.

"Yes, miss, it was me. Now, please, can we go and do what we came to do?"

"OK. But we meet later, yes?"

Hewett was getting bored. This was not how he worked. He left his car, shuffled a few paces, pulled his coat up around his ears and tucked into a doorway. He could hear the music from half a street away.

McGee could hear it too. It sounded like opera, or an anthem. She decided to let him enjoy the end of the track. She tucked back into the shadows.

Hewett knew she was there – and hoped she kept out of his way.

CHAPTER 63

ALEX HAD THREE ROUNDS LEFT. HE WAS COLD, SOAKED and alone. For him, it was just another night in Pazardzhik Prison. This is how he would survive. Using the memory of the place, the hellhole that was his living grave.

He strained his eyes to see. They had to be coming soon. And he needed to leave sooner.

And then the gate began to move. The enormous yellow arms hissed and sighed, pressure in, pressure out, gleaming stainless pistons releasing their grip. He was descending, it was subtle, but for the noise.

Down into the river. Down where he had condemned his wife to die.

Constantin would return for him. He was family. Blood was thicker than water, they said. His brother Stefan would be here soon too. He had played his part like a Shake-spearean actor, plausible to the end. Blood is thicker than water. Where were they?

The gate was dropping now and with it his chance of escape. He edged to the opening, looked through the bars. He could see down into the maelstrom, water everywhere, brown aerated froth was floating on the wind, blowing everywhere. He had never seen anything like it. He had to leave.

He started to climb up, pulling himself out of the steel coffin.

She ran towards him, McCall a second behind. The gate was dropping, slowly, but down it went. She slid across the concrete and grabbed the bars. Alex fell backwards and into the void. She followed.

Now they were both trapped. In a dark space, and about to be submerged. McCall was powerless to help. He turned and saw the others. Cade was walking towards him. "Now what?"

"You mentioned manual operations?"

"I did." Brilliant.

"Dave, Carrie, go and start winding that bloody thing back up."

"What do you want me to do?" McCall looked powerless.

"How accurate is that thing from this distance?" He pointed to the RIB.

"The RIB? Possible."

"No, the case."

"Impossible."

"Then the RIB it is."

McCall leant against the railings, created a strong platform and fired. The first round hit the RIB, drilled a hole through it. The second too, but nearer to the waterline. The third and fourth hit the driver. The boat was now uncontrolled and drifting.

"Shot, sir. Now go and help them wind those two back up again. And when they arrive, shoot him first. The girl is all yours. I think she has a thing for knights on white chargers."

Constantin was clinging to the side, frantically trying to

pull himself into the boat. An errant wave flipped the RIB and pushed the Romanian up and into the main part. He was in. He got to the controls, worked out which bits made it work, then quietly accelerated towards the south bank.

This was déjà vu. The boat drifted into the wall, he grabbed the case, favoured his side, felt the stickiness of the blood on his hip, then clambered up the iron ladder to dry land.

Roberts and Daniel had arrived there too. A triangle of Orion staff – waiting. Each had a different agenda.

"Wait for the moment, Jason. You'll know when it comes."

Constantin tried to adjust his vision. He was limping but heading in the right direction, carrying the case towards the car. Two flickers from the headlights told him he was on target. Nothing to lose. A hundred steps, that's all it was. He could hear the anthem. It stirred him. He picked up the pace, encouraging the blood to flow down his leg, mixing with the sodden material of his trousers and boots.

"Now!"

"Armed police. Put down your weapon. Get down on the ground. Do it! Do it now." McGee was pushing forward, emerging into the light, nimble, up on her toes, coming to a halt, leaning forward slightly, into the shot.

Constantin raised an arm but gripped the case firmly with his other hand.

"Don't shoot. I am unarmed!"

Halford felt for his own weapon. A weapon he shouldn't have. He waited for his own moment.

Roberts had also made the challenge. Steadfastly moving

into the light too. He looked across at McGee. "I'll take it from here, sergeant."

She kept her weapon up in the high ready position, glaring over the green dot straight at the hunched, bedraggled man.

"Bridie. Stand down."

Halford chose the moment. He stepped out of his car, leant across the windscreen and fired.

Hewett moved, reacted to the shot, and fired back. No one had seen him, and for him the chance to finish off Halford was far too valuable to waste. He missed.

Constantin ran towards the Jaguar. Hewett pulled the trigger again. The second round hit its target and hit Constantin who responded without theatrics. He just dropped to the ground. Alive.

He crawled with the case.

Hewett emerged. "Minister. Put your weapon down or you will be shot. I will not ask again."

Daniel looked at Roberts. Roberts looked at McGee. They all looked at Hewett. It took a second, a gaze that seemed to last a lifetime. A triangle of indecision.

Halford lowered his weapon. "I'm here on government business people. Lower your weapons. And I will not be asking you again, Hewett." As Mexican standoffs went it was served with extra habaneros.

He moved forward and bent to pick up the case.

Hewett raised his weapon.

"Touch that and I will kill you. Minister or not."

Halford stood up. "DCI Roberts, as the senior officer in charge, and as your police minister, I suggest you re-think your last statement and make the correct decision here." Halford managed to smile.

Roberts looked at Daniel, handed him his gun, then walked towards Constantin who was very much alive, bleeding heavily, but alive and still gripping onto the case as if his life depended upon it.

Roberts looked down at him, winked, then stamped on his forearm. Then again, and once more for no other reason than he felt like it. He heard the bone begin to break. The scream that the man they had once called The Chemist let out was satisfaction enough for Roberts.

"Karma can be a really nasty bitch when she wants to be, eh?"

He lowered himself to the road, pushed the case away and cuffed his prisoner. It only felt like days since he had first done it. That sense of achievement – at taking someone off the streets – depriving them of their liberty – it had never left him. Twisting the arm behind the older man's back and giving it an extra tug was probably pushing the limits a little. 'Be feral gentlemen.'

So he pulled it again. "That's for Cynthia." And again. "And that's for Steve Hall." Then as he watched the radius poke through the skin, he twisted it once more. The bone gave way. "And that...is a gift from me for the time we met on the tube." He let the pain signals fly around his body. "And I guess that makes us even."

He looked up at Hewett. Then McGee. Made another decision.

"DS McGee, you need to walk away – in fact come and grab this case will you. That's an order." He locked eyes with her, knew she wanted to kill Halford, for like him she had long sensed that he was a one-man pain in the arse that considered himself untouchable.

She reached him, placed the case at Daniel's feet and turned to walk away. She stopped, stepped half a pace to the right, then drove her foot into Constantin's groin. It was a snap kick, fast and perfectly delivered. He screamed and buckled against the handcuffs, worsening the pain in his arm.

"And that is for Nick Fisher!"

Roberts did his best to look the other way, then spoke.

"I know all I need to know about you, Mr Halford. You are Teflon, but one day your past will catch up with you. And as a career police officer, I am bound by the rules and regulations. So, you live to fight another day."

He then turned to look at Hewett.

"But you, sir, are not a police officer. You are not bound by the same rules as me. So, we are going now, some might say it's over to you."

If only he knew.

Roberts pulled Constantin up and onto his feet. He dragged them behind him like most belligerent prisoners do, but soon found momentum when the copper they affectionately called Ginger gave him a twist of encouragement.

McGee tucked in beside him clutching the case, her partner a pace to their right and Daniel brought up the rear. None of them looked back.

"Nice work, guv. And thanks." They got around the corner to Roberts' car when a single shot rang out, the sound of a bull whip, scattering birds into the air and across the river.

He nodded to John Daniel. "Our work here is done team. Nice one, Johnnie. We owe you a drink. Let's go home."

"What about Mr Cade?"

"Oh, Jack will be fine. He's as happy as pig in shit when he's drowning." He thought for a second. "Actually, do me a favour. Go and lodge this bastard at a secure unit. We need to go back to Jack and his group so he can lock up the Gypsy King himself. It's the least we can do."

"Mr Roberts..." It was a weak voice, accented, but strongly defiant and coughing up blood-laced phlegm.

"What? I would have thought you would have zipped that cakehole my son. It had better be important. No cameras around here..."

"You have the wrong man..." He laughed. "The person you are looking for is back there, around that corner...not at the barrier, the one true Gypsy King." He was tumbling on his words. Constantin smiled his own smile; fractured, bleeding and odorous. Then dropped his head and drifted into a blood-loss sleep.

Roberts looked at Daniel. "Make sense?"

"Absolutely. The problem now is, who is he talking about?"

"He means *Hewett*?" Roberts was as unsure as Daniel.

"No. He's far too close. He means Halford?" It seemed unlikely as the other suggestion.

"Our very own police minister, John? No way. We know too much about him."

"Do we? Really? I'm not so sure. He arrived on the scene late in the piece, a bright guy, right place, right time and all that. But a genuine arsehole that no one has a good word to say about. I'm just not sure."

"I guess we'll know in two." Roberts drove, covered a short distance, then spun the car around and headed back to the wharf. When they got back to where the incident had taken place they saw the sight they dreaded. He was lying face down in the concrete, a smear of blood along the pavement where he had tried to drag himself to safety. The Jaguar had gone.

"We should have stayed JD...should have stayed." Roberts punched the nearest wall.

"Now what?"

"Get rid of our prisoner and go hunting for a Minister?"

"Perhaps."

Roberts lifted the head with his shoe, it was wet with blood, across the face, darkening the hair. The entry wound was dark red, relatively small, the edges of the skin had lines emitting from the hole as if the skin had split under immense pressure. The blood stain was very evident, even under streetlamps, crimson against a light-coloured concrete backdrop.

He squatted beside the body, rolled it over, it gave up the fight and flopped onto its back, the face staring emptily at the sky. It looked like the last steak Roberts had prepared for the barbeque; cold, radiating blood and uncooked. He had been a vegetarian from that day onwards.

Then, among the raw and bloody exit wound, what was left of the left eye blinked. The body shuddered. Roberts encouraged it to speak.

"Go on, tell me." The head shook. The other eye opened partially, then the lips started to create words.

"All is not...how it seems, Jason. Get to the bottom of this. Keep your friends close and all that..." It was clear he had minutes, less. It was what the police called a dying declaration. This was the time when a constable would write the speech straight into his pocket notebook and pray that the person making it could sign below.

The man that looked up at him. He had a cold face, a defeated ivory-coloured carapace that simply said 'Tell my loved ones I asked about them.'

Another shudder. And more words. He was drawing the energy from somewhere.

"He did this to me. You never joined the dots did you?" He went quiet again. "Daniel...I apologise." He snorted, a sort of laugh forcing the wound to bleed again.

"Not everything is as I was led to believe. I was told you were the enemy. Trust everyone, trust no one. He told me not to trust you. I shouldn't have taken the law into my own hands that day down by the river. Should have got my people to do it. The thin blue line…The thin…blue…I shouldn't. I just…wanted to do the right thing."

Daniel leaned down, "Who? Who told you not to trust us?"

Constantin called out from the car.

"I told you. Didn't I? The wrong man." He started laughing, which took away some of his pain.

"Shut up!" Daniel was frustrated and angry. "Who? Why? I need to know,road, damn it."

Daniel stared at the face, then looked around him, focusing near and far, working something out in his head. They were missing important information. Daniel's phone began to vibrate just as the prone blond male let out a long sigh and gave up.

When Roberts looked back down onto the road the police minister was dead.

At the barrier, McCall and Francis were taking it in turns with O'Shea to wind the gate back up. Each time it appeared to make progress down, it would slide again. It felt as if the world was working against them.

Inside the gate, things had reached an impasse.

She wanted to kill him at first, then realised they may as well talk whilst they could. She had a lot to learn; he had a lot to tell. She pointed the handgun at him. The green dot was ever present. She knew where he was. One shot would do it.

"You wouldn't kill your own father? Surely?"

"Do you mean like you did? I know about the way you killed your parents. What sort of animal does that?"

"They deserved it. They had no respect for me. Especially her. It was going to happen one day."

"And you killed my mother – your wife. You murdered her in a vile way, deprived her of her dignity....because you could. But you had no reason to treat her this way..."

"I had every reason, girl! Every. Reason!"

"I do not believe you."

"Do you want me to tell you? Are you so brave that you could even begin to understand why I chose to carry out this vile act?"

"Yes. I am."

"Niko slept with so many men. She thought I didn't know. I think she even slept with my own brother."

"This is ridiculous. She would never have done that."

"All women are like this, my dear." His voice was echoing in the chamber, competing with the slushing water.

"But you are different, my beautiful Elena. You have always worshipped your father, held him in such high esteem. I know you better than you know yourself, my dear. If you carry out this act, it will be the end and you will be as guilty as I was. Sins of the father and all that!"

"The reason my mother ran away from you after trying to kill you, to get to London, to be safe."

"Yes, I know. To claim asylum from Bulgaria, but really from me!"

"You think that? Then you have no idea. She told me in a letter, when I was a little girl, she told me she loved my father."

Cade had lowered himself onto the walkway, against the noise of the river and the wind and machinery he could hear every other word. But it all made sense.

He looked back at the three people, all winding the mechanism by hand. They were exhausted.

He knew that Elena held the ace – or rather was

confined in the same space as the most solitary of playing cards. It was now or never. He called out.

"Elena. It's Jack."

Alex immediately moved forward a pace. "Don't listen to him, my girl."

She pointed the pistol at him. He could see enough to know not to move any closer. He had to time his move.

"What? Get us out of here."

"I'm trying, look there's something you need to know. It's really important. It's about your father."

"Talk. He's listening."

Cade shook his head.

"Remember when we first met? And I got you all wrong? That day at the *Oceanside*? Yes? You remember?"

She smiled, still watching Alex like a chess master studies his opponent. "Yes, I remember." How could she forget?

"Well, Elena, you have got it wrong with Alex. He is..."

Alex yelled. "No, Elena. This man is a liar. Do not listen to a word he tells you. I will save us from this place, not him, then we can start again. I should never have sent you away. It was for your own good. Your mother and I were bad for you. I wanted you to grow up strong – and look at you...you make me so proud."

The tennis match had begun in earnest.

"Elena." Cade was shouting now, fighting with nature to be heard. "Do you also remember I flew all the way to the island, in Australia?"

"Yes, how could I forget Jack? We fought like the cats and the dogs."

"And then?"

"And then..." If there had been light, she would have been blushing.

"And then I forgave you."

"Yes, yes, you did. And that night Michael Blake told me something about you, something he never finished." He drew in some more air, could feel himself starting to shake. If he got this wrong, then that would be it.

"OK, so what did he say?"

"You don't need to know El. Listen to me." The Jackdaw was also becoming anxious.

"No, I listen to Jack. It sounds interesting."

"El, Michael Blake told me that he was your real father."

"No!" The yell was loud enough to be heard across the city. It reverberated off the steel walls, the water enhancing it, making it a hundred times worse. "No!"

She fired one shot, straight at him. Then another. The lead alloy projectiles skipped around the gate, missing her and him. The noise was actually more damaging. Both now had a screaming, high-pitched whistle in their ears.

Cade yelled. "Yes, Elena. He *is* your father. Michael Blake. Your mother met him when he worked for the British government, a long time ago. They fell in love, just like you and I did, unexpectedly, against the odds. You could take a DNA test. Either way, you need to know that the man in there with you is not your father. Never was, and never could be. He is a sociopath, Elena. He tells people what they want to hear. He loves only one thing – himself. He is a clever man, but your mother was smarter."

"Jack, she does not need to hear this." For the first time, Alex Stefanescu had the tone of a reasonable man.

"Your mother held the keys to a few very important things. She was an expert in her field. She had the answers Elena. And the man that didn't want those answers to be known, well he ordered her death. And that man was the one they call the Gypsy King."

"And that is Alex. Jack, Alex is my father and the Gypsy

King." Her voice was laced with the accent of her motherland.

"No, you are wrong. Michael was your father. He showed me enough evidence that night in the Whitsundays to convince me – and the King of the Gypsies is a different man altogether."

"You said *was* my father." Her own anxiety was shifting upwards. If it was true.

"I watched him die, about an hour ago. They left us to drown El. It's what they do to people. Only one of us could get away. Your father made sure that was me."

"Jack. Stop this now. Please. El you have always been my girl. Ever since I first held you. I am bad, yes, but for you I would have done anything." He could almost make her out now in the dim light. She was relaxed, a little, holding the gun against her chest.

"Why did Blake let you live – if he was my father then surely you should have let him go, you have no family?"

"That's true. But the men that took your father from his home injected him with a chemical, into his leg. He knew he was going to die a long and very painful death."

"Like I would have done if your mother had done her job properly!" Alex was shouting now, a new sense of energy washing over him. He was pacing, a leopard with his original spots.

"Ignore him, Elena. Listen to me. Alex, I'll make a deal with you. Swap Elena for me. You love her, you hate me."

McCall was listening. This wasn't going to plan.

"Jack, you can't do that." He yelled across the walkway.

Elena heard the voice. That bloody voice, scented, smooth, like a bowl of melted bitter dark chocolate.

Alex thought for a second, suspended over the Thames, his life and hers in the balance, literally. He did love her, that was true, he wasn't her father, that was also true. And he did hate Cade, with a passion.

"OK, I let her go."

"But *I* have the gun, *I* am in charge," said an indignant Petrova.

"Yes, Elena, you are. So why not order Cade into the gate and you come up here with us and run the operation? There's a city that needs some help..." McCall draped his voice around her heart.

She appeared resigned to the suggestion. "OK." She looked at Alex. "But you and I have some things to discuss still. Get me out of here."

Cade joined the other three and took it in turns to wind the over-sized wheel to raise the gate. Water powered through the gap, rushing headlong into the city. Further upstream the lions held their breath, kept their lips sealed and watched out over the river, waiting. It wasn't over yet.

The gate slowly moved upwards, revealing the entrance. The bars were still allowing water to escape. Cade ran towards the capsule with O'Shea, leaving McCall and Francis to lock off the gate. It was halfway between safe and hazardous.

Cade nodded to O'Shea. She held the gun firmly, pointed at the entrance. "If he moves, I shoot him. Correct?"

"One hundred per cent. Twice if you need to."

Elena moved to the side and started climbing. Alex knew he had only one opportunity left. He rushed forward and grabbed her legs and started to pull her back into the gate. She grabbed one of the entrance bars and Cade's hand, as she did so dropping the weapon onto the floor of the gate. Cade leant into the void. Up close and personal.

He grabbed hold of her arms, and the tug of war began. There was no fun involved, this was a fight for her life.

The Yorkshireman was in the entrance doorway,

screaming from the base of his lungs. He had cupped his hands to emphasise his words, not that it made much difference.

"The hydraulics are failing!" He waved his arms frantically, blissfully unaware of the presence of at least three firearms and a caged tiger.

"You need to get out – get away – please. There's too much water. Move!" His gruff voice was lost into the howling gale.

The gate started to drop once more. Gravity was the winner of the human versus machine battle.

"Jack – let go, it's going to drop. We need to move!" Francis was urging his old friend to release her.

She stared back at him – genuine fear illuminated her eyes. She shook her head, gripping Cade's hand, daring herself to let go of the bar. He pulled, she gave in and at the point where Alex had also relented, she suddenly moved forward, leaving Cade to fall into the gate.

Roles. Reversed.

Cade was dancing now, part animal, part lightweight boxer, left and right, finding his footing. And still the capsule edged downwards, faster now.

"Jack!" Petrova had one chance. He turned to look at her.

Looking into his eyes she hissed the words, "Hit him like I hit you!"

It was all he needed. He threw a punch, Alex ducked, another followed, wild, deliberate. Alex countered with a swift blow to Cade's chin, then moved forward to get him in a neck hold – one of his favoured prison tactics. As he took the last step Cade moved to his left, swung his right arm around and drove a flattened fist up and under Alex's ribcage.

The blow was enormous, driven by anger and a desperate

will to live. The damage was instant and although he didn't know it the Jackdaw was already bleeding internally. The same process that Cade would have gone through if the Bulgarian he called El had hit him as hard as she had been trained to.

Cade was moving quickly too, out of the capsule that meant certain death, he pushed himself up on his hands, was grabbed by McCall and Francis, leaving O'Shea to point the weapon into the dark hole that had threatened to consume both men.

He was three quarters of the way out when Alex made his last attempt to drown them both. Lunging towards the exit, he caught Cade by the lower legs and pulled with all of his strength. Cade's fingers were raw, pouring with blood once more. Death because of a thousand cuts.

Alex had him in a vice-like hold. Didn't this man ever give in?

O'Shea screamed at him. "Move out of the way!" She had the means and the motive, all she needed to complete the set was the opportunity.

"Jack, move!"

Cade couldn't speak, he was exhausted. Alex had him pinned. His dark, anthracite eyes focused on Cade. Malevolence personified.

The Englishman grappled, tried to kick him away, but he refused to let go. Cade dropped back into the gate, his hand landing on the top of his right thigh. His fingers brushed against something. He pushed his fingers into the small pouch within the pocket and felt the short stainless steel barrel of a pen. He pulled it out, made a fist with it and spun one hundred and eighty degrees, swinging his arm in an arc towards the Jackdaw's head. The pen drove deep into his temple.

The blow was severe, not enough to kill him but more

than enough to cause bleeding beneath his skull. Soon his right eye would swell, causing the pupil, already naturally black, to blow, swell up and provide a cast-iron symptom for even a first-year medical student to identify.

Cade was running through the water now and springing up and into the entrance. He stopped.

Petrova and O'Shea were shouting at him to leave. The wind was hurling along the Thames like the tempest that it was. Beneath him water poured through the opening and fought with itself as it spun and rose. There were waves on the river, big enough to cause small boats to thrash against their moorings.

Despite the screams of protest Cade went back, leant down towards Alex and pulled the pen from his temple.

"That was a gift from a friend."

He turned and in four paces had jumped up and was pulling himself up onto the walkway when Alex ran again, trying to do the same thing, trying to save his own life.

His hands clamped onto the cold concrete and he gripped and pulled, then pushed himself upwards, looking at O'Shea who had never taken her eyes off him. She pointed the gun at his head and started to press the trigger. 'The best shot comes when you least expect it Carrie.'

She squeezed some more. Closed her eyes, then fired. The gate dropped.

The hydraulics had failed, tonnes of steel crashed down and into the river, submerging it, aligning it with the river bed, forcing water up to the already turbulent surface. It wasn't a slow-motion action, rather a rapid, deafening event.

This was not supposed to happen, ever. Engineers had built in safety measures, overrides, call them what you will. It was not supposed to happen. But then the sheer weight of water hitting the gate was never predicted either.

But it did happen. And Alex Stefanescu, the man the

people spoke of in whispered tones, in quiet corners of smoke-filled bars and bland offices and even government buildings, but above all, the putrid prisons that he had practically run, the man they called the Jackdaw was gone.

Cade was regaining his breath. His hands still bled. Francis was wrapping something around them, trying to keep them from becoming more damaged. McCall was holding Elena, restraining her and sharing his own warmth at the same time and O'Shea remained where she was, staring at the ground.

"Shit, Carrie, that was close. You OK?" Cade was getting himself up, onto one knee, taking a second, then standing. He walked over to her. Then he saw what had transfixed her.

On the concrete walkway, adjacent to where the gate had once been was a pair of severed hands. Each had been sliced cleanly just above the wrist. They made for a surreal sight. Just there. As if they had been placed there by a modern day artist. Two hands, on the floor, almost waiting to do something. Either tap impatiently or walk away like a prop from a horror movie.

To O'Shea, they were still alive.

She started to retch, then walked to the edge and threw up into the river. She had seen some things in her time, but this was a whole new low.

"Get me a bag, Dave." Cade called across to the one-time alcoholic soldier.

"You going to puke as well, Jack?"

"No. I've seen worse. Actually no, photograph them first, then get me a bag."

. . .

In the gate, beneath them, Alex was still alive, pushing himself up and into the air-filled void. He was treading water, trying to find a way out, the river still rising rapidly.

It wasn't a slow death – like the one that killed his wife, Nikolina. Hers was one that she saw coming, watched the tide arriving, had time to think about, heard the water lapping against her ears, could taste the fuel and filth through the tiny hole in the silver tape that they had wrapped around her mouth. Her heart was the last thing to go cold that morning.

Alex knew he was critically injured. He started screaming and shouting. Up on the walkway they heard him.

"That man needs rescuing, for God's sake!" The Yorkshireman, face ruddier than ever, was trying to make sense of the commotion.

"How long would it take to get that gate up?" Cade asked, trying to stay warm, favouring his hands.

"In an emergency like this and for a good man like you, an hour, tops."

"Could he survive, with a pocket of air?"

"He could. If he was a good bugger."

"What if he wasn't? If he'd killed three of my team...and really pissed off your mates in the control room?"

The red-faced manager rubbed his chin in thought. "Well, in that case, it could take days..."

"OK, well, you tried." Cade took a polythene bag from Francis and knelt down to pick up the severed hands.

She was right; they did look alive. If they had grabbed hold of him or formed an offensive hand gesture, it wouldn't have surprised him at all. The left hand still had Stefanescu's favoured wrist watch strapped to it, the sweep second hand quietly minding its own business and telling the time.

The right was a little more untidy, still oozing blood and almost in the shape of a fist. As he turned the bag over he saw it, the deep black tattoo, which came to life in a prison cell, created by mixing whatever they could find, as long as it was black, pushed under his skin and forming the image of a wave. As the hand grew paler, the mark got darker.

The bastard was still trying to be the Alpha male.

Cade was brought back into the here, and now by a phone, pushed towards him by O'Shea. "It's the governor." As nauseous as she looked, it was evident she was enjoying being back in the field.

"Jason. How are you?" His voice was hollow.

"I'm chipper, my old mate. You?" Adrenaline-fuelled.

"Keeping my hand in. You all OK over there on the southside?"

"Well, I've had quieter days. I've got a SOCO on the way and a couple of the team to try to seal off the area. It's like the Wild West over here."

"Can't be any worse than here, mate. I've got three..." He looked up to see O'Shea holding up another finger. "I've got four bodies over here."

Roberts asked the obvious question.

"Stefan and two of what turned out to be his team. All came to an abrupt end at the hands of our overseas team member."

"I knew it. I said that goggle-eyed bastard wasn't to be trusted. Didn't I Jack? Eh?"

"Yes, you did. And you were right. It turns out blood is thicker."

"Three guesses about this side. Go on, have a go, you'll never get it."

"Can I phone a friend?"

"Who would you phone?"

"JD."

"Well, that's not fair he's stood right alongside me. Go

on, tell me who I've got lying on the ground here and who else is in the back of a car with a severely broken arm?"

"With any luck, Constantin is screaming in pain from a peculiar injury. But I'm stuck at that point. Enlighten me."

"Halford. He's been shot, Jack. Dead as the proverbial nail. Hewett was here too, and Bridie. Bridie didn't do it, as much as she might have wanted to. And Hewett left before we got back to the scene, it was all Agatha Christie until JD took a call."

"Who from?"

"Hewett."

"Nice, leaves the scene of the crime then rings in, all concerned, he's always been a great actor."

"A little less subtle, Jack. He said that he didn't kill Halford. Reckons another round hit him. The only person there was him, so it's a case of his word and all that. But he was adamant it was a high velocity round. Kind of explains the noise we heard. JD looked at the entry wound. I know you'll hate me for saying this, Jack, but the minister was hit from your side of the river."

"Sniper?"

"As good as. At least someone who could shoot in these conditions and make it count. Fuck me Jack, the police minister has been shot during our operation. The Home Secretary will have my balls for a bacon sandwich."

"Not sure about that, she hated him too, and from memory she's a vegan."

"Pescatarian. I don't think Sassy Lane is capable of firing one round, let alone one at a target hundreds of metres away in a Force Ten gale."

"I grant you that. But she could have ordered it. You believe Hewett?"

Roberts paused. "Yes, for some reason I do."

"Then we may never know. What's the river like over there?"

"Wet, brown, flowing upstream just the same as your river."

"Arsehole. It seems to be calming a little over here. It will subside once the tide turns again. We may have been lucky for once."

Roberts was distracted. His hearing had always been his finest sense.

"Jack. What's that infernal bloody racket in the background?"

"A million tonnes of water, a hurricane and a rather irate Yorkshireman?"

"No, that screaming sound? It's like a high-pitched bark."

"Oh, that'll be someone screaming Jason. Down in one of the gates, Gate Kilo to be precise."

"Anyone I know?"

"He calls himself the Jackdaw. Europe's most-wanted criminal. Nasty piece of work by all accounts. He's more like a cormorant at the moment, knee deep in river water and has no way of getting out. The ultimate caged animal."

"You know you actually should sound a little more concerned about him, don't you?"

"I should?"

"So other than a captive and very pissed off sea lion, is everyone else alright?"

"Yep, the whole team came through. Sorry, hang on a moment. He's gone quiet." Cade looked around, down at the water, which was beginning to calm. Then he looked at the people he considered colleagues and friends.

"I think he's gone, Jason. Put up a hell of a fight, though. I'd have preferred a one to one with him like they do in the films. Oh, Christ!"

"Jack? Jack?"

"What's happening?" Daniel asked, muscles tensing.

"No idea. Hang on. Jack!" He yelled down the phone.

"It's like that scene in *Love Actually* Jason. Elena's gone in. I'll ring you back."

By the time he had thrown the phone back at O'Shea she had disappeared beneath the surface. The river was hostile at the best of times, but in flood, in the dark and alone, it was lethal.

"What the actual bloody hell?" O'Shea had joined Francis and McCall at the safety barrier.

The Yorkshireman was dialling a number on his phone.

'Not today. I'm nearly bloody well retired! Not today. Do you hear me?'

McCall was ripping his trousers down and off, his jacket too.

"No, Scott! No. You do not go in there."

"Jack. I don't take orders from you, and besides, I have to. I think this was the reason I came. OK." His look said please, his physical stance said 'Don't.'

"No, Scott, the reason you came was because you wanted to purge your soul. Stay here. I'll get the Met to send a boat."

"Jack, she'll be dead by then." It was O'Shea. "God alone knows why she's gone in, but Scott's right. At least let's get some life belts in there."

She threw one over the rail, only to watch it spin out of sight, into the dark. She threw another.

"Lady, will you just wait till you see someone before you hurl all my bloody life preservers over the side!" The Yorkshireman's day had just got worse.

"Jack, she hasn't come up yet." Francis had a torch, commandeered from the Yorkshireman. He was pointing it over the side, scanning the water. "Nothing."

"Then I'm going in. Give me that." McCall grabbed the

torch and the belt, tied it to his midriff and leapt over the side. It looked like another day at the office for the Kiwi.

It was a hell of a jump. He hit the surface hard, then dipped beneath and was gone.

She was at the entrance to the gate. Trying to open her eyes, clinging to the rails with all the strength she had left. It was freezing. The sheer cold was crushing her. Where was he? She hit the rails with her hand.

He could hear her. Banging on the rail. She was there. She had come back, he knew it was her. He reached out, automatically, but without hands he was useless. He had two choices. Leave the air pocket or take a chance. He couldn't even shoot himself. He had never felt so desperately alone. Pazardzhik seemed like the Hilton in comparison.

She was fighting now, losing air rapidly. Then she felt something. A limb, it was him. She grabbed it and started to pull. She opened her eyes, and he was in front of her, floating, his own black eyes staring back. He had a look of realisation, of panic. A haze of red surrounded him.

The tide was dragging them away from the gate, turning them around, disorientating them, draining every last ounce of oxygen from their lungs. She saw Cynthia, drifting by, helpless. Then she saw her mother. An angel in the water. Lighting the path.

For Elena, it was time to make a decision. Let go and save herself or try to save them both, father or not, she still had some questions for him. She tried to kick to the surface, but it was impossible, bubbles left her mouth, she could hear herself screaming. He was too. The Jackdaw was yelling something under the water. It was a blur, the noise of the water and her heartbeat and sheer blind terror.

She began to float upstream with the tide. Wave after

wave battered her. The Thames had never been so turbulent.

Then, from somewhere, she was snatched from the jaws of the final wave. A tanned male hand, strong from years of training, fighting and survival pulled her towards an equally strong torso. The faceless figure held her tightly, then kicked, and kicked and kicked, gaining a few inches with each stroke. She clung to the person as if her life was in resting in his hands. She was seconds away from life.

She was back, on the empty road in New Zealand – Godzone the locals called it. She was back, in the car, on its roof, trapped, alone and dying. Watching the blood drip from its wound; drip, drip, drip, each droplet splattering in nine different directions. She watched each one.

She was watching the Fantail too, with its curious flight and inquisitive face. Hearing the cubes of safety glass popping on the highway, smelling the metallic tang of fresh blood.

The voice spoke to her again.

"It's OK, miss. Truly."

He surfaced first, then her, then the life belt which shot out of the water behind them. He drifted on the current, guiding her to the guardian angel that had arrived in the form of a simple white circle. She grabbed onto it, cleared the water from her eyes.

"You saved me again. You bloody crazy man. Crazy..."

"I'm sure you'll forgive me in the long run, miss."

"Elena, please," she said, shivering violently. She looked up at the barrier, it was vast, dwarfing them. But she was safe. She was with him and she was safe. She leant back against him as he reached for another life belt, thrown by O'Shea.

"Looks like they made it. I think she's finally found her true knight."

"I'm glad." Cade looked at her raised eyebrows and smiled.

"No really Carrie. It wouldn't have worked. She needs a younger man who can keep up with her endless advances."

"You sound envious."

"I've always got you."

"Oh, as chat up lines go, that's up there with the best of the ones I used to get at the Friday night youth club."

"It's a start. Take it or leave it." Cade shivered, it was minus two and a mist was forming on the water. His teeth hurt. "We really should get them some help."

"Dave has already put the call in. He's appeasing the guy from Yorkshire. Apologising for breaking his toys."

"Why do you think she went in? I told her Blake was her real father."

"Sometimes Jack you just don't understand women do you?"

"Next you'll be quoting Mars and Venus."

"Next I'll be giving you a bloody slap. Come on, let's do what we need to do. The place will be crawling with uniforms in no time. I've had enough for one day."

Earlier, the man on the rooftop, across the water, lay prone in the cold night air. He had carried out his instructions, to the letter. The whole operation had taken days to plan. It was his turn to cleanse his soul, he asked for nothing from his client and expected nothing in return.

This was a contract sealed with one man's word to another. No meeting, no follow up, no chain of evidence. Nothing recorded and less written down.

His eye met the black cup on the powerful scope. It didn't steam up, his body was as cold as the weapon. A night shot, in conditions that were far from ideal he saw it as a challenge and an even greater opportunity. He came from the same stock as the man he now focused on. The difference was he had left the clan and joined the enemy – in his case the government. He'd risen through the ranks and had become an outstanding Intelligence Officer and one who had skills to burn.

He had come to hate the government though when they turned upon him and sought to destroy him. And so he became nomadic, a mercenary who sought out opportunities to strike back at governments. He had connections aplenty. The problem was his connections were a web and latterly he had become the fly stuck in the middle.

'This one job will clear you of all of your debts. To this country and your own. You will never have to look over your shoulder again.'

It was that one sentence that drove him to climb the stairs to the top of the building where he found the right platform for himself and his weapon – a suppressed Lobaev M2.

He had personally visited the factory, on Lenin Street, in the Russian town of Kaluzhskaya Oblast. They provided what he requested, and ensured complete discretion, naturally.

He had purchased the rounds, just ten, from another old friend behind what had been for so long a curtain of iron. They were handcrafted. He thought of them as a work of art. The Lapua open-tipped, boat tailed rounds were beautiful, smoother than satin, intricately machined and deadly. He loaded each one, taking time to ensure they were seated perfectly. The magazine was quietly locked into place and a round chambered. He was as quiet as a barn owl.

His gossamer leather glove stretched across his fingers then pressed down slightly onto the trigger, just enough to feel the tension, not enough to release it. He breathed, minimising the cold air that was trying to divulge his presence to another person who shared his art form.

He scanned the horizon, allowed his night vision to settle, then ran the scope across the barrier. Saw the group trying desperately to raise the gate. Focused upon the man kneeling on the floor, holding his hands in pain. He nodded gently. Jack Cade. He'd recognise him anywhere now.

Cade had become one of the few men he trusted. He allowed the scope to remain, the microscopic cross hairs sitting perfectly on his forehead. At eight-hundred-and-sixty metres a second. That was it. All it took for the boat tailed thing of beauty to leave the lightweight rifle, whip across the water, and end Cade's life. In the time it took him to blink. In the time it took him to think about blinking.

He scanned again, warmed up now. No risk of fogging up the glass. Five people, no six. One in the shadows, no, two. Six people, four visible, two in the shadows. One female, pretty, nice eyes, perfect skin, angry persona. She was an ally, too. He'd ignore her as she wasn't a threat and more importantly, wasn't his target.

The males were next. The shadowy one was harder to identify, but the fact that he was hidden meant he was an ally. The two suited men were police, no doubt about that. They bled their professions.

The crawling, fractured-smiled nomad on the concrete was Constantin.

'Look at you, you despicable little bastard. I should use one of these rounds as a practice. Finish off that bitter and twisted smile.'

He breathed again. Waited. Felt the wind buffeting him, watched in awe as nature took on the city. Watched the water pounding against the barrier. Waited. Exhaled. Fired.

He didn't need to make a call 'It is done.' He didn't need to do anything. They trusted his word.

He was moving before the target had dropped to the floor. He was supremely confident. The best rifle in the world had been matched with a highly capable operator. A match made in hell.

Cade heard it. Kneeling there with his hands wrapped against the cold. He swore he heard it. A low-pitched whistle, different to the gust that battered them. It was man-made, rapid, a one-off. He heard it.

When they had achieved what they had set out to do, he asked for a moment, a few minutes to just stand on the walkway and look out across the city. He reflected upon the events of the last few days, weeks and that one day on his past when the girl had entered his life. She had opened up her soul to him; he hadn't even asked. Trust was a two-way street. He made her a promise, then broke it. Promised to care for her. To take the information she had provided and do something positive with it. It had cost Nikolina her life.

Cade knew that the toughest operations came at a cost, financially and often in human terms too. He was, what his old sergeant had once called, eloquently a shit magnet. And he needed a break. Leaning against the railing, it would have been easy to tumble, to fall into the maelstrom and be at peace. But at what cost?

He shook the thoughts clear, took one last look at the city skyline and began to walk away. He stopped when he saw McCall's clothing. Bent down and picked it up. Wrapped the items into a ball and stuck them under his arm. If he hadn't been so attuned to his surroundings, he would have missed the sound.

Of glass onto concrete. Twice.

He looked at the concrete with its anonymous surface and plain colours and saw a sparkling shape smiling back up at him. He picked it up, then the one next to it. They had stopped inches away from the edge. He ran them around in the palm of his hand. Surely not?

He felt in the pocket of the trousers that McCall had discarded without a thought.

"Well, bugger me." Cade couldn't help but smile. "You clever boy."

CHAPTER 64

The Sanctuary, London

ROBERTS HAD INTENDED TO GATHER THE TEAM AT THEIR usual pub on the day that weather records were set to be broken. The day that the Met Office had predicted could be the worst in history. However, Mother Nature held something back in reserve and the lions managed to hold their breath for another day, their Verdigris coating covered only up the eyes.

The Metropolitan Police, London Fire Brigade and Port of London Authority control centres had been overloaded with calls. Try as they might the Op Orion team could not hold back the calls, for as much as they wanted the city and its people not to know it was far too obvious that Old Father Thames was having a dark day. The river was too important to be ignored by a city and its inhabitants, many of whom watched and prayed that the barrier would do its job.

It did, and valiantly. The water levels had never been

higher. Some localised flooding happened east of the barrier, a few boats were damaged, and insurance companies prepared for a deluge of their own.

The storm and the tidal surge had lived to fight another day – the great city of London too. The surge returned back out into the estuary and washed down stream, along the Kent coast, whipping up waves and eroding sand banks and snapping at jetties.

For many Orion staff the day extended and extended, some got home earlier the next day, some bunked down in the office, making a bed out of whatever they could find. It was typical with any police operation that just when you thought you were done, there was always another form to fill or a statement to obtain.

A man in a slate grey suit and a white shirt and screaming lime green tie with matching handkerchief stood outside his local pub. He held his cell phone to his ear, waving to a few of his team that had arrived late – miming that they needed to get a drink in and that's be five minutes.

"Yes, hello Capitan Grigorescu from the Special Intervention Brigade, please. Yes, I'll hold." He paced around the pavement, trying to stay warm whilst a subordinate officer hunted for his boss in the city of Craiova.

"Yes, hello."

"Capitan Grigorescu, it's DCI Jason Roberts, how are you?"

"Wondering why you are phoning me, Jason."

"Would it brighten your day if I said I had Constantin in custody?"

"Oh yes, it would. Tell me where and I will have my staff travel there and arrest him for our charges."

"Good to hear, don't be too kind with him. Secondly, I have another three bodies for you. Two are Alex's men, still trying to ID them as we speak. The other may come as a surprise."

"I am intrigued."

"It's Stefan Stefanescu."

"Oh, that is a great surprise. We thought he was on your side, Jason."

"So did we Capitan, so did we. Send your staff over and I'll have mine meet them at the airport."

The Op Orion team started to drift in to their favourite watering hole. A group of people as eclectic as they could possibly be. Career police officers, former police officers, those that had never quite hung up the handcuffs, the ex-soldier, sat quietly drinking his orange juice, a civilian, and a serving soldier who was destined for a kick up the backside and an off-the-record handshake from his boss twelve thousand miles away.

The soldier sat with the civilian, closer now than they had been allowed over the previous few days. Call it chemistry. Cade was fine with it. Genuinely. Whilst it was good it was great, but he knew he needed to let go of those summertime images and he couldn't think of a finer man to take his place. He would rather consider McCall a friend than an enemy.

She was a lot like her mother and very much like her father – the real one who created her in a wild night in Brussels when her mother was simply doing her job. Nikolina, Niko to her friends was a career Intelligence Officer, the best. Adaptable, gifted, smart and attractive. It was what the Eastern Bloc countries did so well, some even went as far to say they were the greatest export from the countries that had cowered behind the Iron Curtain.

Cade knew that if Niko had survived, the woman he sat next to would have never featured in his life. But she hadn't and O'Shea had. And that was the end of it.

O'Shea's was an insidious friendship, as ivy slowly emerges, climbs, then twists around its host so she had with Cade. They had been so close to making the relationship permanent. A few knew, that needed to know.

John Daniel was one of them. Retired, living a wonderful life on the other side of the world, running a restaurant and serving the best to tourists and locals alike. He had admired Cade from day one, had a few deviations along the way, once where Cade had questioned his true loyalties, however, it seemed that Daniel was a river that ran very deep. His loyalty was without question and in the covert world of that necessity to know he was as airtight as a fresh jar of strawberry jam and as with their seeds he stuck in a person's teeth long after the taste had passed.

He looked across at the man he had come to consider a younger brother, possibly even a son, and he smiled. Cade nodded back, smiled and took a sip of the Talisker *Dark Storm*. Roger, the east Londoner and landlord of The Sanctuary had bought it in especially, his treat he said, kindly.

Cade breathed in the dense air, the old girl hadn't been painted in years, its ceilings a dark shade of ochre and the carpets as sticky as warm tarmac. It wasn't a bad old place really, had even survived the Blitz – and importantly it was theirs. It was a tradition at the end of every operation to meet there and raise a glass, or two. To absent friends, and ex-colleagues, and the victims that had played their part. And to the Queen, naturally.

That left the man leaning on the time-polished wooden

bar top, its brass fittings soaked in overrun pints of local beer and a damp bar towel here and there.

He rubbed his elbow. It was wet and stank of beer. His wife wouldn't mind, she was good like that. And she knew he would always come home.

He had been a detective sergeant when he first met Cade. It seemed so long ago, and yet, at the same time, last week. He looked at him and held his gaze for a second, then nodded and commenced one of his world-famous speeches.

"Right, you bunch of muppets, listen in." They did, glasses were placed on splintered beer mats, potato crisps were left in their packets and all waited to hear the man they called, with affection, the governor.

"You know when this first all started, I was very unfair to blame ex-Inspector Cade for bringing some of the chaos from his world into ours. And I know, that with the benefit of time and hindsight that this was wrong." A few started clapping. Roberts raised his hand. "No, please. I was going to say, in actual fact he is entirely responsible for bringing chaos to our city!" A loud cheer erupted. A few beer mats were thrown, and Elena took the chance to run her hand discreetly across McCall's thigh.

"As I was saying...the last few months have been a mixture of hideous events and total teamwork, and I wouldn't want to work with anyone else. I know Mr Cade and Mr Daniel endorse this. You see, when the team that once called itself the Seventh Wave first rode into town Jack said they'd be a problem, but DCI Jason 'Ginger' Roberts, being a smartarse decided to ignore him."

A pin could have dropped.

"And I was wrong. When I first saw that young Romanian lad lying on the mortuary slab I knew we were dealing with something a little bit tastier than your average villain. And, if I'm honest, that excited me." He took a sip of his ginger wine.

"Ooh, that's nice, you savages should try it sometime." He swallowed it and allowed its heat to warm him through.

"Well, the day has come to stand you all down. We've lost some good people. Cynthia..." They raised a glass. "Steve Hall." Another. "And I never thought I'd say this, but I lost a brave soul too, a covert source of intelligence that I first met when her meat and two veg slipped gracefully onto my chin!" A louder cheer. "It's a long story folks, ask Jack, he's got the film rights. But that source, a woman we'll call Harrier, died a painful and needless death. Let's be under no illusion. These were nasty bastards of the highest order."

He turned to O'Shea, put his hand on her shoulder. "And when I first met this fine lady she had just finished stabbing a DCI with a pencil."

O'Shea stood up. "Hang on a moment, guv. I stabbed Clive Wood with a pencil, God rest his soul. I punched the DCI."

"May the record note the changes to the minutes, please?"

"Indeed, guv, unless you fancy a taste?"

"No Carrie, I don't. I'm happily married, which reminds me I need to Foxtrot Oscar soon. Before I go, I want to also acknowledge you for your outstanding support to the two teams you have worked on. You have literally risked your life, and that doesn't go unnoticed. The Commissioner wishes to catch up soon, he's got a little something for you. Now, moving on, I understand John is heading back to New Zealand in a few days, once he's knocked out a few statements and been to Aqua Scutum to buy a new raincoat. One only hopes it's not the type they wear down on the Embankment late at night...if you get my drift?" He taped the side of his nose with his index finger, then allowed Daniel to reply.

"I am. Jason. Team, it's been a bloody honour. Coming back out of retirement was exactly the right thing for me to do, an itch that needed scratching. The night that double-decker bus flipped south of the city and the morning that poor girl was found in the river..." He stopped and looked at Elena. "I'm so sorry, how insensitive."

"It's OK JD, I forgive you, just spend the rest of your life looking over your shoulder! Or give me a bed at your home in New Zealand. Yes?" She gave him her best raised eyebrow and flirtatious smile, which gained a cheer of approval and caused the senior man to blush.

Elena spoke.

"I have loved working with you Jack, thank you, for caring for my mother, she thought a lot of you I'm sure. You're everything she said you would be. I am very..." She searched for the word. "Grateful. Yes, that is word I am looking for."

She felt a tear of regret and willed it away. The times she had spent with Cade were wonderful and she too had to delete the memories of the past. With luck, she may have a future with the soldier and his pocket full of diamonds.

Cade stood, raised a glass. "To you all. I've been told by none other than the Home Secretary – who has paid for this round – that the Orion team has been so successful it's going to stay as a regular squad, the idea being that it deals with stuff the other units can't. Sounds like the sort of team I'd want to be on. But for now, I shall button up my overcoat, step outside and go and pack my case. I'm heading home to New Zealand soon, but first I'm heading to see my folks, then Spain, catch up with an old uncle who's got a few war stories to tell. Carrie...."

She looked, awkwardly at first, then relaxed. "Jack?"

"I'd like it very much if you would join me."

She stood, awkwardly at first, then straightened out her

back. She took a breath, felt her heartbeat rise, and then replied.

"Do you really think I would travel to another country with the man what has twice allowed me to nearly die?"

Cade knew he had one shot. Adopting a familiar big screen pirate voice he said, after a comedic pause. "Ah, but you didn't die, did you, my love...?"

She went to punch him, hard, on the top of his arm, he held up his hand and watched it splatter blood across the bar. "It seems I am also at great risk of dying if I hang around you much longer! So, what's it to be?"

She looked at Roberts who shrugged, Daniel followed suit.

"OK, but you are paying and if you step out of line just once."

"As if I would expect anything less."

"Watch Big Stan doesn't try to run away with her Jack. She is a very pretty lady." Elena meant every word. She had finally warmed up, borrowed clothes that she would never had chosen did their best to comfort her. McCall, too.

As Cade was leaving, he handed a heavy carrier bag to the soldier.

"Present for you, sergeant. I think you'll find it's all there. Spend it wisely. And look after her and above all enjoy the journey. But never, ever let her drive!" He held his hand out.

McCall stood, carefully shook Cade's hand and allowed his face to alter from craggy into a beam of natural light. Conker-coloured eyes, white teeth, rugged, yet with a heart of gold, a man who put family first and his colleagues a very close second. He had a feeling they would meet up again one day.

"Thank you, brother. Kia kaha. It means..."

"Stay strong. I know. You too."

He hugged Elena, held her just long enough. She whispered in his ear, "Thank you hairdresser car man. I love you. Always."

He laughed, didn't need to force it either. He let her go in more ways than one, gestured for Carrie to link her arm through his and walked out of the pub, onto the cold street where their breath filled the air around them with vapour. They felt alone in a city of millions.

"So, what's it to be Miss O'Shea? New Zealand, London or will you join me in Spain?"

"The gentleman giveth the lady too many options, it seems. How about Old Queen Street tonight then we go from there?"

"Sounds good to me. In fact, as options go it sounds like the best. Do you think your elderly neighbour will be watching from her bedroom?"

"She might be..."

"Well, in that case it would be a shame to disappoint her, after all we did just save her and her people from a fate worse than death."

"Did we, Jack? Really? Or was it just hard work and some sheer bloody luck?"

"Both. But I was always told the harder you work, the luckier you become. Come on, let's go and give Liz a show, shall we?"

"Jack, you are beyond naughty sometimes." O'Shea feigned an awkward smile.

"Says the girl who embarrassed her postman once!"

She was blushing now, and it wasn't the cold that made her cheeks rosy, it was the memory of that morning in the hallway of her apartment block.

New Zealand it was then, and as soon as possible, she was sick of the cold and in her mind she had already packed exactly what she wanted in her suitcase. Spain would be next.

"Jack. Just one question before we get to my place and set the world on fire."

"Go on."

"Me or her?"

"You really expect me to answer that?"

"I do. And I don't mind either way."

"You do. But for the record, you. Quality over quantity any day."

"Seriously Cade I will stab you whilst you sleep you know. Right in the pancreas."

"Crikey, that's very specific. Very painful too, I should imagine, but just think of the make-up sex!"

"You'd be wearing make-up, Jack? Kinky to the end..."

"You have no idea lady..."

She shook her head, smiling, linked her arm through his, dropped her head onto his shoulder and let the frigid city air extract her fears and nightmares. She loved the capital, adored its history and the people, and best of all she loved being there with him as it slowly exorcised her demons.

He was smiling too, and she saw it as they walked past the shopfront of a city icon. It had been a very long time, all good things, and all that.

The team drifted away, mostly to their homes, some to hotels, one to an old girlfriend who was there when he needed to vent, before heading home to his wife, who no longer understood him.

And by eleven they were all gone. Early doors. Another day lay ahead for many of them. The tide never stopped visiting the city, as one threat passed another lay in wait.

Complacency had no place in the teams' vocabulary. They lived to fight another day because they knew how to fight.

Roger pulled the three darts out of the board, placed them back in the holder and closed the small wooden doors. He rolled the eight ball down the green woollen baize, allowing it to ricochet off the bottom cushion and into the bottom pocket. He didn't look back, he'd done it so many times. As the ball dropped into the gulley he wiped down the bar tops, hung up the cloth and then locked the door, turned off the lights and went upstairs to bed.

EPILOGUE

James Cole, the British Prime Minister sat and stared at the package on his desk. It had been laid reverently onto a white cloth and guarded until he had entered his office. He looked, looked away, paced and then spoke.

"Sassy, when I asked Cade for proof that Alex Stefanescu was no longer a threat, did I specifically request that he send me part of his body?"

"Well, to be fair Prime Minister, you did."

He pushed the package with a borrowed ball-point pen, rolled it around until it showed the black tattoo.

"Definitely his?"

"One hundred percent. The fingerprints were checked with our Romanian police colleagues. They've asked for the hand as a memento."

"Sick bastards. How do they sleep at night Sassy?"

"I've no idea, James."

"Ah well, send it to them with my love, won't you. It looks cold, get it a glove." He smiled his trademark smile and walked around the desk. Held her hand.

"I need to do this Sassy, you understand why?"

"I do, but in equal parts I don't James. Ride it out, it won't last forever."

"It will, trust me, this is only the beginning. I'm strong enough, but I'll be damned if I'm going to drag my party down with me. We have managed to keep the wolf pack off our backs, and that's in a large way down to the Orion team. Shielding the press from the dissolution of the monarchy was a master stroke, thank you. But the exit from Europe is a whole new ball game. Thoughts?"

"Let the public decide. That way if they get it wrong in true political style we'll have someone to blame." She shrugged her shoulders and pulled a face.

"OK, I'll bow to your greater knowledge of the people. Hold it back until the twenty-seventh of May."

"State Opening of Parliament?"

"Can you think of a better time? We'll seek a referendum, thus putting the power back in the hands of the people. Her Majesty will be briefed, things will be put in place, at the highest possible level and financial chaos and public disorder will be averted. We've got three months. Get to work now...and Sassy."

"Sir."

"We need to find a new police minister too."

"Of course. Hopefully, the next one will be vetted a little closer than his predecessor."

"Dear God Sass, how did we miss that? A bloody gypsy. Insidiously weaving his way through parliament with one goal. Power and good fortune. If this ever gets out, we are finished. I blame my predecessor."

"Of course. Why wouldn't you? Look Jim, I've met real Roma, they are good people, look at the help we received from our counterparts in Bucharest. We simply cannot tar them all with the same brush. Simply can't happen. We'll score a whole lot more Brownie points if we play to their strengths, say that he was a successful man, regardless of his background, that he made it to the top, despite the challenges etcetera, etcetera."

"Sassy, that bastard was looking to take us all down. Every last one of us. Release a statement to the press that says Harry Halford was a good man, had the country and its people in high regard, died a terrible death because of his beliefs and his job and so on and so forth."

"You mean lie?"

"I mean exactly that."

"And what about the part that says you signed his death warrant?"

"Lock that in a box with the other documents and see that they are burned. They must never be released."

She nodded. "Prime Minister."

"Thank you, Home Secretary."

She turned to walk away. Stopped.

"Have we heard from Hewett?"

"No, but I'm sure he'll be just fine. He'll pop up somewhere, somehow, one day soon. He always does."

"Mexican tonight? Take away? My treat?"

"You, Acting Prime Minister, have yourself a date."

Cole resigned the next day. He was succeeded by Lane, who faced an uncertain political future. Within days she was announced to the public and hours later it had started. A new word would sweep across the British Isles. It was to become the most commonly spoken word in the history of the country. A wave of new opinions, divided families, destabilised financial houses, worried millionaires and their optimistic near cousins the entrepreneurs. One word had created an arena of trepidation among the people of Britain. One word.

Cade and his team had rid the country of a two word crime group – that called itself the Seventh Wave. They had started as misfits, led by a charismatic man who called himself the Jackdaw. As with all groups, they prayed for good fortune and it came in the form of a set of documents the value of which ran into many noughts. What it brought was the threat of wholescale disruption, ruin and riots.

Alex Stefanescu was Europe's most wanted. Past tense. His body had finally surfaced upstream, having been lodged against a wharf for a week or so. His soul had been visited by the ghosts of a thousand or more. Sailors, coal-merchants, spice traders and lightermen had come to pay their respects, drifting through him, mocking him and dragging him down into the darkest reaches of the river.

He emerged onto the surface of a cool, misty and ever-present river. A passing skipper had spotted him and raised the alarm.

By the time divers had recovered the body, across from the old Battersea Power Station, it had bloated hideously. Its head was twice its normal size, eyes bulging, lips tight over teeth, limbs much heavier and a stomach that was grotesque in shape.

Rats had dined on the best parts and urinated on the rest, swimming around him like sharks eyeing up a surfer. To them he was a light lunch – nothing more. He would have despised them.

The media reported on a handless corpse and rumours spread like wildfire that a new criminal group was present in the city. Fingerprints weren't an option, but DNA was and dental records, faxed from a willing dentist in the city of Craiova who said, for the record that he would know his work anywhere and that yes, the teeth belonged to Alex Stefanescu.

The man who considered himself the king of the gypsies had never become the Gypsy King. That title had gone to his brother, real name Luca Stefanescu, the firstborn and brother to Stefan and Alex. Luca had recognised a chance to better himself, had changed his name, entered the United Kingdom and gained an education. What followed was genuine success, where with a university backing he became a young Conservative, studied politics and gained a following. Rising through the ranks, he found himself just a few runs of the ladder away from running a country.

He had set a goal. And he was almost there. A few more years and he could really open up the border, create wealth and opportunity for his people, and above all be worshipped. That was until his little brother had provided evidence of his plans. The government watched and waited and saw that the rumour was true. A country with the reputation of Britain simply couldn't allow it to happen, but equally couldn't endorse murder by one of its own units.

Luca's homeland provided the answer in the form of a former Romanian operator, with a Russian weapon, a Finnish bullet, a car from Germany, and gloves, hand crafted in England by the best in the world. It was a perfect example of cooperation and existing in harmony, at a time when the storm clouds that were gathering sought to rupture the very heart of the European Union.

Luca lay on a metal tray that was as cold as his body. He was drained of life and hope, and his dreams of a better future.

Above him his brother Stefan, eyes of blue and brown marble-cold skin, a man for whom the truth simply didn't exist.

Beneath him, right at the very bottom, at the new Prime Minister's wish was the handless corpse of their brother Alex. His coal-black eyes stared up at the steel tray above him; vacant, filled with hate, a sneer on his rigid face. He was now just another handwritten tag in a fridge full of bodies.

His mother always said he would come to nothing, and at his brutal hand she had made the journey to heaven, torn to pieces, left to die.

At least they would never meet. Instead, she could stand and watch over them, shaking her head in dismay, holding back a tear for each of her boys.

Three brothers. Her three beautiful sons. What had become of them? She was mortified. But now they could cause no more harm, and that meant she could finally rest.

Cade woke before her. Laid for a while, admiring the view. It was something he never thought would happen. Only days earlier they were both stood on a freezing, windswept platform, in the lap of the gods, battling against threats both knew could change many lives. They had survived. They had made it.

They had also survived what many said was the longest journey on the planet, where the next day he had found her asleep on an overly large bed, with the fine cream curtains wafting in the warming breeze. Overhead, a three-bladed fan beat against the air, its rhythmic sound soporific to an already exhausted traveller.

He climbed quietly out of the bed, gently pulled a cotton sheet over her naked body, kissed her gently then left. Outside, the morning was saying goodbye to the night, beginning to announce itself to the world. It was by far his favourite time of the day.

He found his favourite running shoes, just where he had left them, laced them, knotting them twice, selected a playlist on his phone, tucked the earphones in, just so. Then he ran, and as he did so he let go of the demons that had knotted around him over the last few weeks.

Soon he started to feel the resistance of a gentle incline. He acknowledged his senses, isolating themselves once more. His nose was now alive with the scent of the forest, his eyes squinting to avoid the piercing rays and his ears embracing the ever-changing sounds, the most notable of which was the distant pounding of waves upon a shore.

He picked up the pace, feet gently landing on pine needles, crushing them, lifting their scent into the air. Tall trees swayed in time with the ocean breeze. He was alone, and it felt wonderful.

It was quite possibly the most beautiful place in the world.

The story was almost over. A trilogy that had begun on an isolated beach in the Land of the Long White Cloud would also end there, but not before he had completed his final act – every run ended this way. Phone off, dropped onto his shirt, shoes next, left in an orderly pile.

He looked up the beach, about half a mile. A lone figure stopped raking up the seaweed. His powerful tribal-tattooed arm swept the perspiration from his forehead, then waved a greeting.

He waved back – for he was a friend and one who would come to him in a heartbeat. Just say the word, brother.

He ran, timing the entry into the Pacific Ocean, head-first, into the blue, oxygenated bubbles fizzed all around him, the sea crashed above him; he was through the waves, each vying for his attention, tugging, turning, twisting. The sixth wave was powerful, the seventh more so.

He surfaced, blew away the stresses of the chaos and the

almost constant fear of protecting a city and its people. Just let them drift away, trapped in the riptide.

It was good to let go and even better to be home.

In an hour he would be back at his summer house which he called Spindrift, it was his father's favourite name for a boat, but Cade had never been a natural sailor.

He was greeted by fresh coffee, and a smile that said thank you – for last night – possibly even 'I love you'. Not quite, but almost.

Business shirt, blue, checked, crisply ironed. Nothing else.

In the far corner of the kitchen, on the stainless steel worktop, a phone sat in a cradle. A small blue light flashed every half second.

"I see you have a message," she said as she wrapped her arms around him. He was still warm and smelled of the ocean and the forest.

He pressed the button, and an English voice began to speak.

"Hello Mr Cade. You don't know me, but I think you could help. At least they say you can. Can you ring me on this number? As soon as possible? Please."

ACKNOWLEDGMENTS

It was on the heart-breaking morning of saying goodbye to my dear old dad for the very last time, in a hospice in Kent, England, that the inspiration for the Seventh Wave trilogy began. Three years later, *Seventh* was published, followed quickly by its sequel *Seven Degrees*.

I have to thank the 'old man' for giving me the drive to finish the story. "Tell that story son – you need to, and people need to read it."

I must also thank Claire, a six degrees, lifetime, slightly crazy, but such great company friend. Our paths crossed many years ago when as complete strangers we helped a mutual colleague who needed defending at a time of crisis. Claire was 'ex-job' – retired early with injuries sustained on duty and has continued to challenge my writing and my thoughts, but never my patience. Allowing someone to see the writing at its rawest takes courage. Reflecting upon it and providing feedback is equally brave.

To Mum. For your support and love when times were really tough. I know you are desperate to read the final book in the trilogy. And honestly, I can't wait for you to finish it.

Times were tough, often very, but we made it, didn't we? I hope having your son in print means as much to you as it does me.

My children, Stephanie and Andrew. We have a relationship that goes way beyond parent/child. You are both, first and foremost, my friends. And that means that at times we can push the boundaries way beyond where they should be! I love you both equally, it's impossible not to. I hope you enjoy your cameos.

Amanda. My always. Boy, what a year it's been! I put the writing on hold to nurse you back to health, but it was your sheer determination that got you through and I am so in awe of your courage. I am quietly terrified that you won't enjoy this story – to the end. Living under the same roof but never divulging the script has been tough. I love you more.

To my readers across the globe; Australia, New Zealand, Canada, The United States, United Kingdom, even a small town in India. Your feedback and genuine warmth are always so humbling. I hope that one day you can turn this from a door stop into a prized possession, alongside the truly greats of modern fiction.

To Kitty – for believing in an aging old Brit and for daring to challenge a sentence or ten! And on the subject of proof reading. I want to say a huge thank you to Lee, who Mother Nature decreed would have a special skill in the world of error spotting. I won't say what her gift is but needless to say she has eyes as sharp as an eagle.

To the Twitter team. A world of online authors who are there for each other, and me, day and night. Despite the rumours, Twitter has been an incredible platform for me. To name but a few, David Perlmutter, Michael Jenkins, 'Dennis Bisskit' and the many, many great authors who inhabit a website called www.londoncrime.co.uk the brainchild of a truly lovely man who I shall call Jim, for that is his name.

Lastly, on the author front it would be remiss of me, not to mention Donna Siggers. Donna and I met on Twitter. Since then, she has been supportive in so many ways. She's also won awards, and that inspires me to try harder.

To the characters in the series. You know who you are. Some of you are still propping up the thin blue line so require an air of anonymity; some have moved on, but with each of you there is a bond stronger than many could ever imagine. I said last time that you are the mortar in society's brickwork – I really cannot better that. Thank you for your support, great banter, for keeping our loved ones safe and above all thank you for allowing me to craft a character out of you. It's never easy. I hope they meet with your approval!

To Russell, I say this. You may have moved, but you are but a short journey away. Quite how you manage to deal with my endless emails is beyond me. I only hope that one day you might reply. Thanks for the new logo – looks great. Simple, yet great. That's the logo, not you. You are just great. For a Southampton fan. In his late forties.

This final chapter was intended for release in time for Christmas 2018, but fate dealt a few dark cards. In a way, perhaps it was a good thing. I'm positive that the story is better for a break. Coming to the end was cathartic, yet strangely sad. When a writer creates a character, they become a part of their lives – if mine have embedded themselves in your hearts and minds, then my work here is done.

There is no better feedback than listening to someone saying, "I couldn't believe you did that to (insert character name)." Makes me smile.

I intend to bring Jack and the team back before Christmas 2019 in a new, standalone story that I just can't wait to write.

Thank you for supporting me in everything I do.

It would be a travesty if I did not mention two wonderful people, once strangers and yet now friends, confidantes and mentors, occasionally humble students, sounding boards, passionate, eager, energetic and so supportive, they are Rebecca Collins and Adrian Hobart, the directors of Hobeck Books.

I feel we discovered each other when I was about to call time on my hopes and aspirations to finally be recognised as a genuine author and Hobeck were seeking new talent.

The planetary alignment was completed with a shooting star that lit up a velvet sky. I am so thrilled to be working with them and the other members of the Hobeck team. Thank you. x

Lewis

Lewis Hastings is a pseudonym. He was born in 1963 (a by-product of the long, harsh winter of 1962) in Kent, the Garden of England.

By virtue of his father's role as a Prison Officer he became somewhat nomadic, moving from county to county during his formative years. As quickly as he made friends, they became a distant memory.

His school life was a heady cocktail of fun, misery and abject failure which explains why he decided not to pursue a university career. He forged out a highly unsuccessful and miserable career in sales; a way to pay the bills and provide a home for his growing family. In 1988, a cathartic event changed his approach to life, and he spent two frustrating years trying to forge a new career as a Police Officer. By doing this he would in fact continue a family tradition stemming back to the early 1800s.

His career commenced with the Nottinghamshire Constabulary at a time of enormous change and he was soon posted to some of the most beautiful and dangerous locations in the county where he learned the noble art of policing, including community, intelligence and vice work (the latter, whilst challenging, at least offered a secondary income).

In 2003, wearing a different hat, he found himself in New Zealand, soon realising that the age-old maxim about excrement, locations and days of the week still rang true.

Considered a subject matter expert in border related matters, Hastings brings absolute accuracy to all of his plots – having instigated the real life investigation into an international syndicate he can say with authority that this story is very true.

This is his fourth book. The first, an autobiography, *Actually, The World Is Enough* has attracted positive reviews for its ability to make the reader laugh and cry, often in the same sentence.

Hastings' second book, *Seventh,* is a gritty crime thriller and the first part of a trilogy called *The Seventh Wave*.

The third, *Seven Degrees* has authenticity, dark humour and diverse characters which allow it to standalone in a sea of crime thrillers written by current and former law enforcement officers. *Seven of Swords* is the long-awaited finale.

Hastings is married with two children, a lake-loving Labrador, and lives in a house.

$$\overline{}$$

READER REVIEWS

$$\underline{}$$

SEVENTH

'Emotions run high reading this thriller and I feel totally spent now.'

'Expect adrenaline surges, plenty of testosterone, comradory, deceit, empathy and extreme hate in this intense journey that is full of tension, suspense, action, drama and intrigue.'

'Clearly written from the heart.'

'I literally could not put it down.'

'Every page is a delight to read and the story takes you through an amazing journey.'

'A real page turner, I couldn't put it down.'

'This book is a must read.'

SEVEN DEGREES

'A fast paced crime thriller with enough twists to keep readers guessing.'

'...gripping...'

'If book 1 of this trilogy blew me away, then this one blew me harder.'

'...edge of your seat stuff...'

'Fantastic.'

SEVEN OF SWORDS

'Twists and turns in every chapter.'

'Had me gripped from the start...truly magnificent writing.'

'I didn't want it to end!'

'WOW what a read!'

'I implore you to pick up this trilogy.'

'Read it, this will not be a disappointment to you.'

THE ANGEL OF WHITEHALL

'I would recommend this book unequivocally with no reservations, my one issue is that it will ensnare you and leaving it will not be an option until the last page. This is a story destined to be remembered as crossing a threshold of this specific genre. It is that good.'

destined to be remembered as crossing a threshold of this specific genre. It is that good.'

www.ingramcontent.com/pod-product-compliance
Lightning Source LLC
Chambersburg PA
CBHW010344170726
48284CB00009B/2779